THE FAR
PAVILIONS

M.M.KAYE
THE FAR PAVILIONS

VOLUME ONE

ST. MARTIN'S PRESS   NEW YORK

Plan of Kabul Residency drawn by
Reginald Piggott

TO
all those Officers and Men of different races and creeds
who, since 1846, have served with such pride and devotion
in
THE CORPS OF GUIDES
among them
Lieutenant Walter Hamilton V.C.,
my husband Major General Goff Hamilton CB, CBE, DSO,
and his father Colonel Bill Hamilton OBE, DL, JP.

*'We are the Pilgrims, Master: We shall go
Always a little further. It may be
Behind the last blue mountain topped with snow
Across that angry or that glimmering sea,
White on a throne, or guarded in a cave
There lives a prophet who can understand
Why men are born . . .'*

James Elroy Flecker

' 'Tis not too late to seek a newer world.'

Tennyson

Book One

The Twig is Bent

A glossary of Indian words appears on page 1137 of volume two.

I

Ashton Hilary Akbar Pelham-Martyn was born in a camp near the crest of a pass in the Himalayas, and subsequently christened in a patent canvas bucket.

His first cry competed manfully with the snarling call of a leopard on the hillside below, and his first breath had been a lungful of the cold air that blew down from the far rampart of the mountains, bringing with it a clean scent of snow and pine-needles to thin the reek of hot lamp-oil, the smell of blood and sweat, and the pungent odour of pack-ponies.

Isobel had shivered as the icy draught lifted the tent-flap and swayed the flame in the smoke-grimed hurricane lamp, and listening to her son's lusty cries had said weakly: 'He doesn't sound like a pre-mature baby, does he? I suppose I—I must have—miscalculated . . .'

She had: and it was a miscalculation that was to cost her dear. There are few of us, after all, who are called upon to pay for such errors with our lives.

By the standards of the day, which were those of Victoria and her Albert, Isobel Ashton was held to be a shockingly unconventional young woman, and there had been a number of raised eyebrows and censorious comments when she had arrived in the cantonment of Peshawar, on the North-West Frontier of India, in the year of the Great Exhibition, orphaned, unmarried and twenty-one, with the avowed intention of keeping house for her only remaining relative, her bachelor brother William, who had recently been appointed to the newly raised Corps of Guides.

The eyebrows had risen even further when a year later she had married Professor Hilary Pelham-Martyn, the well-known linguist, ethnologist and botanist, and departed with him on a leisurely, planless exploration of the plains and foothills of Hindustan, unaccompanied by so much as a single female attendant.

Hilary was middle-aged and eccentric, and no one—least of all himself—was ever able to decide why he should suddenly have elected to marry a portionless, though admittedly pretty girl, less than half his age and quite unacquainted with the East; or, having remained a bachelor for so many years, married at all. Isobel's reasons, in the opinion of Peshawar society, were more easily explained:

Hilary was rich enough to live as he pleased, and his published works had already made his name known in scholarly circles throughout the civilized world. Miss Ashton, they decided, had done very well for herself.

But Isobel had not married for the sake of money or ambition. Despite her forthright manner she was both impetuous and intensely romantic, and Hilary's mode of life struck her as being the very epitome of Romance. What could be more entrancing than a carefree nomadic existence camping, moving, exploring strange places and the ruins of forgotten empires, sleeping under canvas or the open sky, and giving no thought to the conventions and restriction of the modern world? There was also another, and perhaps more compelling consideration: the need to escape from an intolerable situation.

It had been frustrating in the extreme to arrive unheralded in India only to discover that her brother, far from being pleased to see her, was not only appalled by the prospect of having his sister on his hands, but quite incapable of offering her so much as a roof over her head. The Guides at that time were almost continuously in action against the Frontier tribes and seldom able to live peaceably in their cantonment at Mardan, and both William and the Regiment had been dismayed by Isobel's arrival. Between them they had managed to arrange temporary accommodation for her in the house of a Colonel and Mrs Pemberthy in Peshawar. But this had not been a success.

The Pemberthys were well-meaning but unbearably dull. Moreover, they had made no secret of their disapproval of Miss Ashton's conduct in travelling to the East, unchaperoned, and had done their best by advice and example to erase the unfortunate impression created by her arrival. Isobel soon discovered that she was expected to behave with stultifying decorum. She must not do this and it was inadvisable to do that . . . The list of prohibitions seemed endless.

Edith Pemberthy took no interest in the country where she and her husband had spent the greater part of their lives, and looked upon its people as uncivilized heathens who by the exercise of patience and strictness might be trained to become admirable servants. She could not conceive of there being any real communication with them on any level, and could neither understand nor sympathize with Isobel's eagerness to explore the bazaars and the native city, to ride out into the open country that stretched south to the Indus and the Kabul River or northward to the wild hills of the Khyber.

'There is nothing to see,' said Mrs Pemberthy, 'and the tribesmen are murderous savages—entirely untrustworthy.' Her husband had fully endorsed this view, and eight months under their roof began to feel like eight years to poor Isobel.

She had made no friends, for unfortunately the ladies of the garrison, discussing her over the tea cups, had decided that Miss Ashton was 'fast' and that the most likely motive for her journey to India was the desire to snare herself a husband. A verdict that from constant repetition came to be generally accepted by the station's bachelors, who, much as they might admire her looks, her unaffected manners and her excellent seat on a horse, had no wish to figure as gullible victims of a husband-hunter, and consequently fought shy of her. It is therefore hardly surprising that Isobel should have been heartily sick of Peshawar by the time Professor Pelham-Martyn appeared in the station, accompanied by his long-time friend and travelling companion Sirdar Bahadur Akbar Khan, a motley crew of servants and camp-followers, and four locked *yakdans* containing botanical specimens, the manuscript of a treatise on the origins of Sanskrit and a detailed report, in code, of a variety of official, semi-official and unofficial happenings in the dominions of the East India Company . . .

Hilary Pelham-Martyn bore a strong resemblance to that amiable and equally eccentric gentleman, the late Mr Ashton, and Isobel had adored her father. Possibly this may have had something to do with her immediate interest in the Professor, and the comfortable feeling of security and ease that his company gave her. Everything about him—his mode of life, his intense interest in India and its people, his grizzled, crippled friend Akbar Khan, and his total disregard of the rules that governed the conduct and outlook of such people as the Pemberthys—appealed strongly to Isobel. Paradoxically, he represented both escape and safety, and she had embarked on matrimony as buoyantly, and with as little regard as to the hazards of the future, as she had embarked on the S.S. *Gordon Castle* at Tilbury for the long voyage to India. And this time she had not been disappointed.

Hilary, it is true, treated her more as a favourite daughter than a wife, but this was pleasantly familiar and provided a comfortable leavening of stability and continuity to the haphazard camp life that was to be her portion for the next two years. And, having never previously fallen in love, she had no yardstick by which to measure the affection she felt for her vague, easy-going and unconventional husband, and was as completely content as any human being has a right to be. Hilary permitted her to ride astride, and for two happy years they travelled up and down India, exploring the foothills of the Himalayas and following the Emperor Akbar's road to Kashmir, and returning to spend the winters in the plains among the ruined tombs and palaces of lost cities. For most of that time Isobel had been without any feminine companionship and had not felt the lack of it. There were always books to read or Hilary's botanical specimens to be pressed and catalogued, and she would occupy her evenings with these while her husband and Akbar Khan played chess or argued hotly on involved questions of politics, religion, predestination and race.

Sirdar Bahadur Akbar Khan was a grizzled, crippled, ex-officer of a famous cavalry regiment, who had been wounded at the Battle of Mianee and had retired to his ancestral acres on the banks of the Ravi River to spend the remainder of his days in such peaceful pursuits as cultivation and the study of the Koran. The two men had met when Hilary was camping near Akbar Khan's home village, and had taken an instant liking to each other. They were, in many ways, very similar in character and outlook, and Akbar Khan had become restless and dissatisfied at the prospect of remaining in one place until he died.

'I am an old man, wifeless now; and childless too, for my sons are dead in the service of the Company and my daughter is married. What is there to keep me? Let us travel together,' said Akbar Khan. 'A tent is better than the four walls of a house to one who has had his day.'

They had travelled together ever since and become boon companions. But it had not taken Akbar Khan long to discover that his friend's interest in botany, ruins and the dialects of the country provided an admirable cover for another activity: the compiling of reports on the administration of the East India Company, for the benefit of certain members of Her Majesty's Government who had reason to suspect that all was not as well with India as official sources would have them believe. It was work of which Akbar Khan approved, and to which he had given invaluable assistance, as his knowledge of his fellow countrymen enabled him to weigh the worth of verbal evidence with more accuracy than Hilary. Between them, over the years, they had compiled and sent home folio after folio of fact and warning, much of which was published in the British press and used in debate in both Houses of Parliament—though for all the good it did they might as well have confined themselves to botany, for the public, it seemed, preferred to believe that which disturbed it least and to ignore troublesome information. Which is a failing common to all nations.

The Professor and his friend had worked and travelled together for five years when Hilary unexpectedly added a wife to the caravan, and Akbar Khan had accepted her presence with a placid matter-of-factness that recognized her place in the scheme of things, without considering it particularly important one way or another. He had been the only one of the three who was not disagreeably surprised by the discovery that Isobel was pregnant. It was, after all, the duty of women to produce children, and of course it must be a son.

'We will make him an officer of the Guides, like his uncle,' said Akbar Khan, brooding over the chess board, 'or the Governor of a Province.'

Isobel, like most of her generation, was abysmally ignorant of the processes of birth. She had not discovered her state for some considerable time and then had been startled and more than a little annoyed—it had never occurred to her to be frightened. A baby was going to be a distinct complication in the camp; it would need constant attention, and a nurse and special food and . . . Really, it was too annoying.

Hilary, equally surprised, suggested hopefully that she might be mistaken as to her condition, but being assured she was not, inquired when the child would be born. Isobel had no idea, but she attempted to cast her mind back over the past few months, and having counted on her fingers, frowned and counted again, she ventured an opinion that proved to be wholly inaccurate.

'We'd better make for Peshawar,' decided Hilary. 'There'll be a doctor there. And other women. I suppose it will be all right if we get there a month ahead? Better make it six weeks to be on the safe side.'

Which is how his son came to be born in the middle of nowhere and without the aid of doctor, nurse or such medicines as science possessed.

Apart from one or two sweepers' wives and several veiled and anonymous female relatives of the camp-followers, there was only one other woman in the camp who could be called upon to help: Sita, wife of Hilary's head syce (groom) Daya Ram, a hill-woman from Kangan way who had doubly disgraced herself by bearing and losing five daughters in the past five years—the last of whom had died the previous week, having lived less than three days.

'It seems she cannot bear sons,' said Daya Ram disgustedly. 'But the gods know she should at least have come by enough knowledge to help one into the world.'

So it was poor, shy, bereaved Sita, the groom's wife, who had acted as midwife at Isobel's lying-in. And she had indeed known enough to bring a man-child into the world.

It was not her fault that Isobel died. It was the wind that killed Isobel: that cold wind off the far, high snows beyond the passes. It stirred up the dust and the dead pine-needles and sent them swirling through the tent where the lamp guttered to the draught, and there was dirt in that dust: germs and infection and uncleanness from the camp outside, and from other camps. Dirt that would not have been found in a bedroom in Peshawar cantonment, with an English doctor to care for the young mother.

Three days later a passing missionary, trekking across the mountains on his way to the Punjab, stopped by the camp and was requested to baptize the baby. He had done so in a collapsible canvas bucket, naming him, by his father's wish, Ashton Hilary Akbar, and had left without seeing the child's mother who was said to be feeling 'poorly'—a piece of information that hardly surprised him, since the unfortunate lady could have received no proper attention in such a camp.

Had he been able to delay his departure for another two days he would have been able to officiate at Mrs Pelham-Martyn's funeral, for Isobel died twenty-four hours after her son's christening, and was buried by her husband and her husband's friend on the summit of the pass overlooking their tents, the entire camp attending the ceremony with every evidence of grief.

Hilary too had been grief-stricken. But he had also been aggrieved. What in the name of heaven was he to do with a baby now that Isobel had gone? He knew nothing about babies—apart from the fact that they were given to howling and had to be fed at all hours of the day and night. 'What on earth are we to do with it?' inquired Hilary of Akbar Khan, staring resentfully at his son.

Akbar Khan prodded the infant with a bony finger, and laughed when the baby clung to it. 'Ah, he is a strong, bold boy. He shall be a soldier—a captain of many sabres. Do not trouble yourself on his account, my friend. Daya Ram's wife will feed him as she has done from the day of his birth, having lost her own child, which was surely arranged by Allah who orders all things.'

'But we can't keep him in camp,' objected Hilary. 'We shall have to find someone who is going on leave and get them to take him home. I expect the Pemberthys would know of someone. Or young William. Yes, that's what we'd better do: I've got a brother in England whose wife can take care of him until I get back myself.'

That matter being decided he had taken Akbar Khan's advice and ceased to worry. And as the baby throve and was seldom heard to cry, they came to the conclusion that there was no hurry about going to Peshawar after all, and having cut Isobel's name on a boulder above her grave, they struck camp and headed east towards Garwal.

Hilary never returned to Peshawar; and being deplorably absent-minded, he failed to notify either his brother-in-law William Ashton, or any of his relatives in England, that he was now a father—and a widower. The occasional letter (there were not many) that still arrived addressed to his wife would from time to time remind him of his obligations. But as he was always too occupied to give them his immediate attention, they were put aside to be dealt with at some later date and invariably forgotten; as he came to forget Isobel—and even, on occasions, the fact that he had a son.

'Ash-Baba',* as the baby was known to his foster-mother Sita, and to the entire camp, spent the first eighteen months of his life among the high mountains, and took his first steps on a slippery grass hill-side within sight of the towering peak of Nanda Devi and the long range of her attendant snows. Seeing him toddling about the camp you would have taken him to be Sita's own child, for Isobel had been a brown beauty, honey-skinned, black-haired and grey-eyed; and her son had inherited her colouring. He has also inherited a considerable proportion of her good looks and would, said Akbar Khan approvingly, make a handsome man one day.

The camp never remained long in one place, Hilary being engaged in studying hill dialects and collecting wild flowers. But sterner matters eventually called him from this work, and leaving the hills behind them the camp turned southward and came at last, by way of

* baby; child

Jhansi and Sattara, to the lush greenery and long white beaches of the Coromandal Coast.

The heat of the plains and the humidity of the south did not suit Ash-Baba as the cool air of the hills had done, and Sita, herself a hill-woman, longed for the mountains and would tell him stories of her home in the north among the great ranges of the Hindu Kush. Tales of glaciers and avalanches, of hidden valleys where the rivers teemed with snow trout and the ground was carpeted with flowers; and where fruit blossom scented the air in spring and apples and walnuts ripened in the lazy golden summers. In time these became his favourite stories, and Sita invented a valley which was to be theirs alone and where, one day, they would build a house of mud and pinewood, with a flat roof on which they could spread corn and red peppers to dry, and a garden in which they would grow almond and peach trees and keep a goat and a puppy and a kitten.

Neither she nor any other member of the camp spoke English, and Ash reached the age of four without realizing that the language in which his father occasionally addressed him was, or should have been, his native tongue. But having inherited Hilary's ear for dialects, he picked up a number of tongues in the polyglot camp. Pushtu from Swab Gul, Hindi from Ran Chand, and Tamil, Gujerati and Telegu from the southerners. Though he used, for choice, the Punjabi spoken by Akbar Khan, Sita and Sita's husband Daya Ram. He rarely wore European clothes, since Hilary seldom stayed in places where such things were obtainable. And in any case such garments would have been entirely unsuited to the climate and camp life. He was therefore dressed either in Hindu or Mussulman garb—the difference of opinion between Akbar Khan and Sita as to which he should wear having been settled by compromise: Mussulman one week, Hindu the next. But always the former on a Friday.*

They had spent the autumn of 1855 in the Seeoni hills, ostensibly studying the dialect of the Gonds. And it was here that Hilary had written a report on the events that followed the annexation (he had called it 'theft') by the East India Company of the Princely States of Nagpur, Jhansi and Tanjore. His tale of the Company's dismissal of the unfortunate Commissioner and former Resident of Nagpur, Mr Mansel, who had been ill-advised enough to suggest a more generous settlement with the late Rajah's family (and rash enough to protest

---

* the Mohammedan Sabbath

against the harshness of the action taken) had lost nothing in the telling.

The whole policy of Annexation and Lapse—the taking-over by the Company of any native state where there was no direct heir, in defiance of a centuries-old tradition that permitted a childless man to adopt an heir from among his relations—was, declared Hilary, nothing more than a hypocritical term for an ugly and indefensible act: barefaced robbery and the defrauding of widows and orphans. The rulers in question—and he would point out that Nagpur, Jhansi and Tanjore were only three of the states to fall victims to this iniquitous policy—had been loyal supporters of the Company; yet their loyalty had not prevented their widows and womenfolk being deprived by that same Company of their hereditary rights, together with their jewels and other family heirlooms. In the case of the titular principality of Tanjore, absorbed by right of Lapse on the death of the Rajah, there had been a daughter, though no son; and with commendable courage (considering the treatment meted out to the hapless Mr Mansel) the President, a Mr Forbes, had pleaded the cause of the princess, urging that by the terms of Tanjore's treaty with the Company, the succession had been promised to 'heirs' in general and not specifically to heirs male. But his pleas had been ignored. A strong force of sepoys* had been marched suddenly into the palace and the whole of the property, real or personal, seized; the Company's seals had been put upon all jewels and valuables, the late Rajah's troops disarmed, and his mother's estate sequestered.

There was worse, wrote Hilary, to follow, for it affected the lives and livelihood of many people. Throughout the district, the occupier of every piece of land that had at any time belonged to any previous Rajah of Tanjore was turned out of his possession and ordered to come before the British Commissioner to establish a title, and all those who had depended on the expenditure of the state revenue were panic-stricken at the prospect of being left without employment. Within a week Tanjore, from being the most contented area in the Company's dominions, had been transformed into a hot-bed of disaffection. Its people had venerated their ruling house and were infuriated by its suppression—the very sepoys refusing to receive their pensions. In Jhansi, too, there had been a child of the royal house—a distant cousin only, but one formally adopted by the late Rajah—and

* Indian infantrymen

Lakshmi Bai, the Rajah's lovely widow, had pleaded her husband's long record of loyalty to the Company; but to no avail. Jhansi was declared 'Lapsed to the British Government' and placed under the jurisdiction of the Governor of the North-Western Provinces, its institutions abolished, the establishments of the Rajah's government suspended, and all troops in the service of the state immediately paid off and discharged.

'Nothing,' wrote Hilary, 'could be more calculated to arouse hatred, bitterness and resentment than this brazen and ruthless system of robbery.' But the Great British Public had other matters to think of. The war in the Crimea was proving a costly and harrowing business, and India was far away, out of sight and out of mind. Those few who clicked their tongues disapprovingly over the reports forgot about them a few days later, while the Senior Councillors of the Honorable the East India Company pronounced the writer to be 'a misguided crank' and attempted to discover his identity and prevent his making use of the mails.

They had not succeeded in either task, for Hilary's reports were sent home by unorthodox routes. And though there were officials who regarded his proceedings with suspicion—in particular his close friendship with 'a native'—they lacked evidence. Suspicion was not proof. Hilary continued to move freely about India and took pains to impress upon his son that the greatest sin that man could commit was injustice, and that it must always be fought against, tooth and nail—even when there seemed to be no hope of winning.

'Never forget that, Ashton. Whatever else you are, be just. "Do as you would be done by." That means you must never be unfair. *Never.* Not under any circumstances. Not to anyone. Do you understand?'

Of course he did not, for he was as yet too young. But the lesson was repeated daily until gradually it became borne in upon him what the 'Burra-Sahib'* (he never thought of his father by any other name) meant, for Uncle Akbar too would talk to him of this, telling him stories and quoting from the holy book to illustrate the theme that 'A man is greater than Kings'; and that when he grew up and became a man he would find that this was true. Therefore he must try always to be just in all his dealings, because at this time there

* great man

were many and terrible injustices being done in the land by men who held power and had become drunk with it.

'Why do the people put up with it?' demanded Hilary of Akbar Khan. 'There are millions of them to a handful of the Company. Why don't they do something?—stand up for themselves?'

'They will. One day,' said Akbar Khan placidly.

'Then the sooner the better,' retorted Hilary, adding that, to be fair, there were any number of good Sahibs in the country: Lawrence, Nicholson and Burns; men like Mansel and Forbes, and young Randall in Lunjore, and a hundred others, and that it was ones in Simla and Calcutta who need weeding out—the pompous, greedy and pigheaded old gentlemen with one foot in the grave and heads that had become addled by sun and snobbery and an inflated sense of their own importance. As for the army, there was hardly a senior British officer in India under the age of seventy. 'I am not,' insisted Hilary 'an unpatriotic man. But I cannot see anything admirable in stupidity, injustice and sheer incompetence in high places, and there is too much of all three in the present administration.'

'I will not quarrel with you over that,' said Akbar Khan. 'But it will pass; and your children's children will forget the guilt and remember only the glory, while ours will remember the oppression and deny you the good. Yet there is much good.'

'I know, I know.' Hilary's smile was more than a little wry. 'Perhaps I myself am a pompous and conceited old fool. And perhaps if these fools I complain of were French or Dutch or German I would not mind so much, because then I could say 'what else can you expect?' and feel superior. It is because they are men of my own race that I would have them all good.'

'Only God is that,' said Akbar Khan dryly. 'We, his creatures, are all evil and imperfect, whatever the colour of our skins. But some of us strive for righteousness—and in that there is hope.'

Hilary wrote no more reports on the administrative activities of the East India Company and the Governor-General and Council, but turned instead to those subjects that had always claimed the lion's share of his interest. The resulting manuscripts, unlike his coded reports, were dispatched through the normal channel of the mails, where they were opened and examined, and served to confirm the authorities in their opinion that Professor Pelham-Martyn was, after all, merely an erudite eccentric and entirely above suspicion.

Once again the camp struck its tents, and turning its back upon the palms and temples of the south, moved slowly northward. Ashton Hilary Akbar celebrated his fourth birthday in the capital of the Moguls, the walled city of Delhi, where Hilary had come to complete, correct and dispatch the manuscript of his latest, and last, book. Uncle Akbar marked the occasion by arraying Ash in the finest of Mussulman dress and taking him to pray at the Juma Masjid, the magnificent mosque that the Emperor Shah Jehan had built facing the walls of the *Lal Kila,* the great 'Red Fort' on the banks of the Jumna River.

The mosque had been crowded, for it was a Friday. So crowded that many people who had been unable to find places in the courtyard had climbed to the top of the gateway, and two had fallen because of the press and been killed. 'It was ordained,' said Uncle Akbar, and went on with his prayers. Ash had bowed, knelt and risen in imitation of the other worshippers, and afterwards Uncle Akbar had taught him Shah Jehan's prayer, the *Khutpa,* which begins *'Oh Lord! Do thou great honour to the faith of Islam, and to the professors of that faith, through the perpetual power and majesty of thy slave the Sultan, the son of the Sultan, the Emperor, the son of the Emperor, the Ruler of the two Continents and the Master of the two seas, the Warrior in the cause of God, the Emperor Abdul Muzaffar Shahabuddin Muhammad Shah Jahan Ghazi . . .'*

What, demanded Ash, was a sea? And why only two seas?—and who had ordained that those two people should fall off the gateway?

Sita had countered by dressing her foster-son as a Hindu and taking him to a temple in the city, where in exchange for a few coins a priest in yellow robes had marked his forehead with a small smear of red paste, and he had watched Daya Ram do *pujah* (worship) to an ancient, shapeless shaft of stone, the symbol of the God Shiva.

Akbar Khan had many friends in Delhi, and normally he would have wished to linger there. But this year he was aware of odd and uneasy undercurrents, and the conversation of his friends disturbed him. The city was full of strange rumours and there was a tension and an ominous sense of suppressed excitement in the narrow, noisy streets and crowded bazaars. It gave him a sharp feeling of apprehension and an awareness of impending evil.

'There is some mischief afoot. One can smell it in the very air,' said Akbar Khan. 'It bodes no good for men of your blood, my friend, and I would not have our boy come to any harm. Let us go away from here, to somewhere where the air is cleaner. I do not like cities. They breed foulness as a dunghill breeds flies and maggots, and there is something breeding here that is worse than either.'

'You mean revolt?' said Hilary, undisturbed. 'That is true of half India. And in my opinion the sooner it comes the better: we need an explosion to clear the air and blow those lethargic blockheads in Calcutta and Simla out of their complacency.'

'True. But explosions can kill, and I would not have my boy pay for the errors of his countrymen.'

'You mean *my* boy,' corrected Hilary with a shade of asperity.

'Ours, then. Though he is fonder of me than of you.'

'Only because you spoil him.'

'Not so. It is because I love him, and he knows it. He is the son of your body but of my heart; and I would not have him harmed when the storm breaks—as it will. Have you warned your English friends in the cantonment?'

Hilary said that he had done so many times, but that they did not want to believe it: and the trouble was that not only men in high places, the Members of Council in Calcutta and the civil servants in Simla, knew too little of the minds of those whom they governed, but many army officers were equally ignorant.

'It was not so in the old days,' said Akbar Khan regretfully. 'But the generals are now old and fat and tired, and their officers are moved so frequently that they do not know the customs of their men, or notice that their sepoys are becoming restless. I do not like that tale from Barrackpore. It is true that only one sepoy rebelled, but when he shot down his officer and threatened to shoot the General-Sahib himself, his fellow sepoys watched in silence and did nothing to prevent it. Yet I think it was unwise to disband that regiment after they had hanged the offender, because now there are three hundred more masterless men to add to the disaffection of many others. Trouble will come of it, and I think very soon.'

'I too. And when it does, my countrymen will be both shocked and enraged at such disloyalty and ingratitude. You will see.'

'Perhaps—if we live through it,' said Akbar Khan. 'Wherefore I say, let us go to the hills.'

Hilary packed his boxes and left a number of them in the house of an acquaintance in the cantonment behind the Ridge. He had intended, before leaving Delhi, to write several letters that should have been written years ago. But once again he postponed doing so, for Akbar Khan was impatient to be gone and there would be plenty of time for such tedious business when they reached the peace and quiet of the hills. Besides, having neglected his correspondence for so long, a month or two would make no difference. Consoled by this thought, he shovelled a pile of unanswered letters, including half-a-dozen addressed to his late wife, into a cardboard box marked 'Urgent', and turned to more interesting tasks.

There is a book, published in the spring of 1856 (*Unfamiliar Dialects of Hindustan*, Vol. I, by Prof. H. F. Pelham-Martyn, B.A., D.SC., F.R.G.S., F.S.A., etc.), that is dedicated *'To the dear memory of my wife Isobel'*. The second volume of this work was not published until the autumn of the following year and bore a longer inscription: *'For Ashton Hilary Akbar, hoping it may arouse his interest in a subject that has given endless pleasure to the author—H.F.P-M.'* But by that time both Hilary and Akbar Khan had been six months in their graves, and no one had troubled to inquire who Ashton Hilary Akbar might be.

The camp had moved northward in the direction of the Terai and the foothills of the Doon, and it was here, in early April when the temperature had begun to rise and the nights were no longer cool, that disaster overtook them.

A small party of pilgrims from Hardwar, who had been offered hospitality for a night, brought cholera with them. One of them died in the dark hour before dawn, and his companions fled, abandoning the body which was found by the servants the next morning. By evening three of Hilary's men had taken the disease, and so swiftly did the cholera do its ugly work that none lived to see the dawn. The camp succumbed to panic and many snatched their chattels and vanished, not waiting for their pay. And on the following day Akbar Khan had sickened.

'Go away,' whispered Akbar Khan to Hilary. 'Take the boy and go quickly, lest you too die. Do not grieve for me. I am an old man and a cripple, wifeless and childless. Why should I fear to die? But you have the boy . . . and a son has need of a father.'

'You have been a better father to him than I,' said Hilary, holding his friend's hand.

Akbar Khan smiled. 'That I know, for he has my heart, and I would have taught him—I would have taught him . . . It is too late. Leave quickly.'

'There is nowhere to go,' said Hilary. 'How can one out-distance the black cholera? If we go it will go with us, and I have heard that more than a thousand are dying daily at Hardwar. We are better off here than in the towns, and soon you will be well—you are strong and will recover.'

But Akbar Kahn had died.

Hilary wept for his friend as he had not wept for his wife. And when he had buried him he went to his tent where he wrote a letter to his brother in England and another to his lawyer, and enclosing both with certain other papers and daguerreotypes in his possession, made a small packet of the whole and wrapped it carefully in a square of oiled silk. That done and the packet sealed with wax, he picked up his pen again and began a third letter—that long-overdue letter to Isobel's brother, William Ashton, that he had meant to write years ago and somehow never written. But he had left it too late. The cholera that had killed his friend reached out a bony hand and touched him on the shoulder, and his pen faltered and fell to the floor.

An hour later, rousing himself from a bout of agony, Hilary folded the unfinished page and having slowly and painfully traced an address on it, called for his bearer, Karim Bux. But Karim Bux too was dying, and it was, at long last, Daya Ram's wife, Sita, who came hastening nervously through the dusk of the stricken camp, bringing a hurricane lamp and food for the 'Burra-Sahib'. For the cook and his assistants had run away hours before.

The child had come with her, but when she saw how it was with his father she pushed him outside the reeking tent and would not let him enter.

'That's right,' gasped Hilary, approving the action. 'You're a sensible woman—always said so. Look after him, Sita. Take him to his own people. Don't let him—' He found that he could not finish the sentence and groping weakly for the single sheet of paper and the sealed packet, thrust it at her. 'Money in that tin box—take it. That's right. Should be enough to get you to . . .'

Another convulsion shook him, and Sita, hiding money and papers in the folds of her sari, backed away, and grasping the child's hand hurried him to his own tent and put him to bed—for once, and to his indignation, without the songs and fairy tales that were the normal accompaniments of bedtime.

Hilary died that night, and by mid-afternoon on the following day the cholera had claimed four more lives. Among them, Daya Ram's. Those who remained—by now a mere handful—looted the empty tents of anything of value, and taking the horses and camels, fled southward into the Terai, leaving behind them the newly widowed Sita, for fear that she might have taken the infection from her dead husband, and with her the four-year-old orphan, Ash-Baba.

Years afterwards, when he had forgotten much else, Ash could still remember that night. The heat and the moonlight, the ugly sound of jackals and hyenas quarrelling and snarling within a stone's throw of the little tent where Sita crouched beside him, listening and trembling and patting his shoulder in a vain attempt to soothe his fears and send him to sleep. The flap and croak of gorged vultures roosting in the *sal* trees, the sickening stench of corruption and the dreadful, dragging sense of bewildered desolation at a situation that he could not understand and that no one had explained to him.

He had not been frightened, because he had never yet had cause to be afraid of anything, and Uncle Akbar had taught him that a man must never show fear. Also he was, by temperament, an abnormally courageous child, and life in a camp that moved through jungles, deserts and unexplored mountain ranges had accustomed him to the ways of the wild animals. But he did not know why Sita wept and shivered and why she had not let him approach the 'Burra-Sahib', or understand what had happened to Uncle Akbar and the others. He knew that they were dead, for he had seen death before: tigers that he had been allowed to sit up for in a *machan* with Uncle Akbar and had seen shot. Kills that they had waited above; goats or young buffaloes that a tiger had struck down and partially eaten on the previous day. Black-buck and duck and partridge shot for the pot. These creatures had been dead. But surely Uncle Akbar could not be dead as they were dead? There must be something indestructible—something that remained of men who had walked and talked with one and told one stories, men whom one had loved and looked up to. But where had it gone? It was all very puzzling, and he did not understand.

Sita had dragged thorn branches from the *boma* that had once protected the camp, and piled them in a circle about his tent, heaping them high. And it was as well that she had, for towards midnight a pair of leopards had driven off the jackals and the hyenas to lay claim to the feast, and before dawn a tiger roared in the jungle beyond the *sal* trees, and daylight showed the print of his pugs within a yard of their flimsy barrier of thorn.

There had been no milk that morning, and little food. But Sita had given the child the remains of a chuppatti—the unleavened bread of India—and afterwards she made a bundle of their few belongings, and taking him by the hand led him away from the horror and desolation of the camp.

2

Sita could not have been more than twenty-five years old. But she looked twice that age, for hard work and yearly pregnancies, the bearing of five children and the bitter grief and disappointment of their loss, had combined to age her prematurely. She could neither read nor write and she was not clever, but she possessed courage, loyalty and a loving heart, and it never occurred to her to keep for herself the money Hilary had given her, or to disobey his orders. She had loved Hilary's son from the hour of his birth, and now Hilary had given the boy into her keeping and told her to take him back to his own people. There was no one else to care for Ash-Baba now but herself: he was her responsibility and she would not fail him.

She had no idea who his own people were, or how to find them, but this did not worry her over-much, for she remembered the number of the house in Delhi cantonment where Ash-Baba's father had left the greater part of his luggage, and also the name of the Colonel-Sahib who lived there. She would take the child to Delhi, to Abuthnot Sahib and his Memsahib, who would arrange everything, and as they would certainly need an *ayah* for the boy she, Sita, need not be parted from him. Delhi lay far to the southward but she never doubted that they would reach it in safety, though because the money she had taken from the tin box was more than she had ever seen in her life, she became afraid of attracting undue attention on the road, and dressed Ash in the oldest garments he possessed, warning him that he must on no account talk to strangers.

It was May before they came within sight of the city of the Moguls, for Ash was too heavy for her to carry except for short distances, and though he was a sturdy child he could not cover more than a few miles in one day. The weather too, though usually cool for that season of the year, was getting hotter, and the long, burning days made for slow travel. Ash had accepted their journey without question, for he had never known anything else and a constant change of scene was nothing new. The only stability his life had possessed had been the presence of the same people: Sita, Uncle Akbar and the 'Burra-Sahib'; Daya Ram and Kartar Singh, Swab Gul, Tara Chand, Dunno and a score of others; and though all of them had now gone except Sita, she at least was still here—together with all India and the familiar Indian scene.

They travelled slowly, buying their food in villages by the way and sleeping for preference in the open in order to avoid questions, and they were both very tired by the time the walls and domes and minarets of Delhi showed on the horizon, wraithlike in a dusty, golden evening. Sita had hoped to reach the city before dark, having planned to spend the night with a distant connection of Daya Ram's who kept a grain shop in a side street of the Chandi Chowk, where she could clean and press the English clothes that she had secreted in her bundle, and dress Ash-Baba correctly before taking him to the cantonment. But they had covered nearly six miles that day, and though the walls of Delhi seemed no great distance away, the sun went down while they were still a quarter of a mile short of the bridge of boats by which they must cross the Jumna.

A further half mile separated them from the shop in the city, and soon it would be too dark to see. But they had sufficient food and drink for an evening meal, and as the child was too tired and too sleepy to go further, Sita led him a little way off the road to where a *peepul* tree leaned above a clutter of fallen masonry, and having fed him, spread a blanket among the tree roots and sang him to sleep with an old, old nursery-rhyme of the Punjab, *'Arré Ko-ko, Jarré Ko-ko',* and that best-beloved of lullabies that says—

> *'Nini baba, nini,*
> *Muckan, roti, cheeni,*
> *Roti muckan hogya,*
> *Hamara baba sogya!'**

The night was warm and windless and full of stars, and from where she lay with her arm about the child's small body, Sita could see the lights of Delhi twinkling across the plain, a spangle of gold on the velvet darkness. Jackals howled among the scattered ruins of other and older Delhis, bats and harsh-voiced night birds swooped and called among the branches overhead, and once a hyena laughed hideously from a patch of elephant grass a few yards away, and a mongoose chittered angrily among the shadows. But these were all familiar sounds, as familiar as the tom-toms that beat in the distant

* Sleep baby sleep, Butter, bread, sugar, The bread and butter are finished, My baby is asleep.

city and the shrill hum of the cicadas; and presently Sita drew the end of her *chuddah* over her face and slept.

She awoke in the first flush of dawn, aroused abruptly from sleep by a less familiar sound: a sharp urgent clatter of galloping hooves, the crack of firearms and men's voices, shouting. There were horsemen on the road, approaching from the direction of Meerut and riding like men possessed, or pursued, the dust of their headlong progress streaming out behind them like a trail of white smoke across the dawn-lit plain. They thundered past within a stone's throw of the *peepul* tree, firing wildly into the air and shouting as men shout in a race, and Sita could see their staring eyes and frenzied faces, and the clotted foam that flew from the straining necks and flanks of the galloping horses. They were sowars (troopers) wearing the uniform of one of the Bengal Army's cavalry regiments. Sowars from Meerut. But their uniforms were torn and dusty and disfigured by the dark, unmistakable stains of blood.

A stray bullet ripped through the boughs of the *peepul* tree and Sita cowered down, clutching Ash, who had been woken by the noise. The next moment the riders were past and the dust that whirled up behind them blotted them out in a choking cloud that filled her lungs, making her cough and gasp and cover her face in the folds of her sari. By the time it had blown clear and she could see again, they had reached the river and she heard, faint but clear in the quiet dawn, the hollow thunder of hooves crossing the bridge of boats.

The impression of desperate men who fled in fear of pursuit had been so vivid that Sita snatched up the child, and running with him to the shelter of the elephant grass, crouched there, listening for the hue and cry that must surely follow.

She stayed there for the best part of an hour, hushing the bewildered boy and begging him in whispers to stay still and make no noise; but though she heard no more hoof-beats on the Meerut road, the stillness of the morning lent clarity to a distant crackle of firing and the voices of men shouting under the walls of Delhi. Presently these too ceased or were absorbed into the work-a-day sounds of the awaking city and the normal noises of an Indian morning: the creak of a well-wheel, partridges calling out on the plains and sarus cranes by the river; the harsh cry of a peacock from the standing crops, and the chatter and chirrup of tree-rats, *saht-bai* and weaver-birds. A troop of brown monkeys settled in the branches of the *peepul* tree, and a faint breeze off the river stirred the tall elephant grass and made a dry monotonous rustling that blotted out all other sounds.

'Is it a tiger?' whispered Ash, who had sat up over more than one kill with Uncle Akbar and knew about tigers.

'No—but we must not talk. We must be quiet,' urged Sita. She could not have explained the panic that the yelling horsemen had aroused in her, or what exactly she was afraid of. But her heart was still beating at twice its normal speed and she knew that not even the cholera, or the terrible hours of their last night in camp, had frightened her as the sight of those men had done. Cholera, after all, she knew; and sickness and death and the ways of wild animals. But this was something else. Something inexplicable and terrifying . . .

A country cart drawn by a pair of lethargic bullocks jolted slowly down the road, and the homely, unhurried sound of its passing reassured her. The sun lipped the rim of the far horizon and suddenly it was day, and Sita's breathing slowed and steadied. She stood up cautiously, and peering through the parched grasses saw that the road lay empty in the bright sunlight. Nothing moved upon it—which was in itself unusual, for the Meerut road was normally a busy one and carried the main traffic from Rohilkund and Oude to Delhi. But Sita was unaware of this, and the silence encouraged her, though she was not anxious to follow too closely on the heels of those wild-eyed horsemen, and it seemed wiser to wait awhile. There was still a little food left, but they had finished the milk on the previous night and were both becoming increasingly thirsty.

'Wait here,' she told Ash. 'I will go to the river to fetch water, and I shall not be long. Do not move from here, my heart. Stay still and you will be safe.'

Ash had obeyed her, for he had caught the infection of her panic and for the first time in his life had been frightened. Though he, like Sita, could not have told what he was afraid of.

It had been a long wait, for Sita made a detour and reached the river bank some way above the spot where the road ran on to the bridge of boats, which would have been the shortest way to the water. From here she could see across the sand bars and the wandering channels of the Jumna to the Calcutta Gate and the long line of the wall that stretched away past the Arsenal to the Water Bastion; and also hear, more clearly now, the noise of the city, which sounded from that distance like the hum of an overturned hive of angry bees, magnified a thousand times.

Mixed with that sound were the sharper ones of shots, now a lone one, now a staccato crackle of firing; and the sky above the roof tops was alive with birds—hawks, cawing flocks of crows, and startled pigeons, wheeling and swooping and rising sharply again as though disturbed by something in the streets below. Yes, there was something gravely wrong with Delhi that morning, and it would be better to keep away and not attempt to enter the city until she had some knowledge of what was happening there. It was a pity that there was so little food left, but there would be enough for the child. And at least they would have water.

Sita filled her brass *lotah* in the shallows and stole back to the safety of the elephant grass by the Meerut road, keeping as far as possible to the sparse shelter of *kikar* trees, rocks and clumps of pampas in order to avoid being seen. They would remain here until the evening, she decided, and then cross the bridge after dark, and by-passing the city, make straight for the cantonments. It would be a long walk for Ash-Baba, but if he rested all day . . . She trod out a more comfortable space for him in the heart of the grass patch, and though it had been dusty, airless and intolerably hot, and Ash, having forgotten his fear, had become bored and restless, the heat and the enforced idleness had eventually made him drowsy, and shortly after midday he had fallen asleep.

Sita too had dozed fitfully, soothed by the slow creak of bullock-drawn country carts plodding along the dusty road and the occasional jingle of a passing *ekka*.* Both sounds seemed to betoken the resumption of normal traffic on the Meerut road, so perhaps the danger—if there had been danger—had passed, and what she had witnessed had been no more than messengers hastening to Bahadur Shah, the Mogul, with news of some great event that had aroused the city to excitement and celebration; the news, perhaps, of a victory won by the Company's Bengal Army on some faraway battlefield; or the birth of a son to some fellow monarch—perchance to the *Padishah* Victoria in *Belait* (England)?

These and other comforting conjectures served to blunt the sharp edge of panic, and she could no longer hear the tumult of the city, for though the faint current of air that blew off the wet sand and the winding reaches of the Jumna River was not strong enough to raise the dust that lay thick on the highroad, it was still sufficient to stir

* light two-wheeled trap

the tops of the elephant grass and fill her ears with a soft, murmurous rustling. 'We shall leave when the child awakes,' thought Sita. But even as she thought it the illusion of peace was shattered. A savage tremor swept across the plain like an invisible wave, shuddering through the grass and rocking the very earth beneath her, and on its heels came an appalling crash of sound that split the murmurous silence of the hot afternoon as a thunderbolt will split a pine tree.

The violence of that sound jerked Ash from sleep and brought Sita to her feet, rigid with shock, and peering through the shivering grasses they saw a vast column of smoke rising up above the distant walls of Delhi: an awesome, writhing pillar, mushroom-topped and terrifying in the blaze of the afternoon sunlight. They had no idea what it meant, and never knew that what they had seen was the explosion of the Delhi magazine, blown up by a handful of defenders to prevent it falling into the hands of a rioting mob.

Hours later the smoke still hung there, rose-coloured now in the golden sunset; and when at last Sita and the child ventured out of their hiding place the first rays of the low moon had touched its fading outline with silver.

To turn back now, when they were almost within reach of their goal, was out of the question; though had there been any other way of reaching the cantonments, Sita would have taken it. But she did not dare attempt to ford the Jumna, and there was no other bridge for many miles. They would have to cross by the bridge of boats, and they had done so, hurrying across it in the grey starlight in the wake of a wedding party, to be challenged and halted by armed men on the far side. A lone woman and child being of little account, they had been allowed to pass while the sentries interrogated the wedding guests; and it was from the babble of questions and answers that Sita gained her first information as to the events of the day.

Hilary had been right. And so had Akbar Khan. There had been too many grievances that had been disregarded, too many injustices that had not been recognized and put right, and men would not endure such things for ever. The breaking point had been a petty one: a matter of greased cartridges that had been issued to the Bengal Army for use in the new rifles, of which the grease was suspected of being a mixture of cow and pig fat—the touch of the first destroying the caste of a Hindu and the latter defiling a Mohammedan. But it was an excuse only.

Ever since the day, half a century earlier, when mutiny and bloodshed had followed the Company's attempt to enforce the wearing of a leather stock and a new form of headdress on the troops at Vellore in Madras, the sepoys had suspected a plot aimed at depriving them of caste—that most cherished of all Hindu institutions. The mutiny of Vellore had been put down with swiftness and ferocity, as had other and similar insurrections in the years that followed. But the Company had failed to read the writing on the wall, and were indignant at the outcry against the greased cartridges.

In Barrackpore an angry sepoy, Mangal Pandy of the 34th Native Infantry, having urged his comrades to revolt, had fired at and wounded the British Adjutant. He had subsequently been hanged, while his fellow sepoys who had watched in silence had been deprived of their arms. The regiment itself had been disbanded, and faced with further dissatisfaction the Governor-General had at last issued an order withdrawing the new cartridge. But by that time it was too late, for the sepoys looked upon the order as proof that their suspicions had been correct, and far from easing the tension, it increased it to danger-point. Outbreaks of arson were reported from all over India, but in spite of the explosiveness of the situation and the fact that knowledgeable men were only too well aware of impending disaster, the Commanding Officer of the 3rd Cavalry, stationed at Meerut, had elected to teach his regiment a lesson by insisting that they use the disputed cartridges. Eighty-five of his sowars* having firmly, though courteously, refused to do so, they had been arrested, court-martialled and sentenced to hard-labour for life.

General Hewitt, obese, lethargic and rising seventy, had reluctantly ordered a parade of the entire Meerut Brigade at which the sentences were read aloud, and the eighty-five men publicly stripped of their uniforms and fitted with iron leg-shackles before being led away to life imprisonment. But that long-drawn, inglorious parade proved to be an even greater mistake than the harshness of the sentences, for the sympathy of the watching crowd had been aroused by the sight of the manacled sowars, and all that night men in the barracks and bazaars of Meerut seethed with shame and rage and plotted revenge. With the morning the storm that had threatened for so long broke at last: a mob of furious sepoys attacked the gaol, released the prisoners and turned on the British, and after a day of riot, murder and violence the sowars of the 3rd Cavalry had fired the

* sowars = cavalry soldiers; sepoys = infantry

looted bungalows and ridden to Delhi to raise the standard of revolt and place their sabres at the service of Bahadur Shah, titular King of Delhi and last of the Moguls. It was these men whom Sita had seen in the dawn, and recognized, with terror and foreboding, as the messengers of disaster.

The Mogul, it seemed, had not at first believed them, for there were many British regiments in Meerut, and he had hourly expected to see them hastening in pursuit of the mutineers. Only when none appeared did he become convinced that the troopers of the 3rd Cavalry had spoken no more than the truth when they asserted that all the Sahib-log in Meerut were dead; and this being so, word had gone out for a similar massacre of all Europeans in Delhi. Some of the Sahibs had shut themselves into the magazine, and when it became clear that they could no longer hold it, they had blown it up, and themselves with it. Others had been slaughtered by their troops, or by the mobs which had risen in support of the heroes of Meerut and were still hunting down stray Europeans in the streets of the city . . .

Listening to this tale of the day's doings, Sita had snatched the child away from the light of the flaring torches and dragged him into the shadows, terrified that he might be recognized as *Angrezi* (English) and cut down by the swords of the bridge guard. The roar of the mob and the crash and crackle of burning buildings carried a clearer warning than any words of the dangers to be encountered in the city, and turning from the Calcutta Gate she scurried away into the darkness in the direction of the Water Bastion, keeping to the narrow strip of waste ground that lay between the river and the walls of Delhi.

The ground was rough and strewn with rocks and other pitfalls, and Ash's short legs, trotting beside her, tired early. But by now the moon was up, and the reflected glare of burning houses filled the night with a sunset brightness. They had covered less than half a mile when they came across a strayed donkey wandering aimlessly among the boulders and the rubbish dumps, and appropriated it. Its owner was probably a *dhobi* or a grass-cutter who had tied it insecurely or, hastening to the city to take part in the looting of European-owned shops and houses, had temporarily forgotten it. But to Sita it was a gift from the gods and she accepted it as such. The little creature stood patiently while she placed Ash on its back and mounted behind him, and it had obviously been accustomed to far heavier loads, for at the touch of her heel it trotted briskly forward, keeping to some unseen track that wound between the rocks and scrub and rubbish on the glacis beyond the city ditch.

The donkey's hooves made very little noise on the sandy ground, and Sita's wine-coloured cotton sari was lost among the shadows; but there were men on the walls that night who were suspicious of any sound or movement, and twice harsh voices challenged them and shots ricochetted off the stones at their feet or whined viciously overhead to splash into the river. Then at last they were past the Water Bastion and the Counter-Scarp, and picking their way across the short stretch of open ground that separated the Kashmir Gate from the dark, friendly thickets of the Kudsia Bagh.

A final spatter of shots followed but did not harm them, and ten minutes later they were among trees, with Delhi left behind them—a black, uneven fringe of walls and battlements, rooftops and trees, spiked with the slim minarets of mosques and thrown into sharp silhouette by the glow of the fires. To the right lay the river, while ahead and to the left loomed the long dark line of the Ridge, a natural barrier of rock that lay between the cantonments and the city.

There were always lights in the cantonments, in bungalows, barracks and messes, and the quarters of the camp-followers. The glow they made in the night sky was a familiar sight, but tonight it was much brighter and less constant, waxing and waning as though there were fires there too. The Sahib-log, thought Sita, must have caused bonfires to be lighted around the cantonment area to prevent any attack being launched under cover of darkness, which seemed to her a sensible idea; though it was going to make her own progress more hazardous, for there were armed men on the road that linked the city to the Ridge and the cantonments, hurrying figures on foot and on horseback whom she suspected of being mutineers or looters. The sooner she got the child and herself to the safety of Abuthnot-Sahib's bungalow the better, but it might be wiser to wait here where the trees and thickets offered a hiding place, until there was less activity on the cantonment road.

The donkey jibbed suddenly, almost unseating her. It stood still, blowing loud snuffing breaths of alarm, and when she urged it forward with her heel, it backed instead, so that she was forced to dismount.

'*Dekho!*' (Look!) said Ash, whose eyesight in the dark was almost as good as the donkey's. 'There is someone there in the bushes.'

His voice was interested rather than alarmed, and if he had not spoken before it was only because he had never been much given to talking, except, on occasions, to Akbar Khan. The shots and the shouting had excited him, but no more than that, for Uncle Akbar had taken him out shooting before he could walk, and the only alarming thing about the present situation was Sita's fear; and the fact that she either would not or could not explain their altered circumstances and why everyone he had known in all his short life, everyone but herself, had suddenly deserted him. But like most children the world over, he was resigned to the curious behaviour of grown-ups and accepted it as part of the scheme of things. He knew now that Sita was once again afraid, and this time of the person in the bushes: the donkey was too, and Ash patted the little animal's quivering back and said consolingly: *'Daro mut,'* (Do not fear), 'it is only a memsahib who is asleep.'

The woman in the bushes lay in a curious attitude, as though she had crawled through the tangled undergrowth on hands and knees and had fallen asleep, exhausted. The red light of burning buildings, glinting through the leaves, showed her to be an excessively stout lady wearing a whalebone crinoline and a number of petticoats under a voluminous dress of grey and white striped bombazine which made her appear even stouter. But she was not asleep. She was dead. She must, thought Sita, shrinking back from that vast, silent shape, be one of the Sahib-log who had attempted to escape the massacre in the city and had died of terror or heart-failure, for she bore no sign of any wound. Perhaps she too had been trying to reach the cantonments, and perhaps there were other English fugitives hiding in the shadows—or mutineers, hunting them down.

The latter thought was an alarming one, but a moment's consideration convinced Sita that any sounds of pursuit would be clearly audible among the thickets of the ruined garden, and that no search would be undertaken without torches to light the way. The night was quiet and the only movements she could hear came from the direction of the road. They could safely wait here.

Tethering the donkey so that it could not wander away, she made a nest among the grasses for the child, and having fed him with the last hoarded fragments of a chuppatti, lulled him to sleep with the whispered story of the valley among the mountains where they would one day live in that flat-roofed house among the fruit trees, and keep a goat and a cow, a puppy and a kitten . . . 'And the donkey,' said Ash drowsily. 'We must take the donkey.'

'Assuredly we will take the donkey, he shall help us carry water jars from the river; and wood for our fire, for when night falls it is cool in the high valleys—cool and pleasant, and the wind that blows through the forests smells of pine-cones and snow and makes a sound that says *"Hush—Hush—Hush"* . . .' Ash sighed happily and was asleep.

Sita waited patiently hour after hour until the glow in the sky died down and the stars began to pale, and then smelling the approach of dawn, she roused the sleeping child and stole out of the Kudsia Bagh to complete the last lap of their long journey to the cantonments of Delhi.

There was no one on the road now. It lay grey and empty and deep in dust, and though the air was cool from the river and the long reaches of wet sand, it was tainted with the smell of smoke and a faint reek of corruption, while the silence magnified every small sound: the snap of a dead twig underfoot, the click of a stone struck by the donkey's hooves and Sita's own short uneven breathing. It seemed to her that their progress must be audible a mile away, and she began to urge the donkey to greater speed, kicking its furry sides with her bare heels and exhorting it in a breathless whisper to hurry —hurry.

The last time she and the child had come this way they had driven in a carriage and the distance between the Kashmir Gate and the cantonments had seemed a very short one; but now it seemed endless, and long before they reached the crest of the ridge the sky was grey with the first hint of morning, and the black, shapeless masses to the left and right of the road had resolved themselves into rocks and stunted thorn trees. It was easier once the road began to descend; they made better time on the downward slope, and the silence reassured Sita. If the inhabitants of the cantonment could sleep so peacefully there could be nothing wrong and the trouble must be over—or else it had never reached here.

There were no lights at this hour, and roads, bungalows and gardens lay quiet in the dawn. But the smell of burning was suddenly stronger, and it was not the familiar smell of charcoal or dung fires, but the harsher smell of smouldering beams and thatch, of scorched earth and brickwork.

It was still too dark to make out more than the outline of trees and bungalows, and though the tripping tap of the donkey's hooves was now clearly audible on the harder surface of a made road, no one challenged them, and it seemed that the sentries too were asleep.

The Abuthnots' bungalow lay on the near side of the cantonment in a quiet, tree-shaded road, and Sita found it without much difficulty. Dismounting at the gate she lifted the boy down and began to pull at the knots of her bundle.

'What are you doing?' inquired Ash, interested. He hoped that she meant to produce something for him to eat, for he was hungry. But Sita was unpacking the sailor suit that she had meant to put on him in the house of Daya Ram's cousin, the grain merchant. It was not fitting that the 'Burra-Sahib's' son should be presented to his father's people in the dusty, travel-stained garments of a street-arab, and at least she would see that he was properly clothed. The suit would be crumpled but it was clean, and the shoes well polished; and surely the Memsahib would understand and forgive the lack of pressing?

Ash sighed resignedly and allowed himself to be hurried into the hated sailor suit without protest. He seemed to have grown a lot since he last wore it, for it was uncomfortably tight, and when it came to putting on the strapped European shoes he found it impossible to force his feet into them.

'You are not trying, *piara* (dear),' scolded Sita, almost in tears between weariness and vexation. 'Push hard—harder.'

But it was no use, and she had to let him tread down the heels and wear them as though they had been slippers. The white sailor hat with its wide blue ribbon had not been improved by its long sojourn in the bundle, but she straightened it with an anxious hand and carefully adjusted the elastic band under his chin.

'Now you are altogether a Sahib, Heart-of-my-heart,' whispered Sita, kissing him. She wiped away a tear with the corner of her sari, and tying up his discarded clothing in her bundle, came to her feet and led him up the drive towards the house.

The garden was already silver-grey in the first pale wash of the dawn, and the Abuthnots' bungalow stood out clear-cut and distinct —and quiet. So quiet that as they approached it they heard a quick patter of paws on matting as a dark shape appeared out of the blackness of an open doorway, and scuttling down the verandah, loped away across the lawn. It was not a Sahib's dog, or even one of the pariah-dogs that haunted the cantonment bazaars, but a hyena, its high, humped shoulders and grotesquely stunted hind-quarters unmistakable in the growing light . . .

Sita stood still, her heart once again racing in panic. She could hear the receding rustle of leaves as the hyena vanished among the bushes, and the steady munching of the donkey by the gate. But there was still no sound from the house, or from the servants' quarters behind it, where surely someone should be awake and stirring. Where was the *chowkidar,* the night watchman who should have been guarding the bungalow? Her eye was caught by a small white object that lay on the gravel almost at her feet, and she stooped slowly and picked it up. It was a high-heeled satin shoe such as she had seen the memsahibs wear in the evenings for balls or *burra khanas,** an incongruous object to find lying discarded on the front drive at that hour—or any hour.

Sita's frightened gaze darted over the lawns and flower-beds and she saw for the first time that there were other objects littering the garden: books, pieces of broken china, torn fragments of clothing, a stocking . . . She dropped the satin slipper, and turning, ran back to the gate dragging Ash with her, and thrust him into the shadows of the pepper tree.

'Stay there, *piara,*' ordered Sita in a voice that Ash had never heard her use before. 'Get back—get down into the shadows and do not make a noise. I will see first who is in the bungalow, and then I will come back for you. As you love me, make no sound.'

'Will you bring something to eat?' asked Ash, anxiously, adding with a sigh: 'I'm *so* hungry.'

'Yes, yes. I will find something. I promise you. Only stay quiet.'

Leaving him, she went across the garden, and gathering all her courage, stole up the verandah steps and into the silent house. There was no one there. The dark, empty rooms were littered with broken furniture and the debris left by men who had looted anything of value and wantonly destroyed anything and everything else. The servants' quarters too were deserted, and there had evidently been an attempt to set fire to the bungalow, but the flames had not caught, and behind the broken door of the larder there was still a quantity of food that no one had bothered to steal, perhaps because the caste of the looters prevented them from touching such stuff.

Under other circumstances Sita might have had similar qualms. But now she filled the torn half of a tablecloth with as much as she could conveniently carry. There was bread and cold curry, a bowl of *dal* and the remains of a rice pudding, some boiled potatoes and a

* big dinner-parties

quantity of fresh fruit, a jam tart and half a plum cake as well as several varieties of biscuits. There was also milk, but it was sour, and various tinned foods that were too heavy to carry. But among a welter of broken wine bottles was one that had escaped destruction, and though it was empty there were plenty of corks, and she filled it with cold water from an earthenware *chatti* outside the kitchen and hurried back to Ash.

The sky was growing lighter every minute and soon yesterday's looters, the *budmarshes** from the bazaars, would wake after their night's rioting and come back to see if there was anything they had overlooked. It was unsafe to remain here a moment longer, but first she must strip off that betraying sailor suit; and she did so with hands that trembled with anxiety and haste.

Ash did not understand why she had taken all the trouble to dress him in it only to take it off again, but he was thankful to be out of it, and relieved to see that he would not have to wear it again, for Sita left it lying under the pepper tree. He ate his way solidly through a lump of cold rice pudding while Sita filled her brass *lotah* from a little well among the trampled oleander bushes and drew water in a leather bucket for the donkey, and when that was done they mounted again and set off in the pearl-grey light of a new day towards the Grand Trunk Road that stretches northward towards Kurnal and the Punjab.

The donkey would have kept to the level roads of the cantonment, but now that the sky was brighter Sita could see that most of the bungalows had been gutted by fire, and that smoke from a score of smouldering ruins still rose in ghostly columns above the scorched trees. It was a sight that increased her fears, and rather than cross the cantonment area she turned towards the Ridge and the dark bulk of the Flagstaff Tower, where the Delhi road ran northward to join the Grand Trunk.

Looking back from the crest of the Ridge it was difficult to believe that the once busy cantonment that lay below them was now a desolate shell, for the trees provided a kindly screen and the lazy smoke that drifted up to form a haze above it might have been the smoke of kitchen fires, cooking breakfast for the vanished garrison. On the far side of the Ridge the ground sloped down to merge into the level plain through which the silver ribbon of the Jumna wandered be-

* bad characters; riff-raff

tween white sandbanks and a wide belt of croplands, while a mile and a half away—a shadow on the shadowy plain—lay the domes and walls of Delhi, afloat on the morning mists that were rising off the river. A long white road, straight as a sword blade, led from the Flagstaff Tower to the Kashmir Gate, but at that hour nothing moved on it, not even the wind. The air was still and the world so quiet that Sita could hear, from far, far away, the crowing of a cock in some village beyond the Najafgarh canal.

The Ridge too was deserted, though even here the mute evidence of panic littered the ground: a child's shoe, a doll, a woman's rose-trimmed and beribboned bonnet hanging on a thorn bush, toys, books, bundles and boxes lost in the darkness or discarded in the frenzy of flight, and a dog-cart lying on its side in the ditch with a broken wheel and smashed shafts. The night dew lay thick on everything, bejewelling the wreckage and dipping the grasses in a film of silver; but the first hot breath of the coming day was already drying the dew, and birds had begun to chirp and twitter among the thorn-scrub.

There was no one in the Flagstaff Tower, but here the debris lay thicker, and around it the trampled ground bore signs that a small army of women and children, officers, servants and horse-drawn vehicles had camped there for hours and left only recently; for there were carriage-lamps on the dog-cart, and one of them was still burning. The marks of wheels, hoof-prints and footmarks showed that those who had been there had fled northwards towards Kurnal, and Sita would have followed them, but for one thing . . .

Fifty yards beyond the tower, on the road that led north past the Sudder Bazaar to the cut where it turns right-handed onto the Grand Trunk Road, stood an abandoned cart loaded with what at first sight appeared to be women's clothes. And once again, as on the previous night, the donkey jibbed and would not pass it. It was this that made Sita look closer, and now she saw that there were bodies in the cart: the dead bodies of four Sahibs dressed in scarlet uniforms and hideously mutilated, over which someone had hurriedly thrown a woman's flowered muslin dress and a frilled petticoat in a vain attempt at concealment. The flowers on the dress were forget-me-nots and rosebuds and the petticoat had once been white; but both were now blotched with dark brown stains, for the gay scarlet uniforms had been slashed with sword cuts and were stiff with dried blood.

A single hand, lacking a thumb but still wearing a signet ring that no one had thought to remove, protruded stiffly from among the muslin folds, and staring at it, flinching away, like the animal she rode, from the smell of death, Sita abandoned any idea of following in the wake of the British.

The stories of the men on the bridge, the sight of the dead memsahib in the Kudsia Bagh and even the desolation of the cantonments, had not succeeded in bringing home to her the reality of the situation. It was a rising; riot, arson and *gurrh-burrh*.* She had heard of such outbreaks often enough, though she had never been involved in them. But the Sahib-log had always put them down, and once they were over those who had caused them were hanged or transported, and the Sahib-log were still there, with their power and their numbers greater than before. But the dead men in the cart had been Sahibs—officers of the Company's army—and their fellow Sahibs had been in such fear and haste that they had not even paused to bury their comrades before they fled. They had merely flung some memsahib's clothes onto the cart to hide the faces of the dead and then run away, leaving the bodies to the mercy of crows and vultures and any passing ruffian who might choose to strip them of their uniforms. There could be no safety any longer with the Sahib-log, and she must take Ash-Baba away, somewhere far away from both Delhi and the British . . .

They turned and went back down the road they had just come by and crossed the ruined cantonments, past blackened roofless bungalows, trampled gardens, the gutted barracks and bells of arms, and the quiet cemetery where the British dead lay in neat rows under the alien soil. The donkey's small hooves sounded a hollow, tripping tattoo on the bridge over the Najafgarh canal, and a flight of parrots that had been drinking from a puddle in the dry cut flew up in a green, screaming explosion of sound. But they were clear of the cantonment now and out in the open country; and suddenly the world was no longer grey and still, but yellow with dawn and noisy with birdsong and the chatter of squirrels.

Beyond the canal the path narrowed to a track between sugar cane and tall grass, and presently it met the broad level of the Grand Trunk Road. But instead of turning down it, they crossed over it and followed a field path towards the little village of Dahipur. Without the donkey they could not have gone far, but once out of sight of the

* uproar, tumult

highroad, Sita dismounted and walked, and in this way they put several miles between themselves and Delhi before the sun became too hot. Their progress had been slower than it might have been, for Sita was still actively aware of danger and made constant detours in order to avoid villages and casual wayfarers. It was true that Ash-Baba had inherited his mother's black hair and that the open-air life of the camp had burned his already brown skin as dark as any Indian's, but his eyes were agate-grey, and who was to say that some suspicious passer-by would not recognize him as a white child and kill him for the sake of blood-money? One could also never be certain what a child would say or do, and she would not feel safe until Delhi and the mutineers from Meerut were many days' march behind her.

The crops as yet provided little cover, but the plain was seamed and scored with dry gullies, and there were thickets of thorn and elephant grass that offered adequate hiding-places even for the donkey. Yet here too the English had passed, for a buzzing cloud of flies betrayed the body of an elderly Eurasian, probably a clerk from one of the Government offices, hidden in a patch of grass by the side of the path. He too, like the fat woman in the Kudsia Bagh, had crawled into the grass and died there; but unlike her he had been so sorely wounded that it was astonishing that he should have been able to drag himself so far.

It disturbed Sita to find that others too had attempted to escape across country instead of taking the road to Kurnal. The sight of such wretched fugitives would only serve to bring news of the rising to previously peaceful villages, and kindle scorn of the *feringhis* (foreigners) and support for the rebellious sepoys, and she had hoped by taking this route to out-distance the news from Delhi. Now it seemed as though she had set herself an impossible task, for the man who had died in the grass had quite obviously been there since the previous day, and it looked as though someone must have helped him to get that far—the same person who had carefully spread a handkerchief over his face before leaving him to the flies and the eaters of carrion. Sita dragged the reluctant donkey past, and distracted Ash's attention and her own anguished thoughts by embarking on his favourite story of the secret valley, and of how they would find it someday and live happily ever after.

Towards nightfall they were well off the beaten track, and she judged it safe enough to stop at a village whose twinkling lights promised a bazaar and the prospect of hot food and fresh milk. Ash-

Baba was tired and sleepy and therefore less likely to talk, while the donkey too needed food and water, and she herself was very weary. They slept that night in a lean-to shed belonging to a hospitable cultivator, which they shared with the donkey and the cultivator's cow, Sita representing herself as the wife of a blacksmith from Jullunder way, returning from Agra with an orphaned nephew, the son of her husband's brother. She bought hot food and buffalo-milk in the bazaar, where she heard a variety of frightening rumours—each one worse than the last—and later, when Ash was asleep, she joined a group of gossiping villagers on the edge of the threshing-ground.

Sitting well back among the shadows, she listened to stories of the rising, the tale having reached here that morning, brought by a party of Gujars and confirmed in the late afternoon by five sepoys of the 54th Native Infantry, who had joined the mutineers at the Kashmir Gate on the previous day, and were now on their way to Sirdana and Mazafnagar to carry the news that the Company's power was broken at last, and that once again a Mogul ruled as King in Delhi. The tale had lost nothing in the telling; and hearing it retold by the elders of the village, after all she herself had seen since the men of the 3rd Cavalry galloped past her on the Meerut road, Sita believed it.

All the English in Meerut had been put to the sword, said the elders, confirming the words of the sowars on the bridge of boats, and in Delhi too all had been slain—both in the city and the cantonments. And not only in Delhi and Meerut, either, for the regiments had risen throughout Hind, and soon there would be no *feringhis* left alive in all the land—not so much as a single child. Those who had tried to save themselves by flight were being hunted down and killed, while any who thought to hide themselves in the jungles would be slain by wild beasts—if they did not first perish from hunger and thirst and exposure. Their day was done. They were gone like dust before the wind, and not one would be left to carry the tale of their going. The shame of Plassey* was avenged and the hundred years of subjection at an end—and now there was no need to pay the taxes.

'Is Esh-mitt Sahib also dead, then?' asked an awestruck voice, presumably referring to a local District Officer who was, in all probability, the only white man whom the villagers had ever seen.

* The battle that gained India for Clive and the East India Company in 1757. (There was a legend that the rule of the Company would only last a hundred years from that date.)

'Assuredly. For on Friday—so Durga Dass says—he rode to Delhi to see the Commissioner-Sahib, and did not the sepoy with the pock-marked face say that all the *Angrezi-log* in Delhi were slain? It is certain that he is dead. He and all others of his accursed race.'

Sita listened and believed, and stealing away into the darkness she returned hastily to the bazaar, where she bought a small earthenware bowl and the ingredients for making a brown dye that was equally effective and hard-wearing on the human skin as on cotton cloth. Soaked overnight it had been ready by morning, and long before the village was awake she roused Ash, and leading him out into the dim light of dawn, crouched behind a cactus hedge where she stripped him and applied the dye with a cotton rag, working by touch as much as sight and whispering urgently that he was to tell no one, and to remember that from now on his name was Ashok: 'You will not forget, Heart-of-my-heart? Ashok—promise me you will not forget?'

'Is it a game?' asked Ash, intrigued.

'Yes, yes, a game. We will play that your name is Ashok and that you are my son. My true son: your father being dead—which the gods know is true. What is your name, son?'

'Ashok.'

Sita kissed him passionately, and adjuring him again not to answer questions, took him back to the shed. After eating a frugal meal and paying for their night's lodging, they set out across the fields, and by mid-day the village was far behind them and Delhi and the Meerut road only an ugly memory. 'We will go north. Perhaps to Mardan,' said Sita. 'We shall be safe in the north.'

'In the valley?' asked Ash. 'Are we going to our valley?'

'Not yet, my King. One day surely. But that too lies in the north, so we will go northward.'

It was as well for them that they did so, for behind them the land was ablaze with violence and terror. In Agra and Alipore, Neemuch, Nusserabad and Lucknow, throughout Rohilkhand, Central India and Bundelkhand, in cities and cantonments up and down the country, men rose against the British.

At Cawnpore the Nana, the adopted son of the late Peshwa, whom the authorities had refused to recognize, turned on his oppressors and besieged them in their tragically inadequate entrenchments; and when after twenty days the survivors accepted his offer of safe conduct, and were herded onto river boats that they were told would take them to Allahabad, the boats were set alight and fired upon from the bank. Those who managed to struggle to shore were taken prisoner, the men shot, while some two hundred women and children—all who remained of a garrison that at the beginning of the siege had numbered a thousand—were penned up in a small building, the *Bibi-gurh* (women's house), where they were later hacked to death on the orders of the Nana, and their bodies thrown into a near-by well, the dying with the dead.

In Jhansi that same royal widow whose wrongs Hilary had written of in his last report—Lakshmi-Bai, the beautiful childless Rani who had been refused the right to adopt a son and disinherited by the East India Company—avenged herself for those wrongs by massacring another British garrison unwise enough to surrender to her on her promise of safe conduct.

'Why do the people put up with it?' Hilary had asked Akbar Khan. 'Why don't they do something?' Lakshmi-Bai, the unforgiving, had done something. She had repaid the bitter injustice dealt her by the Governor-General and Council of the Honourable the East India Company with a deed no less unjust. For not only the men, but the wives and children of those who had accepted her offer of safe conduct had been roped together and publicly butchered: children, women and men, in that order . . .

'John Company' had sown the wind. But many who must reap the whirlwind were as blameless and bewildered as Sita and Ash-Baba, blown helplessly before the gale like two small and insignificant sparrows on a wild day of storm.

3

It was October and the leaves were turning gold when they came to Gulkote, a tiny principality near the northern borders of the Punjab, where the plains lose themselves in the foothills that fringe the Pir Panjal.

They had come slowly, and for the most part on foot, for the donkey had been commandeered by a party of sepoys in the last days of May, and the hot weather had made travelling impossible except in the cool of the morning before the sun rose, or after it had set.

The sepoys had been men of the 38th Native Infantry, a regiment that had disintegrated on the day that the sowars of the 3rd Cavalry rode in from Meerut. They had been returning to their homes laden with loot, and were full of tales of the rising, among them the story of how the last of the *feringhis* in Delhi, the two men and fifty women and children who had been imprisoned in the King's palace, had met their end:

'It is necessary to rid the land of all foreigners,' explained the speaker, 'but we of the army refused to turn butcher and slaughter women and babes who were half dead already from fear and hunger and many days of confinement in the dark. Some of the King's household also spoke out against it, saying that it was contrary to the tenets of the Muslim faith to slay women and children or other prisoners of war; but when Miza Majhli tried to save them, the mob cried for his blood, and in the end the King's servants took swords and slew them all.'

'*All?*' faltered Sita. 'But—but what harm would children have done? Could they not at least have spared the little ones?'

'Bah! It is foolish to spare the young of a serpent,' scoffed the sepoy; and Sita quaked anew for Ash-Baba, that embryo serpent playing happily in the dust only a yard or two away.

'That is true,' agreed one of his comrades, 'for they grow up and bred more of their kind. It was well done to rid ourselves of so many who would in their turn have become thieves and oppressors.' Whereupon he commandeered the donkey, and when Sita protested, struck her down with the butt of his musket while a second man picked up Ash, who had rushed to her defence like a small tiger-cat, and flung him into a patch of thorn-scrub. Ash had been severely scratched, and when he crawled out at last bruised, torn and sobbing, it was to find Sita lying unconscious by the roadside and sepoys and donkey already small in the distance.

That had been a black day. But at least the men had not taken Sita's bundle, and there was some consolation in that. Possibly it never occurred to them that the humble possessions of a ragged child and a lone woman could include anything worth taking, and they were not to know that at least half of the coins that Hilary had kept in a tin box under his bed were in a wash-leather bag at the bottom of the bundle. Sita had removed it as soon as she recovered consciousness and could think clearly again, and added it to the other half that she kept in a fold of cloth tied about her waist under her sari. It made a heavy and uncomfortable belt, but was probably safer there than in the bundle; and now that the donkey had been taken, she would in any case have to carry both.

The theft of the donkey had been a grievous blow; as much on sentimental grounds as practical ones, for Ash had grown fond of the little animal and mourned its loss long after even the worst of the scratches had healed and been forgotten. But that incident, and the sepoy's stories, served to underline the dangers of using the roadways that ran between towns and the larger villages, and the wisdom of keeping instead to the cattle tracks of the Mofussil and the little lost villages where life pursued a slow, centuries-old course, and news from the outside world seldom penetrated.

Now and again a ripple from the far-off storm would lap against even such remote fastnesses as these, and they would hear stories of wounded and starving Sahib-log hiding in the jungle or among the rocks, and creeping out to beg food from the meanest passer-by. Once, following a rumour of successful risings throughout Oude and Rohilkund, there had been a tale of mutiny and massacre in Ferozepore and far-off Sialkot, and it was this last that made Sita finally abandon a nebulous plan that she had briefly entertained, of taking Ash-Baba to Mardan where his mother's brother would be stationed with the Guides. For if the regiments in Ferozepore and Sialkot had also mutinied, then what hope would there be for the British in any cantonment town anywhere? If there were still any left alive (which seemed doubtful) they would all soon be dead: all except Ash-Baba, who was now her son Ashok.

Sita never again referred to him as anything but 'my son', and Ash accepted the relationship without question. Within a week he had forgotten that it had begun as a game, or that he had ever called her anything but 'mother'.

As they journeyed further north, skirting the folds of the Sawaliks, the rumours of rising and unrest became fewer, and the talk was only of crops and the harvest and the local problems and gossip of small rural communities whose horizons are bounded by their own fields. The blazing days of June ended in a torrential downpour of rain as the monsoon swept across the parched plains of India, turning the fields to bogs and every ditch and nullah into a river, and reducing each day's journey to a minimum. It was no longer possible to sleep out in the open and shelter had to be found—and paid for.

Sita begrudged the money, for it was a sacred charge and not to be expended lightly. It belonged to Ash-Baba and must be kept for him until he was grown. There was also the danger of appearing too affluent and thereby inviting attack and robbery, so it must be spent in the smallest coins only and to the accompaniment of hard bargaining. She bought, too, a yard of coarse, country-made *puttoo* (tweed) to keep the rain from Ash, though she was well aware that he would have preferred to dispense with this protection and go bare-headed as well as unshod. Ash's paternal grandmother had been a Scotswoman from the west coast of Argyll, and possibly it was her blood in his veins that made him take a particular pleasure in the feel of rain on his face, though it may well have been no more than any child's partiality for splashing through mud and puddles.

Constant exposure to the monsoon had succeeded in washing away most of the dye from his skin, and he was once again a colour that would have been familiar to Hilary and Akbar Khan. But though Sita was aware of this she did not renew the dye, since by now they were close to the foothills of the Himalayas, and hill-folk being fairer-skinned than the men of the south (many of them having light-coloured eyes, blue, grey or hazel, and hair that is as often red or brown as black), her son Ashok aroused no comment and was, indeed, somewhat swarthier than many of the pale-skinned Hindu children with whom he played in the villages by the way. Her fears for his safety were gradually diminishing and she no longer lived in terror that he might betray himself by some unguarded mention of the 'Burra-Sahib' and the old days, because he appeared to have forgotten them.

But Ash had not forgotten: it was just that he did not wish to think or speak of the past. He was, in many ways, a precocious child, for children ripen early in the East, being reckoned men and women at an age when their brothers and sisters in the West are still in the junior forms at school. No one had ever treated him as anything but an equal or kept him immured in a nursery atmosphere. He had had the run of his father's camp from the moment he could crawl, and lived his short life among adults who had, by and large, treated him as an adult—though a privileged one, because they loved him. Had it not been for Hilary and Akbar Khan, he would probably have been spoiled. But though their methods had differed, they had both taken pains to prevent his becoming a pampered brat, Hilary because he could not have endured whining or tantrums and preferred his son to behave from the first as an intelligent human being, and Akbar Khan because he intended the boy to be a commander of armies, a man whom men would one day follow to the death, and such are not the products of a spoilt and over-indulged childhood.

Sita had been the only one who ever spoke to him in baby-talk or sang him childish songs, for Akbar Khan had early impressed it upon him that he was a man and must not allow himself to be molly-coddled. So the songs and the baby-talk had been a secret between Ash and his foster-mother, and it was partly because they shared that secret that he accepted the necessity of keeping other things se-cret, and had not betrayed them both at the start of their ill-fated journey to Delhi. Sita had told him that he must not talk of the 'Burra-Sahib' and Uncle Akbar, or the camp and all the things they were leaving behind them, and he had obeyed her, but as much from shock and bewilderment as obedience to her wishes. The swiftness with which his world had dissolved, and the incomprehensible man-ner of its going, was a black pool of shadow into which he would not look for fear of seeing things he did not want to remember: dreadful things, like Uncle Akbar being thrust into a hole in the ground and the earth piled over him; and the almost worse shock of seeing the 'Burra-Sahib' weeping over that rough mound, when how many times had both he and Uncle Akbar said that tears were only for women?

It was better to turn one's back on such things and refuse to recall them; and Ash had done just that. Sita's urgings had been unneces-sary, for even had she wished him to speak of the past it is unlikely that she could, under any circumstances, have persuaded him to do so. As it was, she imagined that he had forgotten it, and was grateful for the shortness of a child's memory.

Her chief anxiety now was the quest for some peaceful back-water, sufficiently remote from the bustling cities and the highroads of Hind to remain ignorant of such matters as the rise or fall of the Company. A place small enough to escape the eyes of those who would now be in authority, yet large enough to absorb a woman and a child without their arrival attracting attention or arousing curiosity. Somewhere where she could find work and they could settle down and begin life again, and find peace and contentment and freedom from fear. Her own home village did not fall into this category, because there she would be known and her return lead to endless speculation and questioning by her own and her husband's family; and inevitably, the truth would leak out. For the boy's sake she could not risk that: and for her own also. She could hardly conceal Daya Ram's death from his parents, and once that was known, she would be forced to conduct herself as a widow, a childless widow, should; and there were few worse fates in India, for such women were considered to be responsible for their husbands' death, it being believed that some misconduct in a previous life had brought misfortune on their men.

A widow must never wear colours or jewellery, but shave her head and dress only in white. She could not marry again, but must end her days as an unpaid drudge in her husband's family, despised on account of her sex and resented as the bringer of bad luck. It was not surprising that in the days before the law of the Company had forbidden it, many widows had preferred to become suttees and burn themselves alive on their husband's funeral pyres rather than face the bitterness of long years of servitude and humiliation. But a stranger in a strange town could adopt any identity she chose, and who was to know that Sita was a widow—or care? She could pretend that her husband had taken work in the south, or run off and left her. What did it matter? She could hold up her head as the mother of a son, and wear gay colours and glass bangles and her few modest pieces of jewellery. And when she found work she would be working for the boy and herself, and not as an unpaid slave for Daya Ram's family.

Several times during the months that followed their escape from Delhi, Sita thought she had discovered the right place: the haven where they could end their wanderings and find work and safety. But each time there had been something that drove her on: the arrival of an armed band of sepoys from some regiment that had risen against its officers, and who were roaming the country in search of English fugitives; the sight of a family of starving *feringhis,* who had been given shelter by a kindly villager, being dragged out of hiding and put to death by a jeering mob; a passing traveller flaunting a murdered officer's uniform, or half a dozen sowars galloping through the crops . . .

'Aren't we ever going to stop *anywhere?*' inquired Ash wistfully.

June gave place to July, and July to August. And now the crop-lands were behind them and there was only jungle ahead. But Sita and Ash were both used to jungles. The silence and the hot, wet thickets held fewer terrors for them than the villages, and the jungle provided them with edible roots and berries, water and fuel, and shade from the heat as well as shelter from the rain.

Once, walking down a game-track through high grass, they had come face to face with a tiger. But the great beast was full fed and peaceably disposed, and after exchanging a long, surprised stare with the intruders, it had turned aside without haste and vanished into the grass. Sita had not moved for five long minutes, until the scolding chatter of a jungle-cock some thirty yards to their right told her the direction in which the tiger had gone; and then she had turned back and made a detour that took them away from the grass. It was astonishing that they had not lost themselves in those trackless miles of trees and thickets, elephant grass, bamboos, rocks and creepers. But here Sita's unerring sense of direction helped them, and as they were heading for no particular goal, but merely moving hopefully northward, it did not matter very much which path they chose.

By the end of August they had won free of the jungle and were in open country once more, and with September the monsoon slackened. The sun was once again cruelly hot and clouds of mosquitoes rose each evening from the flooded *jheels* and brimming ponds and ditches. But at the edge of the plain and beyond the foothills the high ridges of the Himalayas rose clear and blue above the heat-haze, and the night air held a hint of coolness. Here, in the scattered hamlets, they heard no rumours of strife and insurrection, for now there were few footpaths and no roads, and the land was sparsely populated; the villages consisting of no more than a huddle of huts and a few acres of cultivation, surrounded by miles of rock-strewn grazing ground that was bounded on the one side by jungles and on the other by foothills.

Always, on clear days, they could see the snow peaks, and the sight of them was a constant reminder to Sita that time was running out and that the winter was coming, and that it was necessary for them to find a roof to live under before the cold weather set in. But there was little chance of employment for herself or a hopeful future for Ashok in such country as this, and though she was tired and footsore and desperately weary of travelling she was not tempted to linger in it. They had come a long way since the April morning when they had turned their backs on Hilary's silent camp and set out for Delhi, and they were both sorely in need of rest. And then, in October, when the leaves were turning gold, they came to Gulkote, and Sita realized that here at last was the spot she had been looking for. A place where they could hide and be safe.

The independent State of Gulkote had been too small, too difficult of access and above all too poor to interest the Governor-General and the officials of the East India Company. And as its standing army consisted of less than a hundred soldiers—the majority elderly greybeards equipped with tulwars and rusty jezails—and its ruler appeared to be popular with his subjects and displayed no disposition to be hostile, the Company had left him in peace.

The capital city, from which the state took its name, stood some five thousand feet above sea-level, at the apex of a great triangular plateau among the foothills. It had once been a fortified town and it was still surrounded by a massive wall that enclosed a rabbit warren of houses, a single main street that bisected these from the Lahori Gate on the south to the *Lal Dawaza,* the 'Red Gate', on the north, three temples, a mosque and a maze of narrow alleyways. The whole was overlooked by the Rajah's rambling fortress-palace, the Hawa Mahal—the 'Palace of the Winds' that crowned a towering outcrop of rock some thousand yards beyond the city wall.

The ruling house traced its descent from a Rajput chieftain who had come north in the reign of Sikander Lodi, and stayed to carve out a kingdom for himself and his followers. The kingdom had shrunk with the centuries, until by the time the Punjab fell to the Sikhs under Ranjit Singh, it had been reduced to no more than a handful of villages in a territory that a man on horse-back could traverse in a single day. That it had survived at all was probably due to the fact that its present frontiers were bounded on one side by an unbridged river, on another by a dense track of forest and on the third by a waste of rock-strewn country scored by deep ravines, whose ruler was related to the Rajah; while at its back the wrinkled, wooded foothills swept upwards to meet the white peaks of the Dur Khaima and the great snow-capped range that protects Gulkote from the north. It would have been difficult to move an army against such a strategically placed spot, and as there had never been a sufficiently urgent reason to do so, it had escaped the attentions of the Moguls, Mahrattas, Sikhs and the East India Company, and lived serenely remote from the changing world of the nineteenth century.

The ramshackle town had been in a festive mood on the day that Ash and Sita reached it, there having been a distribution of largess from the palace in the form of food and sweetmeats for the poor, in celebration of the birth of a child to the Senior Rani. It had been a modest celebration, for the child was a daughter, but the citizens were disposed to use it as an excuse for a holiday: feasting, making merry and decorating their houses with garlands and paper flags. Little boys threw *patarkars*—home-made squibs—among the feet of the passers-by in the crowded bazaars, and after dark the thin fire of rockets soared into the night sky to blossom above the rooftops where the women-folk clustered like flocks of chattering birds.

To Sita and Ash, accustomed through long months to silence and solitude—or at best the humble society of small villages—the colour and noise of the jostling, lighthearted crowds were exhilarating beyond words, and they ate of the Rajah's bounty and admired the fireworks, and found lodgings for themselves in the house of a fruit-seller in an alley off the Chandi Bazaar.

'Can we stay here?' asked Ash sleepily, surfeited with sweetmeats and excitement. 'I like it here.'

'I too, little son. Yes, we shall stay here. I will find work and we shall stay and be happy. Yet I wish . . .' Sita stopped on a sigh and did not finish the sentence. Her conscience troubled her, because she had not obeyed the Burra-Sahib's order to return his son to his own people. But she did not know what else she could have done. Perhaps one day, when her boy was a man . . . But for the present they were both weary of wandering, and here they would at least be among the mountains—and safe. An hour or so in the town had convinced her of that last, for in all the talk in the bazaars and the gossip of the loitering, chattering crowds, there had been no word of the troubles that were shaking India, or any mention of mutineers or Sahib-log.

Gulkote was only interested in its own affairs and the latest scandals of the palace. It paid little or no attention to the doings of the world beyond its borders, and at the moment its main topic of conversation (apart from the perennial one of crops and taxes) was the eclipse of the Senior Rani by the concubine, Janoo, a *Nautch*-girl (dancer) from Kashmir, who had acquired such a hold over the jaded monarch that she had recently succeeded in persuading him to marry her.

Janoo-Bai was suspected of practising magic and the black arts. How else could a common dancing-girl have raised herself to the rank of Rani, and ousted from favour the mother of the baby princess, who had reigned undisputed for at least three years? She was known to be both beautiful and ruthless, and the sex of the new baby at the palace was taken as further proof of her malignant powers. 'She is a witch,' said Gulkote. 'Assuredly she is a witch. They at the palace say that it was by her orders that food and sweetmeats were distributed to the hungry to mark the birth of this child, for she rejoices that it is not a son, and would have her rival know it. Now if she herself were to bear a son . . . !'

Sita listened to the talk and was reassured by it; there was nothing here that spelt danger to Ashok, son of Daya Ram, syce, who (so she informed the fruit-seller's wife) had run off with a shameless gipsy woman, leaving her to fend for herself and the child.

Her story had not been questioned, and later she had found work in a shop in Khanna Lal's Gully behind the temple of Ganesh, helping to fashion the gaudy paper and tinsel flowers that are used in garlands and for decorations at weddings and festivals. The work was ill paid, but it sufficed for their needs; and as she had always been quick with her fingers, it was not uncongenial. She was also able to earn a little extra by weaving baskets for the fruit-seller and occasionally helping in the shop.

As soon as they had settled in, Sita dug a hole in the mud floor of their little room and buried the money that Hilary had given her, stamping down the earth and smoothing cow-dung over the whole surface so that no one could tell where it had been disturbed. There remained only the small packet of letters and papers in its oiled-silk wrapping, and this she would have liked to burn. For though she could not read them, she was aware that they must constitute proof of Ash's parentage, and both fear and jealousy urged her to destroy them. If they were found they might lead to his being killed, as the children of the Sahib-log had been killed at Delhi and Jhansi and Cawnpore and a score of other cities, and her own life might well be forfeit for having tried to save him. Even if he escaped that penalty, they still proved that he was not her son; and by now she could not bear the thought of this. Yet she could not bring herself to destroy them, for they too were a sacred trust: the 'Burra-Sahib' had given them into her hand, and were she to burn them his ghost or his God might be angry with her and take revenge for the act. It was better to keep them; but they must never be seen by any other eyes, and if the white ants destroyed them it would not be her fault.

Sita scraped a shallow cavity low down in the wall in the darkest corner of the room, and thrusting the packet into it, covered its hiding place, as she had covered the money, with clay and cow-dung; and having done so, felt that a crushing weight had been lifted off her shoulders and that Ashok was now truly hers.

The boy's grey eyes and ruddy complexion caused no comment in Gulkote, for many of the Rajah's subjects had come from Kashmir, Kulu and the Hindu Kush, and Sita herself was a hill-woman. Ash fraternized with their sons and grandsons and was soon indistinguishable, except to the eye of love, from a hundred other bad little bazaar boys who shouted, frolicked and fought in the streets of Gulkote; and Sita was content. She still believed what the sepoys had told her: that all the English were dead and the rule of the Company broken for ever. Delhi was far away, and beyond the borders of Gulkote lay the Punjab, which had remained relatively quiet; and though an occasional rumour of troubles would drift through the bazaars, these were always vague, garbled and months out of date, and mostly concerned with disasters to the British . . .

None told of the army that had been hurriedly assembled at Ambala. Of the long march of the Guides—eight hundred miles in fourteen days of high summer from Mardan to Delhi—to take part in the siege of that city, of the death of Nicholson, or the surrender of the last Mogul and the slaying of his sons by William Hodson of Hodson's Horse; or that Lucknow was still besieged, and that the great rising that had begun with the revolt of the 3rd Cavalry in Meerut was by no means over.

The *Shaitan-ke-Hawa*—the 'Devil's Wind'—was still blowing strongly through India, but while thousands died, here in sheltered Gulkote the days were slow and peaceful.

*   *   *

Ash had been five years old that October, and it was not until the autumn of the following year of 1858 that Sita learned, through a wandering *sadhu*,* something of what had been happening in the outside world. Delhi and Lucknow re-captured, the Nana Sahib a fugitive, and the valiant Rani of Jhansi killed in battle, dressed as a man and fighting to the last. The Company's rule had been broken, but the *feringhis,* said the *sadhu,* were back in power, stronger than ever and engaged in brutal reprisals against those who had fought them in the great rising. And though the Company was no more, its rule had been replaced by that of the white Rani—Victoria—and all Hind was now a possession of the British Crown, with a British Viceroy and British troops governing the land.

Sita had tried to persuade herself that the man was mistaken, or lying. For if his story was true, she would have to take Ashok back to his people, which by now was a prospect she could no longer face. It *could* not be true . . . or it might not be. She would wait, and do nothing until she was sure. There was no need to do anything yet . . .

She had waited all winter, and in spring there had been news that confirmed everything the *sadhu* had said; but still Sita took no action. Ashok was hers, and she would not, could not, give him up. There had been a time when she could have done so, but that was before she had begun to look on him as her son by right, and see him accepted as such. Besides, it was not as though she were depriving a mother or father of their right: he had lost both, and if anyone had a right to him, surely it was herself? Had she not loved him and cared for him from his birth? Taken him from his mother's womb and fed him at her own breast? He knew no other mother and believed himself to be her child, and she would be robbing no one—*no one.* He was no longer Ash-Baba, but her son, Ashok, and she would burn the papers that lay hidden in the wall and say nothing, and no one would ever know.

So they remained in Gulkote and were happy. But Sita did not burn Hilary's papers, for when it came to the point her fear of what the 'Burra-Sahib's' ghost might do was greater than her fear of what the papers could prove.

Once again there had been feasting and fireworks in the city. But this time it had been in celebration of the birth of a boy to Janoo-Bai the Rani—sometime dancing-girl, and now virtual ruler of Gulkote,

* Hindu holy man

in that she ruled the Rajah to the point where her smallest wish must be gratified.

The Rajah's subjects had been commanded to celebrate and they had done so, though without much enthusiasm; the *Nautch*-girl was not popular with the citizens, and the prospect of a prince of her breeding was displeasing to them. Not that he was the heir, for the Rajah's first wife, who had died in child-birth, had left her lord a son: Lalji, 'the beloved'—the eight-year-old Yuveraj, apple of his father's eye and pride of all Gulkote. But life was uncertain in India and who could say if the boy would live to be a man? His mother, in fifteen years of marriage, had given birth to no less than nine children, all of whom, with the exception of Lalji (and the last—a stillborn daughter), had died in infancy. She herself had not survived that last confinement, and her husband had soon married again, taking as his wife the daughter of a foreign mercenary, a young and lovely girl who became known in Gulkote as the *'Feringhi*-Rani'—the foreign queen.

The *Feringhi*-Rani's father had been a Russian adventurer who had taken service in the armies of various warring Indian princes. Under the last of these, Ranjit Singh, the 'Lion of the Punjab', he had risen to considerable heights; and on the 'Lion's' death, had prudently retired to end his days in the remote and sovereign state of Gulkote. It was rumoured that he had once been an officer of the Cossacks who had been sentenced to life imprisonment for some misdemeanour, but had escaped from his gaolers and found his way to India through the passes of the north. He had certainly shown no desire to return to his native land when Ranjit's death had put an end to his employment in the Punjab, but had lived in comfortable retirement on the accumulated riches of ten years of power, together with a bevy of concubines and his Indian wife, Kumaridevi, the daughter of a Rajput prince whom he had defeated in battle, and whom he had demanded of her father as part of a conqueror's loot— they having seen each other in the sack of the city, and straightway fallen in love.

The *Feringhi*-Rani was this lady's last and only surviving child; born at the cost of her mother's life, since by then the once beautiful princess had been middle-aged and worn out by miscarriages and still-births that were due, in a large part, to the rigours of following her husband on many campaigns. Her daughter had been brought up with a brood of illegitimate half-brothers and sisters, all of whom had considered it a triumph when reports of her beauty had reached the ears of the Rajah of Gulkote, and he had asked for her hand in marriage, knowing that no lesser alliance would have been considered, as on her mother's side her lineage was more royal than his own.

For a time the *Feringhi*-Rani had been happy; none of her half-brothers and sisters or their various mothers had been particularly kind to her, and she had been glad to leave her home for the raffish splendours of the 'Palace of the Winds'. The enmity of the women in the Hawa Mahal had not troubled her over-much, for she was used to the intrigues in Zenanas, and the Rajah was infatuated with her and could refuse her nothing. Nor was she unduly grieved when her father died a year after her marriage, for he had never paid much attention to his numerous offspring. If she had any regrets they were solely on account of her childlessness, though she did not desire children with the single-minded fervour of purely Eastern women, and was in any case sure that it was only a matter of time before they appeared. But the avid interest, jealousy and triumph of the other women over this sore subject (together with their gloating hints that she—'the half-caste'—was barren) piqued her, and she began to worry over it and be impatient for the day when she too should bear a child—a son. Because of course it must be a son.

So far, of all the Rajah's women, only his first wife had born him sons, and of these only one had lived. But one son was no good to a man; he should have many, so that whatever happened, the succession was secure. It was therefore her duty as chief lady of the palace, and his heart, to produce those sons for him, and she was delighted when she at last became pregnant. But perhaps it was her foreign blood that made her react to pregnancy less happily than other women appeared to do, for instead of blooming into further beauty, as they did, she became subject to incessant attacks of vomiting, with the result that she became sallow and haggard, and in a matter of weeks had lost both her beauty and spirits.

The Rajah was genuinely fond of her, but like most men, he did not feel comfortable in the presence of illness and invalids, and preferred to keep out of her way and hope that she would soon recover. It was doubly unfortunate for her that at this juncture, one of his ministers should have given a banquet in his honour at which a troupe of dancing-girls entertained the guests: for among the dancers was the Kashmiri girl, Janoo. An alluring, golden-skinned, dark-eyed witch, as beautiful, and as predatory, as a black panther.

The top of Janoo's head reached no higher than a man's heart, for she was a little woman, and would probably, one day, be a dumpy one. But now she was young, and to the men who watched her swaying to the music of drums and sitars she seemed a living, breathing replica of those voluptuous goddesses who smile from the frescoes of Ajanta or posture in stone on the Black Temple at Konarak. She possessed in abundance that indefinable quality that a generation as yet unborn was to call 'sex-appeal', and she had brains as well as beauty: three invaluable assets that she now used to such good purpose that twenty-four hours later she was installed in the palace, and within a week it was plain to all that the star of the *'Feringhi-Rani'* was setting, and that there was a new favourite to be flattered and propitiated by those who desired favours.

Even then it had never occurred to anyone that this was more than a passing infatuation that would burn itself out as quickly as others had done, for they had not taken the measure of the *Nautch-girl*. But Janoo was ambitious, and she had been instructed from childhood in the art of pleasing and amusing men. She was no longer content with a handful of coins and an occasional trinket; she saw the chance of a throne, played her cards skilfully, and won. The Rajah had married her.

Two weeks later the *Feringhi*-Rani had been brought to bed, but instead of the son who might have restored to her some of her lost prestige, she had borne a small, plain, pallid daughter.

'It is all she is fit for,' said Janoo-Bai scornfully. 'One has only to look at her to see that such a milk-blooded weakling will never be the mother of sons. Now when *my* son is born . . .'

Janoo never doubted for a moment that her first child would be a son. And a son it had been: a strong and lusty boy of whom any father could be proud. Rockets streamed up into the night sky to shower the city with stars while conches blared and gongs boomed in the temples, and the poor fed sumptuously in honour of the new prince, among them young Ashok and his mother Sita, whose clever fingers had fashioned many of the tinselled garlands that decorated the streets that day.

The six-year-old son of Hilary and Isobel had stuffed himself with *halwa* and *jellabies,* shouted and thrown *patarkars* with his friends, and wished that a son could be born to the Rajah every day. He had no complaints against life, but there was no denying that the fare provided by Sita was plain and not overabundant, and the few sweetmeats that came his way were more often than not filched from some stall in the bazaar at the risk of capture and a beating by the incensed owner. He was a strong and well-grown child, tall for his age and as agile as a monkey. The spartan diet of the poor had kept him lean, and the games of tag that he and his friends played in the streets and across the rooftops of the city—not to mention the snatching of sweets and fruit and the headlong flights from pursuit—had hardened his muscles and helped to develop a natural fleetness of foot.

On the other side of the world, in the comfortable upper and middle-class nurseries of Victorian England, children of five and six were still regarded as too young to do more than learn their alphabet with the aid of coloured bricks, and bowl hoops under the careful eye of nursemaids: but in mines and factories and on farms, the children of the poor toiled beside their parents, and in far-off Gulkote, Ash too became a wage-earner.

He was barely six-and-a-half when he went to work as a horse-boy in the stables of Duni Chand, a rich landowner who had a house near the temple of Vishnu and several farms in the country beyond the city limits.

Duni Chand kept a string of horses on which he visited his fields and rode out hawking on the bad-lands by the river, and it was Ash's duty to carry grain and draw water, attend to the harness and lend a hand with anything from cutting grass to curry-combing. The work was arduous and the wages light, but having spent his infancy among horses—his supposed father, Daya Ram, had introduced him to them at an early age—he had never had the least fear of them. It not only pleased him to work with them, but the few annas thus earned gave him an enormous sense of importance. He was a man and a wage-earner and could now, if he so wished, afford to buy *halwa* from the sweetmeat-seller instead of stealing it. This was a step up in the world, and he informed Sita that he had decided to become a syce and earn enough money for the day when they would set out to find their valley. Mohammed Sherif, the head-syce, was reported to earn as much as twelve rupees a month, a vast sum that did not include *dustori*—the one anna on each rupee that he levied on every item of food or equipment purchased for use in the stables, and which more than doubled his salary.

'When I am head-syce,' said Ash grandly, 'we will move to a big house and have a servant to do the cooking, and you will never have to do any more work, Mata-ji.'

It is just possible that he might have carried out his plan and spent his days attached to the stable of some petty nobleman. For as soon as it became apparent that he could ride anything on four legs, Mohammed Sherif, recognizing a born horseman, had permitted him to exercise his charges and taught him many valuable secrets of horsemanship, so that the year he spent in Duni Chand's stables had been a very happy one. But fate, with a certain amount of human assistance, had other plans for Ash; and the fall of a weather-worn slab of sandstone was to change the whole course of his life.

It happened on an April morning, almost three years to the day from the morning when Sita had led him away from the terrible vulture-filled camp in the Terai, and started out on the long road to Delhi. The young crown-prince, Lalji, Yuveraj of Gulkote, rode through the city to make offerings at the Temple of Vishnu. And as he passed under the arch of the ancient Charbagh Gate that stands at the junction of the Chandni Bazaar and the Street of the Coppersmiths, a slab of croping-stone slid from its place and fell into the roadway.

Ash had been standing in the forefront of the crowd, having wriggled his way, eel-like, between the close-packed legs of his elders, and his eye had been caught by a movement overhead. He had seen the slab shift and slip just as the head of the Yuveraj's horse emerged from the shadow of the arch, and almost without thinking (for there had not been time for conscious thought) he leapt at the bridle, and clutching it, checked the startled animal as the heavy slab of sandstone crashed into the street and exploded into a hundred sharp-edged fragments under the prancing hooves. Ash and the horse, together with several spectators, had been gashed by the flying splinters, and there was blood everywhere: on the hot white dust, the gay garments of the crowd and the ceremonial trappings of the horse.

The spectators had screamed and swayed and struggled, and the horse, maddened by pain and noise, would have bolted had not Ash held its head and talked to it and soothed it until the stunned escort, spurring forward, caught the reins from him, and closing up around their prince, shouldered him aside. There followed an interval of surging chaos filled with a clamour of questions and answers while the escort beat back the crowd and stared at the broken coping overhead, and a white-bearded horseman flung Ash a coin—a gold mohur, no less—and said 'Shabash (Bravo), little one! That was well done indeed.'

The crowd, seeing that no one had suffered any serious hurt, yelled their approval, and the procession continued on its way to the accompaniment of frenzied cheers, the Yuveraj sitting straight-backed in the saddle and clutching the reins with hands that were noticeably unsteady. He had kept his seat on the plunging animal with creditable skill, and his future subjects were proud of him. But the small face under the jewelled turban was strained and colourless as he looked back over his shoulder, searching the sea of faces for the boy who had leapt so providentially at his horse's head.

A stranger in the crowd had hoisted Ash up on his shoulder so that he might see the procession depart, and for a brief moment the two children stared at each other, the black frightened eyes of the little prince meeting the interested grey ones of Duni Chand's stable-boy. Then the crowd surged between them, and half a minute later the procession reached the end of the Street of the Coppersmiths and turning it, was lost to sight.

Sita had been gratifyingly impressed by the gold piece, and even more by the tale of the morning's doings. After much discussion, they had decided to take the coin to Burgwan Lal, the jeweller, who was known to be an honest man, and exchange it for a suitable quantity of silver ornaments which Sita could wear until such time as they were in need of ready money. They had neither of them expected to hear any more of the affair—apart from the inevitable comments and congratulations of interested neighbours—but the following morning a stout and supercilious palace official, accompanied by two elderly retainers, knocked on the door of Duni Chand's house. His Highness the Yuveraj, explained the official loftily, desired the immediate attendance of this insignificant brat at the palace, where he would be given living quarters and some minor post in His Highness's household.

'But I can't do that,' protested Ash, dismayed. 'My mother would not like to live alone, and I could not leave her. She would not want—' He was brusquely interrupted:

'What she wants is of no consequence. It is the order of His Highness that you work for him, and you had best make haste and clean yourself. You cannot come in those rags.'

There had been nothing for it but to obey, and Ash had been escorted back to the fruit-seller's shop, where he hurriedly changed into the only other garment he possessed, and comforted the distracted Sita, urging her not to worry for he would be back soon. Very soon—

'Do not cry, mother. There is nothing to cry for. I shall tell the Yuveraj that I would much rather stay here, and because I saved him from injury he will let me return. You will see. Besides, they cannot keep me there against my will.'

Secure in this belief, he hugged her reassuringly and followed the Yuveraj's servants through the city gate and up to the Hawa Mahal—the fortress palace of the Rajahs of Gulkote.

4

The Palace of the Winds was approached by a steep causeway paved with slabs of granite that had been worn into ruts and hollows by the passing of generations of men, elephants and horses. The stone felt cold to Ash's bare feet as he trudged up it in the wake of the Yuveraj's servants, and looking up at the towering walls of rock, he was suddenly afraid.

He did not want to live and work in a fortress. He wanted to stay in the city where his friends lived, and tend Duni Chand's horses and learn wisdom from Mohammed Sherif the head groom. The Hawa Mahal looked a grim and unfriendly place, and the *Badshahi Darwaza,* the King's Gate, by which one entered it, did nothing to mitigate that impression. The great iron-studded doors yawned onto darkness, and there were guards armed with tulwars and jezails lounging in the shadows beyond the stone lintel. The causeway passed under a fretted balcony from where the mouths of cannon gaped down at them, and the sunlight was cut off as though by a sword as they entered a long tunnel, honeycombed on either side by niches, guardrooms and galleries that sloped upwards through the heart of the rock.

The transition from warm sunlight to cold shadow, and the eerie echo under the black vault of the roof, served to intensify Ash's unease, and glancing back over his shoulder to where the great gateway framed a view of the city basking comfortably in the heat haze, he was tempted to run. It seemed to him, suddenly, as though he was entering a prison from which he would never be able to escape, and that if he did not run away now, at once, he would lose freedom and friends and happiness and spend his days penned up behind bars like the talking minah that hung in a cage outside the potter's shop. It was a new and troubling thought, and he shivered as though with cold. But it would obviously be no easy task to dodge past so many guards, and it would be humiliating to be caught and dragged into the palace by force. Besides, he was curious to see the inside of the Hawa Mahal: no one he knew had ever been inside it, and it would be something to boast about to his friends. But as for staying there and working for the Yuveraj, he would not even consider it, and if they thought that they could make him they were wrong. He would escape over the walls and go back to the city, and if they followed him, then he and his mother would both run away. The world was wide, and somewhere among the mountains lay their own valley—that safe place where they could live as they pleased.

The tunnel took a sharp turn to the right and came out into a small open courtyard where there were more guards and more ancient bronze cannon. On the far side of it another gateway led into a vast quadrangle where two of the Rajah's elephants rocked at their pickets in the shade of a *chenar* tree, and a dozen chattering women washed clothes in the green water of a stone tank. Beyond this lay the main bulk of the palace. A fantastic jumble of walls, battlements and wooden balconies, fretted windows, airy turrets and carved galleries—the larger part of it screened from the city below by the outer bastion.

No one knew how old the original fortress was, though legend said that it had defied the armies of Sikundar Dulkhan (Alexander the Great) when that young conqueror swooped down into India from the passes of the north. But a substantial part of the present citadel had been built in the early years of the fifteenth century, by a robber chieftain who required an impregnable stronghold from which he and his followers could sally out to raid the fertile lands beyond the river, and retreat to in time of trouble. In those days it had been known as the *Kala Kila,* the 'Black Fort', not on account of its colour—for it had been built of the same harsh grey stone that formed the towering outcrop of rock upon which it stood—but in reference to its reputation, which was of the darkest. Later, when the territory had fallen to a Rajput adventurer, it had been considerably enlarged, and his son, who built the walled city on the plain below and became the first Rajah of Gulkote, had transformed the *Kala Kila* into a vast, ornately decorated royal residence which on account of its lofty position he re-named the Hawa Mahal—the 'Palace of the Winds'.

It was here that the present Rajah lived in dilapidated splendour in a maze of rooms furnished with Persian carpets, dusty hangings shimmering with gold embroidery, and ornaments of jade or beaten silver, set with rubies and raw turquoise. Here too, in the Queen's rooms of the Zenana Quarters beyond the pierced wooden screens that separated the Hall of Audience from a garden full of fruit trees and roses, lived Janoo-Bai the Rani—her rival, the *Feringhi*-Rani, having died of a fever (though some said of poison) during the previous summer. And in a rabbit-warren of rooms that took up a whole wing of the palace, the little Yuveraj, known more familiarly by his 'milk-name' of Lalji, spent his days among the crowd of attendants, petty officials and hangers-on who had been assigned to his service by his father.

Led into his presence through a bewildering number of passages and ante-chambers, Ash found the heir of Gulkote seated cross-legged on a velvet cushion and engaged in teasing a ruffled cockatoo who looked to be as sour and out of temper as its tormenter. The glittering ceremonial dress of the previous day had been exchanged for tight muslin trousers and a plain linen *achkan,** and in it he looked a good deal younger than he had appeared when mounted on a white stallion in the midst of the procession. Then, he had seemed every inch a prince—and the inches had been considerably increased by a sky-blue turban adorned by a tall aigrette and a flashing clasp of diamonds. But now he was only a small boy. A plump, pasty-faced child who could easily have been taken for two years younger than Ash instead of two years older, and who was not so much cross as frightened.

It was this last that dispelled Ash's awe and put him at his ease, because he too had on occasions taken refuge from fear in a show of ill-temper, and therefore recognized an emotion that was probably hidden from any of the bored adults in the room. It gave him a sudden fellow-feeling for this boy who would one day be Rajah of Gulkote. And an equally sudden urge to take his part against these undiscerning grown-ups who bowed so deferentially and spoke so soothingly in false, flattering voices, while their faces remained cold and sly.

They were not, thought Ash, eyeing them warily, a friendly-looking lot. They were all too fat and sleek and too pleased with themselves, and one of them, a richly dressed young dandy with a handsome dissolute face, who wore a single diamond earring dangling from one ear, was ostentatiously holding a scented handkerchief to his nose as though he feared that this brat from the city might have brought an odour of poverty and the stables with him. Ash looked away and made his bow before royalty, bending low with both hands to his forehead as the custom demanded, but now his gaze was both friendly and interested, and seeing this, the face of the Yuveraj lost some of its ill-temper.

* tight-fitting three-quarter-length coat

'Go away. All of you,' commanded the Yuveraj, imperiously dismissing his attendants with a wave of the royal hand. 'I wish to speak to this boy alone.'

The dandy with the diamond earring leaned down to catch his arm and whisper urgently in his ear, but the Yuveraj pulled away and said loudly and angrily: 'That is fool's talk, Biju Ram. Why should he do me an injury when he has already saved my life? Besides, he is not armed. Go away and don't be so stupid.'

The young man stepped back and bowed with a submissiveness that was sharply at variance with the sudden ugliness of his expression, and Ash was startled to receive a scowl of concentrated venom that seemed out of all proportion to the occasion. Evidently this Biju Ram did not relish being rebuked, and blamed him for being the cause of it; which was manifestly unfair considering he had not said a word—and had never wanted to come here in the first place.

The Yuveraj gestured impatiently and the men withdrew, leaving the two boys to take stock of each other. But Ash still did not speak, and it was the Yuveraj who broke the brief spell of silence that followed. He said abruptly: 'I told my father how you saved my life, and he has said that I may have you for my servant. You will be well paid and I . . . I have no one to play with here. Only women and grown-ups. Will you stay?'

Ash had fully intended to refuse, but now he hesitated and said uncertainly: 'There is my mother . . . I cannot leave her, and I do not think she . . .'

'That is easily arranged. She can live here too and be a waiting-woman to my little sister, the princess. Are you fond of her, then?'

'Of course,' said Ash, astonished. 'She is my mother.'

'So. You are fortunate. I have no mother. She was the Rani, you know. The true Queen. But she died when I was born, so I do not remember her. Perhaps if she had not died . . . My sister Anjuli's mother died too, and they said that it was sorcery, or poison; but then she was a *feringhi,* and always sickly, so perhaps *That One* had no need to use spells or poison or to—' He broke off, looking quickly over his shoulder and then rose abruptly and said 'Come. Let us go out into the garden. There are too many ears here.'

He put the cockatoo back onto its perch and went out through a curtained doorway and past half-a-dozen salaaming retainers into a garden set about with walnut trees and fountains, where a little pavilion reflected itself in a pool full of lily pads and golden carp; Ash following at his heels. At the far side of the garden only a low stone parapet lay between the grass and a sheer drop of two hundred feet onto the floor of the plateau below, while on the other three sides rose the palace: tier upon tier of carved and fretted wood and stone, where a hundred windows looked down upon tree tops and city, and out towards the far horizon.

Lalji sat down on the rim of the pool and began to throw pebbles at the carp, and presently he said: 'Did you see who pushed the stone?'

'What stone?' asked Ash, surprised.

'The one that would have fallen on me had you not checked my horse.'

'Oh that. No one pushed it. It just fell.'

'It was pushed,' insisted Lalji in a harsh whisper. 'Dunmaya, who is—who was my nurse, has always said that if *That One* bore a son she would find some way to make him the heir. And I—I am—' He closed his lips together on the unspoken word, refusing to admit, even to another child, that he was afraid. But the word spoke itself in the quiver of his voice and the unsteadiness of the hands that flung pebbles into the quiet water, and Ash frowned, recalling the movement that had caught his eye before the coping stone slipped, and wondering for the first time why it should have slipped just then, and if it had indeed been a hand that thrust it down.

'Biju Ram says that I am imagining things,' confessed the Yuveraj in a small voice. 'He says that no one would dare. Even *That One* would not. But when the stone fell I remembered what my nurse had said, and I thought . . . Dunmaya says that I must trust no one, but you saved me from the stone, and if you will stay with me perhaps I shall be safe.'

'I don't understand,' said Ash, puzzled. 'Safe from what? You are the Yuveraj and you have servants and guards, and one day you will be Rajah.'

Lalji gave a short, mirthless laugh. 'That was true a little while ago. But now my father has another son. The child of *That One*—the *Nautch*-girl. Dunmaya says she will not rest until she has put him in my place, for she desires the *gadi* (throne) for her own son, and she holds my father in the hollow of her hand—so.' He clenched his fist until the knuckles showed white, and relaxing it, stared down at the pebble that he held, his small face drawn into harsh unchildlike lines.

'I am his son. His eldest son. But he would do anything to please her, and—'

His voice trailed away and was lost in the soft splashing of the fountains. And quite suddenly Ash remembered another voice, someone he had almost forgotten, who had said to him long, long ago in another life and another tongue: 'The worst thing in the world is injustice. That means being unfair.' This was unfair, and so it must not be allowed. Something should be done about it.

'All right. I'll stay,' said Ash, heroically abandoning his happy-go-lucky life in the city and the pleasant future he had planned for himself as head-syce in charge of Duni Chand's horses. The careless years were over.

That evening he sent a message to Sita, who dug up the money and the small sealed packet she had hidden in their room, and tying their scanty possessions into a bundle, set out for the Hawa Mahal; and on the following morning Ash was told to consider himself a member of the Yuveraj's household with a salary of no less than five silver rupees a month, while Sita had been given employment as an extra waiting-woman to the dead *Feringhi*-Rani's little daughter, the Princess Anjuli.

By palace standards, the living quarters allotted to them were humble ones: three small and windowless rooms, one of which was a kitchen. But compared with their single room in the city it seemed to them the height of luxury, and the absence of windows was more than compensated for by the fact that all three doors opened onto a small private courtyard that was protected by an eight-foot wall and shaded by a pine tree. Sita was delighted with it and soon began to look upon it as home, though it grieved her that Ashok could not sleep there. But Ash's duties, which in the main consisted of being in attendance on the Yuveraj for a few hours each day, also required him to sleep in an ante-chamber adjoining the royal bedroom at night.

No one could have described such work as arduous, yet Ash soon came to regard it as irksome to a degree. This was partly due to the temper and vagaries of his youthful master, but mostly on account of the young dandy, Biju Ram, who for some reason had taken a strong dislike to him. Lalji's nickname for Biju Ram was *'Bichchhu'* (scorpion) or more familiarly, *'Bichchhu-ji'*, though it was a name that no one else dared use to his face, for it was all too apt—the dandy being a venomous creature who could turn and sting at the slightest provocation.

In Ash's case no provocation seemed necessary, since Biju Ram appeared to take a positive delight in baiting him. His attentions soon became the bane of the boy's existence, for he lost no opportunity of holding him up to ridicule by making him the butt of endless practical jokes that seemed solely designed to inflict pain and humiliation; and as these tricks were usually lewd as well as cruel, Lalji would snigger at them, and the watching courtiers would break into peals of sycophantic laughter.

Lalji's moods were often ugly and always unpredictable—understandably so, for until the coming of the *Nautch*-girl he had been the spoiled darling of the palace, petted and indulged by his doting father and the adoring Zenana women, and flattered by courtiers and servants alike. His first step-mother, the charming, gentle *Feringhi*-Rani, had grieved for the motherless child, and taking him to her heart, had loved him as though he were her own son. But as neither she nor anyone else had ever attempted to discipline him, it was hardly surprising that the chubby, lovable baby should have grown into a spoilt and overbearing boy, totally unfitted to deal with the changed atmosphere in the palace when the new favourite bore a son and the *Feringhi*-Rani died. For now the little Yuveraj was suddenly of less importance; and even his servants became noticeably less servile, while courtiers who had once flattered and fawned on him hastened to ingratiate themselves with the new power behind the throne.

His rooms and his retinue began to look shabby and neglected, not all his imperious orders were now obeyed, and the continual warnings of his devoted nurse—old Dunmaya, who had been his mother's nurse also and accompanied the Senior Rani to Gulkote when that lady came there as a bride—did nothing to soothe his distress or improve the situation. Dunmaya would have laid down her life for the boy, and her fears for him were probably justified; but the voicing of them, and her constant criticism of his father's growing neglect, only served to increase his unhappiness, and drove him at times to near hysteria. He could not understand what was happening, and it made him frightened rather than angry. But because pride prevented him from showing fear, he took refuge in rage, and those who served him suffered accordingly.

Young as Ash was, something of all this was still apparent to him. But though understanding might help him to excuse much of Lalji's behaviour, it did not make it any easier to bear. Also he did not take kindly to the subservience that the Yuveraj, who had been used to it all his short life, expected from every member of his household; even from those who were elderly grey-beards and grandfathers. Ash had at first been properly impressed by the importance of the heir to the throne, and also with his own duties as this potentate's page, which, in the matter of childhood, he took half seriously and half as a game. Unfortunately, familiarity soon bred contempt and later boredom, and there were times when he hated Lalji and would have run away if it had not been for Sita. But he knew that Sita was happy here, and if he ran away she would have to come with him, not only because he could not leave her behind, but because he suspected that Lalji might treat her unkindly in revenge for his defection. Yet, it was, paradoxically, sympathy for Lalji as much as love for Sita that prevented him from running away.

The two boys had little in common and there were many factors that prevented them from becoming friends: caste, upbringing and environment; heredity and the social gulf that yawned between the heir to a throne and the son of a serving-woman. They were separated, too, by a wide difference in character and temperament; and to a certain extent by the difference in their ages, though this mattered less, for although Lalji was the senior by two years, Ash often felt himself to be the elder by years, and on that account bound to help and protect the weaker vessel from the forces of evil that even the most insensitive must feel stirring in the huge, rambling, ramshackle palace.

Ash had never been insensitive, and though at first he had dismissed Dunmaya's warnings as the babbling of a silly old woman, it had not taken him long to change his mind. The idle, aimless days might drift placidly by, but under that smooth surface ran hidden undercurrents of plot and counterplot, and the wind was not the only thing that whispered in the endless corridors and alcoves of the Hawa Mahal.

Bribery, intrigue and ambition haunted the dusty rooms and lurked behind every door, and even a child could not fail to become aware of it. Yet Ash had taken none of this very seriously until the day when a plate of the Yuveraj's favourite cakes had been found in the little pavilion by the pool in the Yuveraj's private garden . . .

Lalji had been chasing the tame gazelle, and it was Ash who had found them and idly crumbled one into the pool, where the fat carp gobbled it greedily. A few minutes later the fish were floating belly upwards among the lily pads, and Ash, staring at them with shocked, incredulous eyes, realized that they were dead—and what it was that had killed them.

Lalji had an official 'taster' and he normally ate nothing that his taster had not sampled first; but had he found those tempting cakes in the pavilion he would have grabbed and gobbled one as greedily as the carp. Ash snatched them up and carrying them quickly to the parapet at the far side of the garden, dropped them over, plate and all, into the void below. And as the cakes fell, wheeling down in the evening light, a crow swooped and caught one in his beak; and a moment later it too was falling into the gulf, a limp black bundle of feathers.

Ash had told no one of this incident, for though it might have seemed the natural thing to run with it to anyone who would listen, a too early acquaintance with danger had taught him caution, and he felt sure that this was something he had better keep to himself. If he told Lalji it would only add to the boy's fears and send old Dunmaya into a further frenzy of anxiety, and if any inquiries were made it was fairly certain that the real culprit would not be found, and equally certain that some innocent scapegoat would be made to suffer. Ash's experience of life in the palace had already taught him that justice was unlikely to be done if Janoo-Bai had anything to do with it, particularly since her position had recently been further strengthened by the birth of a second son.

It never once occurred to him that the scapegoat might have been himself, or that the cakes in the pavilion could have been intended for him and not, as he supposed, for the Yuveraj.

Ash therefore held his peace; for children can only take the world as they find it, and accept the fact that their elders are all-powerful, if not all-wise. He pushed the incident of the cakes into the back of his mind, and accepting servitude in the Hawa Mahal as a necessary evil that could not at present be avoided, resigned himself to enduring it until such time as the Yuveraj came of age and had no further use for his services. At least he now had plenty to eat and clean clothes to wear; though the promised pay had not materialized, owing to the rapaciousness of the *Nautch*-girl having reduced the Rajah's exchequer to a dangerously low ebb. But it proved a tedious existence, until the coming of Tuku, a little mongoose that had haunted Sita's courtyard and that Ash, in search of distraction, had tamed and trained.

Tuku was the first living thing that was wholly his own, for though he knew that he possessed every scrap of Sita's heart, he could not command her presence when he chose. She had her own duties and was only available at certain hours of the day; but Tuku followed at his heels or rode on his shoulder, slept curled up under his chin at night and came when he called, and Ash loved the graceful, fearless little creature, and felt that Tuku knew it and returned his love. It was a deeply satisfactory comradeship, and it had lasted for over half a year, until a black day when Lalji, feeling tired and cross, had insisted on having Tuku to play with, and having teased him unmercifully, was repaid with a sharp nip. The next two minutes had been a nightmare that haunted Ash for many months and that he was never entirely to forget.

Lalji, his finger dripping blood, had yelled with fright and pain and shrieked to a servant to kill the mongoose at once—at once. It had been done before Ash could intervene. A single slashing blow from a scabarded sword had broken Tuku's back, and he had twitched and whimpered for a moment, and then the life had gone out of him and there was only a limp little scrap of fur in Ash's hands.

It did not seem possible that Tuku was dead: only a minute ago he had been fluffing his tail and chattering crossly at Lalji's impertinences, and now—

Lalji said furiously: 'Don't look at me like that! What does it matter? It was only an animal—a savage, bad-tempered animal. See where he bit me?'

'You were teasing him,' said Ash in a whisper. 'It is you who are the savage, bad-tempered animal.' He wanted to cry—to scream and shriek. Fury welled up in him and he dropped Tuku's small body and sprang at Lalji.

It had been a scuffle rather than a fight. A degrading scuffle in which Lalji spat and kicked and shrieked, until rescued by a dozen servants who had converged upon the room from every direction and dragged the boys apart.

'I'm going,' panted Ash, gripped by a brace of horrified retainers, and glaring defiance. 'I won't stay with you or work for you another minute. I shall go now, and I shall never come back.'

'And I say you shall not go!' screamed Lalji, beside himself with rage. 'You shan't leave without my permission, and if you try to, you'll find you can't. I shall see to that.'

Biju Ram, who as a token gesture towards defending the Yuveraj had picked up a long-barrelled pistol—fortunately unloaded—waved the weapon negligently at Ash and said languidly: 'Your Highness should have the horse-boy branded as one does horses—or mutinous slaves. Then if he should by any chance escape, he would be speedily recognized as your property and returned.'

It is possible that the suggestion was not intended to be taken seriously; but then Lalji was far too angry to think clearly and, blinded by rage, he had seized on it. There had been no one to protest, for by ill luck the only member of his household who might have done so with any chance of success was confined to his bed with a fever. The thing had been done there and then, and by Biju Ram himself. There had been a charcoal brazier in the room, for it was mid-winter and the palace was very cold; and Biju Ram had laughed his giggling laugh and thrust the muzzle of the pistol among the glowing coals. Ash was barely eight years old, but it had taken four men to hold him down, for he was strong and wiry and when he realized what was to happen he fought like a wild-cat, biting and clawing until not one of the four remained unmarked, though it was a useless battle, for the end was never in doubt.

Biju Ram had intended to brand him on the forehead, which could possibly have killed him. But Lalji, for all his fury, still retained a measure of caution, and it occurred to him that as his father might not altogether approve of such proceedings, it might be wiser to mark Ashok in a place less likely to catch the Rajah's eye. Biju Ram was therefore forced to content himself with pressing the mouth of the pistol to the victim's bared breast. There had been an odd sizzling sound and a smell of burnt flesh, and though Ash had resolved that he would die rather than give *Bichchhu* the satisfaction of hearing him cry out, he had been unable to stop himself. His scream of pain had drawn another giggling laugh from the dandy, but its effect upon Lalji was unexpected. It had aroused his better nature, and he had thrown himself at Biju Ram, dragging him back and crying wildly that it was all his own fault and that Ashok was not to blame. At which point Ash had fainted.

'He's dying,' shrieked Lalji, overcome by remorse. 'You've killed him, *Bichchhu.* Do something, one of you. Send for a hakim* . . . fetch Dunmaya. Oh, Ashok, don't die. Please don't die.'

Ash was nowhere near dying, and he had recovered soon enough. The ugly burn had healed cleanly, thanks to the skilful ministrations of Sita and Dunmaya and his own good health, though the scar it left was to last as long as he lived; not as a circle, but as a crescent, for he had flinched sideways as he felt the heat, so that the muzzle had not pressed evenly and Lalji had pulled Biju Ram away before he could rectify this error. 'I would have marked you with the sun,' said Biju Ram, 'but it seems that would have been to do you too much honour, and it is only right that by your cringing you should turn the sun into a mere moon instead'—but he was careful not to say that in front of Lalji, who did not care to be reminded of the episode.

Strangely enough, the two boys had been better friends after that, for Ash was well aware of the heinousness of his offence and knew that in former days he would have been strangled, or trampled to death by the Rajah's elephants. The least he had expected even now was the loss of a limb or an eye, for it was no light crime to lay violent hands on the heir to the throne, and grown men had paid with their lives for lesser offences; so he was relieved that his punishment had been no worse, and astonished that the Yuveraj should have intervened to stop it. The fact that he had not only done so, but publicly admitted himself to be in the wrong, had impressed Ash a great deal, as he was aware what that admission must have cost the Yuveraj.

He missed Tuku unbearably, but he did not attempt to tame another mongoose. Nor did he make any more pets, for he knew that he could never trust Lalji again, and that to let himself become fond of some other creature might only mean providing a useful weapon to be used against him the next time the Yuveraj was out of temper or wished to punish him. Yet despite this (and certainly from no wish of his own) he was to acquire an unexpected substitute for Tuku. Not an animal this time, but a very small human being: Anjuli-Bai, the shy, neglected baby daughter of the unfortunate *Feringhi*-Rani.

It was one of Lalji's good qualities—he had many, and given the right circumstances they might well have outweighed the bad ones—that he was unfailingly kind to his little half-sister. The child was fre-

* doctor

quently to be found in his apartments, for being as yet far too young to be confined to the Zenana Quarters, she came and went as she pleased. She was a thin little creature who appeared to be half-starved and was dressed with a shabbiness that would have been considered disgraceful by many a peasant family—a state of affairs that was directly traceable to the enmity of the *Nautch*-girl, who saw no reason why money or deference should be wasted on the daughter of her dead rival.

Janoo-Bai could not be sure that the child might not develop some of the beauty and charm that had once so captivated the Rajah, and she had no intention of letting him become either fond or proud of his daughter if she could help it; to which end she saw to it that the baby was banished to a distant wing of the palace and cared for by a handful of slovenly unpaid servants who pocketed the meagre household funds for their own use.

The Rajah seldom inquired after his daughter, and in time almost forgot that he had one. Janoo-Bai had assured him that the child was well cared for, and had added some disparaging comments on its lack of good looks, saying that it would make the arranging of a good marriage a difficult matter. 'Such a small, sour-looking little thing,' sighed Janoo-Bai with feigned sympathy, and she had nick-named the child 'Kairi'—that being a small, unripe mango—and laughed with delight when the name was adopted by the palace.

'Kairi-Bai' preferred her half-brother's apartments to her own; they were brighter and better furnished, and besides he sometimes gave her sweets and let her play with his monkeys or the cockatoo and the tame gazelle. His servants too were less impatient with her than her own women, and she had taken a strong fancy to the youngest of them, Ashok, who had found her sobbing quietly in a corner of her brother's garden one day, having been bitten by one of the monkeys, whose tail she had pulled. Ash had taken her to Sita to be soothed and petted, and Sita had bandaged the wound, and having given her a piece of sugar-cane, told her the story of Rama, whose beautiful wife had been stolen by the Demon King of Lanka and rescued with the help of Hanuman, the Monkey God: 'So you see, you must never pull a monkey's tail, because it not only hurts his feelings, but Hanuman would not like it. And now we will pick some marigolds and make a little wreath—see, I will show you how—for you to take to his shrine to show him you are sorry. My son Ashok will take you there.'

The story and the construction of the wreath had successfully distracted the child's attention from her hurts, and she had gone off happily with Ash, holding confidingly to his hand, to make her apologies to Hanuman at the shrine near the elephant lines, where a plaster figure of the Monkey God danced in the gloom. After this she was often to be found in Sita's quarters, though it was not Sita but Ash to whom she attached herself, trotting about after him like some small persistant pariah puppy who has chosen its owner and cannot be snubbed or driven away. In fact, Ash did not try very hard to do either, for Sita told him that he must be especially kind to the forlorn little girl, not because she was a princess, or because she was motherless and neglected, but because she had been born on a day that was doubly auspicious for him: the anniversary of his own birth and the day of their arrival in Gulkote.

It was this more than anything else that made him feel in some way responsible for Kairi, and he resigned himself to being the object of her devotion and was the only person who did not address her by her nickname. He either called her 'Juli' (which was her own version of her given name, for she was still unable to get her tongue round all three syllables) or on rare occasions 'Larla', which means darling, and in general treated her with the tolerant affection he would have accorded to an importunate kitten, protecting her to the best of his ability from the teasing or insolence of the palace servants.

The Yuveraj's attendants had retaliated by jeering at him for being a nursemaid and calling him 'Ayah-ji', until Lalji unexpectedly came to his assistance and turned on them, saying angrily that they would please to remember that the Anjuli-Bai was his sister. After that they had accepted the situation, and in time became so used to it that it was doubtful if anyone noticed it any more; the baby was, in any case, of no importance and would probably not live to grow up, being a scrawny little thing, unlikely to survive the normal ailments of childhood, while as for the boy Ashok, he was of no importance to anyone, not even, it would seem, to the Yuveraj.

But in this last they were wrong. Lalji still trusted him (though he would have found it hard to explain why) and he had no intention of letting him go. The fate of Tuku and the violence that followed it were never referred to again, but Ash soon discovered that Lalji's threat to prevent his leaving the palace had not been an idle one. There was only the one gate into the palace, *Badshai Darwaza:* and after that day he could no longer go through it alone but only, on occasions, in the company of selected servants or officials, who saw to it that he did not stray off on his own or fail to return with them.

'There is an order,' said the sentries blandly, and turned him back. It was the same the next day and every day, and when Ash questioned Lalji, the boy had countered by saying: 'Why should you wish to leave? Are you not comfortable here? If there is anything you lack you have only to tell Ram Dass, and he will send out for it. There is no need for you to go to the bazaars.'

'But I only wish to see my friends,' protested Ash.

'Am I not your friend?' asked the Yuveraj.

There was no answer to that, and Ash never knew who had given the order that he was not to be allowed to leave: the Rajah, or Lalji himself (who said he had not, but was not to be trusted), or perhaps Janoo-Bai, for reasons of her own? But whoever it was, the order was never rescinded, and he was always aware of it. He was a prisoner in the fortress, though he was allowed to go more or less where he chose inside the walls, and as the Hawa Mahal covered a very large area, he could hardly be considered as closely confined. Nor was he friendless, for he had made two good friends in the palace that year, and found at least one ally among the members of Lalji's suite.

Nevertheless, he felt the loss of his liberty keenly, for from the walls and the half-ruined towers and wooden pavilions that crowned them, he could see the world laid out before him like a coloured map, beckoning towards freedom and the far horizons. To the south-west lay the city, with beyond it the wide stretch of the plateau—its far rim sloping steeply down to the river and the rich land of the Punjab, so that sometimes, on clear days, one could even see the plains. But he seldom faced that way, for northward lay the foothills, and behind them, spanning the horizon from east to west, were the true hills and the vast, serrated massif of the Dur Khaima, beautiful and mysterious, robed in forests of rhododendron and *deodar* and crowned with snow.

Ash did not know that he had been born within sight of those snows, or that he had spent his earlier years among the high Himalayas, falling asleep to the sight of them rose-dyed by the sunset or silver under the moon, and waking to see them turn from apricot and amber to dazzling white in the full blaze of the morning. They were part of his subconscious mind, because once, long ago, he had known them by heart as other children know the frieze painted on a nursery wall. But looking at them now, he felt sure that somewhere in the folds of those mountains lay the valley that Sita used to speak of at bedtime: their own valley. That safe hidden place that they would one day reach by long marches over hill-roads and through passes where the wind shrieked between black rocks and green glacier, and the cold glare of snowfields blinded the eyes.

Sita seldom spoke of their valley now; she was too busy during the daytime, and Ash slept in the Yuveraj's quarters at night. But the old bedtime story of his childhood still retained its grip on his imagination, and by now he had forgotten—or perhaps he had never realized —that it was not a real place. It was real to him, and morning and evening, whenever he could steal away from his duties—or, more often, during the long, idle mid-day hours when all the palace dozed and the sun lay hot on the battlements—he would climb up to a little covered balcony that jutted out from the wall of the *Mor Minar*— 'Peacock Tower'—and lying on the warm stone gaze out towards the mountains and think of it. And make plans.

The existence of that balcony was a secret shared only by Kairi, and its discovery had been a happy accident, for it could not be seen from inside the fortress, being hidden from view by the curves of the *Mor Minar*. The *Mor Minar* had been part of the original fort, a guard tower and a look-out, facing the foothills. But both roof and stairway had fallen long ago, and the entrance became blocked by rubble. The balcony was of a later date and had probably been built for the pleasure of some long-dead Rani, for it was no more than a folly, an elegant little pavilion of marble and red sandstone, pierced and carved into the semblance of frozen lace and topped by a hump-backed Hindu dome.

Fragments of wood still adhered to the rusty iron hinges that had once held a door, but the fragile-seeming screens still stood, except where there had once been a window cut in the marble tracery, from which the Rani and her ladies could look out towards the mountains. Here, on the front of the balcony, between the slender arches, there was now only open spaces and fragments of broken carving, below which the wall dropped for forty feet to meet the scrub and the steep rock faces, that in turn plunged downwards for more than four times that distance before merging into the plateau. There were goat tracks through the scrub, but few humans cared to climb so far; and even had they done so they might well have failed to notice the pavilion, for its outlines were lost against the weather-worn bulk of the *Mor Minar*.

Ash and Kairi, pursuing a truant marmoset, had clambered over the rubble that choked the ruined tower, and looking up the topless funnel had spied the fugitive half way up it. There must once have been rooms in the tower, but although no part of the floors remained, there were still traces of the stairway that had led up to them: broken stumps of stone, some barely large enough to provide foothold for the marmoset. But where a monkey can go an active child can often follow, and Ash had had plenty of practice on the rooftops of the city, and possessed an excellent head for heights. Kairi too could climb like a squirrel, and the broken staircase had proved easy enough to negotiate once they had removed the untidy bundles of twigs and egg shells deposited there by generations of owls and jackdaws. They had scrambled up it, and following the marmoset through a doorway, found themselves in a carved and canopied balcony that hung dizzily over empty space, as secure and inaccessible as a swallow's nest.

Ash had been delighted with their find. Here at last was a hidden place to which he could retreat in time of trouble, and from where he could look out across the world and dream of the future—and be alone. The claustrophobic atmosphere of the palace, with its incessant whispers of treachery and intrigue, its cabals and plots and place-seeking, was banished by the clean air that crooned through the marble tracery and kept the little pavilion swept and garnished; and best of all there was no one to dispute his possession of it, for apart from the monkeys and owls, the hill crows and the little yellow-crested bul-buls, no one could have set foot in it for fifty years and by now, in all likelihood, its very existence was forgotten.

Given the choice, Ash would have traded the balcony for permission to visit the city whenever he chose, and had he been given it would not have run away—for Sita's sake, if for nothing else. But deprived of that liberty, it was doubly satisfying to have a safe hiding place where he could escape from the quarrels and the gossip, the tantrums and the talk. The humble quarters that he shared with Sita did not fill this need because any servant sent to find him always came there first, so it was preferable to have a safer place of retreat, one from which he could not be hailed forth to undertake some trivial errand or answer an idle question that had been forgotten by the time he reached the Presence. The discovery of the Queen's balcony made his life in the Hawa Mahal more bearable. And the possession of two such friends as Koda Dad Khan, the *Mir Akhor*—the Master of Horse—and Koda Dad's youngest son, Zarin, almost reconciled him to staying there for ever . . .

Koda Dad was a Pathan who as a youth had left his native Border hills to wander among the northern fringes of the Punjab in search of his fortune. He had come by chance to Gulkote, where his skill at hawking had attracted the attention of the young Rajah, who had newly succeeded to the throne on the death of his father only two months previously. That had been more than thirty years ago, and except for occasional visits to his own Border-country, Koda Dad had never returned home. He had remained in Gulkote in the service of the Rajah, and as *Mir Akhor* was now a man of considerable reputation in the state. There was nothing that he did not know about horses, and it was said of him that he could speak their language and that even the wickedest and most intractable became docile when he spoke to it. He could shoot as well as he could ride, and as his knowledge of hawks and falcony equalled his knowledge of horses, the Rajah himself—no mean authority on both—asked his advice and invariably took it. After his first visit home he had returned with a wife who in due course presented him with three sons, and by now Koda Dad was the proud possessor of several grandsons and would occasionally talk to Ash of these paragons. 'They are myself when I was young; or so says my mother, who sees them often; our home being in the Yusafzai country, which is not far from Hoti Mardan* where my son Awal Shah serves with his Regiment—as does my second son Afzal, also.'

Koda Dad's two eldest sons had taken service under the British in that same Corps of Guides that Ash's Uncle William had belonged to, and now only Zarin Khan, the youngest, still remained with his parents, though he too had set his heart on a military career.

Zarin was nearly six years older than Ash, and by Asian standards a grown man. But apart from the difference in height, the two were very alike in build and colouring, for Zarin, like many Pathans, was grey-eyed and fair-skinned. They might easily have been taken for brothers, and indeed Koda Dad treated them as such, addressing them both as 'my son' and cuffing them with equal impartiality when he considered that they deserved it: an attention that Ash regarded as

* pronounced Ma-darn

an honour, for Koda Dad Khan was a re-incarnation of the friend and hero of his baby days—the shadowy but never-forgotten figure of Uncle Akbar, wise, kind and omniscient.

It was Koda Dad who taught Ash how to fly a hawk and train an unbroken colt, how to spear a tent-peg out of the ground at full gallop with the point of a lance, fire at a moving target and hit it nine times out of ten, and at a stationary one and never miss at all. It was also Koda Dad who lectured him on such matters as the wisdom of keeping his temper and the dangers of impulsiveness, and took him to task for acting or speaking before he thought—a case in point being his attack on the Yuveraj and his threat to leave the palace. 'Had you held your tongue you might have left when you would, instead of getting yourself penned up in this manner,' said Koda Dad severely.

Zarin too had been kind to the boy and treated him as a younger brother, cuffing and encouraging in turn, and best of all, Ash was occasionally permitted to accompany them outside the Hawa Mahal, which was almost as good as going alone, for though they too were instructed to see that he did not run away, their manner, unlike that of the Yuveraj's servants, never smacked of the gaoler, and with them he was able to enjoy the illusion of freedom.

Ash had forgotten the Pushtu he had learnt in his father's camp, but now he learned to speak it again because it was the native tongue of Koda Dad and Zarin and, boy-like, he wished to imitate his heroes in all things. He would speak only in Pushtu when in their company, which amused Koda Dad, though it ruffled Sita, who became as jealous of the old Pathan as she had once been of Akbar Khan. 'He does not worship the gods,' reproved Sita severely. 'Also it is well known that all Pathans live by violence. They are thieves, murderers and cattle killers, and it grieves me, Ashok, that you should spend so much time in the company of barbarians. They will teach you bad ways.'

'Is it bad to ride and shoot and fly a hawk, mother?' countered Ash, who considered that these accomplishments more than made up for such peccadilloes as murder and theft, and had never been able to see why cattle should be regarded as holy, despite all the teachings of Sita and the admonitions of the priests. If it had been horses now —or elephants or tigers—he could have understood it. But cows—

It was difficult for a small boy to keep track of the gods, when there were so many of them: Brahm, Vishnu, Indra and Shiv, who were the same and yet not the same; Mitra, ruler of the day, and Kali of the skulls and blood who was also Parvati the kind and beautiful; Krishna the Beloved, Hanuman the Ape, and pot-bellied Ganesh with his elephant head who was, strangely, the son of Shiv and Parvati. These and a hundred other gods and godlings must all be propitiated by gifts to the priests. Yet Koda Dad said that there was only one god, whose Prophet was Mohammed. Which was certainly simpler, except that it was sometimes difficult to tell who Koda Dad really worshipped—God or Mohammed—for God, according to Koda Dad, lived in the sky, but his followers must not say their prayers unless they faced in the direction of Mecca, a city where Mohammed had been born. And although Koda Dad spoke scornfully of idols and idol-worshippers, he had told Ash about a sacred stone in Mecca that was regarded as holy by all Muslims and accorded a veneration equal to anything offered by the Hindus to the stone emblems of Vishnu. Ash could see little difference between the two: if one was an idol, so was the other.

Thinking the matter over, and unwilling to go against either Sita or Koda Dad, he decided that it might be better to choose his own idol, there being authority for this—or so it seemed to him—in a prayer that he had heard the priest of the city temple intone before the gods:

> *'Oh Lord, forgive three sins that are due to my*
> *human limitations.*
> *Thou art Everywhere, but I worship thee here:*
> *Thou art without form, but I worship thee in these*
> *forms;*
> *Thou needest no praise, yet I offer thee these*
> *prayers and salutations.*
> *Lord, forgive three sins that are due to my*
> *human limitations.'*

That sounded eminently sensible to Ash, and after some deliberation he selected the cluster of snow peaks that faced the Queen's balcony: a crown of pinnacles that lifted high above the distant ranges like the towers and turrets of some fabulous city, and that were known in Gulkote as the Dur Khaima—the Far Pavilions. He found the mountain a more satisfactory object of devotion than the ugly red-daubed *lingam* that Sita made offerings to, and he could also face towards it when he said his prayers, as Koda Dad faced towards Mecca. Besides, reasoned Ash, *someone* must have made it. Perhaps the same someone whom both Sita and her priests and Koda Dad and his maulvies acknowledged? As a manifestation of the powers of that Being it was worthy of veneration. And it was his own. The personally selected interceder, protector and benfactor of Ashok, son of Sita and servant of his Highness the Yuveraj of Gulkote. *'Oh Lord,'* whispered Ash, addressing the Dur Khaima: *'thou art Everywhere, but I worship thee here . . .'*

Once adopted, the beautiful, many-peaked massif acquired a personality of its own, until it almost seemed to Ash that it was a living thing, a goddess with a hundred faces, who, unlike the stone emblems of Vishnu and the shrouded rock in Mecca, took on a different guise with every change and chance of weather and season, and each hour of every day. A gleaming flame in the dawn light and a blaze of silver at mid-day. Gold and rose in the sunset, lilac and lavender in the dusk. Livid against the storm clouds or dark against the stars. And in the months of the monsoon, withdrawing herself behind veil after veil of mist and the steel-grey curtain of the rain.

Nowadays, whenever he visited the Queen's balcony, Ash made a point of taking a handful of grain or a few flowers to lay on the broken ledge as offerings to the Dur Khaima. The birds and squirrels appreciated the grain and in time became surprisingly tame, hopping and scampering over the boy's recumbent form as though he were part of the stonework, and demanding food with the persistence of professional mendicants.

'Where have you been, *piara?*' scolded Sita. 'They have been looking for you, and I told them that you would surely be with the rascally Pathan and his hawks, or in the stables with his good-for-nothing son. Now that you are of the household of the prince it is not seemly that you should go running after such persons.'

'The servants of the Yuveraj would seem to think I am your keeper,' grumbled Koda Dad Khan. 'They come here asking "Where is he? What is he doing? Why is he not here?"'

'Where have you been?' Lalji would demand petulantly: 'Biju and Mohan have been searching everywhere for you. I won't have you going off like this. You are my servant. I wanted to play *chaupur.'*

Ash would apologize and say that he had been wandering in one of the gardens or down at the stables or the elephant lines, and then they would play *chaupur* and the matter would be forgotten—until the next time. The Hawa Mahal was so large that it was easy enough to get lost in it, and Lalji knew that the boy could never go outside it alone and would in the end be found. But he still liked to feel that Ashok was near by, for instinct told him that here was one person who could not be bribed or suborned into playing the traitor; though as there had been no more 'accidents', he was beginning to think that old Dunmaya's fears for his safety were largely imagination and that Biju Ram might be right when he said that no one, not even the *Nautch*-girl, would dare to harm him. If that were so, then there was no longer any reason to keep Ashok in attendance on him; particularly as he did not find the boy such an amusing companion as Pran or Mohan or Biju Ram, who, though probably untrustworthy and a full ten years older than himself (Biju Ram had turned twenty), were always ready to entertain him with amusingly scandalous stories of the Women's Quarters, or initiate him into various pleasurable vices. In fact if it were not for a strong feeling that Ashok was in some way a talisman against danger, he would have been tempted to dismiss him, because there was often something very like scorn in the younger boy's steady grey gaze, and his refusal to be amused by Biju's salacious wit or the entertaining cruelties of Punwa implied a criticism that was lowering to Lalji's self-esteem. Besides, he was becoming jealous of him.

It had started over Anjuli; though that had been a very minor irritation, for she was only a silly baby and a plain one at that. Had she been a pretty or engaging child he might have regarded her as a rival for his father's affections and hated her—as he hated the *Nautch*-girl and the *Nautch*-girl's eldest son, his half-brother, Nandu—but as it was, he remembered the *Feringhi*-Rani's kindness to him, and repaid it by being kind to her daughter and tacitly confirming Ashok in the role of unofficial mentor, bear-leader and protector to that small unripe mango, 'Kairi-Bai'. But he had been displeased when one of his equerries, Hira Lal, had taken a liking to the boy, and even more displeased when Koda Dad Khan, who was something of a legend to the young bloods of the palace, had done the same thing. For Koda Dad had the ear of the Rajah and he had spoken well of the boy.

The ruler of Gulkote was a large, lethargic man whose excessive fondness for wine, women and opium had drained him of strength and given him, in his early fifties, the appearance of a much older man. He was fond of his eldest son, and would have been shocked beyond words at the very idea that anyone could wish to harm his heir, and unhesitatingly condemned to death even the *Nautch*-girl herself had it been proved to him that she had attempted to take the boy's life. But increasing age and weight had made him dislike trouble, and he had discovered that, whenever he paid any attention to Lalji, trouble with the fascinating Janoo-Bai invariably followed. Wherefore in the interests of peace he saw very little of his eldest son, and Lalji, who loved his father with a burning, jealous love, resented the neglect bitterly, as he resented, too, any word spoken to anyone else during his father's all too brief visits.

The Rajah had only spoken to Ash because Koda Dad had remarked that the boy might be worth training, and also because he seemed to remember something about his having once saved Lalji's life, which entitled him to a little attention. For these reasons he had been gracious to Ash, and would sometimes order his attendance when he rode out to try a new falcon on the game-birds that abounded on the flat lands of the plateau. On these occasions Lalji would sulk and scowl and later take some petty and spiteful revenge, such as keeping Ash in attendance on him for hours on end without allowing him to eat or drink or sit until he was dizzy with fatigue, or, more viciously, driving him to rage by some senseless act of cruelty to one of the pet animals in order to have him beaten for the resulting explosion.

Lalji's courtiers, taking their cue from their master, did their best to make life difficult for the upstart horse-boy whose sudden elevation they had always resented, the sole exception to this being Hira Lal, whose duties were vaguely defined as 'Equerry to the Yuveraj'.

Of them all, Hira Lal was the only one who showed Ash any kindness, and he alone never applauded Biju Ram's sadistic foolery or laughed at his prurient jokes. He would yawn instead and toy with the black pearl that dangled from his right ear, fingering it with an abstracted air that somehow managed to convey a blend of boredom, resignation and distaste. The gesture itself was no more than a habit with him, but on such occasions it never failed to infuriate Biju Ram, who suspected (rightly) that the great pearl was worn in deliberate parody of the single earring that he himself affected, and that its rarity—the jewel was the exact shape of a pear and had the subtle, smoky iridescence of a pigeon's feather—only served to make his own diamond-drop look flashy and meretricious by contrast; in the same way as the equerry's sober grey silk *achkans* had a way of making his own more colourful coats appear vulgar and not too well cut.

Hira Lal never seemed to do any work and always appeared to be on the verge of falling asleep, but his lazy-lidded eyes were not nearly as unobservant as they looked, and very little escaped them. He was a good-natured and easy-going man, with a reputation for idleness that was a joke in the palace and gave him something of the standing of a court jester whose utterances need not be taken seriously. 'Do not let them worry you, boy,' he would encourage Ash. 'They are bored, poor mud-heads, and for lack of other amusement must cast about for some creature to torment. To witness another's discomfiture makes them feel more important themselves, even if that someone is only a child or a tame gazelle. If you do not let them see that you care, they will tire of the sport soon enough. Is that not so, *Bichchhu-ji?*'

His use of the nickname was an added insult, and Biju Ram would glare at him from eyes that were narrow slits of fury, while the others would scowl and mutter. But Lalji would pretend not to have heard, for he knew that he could not punish or dismiss Hira Lal, who had been appointed to his service by the Rajah himself (at the instigation, Lalji sometimes suspected, of his hated step-mother, the *Nautch*-girl) so that it was better, on such occasions, to feign deafness. And there was no denying that, spy or no spy, the equerry could be both witty and entertaining; he could crack jokes and invent foolish games that made one laugh on even the dullest day, and life would be a good deal less amusing without him.

Ash too was grateful to Hira Lal, and profited from his advice, which he discovered to be sound. He learned to conceal his emotions and to accept punishment stoically. But although he could in time give a convincing impression of indifference, his emotions were still there, unchanged, and all the stronger because having no outlet they must remain hidden and go deeper. Yet it was Hira Lal who made him see that Lalji should be pitied and not disliked, and how infinitely superior his own position was to that of the angry, bewildered little prince.

'When he oppresses you, it is only to revenge himself for the lack of love that he needs and is not given,' said Hira Lal. 'If he had never had love it would matter less, for many grow up without it and do not know what they have missed. But having had it he has learned what it is to lose it. And it is this that makes him unhappy.

When he has teased and tormented you and had you unjustly punished, you can run to your mother who will console you and weep over your wounds. But there is no one to whom he can run except that old witch of a nurse, Dunmaya, who does nothing but croak warnings and make him frightened of his own shadow. Be patient with him, Ashok, for you are more fortunate than he.'

Ash strove for patience, though it was uphill work. But a clearer understanding of the heir's predicament undoubtedly helped, and for this he was grateful to Hira Lal.

Lalji was married the following year and enmities were forgotten in the bustle and preparation and festivity. The vast, somnolent palace came alive and hummed like a beehive as painters and decorators swarmed in with their buckets of lime wash and colour, and walls, ceilings and archways that were dusty from neglect received coats of bright paint and gilding. The *Nautch*-girl, predictably jealous of all the attention bestowed upon her step-son, had alternately sulked and made scenes, and the bride's relatives had created considerable uproar on the very eve of the wedding by suddenly demanding double the previously agreed bride-price, which had so incensed the groom's father that he had come within an ace of calling the whole thing off. But as this would have brought great shame on all concerned, a compromise had been reached after hours of argument, cajolery and hard bargaining, and the preparations had gone forward.

The bride was the eight-year-old daughter of a small hill Rajah, and after the wedding she would return to her parents until she was old enough for the marriage to be consummated; though this made no difference to the lengthy and elaborate ceremonies. It was a long and tedious business and it cost the Rajah a great deal of money that could have been put to better use alleviating the poverty of his subjects or improving the roads in Gulkote—not that such an idea even crossed the mind of either ruler or subjects, and if it had it would have been unanimously rejected by both in favour of the jollity and entertainment offered by a really lavish wedding.

All Gulkote enjoyed the spectacle and relished the gifts of food and money distributed to the poor, and the sight of so much magnificence. Fireworks, bands, processions by torch-light to the city temple, prancing horsemen and plodding elephants draped in glittering brocade and carrying silver howdahs full of bejewelled guests, enthralled the citizens and drained the treasury. Which troubled the Rajah not a whit, though it angered the *Nautch*-girl, who complained that it was all a great waste of money, and was only placated with a gift of rubies and diamonds from the state regalia.

5

Ash enjoyed the wedding festivities as much as anyone, and for the first time in her short life, the four-year-old Kairi was ordered to take part, as a Princess of Gulkote, in an official ceremony.

As the sister of the Yuveraj, it was her privilege to present the first gifts to the bride; and she had done so dressed in unfamiliar finery and decked with resplendent jewels that had at first delighted her by their colour and glitter, and then tired her by their weight and the way their sharp edges scratched. But as her sole ornament hitherto had been a small mother-of-pearl fish that she wore on a string about her neck as a 'luck-piece' (it had belonged to her mother and once been part of a set of Chinese counters) she had greatly enjoyed the dignity they lent her. It was nice to feel important for once, and she had revelled in that and performed her duties with becoming seriousness.

The ceremonies and festivity had continued for over a week, and when at last they were over and bride and guests had returned to their own homes, Kairi's borrowed finery was whisked away from her and returned to one of the numerous chests that filled the Rajah's treasury, and only tattered decorations, fading wreaths and a smell of stale incense and decaying flowers remained to show that the great occassion had come and gone. The Hawa Mahal and its Rajah relapsed into lethargy, and Janoo-Bai the Rani set about planning far more spectacular alliances for her own small sons.

As for Lalji, now that all the excitement was over he found that the dignity of his married state added nothing to his importance, and that for all the difference it had made to life he might just as well have done without those long, tiring ceremonies. He thought his wife was a stupid little thing and not particularly pretty, and could only hope that she would grow up to look more attractive. Dunmaya said she would; but then Dunmaya would say anything to please him. With the departure of the wedding guests his father had lost interest in him, and once again time hung heavy on his hands and he felt crosser and unhappier than ever. Wherefore he quarrelled with his suite and made life so miserable for Ash that it was some time during those dismal months, in the flat aftermath of the wedding, that

Ash for the first time discussed with Sita the possibility of their leaving Gulkote.

Sita had been aghast at the idea. Not on her own account, for she would have sacrificed anything for his sake; but because she did not believe that he would be better off anywhere else, or that his present mood was anything more than a boy's natural reaction to the churlish behaviour of the Yuveraj, which would pass. Sita was fully aware of the Yuveraj's problems; there were few secrets in the palace, and though it angered her that he should vent his spleen on her beloved son, she, like Hira Lal, could not help feeling a certain sympathy for the motherless, neglected heir whose father was too idle to champion him and whose step-mother prayed for his early death. His fits of ill-temper and sporadic outbursts of cruelty were surely no more than could be expected of a boy caught in such an intolerable web of circumstances, and Ashok must learn to bear with them and try to forgive them. Besides, it was certain that the Yuveraj would never willingly allow him to leave, and he must not even think of running away; it would be impossible, and even if he should succeed, where could they go? Where else could they live in such comfort and security as here, in a Rajah's palace and enjoying the salary and status of royal servants?

'Do they pay you then, mother?' inquired Ash bitterly. 'Me, they do not—though it was promised me. Oh, I am given food and clothing. But never money. And if I ask for it they say, "Later. Another time. Next month." I have not so much as a *pice* to give or spend.'

'But *piara,* we are both fed and clothed,' urged Sita. 'And we have a roof over our heads and a fire to warm ourselves by. Besides, do not forget that the Yuveraj will one day be Rajah, and then you will be rewarded and stand high in his favour. He is only a boy, Ashok, a young, unhappy boy. That is why he is sometimes unjust. But when he is grown he will be wiser. You will see. You have only to be patient and wait a little longer.'

'How much longer? A year? Two years? Three? Oh, mother—!'

'I know, my son. I know. But I—I am not as young as I was, and . . .'

She did not finish the sentence, but Ash looked at her sharply and noticed for the first time, with a curious little stab of fear, that she seemed to have become much thinner of late and that the sprinkling of grey hairs that had grown more noticeable with each year now outnumbered the dark, so that her head was nearer silver than black.

She looked tired too, and he wondered if they made her work too hard in Kairi's wing of the palace. He must talk to Kairi and tell her that his mother must not be worried or overworked. Yet it was he who was worrying her now, and realizing it, he flung his arms about her and hugged her in a sudden spasm of remorse, telling her that of course they would stay—he had only been teasing her, and as long as she was happy here they would remain in the Hawa Mahal.

He did not broach the subject again, and after that he pretended that all was well in the Yuveraj's household and did his best not to let her see that he was disgruntled or unhappy. Kairi, severely lectured for lack of consideration towards his mother, assured him earnestly that Sita's duties were not heavy: 'I think perhaps she only gets tired because she is old,' ventured Kairi, thinking it over. 'Old ladies do get tired, you know. Dunmaya is always saying how tired she is.'

But his mother was not old—not like wrinkled, white-headed Dunmaya, thought Ash; and was once again afraid. Because of that fear he spoke sharply to Kairi, telling her that she was a stupid, brainless baby who did not understand anything and he did not know why he wasted time talking to her or allowed her to follow him about like a mangy kitten, never giving him a moment's peace. 'Miaow! Miaow!— Girls!' said Ash with masculine scorn, and added unkindly that he was thankful that he hadn't any sisters. Whereupon Kairi wept and had to be comforted by being allowed to tie a strand of floss silk about his wrist, which made him her 'bracelet-brother' in accordance with an ancient custom that permits a woman to give or send a bracelet to any man, who, if he accepts it, is thereafter honour-bound to aid and protect her if called upon to do so, as though she were in truth his sister.

But although Kairi's persistent adoration frequently exasperated him, Ash had, in the end, become genuinely fond of the little creature and developed a strong sense of ownership, something that he had not felt since the death of Tuku. Kairi was a more satisfactory pet than even Tuku had been, for she could talk to him. And like Tuku, she loved him and followed him about and depended upon him, so that in time she came to fill the empty place in his heart that had once belonged to the little mongoose. It was good to know that here at least was a creature he could pet and protect without any fear of harm befalling it from Lalji or anyone else. But caution made him warn Kairi not to show her partiality for him too openly: 'I am only your real brother's servant, and so he and the others might not like it,' he explained.

Young as she was, she had understood; and after that she seldom addressed him directly unless they were alone or with Sita. They had devised a way of communicating with each other through the medium of a conversation ostensibly directed at a third person, and such was their rapport that they soon learned to translate the real meaning from an apparently casual sentence addressed to Lalji or one of his household or, more frequently, to a macaw or a pet monkey. It was a game that delighted both of them, and at which they grew so expert that no one save Hira Lal—who seldom missed anything of significance—ever suspected that the little girl's chatter and the boy's occasional remarks had two meanings and were directed at each other. In this way they would openly arrange to meet at certain times, and at certain places for which they had invented code words: either in Sita's courtyard or, more often, in the Queen's balcony, where they would feed the birds and squirrels, discuss the doings of the palace, or sit in companionable silence gazing out at the far snows.

Ash lost one of his few friends that year, for in the autumn Zarin left to join his two elder brothers, who were sowars in the Corps of Guides.

'I have taught him all I know of marksmanship and swordplay, and he was a horseman born,' said Koda Dad. 'It is time he made his own way in the world. Fighting is a man's trade, and there is always war along the Border.'

Koda Dad had seen to it that his son was provided with the finest horse that Gulkote could supply, for vacancies in the Corps were much sought after, and went only to the finest riders and best shots among a long list of applicants. Neither Ash nor Zarin doubted for one moment that a vacancy would be won, and Zarin rode confidently away, assuring Ash that he would return on his first leave.

'And when you are full grown, you shall come to Mardan and be a sowar too,' promised Zarin, 'and we will ride in cavalry charges and see the sack of cities. So look to it that you learn all that my father can teach you, so that you do not disgrace me when you come as a recruit.'

Life in the Hawa Mahal had seemed more irksome than ever after Zarin had gone, and when word came from Mardan that he had won a vacancy in the *rissala* (cavalry) and was now a sowar in the Guides, Ash's restlessness had increased: and with it, a determination to emulate his friend and become a soldier. With this in mind he missed no chance to ride or shoot with Koda Dad; though Sita did her best to discourage this new plan for the future. The very mention of the Guides terrified Sita, and a large part of her hostility towards Koda Dad and his son stemmed from their connection with that Regiment. It had been a severe shock to her to discover that even here in Gulkote, where she had thought herself so safe, Ashok had made friends with men who might one day bring him to the notice of his *Angrezi* uncle, and she had done everything in her power to avert this calamity.

Soldiers, asserted Sita, were brutal, ill-paid men who lived dangerous and disorganized lives, sleeping in tents or on the hard ground with never a roof over their heads or the security of a settled home for their families. Why should Ashok suddenly desire to become a soldier?

She had appeared so upset that Ash had dropped the subject and allowed her to suppose that he had not been serious. He imagined that she had only taken a dislike to it because it had been suggested to him by Koda Dad and Zarin, neither of whom she had ever approved of, and did not suspect that there was any other reason for her opposition. But though he did not mention it again to Sita, he continued to discuss it with Koda Dad, and would often talk of it to Kairi, who despite her tender age and limited understanding, made an admirable and uncritical audience.

Kairi could be relied upon to listen by the hour to anything he had to say, and he found that he did not have to explain things to her, for she seemed to understand him by instinct; though it is doubtful if she remembered any of it for long—except when he spoke of the valley. Kairi preferred that subject to all others, for by now the valley had become as real to her as it was to Ash, and she took it for granted that she would go too and help to build their house. The two children would plan the house together room by room, adding and embellishing, turning it from a cottage to a palace, until—tiring of grandeur—they would demolish it with a wave of a hand and begin it again, this time as a miniature dwelling with low ceilings and a thatched roof. 'Though even that will cost a lot of money,' said Kairi anxiously. 'Tens and tens of rupees'—she still could not count further than ten.

One day she brought him a silver four-anna piece as a beginning, telling him that they should start saving up for the house. The little coin was more money than Ash had held in his hand for a long time, and to him even more than to Kairi it represented something approximating to riches. There were a dozen things he would like to have spent it on, but he hid it instead under a loose stone in the floor of the Queen's balcony, telling her that they would add to it when they could. They never did so, for money was hard to come by in the Hawa Mahal; and though there was always enough to eat, and clothing could be had if one could prove the need of it, Ash looked back on his life in the city as a time of affluence as well as freedom, and recalled with longing his modest wages as a horse-boy in Duni Chand's stables.

It was humiliating to realize that in these days he could not even match Kairi's meagre contribution, and that if he should ever obtain permission to leave the service of the Yuveraj, and overcome Sita's prejudice against soldiering as a career, he would not be able to join Zarin. For Koda Dad told him that the Guides Cavalry was recruited on the *Silladar* system, by which each recruit brought his own horse and also a sum of money with which to buy his equipment, the latter being refunded to him on discharge. Zarin had had both money and a horse, but Ash could see little prospect of acquiring either.

'When I am married, I will give you all the money you need,' consoled Kairi, whose betrothal was already being discussed in the Women's Quarter of the Hawa Mahal.

'What's the good of that?' retorted Ash ungratefully. 'It'll be too late then. You won't be married for years and years—you're only a baby.'

'I shall be six soon,' urged Kairi, 'and Aruna says that this is old enough to be married.'

'Then they will take you away, perhaps days and days of marches from here; and however rich you are, you won't be able to send money back to Gulkote,' said Ash, determined to look on the dark side of things. 'And anyway, your husband might not give you any money.'

'Of course he would. If I were a Maharani I should have crores and crores of rupees to spend—like Janoo-Rani has. And diamonds and pearls and elephants and—'

'And an old, fat, bad-tempered husband who will beat you, and then die years and years before you do, so that you will have to become a suttee and be burned alive with him.'

'Don't say that.' Kairi's voice shook and her small face turned pale, for the Suttee Gate with its pathetic frieze of red hand-prints had always filled her with horror, and she could not bear to pass that tragic reminder of the scores of women who had made those marks— the wives and concubines who had been burned alive with the bodies of dead Rajahs of Gulkote, and who had dipped their palms in red dye and pressed them against the stone as they passed out through the Suttee Gate on their last short journey to the funeral pyre. Such slender, delicate little hands, some of them no bigger than her own. The British had forbidden the barbaric custom of suttee, but everyone knew that in remote and independent states, where white men were seldom seen, it was still practised; and half the population of Gulkote could remember seeing Kairi's grandmother, the old Rani, immolating herself in the flames that consumed the body of her husband, together with three lesser wives and seventeen women of the Zenana.

'If I were you, Juli,' said Ash thinking it over, 'I wouldn't get married at all. It's too dangerous.'

Few Europeans had ever visited Gulkote, for although the state was now officially part of the territory that had come under the jurisdiction of the British Crown after the Sepoy mutiny of 1857, its lack of roads and bridges continued to discourage travellers, and as it had given no trouble, the authorities were content to leave well alone until such time as they had settled the more pressing problems of the sub-continent. In the autumn of '59, the Rajah, with an eye to forestalling interference, had prudently sent his Prime Minister and a deputation of nobles to negotiate a treaty of alliance with the new rulers, but it was not until the spring of '63 that Colonel Frederick Byng of the Political Department paid a formal visit to His Highness of Gulkote, accompanied by several junior secretaries and an escort of Sikh Cavalry under the command of a British officer.

The occasion was one of considerable interest to His Highness's subjects, whose acquaintance with Europeans had so far been limited to that colourful Cossack adventurer, Sergei Vodvichenko, and his hapless, half-caste daughter, the *Feringhi*-Rani. They were curious to see what these Sahib-log looked like and how they would comport themselves. And more than ready to enjoy the festivities that would mark the occasion. It was to be a right royal *tamarsha* (show), and no one looked forward to it with keener anticipation than Ash, though Sita made it clear that she disapproved strongly of foreigners visiting the state, and did her best to dissuade him from attending any of the ceremonies, or even appearing at court during the time that the Englishmen would be present.

'Why should they wish to come here and interfere with us?' complained Sita. 'We do not want *feringhis* here, telling us what we should or should not do and creating worry and trouble for everyone . . . asking questions. Promise me, Ashok, that you will have nothing to do with them.'

Her vehemence puzzled Ash, who had never quite forgotten a certain tall, grey-haired man who had lectured him repeatedly on the crime of being unfair . . . he could remember nothing else about this man except a curious and uncomfortable memory of his face seen fleetingly by lamplight, drained of life and colour; and afterwards the sound of jackals snarling and quarrelling in the moonlight, a sound that had, for some reason, left so strong an impression of fear that even now he could never hear the yelling of a jackal pack without shuddering. But he had early discovered that his mother disliked any mention of the past and could not be persuaded to talk of it. Perhaps the *feringhi* had been unkind to her, and that was why she was so anxious to prevent him from having any truck with the English visitors? It was, however, unreasonable of her to expect him to absent himself from duty for the duration of their stay; this would not be possible, as Lalji would need the services of all in his household during the visit.

But on the eve of Colonel Byng's arrival, Ash was unaccountably taken ill after a meal prepared by his mother, and for the next few days he remained prone on his bed in her quarters, unable to take any interest in anything but the acute discomfort in his head and stomach. Sita nursed him devotedly, accusing herself, with tears and lamentations, of giving him bad food, and while refusing to admit the hakim (doctor) who had been sent by Hira Lal to treat the sufferer, dosed Ash with herbal brews of her own concoction that had the effect of making him drowsy and heavy-headed. By the time he was on his feet again the visitors had gone, and he had to be content with a second-hand account of the junketings, relayed to him by Kairi, Koda Dad and Hira Lal.

'You did not miss very much,' said Hira Lal sardonically. 'The Colonel was old and fat, and his secretaries young and foolish, and only the officer in command of their escort spoke our tongue with any fluency. His Sikhs said that he was a pukka devil—which they meant to be a compliment. Are you well now? Kairi-Bai said she was sure you had been given poison to keep you from seeing the *tamarsha,* but we told her not to be a little owl, for who would care whether you saw it or no? Not Lalji, whatever his foolish little sister may think. Our beloved Yuveraj is too full of his own importance these days to bother his head over such matters.'

This last was true enough, for as his father's heir, Lalji had played a prominent part in the various official functions in honour of Colonel Byng, and enjoyed the limelight. It had been more entertaining and far less tiring than the ceremonies that had attended his wedding, and as part of his father's design to dazzle the barbarians, the clothes and jewels he had been given to wear had been even more magnificent than his wedding finery. Lalji had a fondness for fine clothes and display, and few opportunities for indulging it, so he had thoroughly enjoyed peacocking it at his father's side, decked out in embroidered coats stiff with gold and silver thread, wearing brilliant gauze turbans, ropes of pearls and collars of glittering jewels, and carrying a diamond-hilted sword with velvet scabbard that was sewn with seed pearls.

The fat Englishman who spoke such execrable Hindustani had been most affable, and treated him as though he were already a man grown, and although his father had also presented the *Nautch*-girl's eldest son to the visitors, little Nandu had not created a good impression, for he was a spoilt child and had screamed and whined and been so naughty that the Rajah had lost all patience with him and had him removed half-way through the first reception. He had not been allowed to appear again, so it was Lalji, and Lalji alone, who had sat, stood or ridden by his father's side throughout the four days of festivity; and when it was all over the splendid robes and jewels had not been taken away from him, but left in his charge, and his father had continued to command his presence and treat him with unusual affection.

Lalji was happier than he had ever been before, and his happiness showed itself in a hundred ways. He ceased to tease his little sister or torment his pets, and was gracious and good tempered to all his household. It was a pleasant change from his former tantrums, and only Hira Lal predicted trouble in the future. But then Hira Lal was known to be a cynic. The other members of the Yuveraj's household basked in the relaxed atmosphere created by their young master's change of temper, and saw it as a sign that the boy was becoming a man and preparing at last to put aside childish things. They were also pleasantly surprised at the Rajah's continuous predilection for his son's society: they had not expected it to outlast the departure of the visitors, and were amazed to find that the young Yuveraj now spent a large part of each day in his father's company and was actually being instructed in affairs of state. All of which was deeply gratifying to the *Nautch*-girl's enemies—and they were many—who regarded the situation as a sign of the favourite's declining power (particularly as the child she had lately borne her lord was a small and sickly girl). But as subsequent events were to show they had once again underestimated her.

Janoo-Rani had been thrown into an imperial rage by the removal of her screaming son from the Durbar Hall, and the favourable impression created by his hated half-brother, the heir. She had raged for two days and sulked for a further seven. But, for once, without the anticipated effect. The Rajah had retaliated by avoiding her apartments and keeping to his own part of the palace until such time as she should have recovered her temper, and this unexpected reaction had frightened her as much as it had delighted her enemies.

Janoo looked at herself in the glass and saw in it something that she had hitherto refused to recognize—that she had lost her figure and was becoming stout. Time, childbearing and soft living had taken their toll, and the seductive, golden-skinned girl of a few years ago had gone, leaving in her place a short, plump little woman whose complexion was already beginning to darken and who would soon be fat, but who had, as yet, lost none of her wit or her power to charm. Taking stock of the situation, Janoo had hastily stage-managed a reconciliation, and so successfully that she was soon firmly back in the saddle. But she did not forget that short-lived taste of terror, and now, to the surprise of the court, she set out to win the friendship of her step-son.

It had not been easy, for the boy's jealous hatred of the woman who had supplanted the *Feringhi*-Rani and enslaved his father was a strong growth whose roots went deep. But Lalji had always been fatally susceptible to flattery, and now the *Nautch*-girl fed his vanity with fulsome compliments and extravagant gifts. Reversing her previous policy, she encouraged the Rajah to make much of his eldest son, and in the end she achieved, if not friendship, at least a truce.

'Someone,' said Koda Dad, unimpressed by the Rani's apparent change of heart, 'should remind that boy of the tiger of Teetagunje, who feigned to be a vegetarian and invited the buffalo's child to dine.'

The court too regarded this new situation with a sceptical eye and predicted that it would not last. But as the weeks went by and it was seen that the Rani continued to remain on good terms with her step-son, it lost its novelty and in time came to be accepted as a normal state of affairs; which delighted the Rajah and pleased the majority of the Yuveraj's household—with the exception of old Dunmaya, who could not be brought to trust the *Nautch*-girl, and Hira Lal, who for once found himself in agreement with her. 'Never trust a snake or a harlot,' quoted Hira Lal sardonically.

Ash too had benefited briefly from the changed atmosphere, for Lalji's happiness and high spirits made him wish to make amends for his former unkindness to the boy who had, after all, once saved his life; though Lalji no longer believed that his step-mother had been in any way involved in that incident. It must have been an accident, he felt certain of that now; and also that there had been no need for him to insist on Ashok's presence in the palace, or any valid reason why he should continue to restrict his liberty. The obvious thing to do now would be to permit him to come and go as he chose. But Lalji was nothing if not obstinate and his pride forbade him to go back on any orders he had once given. He resolved, however, to be kinder to Ashok in the future.

For a time it almost seemed that Ash had been reinstated in his original position of companion and confidant to the Yuveraj. But it did not last. He was not aware of having done anything to offend, and he could not understand the reason for his second fall from favour—any more than he had understood the previous, and equally sudden, reinstatement. But the fact remained that once again, and without warning, Lalji turned against him, and from then on treated him with unreasonable and increasing hostility. A trinket mislaid or an ornament broken, a curtain torn or a parrot ailing—these and a dozen other petty mishaps were laid at his door and he was duly punished for them.

'But why *me?*' demanded Ash, bewildered by Lalji's inexplicable change of heart and, as always, taking his troubles to Koda Dad. 'What have I done? It's not fair! Why should he treat me like this? What has happened to him?'

'Allah knows,' shrugged Koda Dad. 'It may be that one of his household became jealous of his renewed favour towards you, and has whispered falsehoods against you to bring you down. The favour of princes breeds envy and makes enemies; and there are some who have no love for you. He they call *"Bichchhu"* for one.'

'Oh, him. Biju Ram has always hated me; though I do not know why he should, for I have done him no harm and I have never stood in his way.'

'Of that I am not so sure,' said Koda Dad.

Ash looked a question, and Koda Dad said dryly: 'Has it never occurred to you that he might be in the pay of the Rani?'

'Biju? But—but that cannot be so,' stammered Ash, aghast. 'He could not . . . not while Lalji holds him in such favour and gives him rich presents and . . . He would not—'

'Why? Was it not the Yuveraj himself who dubbed him *"Bichchhu"?*—and with good reason? I tell you, Biju Ram's blood is as cold as that of his namesake. Moreover, we have a proverb in the country beyond the Khyber, that says "A snake, a scorpion and a Shinwari have no heart to tame" (which Allah knows is true of a Shinwari). Listen, my son; I have heard it whispered in certain quarters of the city, and here too in the Hawa Mahal, that this man is a creature of the Rani's and that she pays him well to do her work. Should this be true—and I think it is—then surely both he and the woman should have every reason to hate you?'

'Yes.' The boy's voice was almost inaudible and he shivered, feeling as though the very ground under his feet was no longer solid. 'Poor Lalji . . . !'

'Poor Lalji, indeed,' agreed Koda Dad soberly. 'Have I not told you many times that life is not always easy for those in high places?'

'Yes; but he had been so much better of late. So much happier; and kinder, too. To everyone, not only me. Yet now all of a sudden I seem to be the only one he is unkind to, and always for things I have not done. It isn't fair, Koda Dad. It isn't *fair.'*

'Bah! that is a child's saying,' grunted Koda Dad. 'Men are not fair—neither the young nor the old. You should have found that out by now, my son. What does Hira Lal say?'

But Hira Lal had only pulled at his earring and said: 'I told you there would be trouble.' And as he refused to add anything to this comment, it could hardly be considered helpful.

A few days later Ash had been accused of damaging Lalji's favourite bow, which had snapped during target practice. He protested that he had not touched it, but was disbelieved and soundly beaten; and it was after this that he had begged permission to resign from the Yuveraj's service and quit the Hawa Mahal. It was not granted. Instead, he was informed that he would not only remain in the service of His Highness, but that in future he would not be permitted under any circumstances to leave the fortress, which meant that he was no longer allowed to accompany Lalji or the Rajah when they rode out to hunt or hawk on the plateau or among the hills; or go into the city with Koda Dad or anyone else. The Hawa Mahal had turned, at last, into the prison that he had visualized on the day that he first entered it: its gates had closed behind him and there was no way of escape.

With the advent of the cold weather Sita contracted a chill and a small dry cough. There was nothing new in this; she had suffered from such things before. But this time she did not seem to throw it off, though she refused to seek advice from the hakim, and assured Ash that it was nothing and would pass as soon as the clean winds of winter rid them of the lingering heat and dampness of the monsoon. Yet already the heat had gone from the plateau and the air that blew off the mountains carried the faint cool tang of pine-needles and snow.

News had come from Zarin in Mardan, but it was not good news. The Guides had been in action against one of the Border tribes, and in the fighting his brother Afzal, Koda Dad's second son, had been killed. 'It is the will of Allah,' said Koda Dad. 'What is written is written. But he was his mother's favourite . . .'

It was a sad autumn for Ash, and would have been sadder but for the staunch support of that small but faithful ally, Kairi-Bai. Neither disapproval nor direct orders had the slightest effect on Kairi, who evaded her women with the ease of long practice and would slip away daily to meet Ash in the balcony on the *Mor Minar,* bringing with her, as often as not, an assortment of fruit or sweetmeats smuggled out from her own meals or stolen from Lalji's.

Lying there and looking out towards the white peaks of the Dur Khaima, the two children would devise endless schemes for Ashok's escape from the palace; or rather, Ash would propound while Kairi listened. But the schemes were not serious, for both knew that Ash would not leave his mother, who was getting daily frailer. She who had always been so hard working and energetic was now often to be found sitting tiredly in her courtyard, her back against the trunk of the pine tree and her hands lying idle in her lap, and by common consent the children were careful not to mention Ash's troubles to her; though there were many troubles, not least of them his knowledge that once again someone was actively attempting to murder the heir of Gulkote.

Three years are a long time in a child's life, and Ash had almost forgotten the poisoned cakes that had been left in Lalji's garden, until suddenly a similar incident recalled them vividly and unpleasantly to his mind.

A box of the special nut-sprinkled *halwa* that Lalji was particularly fond of was found lying on one of the marble seats in the pavilion near the lily pool, and the Yuveraj pounced upon them, supposing them to have been left there by one of his attendants. But even as he did so, Ash recalled in an ugly flash of memory a trio of fat carp floating belly upwards among the lily pads, and springing forward he snatched the box from the Yuveraj's hand.

The action had been purely instinctive, and faced with a furious demand for an explanation he found himself in a trap. Having never told anyone of those cakes, he could not speak of them now without being disbelieved, or accused of concealing an attempt on the Yuveraj's life: either way the truth would not serve him, so he took refuge in a lie and said that the sweets were his own, but were unfit to be eaten, having been handled in error by a sweeper—a man of the lowest caste—and that he had brought them here intending to feed them to the pigeons. Lalji had backed away in horror, and Ash had been punished for bringing them into the garden. Yet that three-year-old memory had not betrayed him, for later that evening he threw one of the sweets to a crow. And the crow had died. But because he had not spoken before, he dared not speak now.

The following week there had been another unnerving incident, involving a cobra that had somehow found its way into Lalji's bedroom. A dozen servants were ready to swear that it could not have been there when the Yuveraj went to bed, but it was certainly there in the small hours of the morning, for something had woken Ash, and within a few minutes of his waking he heard a clock strike two. His pallet lay across the threshold of the Yuveraj's room and no one could pass in without disturbing him: not even a snake. Yet lying awake and listening in the darkness, he had heard something that he could not mistake: the dry rustle and slither of scales moving across the uncarpeted floor.

Ash possessed all the European's horror of snakes, and instinct urged him to be still and make no move that might attract the creature's attention to himself. But the sound had come from inside the Yuveraj's room, and he knew that Lalji was a restless sleeper who might at any moment throw out an arm or turn over with an abruptness that would invite attack. So he rose, shivering with panic, and groped his way over to the curtained doorway that led into an outer room. There was an oil lamp there, its wick turned low, and he set it flaring and woke the servants.

The cobra was investigating the fruit and drink set out on a low table by Lalji's bed, and it was killed to the accompaniment of shrieks from Lalji and considerable uproar from a milling mob of servants, courtiers and guards. No one had ever discovered how it had managed to enter the room, though it was generally supposed to have found its way in through the bathroom sluice, and only Dunmaya saw its appearance as a deliberate plot against her darling.

'She is a foolish old woman, that one,' said Sita, listening to the tale of the night's doings. 'Who would dare to catch a live cobra and carry it through the palace? And if they could do such a thing they would certainly have been seen, for it was not a small snake. Besides, who is there in Gulkote who would wish to harm the boy? Not the Rani; all know how fond she has become of him. She treats him with as much kindness as though he was her own son, and I tell you it is not necessary to have given birth to a child in order to become fond of it. Dunmaya did not bear the Yuveraj, yet she too loves him—even to seeing plots everywhere. She is mad.'

Ash remained silent and did not tell her of those long-ago cakes and the *halwa* that had so recently appeared in the same garden and had also been poisoned, or what Koda Dad had said about the Rani and Biju Ram. He knew that such ugly tales would only frighten her, and he did not intend that she should hear them. But all too soon there came a day when it was no longer possible to keep them from her, for Kairi stumbled upon something that was to alter their lives as drastically as the cholera had done in that terrible spring when Hilary and Akbar Khan had died.

The Princess Anjuli—'Kairi-Bai', the little unripe mango—was barely six years old at that time, and had she been born in any Western country she would still have been considered a baby. But she had not only been born in the east, but in an eastern palace, and a too early experience of the plotting and intrigues of an Indian court had sharpened her wits and made her wise beyond her years.

Mindful of Ashok's warning and knowing him to be out of favour with her brother Lalji, Kairi no longer spoke to him or even glanced his way in public. But the system of secret signs and code words by which they could communicate under the eyes of the whole household without being detected served them well, and it was three days after the incident of the cobra that she ran to the Yuveraj's quarters and managed to convey an urgent signal to Ash. It was one that they were only to use in a dire emergency, and obeying it, Ash had slipped away at the earliest opportunity and made his way to the Queen's balcony, where Kairi had been waiting for him, white-faced and dissolved in tears.

'It's your own fault,' sobbed Kairi. 'She said you threw away some sweets and saved him from a cobra. I truly didn't mean to listen but I was afraid she would be angry if she found me in her garden, and Mian Mittau had flown in there and I had to catch him—I *had* to. So when I heard her coming I hid in the bushes behind the pavilion and I heard . . . I heard what she said. Oh Ashok, she is bad! Bad and wicked. She meant to kill Lalji, and now she is angry with you about the cobra and because of some sweets. She said it showed that you know too much, so they must kill you quickly and she doesn't care how it is done, because it won't show by the time the kites and crows have finished with you, and who will mind about the death of a bazaar brat—that's you Ashok, she meant you. And she told them to throw you over the wall afterwards so that people will think you were climbing and fell off. It's true what I'm telling. They are going to kill you, Ashok. Oh what shall we do—what shall we do?'

Kairi threw herself at him wailing with terror, and Ash put his arms round her and mechanically rocked her to and fro while his thoughts scurried round in frantic circles. Yes, it was true . . . he was sure of that, for Juli could never have invented such a conversation. Janoo-Rani had always meant to kill Lalji and set her own son in his place, and to her certain knowledge he, Ashok, had stood in her way at least three times—four, if she was aware that it was also he who had found and thrown away those cakes. Had she known? He did not think anyone had seen him do that. But it made no difference now. She meant to see that he did not interfere again, and he would be a much easier target than Lalji, for no one would inquire too closely into the death or disappearance of such an unimportant person as the son of a serving-woman in the household of the neglected Kairi-Bai. He had never told Lalji of those cakes, or the truth about the *halwa,* and it was too late to tell him now. Particularly as Lalji had long ago persuaded himself that the falling slab of sandstone had been no more than an accident, and only two days ago had told Dunmaya that she was an evil-minded old troublemaker who deserved to have her tongue cut out, because the old woman had voiced suspicions regarding the cobra. There was no help to be expected from the Yuveraj.

'Juli was right,' thought Ash despairingly. 'It is my own fault for not telling Lalji about it and showing him what those cakes did to the fish years ago, and the sweets poisoning that crow.' He hadn't any proof now; and even if he had it wouldn't help him because Lalji was so sure that the Rani was his friend, and he, Ashok, could not prove that she did it, or tell them what Juli had heard because they would say that she was only a baby and had made it up. But the Rani would know that she hadn't and perhaps kill her too—and his mother as well, in case Sita should ask too many questions if he were killed . . .

Twilight was gathering under the dome of the Queen's balcony, and Kairi had wept herself into exhaustion and now lay still and silent, soothed by the monotonous motion as Ash rocked to and fro and stared above her head at the far-away snows. The breeze was cold with the coming of winter, for October was nearly over and the days were drawing in. The sun had almost vanished and the distant peaks of the Dur Khaima made a frieze of fading rose and amber against an opal sky in which a single star shimmered like one of Janoo-Rani's diamonds.

Ash shivered, and releasing Kairi said abruptly: 'We must go. It will soon be too dark to see, and—and they may be looking for me.' But he did not go until the snows had turned from pink to violet and only the top-most peak of the Far Pavilions—*Tarakalas,* the 'Star Turret'—still held the last of the sunset.

He had brought no rice with him today, but Kairi wore a little bracelet of late rosebuds around one wrist, and he stripped it off and scattered the buds at the edge of the balcony, hoping that the Dur Khaima would understand the emergency and forgive him for not bringing an offering of his own: 'Help me,' prayed Ash to his personal deity. 'Please help me! I don't want to die . . .'

The light faded from the peak and now the whole range was no more than a lilac silhouette against the darkening sky, and there was not one star, but a thousand. As the night wind strengthened it blew the rosebuds away, and Ash was comforted, for it seemed to him that the Dur Khaima had accepted his offering. The two children turned together and groped their way down through the ruined tower and back to Sita's courtyard, hand clutched in hand and eyes and ears strained to catch the smallest sound or movement that would betray a lurker in the shadows.

Sita had been cooking the evening meal, and Ash left Kairi with her and fled back to the Yuveraj's rooms through the maze of corridors and courtyards that formed a third of the Hawa Mahal, his heart thumping wildly and a queer cold feeling between his shoulderblades at that spot where a knife might most easily be driven in. It was an enormous relief to find that he had not been missed because Lalji had received a set of jewelled chessmen from the Rani, and was engaged in a game with Biju Ram.

Half-a-dozen sycophantic courtiers surrounded the chess players and applauded their young master's every move, and at the far end of the room a solitary figure sat cross-legged under a hanging lamp, absorbed in a book and paying no attention to the game. Ash tiptoed over to him and begged in a whisper for a word in private, and Hira Lal's lazy eyes scanned the boy's face for a brief moment before returning to the book.

'No. Tell me here,' said Hira Lal in an unhurried undertone that did not carry to the group of courtiers. 'If it is important, it is better not to go apart, for then someone might follow to find out what it is that you do not wish overheard. Turn your back to them so that they cannot see your face, and do not speak in a whisper. They will never believe that you would talk secrets in so public a place, so you may say what you will.'

Ash obeyed him. He had to have advice, and of all the Yuveraj's household only Hira Lal had befriended him. He would have to trust him now because there was the night to be got through, and he did not know how many of the household were in the *Nautch*-girl's pay: perhaps half of them—or all of them. But not Hira Lal. Instinct told him that he could rely on Hira Lal, and instinct was right. Hira Lal listened without comment, his slim fingers absently toying with his dangling earring while his gaze strayed about the room in a manner calculated to suggest to the group by the chess players that he was bored and paying very little attention. But when Ash had finished, he said quietly: 'You did well to tell me. I will see to it that you come to no harm tonight. But the Rani is a dangerous woman and she can afford to pay highly to achieve her ends. You will have to leave Gulkote—you and your mother both. There is no other way.'

'I cannot'—the boy's voice cracked. 'The Yuveraj would never give me leave and the guards will not let me pass the gate alone.'

'You will not ask for leave. As for the gate, we shall find some other way. Tomorrow go to the Master of Horse and tell him what you have told me. Koda Dad is a wise man and he will devise something. And now I think we have spoken together long enough; that is the second time Biju Ram has looked our way.'

He yawned largely and closing his book with a bang, rose to his feet and said in a carrying voice: 'Horses I can endure, but hawks, no. You must not expect me to show interest in creatures that bite and smell and shed feathers and fleas all over the floor. Grow up, boy, and study the works of the poets. That may improve your mind —if you have a mind.'

He tossed the book to Ash and strolled over to join the group surrounding the chess players. But he was as good as his word. That night one of the Rajah's personal bodyguard shared the ante-chamber with Ash, his presence being explained as a mark of His Highness's disapproval at the laxity that had permitted a cobra to enter his son's bedroom.

There were no alarms in the night; but Ash did not sleep well, and as soon as he could escape next morning he went off to see Koda Dad Khan. Hira Lal had been before him.

'It is all arranged,' said Koda Dad, checking him with an upraised hand. 'We are agreed that you must leave tonight, and as you cannot go through the gate you must go over the wall. For that we shall only need rope; much rope for the drop is a long one. But there is enough and to spare in the stables, so that will be easy. It is the last part that will be difficult, for you will have to climb down the rocks by goat tracks, which are hard enough to find by daylight and will be more so by night. It is fortunate that there is a moon.'

'But—but my mother?' stammered Ash. 'She is not strong and she can't—she could not . . .'

'No, no. She must leave by the gate. There is no order forbidding it. She must say that she wishes to purchase cloth or trinkets in the bazaar, and means to pass a night or two with an old friend. They will not question it, and once she is gone you must pretend to be ill so that you need not sleep in the Yuveraj's quarters tonight. You have only to cough and make believe to have a sore throat, and he will instantly agree to let you sleep elsewhere for he is afraid of infection. Then as soon as the palace is quiet, I myself will let you down on a rope, and after that you will have to get away quickly. Can your mother ride?'

'I don't know. I don't think so. I have never—'

'No matter. The two of you together cannot weigh as much as a full-grown man, and she can mount behind you. Hira Lal will arrange for a horse to be waiting for you among the *chenar* trees by Lal Beg's tomb beyond the city. You know the place. You cannot enter the city, as the gates are closed at night, so your mother must leave it during the afternoon when many people are about and no one notices who goes in or out. Tell her to take food and warm clothing, for the winter is coming and the nights are cold. And when you have her on the horse, ride hard for the north, since they will be sure you will go southward where the climate is kinder and the crops more abundant. With luck they may not search for you for a full day or more, for at first the Yuveraj will think that you are ill, and by the time he finds that you are gone you must be far away. Yet it is not he, but the Rani that you have to fear. She will know very well why you have fled, and desire your death the more—for fear of what you may know and who you might tell. The *Nautch*-girl is a ruthless and dangerous enemy. Do not forget that.'

Ash's young face whitened and he said hoarsely: 'But Juli knows too—Kairi-Bai knows. If the Rani finds out who told me, she will have her killed too. I shall have to take her with me.'

'*Chup!** snapped Koda Dad angrily. 'You talk like a child, Ashok. You must be a man now, and think and act as one. You have only to tell Kairi-Bai to keep her mouth shut, and even the *Nautch*-girl will not suspect her, for the child comes and goes like a sparrow and no one troubles to notice her. But if you run off with the Rajah's daughter, do you think that he would swallow such an affront to his honour? Why, he would hunt you to the death; and there is no man in all Hind who would not think him right and help him to do so. So let us have no more of such foolishness!'

'I'm sorry,' apologized Ash, flushing. 'I didn't think.'

'That has always been your besetting sin, my son,' growled Koda Dad. 'You act first and think afterwards: how many times have I not said so? Well, think now if there is a safe place from where we may

* Be silent!

lower you over the wall on the northern side, because there the ground below is more broken and there are bushes and goat tracks among the rocks. But it will not be easy, for I know of no place on that side where you could not be seen by a man looking out from the wall or a window.'

'There is one,' said Ash slowly. 'A balcony . . .'

So for the first time he went to the Queen's balcony by night, to leave it for the last time; clinging to the end of a rope that Koda Dad Khan and Hira Lal lowered down the forty-foot drop onto the tumbled rocks, where thorn bushes made black patches of shadow in the clear October moonlight, and the wandering goat tracks wound steeply downwards towards the milky levels of the plateau.

He had said goodbye to Kairi earlier that day after Sita had left, and had not expected to see her again. But she had been waiting for him in the Queen's balcony, a small, forlorn shadow in the moon-flooded night.

'They don't know I'm here,' she explained hurriedly, forestalling criticism. 'They think I'm asleep. I left a bundle in my bed in case anyone looked, but they were b-both snoring when I went out and they didn't hear me. Truly they didn't. I wanted to give you a present, because you are my bracelet-brother, and because you are going away. Here—this is for you, Ashok. To—to bring you luck.'

She thrust out a thin, square little palm and the moonlight glinted on a small sliver of mother-of-pearl carved in the semblance of a fish. It was, Ash knew, the only thing she had to give: the sole trinket she possessed and her dearest and greatest treasure. Seen in these terms it was perhaps the most lavish present that anyone could or would ever offer him, and he took it reluctantly, awed by the value of the gift.

'Juli, you shouldn't. I haven't anything to give you.' He was suddenly ashamed that he should have nothing to offer in return. 'I haven't anything at all,' he said bitterly.

'You've got the fish now,' consoled Kairi.

'Yes, I have the fish.'

He looked down at it and found that he could not see it clearly because there were tears in his eyes. But men did not cry. On a sudden inspiration he broke the little slip of mother-of-pearl in two, lengthways, and gave her back half of it. 'There. Now we have each got a luck-charm. And one day, when I come back, we'll stick them together again and—'

'Enough,' interrupted Koda Dad roughly. 'Go back to bed, Kairi-baba. If they find you gone and raise an outcry we shall all be ruined; and the boy must leave at once, for he has a long way to go before moonset. Say goodbye to him now, and go.'

Kairi's small face puckered woefully and the tears that streamed down it drowned the words that she was trying to say, and Ash, embarrassed, said hastily, 'Don't cry, Juli, I'll come back one day, I promise.'

He hugged her briefly and pushing her towards Hira Lal, who was standing silent in the shadows, said urgently: 'See that she gets back safely, won't you, Hira Lal? Her women mustn't know that she has been out tonight, for the Rani might hear of it, and then when it is found that I have gone—'

'Yes, yes, boy. I know. I will see to it. Now go.'

Hira Lal moved out into the moonlight, and as he did so the grey silk of his *achkan* became one with the night sky, and his face and hands took on the neutral tint of the stonework, so that for a moment it seemed to Ash that he was looking at a ghost, and that Hira Lal was already only a memory. The thought sent a chill through him, and for the first time he realized how much he owed to this man who had befriended him. And to Koda Dad and Kairi, and others who had been good to him: falconers, syces, mahouts from the elephant lines; and before that, all the playfellows and acquaintances of his happy days in the city. It was strange that only now, when he was leaving Gulkote, did he see that there had been almost as many good times as bad ones.

The great black pearl that hung from Hira Lal's ear glimmered faintly as its wearer moved, and as the moonlight fell on it, it glinted like a flake of opal—or a falling tear—and Ash stared at it fixedly, willing himself not to cry and wondering when, if ever, he would see it again . . .

Hira Lal said curtly: 'Make haste, boy. It grows late, and you have no time to waste. Go now—and may the gods go with you. *Namaste.*'

'I have let down the loop. Put your foot in it, so, and hold fast to the rope,' directed Koda Dad. 'And when you reach the rocks, be sure of your footing before you let go. From there your way will be more difficult, but if you move slowly and do not slip on the goat tracks you should do well enough. May the All-Merciful permit that you and your mother reach safety. Do not forget us. Farewell, my son. *Khuda Hafiz!'* (God protect you!)

He embraced the boy, and Ash bent to touch his feet with quivering hands and then turned quickly away, making a pretence of adjusting the heavy bundle of clothing for fear that Koda Dad should see the tears in his eyes. Behind him he could hear Kairi sobbing in helpless, childish grief, and, peering downwards he was suddenly appalled by the drop below him and the steep fall of rocks and scrub that plummetted towards the plain.

'Do not look down,' warned Koda Dad. 'Look up!'

Ash jerked his gaze from the gulf at his feet and saw, across the vast moon-washed spaces of the night, the Far Pavilions, their glittering peaks high and serene against the quiet sky. Fixing his gaze upon them he groped with one foot for the dangling loop, and grasping the rope, was lowered from the edge of the balcony, down and down, turning and swaying through dizzy space, while tears stung his eyes and Kairi called from above him in a sobbing whisper that was loud in the night silence: 'Goodbye, Ashok. Goodbye. You will come back, won't you? *Khuda Hafiz! . . . Khuda Hafiz . . . Jeete Raho— Jeete Raho!*'

Her tears fell on his face as she leaned from the edge of the Queen's balcony, and at last his feet touched the rocks at the foot of the wall and he steadied himself, and releasing the rope, saw it drawn up again. For the last time he waved to the three friends who watched from above, and then turning away, scrambled down between the rocks and prickly thorn bushes in search of a faint track he had spied earlier that afternoon when plotting his route from the balcony.

* a Hindu form of blessing, literally 'Live long'

6

The distance from the foot of the wall to the level ground was less than two hundred yards, but it took Ash the best part of an hour to traverse it. Once he had almost come to grief through losing his balance on a steep slope of shale, and it had taken him a long time to crawl back to firmer ground. But after that he had been more cautious, and at long last, scratched, bruised and breathless, with his clothes in tatters but his bundle still intact, he had reached the level ground.

Above him he could see the sheer cliff of the fortress wall and the dark bulk of the Peacock Tower. But the balcony was no longer visible, for it was lost in shadow; and he knew that no one would be there now. Perhaps no one would ever enter it again, unless Juli sometimes went there out of sentiment. But he did not think she would go there often; she was only a baby and in time she would forget, and the way to the balcony be lost—as it had been before he and Juli found it. Everything would change. Lalji would become a man and the *Nautch*-girl would grow old and fat, and lose her beauty and with it her power, Koda Dad would retire and a younger man become Master of Horse. Hira Lal too would grow old, and one day the old Rajah would die and Lalji would be ruler of Gulkote. Only the Dur Khaima would not change. The months, the years, the centuries would pass, and when the Palace of the Winds was no more, the Far Pavilions would still be there, unchanged and unchanging.

Ash knelt on the stony ground and bowed to them for the last time, bending until his forehead touched the dust, as Koda Dad bent when he prayed to Allah. Then, rising, he shouldered his bundle again and set off across the moonlit country towards the grove of *chenars* beyond the city.

Sita had not failed him: and neither had Hira Lal. A sturdy country-bred horse was tethered among the shadows where Sita waited anxiously, clutching a heavy bundle containing the food and clothing for the journey that she had purchased that afternoon in the bazaars. There was a man in charge of the horse, a stranger who gave no name but put a small packet into Ash's hand, saying that it was from Hira Lal.

'He said you might need money and this should help you on your way. The mare is a better animal than she looks,' added the stranger, tightening the girths. 'She will cover many miles a day and you may keep her to a trot for two or three hours at a stretch, for she has drawn a *ghari** and does not tire easily. Your best road is that way—' He pointed with a lean forefinger and then bent to draw a rough map in the moonlit patch of dust: 'Thus. There is no bridge over the river, and the main ferry will be too dangerous, but there is a small one here—to the southward—that is used only by a few farming folk. But even after you have crossed, be careful, for Hira Lal says that the Rani may well pursue you beyond the borders of Gulkote. May the Gods protect you. Ride swiftly'—and as Ash gathered up the reins he sent the horse forward with a slap on its rump.

It was fortunate that Ash not only possessed a good eye for country but had, in the old days, ridden out so frequently on hunting and hawking expeditions with the Rajah, Lalji or Koda Dad. Otherwise he would certainly have lost his way a dozen times before the night was out. But even by moonlight he had been able to follow the route roughly laid out for him by the man who had waited for him among the *chenars* by Lal Beg's tomb, and when the sky lightened to the dawn he recognized a circle of rocks on a hillside from where he had once seen the Rajah shoot a leopard, and knew that he was on the right road.

The drama and excitement of the previous day had exhausted Sita, and she slept soundly, her head against Ash's shoulder, and tied to him by a length of *pagri* (turban) cloth that prevented her from falling. When at last she awoke, aroused by the early sunlight, they could glimpse the river at the far end of a little stony valley between the hills, and Sita had insisted that they eat their morning meal before approaching the ferry, for to appear too early and too eager would only arouse curiosity. 'And because inquiries will soon be made as to all those who have passed this way, we will dress you as a woman, my son,' said Sita. 'Those who come seeking us will ask for a woman and a boy on foot, not two women on horseback.'

Draped in one of Sita's saris and decked with a few cheap brass ornaments, Ash made a very good girl, and Sita warned him to keep his head modestly bent and the sari pulled well forward to hide his face, and to leave the talking to her. The horse had been the only difficulty, for it did not fancy entering the leaky flat-bottomed boat

* cart or carriage

that provided the sole means of crossing the river, and at first the ferryman had demanded an exorbitant sum for transporting it. But though Hira Lal's packet had proved to contain the sum of five rupees in copper and silver coins, Sita had no intention of wasting money and still less of owning to such wealth, and she haggled with the man until the matter had been settled to the satisfaction of both, and the horse coaxed on board.

'Now we are safe,' breathed Sita, looking back from the far bank. But Ash remembered the words of Koda Khan and the man in the *chenar* grove, and he knew that they had only won the first throw. The Rani would make others, using loaded dice; and realizing this, he turned north towards the inhospitable country where the foothills would soon be powdered with snow, instead of southward to the warm air and the lush croplands where, in the circumstances, they would be expected to go.

It seemed to him a very long time—a lifetime—since the day that they had arrived in Gulkote and imagined that here they would find peace and freedom and security. But there had been little freedom or peace in the Hawa Mahal, and no security, and now once again they were homeless and hunted and must search for a safe hiding place. There must be some place, somewhere, where people were not cruel and unjust and interfering—where they could live peacefully, minding their own business and being happy. 'Somewhere where they won't bother about us, but just leave us alone,' thought Ash desperately.

He had had less than three hours' sleep since Kairi had told him what she had overheard in the Rani's garden. He was eleven years old, and very tired.

The nights became colder as they journeyed north, and Sita's cough seemed to be a good deal worse. Though perhaps this was only because Ash was continually with her now, and so noticed it more. Mindful of Hira Lal's warning he had sold the horse as soon as they were well clear of the borders of Gulkote, because he knew that they would be less conspicuous if they travelled on foot. But no sooner had he done so than he regretted it, because Sita could only manage a very short distance each day, and sometimes they covered less than a mile.

He had not realized before how frail she had become, and it worried him. However, they did not always have to go on foot, for with the money Hira Lal had given them, together with the price of the horse, they could afford to travel by tonga or bullock cart. But such journeys, in addition to being undertaken in the company of others, provided an ideal opportunity for questions and gossip, and after enduring a friendly catechism from their fellow-travellers during a long day spent in a bullock cart, and a similar experience from the driver of an *ekka,* they decided it was safer to go slowly on foot.

As the days went by without any sign of pursuit, Sita became less anxious and Ash began to think they had outwitted the Rani and could now relax and start planning for the future. It was obvious that they could not be continually on the move; their purse was not bottomless, and besides, Sita needed rest and quiet and a roof over her head—their own roof, not a different one every night, or the open sky when they failed to reach other shelter. He would have to find work and a hut for them to live in, and the sooner the better, for even at mid-day the air was sharp and chilly, and there was snow on the hills to the north. They had put enough distance between themselves and Gulkote to make it safe enough to stop running, and the Rani would realize that he could do little to harm her now, for even if he were to tell what he knew, who would be interested in the affairs of a small and far-away state, or place any credence in the tales of a vagabond boy?

But Ash had not only underestimated the Rani's agents, but failed to understand the real reason for her determination to destroy him. It was not so much fear of the Rajah, as fear of the British Raj . . .

In the old days of happy independence it would have been enough for Janoo-Rani to know that the boy Ashok had fled the state. But the old days were over and the *Angrezis* were all-powerful in the land, making and unmaking kings. Janoo-Rani still intended to set her son on a throne, and to do that she must first remove his half-brother. The fact that she had made several attempts to do so, and failed, did not worry her unduly; there were other methods and in the end she would find one that succeeded. But it was vital that none save her most trusted confederates should be aware of this, and she had been enraged to discover that one of Lalji's servants, a beggar-brat whom he had introduced into the palace—presumably as a spy—had somehow come to know of it. Well, there was nothing for it but to see that he died before he could carry tales to the Rajah, who had unfortunately taken a fancy to him and might even believe him.

She had given the necessary orders, but before they could be carried out both the boy and his mother had fled; and now Janoo-Rani was not only angry but afraid.

Lalji too had been angry, and he had sent out search parties to arrest the boy and bring him back under guard. But when they failed to find any trace of the runaways he had lost interest, and said that they were well rid of Ashok—a view that the Rani might have endorsed had it not been for the British. But the Rani had not forgotten the unwelcome visit of Colonel Frederick Byng of the Political Department, whom her husband had been compelled to receive with honour, and she had also heard tales of ruling princes who had been deposed by the British Raj for murdering their relatives or rivals. If the boy Ashok were to hear one day that the heir of Gulkote had met with a fatal accident, he might carry tales to those in authority, and then perhaps there would be inquiries; and who knew what might not come to light as a result of officious questioning and inquisitiveness? The boy must not be allowed to live, because as long as he remained alive he was both a danger to her and a stumbling block in the way of her son's advancement. 'At whatever cost, he must be found,' ordered Janoo-Rani. 'He and his mother both, for he will have told her all he knows, and until they are dead we dare not move against the Yuveraj . . .'

Ash obtained work with a blacksmith in a village near the Grand Trunk Road, and with it the use of a ramshackle *godown* (storeroom) behind the forge for himself and Sita. The work was arduous and poorly paid and the room small and windowless and devoid of any furniture. But it was a beginning, and they spent the last of Hira Lal's bounty on a second-hand string bed, a cheap quilt and a set of cooking pots. Sita hid what money remained from the sale of the horse in a hole under her bed, and when Ash was out, dug a second hole in the wall for the sealed packet and the wash-leather bags that she had brought away from her quarters in the Hawa Mahal. She made no attempt to find work for herself, which was unlike her, but seemed content to sit in the sun outside the door of their room, cook their scanty meals and listen of an evening to the tale of Ashok's doings. She had never asked much of life, and she did not regret the Hawa Mahal; she had seen too little of her boy there and knew that he had been unhappy.

Ash was certainly happier now than he had ever been in the service of the Yuveraj, and his meagre wages were at least put into his hand in solid coin; which was more than they had been in the Palace of the Winds. He felt that he was at last a man, and though he had not abandoned his grandiose plans for the future, he would have been content to remain in the village for a year or two. But early in the new year two men had arrived at the village inquiring for a hill-woman and a boy—a grey-eyed boy who, they said, might be disguised as a girl. The pair were wanted for the theft of certain jewellery, the property of the State of Gulkote, and there was a reward of five hundred rupees for their capture and fifty for information that would lead to their arrest . . .

The men had arrived late one evening, and fortunately for Ash had been given lodging for the night in the house of the *tehsildar,** whose young son happened to be a friend of his. This boy had overheard their conversation with his father, and there being no other couple answering to that description in the village, he had crept out into the darkness and woken Ash, who slept on the ground outside Sita's door. Half an hour later the pair were hurrying down a field path in the uncertain starlight, making for the main road where Ash hoped to beg a lift from a passing bullock cart, as it was only too clear that Sita could not go far or fast on foot. They had been lucky, for a kindly tonga driver had taken them up and driven them five miles and more to the outskirts of a small town, where they had taken to the open country, doubling back slowly and painfully to the southward in the hope of throwing their pursuers off the trail.

For the next two months they lived from hand to mouth, continually haunted by the fear of pursuit and never daring to stop in any place where they might attract attention. The larger towns seemed safer than small villages where strangers aroused comment, but work was not easy to find and the living was expensive. Their small hoard of money dwindled, and the close air of the crowded cities did not agree with Sita, who longed for the hills. She had never liked the plains, and now she was afraid of them; and then one evening, gossiping with a group of coolies outside a timber yard, Ash heard again the tale of a rich reward being offered for the capture of two thieves who had stolen a Rajah's jewels, and began to lose heart. Were they never to escape?

'Let us go north again, to the hills,' begged Sita. 'We shall be safe among the hills; there are few roads and many hiding places there.

* village headman

But where can one hide in these flat lands where there are a hundred paths leading to every town?'

So once again they turned northwards, but on foot and very slowly. There was no money now for tongas or bullock carts, and little enough for food, and as they could not afford to pay for lodgings they slept in the streets of towns or under trees in the open country: until there came a day when Sita could go no further . . .

They had spent the previous night in the shelter of an outcrop of rock on the banks of the Jhelum River, within sight of the Kashmir snows; and when the dawn broke over the dew-wet plain the long rampart of the mountains lay high above the morning mists, rose-flushed with the first rays of the coming day. In the clear air of the early morning they seemed no more than a few miles away and as though they could be reached in a mere day's march; but Sita, raising herself on her elbow to gaze longingly at them, knew at last that she would never reach them.

There had been nothing to eat that morning save a handful of parched grain, carefully hoarded against an emergency. Ash ground it between two stones and mixed it to a paste with water, but Sita could not swallow it, and when he wished to move on—their present refuge being too precarious—she shook her head.

'I cannot, *piara,*' whispered Sita. 'I am too tired—too tired.'

'I know, mother darling. I too. But we cannot stay here. It is too dangerous. There is no other cover near by, and if anyone should come this way we should be caught like rats in a trap. And—and I think they may come soon. I . . .' He hesitated, reluctant to add to her trouble, but forced to it because she must understand that they dare not delay. 'I did not tell you before, but yesterday I saw someone I knew in that *serai* where we stopped for a while. A man from Gul-kote. That is why I would not let you stay there. We must walk down-stream and see if we can find a ford, or a boatman who will take us across, and then we can rest for a little. You can lean on me. It will only be a short way, mother dear.'

'I cannot, Heart's-dearest. You must go alone. You will make bet-ter speed without me, and be safer too. They are hunting a woman and a boy travelling together, and I know that I should have parted from you long ago except—except that I could not endure to.'

'That's silly. You know I wouldn't have gone,' said Ash indig-nantly. 'Who would have looked after you if I had? Mother, *please* get up. Please! We'll walk very slowly.'

He knelt beside her pulling at her cold hands and coaxing her. 'You want to get to the mountains, don't you? Well, there they are— look, you can see them plain. You'll be better once you reach them. Your cough will go in the hill air and you'll feel well again, and then we'll look for our valley. You haven't forgotten the valley and the goat and—and the almond tree and . . .' His voice wavered suddenly and he tugged at her hands again, trying to lift her to her feet. 'Only a little way more, I promise.'

But Sita knew that she had come to the end of the road. Her strength was almost spent, and what little she had left must be used for one last, bitter task that must be done quickly, before it was too late. She freed her hands from his grasp and fumbled among the folds of her sari for a sealed packet and four small, heavy, wash-leather bags that she had carried tied about her waist in a length of cloth, and looking at them the tears gathered in her eyes and rolled slowly down her wasted cheeks; the fact that Ashok believed himself to be her son had been so sweet to her that even now, when she knew that the truth might save him, she could not bear to tell him. Yet he must be told. There was no other way in which she could help him to escape; and even this might not serve . . .

'I am not your mother. You are not my son,' whispered Sita, forcing the words through trembling lips. 'You are the son of an *Angrezi* . . . a Sahib . . .'

The words made no sense to Ash, but her tears frightened him more than anything that had ever happened to him during the years of servitude in the Hawa Mahal or the dreadful weeks since their escape: the death of Tuku, the poison and the cobra, the terror of pursuit—nothing had been as bad as this. He put his arms about her and clung to her, begging her not to cry and telling her that he would carry her if she could not walk: he was strong, and if she would hold about his neck he was sure that he could carry her. The things she said made no sense to him, and it was only the sight of the money that at last shocked him into attention. He had never seen so much money before in all his life, and at first it only meant one thing to him: they could afford to hire a cart—to buy one if necessary. His mother need not walk now, and they could out-distance their pursuers and pay for doctors and medicines to make her well. They were rich. 'Why didn't you tell me before, mother?'

'I did not want you to know that you were not my son—my own son,' wept Sita. 'I would have thrown it away had I dared, but—but I did not dare . . . for fear that one day you might have need of it. That day is here, for the Rani's men are close on your heels and if you are to escape them you must leave me and go on alone, and take refuge with your own people where even she will not dare to follow you. You will be safe with them. There is no other way . . .'

'What people? You have always said we had no people. And of course I am your son. You mustn't say things like that. It's only because you are feeling ill and you've had nothing to eat, but now we can buy some food, and a horse and a cart and—'

'Ashok! Listen to me.' Fear and urgency sharpened Sita's voice and her thin hands clutched his wrists with unexpected strength. 'You cannot go back to buy food, and if you show that money they will say you stole it, for it is too great a sum for a boy such as you to possess. You must hide it as I have done, and keep it until you reach your own people. There is much written stuff in the packet, and more on this paper here. You must find someone who can read *Angrezi* and they will tell you who to take it to. Your father wrote it before he died, and—and I would have obeyed his commands and taken you to his people but for the great rising and the slaughter of the Sahib-log in Delhi. But I kept the papers and the money for you, and I did as he asked: I took care of you. He said: 'Look after the boy, Sita.' And that I have done . . . But for love's sake; because alas, alas, I am not your mother. She too was *Angrezi,* but she died at your birth and it was I who took you from her arms and gave you the breast . . . I who cared for you from the first—the very first! But I can do so no longer. So now must I send you back to your own people, for with them you will be safe. And because I can go no further, you must go alone. Do you understand?'

'No,' said Ash. 'You are still my mother and I won't leave you. You can't make me! And I don't believe any of it; any of the rest. Or if it is true, it doesn't matter, for we can burn these papers and then no one will ever know, and I shall still be your son.'

'If you are my son, you will obey me—I do not ask you to do this. As your mother, I command you. Stay with me if you will until I go. It will not be long. But afterwards take the papers and the money and go quickly. Do not destroy them. If you love me, promise that you will not destroy them, but that you will use them and return to your own people. And if you will not do it for love's sake, then do it because I am . . . because I have been your mother. Promise me, Ashok?'

'I—promise,' whispered Ash. She could not be dying . . . it wasn't true. If only he could fetch help—a hakim. Or some hot food: that might revive her. Yet she looked so ill, and supposing he were to leave her and run to the nearest village, and be caught?

He dared not risk it; she was too weak to move and she would die slowly of thirst and starvation. Yet even if he did not go, they would both die, because sooner or later someone would find them here, for there was no other cover for more than a mile in any direction—only the flat, treeless plain and wide reaches of the river. He would never have taken refuge in such a place except that it was dusk when they fled from the *serai,* and not daring to keep to the highroad he had turned towards the open country. They had reached the rocks by the riverside an hour after moonrise and had been forced to stay there because Sita could go no further; yet, recognizing the danger of such an isolated spot, he had meant to leave it at first light and find some safer place of refuge. But now the sun was already shredding away the morning mists and he could see the foothills, and above them the snows were no longer pink and amber but sharply white. The day was here—and his mother was dying . . .

'It isn't true. I won't let it be true!' thought Ash frantically, his arms tight about her as though to hold her safe. But suddenly and hopelessly he knew that it was, and that she was leaving him. Grief and terror and desperation tore at his heart, and he hid his face against her shoulder and wept wildly, as a child weeps, shuddering and gasping. He felt Sita's frail hands patting him and soothing him, and her beloved voice against his ear, murmuring endearments and telling him that he must not cry for he was a man now—he must be brave and strong and outwit his enemies and grow up to be a Burra-Sahib Bahadur, like his father and old Khan Bahadur Akbar Khan for whom he had been named. Did he not remember Uncle Akbar who had taken him to see a tiger shot? He had been no more than a babe then, yet he had not been afraid and they had all been so proud of him. He must be as brave now, and remember that death came in the end for everyone—Rajah and Beggar, Brahmin and Untouchable, man and woman. All passed through the same door and were born again . . .

'I do not die, *piara.* I rest only, and wait to be reborn. And in that next life, if the gods are kind, it may be that we shall meet again. Yes, surely we shall meet again . . . perhaps in that valley—'

She began to talk of it in a slow, halting whisper that struggled for breath, and presently, as his sobs quieted, she turned from that dear familiar tale to the old nursery rhyme with which she had used to sing him to sleep—'*Nini baba, nini, muckan, roti, cheeni,*' crooned Sita. '*Roti muckan hogya; hamara . . . baba . . . sogya—*'

Her voice died away so softly that it was a long time before Ash realized that he was alone.

The blue far-reaching shadows of the early morning shortened into the scanty shade of mid-day, and slowly lengthened again as the afternoon wore away and the sun moved down towards the far horizon.

There were partridges calling out on the plain now, and wild duck quacking on the river, and along the white banks of the Jhelum the mud turtles that had basked all day in the hot sunlight were slipping back into the water. It would be dusk soon, and he would have to go, thought Ash numbly. He had promised to go, and there was nothing left to stay for.

He stood up slowly and with difficulty, for he had crouched all day by Sita's body, holding her stiffening, work-worn hand in his. His muscles were cramped and his mind dazed with grief and shock. He could not remember when he had last eaten, but he did not feel hungry, only very thirsty.

The river was bright with the sunset as he knelt on the wet sand and scooped up the water and drank greedily, and afterwards splashed handfuls of it over his aching head and hot, dry eyes. He had not cried again after Sita died; and he did not cry now, for the boy who had wept so bitterly in the dawn was dead too. He was not yet twelve years old, but he would never be a child again. He had grown up in the short space of a single afternoon and left his childhood behind him for ever. For it was not only his mother whom he had lost that day, but his identity. There was no such person—there never had been—as Ashok, son of Sita who had been the wife of Daya Ram, syce. There was only a boy whose parents were dead and who did not even know his own name or where to find his own kin. An English boy—a *feringhi*. He was a foreigner, and this was not even his own land . . .

The coldness of the water helped to clear his head and he began to wonder what he should do now. He could not go away and leave his mother lying there, for an ugly memory from the almost forgotten past came back to him, and he shivered uncontrollably, recalling a hot night that had been made hideous by the sound of jackals and hyenas quarrelling in the moonlight.

Out on the quiet surface of the river something moved. It was only a piece of driftwood, floating down on the current, but as he watched it slide past him, Ash remembered that his people—no, his mother Sita's people—burnt their dead and cast the ashes into the rivers so that they might be carried at last to the sea.

He could not make a pyre for Sita for there was no fuel. But there was the river. The cool, deep, slow-flowing river that had risen among her own hills, and that would take her gently and carry her to the sea. The setting sun flamed on it with a dazzling brilliance that was brighter than fire, and he turned from it and went back to the shallow cave among the rocks, and wrapping Sita's wasted body in her blanket as though to keep her warm, carried her down to the river and waded through the shallows until the water took her weight. She was stiff already, and so painfully light that the task was easier than he supposed. And when he released her at last she floated away from him, borne up by the blanket.

The current drew her out and down-stream, and he stood waist-deep in the water, straining his eyes to watch her go until at last her small shape was lost in the sun dazzle and he could see it no more. And when the brightness faded and the river turned from gold to opal, she had gone.

Ash turned and waded back to the shore, his legs numbed with cold and his teeth clenched together to keep them from chattering. He was hungry now, but he could not bring himself to eat the paste that he had made for Sita and that she had been unable to swallow, and he threw it away. He would have to find something to eat soon or he would not have the strength to go very far, and he had promised her . . . He lifted the sealed packet and the little wash-leather bags that were heavy with gold and silver coins, and weighed them in his hands, wishing he could leave them and knowing that he must not. They were his and he would have to take them. Removing only a single rupee for his immediate needs, he wrapped them again in the length of cloth and tied it about his waist as Sita had done, concealing it under his ragged garments. The folded sheet of paper with the faded, spidery writing that he could not read he hid in his turban, and now there was nothing left in the shallow cave to show that anyone had ever been there . . . Nothing but the footmarks and a slight depression in the sand where Sita had lain down to sleep on the previous night and where she had died in the dawn. He touched it very gently, as though she were still there and he feared to wake her.

As he did so, the first breath of the night wind blew in from across the river, and eddying about the cave, stirred up the dry silver sand and left it smooth again.

Ashton Hilary Akbar Pelham-Martyn shouldered his bundle and his burdens, and turning his back on the past, set out in the cold twilight to search for his own people.

'It is for a Captain-Sahib. A Captain-Sahib of the Guides,' said the bazaar letter-writer, peering at Hilary's last letter through a pair of scratched spectacles. 'Yes, see—here it says "Mardan". That is by Hoti Mardan, which is up Malakand way. Beyond Attock and the Indus, and across the Kabul River.'

'*The Guides,*' breathed Ash in an awed whisper. He would have made for Mardan long ago had he dared, but he knew that the Rani's men would expect him to go there and would lie in wait for him, for his friendship with Koda Dad's son had been no secret in the Hawa Mahal. But by now the watchers must surely have decided that he was too cunning to make such an obvious move, and they would have left to search elsewhere. Even if they had not, the situation itself had been drastically altered by the fact that he was no longer a friendless bazaar brat, hoping to find shelter with a sowar of the Guides, but a Sahib who could demand protection from his fellow Sahibs. Not only for himself, but for Zarin. And if necessary, for Koda Dad too.

'The Guides,' repeated Ash softly. And suddenly his eyes were bright with excitement and the grey despair that had filled his mind and heart for so many days began to shred away like mist at morning. His luck had changed at last.

'It is the name of a *pulton* (regiment) that is stationed at Mardan,' explained the letter-writer importantly, 'and the Sahib's name is As-esh-taan. Captain Ash-tarn. As for the rest—' he made as though to open the folded paper, but Ash snatched it back, explaining that it was only the Sahib's name and address that he needed, the rest was of no importance.

'If it is a recommendation, it is better to know what has been said,' advised the letter-writer sagely. 'Then if harsh things have been written, one can tear it up and say that one has lost it. Or if it is a good recommendation, it may be sold for much money. Such things fetch good prices in the bazaars. Do you hope to take service with this Sahib, then?'

'No, I—go on a visit to my cousin's wife's brother, who is his servant,' improvised Ash glibly. 'They told me the address, but I had forgotten it and I cannot read *Angrezi*.'

He paid over the half-anna that had been agreed upon and having made sure that he had memorized the name correctly, tucked the paper back among the folds of his turban and spent the other half-anna on a handful of roast *chunna* and a stick of peeled sugar-cane.

Ash had come a long way since the night he left the cave by the Jhelum River. It had not taken him long to discover how much farther and faster he could travel now that he was alone; or how right Sita had been when she had told him that he would be safer by himself, for he had heard of inquiries made in the villages and was aware that the hunt was still up. But since the men who hunted him knew that he would never leave his mother, they still looked for a hill-woman and a grey-eyed boy travelling together, and were not concerned with a single ragged urchin whose colouring, in the north-west of India where the Khyber hills lay along the horizon, was nothing out of the common.

He had not been questioned, but because he was afraid of doing anything that might draw attention to himself, he had not dared to ask for a translation of that paper in any of the smaller towns where such an inquiry might arouse interest. Only when he reached one large enough to boast half-a-dozen letter-writers had he felt safe enough to risk it; and now the name and address on it had turned out to be that of an officer of the Guides—Zarin's regiment. It was almost too good to be true.

Ash remembered that his mother had said she did not know what was written on that paper. But he thought that she must have had some suspicion, and that this perhaps explained her antipathy towards Koda Dad and his son, and her opposition to his plan of joining Zarin one day and enlisting in the same Corps. Yet in the end it was she who had set him on the road to Mardan, where he would see Zarin and become a sowar in the Guides—or even an officer, if this Captain-Sahib should prove to be a relative and prepared to help him. But that last was something he was never to know, for William Ashton was dead.

The Guides had taken part in the Ambeyla expedition, a campaign launched against certain hostile Border tribes in the autumn of the previous year, and William, still unaware that he possessed a nephew, had been killed in action only a few weeks after his sister's son escaped over the walls of the Hawa Mahal. But now it was spring, and the almonds were in bloom and the willows in bud as Ash took the road that leads from Attock to Peshawar.

The Kabul River ran red with the red earth of the Khyber that the spring rains and the melting of the snows in far-off Afghanistan had washed down on the flood, and the fords were impassable, so that he must cross by the bridge of boats at Nowshera. Ash had already made a detour of some dozen miles to avoid crossing the Indus by the Attock ferry, it having occurred to him that it would be an easy matter for a single man to keep a check on all who passed that way: in which he was wise, for there had indeed been a man on watch, an innocent-seeming traveller who appeared to be in no hurry, and who had made friends with the boatman and spent his days idly observing all those who used the ferry. Ash had crossed instead some five miles down-stream, having begged a lift on a farmer's raft, and from there made his way back to the Peshawar road. And now once again providence was kind to him, for in Nowshera a kindly villager on his way to Risalpur with a load of vegetables gave him a lift, and on pretence of being sleepy he burrowed down behind the cabbages and knole-kole and crossed the bridge of boats unseen. So towards evening on that same day—dusty, footsore and very weary—he reached the cantonment of Mardan and asked for Sowar Zarin Khan of the Guides.

The Corps of Guides were back once more in their barracks after months of hard campaigning and harder fighting in the Yusafzai country, and eighteen months of active service had aged Zarin so that he was barely recognizable as the gay youth who had ridden away so light-heartedly from Gulkote. He had grown taller and broader, and acquired an impressive moustache in place of the budding growth that Ash remembered. But he was still the same Zorin, and he had been delighted to see Ashok.

'My father send word that you had left Gulkote, and I knew that you would come here one day,' said Zarin, embracing him. 'You will have to wait until you are full grown before you can enlist as a sowar, but I will speak to my eldest brother, who is now a Jemadar since the battle on the road to Ambeyla, and he will find you work. Is your mother here?'

'She is dead,' said Ash flatly. He found that he could not speak of her even to such an old friend as Zarin. But Zarin appeared to understand: he asked no question and said only, 'I am sorry. She was a good mother to you, and I think it must be hard to lose even a bad one, for each of us has only the one to lose.'

'It seems that I have had two,' said Ash bleakly. And squatting down tiredly to warm himself at Zarin's fire, he told the tale of his escape from the Hawa Mahal and of the things that he had learned from Sita in the cave by the river, producing at last, in proof of the latter, a sheet of paper that bore the address of a dead officer of the Guides.

Zarin could not read the writing, but he too had been startled into belief by the sight of the money, for the coins spoke for themselves and did not need any translation. There were over two hundred of them, of which less than fifty were silver rupees and the rest sovereigns and gold mohurs; and that Sita should have concealed this small fortune for so many years seemed to prove that there must be at least some truth in her story.

'I think we had better show this to my brother,' said Zarin, looking doubtfully at the paper that Ash had thrust into his hand. 'Perhaps he will be able to advise you, for I cannot. It is too dark a matter for me.'

Zarin's brother, the Jemadar, had no such doubts. There was only one course to take. Ashton-Sahib being dead, the whole affair must now be laid before Colonel Browne-Sahib, the Commandant, who would know how to deal with it. He himself, Awal Shah, would accompany the boy Ashok to the Colonel-Sahib's quarters immediately, because if there was any truth in this extraordinary story, the sooner both money and papers were placed in safe hands the better.

'As for you, Zarin, you will say nothing of this to anyone. For if the Rani of Gulkote desires the boy's death, she will revenge herself on those who helped him to escape, and if she should hear that he is with us, she will suspect that our father had a hand in the matter. So it is better for all our sakes that the trail should be lost. I will go now to the Commandant-Sahib, and you, Ashok, will follow me, walking a little behind so that we are not seen to be together, and waiting outside until you are sent for. Come.'

The Jemadar stuffed the evidence into his pocket and strode out into the late sunlight, and Ash followed at a discreet distance and spent the next half hour perched on the edge of a culvert, tossing pebbles into the ditch below, and keeping a watchful eye on the Commandant's windows while the shadows lengthened on the dusty cantonment road and the sharp spring evening filled with the scent of woodsmoke and dung fires.

It was, though he did not know it, his last hour of independence. The last, for many years, of peace and freedom and idleness, and perhaps if he had realized that he might have broken his promise to

Sita and run away while there was still time. Though even if he had escaped the Rani's assassins it is doubtful that he would have got very far, for Colonel Sam Browne, v.c., the Officiating Commandant of the Corps of Guides, having read the unfinished letter that Professor Pelham-Martyn had started to write to his brother-in-law William Ashton, was now engaged in removing the seals from a packet that had been wrapped in oiled silk almost exactly seven years ago. It was already too late for Hilary's son to run away.

Three weeks later Ash was in Bombay, dressed in a hot and uncomfortable suit of European clothes and shod with even more uncomfortable European boots, *en route* for the land of his fathers.

His passage had been arranged and paid for by the officers of his uncle's Regiment, all of whom, after flatly refusing to believe that this beggar-brat could possibly be the nephew of poor William, had eventually been convinced by the evidence in the packet (which included a daguerreotype of Isobel, whose likeness to her son was startling, and another of Ash seated on Sita's lap and taken in Delhi on his fourth birthday—both sitters having been unhesitatingly identified by Zarin), together with a searching verbal and physical examination of the claimant. Once converted, William's friends could not do enough for the nephew of an officer who had served with the Corps since Hodson built the fort at Mardan, and whom everyone had liked. Though his nephew was not in the least grateful for their efforts on his behalf.

Ash had obeyed his foster-mother's last commands and handed over to the Sahib-log the papers and the money she had given him. Having done so, he would have preferred to live in the lines with Zarin and Awal Shah, and earn his living as a stable boy or a grass-cutter until he was old enough to join the Regiment. But this had not been permitted. Why couldn't people leave him alone? thought Ash resentfully. Why, always and everywhere, must there be dictatorial people who gave him unpalatable orders, restricted his liberty and over-rode his wishes—and others, who at a word from an evil and ambitious woman, were even prepared to hunt him across Hind and take his life, though they had no quarrel with him and he had done them no harm? It wasn't fair!

He had been happy in the bazaars of Gulkote and he had not wanted to leave the city and move to the Hawa Mahal. But he had been given no choice. And now it seemed that he must leave his friends and his homeland and go to his father's country; and once again there was no choice—and no appeal. He had walked into a trap as surely as on the day that he had entered the Hawa Mahal, and it was too late to try and escape from it, for the doors were already closing behind him. Perhaps when he grew up he would be allowed to do as he pleased—though in a world filled with oppression, assassins and interfering busy-bodies, he began to think it unlikely. But at least the Sahibs had promised that when the years of servitude in *Belait* were over, he would be permitted to return to Hind.

Colonel Sam Browne, the Commandant, told him that telegrams had been sent to his father's people, who would send him to school and turn him into a Sahib. Also that if he worked hard and did well in examinations (whatever those were) he would obtain a commission in the army and return to Mardan as an officer of the Guides; and it was that hope, rather than his promise to Sita or his fear of the Rani's men, that prevented Ash from making a break for freedom. That, and the fact that he was to travel to England in the care of a Sahib who was taking home two Indian servants; which meant that he would not be entirely alone and friendless. This last had been largely due to a chance remark of Jemadar Awal Shah's.

'It is a pity,' said Awal Shah to his Commanding Officer, 'that the boy will forget the speech and the ways of this land, for a Sahib who can think and talk as one of us, and pass as either a Pathan or a Punjabi without question, would have made his mark in our Regiment. But in *Belait* he will forget and become as other Sahibs; which will be a great loss.'

The Commandant had been much struck by this observation, for although every Englishman in the service of the Government of India was expected to become fluent in one or more of India's languages, very few learned to speak well enough to pass as a native of the country. And those few were for the most part half-castes whose mixed blood debarred them from employment in the higher ranks of the army or the Civil Service—even so gifted a soldier as Colonel George Skinner of Skinner's Horse, the famed 'Sikundar Sahib', having been refused a commission in the Bengal Army because his mother was an Indian lady. But it was plain that William Ashton's nephew was a native of India in all but blood, and one of the few who could go deeper than the skin. As such he might one day prove of inestimable value in a country where accurate information often meant the difference between survival and disaster, and Awal Shah was right: such potentially valuable material ought not to be wasted.

The Commandant brooded over the problem, and eventually hit upon an admirable solution. Colonel Ronald Anderson, the District Commissioner, whose retirement had been enforced by ill-health, would be leaving for England on the following Thursday, taking with him his Pathan bearer, Ala Yar, and his *khansamah* (cook) Mahdoo, whose home was in the hills beyond Abbottabad, both of whom had been in his service for over twenty years. Anderson had been a friend of both John Nicholson and Sir Henry Lawrence, and had in his youth spent several years in Afghanistan on the staff of the ill-fated Macnaghton. He spoke half-a-dozen dialects and had an exhaustive knowledge and a deep love for the North-West Frontier Province and the land beyond its borders, and he would be an ideal person to keep an eye on young Ashton during the long voyage home, and for as many school holidays as the Pelham-Martyns would permit—always supposing he could be persuaded to accept such a task. The Commandant of the Guides Corps had wasted no time, but calling for his horse had ridden off that same day to lay the whole matter before Colonel Anderson. And the retiring Commissioner, intrigued by the story, had instantly consented.

'But of course you will return,' said Zarin, reassuring the anxious Ash. 'Only first it is necessary to acquire learning, and that, they say, must be done in *Belait*. Though I do not myself . . . Well, no matter. But it is even more necessary to remain alive, and it is certain that you are not safe in this country while there is a price upon your head. You cannot be sure that the Rani's spies have lost your trail, but we can at least be sure that they will not follow it across the sea, and that long before you return, both she and they will have forgotten you. I and my brother Awal Shah have been sworn to secrecy and cannot even send news of you to our father, for as letters may be opened and read by the curious, it is better that he should be kept in ignorance rather than risk betraying your whereabouts and your changed fortunes to those who wish you ill. But later, when the *gurrh-burrh* has died down, if the Colonel-Sahib thinks that it is safe to do so, I will write to you to *Belait;* and remember that you do not go there alone. Anderson-Sahib is a good man and one whom you may trust, and he and his servants will see to it that you do not wholly forget us while you learn to be a Sahib—and you will find that the years will go quickly, Ashok.'

Yet there Zarin had been wrong, for they had not gone quickly.

They had crawled by so slowly that every week had seemed a month and every month a year. But he had been right about Colonel Anderson. The ex-District Commissioner had taken a liking to the boy, and during the long, tedious days of the voyage he had managed to teach Ash an astonishing amount of English, having impressed upon him that to be speechless in a foreign land would be a grave disadvantage and, moreover, humiliating to pride.

The point had been taken, and Ash, who had inherited his father's gift for languages, had applied himself with such diligence to the mastering of this new tongue that a year later you would never have known that he had spoken any other, for with the natural imitativeness of youth he had come to speak it with the exact drawl and inflection of upper-crust England—the voice of pedantic tutors and elderly Pelham-Martyns. Yet try as he would, he could not learn to think of himself as one of them, nor did they find it easy to accept him as such.

He was to remain a stranger in a strange land, and England would never be 'Home' to him, because home was Hindustan. He was still—and always would be—Sita's son; and there were endless things about this new life that were not only alien to him, but horrifying. Trivial things in the opinion of Englishmen, but to one brought up in the religion of his foster-mother's people, incredibly shocking. Such as the eating of pork and beef; the one an abomination and the other sacrilege unspeakable—the pig being an unclean animal and the cow a sacred one.

No less appalling was the European habit of using a toothbrush not once but many times, instead of a twig or a small stick that could be plucked daily and discarded after use; saliva, as everyone knows, being of all things the most polluting. Apparently the English did not know, and there were bitter battles before Ash could be brought to accept this and other practices that seemed to him barbaric.

That first year had been a difficult time for all concerned, not least for Ash's relatives, who were equally horrified by the habits and appearance of this young 'heathen' from the East. Rigidly conservative and possessing all the in-bred insularity of their race, they flinched from the prospect of displaying Hilary's son to the critical gaze of their friends and neighbours, and hastily revised their original plans, which had included sending their nephew to the famous public school that had been responsible for the education of seven generations of Pelham-Martyns. Instead, they engaged a resident tutor, together with the weekly attendance of an elderly cleric and a retired Oxford Don, to 'lick him into shape', and thankfully agreed to an arrangement whereby he should spend his holidays with Colonel Anderson.

Pelham Abbas, the seat of Hilary's elder brother, Sir Matthew Pelham-Martyn, Bart, was an imposing property consisting of a large, square Queen Anne house, built on the site of the earlier Tudor one that had been destroyed by Cromwell's men in 1644, and surrounded by terraced lawns, walled gardens, stables and greenhouses. There was also an ornamental lake, an extensive park in which Ash was permitted to ride, a trout stream, and on the far side of a belt of woodland in which Sir Matthew's gamekeeper raised pheasants, a home-farm consisting of some four hundred acres. The house itself was full of family portraits and Regency furniture, and the Pelham-Martyns, who had feared that their uncivilized young nephew might be overawed by it, were disagreeably surprised to discover that he considered it cold and uncomfortable, and not to be compared in either size or magnificence to some Indian palace with an unpronounceable name in which, so he said, he had lived for 'many years'.

It was the first of several surprises, not all of them disagreeable. That the boy should prove to be equally at home with a horse or a gun was something that they had not expected, and for which they were profoundly grateful: 'As long as he can shoot and ride, I suppose he'll scrape past,' said his cousin Humphrey. 'But it is a pity we didn't catch him younger. He doesn't seem to have any of the right ideas.'

Ash's ideas remained unorthodox and frequently led him into trouble; as witness his refusal to eat beef in any form (this was the last and strongest remnant of Sita's training, and the one that took him the longest time to overcome despite the many difficulties involved—not to mention the lectures and punishments it brought down on his head from teachers and schoolmasters, and the anger, resentment and irritation it aroused among his relations). Then, too, he could not see why he should not offer to teach Willie Higgins, the boot-boy, to ride, or invite twelve-year-old Annie Mott, the thin, overworked little scullery maid who always looked half starved, to share his tea in the schoolroom. 'But it's my tea, isn't it Aunt Millicent?' asked Ash. Or: 'But Uncle Matthew gave me Blue Moon for my own horse, so I don't see why . . .'

'They are servants, my dear, and one does not treat servants as equals. They would not understand it,' explained Aunt Millicent, annoyed at being argued with in broken English by this impossible offspring of her eccentric brother-in-law. How *like* Hilary—he had always been a problem, and now that he was dead he was still capable of causing them grave embarrassment.

'But when I was Lalji's servant,' persisted Ash, 'I used to ride his horses, and—'

'That was in India, Ashton. You are in England now, and must learn to behave properly. In England we do not play with the servants or invite them to share our meals. And you will find that Annie is adequately fed in the kitchen.'

'No she's not. She's always hungry, and it isn't fair, because Mrs Mott—'

'That's enough, Ashton. I have said "No", and if I hear any more of this I shall have to give orders that you are to be kept away from the kitchen and not allowed to speak to any of the underservants. Do you understand?'

Ash did not. But then neither did his relatives. Later on, when he had learned to read and write in English as well as speak it, his uncle, in a praiseworthy attempt to encourage industry and lighten the tedium of lessons, had given him a dozen books on India, saying that they would of course be of special interest to him. The books had included several of Hilary's later works, together with such stirring tales as *The Conquest of Bengal,* Sleeman's account of the suppression of Thuggery, and Sir John Kaye's *History of the Sepoy War.* And Ash had certainly been interested; though not in the way that his uncle had intended. He found his father's books too dry and erudite, and his reactions to the others had seriously annoyed Sir Matthew, who had been rash enough to request his opinion on them.

'But you asked me what I thought!' protested Ash in some indignation. 'And that is what I think. After all, it was their country and they weren't doing you—I mean us—any harm. I don't think it was fair.'

'Shades of Hilary!' thought Sir Matthew with exasperation, and he explained tartly that, on the contrary, they had been doing a great deal of harm—what with murdering, oppressing and making war on each other, strangling harmless travellers in honour of some heathen goddess, burning widows alive, and generally obstructing trade and progress. Such horrors could not be allowed to continue unchecked, and it was both the duty and responsibility of Britain, as a Christian nation, to put a stop to these barbarities and bring peace and tranquillity to the suffering millions of India.

'But *why* was it your responsibility?' asked Ash, genuinely puzzled. 'I don't see that it had anything to do with you—I mean with us. India isn't even anywhere *near* us. It's at the other side of the world.'

'My dear boy, you have not been giving proper attention to your books,' said Sir Matthew, striving for patience. 'If you had read more carefully you would have learned that we had been granted trading posts there. And trade is not only vital to us, but to the prosperity of the entire world. We could not permit it to be disrupted by continual vicious and petty wars between rival princes. It was necessary to preserve order, and that we have done. We have, under God's providence, been able to bring peace and prosperity to that unhappy country, and bestow the blessings of progress on a people who have for centuries suffered atrocious persecution and oppression at the hands of greedy priests and quarrelling overlords. It is something we may be proud of, and it has not been without grave cost to ourselves in labour and lives. But one cannot hold back the march of progress. This is the nineteenth century, and the world is becoming too small to permit large portions of it to remain in a state of medieval depravity and barbarism.'

Ash had a sudden vision of the white pinacles of the Dur Khaima and the wide sweep of the plateau across which he had ridden out hawking with Lalji and Koda Dad, and his heart sank: it was terrible to think that one day there might be no wild, beautiful places left where one could escape from the things that Uncle Matthew and his friends called 'Progress'. He had formed an unfavourable opinion of Progress, and he did not continue the conversation, it being obvious to him that he and his uncle would never see eye to eye on such subjects.

Ash was aware (as Uncle Matthew was not) of a great many things in Pelham Abbas that were in need of reform: the waste and extravagance, and the feuds that raged in the servants' hall; the tyranny of the upper servants and the miserably inadequate wages that were considered sufficient payment for long hours of gruelling work; the unheated attics in which such despised underlings as kitchen and scullery maids, boot-boys and under-footmen slept; the long flights of uncomfortable stairs that the housemaids must toil up and down a dozen times a day carrying cans of boiling water, slop-pails or loaded trays, with the dread shadow of instant expulsion without recompense or reference hanging over them should they commit any fault. The only difference that Ash could see between the status of the Pelham Abbas servants and those in the Hawa Mahal was that the latter led pleasanter and more idle lives. Yet he wondered what his uncle would think if Hira Lal or Koda Dad—who were both wise and incorruptible men—were suddenly to appear before the gates of Pelham Abbas accompanied by the guns, war elephants and armed soldiers of the Gulkote State Forces, and take over the management of the house and estates, setting them to rights according to ideas of their own? Would Uncle Matthew gratefully accept their domination and willingly obey their orders because they were running his house and his affairs better than he could run them himself? Ash doubted it. People everywhere preferred to make their own mistakes, and resented strangers (even efficient and well-meaning ones) interfering with their affairs.

He resented it himself. He hadn't wanted to come to *Belait* and learn to be a Sahib. He would far rather have stayed in Mardan and become a sowar like Zarin. But he had not been given the choice, and felt in consequence that he understood more about the feelings of subject races than his Uncle Matthew, who had spoken so patronizingly of 'bestowing the benefits of peace and prosperity on the suffering millions of India'.

'I suppose they look on me as one of the "suffering millions",' thought Ash bitterly, 'but I'd rather be back there, and working as a coolie, than here, being told what to do all day.'

The holidays had been oases in a dry wilderness of lessons, and but for them he often felt that he would not have been able to endure this new life; for although he was encouraged to walk and ride in the park, it was never alone but always under the watchful eye of his tutor or a groom. And as the park was surrounded by a high stone wall and he was not allowed beyond the lodge gates, his world was in many ways as restricted as that of a prisoner or a mental patient. Yet the loss of freedom had not been the worst thing in those years, for Ash had experienced much the same restriction in the Hawa Mahal. But then Sita had been there, and he had had friends; and at least Lalji had been young.

The age of his present gaolers irked him, and after the colourful muddle of an Indian court he found the decorous and inflexible ritual of Victorian country-house life dreary and meaningless—and alien beyond words. But since his pocket money, like the servants' wages, was too meagre to permit him to think of escape—and in any case, England was an island and India was six thousand miles away—there was nothing he could do about it except endure it, and wait for the day when he could go back to join the Corps of Guides. Only obedience and hard work could hasten that day; so he had been obedient and had worked hard at his lessons, and his reward had been the end of tutors and life at Pelham Abbas, and four years at the school his father and grandfather and great-grandfather had attended before him.

Nothing in Ash's formative years had prepared him for life in an English public school, and he detested every aspect of it: the regimentation, the monotony and the lack of privacy, the necessity to conform and the bullying and brutality that were meted out to weaklings and all whose opinions differed from those of the majority; the compulsory games and the reverence paid to such gods as the Head of Games and the Captain of Cricket. He was not given to talking of himself, but the fact that one of his names was Akbar had elicited questions, and his replies having revealed something of his background, he had promptly been nicknamed 'Pandy', a name applied for many years by British soldiers to all Indians, whom they termed 'Pandies' in reference to the Sepoy, Mangal Pandy, who had fired the first shot of the Indian Mutiny.

'Young Pandy Martyn' had been treated as a species of foreign barbarian who must be taught how to behave in a civilized country, and the process had been a painful one. Ash had not accepted it in the proper spirit, but attacked his tormentors with teeth, nails and feet in the manner of the Gulkote bazaars, which was apparently not only uncivilized but 'unsporting'—though it did not appear to be unsporting for five or six of his opponents to set upon him at once when it became clear that in the matter of muscle he was a match for any two of them. But numbers invariably triumphed, and for a time he had again seriously contemplated flight; only to reject it once more as impractical. He would have to endure this as he had endured the lesser evils of Pelham Abbas. But at least he would show these *feringhis* that on their playing fields he could be as good or better than they.

Koda Dad's training in marksmanship having encouraged a naturally good eye, it had not taken long for Ash's schoolmates to discover that 'young Pandy' could more than hold his own at any form of sport, and it had made a great deal of difference to their attitude towards him—particularly once he had learnt to box. When he eventually graduated from the Second Eleven to the First, played fives and football for his House and later for the school, he became the object of considerable hero-worship among the junior forms; though his contemporaries found him difficult to know. Not unfriendly, but apparently uninterested in any of the things that they had always believed in, such as the supremacy of the Anglo-Saxon races, the importance of being well-bred, and the Divine Right of the British to govern and control all coloured (and therefore unenlightened) peoples.

Even Colonel Anderson, in most matters so wise and understanding, had little sympathy with Ash's views, for his own opinions inclined more in the direction of Sir Matthew's. He too had pointed out that with the triumph of the steam-engine and the improvement of medical standards, the world was becoming smaller and more overcrowded every year. It was no longer possible for either nations or individuals to go their own way and do exactly as they pleased, for if everyone were free to do as they liked, the result would not be contentment, but anarchy and chaos. 'You'll have to find a desert island, Ash, if you want to live your life without anyone else interfering with it. And I don't suppose there are many of those left.'

The English climate had not improved Colonel Anderson's health as much as had been hoped, but though he had been forced to resign himself to a life of semi-invalidism he continued to take an active interest in Ash, who still spent the greater part of the school holidays under his roof. The Colonel's house was a small one on the outskirts of Torquay, and though in no way comparable to Pelham Abbas, Ash would have preferred to spend all his free time there, since those portions of the holidays that had to be spent in his uncle's house continued to be a severe trial to both of them. Sir Matthew being annoyed to find that, except in the matter of sport, his nephew showed no signs of turning into a credit to him and every sign of being as intransigent as his father Hilary had been, while Ash, on his part, was equally baffled and exasperated by his uncle, his relatives and his relatives' friends. Why, for instance, would they persist in asking for his views, and then be affronted when he gave them? 'What do *you* think, Ashton?' might be a well-meaning remark, but it was also a singularly stupid one if he were not expected to give an honest reply.

He would never understand the English—or feel at home in their country.

Colonel Anderson never asked stupid questions and his conversation was astringent and stimulating. He loved India with the single-minded devotion that some men give to their work—or their wives—and would talk by the hour of its history, culture, problems and politics, and the knowledge and guile that must be acquired by those who aspired to serve and govern its peoples. On these occasions he invariably spoke in Hindustani or Pushtu, and as neither Ala Yar or Mahdoo ever addressed his protégé in English, he was able to report to Mardan that the boy still spoke both languages as fluently as ever.

The Colonel had been ill in the winter of 1868, so Ash had spent the Christmas holidays at Pelham Abbas, where his education—if it could be called that—had taken a new turn. He had been seduced by a recently engaged housemaid, one Lily Briggs, a bold, brassy-haired girl some five years his senior, who had already caused considerable rivalry and dissension among the men in the servants' hall.

Lily had a loose mouth and a roving eye, and she had formed a habit of coming in last thing at night in her dressing-gown to make sure that Ash's bedroom windows were open and his curtains properly drawn. Her heavy corn-coloured plaits fell almost to her knee, and one night she combed them out and sat on the edge of Ash's bed to show him, she said, that she could sit on her hair. From there things had moved very fast and Ash was never quite sure how she had come to be in his bed, or who had put out the light; but it had been wildly exciting. His own inexperience had been more than compensated for by Lily's extreme proficiency, and he had proved such an apt pupil that she had enjoyed herself immensely and contrived to spend the next six nights in his bed. She would certainly have spent the seventh there as well had they not been discovered by Mrs Parrot, the housekeeper, in flagrante delicto—though that was not precisely the term Mrs Parrot had used when reporting the incident to Ash's Aunt Millicent . . .

Lily Briggs was dismissed without a character, while Ash received a sound thrashing and a lecture on the evils of concupiscence from Uncle Matthew, and a black eye and a split lip from the second footman, who had been one of the faithless Lily's most fervent admirers. The remainder of that holiday passed without incident and the next one saw him back with Colonel Anderson.

Once or twice a year there would be a letter from Zarin. But on the whole these contained little news; Zarin could not write, and the bazaar letter-writer he employed had a flowery style and a habit of beginning and ending every letter with polite and protracted inquiries as to the recipient's health, and long-winded prayers to 'the Almighty God' for his continued well-being. Sandwiched in between would be a few disconnected items of news, and by this means Ash learned that Zarin was to be married to a second cousin of Awal Shah's wife; that a young squadron officer, Lieutenant Ommaney, had been murdered by a fanatic while attending band practice in Mardan; and that the Guides had been out against the Utman Khel, who had been raiding villages in British territory.

Sometime during those early years Zarin's mother died, and shortly afterwards Koda Dad Khan resigned his post and left Gulkote. The Rajah had been loth to part with his old and trusted servant, but Koda Dad had pleaded ill-health and his desire to end his days among his kinsmen in the village where he had been born. His true reason, however, had been a lively distrust of Janoo-Rani, who had made no secret of the fact that she suspected him of complicity in Ashok's escape. She had done her best to poison the Rajah's mind against him, but without success. The Rajah valued the old man and had been curt with Janoo-Rani, and Koda Dad knew that he had nothing to fear from her while he enjoyed her husband's favour and protection.

But there came a day when the Rajah decided to journey to Calcutta in order to see the Viceroy and personally press his claim to the neighbouring state of Karidarra, whose late ruler, a distant cousin, had left no heir. He announced that his eldest son, the Yuveraj, would accompany him, and that during his absence the Rani would act as Regent—a piece of folly which (in Koda Dad's opinion) many people besides himself might have cause to regret. The list of officials who were to travel to Calcutta in the Rajah's suite did not include the Master of Horse; and noting that omission, Koda Dad knew that the time had come for him to leave Gulkote.

He was not sorry to go, because now that his wife was dead and his sons were soldiering in the north, there was little to stay for: a few friends, his horses and his hawks, that was all. The Rajah had been more than generous to him, and he had ridden away on the finest horse in the royal stables, with his favourite hawk on his wrist and his saddle-bags crammed with enough coins to ensure a comfortable old age. 'You are wise to leave,' said Hira Lal. 'Were it not for the Yuveraj—who, the gods know, needs at least one servant who is not in the pay of the *Nautch*-girl—I would follow your example. But then I am to go to Calcutta with him; and I do not think she suspects me, for I have been very careful.'

But it seemed that Hira Lal had not been careful enough. He had allowed himself to forget that Lalji, spoilt, vain and gullible, had never been capable of distinguishing between his friends and his enemies, and could be counted upon to prefer the latter because they pandered to him and flattered him. Lalji's chosen favourites, Biju and Puran, were both spies of the Rani, and they had always distrusted Hira Lal. One hot night on the long journey to Calcutta, Hira Lal had apparently left his tent in search of air and been attacked and carried off by a tiger. There had been no signs of a struggle, but a fragment of his blood-stained clothing had been found caught on a thorn bush a hundred yards from the camp; and there was known to be a man-eating tiger in the territory. The Rajah had offered a hundred rupees for the recovery of his body, but the surrounding country was full of thickets, elephant grass and deep ravines, and no further trace of him had been found.

Hira Lal had vanished. But as Koda Dad's friends were not addicted to writing him letters, he never heard the tale—or anything further from Gulkote. And neither did Ash, since Koda Dad's departure from the state had severed his last link with it. Inevitably, the past retreated, for life in England allowed him little time for retrospect. There was always work to be done and games to be played, school to be endured and holidays to be enjoyed, and in time the memory of Gulkote became shadowy and a little unreal, and he seldom thought of it, though at the back of his mind—ignored but ever-present—there lurked a curious feeling of emptiness and loss, a haunting sense of being incomplete because something that was vitally necessary to him had gone out of his life. He had no idea how long that feeling had been there, and he made no attempt to analyse it for fear that it might lead him back to the day of Sita's death. But he was convinced that just as soon as he returned to his own country and saw Zarin and Koda Dad again, it would vanish; and in the meantime he accepted it much as a man with one arm or one leg accepts his disability and learns to live with it; and to ignore it.

He made no close friends and was never particularly popular among his contemporaries, who found him difficult to know and continued to regard him as something of a freak—a 'loner'. But in a world where the ability to hit a ball or out-run one's fellows was prized above scholarship, his prowess at sports at least earned him their respect (and in the case of his juniors a large measure of admiration), and in his last year at school he had a batting average of fifty-two point nought three, took seven wickets for sixteen in a house match, made a century at Lord's and passed into the new Royal Military Academy at Sandhurst by a comfortable margin.

It was a come-down, after those three final terms, to find himself once more in the position of an obscure 'new boy' at the bottom of a ladder. But on the whole he preferred the R.M.A. to his public school, and did well there; well enough, at all events, for some of his fellow cadets to try and dissuade him from going into the Indian Army—especially now that the purchase of commissions was to be abolished, which meant that the sons of rich men would in future be obliged to rely on ability instead of their purses to obtain promotion. Thus handicapped, few gentlemen would now care to plump for an army career, and Ash's advisers prophesied (correctly as it happened) a disastrous drop in cadets; their own term being the last to enter before the new rule came into force. It was going to be bad enough in a decent regiment, let alone going off to soldier among a lot of pushing, provincial nobodies. 'And you don't want to do that, you know. After all, it's not as if you were short of the ready, so why go off and bury yourself in some colonial backwoods among a lot of blacks and second-raters? My pater says . . .'

Ash had retorted with some heat that if the speaker and his father and his friends really thought along these lines, then the sooner the British cleared out of India and left her to run her own affairs the better, for she could probably do so more successfully with her own first-raters than with anyone else's second-raters.

'Pandy's up on his elephant again!' jeered his Company (the nickname had followed him to the Military Academy). But a Senior Instructor, who had overheard the exchange and repeated it to the Company Commander, had been inclined to agree with him.

'It's the old Horse Guards' attitude,' said the Senior Instructor. 'All those fellows were as caste-ridden as Hindus, and used to regard an India Army officer as some form of Untouchable. Why, old Cardigan wouldn't even eat in mess with one. But if we want to have an Empire, we need our best material to serve overseas, not our worst. And thanks be to God there are still enough of the former who are prepared to go.'

'Would you class young Pandy Martyn among the best?' inquired the Company Commander sceptically. 'Damned if I would. If you want my opinion, he's as wild as a hawk and liable to fly off at a tangent at any moment. Doesn't take any too kindly to discipline either, for all that surface appearance of docility. I don't trust the type. The army's no place for Radicals—especially the Indian Army. In fact they're a downright danger, and if I had any say in it I'd keep 'em out of it. And that goes for young Pandy!'

'Nonsense. He'll probably end up as another Nicholson. Or a Hodson, anyway.'

'That's just what I'm afraid of—or would be, if I were his future C.O. Both those two were mountebanks. Useful ones, I grant you. But only because of the particular circumstances. It was probably fortunate that they died when they did. From all one hears, they must have been quite insufferable.'

'Oh, well, perhaps you're right,' conceded the Senior Instructor, losing interest in the subject.

As at school, Ash made no close friends at Sandhurst, though he was liked, and to a great extent admired—the latter again almost solely on account of his success as an athlete. He won the Pentathlon, played football, cricket and fives for the Academy, took first place in the riding events and marksmanship, and passed out twenty-seventh in a list of two hundred and four cadets.

Uncle Matthew and Aunt Millicent, Cousin Humphrey and two elderly female Pelham-Martyns attended the Passing-Out Parade. But Colonel Anderson had not been present. He had died in the previous week, leaving a small legacy to each of his two Indian servants, in addition to a sum sufficient to cover their return to their own country, and a letter to Ash asking him to see that they reached their homes in safety. His house and its contents had been left to a nephew, and Ash, Ala Yar and Mahdoo had spent their last month in England at Pelham Abbas; embarking at the end of June on the S.S. *Canterbury Castle,* for Bombay. The years of exile were over, and for all three of them, home lay ahead.

'It will be good to see Lahore again,' said Mahdoo. 'There be many larger cities in *Belait,* but save only in the matter of size, none can rival Lahore.'

'Or Peshawar—or Kabul,' grunted Ala Yar. 'It will be pleasant to purchase proper food in the bazaars once more and to smell the morning among the Khyber hills.'

Ash said nothing. He leaned upon the rail and watched the foam-streaked water widen between the ship and the shore, and saw life opening before him like a vast sunlit plain stretching away and away towards unimaginable horizons. A plain across which he could travel at will, choosing his own path and taking his own time.

He was free at last. He was going home, and the future was his to do what he liked with. The Regiment first: the Guides and Zarin and soldiering among the wild hills of the North-West Frontier . . . perhaps one day he would command the Corps; and after that a Division. In time—who knew?—he might even become *Jung-i-Lat Sahib*—Commander-in-Chief of all the armies in Hind—but that would be a long way ahead . . . he would be old then and all this would be in the past. He did not have to think of the past just now: only of the future . . .

Book Two

Belinda

8

Ash had returned to India in the late summer of 1871.

It was a year that had not been without interest to many millions of people. France had seen the capitulation of Paris, heard Prince William of Prussia proclaimed Emperor of Germany at Versailles, and once again declared herself a Republic. In England, Parliament had finally legalized trade unions, and an end had been put to the long-established and iniquitous system by which commissions in the British Army could be purchased by the highest bidder, irrespective of merit. But none of these events had been of any interest to Ashton Hilary Akbar, compared to the fact that he was returning at last to the land of his birth after seven long years in exile.

He was home again. He was in his nineteenth year—and he was engaged to be married . . .

Until recently, Ash had had very little to do with girls of his own class, for after Lily Briggs the well-bred and well-behaved sisters and cousins of his schoolmates had seemed painfully prim and colourless, and he had gone out of his way to avoid them. Lily had had her successors, but they had made no lasting impression and already their names and faces were becoming dim, for his heart had never again been involved. As a cadet he had gained the quite unfounded reputation of being a misogynist by refusing invitations to tea-parties, picnics and dances, and announcing grandly that he 'had no time for women'. But there had been plenty of time—hours and days and weeks of it—on the long sea voyage from London to Bombay. And Miss Belinda Harlowe was not only a young lady, but far and away the prettiest girl on board.

There was nothing prim or colourless about Belinda. She was as pink and white and gold as Ash's romanticized memory of Lily, as gay as Dolly Develaine of 'The Seaside Follies' and as seductively shaped as Ivy Markins, who had worked in a hat shop in Camberley and been so generous with her favours. She was also sweet and innocent and young (two years younger than Ash) and, in addition to a charming, wilful face that was set off to admiration by a wealth of pale gold ringlets, was the fortunate possessor of a small straight nose that wrinkled deliciously when she laughed, a pair of large cornflower-blue eyes that sparkled with interest and eagerness for life, and a kissable mouth made more inviting by the fact that a dimple hovered near each corner.

None of these assets would have aroused much emotion in Ash (beyond a natural feeling of admiration for a pretty girl), had he not discovered that Miss Harlowe, who like himself had been born in India, was delighted at the prospect of returning there. She had said as much one evening during dinner, when the *Canterbury Castle* had been at sea for close on ten days, and several of the older ladies, including Belinda's mother, had been lamenting the fact that they were journeying east once more. They had been cataloguing the many discomforts of life in India—the heat, the dust, the disease, the appalling state of the roads and the difficulties of travel—when Belinda had intervened with a laughing protest:

'Oh no, Mama! How can you say such things? Why, it's a delightful country. I can remember it clearly—that lovely cool bungalow with the purple creeper climbing over the porch, and all the gorgeous flowers in the garden; the ones like spotted lilies and those tall scarlet ones that were always covered with butterflies. And riding my pony on the Mall and seeing lines of camels, and being carried in a dandy when we went up to the hills for the summer—those great tall pine trees and the yellow wild roses that smelled so sweet . . . and the snows: miles and miles of snow mountains. You've no *idea* how ugly Nelbury and Aunt Lizzie's house seemed after that; and her servants were always scolding me, instead of spoiling me like Ayah and Abdul and my syce. I can't wait to get back.'

This artless speech had displeased a Mrs Chiverton, who evidently deciding that young Miss Harlowe was a forward chit who had no business to intervene in a conversation between her elders, remarked dampingly that no one who had endured the horrors of the Mutiny would ever be able to trust an Indian again, and that she envied dear Belinda's happy ignorance of the dangers that must face any sensitive Englishwoman forced by circumstances and a sense of duty to live in that barbarous land. At which Belinda, wholly unabashed, had laughed, and throwing a sparkling glance around the men seated about the long table, said sweetly: 'But only think how many brave men we have to defend us. One could not be afraid. Besides I'm sure that nothing of that nature could happen again'—and leaning forward she appealed to Ash, who was seated on the opposite side of the table and had been listening with interest—'don't you agree, Mr Pelham-Martyn?'

'I don't know,' replied Ash, incurably honest. 'I suppose that will depend on us.'

'On *us?*' repeated Mrs Chiverton in a tone that told Ash he had made a suggestion that she not only found totally unacceptable, but coming from such a very junior officer, positively insulting.

Ash hesitated, unwilling to offend her further, but Miss Harlowe had rushed gaily in where an ensign feared to tread: 'He means that provided we deal justly with them, they will have no reason to rise against us;' here she turned to him again and added: 'That was what you meant, wasn't it?'

It was not exactly what Ash had meant, but it was Belinda's use of the word 'justly' that made him cease from that moment to see her only as a pretty girl; and after that, despite the fact that strict chaperoning, a plethora of admirers and the crowded conditions that prevailed on shipboard made it well-nigh impossible to have any speech with her alone, he seized every opportunity that offered to talk to her or listen to her talk to him, of the land to which both were returning with such high hopes and happy anticipation.

Belinda's mother, Mrs Archibald Harlowe, was a stout, well-meaning and fluffy-minded woman who had once been as pretty as her daughter; but the climate and conditions that prevailed in India, together with her distrust of 'the natives' and fear of a second Mutiny, had not suited her health or her temperament. The heat and constant pregnancies had thickened a once admirable figure, her husband, now in his late sixties, was still only a Major in an Indian infantry regiment, three of the seven children she had borne him had died in infancy, and a year ago she had been forced to take her five-year-old twins, Harry and Teddy, home to England to leave them in the care of her sister Lizzie—for India was still regarded as a death trap for the young; cantonment cemeteries up and down the country being crowded with the graves of children who had died of cholera, heatstroke, typhoid or snake-bite.

Nothing would have pleased Mrs Harlowe more than to be able to stay in England with her darling boys, but after exhaustive discussions with her sister the two ladies had agreed that it was her plain duty to return to India: not her duty to her husband, but to her daughter Belinda, who at the age of seven had also been consigned to Lizzie's care. That had been ten years ago, and as Lizzie pointed out, the girl's chances of making an advantageous match in a small provincial town such as Nelbury were slight. In British India, however, eligible bachelors were two-a-penny, so it was only sensible to give Belinda the chance to meet and marry some suitable gentleman, after which her Mama would be able to return to her precious boys, and make her home with dear Lizzie until such time as Archie gained command of his regiment or was retired.

No one (with the possible exception of Major Harlowe) could have found fault with this programme, and Mrs Harlowe's confidence in her decision had been speedily vindicated when no less than eleven gentlemen out of the twenty-nine who had taken passages on the S.S. *Canterbury Castle* began to pay marked attention to her pretty daughter. True, these were for the most part mere boys; either penniless ensigns, junior Civil Servants or youthful recruits to Trade, and the five other unmarried ladies on board were not remarkable for good looks. But the gentlemen did include an infantry Captain in his mid-thirties, a rich middle-aged widower who was the senior partner in a firm of jute exporters, and young Ensign Pelham-Martyn, who (according to Mrs Chiverton, the ship's gossip) was not only the nephew of a baronet, but sole heir to a more than comfortable fortune left him by his father, who had been a distinguished scholar with a world-wide reputation.

From the purely financial aspect, Mrs Harlowe considered that Mr Joseph Tilbery, the widower, was probably the most eligible prospect. But though his attentions to her daughter had been marked, he had not as yet made any declaration, and Belinda herself had been heard to refer to both him and the infantry Captain as 'old fogies'. The ensigns and young Civil Servants were much more to her taste, and she flirted with them light-heartedly and enjoyed herself enormously, playing off one against the other and revelling in being young and pretty and admired.

The heady atmosphere of that long voyage had been further heightened for her by a romantic event—a wedding at sea. Admittedly the bride and bridegroom had neither of them been handsome nor in the first blush of youth, and as both were travelling steerage she had not previously laid eyes upon them. But the Captain, having been prevailed upon to exercise the powers invested in him as master of an ocean-going vessel, had married Sergeant Alfred Biggs of the Supply Corps, returning from leave, to Miss Mabel Timmins, travelling to Bombay to join a brother working for the Bombay-and-Baroda Railway, the wedding taking place in the First-Class Saloon in the presence of every passenger on board who could be crammed into it, and being followed by speeches and toasts drunk in champagne donated by the Captain. Later on, the entire company had danced on deck, and no less than three of Belinda's suitors had begged her to follow the bride's admirable example and spend the remainder of the voyage on honeymoon.

In the circumstances, it is hardly surprising that if the other young ladies were unfriendly and their mothers openly disapproving, Belinda did not notice it. She had been cooped up in her aunt's house for ten long years, minding her lessons, stitching away at interminable samplers and saying 'Yes, Aunt Lizzie' and 'No, Aunt Lizzie', and the only young men she met (at strictly chaperoned parties) were the sons of her aunt's friends: awkward, gawking schoolboys who had known her since she was in pinafores and treated her as a sister. The transition from that confined and stultifying atmosphere to the delightful freedom of life on an ocean liner and the attentions of a dozen admiring young gentlemen was an exhilarating experience, and Belinda revelled in it and was perhaps as completely happy as anyone can hope to be in the course of one lifetime. Her only difficulty had been to decide which of her many admirers she preferred, but by the time the ship reached Alexandria she was no longer in any doubt.

Ashton Pelham-Martyn might not be as handsome as George Garforth (who, though gauche and really tediously shy, possessed a Grecian profile and Byronic curls); nor was he as witty or amusing as Ensign Augustus Blain, or as rich as Mr Joseph Tilbery of Tilbery, Patterson & Company. He was, in fact, rather a silent young man, except when he talked about India, which she encouraged him to do whenever her importunate admirers allowed her any private conversation with him, for he made it sound like her childhood memories of it: a magic place. He could, she found, be excessively charming when he chose, and there was something about him that she found fascinating: something different and exciting . . . and a little disquieting: the difference that lies between a wild hawk and a tame cage-bird. He was also undeniably good-looking in a dark, thin-faced way, and moreover a certain air of romantic mystery hung about him; there was some story of his having been brought up in an Indian palace, and that old gossip, Mrs Chiverton, had unkindly hinted that the swarthiness of his complexion and the darkness of his hair and lashes was possibly the result of mixed blood. But then everyone knew that Mrs Chiverton was a cat and would have been only too pleased if he had taken some notice of her own exceedingly plain daughter, Amy.

Belinda turned her sunniest smiles on Ensign Pelham-Martyn, who ended by falling helplessly and hopelessly in love, and by the last day of the voyage had summoned up enough courage to approach Mrs Harlowe and ask her permission to propose for her daughter's hand.

Ash had been in dread of a rebuff on the score of his youth and his unworthiness, and he could not believe his good fortune when Belinda's mother assured him that she had no objection at all to his doing so, and was certain that dear Bella's Papa would agree with her, as he too believed in early marriages. Though the latter statement was far from being true, for Major Harlowe, like most older army officers, strongly disapproved of young officers ruining their prospects and reducing their usefulness to their regiments by getting tied up too early to some girl who would inevitably take their attention off their work, and involve them in domestic trivia to the detriment of the men under their command.

The Major himself had been more than twice his wife's age and nearer forty than thirty when he married; but although Mrs Harlowe was not ignorant of his views, she had no hesitation in pledging his consent, for she had managed to convince herself that Archie must certainly wish to see his only daughter so suitably bestowed. After all, it was not as though the young people would have to live on an ensign's pay; Ashton's allowance was more than generous, and in a little more than two years' time he would come of age and inherit the whole of his father's fortune. So of course Archie must consent. Ashton might be still in his teens, but anyone could see that he was old for his age. Such a quiet, well-mannered young man. So devoted to Belinda—and so *very* eligible.

Mrs Harlowe shed a few emotional tears, and half an hour later, in a quiet corner of the forward deck while the sun was setting and their fellow passengers were changing for dinner, Ash proposed to Belinda and was accepted.

The engagement was supposed to be kept secret, but somehow it leaked out, and dinner was barely over before Ash found himself receiving the envious congratulations of his rivals and an assortment of chilly stares from the ladies; most of whom had already declared

Miss Harlowe to be a shocking flirt and were now convinced that her mama, far from being the foolish but good-natured creature they had supposed, was nothing more than a shameless, scheming, cradle-snatcher.

Mr Tilbery and the infantry Captain had been particularly frosty, but only George Garforth had registered an active protest.

George had turned as white as a sheet, and after attempting to drown his disappointment in drink had offered to fight the successful suitor, though, luckily for all concerned, he had been taken ignominiously ill before his challenge could be accepted. Belinda had retired early, and George having been carried to his cabin, Ash had gone up to the deserted deck, where he had spent the night lying in a deck chair under the stars, dizzy with champagne and happiness.

It had been a wonderful night, and watching the dear, familiar constellations of his childhood wheel overhead, it seemed to Ash that whatever else he might forget, he would remember this night forever —and that he would never be so happy again. His first love-affair had ended in disaster, and it had taken him a full six months to realize that Lily Briggs, far from being a golden goddess who had miraculously fallen in love with him, was nothing more than an amoral slut who had amused herself by seducing a schoolboy. Yet because she had been the first woman he had ever slept with, he knew that he would never quite forget her. Her successors had been no more than brief, sordid adventures in sex, and soon he would not even be able to remember their names, and could only be sorry that he had ever known any of them. To have done so seemed in some way a betrayal of Belinda; but at least she need never know about them, and there were so many other things that he could tell her about: the whole fantastic story of his childhood, and all the secrets and sorrows and enchantments of those years.

He would have told her all this before had it been possible, but with half-a-dozen jealous rivals competing for her attention there had been no chance of doing so, and there had been many occasions when he had felt like murdering Gus Blaine or that pompous old fool Mr Tilbery—or, for that matter, the entire roster of Belinda's beaux. Yet with so many to choose from, she had, incredibly, chosen him. He was the luckiest man in the world, and tomorrow—no, today, for it was well after midnight—he would be back in his own land at last. Soon now he would cross the Ravi River again and see the mountains, and Zarin . . .

Zarin—

Ash found himself wondering a little uneasily if Zarin would have changed very much during the past years, and if he would even be able to recognize him on sight. There had been nothing of the old Zarin in those stilted, flowery letters that had come so infrequently and told him so little. He knew that Zarin was now a Daffadar and the father of three children, but that was all. The rest had merely been a brief chronicle of regimental events and he no longer knew how Zarin thought or felt. Would they be able to take up the old relationship where they had left it seven years ago?

It had never occurred to him before that they might not, but now, quite suddenly, a doubt crept in, for he remembered that their positions would be reversed. He was returning as a British officer and Zarin Khan, that 'elder brother' whom he had admired and envied and striven to emulate, would be under his command. How much difference was that going to make? None, if he could help it; but circumstances might make a great deal—such things as regimental custom and etiquette. And then there would be his fellow officers, and even Belinda . . . no, not Belinda: she loved him, and so she would feel as he felt. But it might be difficult at first for both Zarin and himself.

He wished now that it had been possible for them to meet on neutral ground instead of in the strictly military atmosphere of Mardan, where they would be under the critical eye of a dozen men who knew something of his story and would watch to see how he comported himself. However, it was too late to worry about that, and he would just have to behave circumspectly and try to remember not to rush his fences (always, according to both Koda Dad and Uncle Matthew, his besetting sin). In the meantime there was the long journey north, and the dismal prospect of parting with Ala Yar and Mahdoo, this last being the one black cloud on his bright horizon.

Recalling it now he was conscious of a sharp pang of guilt, because there was no blinking the fact that his preoccupation with Belinda had made him neglect them of late, and beyond an occasional stroll with one or other in the early morning before the passengers were astir, and a few words each day when Ala Yar came to his cabin to lay out clean linen or put studs in his shirt, he had seen very little of them. And it was too late to make amends now, for tomorrow—today—they would say goodbye to him. The three of them would be going their separate ways, and he knew that for his part he would miss both of them more than he could say. They were a link between the old days of his childhood and the new days and the new life that would begin when the sun rose, which would be very soon now, for already the stars were losing their brightness and to the East the sky was faintly green with the first, far-off glimmer of the dawn.

Bombay was still below the horizon, but the dawn wind carried the scent of the city far out to sea, and Ash could smell the mingled odours of dust and sewage, of crowded bazaars and rotting vegetation and a faint scent of flowers—frangipani, marigold, jasmine and orange blossom. The smell of home.

9

Daffadar Zarin Khan of the Guides had asked for three weeks' leave 'on urgent private affairs', and travelled to Bombay at his own expense to meet the S.S. *Canterbury Castle,* bringing with him a bearer for Ash: one Gul Baz, a Pathan, who had been specially selected for the post by Awal Shah.

The years had left few marks on Zarin, and at a casual glance there was little difference between the man who stood watching the ship approach and the young sowar who had waved farewell to a disconsolate boy nearly seven years ago. He was taller now and broader, and his moustache was more luxuriant. There were also lines about his mouth and eyes that had not been there before, and in place of the sand-coloured uniform and puttees he had been wearing when Ash had last seen him, he wore the holiday dress of a Pathan: voluminous trousers, a flowered waistcoat and a flowing white shirt.

The sun blazed down on the grimy dock with its jostling jabbering crowd of coolies, port officials, hotel touts and friends and relatives who had gathered to meet the ship, and as the tugs manoeuvred her alongside and the gang-planks ran out, Zarin's eyes scanned the lines of faces that peered down from the deck rails, and it occurred to him for the first time that although Ashok should have small difficulty in recognizing him, he himself might find it less easy to identify a boy who would now be a man. But almost in the same moment his gaze checked and he drew a quick breath of relief. Yes, that must surely be Ashok. There could be no mistaking him.

He was not as tall as Zarin had expected him to be, being just under six foot; but a fair enough height, and with the lean good looks of a northerner or a Pathan. His dress proclaimed him a Sahib, yet his complexion, which had always been swarthy, was now as dark as an Asiatic's from the suns of the long lazy days on shipboard, and his hair as black. Put him in the proper clothing and he could still pass as a Pathan or a hillman, decided Zarin with a wry grin—always provided the years had not changed him in too many other ways.

This was something that only time would show, for though he had written with great frequency and his letters, except for the earlier ones, had been in Urdu script (Colonel Anderson having tutored him in this) they had had to be translated to Zarin by a munshi, and had lost much in the process. But at least they proved that the boy had not forgotten his friends. It remained to be seen if it were possible for them to adjust to a new relationship. He could see that Ashok was not expecting anyone to meet him, for unlike the majority of his fellow passengers he was not scanning the faces of the crowd in search of familiar features, but gazing above them towards the rooftops and the lush green gardens of the beautiful, flamboyant city. Even from that distance Zarin could see his expression; and reading it, was satisfied. It was indeed Ashok and not a stranger who had returned home.

'There is Pelham-Sahib,' said Zarin, pointing him out to Gul Baz. He raised a hand to signal to his friend, and then dropped it without doing so. For a woman had come to stand beside Ashok, a very young woman who took his arm and clung to it as though by right, laughing up into his face and demanding his attention. Ashok turned immediately and his expression changed; and noting it, Zarin's brows twitched together in a frown. A memsahib . . . a young memsahib. This was one complication he had not bargained for.

From the first, it had been the memsahibs who had created distrust and raised social barriers between white men and brown in the territories of the Raj. In the old days—the brave days of 'John Company' that had seen the birth of the Bengal Army—there had been few memsahibs in India, because the climate had not been considered suitable for them, while the length and discomfort of voyages by sailing ship had discouraged many of them and kept them away. Deprived of their society the Sahibs had married or taken mistresses from the local population, and had in consequence come to know and understand the country and its people—and to speak its languages with great fluency. There had been friendship and brotherhood between white men and brown in those days, and a great measure of mutual respect. But when the harnessing of steam had made sea voyages quicker and more comfortable, the memsahibs had flocked to India—bringing with them a full complement of snobbery, insularity and intolerance.

Indians who had hitherto been treated as equals became 'natives' and the term itself lost its dictionary definition and became an opprobrious word, signifying members of an inferior—and coloured—race. The memsahibs preferred not to have any social contact with 'natives', though they were not above accepting the lavish hospitality of Indian princes, and prided themselves on being patient with their numerous household servants. But they rarely invited Indians into their homes, or exerted themselves to make friends among them; and few showed any interest in the history and culture of the land which the majority looked upon as heathen and barbaric. Their menfolk no longer married Indian brides or kept Indian mistresses, and the memsahibs reserved their greatest scorn for the numerous half-castes that their own countrymen had fathered in happier times, referring to them contemptuously as 'Eurasians' or 'Blacky-whites', and ostracizing anyone whom they suspected of having what came to be termed 'a touch of the tar-brush'. There were of course many exceptions, but they were swamped by the bigoted majority, and as social contact between the races dwindled, sympathy and understanding waned, and a large part of the camaraderie of the old days was lost, to be replaced by distrust, suspicion and resentment.

Zarin Khan, standing in the hot sunlight on the dock at Bombay and watching his one-time friend solicitously helping a yellow-haired girl down the gang-way, felt his heart sink. He did not know what the years in *Belait* might have done to Ashok, but he had not expected any complications of this kind, and he could only hope that it might prove to be no more than a passing affair that would burn itself out in a matter of weeks. But he did not like the complacent and proprietary expression on the face of the short stout memsahib, undoubtedly the girl's mother, whom he now recognized as the wife of Harlowe Sahib, second-in-command of a regiment at present stationed at Peshawar. It boded no good, and Peshawar being less than four hours' ride from Mardan, the girl would be able to keep Ashok dancing attendance upon her at a time when his attention should be concentrated upon more important matters. Zarin frowned and was suddenly unsure of his welcome.

Major Harlowe had been unable to meet his family in Bombay, for the Frontier regiments were preparing for autumn manoeuvres and he had too much work on his hands to permit him to take leave at this time. But he had sent his bearer and his wife's *ayah* to see to their comfort on the long journey north, and felt sure that they would find an acquaintance or two on the train and not be too dull.

'Of course we shall not be dull,' cried Belinda, looking about her with sparkling eyes. 'Ash will be with us. Besides, there will be so much to see. Jungles and tigers and elephants and—oh, do look at that adorable baby; it's only wearing a bangle. Just imagine taking one's baby out in England dressed in nothing but a bangle! Why has Mr Tilbery got all those garlands round his neck? How comical he looks, all smothered in flowers and tinsel. Mrs Chiverton has got some on too: I wish—Ash, there's a native over there who keeps staring at us. The tall one in a white turban with gold ends. I believe he knows you.'

Ash turned to look, and stood suddenly still. *Zarin . . .*

The years rolled back and for a brief moment he was a boy again, listening to Zarin telling him why he must go to England and assuring him that he would one day return: *'the years will pass quickly, Ashok.'* They had not passed quickly; but they had passed. He had come home again, and here, waiting for him as he had promised, was Zarin. He tried to call to him but there was a lump in his throat and he could only smile foolishly.

'What's the matter, Ash?' inquired Belinda, tugging at his coat-sleeve. 'Why are you looking like that? Who is that man?'

Ash found his voice: 'Zarin. It's Zarin—'

He brushed her hand from his arm and broke into a run, leaving Belinda to stare after him, startled and more than a little shocked by the sight of her betrothed publicly embracing a strange native with a fervour that she would have considered excessive even if they had been Frenchmen. Why, they were actually *hugging* each other. Belinda turned away abruptly, scarlet-cheeked with embarrassment, and met the malicious gaze of Amy Chiverton who had also been a witness to the encounter.

'Mama always said that there was something fishy about Mr Pelham-Martyn,' remarked Miss Chiverton spitefully. 'Do you suppose that man is his half-brother, or a cousin or something? They are certainly *very* alike. Oh, I forgot you were engaged to him. How dreadful of me. I'm *so* sorry. But of course I was joking. I expect it's only one of his old servants come to meet him. Ours have come too. I expect yours are here as well.'

But surely one did not embrace one's old servants? thought Belinda; and anyway, the man was far from old. She turned to look at them again and saw with a sharp pang of unease that in one respect Amy Chiverton had been right. The two men were not unlike, and if Ashton were to grow a moustache they could almost pass as brothers . . .

'Really, Belinda dear,' scolded Mrs Harlowe, hurrying back from saying her goodbyes to a Colonel and Mrs Philpot who had occupied the next door cabin. 'How many times have I told you that you must not stand about in the sun without a parasol? You will ruin your complexion. Where is Ashton?'

'He—he had to see someone about his luggage,' lied Belinda, catching her mother's arm and pulling her away in the direction of the customs shed. 'He will only be a moment. Let us get into the shade.'

It was suddenly unbearable to her that Mama should see Ashton and that native hugging each other, for although Mama would never dream of saying—or even thinking—the sort of things that Amy Chiverton had just said, she would certainly be disapproving, and just at that moment Belinda felt that she could not bear to listen to anything else on the subject. Ashton would probably have some perfectly reasonable explanation, but he should never have abandoned her like that. He had no right to run off and leave her alone and unattended among a crowd of jostling coolies, just as though she was someone of no importance at all. If *this* was the way he intended to treat her—

Belinda's blue eyes filled with angry tears, and all at once the bustling, colourful scene about her lost its charm and she was aware only of the heat and noise and discomfort, and the fact that the bodice of her flowered muslin dress was already drenched with sweat and clinging unattractively to her shoulder blades. Ash had behaved abominably and India was horrid.

For the moment, at least, Ash had forgotten all about her. And forgotten too, as he laughed and exclaimed and embraced his friend, that he was now a Sahib and an officer.

'Zarin—Zarin. Why didn't anyone tell me that you would be here?'

'They did not know. I asked for leave and came away, not telling anyone where I meant to go.'

'Not even Awal Shah? How is he? Did you recognize me at once, or weren't you sure? Have I changed very much? You have not, Zarin. You haven't changed at all. Well, a little perhaps. But not enough to matter. Tell me about your father—is he well? Shall I see him in Mardan?'

'I do not think so. He is well, but his village lies two *koss** beyond the Border and he seldom leaves it for he is getting old.'

* 1 *koss* = 2 miles

'Then we must take leave and visit him. Oh Zarin, it is so good to see you. It is so good to be back.'

'I too am glad. There have been times when I feared that you might grow away from us and be reluctant to return, but I see now that you are still the same Ashok with whom I flew kites and stole melons in the days when we lived in the Hawa Mahal. I should have known that you would not change. Have the years in *Belait* seemed very long?'

'Yes,' said Ash shortly. 'But they are over, thank God. Tell me about yourself and the Regiment.'

The talk turned to the Guides and the rumours of a winter campaign against certain of the Frontier tribes who had been raiding villages and stealing women and cattle, and presently Zarin presented Gul Baz and was introduced in his turn to Ala Yar and Mahdoo. One or two of the departing passengers paused curiously, surprised by the sight of young Pelham-Martyn laughing and chattering with such joyous animation to a group of 'natives', for he had been anything but talkative on board and had, in fact, been voted a dull dog; though his success with the little Harlowe girl suggested that there must be more to him than met the eye. There was certainly no trace of reserve in his manners at the present moment, and those of his fellow passengers whose attention had been briefly attracted to the strangely assorted group raised their eyebrows in astonished disapproval and hurried on again, feeling vaguely affronted.

The crowds on the quayside began to thin and the mountains of luggage to dwindle, and still Belinda and her mother waited impatiently for Ash to return. Their companions of the last two months piled into carriages and were driven away in the direction of the city, and above their heads the sun beat down on the corrugated iron roof of the customs shed, and the temperature soared. But Ash had lost all count of time. There had been so much to talk of and to tell; and when at last Zarin dispatched Gul Baz to seek out his luggage and engage coolies to carry it from the dock, Ala Yar had announced unexpectedly that both he and Mahdoo would be accompanying Ash to Mardan.

'You will not require that new bearer,' said Ala Yar, 'for before he died I made a promise to Anderson-Sahib that I would see to your welfare. Mahdoo too wishes to take service with you. We have discussed the matter between us, and though we are both old men we do not desire to retire and sit idle. Nor do we wish to seek employment with some new Sahib whose ways will be strange to us. Therefore I will be your bearer and Mahdoo your cook; and there is no need to trouble yourself over the matter of payment, as Anderson-Sahib made ample provision for us both and our needs are small. A few rupees will suffice.'

No argument could move either old gentleman from this decision, and when Zarin pointed out that a junior subaltern living in the mess would have no need of a cook, Mahdoo said placidly that in that case he would be a *khidmatgar* (butler); what did it matter? But he and Ala Yar had served together for many years and were used to each other's ways—and to Ash-Sahib's too—and they preferred to remain together.

Nothing could have suited Ash better, for the prospect of parting with them had been the only thing that marred his return to India, and he was delighted to agree to this arrangement, and to the suggestion that Gul Baz should be retained as 'assistant bearer'. 'I will send him to the station to buy the tickets and to reserve a compartment for us as near to yours as may be,' said Zarin: 'No, we cannot travel with you . . . Or you with us. It would not be fitting. You are now a Sahib, and if you do not behave as one it will cause trouble for us all, for there are many who would not understand it.'

'He is right,' agreed Ala Yar. 'And there are also the memsahibs to be thought of.'

'Oh, to hell with—' began Ash and stopped on a gasp. '*Belinda!* Oh God, I forgot her. Look—I'll meet you at the station, Zarin. Tell Gul Baz to bring along my luggage. Ala Yar, you've got the keys haven't you? You know my gear. I must go—'

He ran back to where he had left Belinda, but she had gone. So too had all the other passengers, together with their baggage and those who had come to meet them. The S.S. *Canterbury Castle* lay silent and apparently deserted in the mid-day heat, and an official in the customs shed informed Ash that two ladies who had been waiting there for the best part of an hour had only just left. No, he did not know where they had gone: probably to a hotel on Malabar Hill, or to the Yacht Club, or the Byculla. One of the *ghari-wallahs** outside might be able to tell him. Both ladies, added the official unkindly, had appeared upset.

Ash hired a tonga and set off in pursuit, but as the pony proved to

* drivers of horse-drawn vehicles

be a jaded animal and incapable of any speed, he failed to overtake them. Having spent an anxious and exhausting afternoon driving about Bombay making fruitless inquiries at a number of hotels and clubs, he was left with no alternative but to make for the railway station and await them there.

The mail train was not due to leave until the late evening, so he spent the intervening hours loitering unhappily in the entrance hall and anathematizing himself for a selfish, unthinking clod who was in every way unworthy of such a superlatively lovely creature as Belinda. Only last night he had told her that if she would entrust her future to him, he would love and cherish her for ever and do everything in his power to make her happy. Yet at the first test he had failed her. What must she be thinking of him and where had she gone?

Belinda and her mother had, in fact, gone to the house of an acquaintance who lived within easy reach of the harbour, where they had spent the day; it being too hot, in Mrs Harlowe's opinion, for sight-seeing, and of course there was no question of Belinda being allowed to go out alone. They left for the station after an early supper and arrived to find Ash on the platform, though unfortunately for him, not alone. His luck was plainly out that day, because had they arrived five minutes earlier he would still have been standing forlornly by the ticket office. But Ala Yar had friends in the city and he had taken Zarin and Mahdoo to visit them, leaving Gul Baz to make all the necessary arrangements at the station. The three men had driven up in a tonga not five minutes before the arrival of Mrs Harlowe and her daughter, which could not have been more unfortunate, as seeing them in animated conversation with her betrothed, Belinda not unnaturally concluded that he had spent the day with them, preferring their company to her own and making no attempt to find her.

Anger and unshed tears formed a hot hard lump in her throat, and despite her training and the fact that the platform was crowded with travellers, baggage coolies, and vendors of food and drink, if she had possessed an engagement ring she would at that moment have torn it off and flung it in Ash's face. Deprived of such an outlet for her wounded feelings, she was preparing to sweep past him with her head in the air, when unkind fate sent her a weapon that few women, in these circumstances, could have resisted making use of.

It was to prove, in the long run, one of those trivial incidents that can change the character and course of events in the lives of many more people than those immediately involved, though no one, least of all Belinda, could be expected to know that. She merely saw a chance of repaying Ash in his own coin, and took it; and young George Garforth—he of the Grecian profile and Byronic curls—hurrying down the platform in search of his carriage, found himself being greeted with every appearance of delight by the girl to whom he had already lost his heart. Overcome by this reception, he now lost his head as well.

A combination of love, shyness and an acute sense of inferiority had hitherto prevented him from expressing his devotion, and though Belinda admired his looks, she considered him deplorably dull and had agreed wholeheartedly with Amy Chiverton's malicious observation that 'poor Mr Garforth would have made an excellent tailor's dummy'. Such looks ought, by rights, to have bestowed confidence, if not conceit, on their owner. But George Garforth quite obviously lacked any trace of either quality, and was not only painfully unsure of himself, but apt, at times, to be unbelievably gauche, pushing himself forward in an unseemly manner at quite the wrong moments, and then retreating in scarlet-faced confusion that created even further embarrassment. Ash, who rather liked him, had once said, 'The trouble with George is that he was born with one skin too few, so everything seems to touch him on the raw.'

Belinda had certainly done so. On the only occasion that George had nerved himself to make a bid for her attention, he had set about it in a manner calculated to irritate the mildest of girls, and she had been compelled to give him a sharp set-down that had sent him back into his shell, sore, blushing and humiliated. Yet here she was, advancing on him with an outstretched hand and a smile of such dazzling sweetness that poor George stopped in his tracks and cast an involuntary look over his shoulder to see who could be standing behind him.

'Why, Mr Garforth. What a pleasant surprise. Are you travelling on this train? I do hope so. It will make the journey so much pleasanter if we have friends on board.'

George stared at her as though he could not believe his ears, and then dropping the packet of letters he held, he clutched her proffered hand with the fervour of a drowning man catching at a rope. The blood drained out of his face and his tongue seemed to tie itself into knots, but his inability to answer her did not appear to offend his divinity, for having freed her hand from his grasp she tucked it confidingly under his arm and begged his escort to her carriage.

'If I had known that you would be on this train, I should not have worried,' declared Belinda gaily. 'But I confess I was a trifle hurt that you had not even said goodbye to me this morning. I looked for you everywhere, but the dock was so hot and crowded.'

'D-did you?' stammered George, finding his voice. 'Did—did you really?'

They were approaching Ash and his disreputable friends, and Belinda laughed up into her escort's pallid face, and giving his arm a little squeeze, said: 'Yes, *really*.'

The colour rushed back into George's face, and he took a deep breath that seemed to fill not only his lungs but his whole body with a heady exhilaration that no wine had ever given him before. All at once he felt taller and broader, and for the first time in his life, full of confidence.

'I *say!*' said George. He began to laugh, and Ash looked round and saw them arm in arm, laughing together as though neither had a care in the world. He started forward and Belinda said carelessly: 'Oh, hallo, Ashton,' and passed by with a casual little inclination of the head that was infinitely more wounding than any cut direct.

Ash followed them to the Harlowes' carriage where he found himself compelled to make his apologies and explanations to Mrs Harlowe, as Belinda seemed far too occupied with George to pay much attention to what he was saying—beyond telling him graciously that there was no need for him to apologize, it did not matter at all. Which not only took the wind out of his sails, but left him feeling uncommonly foolish.

He was to feel a good deal worse in the days that followed, for Belinda continued to treat him with maddening politeness when he presented himself at her carriage during the leisurely and frequent stops at wayside stations, and never once invited him to sit with them in their carriage, or take her strolling on the platform during the evening halts. This behaviour afflicted Ash and alarmed poor Mrs Harlowe, but its effect upon George was little short of electrifying. No one who had travelled out with him on the S.S. *Canterbury Castle* would have believed that the gauche, tongue-tied and over-sensitive youth of the voyage could have blossomed so swiftly into this talkative and assured young man, who squared his shoulders and threw out his chest as he walked in the twilight with Belinda on his arm, or monopolized the conversation in the carriage.

Ash himself was far too crushed and remorseful to take offence at his love's behaviour, or even notice George's growing jealousy and truculence, for he had already convicted himself of almost every crime in a lover's calendar, and felt that no punishment could be too severe—except the unthinkable one of losing her. As for Zarin, finding that he could do nothing to lighten Ashok's mood, he abandoned the attempt, and consoled himself with the more congenial company of his fellow-countrymen until such time as his friend should come to his senses. The journey that both had looked forward to had become slow and tedious, and Ash had no attention to spare for the vast landscape that streamed past his window, though it was seven long years since he had last seen it, and for the greater part of those years had dreamed of little else than seeing it again.

The tree-clad gorges and lush greenness of the south gave place to the parched emptiness of rock and sand: to jungle and cropland, little lost villages and the ruins of dead and gone cities, and wide, winding rivers where crocodiles and mud-turtles basked on the sand bars and white egrets fished in the shallows. At night-fall the thickets and the elephant grass shimmered with fire-flies, and at dawn peacocks cried from every cane-brake and the yellow sky mirrored itself in ponds and ditches that were starred with water-lilies. But Ash lay on his back and stared at the ceiling, rehearsing speeches to soften Belinda's heart, or replying to the conversational efforts of his travelling companions—an enthusiastic young man in the Political Department and a middle-aged Forest-Officer—very much at random.

Mrs Harlowe was also not enjoying the journey, which was only to be expected. Experience had taught her that travelling in India by whatever means was bound to be hot, dusty and excessively uncomfortable; but on the present occasion it was neither the tediousness or the discomfort that was upsetting her, but Ashton and Belinda, whose behaviour had plainly demonstrated that both were still little more than children. A great many girls married at seventeen—she herself had done so; but they married grown men who could be relied upon to take care of them, not thoughtless and irresponsible boys in their teens, which Ashton had shown himself to be when he ran off and left Belinda alone and unprotected on a crowded quayside while he gossiped for over an hour with a parcel of natives.

His excuse for this behaviour had merely made matters worse. To explain that one of them (and a mere daffadar at that—not even an Indian officer) was an old friend who had travelled from the Khyber to Bombay to meet him, and that he had been so pleased to see him that he had 'lost all count of time', might reflect credit on his honesty, but it certainly proved him to be lacking in wisdom and tact, and Mrs Harlowe fully sympathized with her daughter's rejection of such a clumsily phrased apology. Ashton really should have known better. And know better, too, than to be on such exceedingly friendly terms with sepoys and servants. Such behaviour was not at all the thing, and only went to prove that he did not yet know how to conduct himself—and also that she herself knew far too little about him. She had, in fact, allowed his eligibility in the matter of birth and fortune, and her anxiety to see her daughter swiftly and safely bestowed, to override good sense and caution. And now Belinda was flirting shamelessly with another, and quite ineligible young man, and really she felt distracted with worry. It was all most upsetting, and she did not know *what* Archie was going to say when he heard . . .

Poor, foolish, conscience-stricken Mrs Harlowe took refuge in tears and an attack of vapours, and three days of this atmosphere proved more than enough for Belinda, who began to discover that a sense of outrage was not equal to sustaining her through the boredom of endless hours penned up in a hot and dusty railway carriage, with nothing to do but listen to Mama's tearful observations on the subject of Ashton, early engagements and what Papa was likely to say about it all. Of course Ashton had behaved abominably, but he had been punished enough. Besides, she was beginning to tire of George Garforth's increasing bumptiousness and the protective and proprietary airs he had begun to adopt towards her, and thought that it was really time she put him in his place.

When the train next stopped at a station and Ash as usual knocked humbly at the door, he was admitted, and the unhappy George found himself suddenly relegated to the position of odd-man-out and left to hang about the platform, or make laborious conversation with his divinity's mother. But for Ash and Belinda the rest of the journey passed pleasantly enough—apart from a tiff in Delhi, where the railway stopped and anyone wishing to travel further northward must proceed in the manner of an older day by dâk-*ghari*,* palanquin, bullock cart or on foot. The travellers had put up

* mail carriage (*dâk* literally post, mail, posting-house)

at Delhi dâk-bungalow, and Ash, after two afternoons devoted to sightseeing, had absented himself for an entire day.

He had, in fact, been absent for a full twenty-four hours, but fortunately neither Mrs nor Miss Harlowe was aware of this, for Ash was learning wisdom, and this time he had accounted for his absence by producing a very pretty pearl and diamond ring, explaining that he had had to visit at least twenty or thirty shops in the old city and along the Chandi Chowk, Delhi's famous 'Silver Street', before finding something good enough to give Belinda. Both ladies had been charmed with the ring; though it could not of course be worn until Ash had spoken to Belinda's Papa. And as George Garforth had taken advantage of Ash's absence to take them for a picnic to the Kutab Minar, they had passed the day very pleasantly. Ash was forgiven, and neither Belinda nor her mother had thought to ask him any further questions, which was just as well, for he had, in point of fact, spent less than half an hour over the purchase of the ring and the rest of the time in quite another fashion.

Mahdoo had relations in Delhi, and on the previous night Ash had donned the dress of a Pathan (borrowed for the occasion from Gul Baz) and roistered in the city until dawn, eating and drinking and merry-making with Mahdoo's relatives, and later sampling the night-life of the crowded bazaars with Zarin. He was filled with an exhilarating sense of freedom, as though he had broken out of gaol. The Western veneer so painfully acquired during the cold years at school and Pelham Abbas fell away from him as easily as though it had been no more than a winter overcoat, discarded on the first warm day of spring, and he slipped back effortlessly into the ways and speech of his childhood. The rich, spicy food tasted ambrosial after a diet of boiled beef and carrots, watery cabbage and suet puddings, while the heat and smell and noise of the city was an intoxication and a deep delight. England, Sahib-hood, the Guides, Belinda—all were forgotten, and he was once more Sita's son Ashok, who had come home and inherited a kingdom.

Having no idea which temple Sita had taken him to (even if he had, he would not have been able to enter it in his present guise) he gave alms to several ash-smeared *sadhus* and a dozen Hindu beggars in her name, and the following morning, in company with Zarin, Ala Yar, Mahdoo and Gul Baz, he joined a vast congregation in the great courtyard of the Juma Masjid and said a prayer for her and for Uncle Akbar—the one an orthodox Hindu and the other a devout

Mussulman—in the belief that the One God, to whom all creeds are one, would hear and not be offended.

There had been a group of tourists in the gallery above the great gate, European men and women who had looked down at the worshipping throng below, laughing and talking the while as though they were watching the antics of animals in a zoo. Their plangent voices cut through the murmured prayers, and Ash was wondering angrily what they would think if a group of Indians behaved in a similar manner during a service in Westminster Abbey, when he was disconcerted to see that one of them was Mrs Harlowe and another his betrothed. 'It's only ignorance . . . they don't mean any harm; they don't understand,' he excused them to himself.

The red-walled city of the Moguls was as intriguing by day as it was exciting by night, but towards evening his conscience belatedly reminded him of the enormity of his behaviour and its probable consequences, and he reluctantly changed back into his own clothing and spent half an hour in a jeweller's shop in the Chandi Chowk before presenting himself at the dâk-bungalow.

Only a handful of passengers who had travelled on the mail-train from Bombay were going further north into the Punjab, and the remainder of the journey had been undertaken in dâk-*gharis,* rickety horse-drawn vehicles that resembled closed boxes on wheels. This time Ash had only one companion to share his carriage with him, but as it turned out to be George Garforth he would have been happier on his own or with a full complement of passengers.

George had no intention of relinquishing the hopes that Belinda had encouraged by her treatment of him during the first three days out from Bombay. The fact that she considered herself engaged to Ashton Pelham-Martyn made no difference to his feelings for her (beyond adding jealousy and despair to the other emotions he was suffering on her behalf) and as he saw no reason why he should not discuss the subject of his wounded heart with her betrothed, Ash found himself listening to a good deal of talk from his love-sick rival, and was often hard put to it to keep his temper.

It was sad that Belinda, by encouraging George to talk about himself, should have released such an uninhibited torrent of speech, for once having got the bit between his teeth, George showed every sign of bolting. But as Ash could see no way of stopping him that did not involve unpleasantness, he merely took the easier way of spending a large part of each day in the company of Zarin, Ala Yar and Mahdoo; not only because he found their society infinitely preferable to Mr Garforth's, but because it was no longer possible for him to get Belinda to himself—her Mama having invited an old acquaintance, a Mrs Viccary, to share their dâk-*ghari*.

The presence of a third, and middle-aged lady, effectively put an end to any hope of his being invited to pass an occasional hour or so in the Harlowes' carriage, or of spending much time alone with them at the various stopping places where rooms and meals were available and the horses were changed. Yet in spite of this disappointment he did not, as might have been expected, take a strong dislike to the interloper, for Mrs Viccary turned out to be a delightful person, wise, tolerant and understanding, with a talent for making friends and a genuine interest in other people that made her very easy to talk to. As she was also an excellent and sympathetic listener, it was not long before Ash found himself telling her more of his history than he was ever to tell Belinda; which surprised him—though it did not surprise her.

Edith Viccary was used to receiving confidences (and had never been known to betray one, which probably accounted for the fact that she received so many). Moreover in the present instance, having listened to a voluble account of young Mr Pelham-Martyn's prospects, relatives and background from his prospective mother-in-law, she had exerted herself to draw him out, as she not only fully understood but shared his passion for his adopted country, which was, in a sense, her own, because she too had been born in it. She had also by now spent the greater part of her life there, for having been sent home to England at the age of eight, she had come back as a young lady of sixteen to rejoin her parents who were at that time stationed at Delhi; and it was there in the capital city of the Moguls that a year later she met and married a young engineer, Charles Viccary.

That had been in the winter of 1849, and since then her husband's work had taken her to most parts of the vast sub-continent in which men of both their families, Carrolls and Viccarys, had served for three successive generations—initially in the East India Company and later under the Crown. And the more she saw of it, the more she came to love the land, and to appreciate its peoples, among whom she was proud to number many close friends, for unlike Mrs Harlowe, she had set herself to master at least four of India's main languages and learned to speak them with enviable fluency. When cholera deprived her of her only child, and the great Sepoy Rising of '57 took the lives of her parents, and of her sister Sarah and Sarah's three small children who died in the terrible *Bibi-gurh* at Cawnpore, she did not give way to despair or lose her sense of proportion and justice; and even during the bitter aftermath of the Mutiny she did not allow herself to hate.

In this, as in all else, she was by no means unique. But as she happened to be the first of her kind whom Ash had met, it was Edith Viccary who was responsible for erasing forever an uneasy suspicion that he had lately begun to entertain—that Mrs Harlowe and those of her fellow-sightseers who had laughed and talked so loudly during the prayers at the Juma Masjid were typical of all the British-born 'memsahibs' in India. For this alone he would have been willing to forgive her almost anything—even for being the unwitting cause of preventing him from seeing as much of Belinda as he had hoped to do on the journey north.

Apart from that deprivation, the days passed pleasantly. It was good to be with Zarin again and listen to familiar talk while the remembered scenes unrolled beyond the windows; to eat the food that Gul Baz bought from the stalls of vendors in the villages—curries and dals, rice, chuppattis and sticky sweetmeats shimmering with beaten silver—served as often as not on green leaves, and washed down with draughts of buffalo milk or water from the wells that were to be found at every hamlet. The names of towns and rivers and the aspect of every little village was suddenly familiar to him, for this was the country across which he and Sita had wandered in the months that followed their escape from Gulkote.

Karnal, Ambala, Ludhiana, Jullundar, Amritsar and Lahore, the Sutlej and the Ravi Rivers. He knew them all . . . The temperature at mid-morning and for the best part of the afternoon remained uncomfortably high, and the sun still blistered the paintwork on the roofs and sides of the *gharies*. But as the teams of starveling ponies rattled them forward across the rich croplands of the Punjab, the air became noticeably cooler, and there came a day when Ash, descending in the early dawn to stretch his legs on the quiet roadside, saw above the far horizon to the north a long, jagged line of pale rose glowing bright against the cool green of the sky: and knew that he was looking at the snow peaks of the Himalayas.

His heart seemed to turn over as he looked, and his eyes filled with tears. And all at once he wanted to laugh and cry and to shout aloud—or to pray, as Zarin and Ala Yar and a dozen of their coreligionists were doing. Only it was not towards Mecca that he would face, but to the mountains. His own mountains, in whose shadow he had been born—to the Dur Khaima to which he had prayed as a child. Somewhere over there lay the Far Pavilions, with *Tarakalas*, the 'Star Tower', catching the first rays of the sunrise. And somewhere, too, the valley that Sita had so longed to reach before she died, and that he himself would reach one day.

They had stopped for the previous night on the outskirts of a little village, and there was a food-stall near by. Ash bought a handful of cooked rice, and remembering the offerings he used to make to the Dur Khaima in the Queen's balcony at Gulkote, he strewed it on the dew-wet ground. Perhaps it would bring him luck. A grey-headed plains crow and a famished pariah dog swooped upon the feast, and the sight of the emaciated mongrel recalled him abruptly from the past. Gulkote and the Dur Khaima were forgotten, and it was Ashton Pelham-Martyn and not Ashok who bought half-a-dozen chuppattis and fed them to a starving dog; and Isobel's son, not Sita's, who boarded the *ghari* again, hands in pockets and whistling 'John Peel' as the sun rose above the horizon and flooded the plains with brilliant light.

'Ah! This smells like my own country again,' said Ala Yar, snuffing the wind like an elderly horse that scents its stable. 'Now it will not matter so much if these *gharis* should break down, for if need be we can walk the rest of the way.' (Ala Yar distrusted hired vehicles and was convinced that the frequent halts were due to faulty driving.)

The *gharis* did not break down, but a culvert and half a mile of road that had been swept away by the flooding of a river caused a delay of two days, and the travellers were forced to put up in a near-by dâk-bungalow until the road was mended.

There is little doubt that but for George Garforth, Ash would not have been able to resist the temptation to play truant in the company of Zarin and Ala Yar. But he had not forgotten Belinda's graciousness to George during those three dismal days after leaving Bombay, or that George had been quick to step into the breach when he, Ash, had absented himself in Delhi, so to Zarin's disgust he spent every possible moment in her company during that two days' delay.

Mr Garforth had been equally assiduous, though once again he had been compelled to spend most of the time talking to Mrs Harlowe rather than to her daughter. He had, however, won golden opinions from that lady by holding her knitting wool and telling her at length about his childhood. She had always considered George Garforth to be a very personable and presentable young man, but Byronic features, chestnut curls and melting brown eyes did not compensate for lack of means, and it had to be owned that Mr Garforth's prospects, for the moment anyway, were not bright.

As a new and very junior member of a firm which dealt in beer, wines and spirits, his salary was modest and his social position even more so; for except in the great ports such as Calcutta, Bombay and Madras, where Commerce was King, Anglo-Indian society ranked the 'boxwallah' (a scornful term applied to all who engaged in trade) well below the level of those two ruling castes, the army and the Civil Service, and in such a military stronghold as Peshawar, a junior 'boxwallah' would count for very little indeed; which was a pity, thought Mrs Harlowe, because if only things had been different she would have been far happier with George Garforth as a son-in-law than with Ashton Pelham-Martyn, who was so . . . who was so . . . It was difficult to explain what she felt about Ashton. On board he had seemed such a quiet and dependable young man, and the fact that he was rich (or, at least, so comfortably off) and that as his uncle had only the one son, there was always the chance that Ashton might one day inherit a baronetcy, had made him appear an excellent matrimonial prospect; but ever since that dreadful day in Bombay she had been beset by doubts.

If only George had been as eligible as Ashton, sighed Mrs Harlowe, how much happier she would feel about dear Bella's future. George, for all his spectacular looks, was so comfortably normal and uncomplicated, and his parents certainly seemed to be well off; his description of his home made it plain that they lived in far greater style than she herself had ever been accustomed to. Two carriages, no less—it made one wonder if he were not a better prospect than he appeared. His father, he had told her, was Irish by extraction, and his maternal grandmother a Greek lady of title (which would account for the romantic profile), and though he himself had wanted to go into the army, his mother had been so set against it that to please her he had given up the idea and agreed instead to go in for commerce. The romance of the East had appealed to his adventurous spirit and led to his accepting a post in the firm of Brown & Macdonald, in preference to some well-paid sinecure obtained for him through family influence in England; for, fond as he was of his parents, George had confessed that he preferred to stand on his own feet and start at the bottom of the ladder, a sentiment that won Mrs Harlowe's full approval.

What a nice boy he was. Now Ashton never mentioned his parents, and what little he had told her of his childhood was so exceedingly odd that she had been forced to discourage him from saying any more, and had told him (tactfully of course) that the less he said about it the better as such a story was likely to be . . . well . . . misunderstood. A Hindu foster-mother, the wife of a common syce, whom he actually spoke of as 'my mother' as though she had been the real one! Mrs Harlowe shuddered at the thought of what people would say if they knew, and wished she had not been so precipitate over agreeing to his betrothal to Belinda. She would never have done such a thing if it had not been for little Harry and Teddy and her longing to be with them again. People did not understand how terrible it was to be separated from one's children for years at a time. Even Archie did not. She had only wanted Belinda to be safely and happily married and she did so hope Archie was not going to be cross. After all, she had done it for the best. The best for Harry and Teddy . . .

By dusk on the second day the repairs to the road were completed and the passengers rounded up and re-embarked, and shortly after moon-rise the *gharis* rattled forward upon the last leg of the journey to Jhelum, where there was a British military cantonment of some size.

The Jhelum River was running high and swiftly, swollen by heavy autumn rains in far-away Kashmir, and there was nothing in the sight of that turbulent brown flood to remind Ash of the quiet river that had carried Sita away from him so many years ago. The town itself, together with the cantonments, lay on the far side, but as there had been a military exercise that day, there were a number of British officers idling on the near bank waiting for boats to ferry them back, and Belinda viewed the younger ones with lively interest and thought how very different (and how much more exciting) these cheerful, sunburned young officers were from the stolid and soberly clad townsmen of Nelbury, who, viewed in retrospect, might have belonged to a different race from these gaily uniformed men whom the furnace summers and bitter Khyber winters, warfare, responsibility and hard exercise had welded into a type that had become as instantly recognizable as a Red Indian or the cowboys of Texas.

The very sight of them served to restore Belinda's spirits, which had sunk considerably during the last day or two. The mounting tedium and discomfort of the dusty, interminable journey had depressed her, and the group of young officers on the bank was a welcome reminder that civilization and gaiety had not been left behind. No pretty girl need ever feel bored or neglected with so many men to squire her to picnics and partner her at dances, and it was almost a pity that she had engaged herself to marry Ashton. But then she was in love with him, and so of course she wished to marry him; though perhaps not too soon. It would be pleasant to be free for a few years longer and to enjoy all the delights of being courted by half-a-dozen young men instead of only one; and it wasn't as though Ash would even be in the same station. He would be miles away in Mardan and probably unable to ride over and see her more than once a week at most, yet as an engaged girl she would be unable to accept invitations from other men; that would be considered shockingly fast.

Belinda sighed, admiring the scarlet coats and luxuriant moustaches of the young officers, and somewhat naturally did not spare a look for the older ones, as she was not expecting to see her father. Even if she had been, she would not have recognized him. The man she dimly remembered had seemed a giant to his seven-year-old daughter, while the small and elderly gentleman who now appeared at the door of their *ghari* was an unimpressive figure, and Belinda was as shocked as she was startled when her mother uttered a piercing cry of 'Archie!' and warmly embraced the stranger. Could this really be the alarming autocrat of whom her resolute Aunt Lizzie and her stout and voluble Mama had so often said, 'Your Papa would never permit it'?

But if Belinda was disappointed in her Papa, it was plain that he was far from disappointed in his daughter. She was, he told her, the very image of her dear Mama at the same age, and it was the greatest pity that the Brigade would be going off on manoeuvres so soon, for he was afraid she might find Peshawar a trifle slow with all the young sparks away under canvas. But by Christmas the regiments would all be back in cantonments, and after that she would have nothing to complain of, as Peshawar was a very gay station.

Major Harlowe pinched his daughter's chin, and added that he could see they would soon have all the young fellows lining up to take his pretty little puss out riding and dancing—a remark that caused Belinda to blush uncomfortably and her mother to hope that Edith Viccary would not say anything indiscreet, or Ashton put in an appearance before she had been able to explain matters to Archie. It was really *very* vexing that Archie should have elected to meet them at Jhelum, for she had counted upon being able to choose her time and broach the subject of Belinda's engagement in the privacy of their own bungalow before there was any chance of his meeting Mr Pelham-Martyn, who would be parting company with them at Nowshera.

The next quarter of an hour had proved a difficult one, but Mrs Viccary had said nothing untoward, and when Ash put in an appearance he was so closely followed by George Garforth that it had been possible for Mrs Harlowe to introduce both young men as shipboard acquaintances, and to get rid of them on the excuse that she and her husband and dear Bella had so much to say to each other after so long a separation . . . she was *sure* they would understand.

Ash certainly understood that this was not the time or the place for him to present himself to Major Harlowe in the character of a future son-in-law, and he had retired to the dining room of the dâk-bungalow to eat a four-course meal while Zarin arranged transport and accommodation for the rest of the journey, and George prowled up and down the verandah in the hope of catching a last glance from Belinda's blue eyes.

'I can't understand you,' said George bitterly, joining Ash at the table when the Harlowes had finally departed. 'If I had only had the luck to be in your shoes, I'd be with them now, tackling the old man and staking my claim before the whole world. You don't deserve that angel, and it'll serve you right if some other fellow cuts you out. I bet you there'll be dozens of them hanging about her in Peshawar.'

'There were at least a dozen on the boat,' observed Ash amicably. 'And if you think this is a good place to line up before a complete stranger and demand his daughter's hand in marriage, *you're* the one who must be mad. Damn it, he hasn't seen her since she was in short socks. I can't embark on a subject like that five minutes after he's met her; and in a crowded dâk-bungalow at that. Talk sense.'

'I believe I *am* mad,' groaned George, striking his forehead in a manner that would have done credit to Henry Irving. 'But I can't help loving her. I know it's hopeless, but that doesn't make any difference. I love her, and if you let her down—'

'Oh, stow it, George!' interrupted Ash impatiently. 'You've just announced that she'll probably throw me over for someone else, and you can't have it both ways. Tell a *khidmatgar* to get you something to eat and let me get on with my dinner.'

He sympathized with the unsuccessful suitor, and as the accepted one, felt in honour bound to treat him kindly; but George's dramatics were beginning to pall, and Ash could only regret that he would be stationed in Peshawar where, if he intended to haunt the Harlowes' bungalow, they were bound to meet. As for any fears that Belinda might change her mind, Ash had none. She had assured him of her love, and to have harboured any doubts on that score would have seemed to him a lack of trust and an insult to them both. By which it can be seen that he was still young enough to be pompous in the matter of his emotions.

He was also sufficiently lacking in vanity to feel no surprise when neither Belinda nor Mrs Harlowe made any move to single him out for attention, or bring him to the notice of his future father-in-law when they met on the road at the various dâk-bungalows between Jhelum and Nowshera where the dâk-*gharis* changed horses while their passengers ate, and where they put up at night. George might say what he liked (and he said a good deal, since they were still, unfortunately, sharing the same dâk-*ghari*) but it seemed only reasonable to Ash that a daughter who had been separated from her father for so many years should hesitate to spoil their meeting by informing him that she planned to leave him before too long. Once the Harlowes were safely settled into their own house and had recovered from the fatigue of the journey, Belinda would be sure to write and let him know when he might call, and he would ride over to Peshawar and talk the whole matter over with her father—and perhaps—who knew? —they might even be married by the spring.

It must be owned that such an idea had not previously occurred to him, for he had imagined that Belinda's Papa would insist that they wait until he came of age, and he had not been prepared to quarrel with that. But his meeting with Major Harlowe had made him begin to revise his plans. Ash too had pictured someone far more formidable than the undersized and—it must be admitted—insignificant-looking gentleman to whom he had been introduced at Jhelum, but now that he had seen the Major, he was no longer surprised that Mrs Harlowe should have taken it upon herself to consent to the engagement instead of telling him (which he had fully expected her to do) that he must wait until he had seen Belinda's Papa, because if looks were anything to go by, Major Archibald Harlowe was the kind of man who would allow himself to be over-ruled by the opinions of his women-folk; in which case they might well be able to talk him into allowing an early wedding. It was an exciting prospect, and Ash gave himself up to day dreams.

Major Harlowe, for his part, had paid no particular attention to Ensign Pelham-Martyn beyond vaguely noting that his pretty little daughter seemed to have attracted two personable young admirers. He had acknowledged his wife's introductions to Ash and Mr Garforth, and promptly forgotten their names, though he would nod amiably to them whenever they met at one of the staging posts on the road, and twit his daughter on having acquired two beaux already.

The road wound through the desolate Salt Ranges that lay between Jhelum and the great cantonment of Rawalpindi, and swept onward, past the ruins of Taxila and among low rocky hills that showed above a barren plain like the bones of starving cattle, to end on the banks of the Indus under the grim shadow of Attock Fort. Here the travellers descended, and having paid off their drivers, crossed the river by ferry and continued their journey in fresh relays of dâk-*gharis* along a road that ran parallel to the Kabul River. The autumn rains had turned the river to a swirling, rust-stained torrent, but the plains were still parched and dusty, and beyond the swollen river the land stretched away towards the hills, lion-coloured and rock-strewn, its trees and fields dried to a uniform gold by the furnace heat of the summer months.

The hills were nearer now, and the horizon no longer limitless but bounded by bleak folds and ridges of rock that changed colour with every hour of the day: at one moment seeming fifty miles away and as blue and transparent as glass, and at another a mere furlong distant, rust-brown and streaked with the black shadows of innumerable gullies. Behind them the Border hills and the mountains of Malakand rose up in ridge after ridge like frozen waves breaking on the rim of the plain, guardians of a harsh land inhabited by a score of turbulent tribes who recognized no law save that of force, lived in fortified villages and indulged in savage blood-feuds, and waged perpetual war either with each other or the British. For this was the North–West Frontier: the Gateway of India through which Alexander of Macedon and his conquering Legions had marched when the world was young. Beyond its inhospitable passes lay the Kingdom of Sher Ali, Amir of Afghanistan. And beyond that, the vast and menacing Empire of the Tsars.

To Belinda, the countryside seemed depressingly bleak and empty, but at least there was no lack of traffic on the Peshawar road, and looking out from the window of the dâk-*ghari* she could see an occasional Englishman on horseback or driving a trap, as well as the now familiar country carts and plodding pedestrians; and once a column of British soldiers on the march tramped past, a file of laden baggage elephants rolling in their wake, and the thick dust dimming their scarlet coats to an indeterminate and rusty grey.

There were camels too, creatures that she could remember seeing as a child: long lines of them carrying enormous loads that jolted and swayed like bumboats in a choppy sea, high above the inevitable goats and cattle that were being herded from one village to the next. As they neared the outskirts of Nowshera the traffic thickened and the drivers of phaetons and *tikka-gharis,* tongas and *ekkas,* whipped up their ponies for a final burst of speed and raced each other into the town, scattering pedestrians like startled chickens and raising a smothering cloud of dust that set their passengers choking. The town was a small one with a dâk-bungalow that differed very little from a dozen others on the road, and it was not until Ash came to say goodbye that Belinda realized that this was where he must leave them.

He stood hat in hand in the late evening sunlight, gazing at her with his heart in his eyes and finding that it was impossible to say any of the things he had meant to say, because her parents were listening and it was plain to him from Mrs Harlowe's flustered manner and her husband's polite indifference that nothing had as yet been said on the subject of an engagement. In the circumstances he could only press Belinda's hand, and assure her that he would ride over to Peshawar at the first opportunity to give himself the pleasure of calling upon her. Mrs Harlowe said that they would be happy to see him; though not for a week or so, for what with all the unpacking . . . perhaps next month? and her husband said vaguely: 'Of course, of course,' adding that around Christmas most of the young fellows managed to get a few days' leave from their regiments and he dared say that Mr—er—er? would be able to do so too and must certainly look them up. Belinda blushed and murmured something to the effect that she hoped Mr Pelham-Martyn would be able to visit Peshawar long before Christmas, and at this point the driver of the

Harlowes' *ghari,* who had been superintending a change of horses, announced that he was now ready to take the road.

Major Harlowe embarked his family once more, the doors slammed shut, a whip cracked and they were gone in a cloud of dust, leaving Ash standing in the roadway feeling depressed and inadequate and wishing that he had summoned up enough courage to kiss Belinda before them all and thereby force the issue. Mrs Harlowe's reference to 'sometime next month' had not been encouraging, but it was her husband's remark about 'a few days' leave at Christmas' that had given him a really disagreeable jolt, for he had looked forward to riding over to Peshawar within a day or two of his arrival, and until that moment it had not occurred to him that leave to do so might not be granted to a newly joined subaltern; or not unless he could give some particularly pressing reason for requesting it, and he could hardly discuss the subject of his engagement to Belinda with his Adjutant or the Commanding Officer before it had even been mentioned to her father. He could only hope that once Mrs Harlowe had explained matters to her husband, Major Harlowe might demand his presence in Peshawar, or else ride over himself to Mardan. But that would depend largely on his reception of the news, and Ash was suddenly a lot less confident that he would approve it.

'The Regiment have sent a tonga,' said Zarin, appearing abruptly at his side. 'It will not take us all, so I told Gul Baz to hire a second for himself and Mahdoo, and they have gone on ahead with the baggage. The day grows late and there is more than ten *koss* to be covered before we see Mardan. Let us go.'

10

Night falls swiftly in the East, for there is no lingering dusk to soften the transition from daylight to darkness. The Kabul River had been gold with the sunset as Ash and his three companions crossed the bridge of boats at Nowshera, but long before they reached Mardan the moon was high and the shadow of the little star-shaped fort that Hodson built in the years before the Great Mutiny lay black on the milk-white plain.

In the old days, when the Land-of-the-Five-Rivers (the Punjab) was still a Sikh province, and the only British troops within its borders were East India Company regiments stationed at Lahore to uphold the authority of a British Resident, the idea of an elite and highly mobile force, capable of moving to any trouble-spot at a moment's notice, had been conceived by Sir Henry Lawrence, that great and wise administrator who was to die a hero's death during the Mutiny, in the beleaguered Residency at Lucknow.

This 'fire-brigade' would consist of one troop of cavalry and two companies of infantry, unhampered by tradition and run on entirely new lines, in that it would combine soldiering with early and accurate intelligence work, and its members—handpicked men commanded by handpicked officers—would wear a loose, comfortable, khaki-coloured uniform that would blend into the dusty background of the Frontier hills, instead of the regulation scarlet coat and tight stock in which a majority of regiments marched, sweltered and suffered in temperatures that made such clothing a torment—and which could be seen from miles away. As a further break with tradition, Sir Henry had named his brain-child 'The Corps of Guides' and entrusted the raising of it to one Harry Lumsden, a young man possessed of exceptional ability, character and courage, who had fully justified the choice.

The original headquarters of the new Corps had been at Peshawar, and at first its duties had consisted of dealing with the marauding Frontier tribes, who preyed on the peaceful villagers, carrying off women, children and cattle into the inhospitable Border hills, in defiance of the Sikh Durbar who were nominally in control of the Punjab and in whose name a handful of British officials exercised authority. Later on the Corps had been sent south to fight in the plains round Ferzapore, Mooltan and Lahore, and had served with distinction in the bloody battles of the Second Sikh War.

It was only when the war had ended and the Punjab been annexed by the Company's Government that the Guides had returned once more to the Frontier—though not to Peshawar. The Border having become more settled, they had selected a site near the Kalpani River where the tracks from Swat and Buner meet, and exchanged their tents for a mud-walled fort at Mardan on the plain of Yusafzai. It had been a desolate and treeless spot when Hodson had begun work on the fort, and his wife, Sophia, writing home in January of 1854, had said of it: 'Picture to yourself an immense plain, flat as a billiard table but not as green, with here and there a dotting of camel-thorn about eighteen inches high by way of vegetation. This, far as the eye can see on the west and south of us, but on the north the everlasting snows of the mighty Himalayas above the lower range which is close to our camp.'

The view had not changed: but the Corps had grown in size and the Guides had planted trees to shade their cantonment, and on this autumn night the garden that Hodson had made for his wife and their only and dearly loved child, who was to die in infancy, was sweet with the scent of jasmine and roses. In the cemetery where the dead of the Ambeyla campaign lay buried, a dozen tombstones gleamed white in the moonlight; and near by, at the junction of three roads, a mulberry tree threw a black patch of shadow above the place where Colonel Spottiswood, Commanding Officer of the Bengal Infantry Regiment that had been sent to relieve the Guides in the black year of 1857, shot himself when his beloved regiment mutinied.

The familiar scents and sounds of the cantonment drifted out to Ash like a greeting. The smell of horses and wood-smoke, of water on parched ground and spiced food cooking over charcoal fires, the stamp and whicker of cavalry chargers tethered in the lines, and the beehive hum of men gossiping after a hard day's work. In the Officers' Mess half-a-dozen voices were singing a popular music-hall ballad to the strains of a tinny piano, and somewhere in the bazaar a tom-tom beat a montonous counterpoint to the doleful howling of pariah dogs baying the moon. A conch brayed in a temple and from far out on the milky plain beyond the river came the mournful cry of a jackal pack.

'It is good to be back,' said Zarin, sniffing the night air with approval. 'This is better than the heat and noise of the south and the racket of trains.'

Ash made no reply. He was looking about him and realizing that this small, man-made oasis between the foothills of the Himalayas and the wide sweep of the plain would be his home for many years. From here he would ride out with his Regiment to keep the peace of the Border and to fight battles among those hills that showed like folds of crumpled cloth in the moonlight, or to dance, hunt and race in any one of a dozen gay stations from Delhi to Peshawar; but for whatever reason he left it, either on duty or for pleasure, as long as he served with the Guides he would always come back to Mardan . . .

He turned to grin at Zarin and was about to speak when a figure detached itself from the shadow of a neem tree by the roadside, and moving out into the moonlight, brought the tonga to a halt.

'Who is it?' asked Ash in the vernacular—but even as he spoke the memory of another moonlight night came back to him, and without waiting for an answer he leapt from the tonga and was in the dusty road, stooping to touch the feet of an old man who stood by the horse's head.

'*Koda Dad!*—it is you, my father.' There was a break in Ash's voice and the past came back to him as though lit by bright flashes of lightning.

The old man laughed and embraced him. 'So you have not forgotten me, my son. That is good, for I do not think I should have known you. The little boy has grown into a tall strong man—almost as tall as I; or is it that old age has shrivelled me somewhat? My sons sent word that you were coming, so I made the journey to Mardan, and Awal Shah and I have waited by the roadside these last three nights, not knowing when you could come.'

Awal Shah stepped out of the shadows and brought his hand up to a salute; his father and Zarin might forget that Ash was an officer, but Jemadar Awal Shah would not.

'Salaam, Sahib,' said Awal Shah. 'The *gharis* being delayed, it was not known when you would reach here. But my father wished to see you before you made your salaams to the Colonel Sahib. Therefore we waited.'

'Yes, yes,' nodded Koda Dad, 'for tomorrow will not do. Tomorrow you will be an officer-Sahib with many duties to perform, and your time will not be your own. But tonight, before you have reported yourself to those in authority, you are still Ashok and may, if you will, spare half an hour to speak to an old man.'

'Willingly, my father. Tell the tonga-wallah to wait, Zarin. Do we go to your quarters, Jemadar Sahib?'

'No. That would not be wise or fitting. But we have brought food, and there is a place behind these trees where we can sit and talk together and be out of sight of the road.'

The Jemadar turned and led the way to a small patch of ground, blackened by the ashes of old camp fires, where a handful of charcoal glowed red among the roots of the neem tree. Someone had set out several covered *dechis* (cooking pots) and a hookah, and Koda Dad Khan squatted down comfortably in the shadows, grunting approval as Ash followed his example, for few Europeans find it easy to adopt that characteristically Eastern pose—the cut of Western clothes discourages such attitudes, nor are Western men accustomed from youth to squat on their hunkers while eating, talking or idling. But Colonel Anderson, like Awal Shah and the Commandant of the Guides, had had his own ideas as to the education and training of Ashton Pelham-Martyn, and he had seen to it that the boy did not forget things that might one day be of use to the man.

'My son Zarin sent a message from Delhi to tell his brother that all was well and that you had not become a stranger to us. Therefore I came over the Border to welcome you back,' said Koda Dad, taking a long pull at the hookah.

'And what if he had sent word that I had become altogether a Sahib?' inquired Ash, accepting a chuppatti heaped with *pilau* and falling to with a good appetite.

'Then I should not have come, since there would have been nothing that needed saying. But now there are things that must be said.'

There was that in his voice that made Ash say sharply: 'What things? Is it bad news? Are you in trouble?'

'No, no. It is only that Zarin and Ala Yar both say that you are still in many ways the Ashok of Gulkote days; which is good news. But—' The old man paused to glance at his sons, who nodded as though in agreement with a spoken question, and Ash looked from Koda Dad to Zarin and from Zarin to Awal Shah, and seeing the same expression on all three faces, said abruptly, 'What is it?'

'Nothing that need disturb you,' said Koda Dad tranquilly. 'It is only that here in Mardan, or wheresoever the Guides are sent, you and my son can no longer be the Zarin and Ashok of the old days, for it would not be fitting that a daffadar and an *Angrezi* officer should behave as blood-brothers. It would cause too much talk. And also—who knows?—the fear of favouritism among the men; there being Pathans of many different clans in the Guides, and also many men of different faiths, such as Sikhs and Hindus, all of them equal in the sight of their officers, which is just and right. Therefore only when you and Zarin are alone, or on leave, can you be yourselves as once you were; but not here or now, in the presence of the Regiment. Is it understood?'

The last three words were spoken quite softly, but they were less a question than a command, and the tone was a reminder of the old days when a Master of Horse had befriended a lonely little boy in the service of a spoilt princeling, cuffing him when he needed it, consoling him in his misfortunes, and treating him in all ways as a son. Ash recognized it and reacted to it in the same spirit, though with reluctance. It seemed absurd to him that he should not be able to treat Zarin as a friend and brother without giving rise to criticism. But then he found a great many things that his elders and betters did absurd, and had seldom found any profit in arguing with them. In the circumstances Koda Dad's advice was probably sound and must be accepted, so he said slowly: 'It is understood. But . . .'

'There are no buts,' interrupted Awal Shah sharply. 'My father and I have discussed this between us, and we are agreed. Zarin also. The past is the past, and it is best that it should be forgotten. The Hindu boy from Gulkote is dead and in his place is a Sahib—an officer-Sahib of the Guides. You cannot alter that; or try to be two people in one skin.'

'I am that already,' said Ash wryly. 'Your brother helped to make me so when he told me that it would be best for me to go to *Belait* to the care of my father's people, and to learn to become a Sahib. Well, I have learned. Yet I am still Ashok, and I cannot alter that either, for having been a child of this land for eleven years I am tied to it by something as strong as the tie of blood, and shall always be two people in one skin—which is not a comfortable thing to be.'

His voice held a sudden note of bitterness and Koda Dad laid a consoling hand on his shoulder and said gently: 'That I understand. But you will find it easier if you keep the two separate and do not try to be both at one time. And some day—who knows?—you may discover in yourself a third person who is neither Ashok nor Pelham-

Sahib, but someone whole and complete: yourself. Now let us talk of other things. Give me the hookah.'

Awal Shah pushed the pipe towards him, and the familiar bubbling purr and the scent of country-grown tobacco took Ash back to long-ago evenings in Koda Dad's quarters in the Palace of the Winds. But as the pipe circulated it was not of the past that the old man spoke, but of the present and the future. His talk was of the Border, which had been unusually peaceful of late, and as they spoke the moon swung clear of the surrounding tree-tops and drowned the red glow of the coals in a flood of cold, clear light. From the direction of the road came a sharp jangle of bells as the tonga-pony shook its head restlessly, impatient for its stable, and presently its driver coughed discreetly to indicate that time was passing and that he had already wasted the best part of an hour.

'It grows late,' said Koda Dad, 'and if I am to get any sleep I must go, for tomorrow I set out for my own village before sunrise. No, no, my mind is made up. I wished only to see you, Ashok, and that being done I return to my own house—' His hand pressed heavily on Ash's shoulder as he levered himself to his feet. 'Old men become like horses; they like their own stable best. Farewell, my son. It is good to have seen you again; and when next you obtain leave, Zarin shall bring you across the Border to visit me.'

He embraced Ash and left, striding stiffly away into the shadows and disdaining the proffered help of his eldest son, who spoke briefly to Zarin, saluted Ash and followed in the wake of his father.

Zarin scuffed out the remnants of the fire and gathering up the cooking pots and the hookah, said: 'I too must go now. Our holiday is over and my father is right—we would do better not to arrive together. The tonga will take you to the Adjutant Sahib's quarters where you should report your arrival. We shall see each other; but only in the way of work.'

'But there will be other holidays.'

'*Beshak!*' (without doubt). 'When we are on leave we can be what we choose. But here we are on duty in the service of the Sirkar. Salaam, Sahib.'

He vanished among the tree shadows and Ash went slowly back to the road where the tonga waited in the moonlight, and was bowled away into the fort to report himself to the Adjutant.

Those first days in Mardan had not been entirely happy ones for Ash, a circumstance that probably accounted for much that was to happen in the future, since it altered, at the outset, his approach to army life, and intensified an inborn impatience for rules and regulations, and a critical attitude to the arbitrary decisions of his elders and betters.

He should of course have foreseen it all, though the fact that he had not done so was not entirely his own fault. At least three other people must be held partly responsible: his Uncle Matthew, who had naturally never dreamt of warning his nephew against engaging himself to be married before he had so much as joined his regiment, Colonel Anderson, who had given him a great deal of good advice but (himself a confirmed bachelor) had neglected to touch on matrimony, and Mrs Harlowe, who should have scouted the idea instead of welcoming it with such alacrity and instantly pledging her own and her husband's consent. In the circumstances Ash could hardly be blamed for thinking that lack of means, not years, was the sole reason why young officers were discouraged from marrying at the outset of their careers, and as this did not apply to him, that there could be no serious objection to his betrothal.

He was very speedily disillusioned, for Mrs Harlowe's worst fears had been realized. Her husband had taken an exceedingly poor view of the whole affair; and so too, when he heard of it, had the Commandant of the Guides. Ash's intention of riding over to Peshawar at the first opportunity had been forestalled by Major Harlowe, who had driven to Mardan two days after his arrival and had a private talk with the Commandant.

Both men had been in complete agreement on the subject of early marriages and the fatal consequences attending young officers who acquired wives before they had, metaphorically speaking, cut their wisdom teeth. Ash had been sent for and treated to an embarrassing lecture that had left him feeling bruised and humiliated and, worse, infuriatingly callow. He had not been refused permission to see Belinda—it would perhaps have been kinder if he had been—but Major Harlowe had made it painfully clear that there could be no question of an engagement, official or otherwise, and that the matter must not be raised again for several years, by which time it was to be hoped that both young people would have learnt wisdom and acquired more sensible views on life (and, by implication, Belinda would have met and married some older and more suitable man). Provided that was clearly understood, Major Harlowe would have no objection to Mr Pelham-Martyn calling on his family, if at any time he should happen to be in Peshawar.

'You must not think me hard-hearted, my boy,' said Belinda's father. 'I know just how you feel. But really, you know, it will not do. I am aware that financially you are well able to support a wife, but that don't alter the fact that you are both far too young to be thinking of marriage. Or if Bella is not, you are. Cut your milk teeth first my boy, and learn your trade; and if you have any sense you'll give yourself at least another eight or ten years before you tie yourself to petticoats and perambulators. That's my advice.'

It was also the Commandant's. When Ash had attempted to argue his cause, he had been tersely instructed not to be a young fool, and that if he felt himself unable to support life without Miss Harlowe, then he was obviously unsuited to such a Corps as the Guides, and had better arrange a transfer to some more sedentary branch of the service as soon as possible. In the meantime, as it seemed that there had been some talk of an engagement, he had permission to take leave the following weekend in order to ride over to Peshawar and put matters straight with Miss Harlowe.

Ash had been prepared for a certain amount of opposition to his matrimonial plans and would undoubtedly have settled for a long engagement, but it had never crossed his mind that Belinda's father and his own Commanding Officer would refuse to recognize any engagement at all. After all, it was not as though he were a fortune-hunter or a penniless nobody; compared with the average Indian Army officer he could be considered extremely well-off, and it was therefore palpably unjust that his proposal to Belinda should be dismissed in this cavalier fashion.

Suddenly convinced that he could not possibly live without her, he decided on the instant that there was nothing for it but to elope. If he and Belinda were to run away together, her father would consent to the marriage in order to avoid a scandal, and if the Guides refused to keep him, well, there were plenty of other regiments.

Looking back on it, Ash could never remember very much about that first week in Mardan: there had been so much to learn and so much to do. But though the days had been full of interest, the nights had turned into a long battle for sleep, for it was only then that he had leisure to think of Belinda.

He would lie awake in the darkness evolving wild plans, and when at last he slept it was always to dream of riding headlong across a stony plain between low barren hills, with a girl on the crupper behind him who clung to him and urged him to ride faster—faster. A girl whose face he could not see, but who was of course Belinda; though the long hair that streamed out behind her like a flag in the wind, impeding his view of their pursuers, was not yellow but black. He would hear the thunder of following hoof-beats coming louder and nearer, and would wake sweating with terror—to find that the sound of galloping horses was his own heart-beats thumping as though he had been running a race.

It was disturbing, too, to realize that although he was back once more in the land of his birth and able to see and speak with Zarin and Koda Dad again, he had not after all lost that nagging sense of emptiness that had haunted his years in exile. It was still there, but he felt sure that if Belinda would only agree to defy her father and marry him, with or without permission, he would be free of it for ever—together with all restlessness and anxiety and doubt. It was the nights that made the week seem long. Yet almost before he knew it, it was Saturday.

He left Mardan well before sunrise, accompanied by Gul Baz, and they breakfasted a mile beyond Nowshera on chuppattis and dal curry bought from a food-vendor by the side of the Peshawar road. Parrots screamed and preened among the branches of the shade-trees lining the road and Gul Baz, though now in his thirtieth year, so far forgot himself as to break into song, and Ash recovered his spirits and was suddenly full of optimism. Somehow and in some way his problems would be solved, and tomorrow when he rode back to Mardan the future would be clear and everything settled.

Ash had sent a brief letter to Belinda, telling her that he would be riding over to Peshawar and hoped to reach there by mid-day, and a longer and more formal one to Mrs Harlowe, asking permission to call. But though he arrived at their bungalow a little earlier than he expected he found it empty but for a portly Mohammedan bearer, who informed him that the Major-Sahib had gone into camp with his regiment on the previous day, and the memsahibs were out shopping and would not be back until three o'clock, as they were taking *tiffin* with the Deputy Commissioner's memsahib. There was, however, a note for Ash . . .

They were so sorry, wrote Belinda, to be out, but the luncheon engagement was one that could not be missed, and as Mohan Lal's shop had announced the arrival of a new consignment of dress materials and printed cottons from Calcutta, there was no help for it but to leave early. She was sure Ash would understand, and Mama hoped that he would take tea with them at four o'clock.

The note contained three spelling mistakes and had obviously been written in a hurry, but it was the first that Ash had ever received from her, and as she had signed herself his affectionate Belinda, he stowed it carefully away in the breast-pocket of his coat, and leaving a message to say that he would return at tea time, remounted his horse and rode slowly away to the dâk-bungalow. There he engaged a room for the night, left Gul Baz and the horses, and having sent for a tonga, had himself driven to the Club. At least it would be cool there and probably quiet—which was more than could be said for the dâk-bungalow. But it proved to be an unfortunate choice.

The Club was certainly cool and comfortable, and it was empty except for a sprinkling of bored *khidmatgars* and two middle-aged Englishwomen who were drinking coffee in a corner of the lounge. Ash retired to the opposite corner with a mug of beer and a six-month-old copy of *Punch,* but the quacking voices of the two women made it impossible to concentrate, and presently he rose abruptly, and marching out of the lounge, took refuge in the bar where, owing to the fact that most of the garrison were out on manoeuvres, he found himself the sole occupant and was alone with his thoughts, none of which were particularly pleasant.

It was a measure of his disquiet that barely a quarter of an hour later he greeted the appearance of George Garforth with something approaching relief, though normally he would have been at pains to avoid George's company, and within minutes was regretting that he had not done so. For George, having accepted his offer of a drink, had immediately embarked on a harrowing description of Belinda's impact on Peshawar society and the compliments paid to her by several eligible bachelors who, asserted George, should know better than to pester such a young and innocent creature with their loathsome attentions.

'It's downright disgusting, when you think that Foley and Robinson are both old enough to be her father—or her uncles, anyway,' said George bitterly. 'As for Claude Parberry, anyone can see that he is nothing but a *roué* and not to be trusted to take one's sister out riding. I can't think why her mother permits it: or why you do.'

He glowered resentfully at Ash, and having refreshed himself with a long pull at his glass, cheered up slightly and remarked that he happened to know that Belinda was merely embarrassed by the attention of these officers—he would not call them 'gentlemen'—but the poor child was too inexperienced to know how to deal with them as they deserved. He could only wish she would give him the right to do so, said George, adding truculently that he felt it only fair to warn Ash that she might yet do so.

'I may as well tell you,' declared George loudly, 'that as she is not wearing your ring, I do not regard her as irrevocably bound to you, and I shall do my best to make her change her mind. After all, "All's fair in love and war" you know, and I was in love with Belinda before you were. Have another drink?'

Ash refused, saying curtly that he had ordered lunch and did not intend to keep it waiting. But George was impervious to snubs and merely said that he too was feeling peckish and would join him. The meal was hardly a convivial one; Ash did not talk at all while George never stopped talking, and judging from his conversation, he appeared to be very much *persona grata* at the Harlowes' bungalow. He had already squired Belinda to a picnic in addition to accompanying her and her mother on a shopping expedition, and that very evening was to dine with them and go on afterwards to the 'Saturday Hop' at the Club.

'Belinda says I am quite the best dancer in Peshawar,' observed George complacently. 'I daresay I—' he broke off abruptly as a new and obviously disagreeable thought struck him. 'Oh, I suppose you are going to be there tonight. Well, you won't find many people there. I believe it's no end of a crush when the military are in town, but as most of 'em are marching around the Kajuri Plain just now, the hops are pretty small affairs. I can't think why Belinda didn't mention that you'd be coming. But perhaps you don't dance? I believe some of the fellows don't, but for my part—'

George continued to talk his way steadily through four courses, and Ash was profoundly relieved when at last he took himself off. A post-luncheon silence descended upon the Club, and he returned to the deserted lounge and the unread copy of *Punch,* and watched the hands of the clock crawl slowly round the dial until at last it was time to leave.

Mrs Harlowe was waiting for him in her drawing-room, and although she greeted him kindly enough, she appeared ill at ease and plunged at once into a disjointed flood of small talk. It was plain that she did not intend to discuss personal matters and was determined to treat his visit as nothing more than a social call, and she was becoming a little breathless by the time her daughter tripped in, wearing white muslin and looking enchantingly young and pretty.

Framed in the doorway of that common-place bungalow drawing-room with its drab-coloured chintzes, numdah rugs and Benares-brass trays, Belinda glowed like a freshly blown rose in an English garden, and Ash forgot the proprieties and the fact that her mother was present, and ignoring her outstretched hand, caught her in his arms and would have kissed her if she had not turned her head away and twisted free.

'Ashton!' Belinda's hands flew to her hair, patting her curls into place as she backed away from him, blushing vividly, and uncertain whether to laugh or be scandalized: 'Whatever will Mama think? If you are going to behave so abominably I shall go away. Now do sit down and be sensible. No, not over there. Here, beside Mama. We both want to hear about your Regiment and Mardan and what you have been doing with yourself.'

Ash opened his mouth to protest that he had not come to talk about such things, but he was foiled by Mrs Harlowe, who rang for tea; and in the presence of a hovering *khidmatgar* there was nothing for it but to give a brief account of his doings, while Belinda poured and the *khidmatgar* proffered plates of cakes and sandwiches.

Listening to his own voice, it seemed to Ash that the day had taken on a queer dream-like quality in which nothing was real. Their whole future, his and Belinda's, was at stake; yet here they sat, sipping tea and nibbling egg sandwiches, and talking trivialities as though nothing else mattered. The entire day had been a nightmare from the moment that he had arrived at the Harlowes' bungalow and learnt that Belinda had left to go shopping: George's unwelcome conversation, the long, slow hours of waiting, Mrs Hawlowe's nervous chatter, and now this. The room seemed to be full of an invisible glue in which he struggled feebly like a fly trapped in a pot of jam, while Mrs Harlowe talked of Zenana Missions and Belinda gleefully listed the various gay functions she had attended during the past week, and drew his attention to the impressive array of engraved cards that stood ranged on the chimney-piece.

Ash glanced at them and said abruptly: 'I saw George Garforth at the Club. He says he has seen you fairly frequently during the past week.'

Belinda laughed and made a little moue. 'If he has, it is only because nearly all the presentable men are out in camp, so he is almost the only one left who can be trusted not to tread on one's dress at a dance. Do you dance, Ashton? I do hope so, for I find I enjoy it more than anything.'

'Then perhaps you will give me some dances tonight,' said Ash. 'I understand that there is to be a dance at the Club, and though I cannot undertake to dance as well as George, I will at least try not to tread on your dress.'

'Oh, but—' Belinda stopped and looked appealingly at her mother, and poor Mrs Harlowe, distracted by the whole situation and finding herself quite incapable of dealing with it, issued a flustered invitation to Ash to join their party that evening, which she had certainly not meant to do. She had only asked him to tea in order to give the young couple an opportunity to talk the matter over in the garden and decide—as of course they must decide—that there was no point in continuing the association and that it would be better to part. Belinda could then return Ashton's ring, and after that the poor boy would naturally wish to leave Peshawar immediately, as the very *last* thing he would want to do would be to return an hour or so later in order to dine with them. She could not imagine why she had invited him to do so, but perhaps he would have the sense to refuse.

Ash had disappointed her: he had accepted with alacrity, under the mistaken impression that the invitation showed Mrs Harlowe to be still on his side and prepared to support his suit; and when she suggested that Belinda might like to show him the garden, he took it as a further proof of her goodwill. Once again, as on the Peshawar road in the early morning, his spirits soared, and he followed Belinda out into the garden and kissed her behind a kindly screen of pepper trees, feeling light-headed with love and optimism. But what followed was worse than anything that he had endured or imagined in the dismal days since his interview with Major Harlowe and the Commanding Officer . . .

Belinda had certainly returned his kiss, but having done so she had also returned his ring and had left him in no doubt as to her parents' opposition to the engagement. Ash learnt that Mrs Harlowe, far from supporting his suit, had gone over to the enemy and was now fully persuaded as to the folly of the whole affair. There was no question of either parent relenting, and as Belinda herself would not be of age for another four years, there was nothing to be gained by arguing or protesting.

Her reaction to Ash's suggestion that they elope had been blank dismay and an emphatic refusal to consider it for a moment. 'I wouldn't *dream* of doing anything so—so silly and outrageous. Really, Ashton, I think you must be mad. You'd be dismissed from your Regiment and everyone would know why, and there'd be a vulgar scandal and you'd be disgraced; and so would I. I'd never be able to hold up my head again, and I think you are quite horrid to—to even *mention* such a thing to me.'

Belinda burst into tears, and only the most abject of apologies on Ash's part had prevented her from running back to the house and refusing to see him again. But though she had eventually agreed to forgive him, the damage had been done, and she would not agree to any private contract between them. 'It's not that I don't love you any more,' explained Belinda tearfully. 'I do, and I would marry you tomorrow if Papa approved. But how can I know what I shall feel like when I'm twenty-one?—or if you will still be in love with me by then?'

'I shall always be in love with you!' vowed Ash passionately.

'Well, if you are, and if I am still in love with you, then of course we shall get married because we shall have proved that we must be the right people for each other.'

Ash insisted that he already knew that, and for his part he would be willing to wait for any length of time if only she would promise faithfully to marry him some day. But Belinda would not promise anything. Nor would she take back the ring. Ashton must keep it, and perhaps one day when they were both older, if her parents and his Commanding Officer approved and if they themselves were still of the same mind—

'If—if—if,' interrupted Ash savagely. 'Is that all you can offer me? "If your parents approve", "If my C.O. permits". But what about *us* my darling?—you and me? It's *our* life and *our* love and *our* future that is being decided. If you loved me—'

He stopped, defeated. Belinda was looking hurt and upset and it was obvious that if he were to continue in this strain it would only lead to another quarrel and more tears, and the possibility of an immediate and permanent break. That last was something he could not bear to contemplate, so he reached for her hand, and kissing it, said contritely: 'I'm sorry, darling. I shouldn't have said that. I know you love me and that none of this is your fault. I'll keep your ring for you, and one day, when I've proved myself worthy of you, I shall ask you to take it back again. You know that, don't you?'

'Oh, Ashton, of course I do. And I'm sorry too. But Papa says— Oh well, don't let's talk about that any more, because it doesn't do any good.'

Belinda dabbed her eyes with a sodden scrap of lace and cambric and looked so forlorn that Ash would have kissed her again. But she would not let him do so, on the grounds that having returned his ring and thereby formally ended their betrothal, it would not be proper. She hoped, however, that they could remain friends, and that he would not feel obliged to change his mind about joining the party that evening, for she was sure that he would dance delightfully; and in any case, an extra man was always useful. On which deflating note the conversation ended and Ash escorted her back to the bungalow with a face of doom and a strong desire to cut his throat—or get drunk.

The reflection that his presence that evening as an extra man would be 'useful' was not calculated to soothe the feelings of a rejected suitor. But as he could not bring himself to forgo even a moment of Belinda's company, he swallowed his pride and attended the party.

He had not expected to enjoy it, but it had proved a surprisingly pleasant evening. Belinda had danced with him three times and been kind enough to commend his waltzing, and emboldened by this success, he had begged as a keepsake the yellow rose-bud she wore at her breast. She would not give it to him (George had already made the same request and been refused, and besides, Mama would be sure to notice), but she had allowed him to take her for a stroll on the lantern-lit terrace, which prevented him from feeling unduly depressed by the fact that she had also given three dances to George Garforth, and two waltzes and the supper dance to a tall, chinless young man who was, apparently, an aide-de-camp to some high-ranking General. But then Belinda in a ball-gown was such a be-witching sight that Ash felt himself quite unworthy of her and even deeper in love than before—if that were possible. The thought of having to wait for her, even if it should mean serving seven years, as Jacob had for Rachel, no longer seemed an intolerable injustice, but only reasonable and right. Such dazzling prizes should be earned, not snatched carelessly and in haste.

Mrs Harlowe, who had feared that the presence of Belinda's discarded lover would cast a gloom over her party, was relieved to find that his behaviour could not be faulted, and that he had actually contributed a great deal to the evening's success, being pronounced a delightful young man and an asset to any party. While as for Belinda herself, the impression that Ash had made on the other young women present had not been lost upon her. Being confident of his devotion it pleased her to know that she possessed something that others found desirable, and on parting with him she returned the pressure of his hand with so much warmth and such a speaking look from her blue eyes that he went back to the dâk-bungalow walking on air.

Her mother too had been unexpectedly kind and had actually said that she hoped he would call on them when next he was in Peshawar, though she was sorry that prior engagements would prevent them from seeing him on the following day. But this had not depressed him, for as their carriage drove away down the dark cantonment road, Ash looked down at the thing that Belinda had pressed into his palm under cover of the conventional farewell, and was comforted and uplifted to find that he held a much crushed and faded yellow rose-bud.

II

Mardan looked friendly and familiar in the evening light, and Ash was surprised to find himself glad to get back to it. The sounds and smells of the cavalry lines, the little star-shaped fort and the long line of the Yusafzai hills, rose-red in the sunset, already seemed like home to him; and though he had not expected to be back until late, Ala Yar was waiting on the verandah, ready to talk or be silent as the mood took him.

In the months that followed there had been little time in which to brood over Belinda and the unsatisfactory state of their love-affair, and there were even days—sometimes several in succession—when he did not think of her at all; and if he dreamed of her at night he did not remember it by morning. For Ash was discovering, as others had done before him, that the ways of the Indian Army (and in particular the ways of the Corps of Guides) differed a great deal from the pattern laid down by the Military Academy at Sandhurst. That difference was very much to his taste, and had it not been for Belinda, he would have had nothing to complain of and much to commend.

As a junior officer of the Guides he was expected to devote a part of each day to the study of Pushtu and Hindustani, the former being the language of the Border and the latter the lingua-franca of India and the Indian Army. But though he needed no instruction in either, he had still not learned to read or write them with the same facility with which he used the spoken word, and now he studied hard under an elderly munshi (teacher) and being Hilary's son made rapid progress. Which, it may here be noted, availed him little, for when he subsequently sat for the written examination in the Higher Standard, he failed to pass, to his own bewilderment and the fury of his munshi who took the matter up with the Commandant, asserting angrily that it was impossible for Pelham-Sahib to have failed; never before had he taught such a pupil and there must be some fault on the part of the examiners—a misprint perhaps? The papers were not returnable, but the Commandant had a friend in Calcutta who on the promise that no action would be taken, borrowed them from the files, only to discover, scrawled across them in red ink, the terse comment: *Flawless. This officer has obviously used a crib.*

'Tell the boy to make a few errors next time,' advised the Commandant's friend. But Ash never sat for an examination again.

November saw the beginning of squadron training, and he exchanged his hot, high room in the fort for a tent on the plains beyond the river. Camp life, with its long hours in the saddle and frosty nights under canvas or the open sky, was far more to his taste than the routine of the cantonment; and after sundown when the tired squadron had finished their evening meal and his fellow officers, sated with fresh air and hard exercise, had fallen asleep, Ash would join a group around one of the fires and listen to the talk.

This to him was almost the best part of the day, and during it he learned a great deal more about his men than he would ever have learned in the normal course of his duties, not only about their families and personal problems, but the dissimilarities in their characters. For men who are relaxed and at ease show a different side of themselves from that which appears when they are on duty; and as the firelight faded and the ring of faces became shadowy and unrecognizable, they would discuss many things that would not normally have been raised in the presence of a *feringhi*. The talk would range widely, from tribal matters to theology; and once a Pathan sowar who had recently met and conversed with a missionary (to the mystification and deep misunderstanding of them both) had demanded of Ash an explanation of the Trinity: 'For the Missionary-Sahib,' said the sowar, 'says that he too believes that there is only the One God, but that his god is three gods in one person. Now, how can that be?'

Ash hesitated for a moment, and then, picking up the lid of a biscuit-tin that someone had been using as a plate, poured a drop of water into three of the corners and said: 'Look—here are three things, are there not? Each separate to itself.' The assembly having looked and agreed, he tilted the tin so that the three drops ran together and formed a single and larger one: 'Now tell me, which is which of the three? There is now only one, yet all three are in that one.' His audience had applauded and the tin was handed round to be peered at and argued over, and Ash achieved an overnight reputation for great wisdom.

He was sorry when the camp broke up and they returned to the cantonment, but apart from the blow to his hopes of an early marriage, he thoroughly enjoyed his first cold weather in Mardan. He got on well with his fellow officers and was on excellent terms with his men—all of whom, by the mysterious grapevines of India (for neither Zarin nor Awal Shah had talked), knew something of his story and took a keen and faintly proprietary interest in his progress. Because of this his troop soon acquired the reputation of being the smartest and best disciplined in its squadron, for which Ash received more credit than he deserved, as it was his background rather than any special talent for leadership or force of character that was responsible for this state of affairs. The men knew that 'Pelham-Sahib' not only spoke but thought as they did, and therefore could not be fooled by lies or tricks such as might serve occasionally with other Sahibs. They knew too that it was safe to bring him their private disputes, because he could be counted upon to make allowances for certain factors that would for ever be beyond the comprehension of those born and bred in the West. It was Ash, for example, who while out on detachment with his troop gave a judgment that was remembered and appreciated for many years on the Border . . .

His men had been told to keep a look out for a grey polo pony stolen from an officer stationed at Risalpur, and on the following night a missionary doctor, riding a grey horse, had jogged past in the moonlight and been challenged by a sentry. The horse had taken fright and bolted, and the sentry, supposing this to be the action of a thief putting spurs to his steed, fired at the doctor and fortunately missed. But the shot had gone uncomfortably close and the doctor, an elderly and choleric gentleman, had been exceedingly angry and lodged a complaint against the sentry. The man had come up for judgement the next morning and Ash, using the judiciary powers of a detachment commander, had sentenced him to fifteen days' detention with loss of pay: two days for firing at a Sahib, and the remainder for having missed him when he did. The sentence had been received with considerable acclamation, and the fact that the Commandant had later put it aside on the grounds that the sowar in question had acted in good faith did nothing to affect the popularity of the verdict; the men being well aware that Ash could not have enforced it and had merely taken this way of showing his disapproval of poor marksmanship. His seniors, however, had not been amused.

'We shall have to watch that young man,' said his Squadron Commander. 'Good stuff in him, but he lacks balance.'

'*Too rash, too unadvised, too sudden*,' quoted Lieutenant Battye. 'I agree. But he'll learn.'

'I suppose so; though there are times when I have my doubts about it. If only he had a cooler head and a bit more steadiness, he'd be first-class material for a Corps like this. But he's too apt to go off at half-cock. Frankly, he worries me, Wigram.'

'Why? The men think the world of him. He can do anything with them.'

'I know. They treat him as though he were some sort of minor deity, and I believe they'd follow him anywhere.'

'Well, what's wrong with that?' demanded the Lieutenant, puzzled by his senior's tone of voice.

The Squadron Commander frowned and tugged unhappily at his moustache, looking baffled and irritated: 'On the face of it, nothing. All the same, and just between the two of us, I'm not at all sure that in a crisis he wouldn't leap before he looked and lead them into something he couldn't get them out of. He's got plenty of courage, I'll grant you that. Possibly too much. But he seems to me to be guided too often by his emotions and not enough by . . . And there's another thing: in a pinch, and supposing he had to make a decision, which way would his loyalties lie? With England or India?'

'Good God,' gasped the Lieutenant, genuinely shocked. 'You aren't suggesting he'd turn traitor, are you?'

'No, no, of course not. Well . . . not exactly. But with a fellow like that—with that background I mean—there's no knowing how it might look to him. It's a deal simpler for you and me, Wigram, for we are always going to assume that our side of any question is the right one; because it's ours. But which *is* his side? See what I mean?'

'Can't say that I do,' admitted the Lieutenant uneasily. 'After all, it's not as though he had any Indian blood in him, is it? Both his parents were as British as—as beer. And just because he was born out here—Well, I mean, dozens of fellows were. You were, for one.'

'Yes, but I never once thought of myself as an Indian! Well he did, and that's the difference. Oh well, time will show. But I'm not at all sure that we didn't make a hell of a mistake in fetching him back to this country.'

'Couldn't have stopped him,' said the Lieutenant with conviction. 'He'd have got back even if he'd had to walk—or swim. Seems to look upon it as his home.'

'Exactly what I've been saying—but it isn't: not really. And one day he's going to find that out, and when he does, he'll realize that he doesn't belong anywhere—unless it's in Limbo, which as far as I remember is somewhere on the fringes of Hell. I tell you, Wigs, I wouldn't be in that boy's shoes for all the tea in China; and I probably wouldn't have cared a damn about it if he'd managed to get back here off his own bat, because that would have been his own affair. As it is, we—the Corps—saddled ourselves with the responsibility for it, so it's ours too, and that's what worries me. Though mark you, I like the boy.'

'Oh, he's all right,' said the Lieutenant easily. 'A bit difficult to get to know, if you know what I mean. You get just so far and no further. But there's no denying that he's the best all-rounder on the sports side that we've had in years, and we ought to knock spots off the rest of the Brigade at next month's gymkhana.'

Neither Awal Shah nor Zarin were in Ash's squadron, and he saw comparatively little of them in Mardan, though whenever possible one or other of them would accompany him out shooting. When neither of them could do so, he would either go alone or take one of his sowars—Malik Shah or Lal Mast, tribesmen from the country beyond the Panjkora, whose company he enjoyed and from whom he had learned much.

Malik Shah was an excellent *shikari* who could stalk a herd of gurral so cunningly that not one would see him until he was well within range; and in this his cousin, Lal Mast (the relationship was so remote that it was impossible to work out the degree), was almost his equal. But though Ash spent many hours in the hills with one or other of them when Zarin was otherwise occupied, he never learned to move as skilfully or as silently as they did, or mastered completely their trick of melting into the landscape and becoming so much a part of it that one would have sworn that there was no human being within miles.

'It has to be learned when young,' said Malik Shah consolingly, as the buck they had been stalking threw up its head and bounded away across the plain. 'In my country, to move unseen, taking advantage of every stick and stone or blade of grass, may often mean the difference between living and dying; for we are all good shots and we make many enemies. But with you, Sahib, it is different; you have never had to lie as still as a stone, or slither from rock to rock as silently as a snake because an enemy waits for you on the far slope—

or you yourself stalk one for his life. Had I a gun such as this one' (he had been shooting with his army-issue carbine) 'I should make myself master of our valley and a score of villages among the hills. Wait here, Sahib, and I will drive the buck this way again—between that nullah and those thorn bushes yonder. That should give you a good shot.'

Ash acquired a number of friends among the villages and spent many nights as the guest of headmen beyond the Border, where few if any of the inhabitants had ever seen a white man before. The men of his own troop were drawn largely from the Border tribes: Yusafzai, Orakzai and Khattak, with a sprinkling of Afridis. But the Guides also recruited a large number of Sikhs, as well as Hindus from the Punjab, Gurkhas from Nepal, Dogras, Farsiwans (Persians) and Punjabi Mussulmans; and Ash would sometimes head southward across the Indus to shoot snipe and *chinkara* in the company of Risalder Kirwan Singh of the Sikhs, or Bika Ram, one of the Hindu non-commissioned officers; cheerful men whose talk reminded him of the play-fellows of his youth—those merry companions of his careless, carefree years in the bazaars of Gulkote city. Yes, it was a good time—or would have been, if it had not been for Belinda.

For Belinda's sake Ash would willingly have spent all his free time dancing attendance upon her in Peshawar. But Major Harlowe would not permit him to visit her more than once a month, and then only to take tea; and even Mrs Viccary, who was often a fellow-guest on these occasions, and would ask him back to dine and listen sympathetically to his woes, refused to concede that the Major's behaviour was unreasonable, advising him instead to try putting himself in the anxious father's place. Only at Christmas time (proverbially a season of Peace and Goodwill) had there been any relaxation of this rule, but by then the Peshawar Brigade were back from the Kajuri Plain and Belinda was involved in a festive whirl of parties, race-meetings and balls.

Ash rode over to deliver his Christmas presents at the Harlowes' bungalow, and to enter his name for the Boxing Day Point-to-Point, which to Belinda's delight he subsequently won by a short head. She seemed for some reason to regard the exploit as reflecting credit upon herself, and rewarded him with two waltzes and the supper-dance at the Boxing Day Ball that night. As a result, he enjoyed the evening, and in the course of it had a long talk with Mrs Viccary, danced with several other young ladies and made himself so pleasant to their mamas that he was later to receive a flattering number of invitations to other parties and balls. But in the event, he never attended another dance in Peshawar. He saw the New Year of 1872 in with Zarin, and in very different surroundings, for they took two days' casual leave and spent them with Koda Dad.

January and February were icy months that year: snow whitened the Border Hills, the Regiment donned poshteens (sheepskin jerkins) to keep out the cold, and Ala Yar kept a log fire burning in Ash's room in the fort where the Munshi came daily to instruct the Sahib in reading and writing. By early April the poplars and willows along the Peshawar road were in bud and the orchards were once again bright with almond blossom; and as spring came and went there was still no sign of trouble on the Frontier and—outwardly at least—the tribes remained at peace with one another and the British.

In Mardan the Guides played a new game called polo, fought mock battles on the plain and instructed their new recruits as they had done for many seasons, and the routine of the Regiment became as familiar to Ash as the walls of his room or the view from the mess verandah. Day began with the scalding mug of tea, sweetened with *gur* and tasting faintly of woodsmoke, that Ala Yar brought to his bedside; and while he shaved and dressed, the old Pathan would discuss the doings of the previous day and tell him the news of Mardan and the Border and the gossip of the bazaars. After that came musketry on the ranges, breakfast in mess, stables, a session in the office, and, at intervals, durbar—the regimental parliament where complaints, requests for leave, and all matters pertaining to policy and justice came up before a *panchayat* ('five elders'). This last being the system by which Indian villages have governed themselves from time immemorial. Here the *panchayat* consisted of the Commanding Officer, the Second-in-Command, the Adjutant and the two senior Indian officers, the men attending not as spectators, but to see that justice was done, for under the *Silladar* system every man in the Regiment was to all intents and purposes a shareholder in a private company, owning his own horse and his gear, as an apprentice owns the tools of his trade. The Guides were none of them landless men, but came of yeoman stock. They enlisted for honour and the love of fighting (and for loot if loot was to be had) and when they had had their fill of military service they would retire to farm their own acres —and send their sons to join the Regiment.

When work was over, Ash spent most of his free time out shooting, and divided the remainder between polo and hawking. Once every week he would write to Belinda (who was not permitted to reply) and once every month he would ride over to Peshawar to pay the formal afternoon call allowed by Major Harlowe.

There had been a time when he had fondly imagined that it would be a simple matter to beat this restriction by attending various Peshawar functions at which Belinda was bound to be present, such as Club dances, hunts or race meetings. But this had not proved a success; she had been far too strictly chaperoned to allow him to have any speech with her, and to have to watch while she rode and talked with other men, or danced with George Garforth (still, apparently, a favoured partner), had been so depressing that it was almost a relief when his Commanding Officer, hearing of these visits, had vetoed them and placed Peshawar out of bounds to him except for the one day a month permitted by Belinda's father.

Ash became savagely jealous of George, which was an unnecessary waste of emotion. Belinda's parents might permit Mr Garforth to call with great frequency, and have no objection to her dancing or riding with him; but they were shrewd enough to realize that she stood in no danger of falling in love with him, and in the normal course of events would probably not have invited him to their house at all, as Mr Garforth's position in the social hierarchy of Peshawar was a humble one. But the fact that his arrival had coincided with the autumn manoeuvres and a resulting shortage of dancing partners had been greatly to his advantage, while his good looks had made an instant impression on every young lady in the station. This, coupled with his newly acquired confidence and his talk of a titled grandmother (the daughter, it was rumoured, of a liaison between a beautiful Greek countess and no less a person than George Gordon, Lord Byron), lifted him out of the ruck, and Belinda would not have been human had she failed to take pleasure in the fact that a man whom other girls admired had eyes only for herself. Besides, as she had once told Ash, George was such an excellent dancer.

She therefore continued to see a great deal of him even after the Regiments returned to Peshawar, for her father not only had no objection to her being squired about by a young man whom she would never consider marrying, but hoped that it might help her to forget that ridiculous engagement. As for George's feelings, he did not give that a moment's thought; according to Major Harlowe, every young man at one time or another fell in love and had his heart broken, and the majority of them did it half-a-dozen times over. Nor was he disposed to waste any concern over Ash's feelings either: marriage, indeed—at nineteen—the boy must be half-witted. Either that or his early up-bringing had warped his thinking, for had he indeed been a native of this country he could have married at fifteen without causing any comment. But then Ashton was British and should behave as such.

Ash was trying his best to do so, but he found it hard going. The very qualities that nine years ago Awal Shah and the then Commandant of the Guides, and later Colonel Anderson, had regarded as valuable future assets were proving to have their drawbacks, and Ash often envied his fellow officers, who could make decisions with such cheerful confidence. To them so many matters were either right or wrong, necessary or unnecessary, the obvious, or the sensible, or the just course to pursue: it was as simple as that. But it was not always so to Ash, who was apt to look at a question as much from the viewpoint of Lance-Naik Chaudri Ram or Sowar Malik Shah as from that of a product of the British public-school system and a cadet of the Royal Military Academy; which tended to complicate matters rather than simplify them, for to know what was going on in the mind of a sowar up for judgement, and to understand only too well the mental processes that had led the culprit to commit whatever crime he was accused of, did not always help towards giving a quick and clear-cut verdict.

Too often, Ash's sympathies lay with a man for no better reason than he himself could and frequently did think as a native of the country. And there is a wide and fundamental difference between the reasoning of East and West—a fact that has before now confounded many a well-meaning missionary and zealous administrator, and led them to condemn whole nations as immoral and corrupt because their laws and standards, habits and customs, differ from those evolved by the Christian West.

'A Sahib, for instance,' explained the Munshi, attempting to illustrate that difference to his pupils, 'will always give a truthful answer in reply to a question, without considering first whether or not a lie might have served better. Now with us it is the reverse; which in the end causes less trouble. We of this country recognize that truth can often be most dangerous and therefore should on no account be scattered carelessly abroad, like husks for the chickens, but used only with great caution.'

His pupils, junior officers who had been brought up by parents and tutors to consider lying a deadly sin, were shocked by this open admission on the part of an elderly teacher that in India a lie was regarded as entirely permissible (and for reasons that seemed to an Englishman both sly and cynical). They would learn better in time, as other British officers, officials and businessmen had learned before them. And as their understanding increased, their usefulness to their country and to the Empire that their country governed would increase proportionately. But the chances were that with the best will in the world they would never fully understand more than a little of the motives and processes of thought that dictated Asiatic reasoning: the tip of the iceberg only. Some few would learn to see further, and many would imagine that they could, though there would be many more who were unwilling or incapable of making the effort to do so. But blood and environment, custom, culture and religion divided them, and the bridges between those gulfs were still too few; or at best, slender and insubstantial structures that were apt to break down at unexpected moments if overmuch reliance were placed upon them.

Ash would have found life easier if, like his fellow officers, he could have concentrated upon building and making use of such bridges, instead of standing with one foot on each bank, uneasily balanced between the two and unable to throw his full weight onto either. It was an invidious position and he did not relish it.

His happiest times were when he was out with Zarin, though even Zarin had changed. The old relationship that both had imagined they had recaptured, and could keep, was being altered by circumstances beyond the control of either of them. Zarin found it increasingly difficult to forget that Ash was a Sahib and an officer set in authority over him, and this inevitably raised a barrier between them: a flimsy one it is true, and Ash, for his part, was barely aware of it. But because of those years in England, his official position in the Regiment and some of the things he would say or do, Zarin was no longer quite sure what his friend's reactions would be in certain circumstances, and therefore felt it safer to walk a little warily. For Ashok was also 'Pelham-Sahib', and who could be certain which one, at any given moment, would be in the saddle?—Sita's son, or the British officer?

Where Zarin was concerned, Ash would have preferred to be the former only; but he too had realized that the relationship between them could never be quite the same again. The lordly elder brother and the hero-worshipping small boy of the Gulkote days had both, inevitably, outgrown the past. And in growing up they had drawn level with each other. Their friendship remained, but it had changed its quality and now contained hidden reservations that had not been there before.

Only Koda Dad had not changed; and whenever possible Ash would cross the Border to visit him and spend long hours in his company, riding or hawking or merely squatting comfortably by his fireside while the old man discussed the present or reminisced about the past. It was only with Koda Dad that he felt completely relaxed and at ease, for though he would have hotly denied that there was any change in his relationship with Zarin, he knew that something was there: 'a cloud no bigger than a man's hand'.

Neither Ala Yar nor Mahdoo, or Awal Shah either, would ever treat him as anything but a Sahib, since none of them had known him in the days when he was merely Ashok. But Koda Dad had never had any contact with the 'Sahib-log', and in his long life had seen very few of them: a handful at most. All that he knew of them had been learned at secondhand, so their influence on him had been minimal, and the fact that Ashok's parents had been *Angrezis,* and that he was therefore a Sahib by right of blood, in no way altered Koda Dad's feelings towards him. The boy was the same boy, and no child could be held responsible for his parentage. To Koda Dad, Ash would always be Ashok and not Pelham-Sahib.

Regimental routine changed with the coming of the hot weather; officers and men now rose before dawn in order to make use of the coolest hours of the day, and during the fierce heat of the morning and early afternoon they remained indoors, emerging again as the sun began to slide once more towards the horizon. Ash no longer rode over to Peshawar, for Mrs Harlowe and her daughter had retreated to the cool of the hills, and he could only keep in touch with Belinda by letter (his letters, not hers). Once, as a great concession, Belinda had been allowed to reply, but the stilted little note, obviously written under Mrs Harlowe's eye, told him nothing except that Belinda appeared to be having an exceedingly gay time in Murree, which was not the sort of news he really wished to hear. She had mentioned no names, but he learned by chance from an officer in Razmak that the firm of Brown & MacDonald, who employed

George Garforth, had a branch in Murree, and that George, having suffered an attack of heat-stroke in Peshawar, had been transferred there for the summer.

The thought of his rival picnicking in the pine-woods with Belinda and partnering her to dances was intolerable. But there was nothing he could do about it, for when he applied for permission to take hot-weather leave in Murree, the Adjutant had brusquely informed him that if he wished to go on leave he could go and shoot in Kashmir—and via Abbottabad, not Murree—which would do him a deal more good than poodle-faking at tea-parties.

Zarin had been equally unsympathetic. In his opinion, to go running like a tame puppy-dog, begging for scraps, after a woman who would neither marry or bed with one, was both undignified and a waste of time that might be put to better use. He advised Ash to abandon any thought of marriage for at least five years, and suggested instead a visit to one of the better-known houses of ill-fame in Peshawar or Rawalpindi.

Ash was strongly tempted to accept, and it would probably have done him a great deal of good, for the life of an unmarried subaltern in the Indian Army was a monastic one. The majority of his fellow-officers, similarly placed, kept their sexual appetites within bounds by taking violent exercise, while the remainder risked contracting unpleasant diseases and being robbed of their valuables by paying surreptitious visits to brothels in the bazaar, or indulging in less orthodox affairs with local youths after the fashion of the Frontier tribesmen, who have never seen anything wrong in such behaviour. Ash, however, had no leanings towards homosexuality, and being enamoured of Belinda he could not bring himself to purchase the favour of harlots—even those of such notable charmers as Masumah, the wittiest, prettiest *kasbi* in Peshawar. He went fishing in the Kangan Valley instead.

By September the nights were cooler, even though the days were still intolerably hot. But by the middle of October there was a freshness in the air, and once again duck and teal appeared on the *jheels* and the quieter reaches of the rivers, and long lines of geese flew high overhead, making for their winter feeding-grounds in central and southern India. Zarin was promoted to Jemadar, and Belinda and her mother arrived back in Peshawar.

Ash rode over to take tea with the Harlowes. He had not seen Belinda since the spring, nearly six months ago—though it seemed to him more like six years, and might almost have been so, for she had altered a great deal. She was still as pretty as ever, but she no longer looked like a gay, heedless school-girl who had only recently escaped from her lesson-books and was revelling in newly acquired freedom and her first heady taste of life. She had acquired a good deal of assurance and was suddenly very much a young lady. And although she was just as gay, it seemed to Ash that her gaiety was no longer spontaneous, and that her laugh and the pretty airs and graces, that had once been wholly charming and unselfconscious, now held a trace of artificiality.

The change in her disturbed him and he tried without success to convince himself that he had imagined it, or that after so long a parting Belinda felt shy and possibly a little awkward at seeing him again, and that once this had worn off she would be her own sweet, familiar self again.

The only gleam of consolation in that dismal afternoon was the fact that George Garforth, who had also been invited, had received even less attention from Belinda than he himself had done. On the other hand, George was obviously very much at home in Mrs Harlowe's drawing-room, and on excellent terms with her (she had addressed him on several occasions as her 'dear boy') while politeness had compelled Belinda to devote most of her attention to entertaining a stout and elderly civilian who rejoiced in the name of Podmore-Smyth and was a friend of her father's.

It would be interesting to know what course Ash's life might have taken if he had never met Belinda, or having met her, had avoided provoking her into flirting with George Garforth. Only one of the three was to avoid suffering from the fact that the threads of their separate lives had become entangled, and now both George and Belinda were to play a part—though admittedly a very small one—in setting in train something that was to make all the difference to Ash's future, since both were responsible for the state of mind in which he had returned from Peshawar, and it was the thought of them that had later driven him out to walk in the moonlight.

He had gone to bed early, and when at last he fell asleep it was only to dream the same dream that had haunted his sleep during his first week in Mardan. Once again he found himself riding for his life —and Belinda's—across a stony plain between low, barren hills, while behind him the thud of pursuing hoof-beats grew louder and nearer until he awoke to find that the sound was no more than the hammering of his own heart . . .

The night was fresh and cool, but his body was wet with sweat, and he threw off his blanket and lay still, waiting for his racing heartbeats to slow down to their proper pace, and still subconsciously listening for sounds of pursuit. Beyond the open window the fort lay bathed in moonlight, but even the pariah dogs and jackals were silent, and except for the sentries the whole cantonment seemed asleep. Ash got up and went out onto the verandah and presently, seized by a sudden spasm of restlessness, he returned to don a dressing gown and a pair of *chupplis*—the heavy leather sandals that are the common footwear of the Border—and went out to walk off his disquiet in the night air. The sentry recognized him and let him pass with a murmured word in place of the conventional challenge, and he turned towards the parade ground and the open country that stretched away beyond it to meet the hills, his shadow dark before him on the dusty road.

There were a number of piquets encircling Mardan to give warning in case of an attack, but knowing the precise location of each one, Ash found little difficulty in avoiding them, and soon he had left the cantonment behind him and was striding out towards the hills. The plain was seamed with gullies and dotted with camel-thorn, boulders and sudden outcrops of rock, and the iron studs on the soles of his *chupplis* clicked on the stony ground and made a sound that was magnified out of all proportion by the silence. The noise disturbed his train of thought and became an active irritation, but eventually he came on a goat track where the dust lay inches deep, and after that he moved without sound.

The track wandered out across the plain in the aimless manner of goat tracks, and he kept to it for the best part of a mile, before turning aside to sit above it on the crest of a small hillock where a flat-topped rock, shaded by pampas grass and a pile of boulders, offered an inviting seat. The hillock was barely more than a mound, but seated on the rock with his back against a boulder, Ash looked out across the moon-washed levels and had the illusion that he was sitting high above the plain—as high and secluded as in the Queen's balcony on the Peacock Tower.

There had been a light fall of rain on the previous day, and in the clean, cold air even the peaks of the far mountains seemed very near: a day's march at most—or an hour's. Looking at them, Ash stopped thinking of Belinda and George and thought instead of other things: of another moonlight night, long ago, when he had made his way across just such a plain as this one towards a grove of *chenar* trees by the Gulkote road. He wondered what had become of Hira Lal. He would like to meet Hira Lal again, and repay a part of the debt he owed him for the horse and the money. One of these days he must take leave and . . . His thoughts came suddenly back from the past and his eyes narrowed and became intent.

Something was moving out on the plain and it could not be cattle, for there was no village near enough. Presumably, some kind of deer; *chinkara* perhaps? It was difficult to tell, for moonlight played tricks with one's eyesight. But as they were moving towards him and there was no wind to carry his scent to them, he would know soon enough. He had only to remain still and they would pass very close, for his clothing was the same colour as the rock, and sitting motionless in the shadows he would be almost invisible even to the keen eyes of a wild creature.

His interest was at first no more than idle. But all at once it ceased to be so, for the moonlight glinted on something that was not horns, but metal. He had been watching men, not wild game: armed men who carried muskets.

As they came nearer Ash could see that there were only three of them, and the sudden tension of his nerves relaxed. He had imagined for a moment that they might be a party of raiders from across the Border, swooping down to attack some sleeping village and carry off cattle and women. But three men could not do much harm and possibly they were only *Powindahs*—wandering, gipsy-like folk who live in tents and are always on the move. He did not think this very likely, for now that the days were pleasantly cool again, few men would choose to travel on foot by night. But whoever they were he preferred not to meet them, as their reasons for being abroad at such an hour were almost certainly discreditable, and cattle-thieves and outlaws were apt to shoot first and ask questions afterwards. He therefore stayed very still and was grateful for the lengthening shadows, and for the fact that the moon was behind him and shining straight into the eyes of the advancing men.

Secure in the knowledge that if he did not move they were unlikely to see him, he was able to relax and watch them approach with curiosity and a touch of impatience. He was beginning to feel chilly and he wished that the strangers would quicken their pace, for until they had passed and were well out of range, he himself would not be able to leave. Ash yawned—and a split second later was tense and listening.

The sound he had heard was a very small one, but it had not been made by the men who were moving towards him. It had come from much nearer and from somewhere behind him: at a guess, from not more than twenty or thirty yards away—though in that windless silence any sound would carry a considerable distance. This one had been no more than the rattle of a displaced pebble; but except for the mound on which he sat the plain for several hundred yards in every direction was as flat as a board, and no pebble could have dislodged itself, or struck against another with that degree of force, without assistance. He held his breath to listen and heard another sound that was as easy to recognize as the first had been: the click of an iron-studded *chuppli* striking against a stone. There was at least one other man approaching the mound, but from a different direction.

Several separate possibilities flashed through Ash's mind, all of them unpleasant. Blood-feuds bedevilled the Border country, and the man or men behind him might be laying a trap for those ahead. Or was he himself the quarry and had he perhaps been seen and followed by someone who had cause to hate the Guides? It had been a mistake to come out unarmed. But it was too late to regret that now, for once again metal clicked on stone and a pebble rattled, and Ash turned his head cautiously in the direction of the sound and waited with every nerve and muscle in his body tensed and ready.

There was a rustle close by as someone brushed against a thorn bush below the mound, and a moment later a lone man hurried past and went on without turning. He had gone too quickly for Ash to gain more than a fleeting impression of a tall figure, muffled in a coarse woollen blanket and further protected from the night air by a length of cloth wound about his head and neck. Once past he was only a hurrying shape in the moonlight, and if he were armed it was certainly not with a musket, though the blanket probably concealed a Pathan knife. It was also clear that he had neither seen Ash nor suspected his presence. Yet there had been an indefinable suggestion of furtiveness about him—in the hunch of his shoulders and the way his head turned sharply from left to right, giving an impression of nervous haste and the fear of being followed.

The four men met some fifty yards from the mound and stood talking together for several minutes. Presently they squatted down on their hunkers to continue the conversation in more comfort, and Ash saw the flash of flint on tinder as a hookah was lit and passed round. They were too far away for him to be able to catch more than a faint murmur of voices and an occasional laugh, yet he knew that if he attempted to leave they would see him, and he did not think they would take at all kindly to the idea that they had been spied upon. The very fact that they had chosen to meet at such an hour and in such a place was a clear indication that their business was not one they wished to advertise, and in the circumstances it seemed safer to stay where he was.

He had stayed there for the better part of an hour, becoming colder and crosser with every passing minute, and cursing himself for being such a fool as to indulge in nocturnal rambles. But at last the long wait was over and the four rose to their feet and went their separate ways: three of them heading back towards the hills while the fourth man returned the way he had come, passing again within a few feet of the mound. This time the moon was full on his face instead of behind him, but he had wrapped the loose end of his headcloth about his mouth and chin so that only a hawk-like nose and a pair of deep-set eyes were visible. Yet despite this, something about him struck Ash as familiar. The man was someone he knew: he was quite certain of that, though he did not know why he should be; but before he had time to think it out the man had passed him and gone.

Ash waited for a moment or two before turning to peer cautiously around the boulders and watch the tall figure hurrying away in the direction of Mardan, and only when he could see it no longer did he get to his feet, cramped and cold and with all thoughts of Belinda driven out of his head, and set out on the long walk homeward to the fort.

Looking back on it next morning in the brilliant light of a blue and gold autumn day, the incident lost the sinister overtones that moonlight had lent it, and appeared singularly innocuous. The four men had probably only met to discuss some urgent matter of purely tribal interest, and if they preferred to do so by night that was their affair. Ash put the whole thing out of his mind, and would probably never have thought of it again but for a chance encounter in the dusk some six days later . . .

There had been no polo on that particular evening, so he had taken a gun and gone after partridge in the scrub-land along the

river, and returning shortly after sunset he met a man on the cantonment road by the cavalry lines: a sowar of his own squadron. The
light was fading fast and it was only when they were almost abreast
that Ash recognizcd him. Returning the man's salute, he walked on,
and then stopped and turned, checked by a sudden memory. It was
partly the man's gait—he had a trick of hitching one shoulder very
slightly to match his stride. But there was something else: an old scar
that divided his right eyebrow into two and that Ash had seen, without realizing it, on the upper part of a face glimpsed briefly in bright
moonlight.

'Dilasha Khan.'

'Sahib?' The man turned and came back. He was an Afridi-
Pathan, and his tribe was one of many who in theory owe allegiance
to the Amir of Afghanistan, but in practice acknowledge no law save
their own. Recalling this, it occurred to Ash that the men Dilasah
Khan had gone out to meet were almost certainly kinsmen bringing
him news from his village, and that in all probability it concerned
some blood-feud with a neighbouring tribe, one or more of whose
members might be serving with him in the Guides.

British territory was held to be neutral ground and no blood-feud
might be carried into it. But one step beyond the Border things were
different, and Dilasah's fellow tribesmen might not wish to be
tracked there. In any case, he had not been breaking the law, so it
was hardly fair, thought Ash, to catechize him about something that
he obviously wished to keep private. As he himself had suffered from
similar interference in his time, and resented it, he did not say what
he had meant to; which was, perhaps, a mistake, for if Dilasah had
taken fright he might have changed his mind and his plans, and
thereby saved, amongst other things, his own life. Though as his
creed taught him that his fate was tied about his neck and could not
be avoided, he would presumably have refused to believe that any
action of his own, or anyone else's, could have altered it.

In the event, Ash said nothing of having seen him out on the plain
by night, and spoke instead of some trivial matter concerned with the
riding school, before sending the man on his way. But the incident,
now that it had been recalled, refused to be dismissed from his mind,
and for some unknown reason it nagged at him with the persistence
of a fly that keeps settling on the face of a drowsing man. Because of
this he paid more attention to Sowar Dilasah Khan than he would

otherwise have done, and decided that he did not like him. The man was a good soldier and a more than adequate horseman, and there was no fault to be found with him on that level. But there was something about him that Ash could only define as 'shifty'. Something in his manner which was tinged with obsequiousness (a most uncharacteristic quality in a tribesman) and in the way his eyes slid away, avoiding a direct gaze.

'I don't trust that fellow Dilasah,' confessed Ash, discussing the troop with his Squadron Commander. 'I've seen one or two horses with that sort of look in their eyes, and I wouldn't have one if it was being given away with a pound of tea.'

'Dilasah? Oh, nonsense,' said the Squadron Commander. 'Why, what's he been up to?'

'Nothing. It's just that . . . I don't know. He gives me an uncomfortable feeling between my shoulder blades, that's all. I saw him out on the plain one night—'

Ash described the incident and the Squadron Commander laughed and dismissed it with a shrug of the shoulders and an interpretation that was similar to Ash's original one: 'Ten to one there's been a row between his lot and the next-door village, and they were merely warning him to watch out for himself next time he goes on leave, because his cousin Habib has just shot their headman's son, Ali, and Ali's relations will be gunning for all or any of Habib's. Bet you it's that.'

'I thought so too at first, but it can't have been, because he went out to meet them. That means that it was all arranged beforehand. The meeting, I mean.'

'Well, why not? They'd probably sent a message to say that they had news for him. If it was about a killing, they wouldn't have risked saying more than that.'

'I expect you're right. All the same, I've a feeling we ought to watch that fellow.'

'You do that,' agreed the Squadron Commander cordially. His tone conveyed a distinct suggestion of 'run away and play' and Ash flushed and dropped the subject. But he did not forget it and he was sufficiently interested to ask Ala Yar to make a few inquiries into the history and background of Sowar Dilasah Khan.

'There are five others of his clan in the *rissala* (cavalry),' reported Ala Yar. 'All proud, fierce men—Afridis who have joined the Guides for *izzat* (honour) and because they love a fight. And also perhaps because their clan is rent by many blood-feuds, and here they cannot be ambushed and shot down without warning. There are two of them in your own troop: Malik Shah and Lal Mast.'

'I know that. And they are both good men—the best. I have been out on *shikar* with Malik half a dozen times, and as for Lal Mast—'

Ala Yar held up a hand: 'Hear me out. I had not finished. Their clan is a small one and so they are all in some way tied by blood—third, fourth and it may be fifteenth cousins a dozen times removed. Yet it is a fact that not one of them has any liking for their kinsman, Dilasah. They say he is a cheat and sly; and like yourself, they distrust him.'

'Why? In what way?'

'Oh, for a dozen small things done in childhood. You know how it is with children: one of their number lies or cheats or runs tale-bearing to those in authority, and for this his playmates hold him in dislike. Even when they grow up and become men, the dislike remains. The others were not pleased when he joined the Guides, and they say that they do not understand why he did so, for it was unlike him. But he came with a good horse and rode it well, and he is also a fine marksman; he won his place fairly in competition with others, and as his officers speak well of him his kinsmen can have no complaint and from pride in their clan they will stand by him. Nevertheless they still dislike him, for he has at one time or another done each of them an ill turn—boy's tricks only; but men, as I have said, do not forget. Ask Malik or Lal Mast, next time you go out shooting with them.'

Ash had done so. But he had learned no more than Ala Yar had told him.

'Dilasah? He is a serpent,' said Malik Shah. 'His blood runs slow and his tongue drips poison. When we were boys—' He told a long tale of a childhood escapade that had ended in punishment and tears for all save Dilasah, who had instigated the whole affair and then betrayed his playfellows to authority and avoided the consequences by some spirited lying. It was plain that the episode still rankled, yet Malik admitted that a year in the Regiment had improved Dilasah out of all knowledge: 'He has made a good soldier, and when we of the Guides are again called upon to fight battles, he may even bring credit upon us, and on his clan also. Still, it is strange that he should have wished to serve under the Sirkar and submit himself to discipline, for I would have said that he was the last man to choose this way of life. Yet—who knows?—he may have done some killing that has made life in our hills too dangerous for him, and so has sought safety here for a while. He would not be the only one to do so!'

Malik laughed, and Ash, who knew that last was true enough, did not pursue the subject. But less than a week later it became all too clear why Dilasah Khan had enlisted in the Guides. And equally clear that his kinsmen's distrust and Ash's suspicions had been well founded.

12

There had been no moon on the night that Dilasah disappeared from Mardan, taking with him his own and one other Government-issue cavalry carbine. Nor had anyone seen him go, for he, like Malik, could move like a shadow when he chose.

He had been on sentry duty in the last watch before dawn, one of two men who were patrolling the lines, and the fact that he had not knifed his fellow sentry was probably due to a dislike of being involved in further blood-feuds rather than any respect for human life. But the man had suffered a bad case of concussion and it was some time before he could tell his story. He had naturally not expected any attack from such a quarter and could not remember being hit; but it was obvious that Dilasah had felled him with the butt of his carbine before gagging and binding him with his own turban, and dragging him away into the shadows out of earshot of the sleeping camp. The aggressor had then made off into the darkness, and must have had at least an hour's start before the groans of the bound man at last aroused someone to investigate, for although patrols on horseback had galloped out to scour the countryside and track him down, they failed to find him.

By nightfall there was still no sign of him, and the following morning the Commandant demanded to know how many other members of his clan were serving with the Regiment. These were summoned to his office and ordered to remove every piece of uniform or equipment that was the property of the Corps, and they had obeyed in silence, each in turn adding to the pile on the matting-covered floor before returning to his place to stand rigidly at attention.

'Now go,' said the Commandant. 'And do not let me see your faces again until you have brought back both rifles.'

The men had gone without a word, and no one had questioned the Commanding Officer's action except Ash, to whom it had come as the culmination of a particularly harrowing week.

'But he can't do that,' stormed Ash to his Squadron Commander, white-lipped with anger. 'What's it got to do with them? It wasn't *their* fault. Why—why they don't even like the man! They never have.'

'They belong to the same clan,' explained the Squadron Commander patiently, 'and the C.O.'s a very shrewd bird who knows what he's doing. He wants those carbines back because we can't afford to have that kind of weapon being used in the passes—and because we can't afford to allow one of our fellows to get away with this kind of thing either. It might give a lot of other men ideas. No; he's done the only thing he can. It's a question of *izzat*. Dilasah has let his clan down and his fellow clansmen will get those carbines back for their own sakes. You'll see. They've probably got a pretty good idea where he's heading for, and the chances are that they'll be back inside forty-eight hours with the rifles.'

'What if they are?' demanded Ash. 'They've had their uniforms stripped off them and they've been flung out—punished and publicly disgraced for something that had nothing whatever to do with them. If there was any justice, *I'm* the one who ought to be punished—or *you!* I knew that man was up to no good, and so did you. I warned you, and you brushed it off as though I'd brought you some footling fairy-story. But I could still have done something to prevent this, and Malik and the others couldn't. It isn't fair!'

'Oh for God's sake grow up, Pandy,' snapped the Squadron Commander, losing his patience: 'You're behaving like a child of two. What's got into you? You've been going round like a bear with a sore head for the last few days. Aren't you feeling well?'

'I'm perfectly well, thank you,' retorted Ash angrily. 'But I don't like injustice and I'm going to see the C.O. myself.'

'Well, rather you than me. He's not in a particularly good mood at the moment, and after you've heard what he has to say you'll wish you'd had more sense.'

But Ash was beyond the reach of reason, not only on account of Dilasah Khan's defection and the dismissal of his fellow clansmen. That had merely been the last, and by no means worst incident, in a week that he was to look back on as the blackest period of his life. Ever afterwards, nothing would ever seem so bad again, because he himself was never again to be the same kind of person that he had been until then . . .

It had begun with the arrival of a letter by the morning post, and he had not even recognized the writing on the envelope, but had opened it casually in the mess, expecting it to contain only another invitation to a dinner-party or a dance. Mrs Harlowe's well-meant letter, informing him that her daughter was engaged to be married, had been as unexpected as the first shock of an earthquake.

Belinda was so very, *very* happy, wrote Mrs Harlowe, and she did *so* hope that he would do nothing to spoil that happiness, but be sensible about it and not enact them any tragedies, for it must have become plain to him by now that he and Belinda were *quite* unsuited to each other, and in any case he was much too young to be thinking of marrying and settling down. Ambrose was in every way a far more suitable husband for Belinda, and she felt sure that Ashton would be unselfish enough to rejoice in her daughter's great happiness and wish her the best of good fortune in the future. Belinda had asked her to break the news to him, as owing to all the foolish talk there had been between them, the dear child felt that he might prefer it that way . . .

Ash sat staring at the letter for so long that eventually one of his friends had inquired if he were feeling all right, and had had to repeat the question three times before receiving an answer.

'Yes—I mean, no. It's nothing,' said Ash confusedly.

'Bad news?' asked Wigram Battye sympathetically.

'No. Only a headache—touch of the sun, I expect. Think I'll go and lie down,' said Ash. And added unexpectedly: 'I don't believe it!'

'Believe what? I say, old fellow, hadn't you better see the M.O.? You're looking like death,' observed Wigram candidly. 'If it is sunstroke—'

'Oh, don't be an ass,' said Ash unkindly, and went back to his room to sit on the edge of his bed and re-read Mrs Harlowe's letter.

He read it half-a-dozen times, and each time it seemed to be less believable. If Belinda had really been falling in love with someone else, surely he would have sensed it when he last saw her—which was barely three weeks ago? But her last words to him had given no indication of any drastic change of heart, and he did not believe that after all that there had been between them, she would have asked her mother to write such a letter. If it were true, she would have written to him herself; she had always been honest with him. *Ambrose*—Who the hell was Ambrose? It was all a plot on the part of her parents. A plot to separate them. Either that, or they were forcing Belinda into a distasteful marriage against her will.

Mrs Harlowe's letter had arrived on a Friday, and there were still eight days to go before Ash was officially allowed to see Belinda again. But on the following day he defied orders and rode over to Peshawar.

Once again, as on the occasion of his first visit, the Harlowes' bungalow was empty and a servant informed him that the Sahib and the memsahibs were out to lunch and not expected back until mid-afternoon. Ash retired, as he had done before, to the Club; and here too, history repeated itself, for though the Club was far from empty and the lawns and terraces were packed with a gay and chattering Saturday morning crowd, the first person to accost him was George Garforth.

'Ash!' cried George grabbing at him as he passed. 'Mus' talk to you. Don't go. Have a drink—'

Ash had no desire at all to talk to George—or to anyone else, apart from Belinda. But two things prevented him from disengaging himself and walking away. The first, that George was tipsy, and the second that here was someone who would certainly know if there was any truth in this tale of an engagement. Though the very fact that George was drunk—and at this hour of the morning—made his heart shrink with foreboding.

'Jus' the fellow I wanted to shee,' babbled George hoarsely. 'Wan' t' talk to you, Ash. Only one I can talk to. But not here . . . too many people here . . . too many b-bloody stuck-up snobs sitting around and listening. Le's go t' my bungalow for *t-tiffin*.'

In the circumstances it seemed a sensible suggestion, for Ash could think of nothing worse than having to listen to what George had to say (if, as seemed only too likely, it concerned Belinda) in the presence of half the members of the Peshawar Club. In any case, the sooner Mr Garforth removed himself from such a public spot the better, for his behaviour was obviously attracting a considerable amount of attention. Far too many people were staring at him in patent disapproval and whispering to their neighbours, and it was plainly only a question of time before the Secretary or some irate member requested him to leave—a disgrace that to someone of George's over-sensitive temperament would cause a degree of suffering and humiliation out of all proportion to the offence. Ash sent for a tonga and took the inebriated Mr Garforth back to his bungalow, which turned out to be a large, square building, part office, that was owned by his firm.

George's portion of it was a modest one, consisting of a small back-bedroom with an adjoining bathroom and one end of a verandah (screened off from the remainder by a *chik**) that did duty as a

---

* sun-blind made of split cane

combined sitting-room and dining-room. The whole bore a depressing resemblance to a dâk-bungalow, but the servant who appeared at the sound of the tonga bell was able to produce a three-course lunch, accompanied by two bottles of Brown & MacDonald's light ale, so that despite his forebodings Ash contrived to make a tolerable meal. His host, on the other hand, rejected every dish with expressions of loathing, and sat slumped in his chair muttering belligerently and scowling at the *khidmatgar*. It was only when the table was eventually cleared and the servant went away that he abandoned this truculence in a startling manner.

The verandah *chik* had no sooner dropped into place behind the departing *khidmatgar* than George leant forward, and laying his folded arms on the table, dropped his head onto them and burst into tears.

Ash retired precipitately to the dusty compound where a solitary neem tree provided an oasis of shade in the mid-day glare. He would have liked to walk back to the Club, but he could not bring himself to abandon George at this particular juncture, even though he was by now fairly certain that the cause of both drunkenness and grief must be Belinda's engagement, and he was no longer sure that he wanted to hear what George had to say on the subject. He sat down on a root of the neem tree, feeling angry with himself and angrier with George, and waited. The harsh, gulping sobs were not a pleasant sound to listen to, but they stopped at last and he heard George blow his nose and stumble away to the bedroom where, judging from the noise of splashing, he appeared to be emptying the contents of the water *chatti* over his head.

Ash rose and came back to his chair on the verandah, and presently George reappeared wearing a towel around his shoulders and with his hair dripping water. He poured himself out a cup of black coffee from the pot that the *khidmatgar* had left on a tray, and subsided heavily into a sagging cane chair where he sat sipping the hot liquid and looking utterly demoralized. There seemed to be nothing left of the talkative and bumptious young man who for over a year had been such a success at tea-parties and Club dances. Even his good looks had vanished, for his pallid face was puffy and unshaven and his eyes red with weeping, while his sodden hair had lost its Byronic curls and straggled limply down his neck and forehead.

Confronted by this spectacle Ash's irritation became diluted with sympathy, and resigning himself to the role of confidante and comforter, he got up and helped himself to coffee and said with an effort: 'You'd better tell me about it. I suppose it's this engagement.'

'What engagement?' asked George tonelessly.

Ash's heart gave a leap that set his pulses racing, and the coffee slopped all over the floor. So he had been right after all. Mrs Harlowe had lied to him, and it wasn't true.

'Belinda's of course. I thought that was why—I mean . . .' He was incoherent with relief. 'I'd heard she was engaged to be married.'

'Oh that,' said George, dismissing it as something of no account.

'Then it isn't true? Her mother said—'

'It wasn't really her,' gulped George. 'She—Mrs Harlowe—tried to be nice about it, I think. She really did like me, you know. But Belinda . . . I—I wouldn't have believed that *anyone* . . . no, that isn't true; I suppose it was just because I did believe it that I tried to keep it quiet. I should have known that someone would find out one day.'

'Find out what? What the blazes are you mumbling about, George? Is she engaged or isn't she?'

'Who? Oh, Belinda. Yes. They got engaged after the Bachelors' Ball, I believe. Look, Ash, do you mind if I talk to you about something? You see, I don't know what to do. Whether to stick it out, or give in my notice and quit, or . . . I can't stay on here. I won't. I'd—I'd rather shoot myself. She'll tell everyone—she's started already. Didn't you see the way they were all staring at me and whispering at the Club this morning? You must have noticed. And it will get worse. Much worse. I don't think I can—'

But Ash was not listening. He had put down his cup with a hand that was noticeably unsteady and now he sat down with some suddenness. He did not want to hear anything more or to talk to anyone. Not to George, anyway. And yet . . .

He said abruptly: 'But that can't be true. The Bachelors' Ball was right at the beginning of the month. That's nearly six weeks ago, and I've seen her since then. I had tea with her, and if it was true she would have told me then. Or her mother would. Or someone.'

'They didn't want to announce it too soon. They kept it quiet until his new appointment came through—I suppose it sounded grander then. Marrying a Resident, you know.'

'A *Resident*? But—' Ash broke off and scowled at George, who must be even drunker than he had thought, because a Residency was a senior appointment: a 'plum job' of the Indian Civil Service. Only men who had served that department for many years were sent to represent their Government in some independent native state with the title of 'Resident'.

'Bholapore—one of those states somewhere down south,' said George indifferently. 'It was in the papers last week.'

'Bholapore?' repeated Ash stupidly. 'But—Oh, you must have made a mistake. You're drunk. That's what it is. How would Belinda ever meet anyone like that, let alone get engaged to him?'

'Well, she has,' said George flatly and as though it did not matter very much. 'Friend of her father's. You must have noticed him: stout party with a red face and grey whiskers. He was having tea with them the last time you were here, and Belinda was all over him.'

'*Podmore-Smyth!*' gasped Ash, appalled.

'That's the fellow. Pompous old bore, but I'm told he's no end of a catch. Sure to be knighted before long and end up as a Lieutenant-Governor, and all that. His wife only died last year, and his daughters are older than Belinda, but she doesn't seem to mind that. He's got a lot of money of course—his father was one of those Calcutta Nabobs, so he's simply rolling in it. And I suppose she likes the idea of being Lady Podmore-Smyth. Or Her Excellency the Governess. Or possibly even Baroness Podmore of Poop one day.' George gave a hollow crack of laughter and helped himself to more coffee.

'I don't believe it,' said Ash violently. 'You're making it up. She wouldn't do a thing like that. Not Belinda. You don't know her like I do. She's sweet and honest and—'

'She's honest, all right,' agreed George bitterly. His lip quivered and once again his eyes filled with tears.

Ash disregarded them: 'If she's engaged to him it's because she's been forced into it. Her parents are behind this—that dried-up old stick of a father and her idiotic, gossiping mother. Well, if they think I'm going to let them ruin Belinda's life and mine, they're wrong.'

'You're the one who's wrong,' said George. 'Her parents didn't like it above half, but she coaxed them round. She's a taking little thing, as you should know by now. But then you don't really know her at all. Neither did I. I thought I did, and I would never have believed . . . Oh God, what am I going to do?'

The tears brimmed over and trickled down his cheeks, but he made no attempt to brush them away or any effort to control them. He merely sat there slumped in his chair and staring into vacancy, with his jaw slack and his fingers clenching and unclenching on the coffee cup. He was an embarassing sight and his unashamed misery exasperated Ash. What right had George to behave like this? It was not as though Belinda had even been engaged to him, or ever would have been. Ash told him so with considerable sharpness, and found a perverse comfort in doing so. But though he had not minced his words they drew no answering spark of anger from George.

'It's not that,' said George dully. 'You don't understand. Of course I knew she'd never marry me; I'm not a fool. I was too young and I hadn't any prospects. I hadn't . . . *anything!* I suppose that's why I invented all that stuff. To make myself more interesting . . . But I never thought—I didn't dream that she'd take it like that if she found out.'

'Found out *what?*' demanded Ash, justifiably bewildered. 'For God's sake, George, pull yourself together and stop babbling! What is all this about? What did she find out?'

'About me. You see I—I've told a lot of lies about myself. And that woman Mrs Gidney, who Belinda's mother is so thick with, has a friend in Rangoon who knows someone who—Well, it was like this . . .'

It was a simple and rather sordid little story, and no one came out of it very well. Mrs Gidney, writing to a dear friend in Rangoon, had happened to mention George's name and comment on his romantic ancestry, and by an unfortunate coincidence the friend was acquainted with a certain Mr Frisby in the teak trade. And that was how it had all come out . . .

George's grandmother, far from being a Greek countess, had been an Indian woman of humble parentage whose union with his grandfather—a colour-sergeant in a British regiment stationed in Agra—had been of a strictly temporary nature, but had resulted in the birth of a daughter who had eventually been placed in a home for the orphaned or abandoned children of mixed parentage. At the age of fifteen the child had been found employment as a nursemaid in an army family, and subsequently married a young corporal in her master's regiment, one Alfred Garforth. Their son George, who had been born in Bareilly, was the only one in the family to survive the Mutiny of 1857, his parents, his baby brother and three small sisters having all been murdered in the space of fifteen frenzied minutes.

George had been spending the day with the family of a friendly storekeeper who had escaped the massacre, and during the few years that remained before the regiment returned to England, the same kindly couple had given him a home, for as his father too had been an orphan, there were no relations to take care of the boy. It was during this period that little George learned from his playmates that a 'half-caste' was an object of scorn. There were several such among the barrack children, and they and he were teased and despised by those whose parents and grandparents were white, and looked down upon with almost equal scorn by Indian children with parents and grandparents who were brown.

'Yer grandma was a sweeper-woman!' or 'Yah, yah, yer a bleedin' blacky-white,' were familiar taunts in scuffles among the barrack children, while the vocabulary of the bazaar children could be even more wounding. Yet George, by the irony of fate, was fairer than many of his white tormentors, and had he possessed a tougher character, or been less good-looking, he might have lived down the unknown grandmother. But he was not only a very pretty little boy, but a painfully timid one, a combination that endeared him to adults but made his own generation yearn to kick him—which they did with enthusiasm and on every possible occasion.

George developed a bad stammer and burning hatred of his schoolmates and the barracks and anything and everything to do with the army, and when the regiment sailed for England, taking him with them, it was only the kindness of the storekeeper and his wife, Fred and Annie Mullens, that saved him from being sent to an army orphanage, for they had arranged for him to be educated at their expense at a small boarding school near Bristol that catered exclusively for children whose parents were overseas. A large number of these children spent both holidays and term time at the school, and nearly all of them had been born abroad, which was George's misfortune, for they too spoke of 'half-castes' with scorn, and one of their number who had the misfortune to be black-eyed and dark-complexioned was cruelly teased on this score—George, to his shame, joining in with the best of them. For with the possible exception of the Headmaster, no one at the school knew anything about him, and he was therefore able to invent a family-tree for himself.

At first this was a comparatively modest affair. But as he grew older he enlarged it, adding mythical grandparents and great-grandparents and a variety of picturesque ancestors. And because he was always afraid that one day his eyes would become darker and his skin betray him by turning brown (as his baby curls, once blond, had done) he gave himself an Irish father—the Irish being prone to black hair—and added a Greek grandmother for good measure. Later he was to discover that a majority of waiters and small shopkeepers in Soho were immigrants from Greece, and as by then he could hardly change this mythical woman's nationality, he decided to make her a countess.

Towards the end of his school-days his benefactor, Mr Mullens, who had a friend in Brown & MacDonalds', arranged for his protégé to enter that firm as a clerk, imagining that by doing so he had done young George an excellent turn and started him on what might one day prove to be a profitable career in the wine business. Unfortunately, the news had been anything but welcome to George, who left to himself would never have returned to India, but he lacked both the courage and the means to refuse such an offer. When he had served his apprenticeship and was eventually ordered to Peshawar, the only bright spot on his horizon was the fact that close on four hundred miles separated Peshawar from Bareilly, and that he would not, in any case, be expected to visit Mr and Mrs Mullens; for barely a month before his departure he heard that Mr Mullens had died of enteric and his broken-hearted widow had sold the store and sailed for Rangoon, where her son-in-law was doing well in the teak trade.

Mr Mullens, charitable to the last, had left George fifty pounds and a gold watch, and George spent the money on clothes and told his landlady that the watch had been his grandfather's. His Irish grandfather—the O'Garforth of Castle Garforth . . .

'I didn't think they would ever find out,' confessed George miserably. 'But Mrs Gidney has a friend whose husband is in the teak trade and knows old man Mullens's son-in-law, and it seems that the friend met Mrs Mullens one day and they began talking about the Mutiny and all that, and Mrs Mullens told her about me and how her husband paid for my schooling and got me this job, and how well I was doing, and—Well, just about *everything*. She even had a photograph of me. I'd forgotten that. I sent it to them my last term at school. I used to write to them, you know. And then this friend wrote to Mrs Gidney . . .'

Mrs Gidney had apparently conceived it her duty to 'warn' her dear friend Mrs Harlowe, and Mrs Harlowe, greatly upset by George's duplicity, had somewhat naturally told her daughter. But where the two older ladies had merely been shocked, Belinda had been outraged, not so much because she had been lied to, but because she considered that she had been made to look foolish. After all it was she and her mother who had, in effect, sponsored George and helped to launch him on Peshawar society, because although his looks alone would have attracted a certain amount of attention, they would never have obtained for him the social recognition that Mrs Harlowe's partiality and her daughter's friendship for him had bestowed on him from the start. Besides, Belinda had more than half believed that romantic tale of a liaison between his mythical great-grandmother and Lord Byron (though to give George his due, this was one rumour for which he was not responsible), but though she had found nothing shocking in an illegitimate grandmama born of such exalted parents —in fact, quite the reverse—the bastard daughter of a colour-sergeant and a low-caste Hindu woman was a very different affair, and sordid in the extreme. Why, George's mother was nothing more than a half-caste—an illegitimate Eurasian who had married a corporal in a line regiment—and George himself had more than a 'touch of the tar-brush', for he was one quarter Indian; and low-caste Indian at that. This—*this* was the man that she, Belinda, had helped to foist onto Peshawar society and had danced and dined with and bestowed her smiles on. Now all the other girls were going to laugh at her, and she would never live it down. Never.

'She was so *angry*,' whispered George. 'She said such terrible things—that all half-castes told lies and she never wanted to see me again, and . . . and if I ever spoke to her again she'd c-cut me d-dead. I didn't know anyone could be so cruel. She didn't even look p-pretty any more . . . she looked ugly. And her voice . . . Her mother k-kept saying "You don't mean that, dear. You can't mean that." But she did. And now she's started t-telling people. I know she has, because they look at me as though I was s-some sort of insect and . . . What am I going to do, Ash? I'd k-kill myself if I could, but I haven't got the g-guts to do it. Not even when I'm drunk. But I can't stay here any longer. I can't! D-do you think that if I made a c-clean breast of it to my boss he'd send me s-somewhere else? If I *begged* him to?'

Ash did not answer. He was feeling dazed and sick, and in spite of everything, disbelieving. He would not and could not believe it of Belinda. Of George, yes. The story explained a great deal about George: his appalling sensitiveness and lack of confidence; that abrupt transformation from tongue-tied timidity to brashness and truculence when Belinda set out to charm him and Mrs Harlowe treated him with consideration and kindness, and he began to believe in himself at last; and most of all, his complete moral and physical collapse now that his make-believe world had been exposed as a sham. But Belinda could never have behaved in the manner he described. George was inventing again and allowing his guilty conscience to put into her mouth sentiments that he had already applied to himself. Because these were the sort of things he was afraid she might say, he was punishing himself by pretending she had actually said them—and quite possibly, too, that she was engaged to Mr Podmore-Smyth, which was something else that he, Ash, was not prepared to believe until he heard it from her own mouth. Then if her parents were really putting pressure on her to force her into marrying some dirty old man in his dotage, he would expose them for what they were.

He stood up and jerked the *chik* aside, and shouted for the servant to call him a tonga.

'You aren't going?' gasped George, in a panic. 'Don't go yet. Please don't go! If you leave me I'll—I'll only get drunk again, and it's worse when I'm drunk. Besides, b-brandy only makes me feel braver. I might g-go out and d-do something stupid. Like going to the Club this morning and m-making a fool of myself.'

'Then don't get drunk,' snapped Ash, exasperated. 'And for God's sake, George, stop feeling so damn' sorry for yourself. You don't have to go to pieces just because you've been found out telling a pack of silly taradiddles about your grandmother. Who the hell cares what your grandmother was or wasn't? You are still you, aren't you? It's sheer poppycock to pretend that people only liked you because they thought your grandmother was a Greek or an Italian or whatever it was. And if you imagine for one minute that Belinda or anyone else is going to spread around any stories about her, you must be mad. You know what it is, George?—you've exaggerated the whole thing out of all proportion, and been so busy being sorry for yourself that you haven't even stopped for a minute to think about it sensibly.'

'You didn't hear what Belinda s-said to me,' gulped George. 'If you'd heard her—'

'I daresay she was damned angry with you for telling her a lot of fatuous lies, and only wanted to punish you for that. Try and use your head for half a second and stop behaving like a hysterical rabbit. If Belinda is what I believe her to be she'll keep quiet about it for your sake, and if she's what you like to think she is, she'll keep it even quieter for her own—and that goes for her mother and Mrs Gidney too, for I don't suppose either of them will care to advertise the fact that they've been a pair of gullible old tabbies.'

'I never thought of that,' admitted George, cheering up slightly. 'Yes, I suppose . . .' His shoulders slumped again. 'But then no one spoke to me at the Club this morning except Mrs Viccary. The rest just looked at me and whispered and sniggered and—'

'Oh, stow it, George,' interrupted Ash angrily. 'You turn up at the Club on a Saturday morning as drunk as an owl and are surprised because people notice it. For the love of God, stop dramatizing yourself and try to keep a sense of proportion.'

He reached for his hat as a clatter of hooves and the jangle of a bell announced the arrival of a tonga, and George said wistfully: 'I'd hoped you'd stay on a b-bit and—and advise me. It's been awful just sitting here alone and thinking; and if I could just talk about it—'

'You've talked about it for over an hour,' observed Ash tartly. 'And if you really want my advice, you'll forget all about this and shut up about your great-aunts or grandmothers or whoever they were, and just go on behaving as though nothing had happened, instead of making a public exhibition of yourself and inviting comment. No one else is ever going to hear about it if only you'll keep your head and shut your mouth.'

'You—you really think so?' stammered George. 'Perhaps you're right. Perhaps it won't ever get out. I d-don't think I could bear it if it did. If it does . . . Ash, honestly now, w-what would you do, if you were me?'

'Shoot myself,' said Ash unkindly. 'Goodbye George.'

He leapt down the verandah steps and was driven back to the Club where he collected his horse and rode over to the Harlowes' bungalow; and for once luck seemed to be with him, for Belinda's parents were still out, while she herself had returned and was resting. The bearer, roused from his afternoon nap, was loath to disturb her, but when Ash threatened to walk in on her himself he hurried away and tapped on her door, telling her that a Sahib had called to see her and would not go away until he had done so. But when Belinda entered the drawing-room some five minutes later it was instantly and painfully clear that she had expected to see someone entirely different. She ran gaily into the room and then stopped dead, the

smile wiped from her pretty face and her eyes widening in apprehension and anger.

'*Ashton!* What are you doing here?'

Something in her voice and expression daunted Ash and he said
uncertainly, stammering a little, as George too had stammered: 'I—I
had to see you, darling. Your m-mother wrote to me. She said you
were . . . you were engaged to be married. It isn't true is it?'

Belinda did not answer the question. She said instead: 'You
shouldn't have come here. You know quite well you should not.
Please go, Ashton. Papa will only be angry if he comes back and
finds you here. Abdul should never have let you in. Now *do* go.'

'Is it true?' repeated Ash, ignoring the appeal.

Belinda stamped her foot: 'I asked you to go, Ashton. You've no
right to come forcing your way in here and cross-questioning me
when you know I'm alone and—' She shrank away as Ash came towards her, but he walked past her without touching her, and closing
the door, locked it and put the key into his pocket and went back to
stand between her and the french windows, blocking her retreat.

Belinda opened her mouth to call the bearer and then closed it
again, daunted by the prospect of embroiling one of the servants in
such an embarrassing situation. An interview with Ashton, however
distasteful, seemed the lesser of two evils—and as she would probably
have to endure one sooner or later, she might as well get it over now.
So she smiled at him and said coaxingly: 'Please don't let's have a
scene, Ashton. I know you must feel badly about it. That's why I
asked Mama to write—because I couldn't bear to be the one to hurt
you. But you must have realized by now that when we first met we
were both much too young to know our own minds, and that we'd
grow out of it, just like Papa said.'

'Are you going to marry that man Podmore?' asked Ash stonily.

'If you mean Mr Podmore-Smyth, yes, I am. And you needn't use
that tone of voice either, because—'

'But my darling, you can't let yourself be bullied into this. Do you
think I don't know that this is all your father's doing? You were in
love with *me*—you were going to marry me—and now he's forcing
you into this. Why don't you stand up for yourself? Oh Belinda, darling, can't you *see?*'

'Yes, I can,' said Belinda crossly. 'I can see that you don't know
anything about it, for if you must know, Papa was very much against
it. And Mama too. But I'm not seventeen any longer: I shall be nine-

teen this year and quite old enough to know my own mind, so there was really nothing they could do about it, and in the end they had to agree, because Ambrose—'

'Are you trying to pretend that you're in love with him?' interrupted Ash harshly.

'Of course I'm in love with him. You don't suppose that I'd marry him if I wasn't?'

'You can't be. It isn't true. That fat, prosing, pompous old man who's the same age as your father . . .'

The blood rushed up into Belinda's face and quite suddenly Ash remembered what George had said about her losing her prettiness and looking ugly. She had lost it now and her voice was strident and furious:

'He's not as old as my father! He's not. How *dare* you talk to me like that? You're jealous of him because he's a man of the world—because he's mature and interesting and successful. Someone I can rely on and look up to, and not a silly, callow boy who—' She checked and bit her lip, and controlling herself with an effort said in a more reasonable voice: 'I'm sorry, Ashton. But it makes me so angry when people say things like that. After all, you were just as angry when Papa thought you were too young. You said age had nothing to do with it, remember? and it's true. Ambrose understands me, and he's kind and generous and clever and everyone says that he's bound to be a Governor. He might even be Viceroy one day.'

'And I gather he's rich as well.'

Belinda missed the sarcasm and accepting the comment at its face value said happily: 'Yes, he is. He's given me such lovely presents. Look.'

She held out her left hand in unaffected pleasure and Ash saw with a pang that it was adorned with a band of enormous diamonds, any one of which was at least twice the size of the pearls in that pretty but unpretentious ring that he had bought for her in Delhi over a year and a half ago. It seemed much longer than that; five years at least. Too long for Belinda, who was going to marry a man old enough to be her father. A fat, rich, successful widower who could give her diamonds and make her Lady Podmore-Smyth—and present her with two ready-made step-children the same age as herself.

There appeared to be nothing left to say. The sight of those diamonds on Belinda's finger proved that all the arguments and pleas that he had meant to use would be a waste of time, and all he could do now was to wish her happiness and go. It was strange to think that he had planned to spend his whole life with her and that now he was probably seeing her for the last time. Outwardly she was as pink and white and pretty as ever, yet it was obvious that he had really never known what went on inside that golden head, but had fallen in love with someone who had existed largely in his imagination.

He said slowly: 'I suppose I've been doing it too. Inventing stories to suit myself and make me feel more comfortable, just like George did.'

Belinda stiffened, and once again, and shockingly, her face was scarlet with anger and her voice high-pitched and shrewish: 'Don't you speak to me about George. He's nothing but a low-bred, lying hypocrite. All those stories about a Greek grandmother—'

Something in Ash's face checked her and she broke off and gave a shrill laugh that was as ugly as her voice: 'Oh, I forgot you wouldn't know about that. Well, I'll tell you. She was no more Greek than I am. She was a bazaar woman and if he thinks I'm going to keep my mouth shut, he's mistaken.'

Ash said haltingly, through stiff lips: 'You can't. You don't mean it . . . You couldn't . . .'

Belinda laughed again, her eyes bright with anger and malice. 'Oh, yes I could. And I have, too. Do you think I'm going to sit and wait until someone else finds out and starts telling everyone, and people begin laughing at me and Mama behind our backs, and sympathizing with us for being taken in? I'd rather die! I shall tell them myself; I shall tell them that I always suspected it and that I trapped him into admitting it, and—'

Her voice was shaking with resentment and wounded vanity, and Ash could only stare at her, appalled, while her pretty pink mouth went on and on manufacturing malice and pouring out spite as though she could not stop herself. Had he been older and wiser, and less badly hurt himself, he might have recognized it for what it was: a tantrum thrown by a spoilt child who has been courted and flattered and over-indulged to a point where good sense and youthful high-spirits have turned to conceit and vanity, and any opposition— any fancied slight—is magnified into an unforgivable injury.

Belinda was young and not very wise. She had been foolish enough to accept the compliments of her beaux at their face value, and after a heady year as a reigning belle had come to expect adulation, approval and envy as her due. She had, in fact, become insufferably set up in her own esteem, and having flaunted the handsome George as one of her conquests, she could not endure the thought of what several jealous young ladies would have to say when they discovered how she had been hoodwinked. How *dare* George lie to her and make a fool of her?—that, in effect, was her instinctive reaction to Mrs Gidney's disclosures. The pathos of George's lies and posturing, the personal tragedy that underlay it and the humiliation that he must now be suffering were aspects of the affair that she had not even thought of, for in the shock of discovery she could only think of how it might affect Miss Belinda Harlowe.

Ash was the first person apart from her Mama and George himself to whom she had been able to unburden herself of all the pent-up forces of resentment and wounded vanity that had been accumulating within her ever since she learned of George's duplicity, and she found it a great relief. But to Ash, listening to the angry spate of words, it was the final betrayal: the collapse of all that he had believed her to be—sweet, kind, innocent and good. The owner of this shrewish voice was none of those things. She was a worldly and grasping woman who was prepared to marry an old, fat man for the sake of money and position. A heartless snob who could judge a man and condemn him for the sins of his grandparents, and an evil-tongued virago who was not above ruining a man's reputation in order to save a few scratches on her own.

He had not spoken or made any attempt to interrupt the tirade, but his disgust must have shown plainly on his face, for Belinda's voice rose suddenly and her hand darted out with the swiftness of a cat's paw to slap his cheek with a violence that jerked his head back and made her palm tingle.

The action took them both by surprise, and for a frozen moment they stared at each other in mutual horror, too startled to speak. Then Ash said grandly: 'Thank you,' and Belinda burst into tears and whirling round, ran to the door, which was, of course, locked.

It was at this juncture that the crunch of wheels on gravel announced the inopportune return of Major and Mrs Harlowe, and the next ten minutes had been, to say the least of it, confused. By the time Ash had been able to get the key out of his pocket and unlock the door, Belinda was in hysterics, and her startled parents were greeted by the sight of a sobbing, screaming daughter bursting out of the drawing-room to rush wildly across the hall and into her bedroom, slamming the door behind her with a bang that reverberated through the bungalow.

Major Harlowe had been the first to recover himself, and what he had had to say on the subject of Ash's manners and general disposition had made unpleasant hearing. Mrs Harlowe had contributed nothing to the interview, having hurried away to comfort her afflicted daughter, and her husband's trenchant summing-up of Ash's character had been conducted against a background of muffled wails and agitated maternal appeals to know what that 'horrid boy' had been doing.

'I intend to take this up with your Commanding Officer,' announced Major Harlowe in conclusion, 'and I am warning you that if I ever catch you so much as attempting to speak to my daughter again, I shall take great pleasure in giving you the thrashing you so richly deserve. Now get out.'

He had given Ash no opportunity to speak, and even if he had done so there was very little to be said that would not have exacerbated the situation still further; apart from an abject apology, which might possibly have been accepted, though it would not have changed anything. But Ash had no intention of apologizing. The boot, he considered, should be on the other foot, and he had confirmed the Major's opinion of him by looking that irate gentleman up and down in a manner that could hardly have been bettered by his Uncle Matthew, and leaving without so much as a word of explanation or regret.

'Insufferable young puppy,' fumed the Major, justifiably incensed; and he retired to his study to compose a forceful letter to the Commandant of the Corps of Guides, while Ash rode back to Mardan with his mind in a turmoil of anger and disgust and sheer, concentrated bitterness.

It was not Belinda's engagement that stuck in his throat. He could have found excuses for that: the Victorian age approved the marriage of young girls to much older men, and it was no uncommon thing for a girl of sixteen or seventeen to marry a man of forty. Mr Podmore-Smyth, whatever his physical disadvantages, was rich, respected and successful, and Belinda had probably been flattered by his attentions and ended by mistaking her admiration for his qualities as something much warmer, and persuading herself that it was love. She was, after all, young and impressionable, and she had always been impulsive. Ash might have forgiven her engagement, but he could neither excuse nor condone her behaviour in the matter of George.

George had undoubtedly told a lot of silly lies, but the revenge Belinda was taking on him was cruelly unjust, for it was not as though he had intended to marry her under false pretences. He knew very well that neither she nor her parents would ever have seriously considered him as a possible husband, and the most he had hoped to do was to make himself more interesting in her eyes and be accepted as an equal by the narrow, insular society of the cantonment. Yet now she was planning to expose him as a liar and a half-caste to that same society, knowing full well that although they might forgive the first, they would neither forgive nor forget the second. George would be ruined socially, for Anglo-India was intensely parochial and the story would follow him up and down the country. Wherever he went there would always be someone who knew it, or had heard it from someone else, and the virtuous middle-class matrons would whisper behind their fans while their daughters snubbed him and their menfolk laughed—and blackballed him at their Clubs.

'It's not fair!' thought Ash passionately. What did it matter who a man's grandmother was? Or his father or mother, if it came to that? He wished now that he had swallowed his pride and his bile and put in a plea for George to Belinda's father. He ought to have spoken up and told that old puffing-billy what his daughter was up to, and that she must be stopped. Except that it was already too late for that, as according to her she had already told several people, and for all he knew, her father might agree with her. Her mother and that tattling woman Mrs Gidney obviously did, and so, presumably, would their friends and acquaintances, all of whom would sympathize with that conceited little bitch, Belinda, and turn on poor George like a pack of wolves. The ugliness and injustice of it stuck in Ash's throat and choked him, and he felt physically ill with disgust.

He had arrived back in Mardan in a black rage and blacker disillusionment. And a few days later Dilasah had absconded with the carbines, and five sowars of his clan, including Malik Shah and Lal Mast, had been stripped of their uniforms and expelled from the Regiment with orders to bring back the stolen carbines or never again show their faces in Mardan . . .

Ash had intended to demand an interview with the Commandant in order to protest against the action that had been taken. But he had been forestalled by the belated arrival of a letter from Major Harlowe, and had been sent for instead to explain himself. The dressing-down he had received from Belinda's father had been nothing to the one he received from his C.O., though most of it went over his head, for once again he was obsessed with an injustice. It was not *fair* that five men of Dilasah Khan's tribe, with impeccable records—men who had never even liked Dilasah, let alone helped him!—should be driven out of the Guides like criminals. He could barely wait for the Commandant to finish speaking before making his own protest; and the fact that he had obviously paid little attention to anything that had been said to him did nothing to improve his case, or the Commandant's temper.

'If anyone is responsible, it's me,' declared Ash with a fine disregard for grammar. *'I'm* the one who ought to be sacked or sent after Dilasah, because I knew there was something wrong somewhere, and I ought to have seen that he didn't get a chance to do anything like this. But Malik and the others had nothing whatever to do with it, and it's not fair that their faces should be blackened in this way. It's not their fault that he belongs to their tribe, and it's downright unjust that—'

He got no further. The Commandant told him in one brief, blistering sentence what others had previously told him at greater length but with less clarity, and dismissed him from the Presence. Ash took his troubles to Zarin, but once again received no encouragement from that quarter, for Zarin considered the Commandant's action to be a wise one. So too did Risaldar Awal Shah.

'How else will he get our rifles back?' demanded Awal Shah. 'We of the whole Guide Corps have scoured the countryside and have not caught so much as a glimpse of Dilasah. But it may be that his own kin will be able to read his mind and follow his trail, and in two days, or three, they will return with the rifles. Thus their honour and ours will be saved.'

Zarin grunted in agreement, and Koda Dad, who happened to be paying a rare visit to his sons, not only sided with them but took Ash to task.

'You talk like a Sahib,' said Koda Dad crossly. 'To prate of injustice in such a matter is foolishness. The Commandant-Sahib is wiser, for he is thinking not as an *Angrezi* but as a Pathan, while you—you who were once Ashok—are looking at this as though you had never been anything but Pelham-Sahib. *Chut!* how many times have I not told you that it is only children who cry "it is not fair"—children and

Sahib-log? Now at last,' added Koda Dad acidly, 'I see that you are indeed a Sahib.'

Ash returned to his quarters sore and discomforted, and as angry as before. Yet even then he might have saved himself from folly if it had not been for George—for George and Belinda . . .

Walking into the mess that night, Ash met one of his fellow subalterns, newly returned from a visit to Headquarters in Peshawar.

'Heard the news about that fellow Garforth?' inquired Cooke-Collis.

'No. And I don't want to, thanks all the same,' retorted Ash rudely. He had not expected the story to spread quite so quickly, and the thought of having to listen to some second-hand or third-hand version of it sickened him.

'Why, didn't you like him?'

Ash ignored the question, and turning his back, hailed a *khidmatgar* and ordered himself a double brandy. But Cooke-Collis was not so easily put off: 'Think I'll have one too. *Hamare waste bhi,** Iman Din. I need it, by jove. Nasty business at any time, but when it's someone you know, it's a bit of a shock, even if you didn't know them very well, and I didn't really; though I'd met him at several dinner-parties and dances and all that sort of thing, because he got asked all over the place. Very popular with the ladies, even though he was only a junior boxwallah. Not that I've anything against boxwallahs, you know; daresay they're a very pleasant lot. But Garforth was the only one you seemed to meet almost everywhere, and I won't deny that it was a nasty shock to hear that he—'

'Was a half-caste,' finished Ash impatiently. 'Yes, I know. And I don't see that it is any concern of yours or anyone else's, so you needn't go on about it.'

'Was he a half-caste? I didn't know that. Are you sure? He didn't look it.'

'Then what on earth are you talking about?' demanded Ash, angry with himself for betraying George's secret to someone who obviously did not know it and would now inevitably hand it on.

'Garforth, of course. He shot himself this afternoon.'

'*What?*' Ash's voice cracked. 'I don't believe it.'

'Perfectly true, I'm afraid. I don't know what he'd been up to, but it seems that several people cut him at the Club last night. Then this

* for me too

morning he got a couple of letters cancelling invitations that he had already accepted, so at lunch time he took two bottles of brandy from the shop, drank 'em both and then shot himself, poor devil. I got it from Billy Carddock who'd just met the doctor coming away from the firm's bungalow. He said they'd no idea what was behind it.'

'I was,' whispered Ash, his face grey and drawn with shock: 'He asked me what I'd do if I were in his place, and I told him . . . I told him—' He shuddered, and pushing the unbearable thought away, said aloud: 'Belinda was behind it. Belinda and all those narrow-minded, bigoted, bourgeois snobs who purred over him while they thought his grandmother was a countess and cut him when they found out that she was only a bazaar woman from Agra. The——, ——!' The end of the softly spoken sentence was in the vernacular and happily unintelligible to young Mr Cooke-Collis, but its virulent obscenity startled the *khidmatgar* into dropping a box of cigars, and drew a shocked protest from a senior Major who happened to be standing within earshot.

'Here, I say,' objected the Major. 'You can't talk like that in mess, Ashton. If you must spout filth, go and do it somewhere else, will you.'

'Don't worry,' said Ash, his voice deceptively gentle. 'I'm going.'

He lifted his glass as though drinking a toast, and having drained it, tossed it over his shoulder in the manner of an earlier day when it had been the custom in some regiments to drink a young queen's health in broken glass. The crash brought conversation to a stop, and in the brief lull that followed, Ash turned on his heel and walked out of the mess.

'Silly young ass,' observed the Major without heat. 'I shall have to give him a talking-to in the morning.'

But Ash was not there in the morning.

His room was empty and his bed had not been slept in, and the sentry who had come on duty at midnight reported that Pelham-Sahib had left the fort shortly after that hour, saying that he could not sleep and would walk for a while. He had been wearing a poshteen and a pair of Pathan trousers, and as far as the sentry could remember had not been carrying anything. His horses were still in the stables, and Ala Yar, questioned by the Adjutant, said that apart from the poshteen and a pair of *chupplis* and some money, the only thing missing from his room was a set of Pathan clothing and an

Afghan knife that his Sahib always kept in a locked box on top of the *almirah* (cupboard). The box had not been in its accustomed place when he, Ala Yar, had brought in his Sahib's *chota hazri* (small breakfast) that morning; it had been on the floor, open and empty. As for the money it was a matter of a few rupees only, and it was certain that no thief had taken it, for his Sahib's gold cuff-links and silver-backed brushes lay on the dressing table where no one could have failed to see them. It was Ala Yar's opinion that his Sahib, being troubled in his mind, had taken leave and followed after the father of Risaldar Awal Shah and Jemadar Zarin Khan, who had been visiting his sons and had left in the late afternoon of the previous day to return to his village.

'Koda Dad Khan is as a father to my Sahib, who has a great affection for him,' said Ala Yar. 'But yesterday there was some small disagreement between them, and it may be my Sahib desires to mend matters and make his peace with the old man, and when he has done so he will return swiftly. No harm will befall him beyond the Border.'

'That's all very well, but he's got no damned business to be beyond the Border—now or at any other time,' retorted the Adjutant, forgetting for a moment whom he was addressing. 'Just you wait until I get my hands on that young—' He recollected himself and dismissed Ala Yar, who returned to the Sahib's quarters to remove the *chota hazri* tray that he had placed on the bedside table in the dawn, and in the agitation of the morning omitted to remove. It was only then that he saw the letter underneath it, for in the dim light of the early morning the envelope had now shown up against the clean cloth that he himself changed daily on the Sahib's table.

Ala Yar had learned to read a little English during his years in *Belait,* and ten minutes later, having deciphered the address, he was in the Commandant's office.

Ash had indeed gone over the Border. But not to visit Koda Dad. He had gone to join Malik Shah and Lal Mast and their fellow clansmen, who had been sent to track down Dilasah and bring back the two stolen rifles. And though search parties were sent out to bring him in, they could find no trace of him. He had vanished as completely as Dilasah had done, and nothing more was heard of him for almost two years.

That afternoon Zarin had gone to the Commandant and asked for special leave so that he might go in search of Pelham-Sahib. But this had been refused, and a few hours later, after a long talk with Mahdoo and a shorter and slightly acrimonious one with Zarin, Ala Yar had gone instead.

'I am the Sahib's servant, and he has not yet dismissed me from his service,' said Ala Yar. 'There is also the promise that I made to Anderson-Sahib that I would see to it that the boy came to no harm, and as you cannot go after him, I must do so. That is all.'

'I would go if I could,' growled Zarin. 'But I too am a servant. I serve the Sirkar and I cannot do as I please.'

'I know. Therefore I go in your stead.'

'You are an old fool,' said Zarin angrily.

'Maybe,' agreed Ala Yar without rancour.

He left Mardan an hour before sunset, and Mahdoo accompanied him for a mile along the track that leads towards Afghanistan and stood to watch him grow smaller and smaller against the vast, desolate background of the plain and the Border hills, until at last the sun went down and the dusty purple twilight hid him from sight.

Book Three

World out of Time

13

'There are men out there. Beyond the nullah, to the left,' said one of the sentries, peering out at the moonlit plain. 'Look—they are moving this way.'

His companion turned to stare in the direction of the pointing finger, and after a moment or two laughed and shook his head. 'Gazelle. This drought has made the *chinkara* so bold that they do not fear to approach within a stone's throw. But if those clouds yonder do not fail us, there should soon be grass in plenty.'

The summer of 1874 had been a particularly trying one. The monsoon had been late and scanty and the plains around Mardan were burned to a dry golden-brown in which no trace of green showed. Dust-devils danced all day among the mirages and the parched thorn bushes, and the rivers ran low and sluggishly between banks of blinding white sand.

There was no grass on the hills either, and most of the game had moved up the far valleys in search of food. Only a few wild pig and *chinkara* had remained, and these plundered the fields of the villagers by night, and would occasionally even venture into the cantonment to eat the shrubs in Hodson's garden, or nibble the leaves of the mulberry tree that marked the place where Colonel Spottiswood had killed himself over seventeen years ago. The sentries had become so accustomed to the sight of them that a dark shape skirting the parade ground or moving among the shadows no longer brought a challenge followed by the crack of a carbine; and in any case, the section of Frontier adjacent to Mardan had been quiet for so long that men were becoming used to peace.

There had been no 'Border incidents' for over five years, and the Guides had had no active soldiering to occupy them. They had provided an escort under Jemadar Siffat Khan to accompany a new Envoy on a mission to Kashgar, and a year later two of the escort had carried the completed treaty from Kashgar to Calcutta in sixty days. A sepoy of the Guides Infantry had been detailed to accompany a messenger across the Oxus and from there, by way of Badakshan and Kabul, to India, and a sowar of the Cavalry, who had been sent to Persia with a British officer bound on a special mission, had been killed on the road to Teheran while defending the baggage from a gang of robbers. The Corps itself had taken part in a year-long 'camp of exercise' at Hasan Abdal, from where it had returned to Mardan in February of that year, to occupy itself with the normal routine of cantonment life, and pray throughout that hot weather for rain to temper the remorseless heat.

September had been as scorching as July, but now October was almost out, and the mercury in the thermometer that hung in the mess verandah retreated daily. Men went abroad again at midday, and the wind that blew off the mountains at sunset carried a refreshing edge of coolness. But apart from a few brief and isolated showers there had been no sign of the autumn rains—until tonight, when for the first time in many months there were clouds in the sky . . .

'This time—*Shukr Allah**—they will not fail us,' said the sentry devoutly. 'The wind is behind them and I can smell rain.'

'I too,' said his companion. The two men sniffed appreciatively, and as a sudden gust whirled up the dust and obscured any further movement on the plain, they turned together and continued on their rounds.

The wind had been blowing only fitfully since moonrise, but now it steadied and blew strongly, driving the banked clouds before it until presently they reached the moon and blotted it out. A quarter of an hour later the first swollen drops of rain splashed down out of the darkness: forerunners of a lashing torrent that within seconds turned the dust of the long, scorching summer into a sea of mud, and transformed every dry nullah and ditch into a fully fledged river.

Under cover of darkness and that raging bedlam of noise and water, the handful of men that one of the sentries had mistaken for *chinkara* passed the outposts unseen. But head-down against the wind-driven rain, they missed their way and were challenged by the guard on the gate of the fort.

It had been no part of their plan to be dragged before Authority that night. They had hoped to reach the cavalry lines without being detected, and to lie up there until morning; but as it was, the havildar in charge of the guard had sent for the Indian officer on duty, who in turn sent for the Duty Officer; and presently the Adjutant was fetched from the mess where he had been playing whist, and the Second-in-Command, who had retired early, aroused from his bed.

The Commandant had also retired early, but not to sleep. He had

* thanks be to God

been writing his weekly letters home when he was interrupted by the entrance of two of his officers, accompanied by as sorry an object as had ever been seen in that room. A gaunt, bearded tribesman with a bandaged head, from whose tattered blanket, worn cloak-wise in the manner of the Frontier, a dozen little rivulets poured onto the Commandant's cherished Shiraz carpet. The bandage too leaked a steady red-stained trickle down one hollow and unshaven cheek, and the blanket that clung wetly to the man's scare-crow body failed to conceal that he held something long and bulky under its sodden folds. He let his arms drop, and the carbines that he had been carrying slid down and fell with a clatter into the circle of light shed by the oil lamp on the writing table.

'There they are, sir,' said Ash. 'I'm sorry . . . we took so long . . . about it, but . . . it wasn't as easy as . . . we'd thought.'

The Commandant stared at him and did not speak. He found it difficult to believe that this was the boy who had stormed into his office nearly two years ago. This was a man. A tall one, for he had come late to his full height, and lean with the leanness of hard muscle and harder living. His eyes were sunk deep in his head, and he was ragged, unkempt and wounded, and dazed with fatigue. But he held himself erect and forced his tongue to the English that it had not spoken for so long:

'I must . . . apologize, sir,' said Ash haltingly, the words blurred by exhaustion, 'for . . . letting you see us like—like this. We didn't mean . . . We meant to spend the night with Zarin and—make ourselves presentable, and in the morning . . . But the storm—' His voice failed and he made a vague and entirely oriental gesture with one hand.

The Commandant turned to the Adjutant and said curtly: 'Are the others out there?'

'Yes, sir. All except Malik Shah.'

'He's dead,' said Ash tiredly.

'And Dilasah Khan?'

'He too. We got back most of the ammunition. He hadn't used much of it. Lal Mast has it . . .' Ash stared down at the carbines for a long moment, and said with sudden bitterness: 'I hope they're worth it. They cost three lives. That is a high price to pay for anything.'

'For honour?' suggested the Commandant in the same curt voice.

'Oh—*honour!*' said Ash; and laughed mirthlessly. 'Malik and Ala Yar . . . Ala Yar.' His voice broke and his eyes were suddenly full of tears. He said harshly: 'May I go now, sir?' And almost as he spoke he fell forward, as a tree falls, and lay sprawled and unconscious across the cavalry carbines that had been stolen two years ago and recovered at the cost of three lives. One of them Ala Yar's . . .

'He'll have to be cashiered, of course,' said the Second-in-Command.

His tone made the remark less an assertion than a query, and his Commanding Officer, who had been drawing complicated patterns on the blotting paper, looked up sharply.

'Well, I mean—it seems a pity,' said the Major defensively. 'After all, when you come to think of it, it was a damned fine show. I've been talking to Lal Mast and the others and they—'

'So, oddly enough, have I,' interrupted the Commandant with some asperity. 'And if you intend to play Devil's Advocate, you're wasting your time. I don't need one.'

Two days had passed since Ash and his four companions had stumbled into Mardan, but the rain was still falling and the little fort was loud with the sound of water drumming upon the flat roofs, cascading from pipes and gutters, and splashing into the inch-deep lake that had replaced the dusty paths and parched lawns of the previous week. Malik Shah's family were to be awarded a pension, and his four fellow-tribesmen had been congratulated and reinstated, their uniforms returned and two years' back-pay handed over to them. But Lieutenant Pelham-Martyn, who faced a charge of Absent Without Leave for the space of twenty-three months and two days, was technically under close arrest—though in actual fact confined to bed in the quarters of the Medical Officer, Ambrose Kelly, with a high fever due to a head wound that had become septic. His fate and his future were still under discussion.

'You mean you agree with me?' demanded the Major, startled.

'Of course I do. Why else should I have bothered to go over to Peshawar yesterday? You don't suppose I spent over an hour jawing with the Commissioner, and two more arguing with an assortment of brass-hats, just for the fun of it, do you? Ashton's an insubordinate young bastard, but he's too valuable to throw away. Look—what's the most useful thing to any military commander who is planning a campaign or trying to keep order in a country like this? Information!

Early and accurate information is worth more than all the guns and ammunition one could ask for, and that's why I'm going to fight like a steer to keep that young idiot. I don't imagine any other Corps could get away with it; but then we're not like any other Corps. We've always been pretty unorthodox, and if one of our officers can spend a couple of years on the other side of the Border without being spotted as an Englishman or shot as a spy, he's too bloody useful to lose and that's all there is to it. Though mark you, what he really deserves is a Court Martial. *And* they'd cashier him.'

'But what the hell are we going to do with him?' demanded the Major. 'We can't just let him stay on here as though nothing had happened, can we?'

'No, of course not. The sooner he leaves Mardan the better. I propose to see if I can't get him transferred to another unit for a couple of years. Preferably a British one, where he can cool his heels and mix with his own people for a change. He needs to get right away from his friends and the Frontier for a while; and it won't do him any harm to go somewhere down south.'

'He'll probably get into even more trouble there,' observed the Major pessimistically. 'After all, he was brought up as a Hindu, wasn't he?'

'What of it? The point is, he can't stay here just now. It would have a bad effect on discipline.'

Which is why Ashton Pelham-Martyn came to be stationed in Rawalpindi that winter.

If his Commanding Officer had had his way, Ash would have been sent somewhere a good deal further off. For although Rawalpindi is hardly true Frontier country (which in the north-west is held to start at Hasan Abdal, once a posting-stage of the Mogul Emperors on their journeys to Kashmir) it lies only one hundred and thirteen miles to the south-east of Mardan. But as the main object of those in authority had been to remove the offender from his regiment as soon as possible, and as the 'Pindi Brigade had been unable to provide an immediate vacancy (Ash would have been surprised to learn how many strings had been pulled to engineer that unorthodox posting), it would have to do for the present. Meanwhile the Commandant of the Guides had been promised that at the first opportunity Mr Pelham-Martyn would be moved further down south, and that on no account whatever would he be permitted to put so much as a foot inside the North-West Frontier Province, or go back across the Indus.

In the unlikely event of there being anyone there who could recall having seen him when he stopped at the 'Pindi dâk-bungalow on his way from Bombay to Mardan, over three years ago, they would certainly not have known him now, for he had changed beyond recognition—and not only outwardly. As a child in the Gulkote days he would, by European standards, have been considered old for his age; the city and the Hawa Mahal made few concessions to youth, and he had made an early acquaintance with the facts of life and death and evil. Yet later on, as a boy among boys of his own blood, he had seemed curiously young, for he had retained a child's way of looking at a problem and seeing it in the simplest possible terms, without realizing—or perhaps merely ignoring—the fact that every question is likely to have more than two sides to it.

Arriving back in Rawalpindi that winter he was still only twenty-two. But he had grown up at last—though he was always to retain a trace of the child and the boy and the young man he had once been, and despite the strictures of Koda Dad, to continue to see things as 'fair' or 'unfair'. But he had learned many things in the land beyond the Border, not least among them to ride his temper on a tight rein, to think more carefully before he spoke, to curb his impatience and (surprisingly enough) to laugh.

Superficially, the change in him was more noticeable. For though he had removed both beard and moustache, the boyish look had gone for ever and his face bore deep, unyouthful lines that had been etched there by hunger and grief and hard living. It also bore a long, angry-looking scar that ran up into his hair above his left temple, pulling up one eyebrow and giving him a quizzical look which oddly enough was far from unattractive, and looking at him now one would have said he was a remarkably handsome man—and also, in some indefinable way, a dangerous one: someone to be reckoned with . . .

Accompanied by Gul Baz and Mahdoo, who was very shrivelled now and beginning to feel his years, Ash arrived in Rawalpindi to find that he had been allotted a half share in part of a small, dilapidated bungalow largely given over to offices and the storing of files. The quarters were cramped and dark, but compared with the places he had slept in during the past two years they seemed palatial; and having lived cheek-by-jowl with his fellow men for months on end, he had no objection at all to sharing them. The cantonment suffered from a chronic shortage of accommodation, and he was, in fact, lucky not to be sharing a tent. And even luckier, as it turned out, in his stable-companion; though a gangling young ensign almost four years his junior, newly arrived from Home and addicted to writing bad verse, was probably the last person whom Ash himself would have selected for a roommate. Yet surprisingly, it proved to be a great success. The two had taken to each other from the outset and were soon to find that they had a great deal in common.

Ensign Walter Richard Pollock Hamilton of the 70th Foot was at that time only a year younger than Ash had been when he landed at Bombay. And like Ash, he saw India as a wonderful and mysterious country, full of endless possibilities for excitement and adventure. He was a pleasant youth, good-tempered, high-spirited and intensely romantic—and he too had fallen desperately in love with a yellow-haired chit of sixteen during the voyage from England. The girl had had no objection to flirting with the tall handsome boy, but his suit had been rejected out of hand on the score of his youth, and two days out of Bombay she had become engaged to an elderly gentleman who must have been at least twice her age: 'Thirty, if he was a day,' declared Walter disgustedly. 'And a civilian too. Some dreary fellow in the Political Department. Would you believe it, now?'

'Only too easily,' said Ash. 'Belinda, let me tell you—'

But that story, as he told it now, was no longer a tragic one, and any bitterness that remained was solely on George Garforth's account. For this was something else that had altered during the past two years; and looking back on his abortive romance, Ash could not only recognize it for the foolish and ephemeral thing it had been, but also see the comic side of it. Retold to Walter, the chronicle of his misfortune lost all trace of tragedy, and eventually became so hilarious that the ghost of Belinda was exorcized for ever, swept away on a gale of laughter into the limbo that is reserved for forgotten love-affairs. Walter's flirtatious sixteen-year-old had followed her there, and he celebrated the fact by writing a ribald poem entitled 'Ode to Forsaken Subalterns', that would have surprised and pained his fond relatives—who were used to more elevated out-pourings from 'dear Wally'.

Wally rather fancied himself as a writer of verse. It was the only thing in which his sense of humour failed him, and his letters home were apt to contain deplorably amateur poems that were passed round the family circle and greatly admired by doting aunts and similar biased and unqualified critics, who considered them to be quite as good as 'dear Mr Tennyson's'. And wrote to say so. The 'Ode', however, was in a very different style from any of his previous effusions, and Ash translated it into Urdu and had it set to music by a Kashmiri singer of his acquaintance. It subsequently achieved quite a success in the 'Pindi bazaar, and versions of it (the more colourful ones) were sung for many years throughout the Punjab.

Wally himself was no mean singer, though the songs he sang were less secular. He had been a member of his school choir for several years, and nowadays, when he felt the urge to sing (which was often, for he sang whenever he was happy or exhilarated), he would launch into one of the more militant hymns of his youth: 'Fight the good fight', 'Onward Christian Soldiers!', 'Forward be our watchword!' or 'For all the Saints'—the last being a special favourite. There was no irreverence in this: Wally approved the sentiments and genuinely liked the familiar melodies (he said they were 'corking tunes') and could see no reason why hymns should only be sung in church; particularly the ones that conjured up for him visions of banners and trumpets and legions of armed men charging into battle to smite the troops of Midian. His fondness for these stirring anthems meant that the day in the bungalow invariably began with the sound of a baritone voice, accompanied by much splashing of bath water, announcing melodiously that 'Time like an ever-rolling stream bears all its sons away', or, alternatively, demanding 'Oh, let thy soldiers, faithful true and bold, fight as the Saints who nobly fought of old, and win with them the Victor's crown of gold—Alle—luia! *Al—le—lu—ia!*' Similar hymns frequently enlivened the evening rides, and once Wally had raced down the polo ground and scored the winning goal in the last two seconds of a hard-fought match, chanting 'Forward into battle see our banners go!'

These and other 'Wally-isms', such as his occasional use of brogue, were an endless source of amusement to Ash. Though it is probable that in anyone else he would have found them tiresome or dismissed them, scornfully, as affectation. But then Wally was . . . Wally—*fidus Achates*.

Apart from Zarin, who had been more like an elder brother to him, Ash had never had a really close friend. He seemed to have no talent for friendship with those of his own blood. At school and the Military Academy, and later in the Regiment, he had always been something of a loner; an observer rather than a participant; and even at the height of his popularity as an athlete, no one had been able to claim that they knew him well or were on particularly friendly terms with him, though many would have liked to do so. But then he had never cared whether he was liked or not, and though, on the whole, he had been, it had been a luke-warm emotion, which was largely his own fault. Yet now, and entirely unexpectedly, he had found the friend that he had missed in those earlier years.

From the moment of their meeting he had felt at ease with Walter; so much so, that he had told him what he had told no one else, not even Zarin—the full tale of the grim tracking-down of Dilasah Khan and the death of Ala Yar and Malik. The savage revenge that the hunters had taken on the thief and killer, the long, terrible journey back through territory held by hostile tribes who had hunted the hunters, and the ambush that had been laid for them on the very fringe of the Border by several men of the Utman Khel who had seen and coveted the carbines, and from which they had barely escaped with their lives after Ash and Lal Mast had been wounded . . .

It was a story that the Commandant of the Guides had heard, in part, from the four men of Dilasah's tribe, though not from Ash, who had initially been too ill to be interrogated, and had later confined himself to answering questions in the fewest possible words. Ash's official account of those two years had been colourless in the extreme. But the full story was anything but colourless, and Walter—himself the stuff of which heroes are made—had listened enthralled and become a hero-worshipper in his turn. There was no one like Ash! And, naturally, no regiment like the Guides.

Walter had always meant to be a soldier. The heroes of his childhood had been Joshua and David, Alexander the Great and Rupert of the Rhine, and all his dreams were of military glory. They were very private dreams and he had never imagined himself being able to talk of them to anyone. Yet he had talked of them to Ash, and without embarrassment, and taken a good deal of ribbing on the subject with unimpaired good temper.

'The trouble with you, Wally,' said Ash, 'is that you've been born too late. You ought to have been a cavalier. Or one of Henry's knights at Agincourt. But there are no worlds left to conquer now—and precious little glamour or chivalry about modern warfare.'

'Perhaps not in Europe,' agreed Wally, 'but that's why I wanted to come out here. It's different in India.'

'Don't you believe it.'

'But it *is!* It must be, in a country where guns are still dragged by elephants and the rank and file of a Regiment like yours have competed for the honour of serving in it. Your sowars and sepoys are not pressed men, or riff-raff from the slums of big cities like Lahore and Peshawar. They're yeomen—gentlemen adventurers who have enlisted for honour. It's magnificent.'

'I can see that you are a hopeless idealist,' said Ash drily.

'And it's a misbegotten cynic you are,' retorted Wally. 'Haven't you ever wanted to storm an impregnable position or defend an impossible one? I have. I'd like to lead a cavalry charge, or a forlorn hope. And I'd like my countrymen to remember me as they remember men like Philip Sidney and Sir John Moore. And him over there: *"Nikalseyne"*—'

They had been riding across the open country west of 'Pindi, and Wally flung out an arm to point at a rocky hillock on the horizon, crowned by a granite obelisk that commemorated the name of John Nicholson, killed while leading an assault during the battle for Delhi, seventeen years ago. 'That's the way I'd like to die. Gloriously—with a sword in my hand and at the head of my men.'

Ash observed dampingly that Nicholson's men had failed to follow him, and that he had in fact lingered on in agony for at least three days after being shot.

'What if he did? That's not the way he'll be remembered. Alexander said it all more than two thousand years ago'—there was a glow in the boy's eyes and his face had flushed like a girl's—' *"It is a lovely thing to live with courage, and to die leaving behind an everlasting renown."* I read that when I was ten, and I've never forgotten it. That's exactly—'

He broke off as a sudden shiver made his teeth chatter, and Ash said: 'Goose walking over your grave—and serve you right. Speaking for myself, I'd rather play safe and live to a ripe and undistinguished old age.'

'Oh, rats!' retorted Wally scornfully, firm in the conviction that his friend was a hero. 'It's getting damned chilly out here. Race you to the road.'

Ash was no stranger to hero-worship. He had received a good deal of it from his juniors in the days when he had been a member of the first eleven at his school, and later when he had played for the Military Academy; and once, long ago, from a little girl; 'a small sour-looking little thing like an unripe mango'. He had never taken it very seriously and had in general found it either irritating or embarrassing; and on occasions, both. But Wally's admiration was different, and it warmed his heart because it was a tribute from a friend, and not slavish adulation for mere physical prowess and skill at games, regardless of whether the possessor of it was, in himself, an admirable or a despicable character; or a dull one.

The two became known in Rawalpindi as 'The Inseparables' and if one were seen without the other there was always someone to call out: 'Hullo David—what have you done with Jonathan?' or 'Blowed if it ain't Wally! I didn't recognize you without Pandy—you look improperly dressed.' These and other equally foolish pleasantries had at first attracted the disapproving attention of several senior officers, none of whom would have objected very much to their juniors keeping half-caste mistresses or visiting the harlot's quarter of the bazaar (always provided they were discreet about it) but who had a horror of what they termed 'unnatural vice'.

To these grey-beards any close friendship between young men was suspect, and they feared the worst; but careful inquiry revealed nothing half-caste mistresses or visiting the harlots' quarter of the bazaar officer. In that respect at least, both were unquestionably 'normal'— as Lalun, for one (the most alluring and expensive courtesan in the city), could have testified. Not that their visits to such establishments were very frequent; their tastes lay in other directions, and Lalun and her kind merely represented experience: one of many. Together they rode, raced and played polo, shot partridge on the plains and *chikor* among the hills, fished or went swimming in the rivers, and spent far more than they could afford on buying horses.

They read voraciously—military history, memoirs, poetry, essays, novels: De Quincey, Dickens, Thackeray and Walter Scott; Shakespeare, Euripides and Marlowe; Gibbon's *Decline and Fall,* Balzac's *La Comédie Humaine* and Darwin's *Descent of Man* . . . Tacitus and the Koran, and as much of the literature of the country as they could get their hands on—their tastes were catholic and all was grist to their mill. Wally was working for his Lieutenancy and Ash coached him in Pushtu and Hindustani, and talked to him by the hour of India and its peoples; not the British India of cantonments and Clubs, or the artificial world of hill stations and horse shows, but that other India: that mixture of glamour and tawdriness, viciousness and nobility. A land full of gods and gold and famine. Ugly as a rotting corpse and beautiful beyond belief . . .

'I still think of it as my own country, and that I belong here,' confessed Ash, 'even though I've learned that feeling one belongs doesn't mean much, unless one is accepted as belonging; which I am not—except by Koda Dad, and sometimes by strangers who don't know my history. To those who do, it seems I am and always will be a "Sahib". Though when I was young I was, or thought I was, a Hindu for almost seven years—a life-time, to a child. In those days it never occurred to me or to anyone else that I was not one, yet now no high-caste Hindu would care to sit at the same table with me, and many would have to throw away their food if my shadow fell on it, and wash themselves if I so much as touched them. Even the humblest would break any dish or cup that I had eaten or drunk from, so that no one else would be defiled by using it. That sort of thing isn't so with Mohammedans, of course; but when we were hunting Dilasah Khan and I lived and fought and thought as one of them, I don't think that any of the men who knew who I was ever really forgot it. And as I can't seem to learn to think of myself as a Sahib or an Englishman, I presume that I am what the Foreign Office would call "A stateless person". A citizen of no-man's-land.'

' "That Paradise of Fools, to few unknown",' quoted Wally.

'What's that?'

'Limbo—according to Milton.'

'Oh. Yes, you may be right. Though I wouldn't have described it as a Paradise, myself.'

'It might have its advantages,' suggested Wally.

'Maybe. But I admit I can't think of any,' said Ash wryly.

Once, sitting out in the warm moonlight among the ruins of Taxila (the 'Pindi Brigade was in camp), he had spoken of Sita, which was another thing that he had never been able to do before. Not even to Zarin and Koda Dad, who had known her.

'. . . so you see, Wally,' concluded Ash reflectively, 'whatever people say, she was my real mother. I never knew the other one and somehow I can't believe in her; though I've seen a picture of her of course. She must have been a very pretty woman, and I don't suppose that Mata-ji—Sita—was pretty. But then she always looked beautiful to me, and I suppose it's because of her that I feel that this country, and not England, is my own. Anyway, Englishmen don't talk about their mothers. It's considered to be either "soppy" or "bad form"—I forget which.'

'Both, I think,' said Wally, and added smugly: 'Though I'm allowed to, of course. It's one of the privileges of being Irish. Sentiment is expected of us. It's a great relief. Your foster-mother must have been a remarkable woman.'

'She was. I didn't realize just how remarkable until much later on. One takes such a lot for granted when one is young. She had more courage than anyone I have ever known. The best kind of courage, for she was always afraid. I know that now, though I didn't then. And she was such a little woman. She was so small that I . . .'

He broke off and sat staring out across the plain, remembering how easy it had been for an eleven-year-old boy to lift her in his arms and carry her down to the river . . .

The night wind smelt of wood-smoke from the camp fires, and very faintly of pine trees from the near-by foothills that lay like wrinkled velvet in the moonlight. Perhaps it was that last that had recalled the ghost of Sita. 'She used to talk to me about a valley in the mountains,' said Ash slowly. 'I suppose it must have been her home, where she was born. She was a hill-woman, you know. We were going to go and live there one day and build a house and plant fruit trees and keep a goat and a donkey. I wish I knew where it was.'

'Didn't she ever tell you?' asked Wally.

'She may have done once. If she did, I've forgotten. But I imagine it's somewhere in the Pir Panjal; though I always used to think it must be in the mountains below the Dur Khaima. You don't know about the Dur Khaima, do you? It's the highest mountain in the range you can see from Gulkote: a great crown of snow peaks. I used to say my prayers to it. Silly, isn't it?'

'Not really. Did you ever read *Aurora Leigh?*—"*Earth's crammed with heaven, and every common bush afire with God; but only he who sees takes off his shoes.*" You were merely taking off your shoes —that's all. And you aren't the only one either: millions of people must have felt the same, for there are holy mountains all over the world. And then there was David, of course: "*Levavi oculos*"—'

Ash laughed. 'I know. It's funny you should say that. I used to think of the Dur Khaima every time we sang that in chapel.' He turned to face the foothills and faraway line of the mountains that rose up behind them, dark against the stars, and quoted in an undertone: ' "I will lift up mine eyes unto the hills, from whence cometh my help." D'you know, Wally, when I first came to England and didn't know any better, I tried to find out in what direction the Himalayas lay so that I could face that way when I said my prayers, like Koda Dad and Zarin, who always faced towards Mecca. I remember my aunt was simply horrified. She told the vicar that I was not only a heathen, but a devil-worshipper.'

'You can see her point,' said Wally tolerantly. 'Now I was luckier. Fortunately for me, my family never discovered that for years I thought I was praying to my godfather. Well, you can see how it was —"God-the-Father"—it was perfectly obvious to me. Particularly as the old boy had an impressive set of white whiskers and a gold watch-chain, and every one was terrified of him. I can tell you it gave me no end of a jolt when I finally discovered that he wasn't really God and that I'd been sending my petitions to the wrong address. All those years of earnest supplication straight down the drain. It was a disaster, so it was.'

Ash's shout of laughter woke the occupant of the nearest tent, and an irate voice urged them to shut up and let a fellow sleep.

Wally grinned and lowered his voice. 'No, seriously now, it was the waste that worried me most. But I've come to the conclusion that it's the intention that counts. My prayers had been perfectly genuine, as I expect yours were too, so the fact that they were wrongly addressed was an error for which I do not believe the Almighty will hold us responsible.'

'I hope you're right. Do you still say your prayers, Wally?'

'Of course,' said Wally, genuinely surprised. 'Don't you?'

'Sometimes. Though I'm not sure who I address them to.' Ash stood up and slapped the dust and dried grass from his clothes. 'Come on, Galahad, it's time we turned in. This bloody exercise is due to start at 3 a.m.'

In the circumstances it was hardly surprising that Wally should have set his heart on joining the Guides, though there was, as yet, very little that he could do about it because he must first pass for his Lieutenancy. Ash had been in some doubt whether a good word from him might not hinder rather than help his friend's chances of being offered a vacancy, so he had used a more oblique method and introduced him to Lieutenant Wigram Battye of the Guides, who had twice been over to Rawalpindi on duty. And, later on, to Zarin.

Zarin had taken short leave in the heat of June and ridden into 'Pindi bringing messages from his father and brother, and news of the Regiment and the Frontier. He had not been able to stay for long as the monsoon was due at any moment, and once it broke, the fords would be impassable and travelling become a slow business; but he had stayed long enough to gain an excellent impression of Ashok's new friend. Ash had made certain that Zarin should see for himself that the boy was an admirable shot and a born rider, and had encouraged the two to talk, knowing that under his own unorthodox tutorage, and the more scholarly methods of a Munshi, Wally had already made great strides in the two main tongues of the Frontier. And though Ash had said nothing in his praise, Mahdoo had said a great deal:

'That is a good Sahib,' said Mahdoo, gossiping with Zarin on the back verandah. 'One of the old kind, such as Anderson-Sahib was in his youth. Courteous and kind, and with the bearing and courage of a king. Our boy has become a changed man since they met. Cheerful again, and full of laughter and jokes. Yes, good boys both.'

Zarin had learnt to respect the old man's judgement, and Wally's own character and personality did the rest. Wigram Battye too watched and listened and approved; and both he and Zarin carried favourable reports back to Mardan, with the result that the Guides, always on the look-out for good material, took note of Ensign Walter Hamilton of the 70th Foot as a possible future addition to their Corps.

The hot weather that year had not been as abominable as the previous one, but it was Wally's first and he suffered all the torments that can beset the novice undergoing his first experience of soaring temperatures. Prickly-heat, boils and sandfly-fever, dysentery, dengi and other hot-weather maladies plagued him by turn, and eventually he went down with a severe attack of heat-stroke and spent several days in a darkened room, convinced that he was dying—and with nothing done of all the many things he had hoped to do. On the advice of the M.O., his Colonel had packed him off to the hills to recuperate, and Ash had managed to get leave and gone with him.

Accompanied by Mahdoo and Gul Baz, the two had left by tonga for Muree, where rooms had been booked for them in one of the hotels that at this time of year were full of summer visitors escaping from the blazing heat of the plains.

Wally celebrated his own escape by falling in love with three young ladies at once: a pretty girl who sat with her mother at a nearby table in the dining-room, and the twin daughters of a High-Court Judge who had hired a cottage in the hotel grounds. His inability to choose between them prevented any of these affairs from becoming serious, but they inspired him to write a good deal of love-lorn verse, all of it deplorable, and led him to accept so many invitations to dine, dance or take tea that if Ash had not intervened, his chances of enjoying the rest and quiet advocated by the doctor would have been minimal. But Ash had no intention of wasting his leave dancing attendance on 'a bunch of bird-witted girls and giddy grass-widows', and said so with considerable force—adding a rider to the effect that in his opinion the objects of Wally's divided devotion were three of the most insipid damsels this side of Suez, and his doggerel was worthy of them.

'The trouble with you,' retorted the incensed poet, touched on the raw, 'is that you have no soul. And what's more, if you're going to go on posing as a misogynist for the rest of your life just because some silly chit gave your fresh young illusions a black eye and a bloody nose a few years ago, you haven't any sense either. It's about time you got over Bertha or Bella or Belinda or whatever her name was, and realized that there are other women in the world—and very charming ones too. Not,' conceded Wally generously, 'that you have to marry them, of course. I don't think, myself, that a soldier should get married until he's at least thirty-five.'

' "A Daniel come to judgement"!' mocked Ash. 'Well, in that case, the sooner we remove ourselves from temptation the better.'

They removed themselves to Kashmir, leaving most of their luggage behind in the hotel and hiring hill ponies for the long trek between Murree and Baramullah, from where they turned aside to shoot duck on the Wula Lake and red bear and *barasingh* in the mountains above it.

It was Wally's first experience of high mountains, and gazing at the white crest of Nanga Parbat, the 'Naked Mountain', rising tall and stately above the long range of snows that ring Lalla Rookh's fabled valley, he could understand the awe that had moved Ash as a small boy to pray to the Dur Khaima. The whole country seemed extravagantly beautiful to him, from the lotus-strewn lakes and the winding, willow-fringed rivers, to the vast forests of deodar and chestnut that swept upwards to meet the shale and the great glaciers that lay above the snow line. He was loth to leave it, and 'Pindi seemed hotter and dustier and more unpleasant than ever as their tonga rattled along the cantonment road on the last day of leave, bringing them back once more to their bungalow. But the mountain air and the long days spent in the open had done their work. He returned fit and well, and suffered no more illness during the remainder of that hot weather.

The heat had not worried Ash, but desk work bored him to distraction and there was always too much of that in Rawalpindi. Zarin, riding over from Mardan, told him that the Guides were to provide an escort for the eldest son of the *Padishah* (the Queen) when he visited Lahore during his tour of India in the coming cold weather.

'It's a great honour,' said Zarin, 'and I grieve that you will have no share in it. How much longer do they mean to keep you here, tied to a desk? It is nearly a year now. Soon it will be three years since you last served with the Guide Corps, and that is far too long. It is time you came back to us.'

But the authorities did not agree with this view. They had made a promise to send Lieutenant Pelham-Martyn further away from the Frontier as soon as a suitable opportunity presented itself, and now, nearly eleven months later, they roused themselves from the lethargy induced by the hot weather, and redeemed it.

A letter had come from the Governor of the Punjab's First Secretary requesting them, on behalf of His Excellency, to nominate a suitable British officer to escort the two sisters of His Highness the Maharajah of Karidkote, to Rajputana, to be married to the Rana of Bhithor. The officer's principal duty on the march would consist of seeing that His Highness's sisters were received with due honour and the proper salutes by any British garrisons on the route, and that their camp was adequately provisioned. On arrival in Bhitor he would be expected to see that the agreed bride-price was paid and the brides safely married, before accompanying the camp back to the borders of Karidkote. Taking all this into account, and bearing in mind that the camp was likely to be a large one, it was essential that the officer selected should not only be a fluent linguist, but have a thorough knowledge of the native character and the customs of the country.

It was that final paragraph that had brought Lieutenant Pelham-Martyn's name to mind; and the fact that the assignment would certainly take him well away from the North-West Frontier had served to clinch the matter. Ash himself had not been invited to express any opinions or allowed the option of refusing the appointment. He had merely been sent for and given his orders.

'What they appear to want,' said Ash disgustedly, describing the interview to Wally, 'is someone to act as a combination of sheep-dog, supply officer and nursemaid to a parcel of squealing women and palace parasites; and I'm it. Oh well, bang goes polo for this season. Who'd be a peace-time soldier?'

'Faith, if you ask me, it's a lucky divil you are,' said Wally enviously. 'I only wish they'd chosen me. Just think of it—jaunting off across India in charge of a pair of beautiful princesses.'

'Pair of bun-faced dowds, more likely,' returned Ash sourly. 'Bet you anything they're fat, spoilt and spotty—and still in the schoolroom.'

'Blather! All princesses are ravishingly beautiful. Or they should be, anyway. I can just picture them: rings on their fingers and bells on their toes, and hair like Rapunzel's—no, she was a blonde, wasn't she? They'll be brunettes. I adore brunettes. You wouldn't be asking if I could go along with you, would you now? As a sort of right-hand-man: head cook and bottle-washer? You're sure to need one.'

'Like rabies,' observed Ash inelegantly.

Fifteen days later he said goodbye to Wally, and accompanied by Mahdoo and Gul Baz, his head-syce Kulu Ram, a grass-cutter and half-a-dozen lesser retainers, set out for Deenagunj, a small town in British India where the wedding party, at present under the charge of a local District Officer, awaited his arrival.

14

Deenagunj lay on the fringe of the foothills, a day's march from the border of the independent State of Karidkote and some twenty miles from the nearest British garrison.

Barely more than a village, it was indistinguishable from a hundred other little towns in the northern half of the territory that is watered by the Chenab, the Ravi and the Beas Rivers, and its population seldom rose above two thousand. At the present moment, however, this figure had been disastrously increased, the Governor's secretary having under-stated the case when he expressed the opinion that the bridal camp was 'likely to be a large one', as it was, in point of fact, enormous.

The assembly sent by the Maharajah of Karidkote to escort his sisters to their wedding outnumbered the citizens of Deenagunj by almost four to one, and Ash arrived to find the town a mere annex to the camp, the bazaar sold out of all foodstuffs and fodder and rapidly running short of water, the city-fathers in a state of near hysteria and the District Officer, nominally in control of the camp, down with malaria.

It was a situation that might well have daunted a great many older and more experienced men than Ash. But the authorities had, after all, not chosen so badly when they nominated Lieutenant Pelham-Martyn (temporarily elevated to the rank of Captain by virtue of his office) for this particular mission. The uproar and confusion that would have conveyed, to an alien eye, an impression of riot, aroused no dismay in one who had been brought up in the bazaars of an Indian city and become accustomed at an early age to the extravagance, muddle and intrigue of life in the palace of an Indian prince.

The size and disorganization of the camp did not strike Ash as in any way remarkable, for he had not forgotten Lalji's wedding and the army of attendants that had accompanied the bride to Gulkote and settled like a swarm of locusts on the city and the Hawa Mahal. Yet Lalji's bride had only been the daughter of some small hill Rajah, while the brother of the Karidkote princesses was a full-blown Maharajah and ruler of no small state, so it was only to be expected that their escort would be proportionately larger. All that was needed was someone to take decisions and to give the necessary orders, and Ash had not served with the Guides and been tutored by Koda Dad's two sons for nothing. This was familiar ground.

He sent Gul Baz to find a guide who could take them to the District Officer, and presently they were riding through the mêlée, led by an elderly individual in uniform—presumably that of the Karidkote State Forces—who laid about him with the scabbard of a rusty tulwar as he cleared a passage for them between the shifting, shouting crowd of men and animals.

The District Officer's tent had been pitched under a *sal* tree and its occupant lay prone on a camp bed, shivering helplessly in the grip of fever. His temperature was a hundred and three (which was much the same as that in the tent) and he was unfeignedly glad to see his replacement. Mr Carter was both young and new to the district, and as it was also his first experience of malaria, it is hardly surprising that he should regard the whole situation as some form of nightmare. The endless stream of petitions, complaints and accusations, the chaos and the heat and the noise—particularly the noise—made his head feel as though it was an anvil on which iron hammers beat unceasingly, and the sight of Ash, who would relieve him of responsibility, was as welcome as water in a desert.

'Sorry about this,' croaked the District Officer. 'Devilish nuisance. Afraid you'll find things are in a . . . bit of a mess here. Undisciplined beggars . . . better get 'em on the move again, soon as you can . . . before there's a scrimmage. There's this business about the boy, too . . . Jhoti—H.H.'s brother. The Heir Apparent. Arrived last night. Ought to tell you—'

He did his best to give Ash an outline of the position and some idea of the responsibilities and problems involved, but it was plain that he found it almost impossible to marshal his thoughts or make his tongue obey him, and he eventually abandoned the effort and sent instead for a native clerk, who reeled off a tally of the dowry contained in a score of iron-bound chests and the amount of ready money available for the journey, produced lists of men, waiting-women, baggage-animals, tents, supplies and camp-followers, but admitted that the numbers were only approximate and the actual total was probably somewhat higher. Even on paper the entourage was formidable enough, for it included a battery of artillery and two regiments of the Maharajah's soldiery, together with twenty-five elephants, five hundred camels, innumerable horses and at least six thousand camp-followers.

'No need to have sent so many. Bit of swank—that's all,' whispered the District Officer hoarsely. 'But then he's only a boy still. Not seventeen yet . . . H.H., I mean. Father died a few years ago, and this . . . this is his chance to show off to the others—fellow princes. And to us, of course. Waste of money, but no arguing with him. Difficult young man . . . tricky . . .'

It appeared that the young Maharajah had escorted his sisters as far as the border of his state, and then turned back to go hunting, leaving the cumbersome camp in charge of the District Officer, whose orders were to accompany it as far as Deenagunj, where he would hand it over to Captain Pelham-Martyn of the Guides Cavalry. But neither His Excellency the Governor of the Punjab nor the military authorities at Rawalpindi had realized how large that camp would be. Nor had they known that there would be a last-minute addition to the party in the person of His Highness's ten-year-old brother, Jhoti.

'Don't know why they sent him. Though I can guess,' mumbled the District Officer. 'Nuisance, though . . . didn't even know he was here until last night . . . More responsibility. Oh well—your pigeon now, thank God! Sorry for you . . .'

There were a good many other formalities that had to be completed, and by the time these had been dealt with the day was far advanced. But the sick man insisted upon leaving, not only because he craved for quiet and for clean air to breathe, but because he recognized the pitfalls of divided authority. The camp was no longer 'his pigeon' and therefore the sooner he left it the better. His servants transferred him to a waiting palanquin and jogged away into the dusty glow of the late afternoon, and Ash went out to take over control of his command.

That first evening had been a chaotic one. No sooner had the District Officer's palanquin disappeared from sight than a clamouring horde converged upon his successor with demands for payment of bills, accusations of theft, brutality and other forms of *zulum* (oppression), and loud-voiced complaints on a score of matters ranging from inadequate accommodation to a dispute between the camel-drivers and the mahouts from the elephant lines over an allocation of fodder. Their behaviour was understandable, for the age and rank of the new Sahib who had taken over from 'Carter-Sahib' presupposed inexperience, and judging solely by this yardstick, it seemed to the camp (and also to the city-fathers) that the Sirkar had sent an almost insultingly inadequate representative to act as 'sheep-dog, supply-officer and nursemaid'. They therefore reacted to this belief in a predictable manner, and discovered their mistake in something under five minutes.

'I addressed them,' wrote Ash, describing the scene in a letter to Wally, 'and after that we managed to get things straightened out all right.' Which is probably as good a description as any, though it hardly conveyed the impact that his words and personality had on the noisy gathering in the Karidkote camp. No Sahib of their acquaintance had ever possessed such a fluent and picturesque command of their language as this young Sahib—or been able to compress so much authority and sound commonsense into half-a-dozen trenchantly phrased sentences. The few *Angrezi-log* whom they had previously come across were either polite officials, earnestly striving to understand a point of view that was alien to them, or, on occasions, some less polite Sahib on survey or *shikar,* who lost his temper and shouted at them when crossed. Pelham-Sahib had done none of these things. He had spoken to them in the manner of an experienced *sirdar* (headman), wise in the ways of his fellow men and the customs of the district, and used to being obeyed. Ash, it will be seen, had learned much from the regimental durbars.

The camp listened and approved: this was someone who understood them and whom they could understand. By the time the tents were struck on the following morning and they were ready to move on, the townsmen's accounts had been paid, a majority of the disputes settled, and Ash had managed to meet and exchange courtesies with most of the senior members of the bridal party; though he had not had time to sort them out, and retained only a confused impression of scores of faces momentarily concealed by hands pressed palm to palm in the traditional Hindu gesture of greeting. Later he must get to know them all, but at the moment the most important thing was to get the camp on the move. The District Officer's advice on that head had been sound, and Ash resolved to hurry them forward with as much speed as they could make, and if possible avoid stopping for more than one or two nights in any one place, so that they did not repeat the mistake of wearing out their welcome as they had done at Deenagunj. Close on eight thousand humans and more than half as many baggage animals were worse than a plague of locusts, and it was clear that without planning and forethought their effect upon the country they passed through could be quite as devastating, and equally disastrous.

He found little attention to spare for individuals on that first day's march, for he rode up and down the long column, taking note of its numbers and composition and estimating their capacity for speed, thereby unconsciously enacting one of the roles that he had mentioned to Wally—that of sheep-dog. This was easy enough to do, for progress was slow. The mile-long column moved at a foot's pace, plodding through the dust at the same leisurely pace as the elephants and stopping at frequent intervals to rest, talk or argue, to wait for stragglers or draw water from the wayside wells. At least a third of the elephants were baggage animals, while the remainder, with the exception of four state elephants, carried a large number of the Karidkote forces and a weird assortment of weapons that included the heavy iron cannons of the artillery.

The four state elephants bore magnificent howdahs of beaten gold and silver in which the Rajkumaries* and their ladies, together with their younger brother and certain senior members of the bridal party, would ride in procession on the day of the wedding, and it had also been expected that the brides would travel in them on the journey. But the slow, rolling stride of the great beasts made the howdahs sway, and the youngest bride (who was also the most important one, being the Maharajah's full sister) complained that it made her feel ill, and demanded that both she and her sister, from whom she refused to be parted, be transferred to a *ruth*—a bullock-drawn cart with a domed roof and embroidered curtains.

'Her Highness is very nervous,' explained the chief eunuch, apologizing to Ash for the delay caused by this alteration in the travelling arrangements. 'She has never before been outside the Zenana walls, and she pines for her home, and is greatly afraid.'

They covered less than nine miles that first day—scarcely three as the crow flies, for their road wound and twisted downwards between low, scrub-covered hills that were barely more than folds in the ground. It was clear that they might often do less, and Ash, poring over the large-scale survey map that evening and calculating their weekly advance at an average of fifty to sixty miles, realized that at this rate it was going to be many months before he saw Rawalpindi again. The thought did not depress him, for this nomadic open-air

* Princesses

life with its constant change of scene was going to be very much to his taste, and he found it exhilarating to be free from supervision and senior officers, in sole charge of several thousand people and answerable to no one.

Halfway through the following day he belatedly recalled that the Maharajah's young brother had arrived, but on inquiring if he might pay his respects to the little prince, he was told that His Highness was unwell (the result, it was reported, of eating too many sweetmeats) and that it would be better to wait a day or two. The Sahib would be informed as soon as the child was feeling fully recovered. In the meantime, as a special mark of favour, he had been asked to meet the prince's sisters.

The brides' tent was the largest in the camp, and as it was always the first to be pitched, the remainder formed a series of circles about it, those in the inner ring being occupied by ladies-in-waiting, serving women and eunuchs, and the next by high officials, palace guards, and the little prince and his personal servants. By rights, Ash's tent should have been included in the latter circle, but he preferred a quieter and less central position, and had arranged for it to be pitched on the outskirts of the camp, which on this particular evening was some considerable distance from the brides' pavilion. He had been escorted to the meeting by two officers of the guard and an elderly gentleman who had been introduced to him on the previous evening as the Rao Sahib, a brother of the late Maharajah and uncle to the two princesses.

The custom of purdah—the veiling and seclusion of women—was adopted by Hindu India from Mohammedan conquerors and does not go far back into the roots of the country, so the fact that Ash was permitted to meet his two charges was not really surprising. As a Sahib and a foreigner, and more particularly as the representative of the Raj whose duty it was to see to their safety and comfort on the journey, he merited special treatment and was therefore accorded the honour of speaking with them; a privilege that would not have been accorded to any other man who was not a near relative. The interview, however, had been a brief one, and by no means private, having been conducted in the presence of their uncle and a second elderly kinsman, Maldeo Rai, as well as their duenna and distant cousin Unpora-Bai, several waiting women, a eunuch and half-a-dozen children. The decencies were preserved by the fact that the brides' faces, and that of Unpora-Bai, were partially covered by the fringed and embroidered saris that they held in such a way that only their eyes and a small segment of forehead were visible. But as the saris were of the finest silk gauze from Benares, this was more a token gesture than anything else, and Ash was able to gain a fairly accurate idea of their looks.

'You were quite right about them,' he wrote to Wally in a lengthy postscript to the letter describing his arrival in camp, 'they are as pretty as pictures. Or the younger one is, anyway. She's not yet fourteen, and just like that miniature of Shah Jehan's Empress, the lady of the Taj. I managed to get a good look at her because one of the children tried to catch her attention by tugging at her sari, and twitched it out of her hand. She's the prettiest thing you ever saw, and it's thankful I am that you can't see her, you susceptible Celt, for you'd fall in love with her on the spot and there would be no holding you. You'd be rhyming heart, part and cupid's dart all the way from here to Bhithor, and I'm not sure I could endure it. Thank God I'm a soured and unimpressionable misanthropist! The other sister kept a bit in the background and is quite old, at least eighteen, which in this country is practically on the shelf, and I can't think what they were about not to marry her off years ago; except that I gather she is only the daughter of some secondary wife, or possibly a concubine of the late Maharajah's, and from what I could see of her I wouldn't say she was exactly the Indian idea of a beauty. Or mine either, for that matter. Much too tall and with one of those rather square faces. I prefer oval ones, myself. But her eyes are magnificent—"like the fishpools in Heshbon by the gate of Beth-Rabbin"—not black like her sister's but the colour of peat-water, with little gold flecks in them. Don't you wish you were in my shoes?'

Ash might choose to describe himself as soured and unimpressionable, but the fact that the Karidkote princesses were far from unattractive undoubtedly added a fillip to the situation; though as he was unlikely to see very much of them their personal appearance, one way or another, was a matter of little importance. Nevertheless, the thought that he was escorting two charming young creatures to their wedding instead of the 'pair of dowds' that he had visualized made the whole affair seem more romantic. It even lent a redeeming touch of glamour to the din and dirt and inconvenience of the enormous camp, and he strolled back to his tent humming the old nursery rhyme that tells of a lady who rode to Banbury Cross 'with rings on her fingers and bells on her toes', and mentally recalling the names of legendary beauties whose stories are chronicled in Tod's *Rajasthan:* Humayan's wife, the fourteen-year-old Hamedu; lovely Padmini, 'the fairest of all flesh on earth', whose fatal beauty had led to the first and most terrible Sack of Chitor; Mumtaz Mahal, 'Splendour of the Palace', to whose memory her grieving husband had raised that wonder in white marble, the Taj Mahal. Perhaps Wally was right after all, and all princesses were beautiful.

Ash had been far too interested in the brides to spare more than a cursory glance at the remainder of the company, several of whom would have repaid a little more of his attention. And as the next day's march was to end on the outskirts of a town where there was a small garrison of British troops, he had ridden on ahead to speak to the officer in command, and seen little of anyone in the camp during that day, for the Garrison Commander had invited him to dine in mess.

Unlike Wally, his host that night appeared to think that a British officer landed with Ash's present task was greatly to be pitied, and had said as much over the port and cigars. 'Can't say I envy you the job,' said the Garrison Commander. 'Thank God I'm never likely to be told off to do anything in that line! It must be nearly impossible to live in among that lot without putting your foot in it twenty times a day, and frankly, I can't think how you manage it.'

'Manage what?' inquired Ash, puzzled.

'Coping with this caste business. It's no problem with Mussulmans, who don't seem to mind who they eat and drink with or give a damn who cooks or serves the stuff, and don't appear to have too many religious taboos. But caste Hindus can pose the most appalling problems, as I've learnt to my cost. They're so hedged about with complicated rules and customs and restrictions imposed upon them by their religion, that a stranger in their midst has to walk like Agag to avoid offending them—or at the very least, embarrassing them. I don't mind telling you that I find it a devil of a problem.'

The speaker had gone on to illustrate the pitfalls of the caste system with a long story about a sepoy who had been wounded in battle and left for dead, but recovering, had wandered for days in the jungle, famished, delirious and half mad with thirst, and eventually been found by a little girl who had been herding goats, and who had given him a drink of milk that had undoubtedly saved his life, for he had been at his last gasp. Not long afterwards he had come across some men of his own regiment who had carried him to the nearest hospital, where he had lain gravely ill for many months before being discharged and returning to duty. Several years later he had obtained leave to go to his home, and on arriving there had told his story. His father had immediately said that from his description of the child she could have been an 'untouchable', and if so, his son was defiled and must not stay in his own home, for his presence would pollute it. No arguments had been of any use, and not only his own family but the entire village recoiled from him as an outcaste and unclean. Only after costly ceremonies (for the performance of which the priests demanded every anna of his life's savings) was he declared 'purified' and allowed to enter his family home again.

'And all this,' said the Garrison Commander, summing up, 'because the poor devil had once, when crazed with wounds and thirst and at his last gasp, accepted a cup of milk from the hands of a child who might possibly have been an "untouchable". Apparently he ought to have preferred death to the remote possibility of defilement. Can you beat it? And I assure you that the story is true, because a cousin of mine had it from the sepoy himself. Just shows you what we're up against in this country. But I suppose you've found that out for yourself by now.'

Ash had found it out many years ago. But he refrained from saying so and merely said that he thought that in these matters a fanatical regard for the letter-of-the-law and an obsessive terror of pollution was, in general, confined to the priests (who benefited greatly from it) and to the middle classes, both upper and lower. The nobility tended to be less hag-ridden by it, while royalty, secure in the knowledge of their own superiority over men of lesser birth, usually felt free to stretch the rules to suit themselves—fortified no doubt by the knowledge that if they overstepped the mark they could well afford to pay the Brahmins to put them right again with the gods. 'It isn't so much that they are more broad-minded,' said Ash, 'but they are firm believers in the Divine Right of Kings; which is not surprising when one thinks that a number of the princely houses claim to be descended from a god—or from the sun or the moon. If you believe that, you can't really feel that you are quite like other men, so you can afford to do things that people with less exalted ancestors wouldn't dare do. Not that the great are irreligious—far from it. They can be just as devout. But possibly less bigoted.'

'You may be right,' acknowledged the Garrison Commander. 'But then I have to admit that I don't know any of the ruling princes. Have some more port?'

The conversation had switched to pig-sticking and horses, and Ash had not returned to his tent until well after midnight.

The following morning had dawned wet and windy, so that he was able to sleep late, for under such conditions the camp took longer than usual to get on the move. And because of the weather, he again had little opportunity to take note of his fellow-travellers, who unlike himself were shrouded and unidentifiable under cloaks or blankets worn to keep out the wet. Not that this worried him, as there would be plenty of time later on, and he was more than content to jog along in silence; even the discomfort of spending the day in a damp saddle, head down against a gusty wind that tugged at his sodden cloak and drove the rain into his eyes, being infinitely preferable to being tied to an office desk in Rawalpindi. The almost total lack of paper-work was, in his opinion, one of the main advantages of this present assignment, another being that any problems that arose were likely to be familiar ones, differing only in degree from those that cropped up frequently at regimental durbars, and just as easily dealt with.

But in this he was mistaken, for that self-same evening he was to come up against one that was not only unfamiliar, but very difficult to deal with. And, potentially, extremely dangerous.

The fact that he was entirely unprepared for it was largely his own fault, though insufficient consultation between Army Headquarters in Rawalpindi and the Commandant of the Corps of Guides, together with inadequate briefing by the Political Department and the illness of the District Officer, could also be held responsible. But it was Ash's original attitude to his appointment—that disgusted dismissal of it as a mere matter of playing sheep-dog and chaperone to 'a pair of dowds and a parcel of squealing women'—that had led him into the old error of his early school-days: neglecting to do his homework.

He had no one to blame but himself, since he had, quite simply, not bothered to find out anything about the background and history of the state whose princesses he was to escort to their wedding, while the authorities in Rawalpindi, for their part, had given him no information on that head because they assumed that Mr Carter, the District Officer, would deal fully with it; and they could hardly have been expected to know that an attack of malaria would prevent the District Officer from doing anything of the sort. But as a result, Ash had entered on his command in a blithe state of ignorance and wholly unaware of the pitfalls that lay ahead. Even the information that a young brother of the Maharajah's had elected to join the camp at the last possible moment, and would be travelling with them, had not struck him as particularly interesting. After all, why shouldn't the child accompany his sisters to their wedding? He had dismissed young Jhoti's presence as something of no importance, and beyond sending a polite inquiry as to his health, gave the matter no more thought. But that evening, as darkness fell, a servant brought him a message to say that the little prince was now fully recovered from his indisposition and would like to see him.

The rain had stopped some hours before and the sky was clear again as Ash, wearing mess dress in honour of the occasion, was once more conducted through the roaring, lamp-lit camp to a tent near that of the princesses, where a sentry armed with an ancient tul-war provided a token guard and a yawning servant waited to usher him into the Presence. A solitary hurricane lamp hung on an iron pole outside, but passing in under the tent-flap Ash was met by a blaze of light that momentarily dazzled him, for the interior of the tent was lit by half-a-dozen European-style lamps that had been de-signed to carry shades of silk or velvet, but that now stood, un-shaded, on low tables set in a half-circle about a pile of cushions on which sat a plump, pallid little boy.

He was a handsome child, despite his plumpness and his pasty complexion, and Ash, blinking in the glare, was suddenly reminded of Lalji as he had seen him on that first day in the Hawa Mahal. This child must be about the same age as Lalji had been then, and was sufficiently like Ash's memory of the Yuveraj for the two to be brothers, though Lalji, thought Ash, had been a far less personable child than this one, and he would certainly not have risen to his feet to greet his visitor, as Jhoti was doing. The resemblance was mainly a matter of dress and expression, for Lalji had worn similar clothes and he too had looked sour and cross—and very frightened.

It occurred to Ash, bowing in acknowledgement of the boy's greeting, that if (as Wally maintained) all princesses were beautiful, it was a pity that all young princes should be plump and cross and frightened. Or, at least, all the ones that he himself had met so far.

The absurdity of this reflection made him grin and he was still smiling when he straightened up . . . to find himself looking directly at a face that even after all these years he recognized instantly and with a paralysing sensation of shock—the face of a man who stood immediately behind the little prince and less than three paces away, and whose narrow eyes held the same slyness, the same chilling look of calculation and malice that had been so familiar in the days when their owner had been Lalji's favourite courtier and the *Nautch*-girl's spy.

It was Biju Ram.

The smile on Ash's face stiffened into a fixed grimace and he felt his heart jerk and miss a beat. It was not possible—he must be mistaken. Yet he knew that he was not. And in the same instant he knew too, and without any shadow of doubt, why the boy Jhoti reminded him of Lalji. Because Jhoti was either Lalji's brother or his first cousin.

He could not be Nandu: he was too young for that. But there had been at least two more children, and for all he knew the *Nautch*-girl might have borne many others later on. Or could this be Lalji's son . . . ? No, that was not likely. A cousin, then?—a child or grandchild of one of the brothers of the old Rajah of Gulkote . . . ?

Ash became aware that several people were beginning to look at him curiously, and also that there was no trace of recognition in Biju Ram's narrow-eyed gaze. That slyness was habitual; and so was the malice. As for the look of calculation, it probably only meant that Biju Ram was assessing the calibre of the new Sahib and wondering if it would be necessary to placate him, because in no circumstances could he have recognized this Sahib as the 'horse-boy' who had saved the life of the Yuveraj of Gulkote so many years ago.

Ash forced himself to look away and to reply to the polite questions of the little prince; and presently his pulse steadied and he was able to glance casually about the tent and assure himself that there was no one else there whom he knew. There were at least two. But even then he could surely not be in any danger of discovery, for apart from Koda Dad (and he would never have told), no one else in Gulkote could have learned that Sita's son was an *Angrezi*. There was nothing to connect the boy Ashok with a Captain Ashton Pelham-Martyn of the Guides, and little enough resemblance between the two. It was only Biju Ram who had not altered. True, he was much fatter and beginning to grow a little grey, and the lines that dissipation had already begun to draw on his face when he was a young man were deeper now; but that was all. He was still smooth and spruce and sly, and he still wore a large diamond drop in one ear. But why was he here, and what was the relationship between the

Yuveraj of Gulkote and the ten-year-old Jhoti? And who, or what, was the child frightened of?

Ash had seen fear too often not to recognize it, and the signs were all there: the wide, over-bright eyes and the swift glances that flickered to left and right and back over the shoulder; the tensed muscles and jerking turn of the head, and the uncontrollable quiver and clench of the hands.

This was how Lalji too had looked; and with good reason. But then this child was not heir to a throne. He was merely a younger brother, so it seemed inconceivable that anyone should wish to harm him. A more likely explanation was that he had run away to join the wedding party against the wishes of his elders, and was only now beginning to assess the possible consequence of his escapade.

'He's probably only a spoilt brat who has gone too far and is now scared of being spanked,' thought Ash. 'And if he is playing truant, I'll bet anything that Biju Ram put him up to it . . . I must find out about his family. About all of them. I should have done it before . . .'

The little prince had begun on introductions, and Ash found himself greeting Biju Ram and exchanging the few formal sentences suitable to the occasion before passing on to the next in line. Ten minutes later the interview was over and he was outside in the semi-darkness, and shivering a little, not only because the night air struck cool after the heat in the overlighted tent. He drew a deep, shuddering breath of relief as though he had escaped from a trap, and was ashamed to discover that his palms were sore where his nails had pressed into them—though he had not even realized until this moment that he had been holding his hands tightly clenched.

That night his tent had been pitched under a banyan tree, some fifty yards beyond the perimeter of the camp and screened from it by the cluster of smaller tents that housed his personal servants. Passing these, he changed his mind about sending for one of the Karidkote clerks, because Mahdoo was sitting out in the open smoking his hookah, and it occurred to Ash that by this time the old man had probably picked up as much information about the royal family of Karidkote as any denizen of that state. Mahdoo enjoyed gossiping, and as he came into contact with many people whom Ash did not meet, he heard things that are not usually spoken of to Sahibs.

Ash paused beside the old man and said in an undertone: 'Come and talk with me in my tent, Cha-cha (uncle), I need advice. There are also many things that it may be you can tell me. Give me your hand. I will carry the hookah.'

A hurricane lamp with the wick turned low had been left hanging in Ash's tent, but he preferred to sit outside under the narrow awning, from where he could look out past the dense shadows of the banyan tree to the wide plain that lay beyond it, dim in the starlight. Mahdoo squatted comfortably on his hunkers while Ash, impeded by mess dress, had to content himself with a camp chair.

'What is it that you would know, *beta* (son)?' inquired the old man, using the familiar address of long ago, which was something that he did very rarely in these days.

Ash did not reply to the question immediately, but was silent for a space, listening to the soothing bubble of the hookah and arranging his thoughts. At last he said slowly: 'Firstly, I would know what connection there is between this Maharajah of Karidkote, whose sisters we take to their wedding and whose brother travels with us, and a certain Rajah of Gulkote. There must be one, I am sure of that.'

'But of course,' said Mahdoo, surprised. 'They are one and the same. The territories of His Highness of Karidarra adjoined those of his cousin the Rajah of Gulkote, and when His Highness died, leaving no heir, the Rajah left for Calcutta to lay claim before the *Lat*-Sahib himself to the lands and titles of his cousin. There being no one nearer in blood, it was granted to him, and the two states were merged into one and re-named Karidkote. How is it that you did not know this?'

'Because I am blind—and a fool!' Ash's voice was barely more than a whisper, but it held a concentrated bitterness that startled Mahdoo. 'I was angry because I knew that the Generals in Rawalpindi were only using this appointment as a pretext to send me further away from my friends and the Frontier, so I would not even take the trouble to ask questions, or to find out anything. Anything at all!'

'But why should it matter to you who these princely folk are? What difference does it make?' asked the old man, troubled by Ash's vehemence. Mahdoo had never been told the story of Gulkote. Colonel Anderson had advised against it on the grounds that the fewer people who knew that tale the better, as the boy's life might depend on his trail being lost. It was the one thing that Ash had been forbidden to mention before Ala Yar or Mahdoo, and he did not wish to go into it now. He said instead:

'One should know all that one can about those under one's charge, for fear of . . . of giving offence through ignorance. But tonight I have been made to realize that I know nothing at all. Not even . . . When did the old Rajah die, Mahdoo? And who is this old man whom they say is his brother?'

'The Rao-Sahib? He is a half-brother only: the elder son by some two years, though being the son of a concubine he could not inherit the *gadi* (throne), which went to a younger son whose mother was the Rani. But all the family have always held him in great affection and respect. As for the Rajah—the Maharajah—he died some three years ago, I think. It is his son, the brother of the Rajkumaries, who now sits on the *gadi* in his place.'

'Lalji,' said Ash in a whisper.

'Who?'

'The eldest son. That was his milk-name. But he would have been—' Ash stopped, remembering suddenly that the District Officer had spoken of the Maharajah of Karidkote as only a boy and 'not yet seventeen'.

'Nay, nay. This is not the son of the first wife, but a younger one: the second son. The first one died of a fall some years before his father. It is said that he was playing with a monkey on the walls of the palace and fell and was killed. It was an accident,' said Mahdoo; and added softly: '—or so they say.'

'*An accident*,' thought Ash. The same kind of accident that had so nearly happened before. Had it been Biju Ram who pushed him over to his death? Or Panwa, or . . . Poor Lalji! Ash shuddered, visualizing that last hideous moment of terror and the long, long fall onto the rocks below. Poor Lalji—poor little Yuveraj. So they had done for him at last and the *Nautch*-girl had won. It was her son, Nandu, the spoilt brat who had been banished, shrieking, on the occasion of Colonel Byng's visit to Gulkote, who was now Maharajah of the new State of Karidkote. And Lalji was dead . . .

'It seems that the family has suffered many misfortunes of late years,' said Mahdoo reflectively, and sucked again on his pipe: 'The old Maharajah also met his death from a fall. I am told that he was out hawking when his horse bolted and fell into a nullah, breaking both their necks. They think the horse must have been stung by a bee. It was very sad for his new bride—did I tell you that he had recently taken another wife?—yes, indeed, his fourth, the first two being dead. They say she was young and very beautiful: the daughter

of a rich *zemindar* . . .' The hookah bubbled again and it seemed to
Ash as though the sound was a malicious chuckle, laden with sly in-
nuendo. 'It is said,' continued Mahdoo softly, 'that the third Rani
was greatly angered, and had threatened to kill herself. But there was
no need, for her husband died and the new bride burned with him on
his pyre.'

'Suttee? But that has been forbidden,' said Ash sharply. 'It is
against the law.'

'Maybe, child. But the princes are still a law unto themselves, and
in many states they do as they wish and no one hears until it is too
late. The girl was in ashes long before anyone could interfere. It
seems that the Senior Rani would have joined her on the pyre had
her women not locked her in a room from which she could not escape, and sent a word to Political Sahib, who was on tour and could
not be reached in time to prevent the Junior Rani from becoming a
suttee.'

'Very convenient for the Senior Rani—who I presume became the
power behind the throne in Karidkote,' observed Ash dryly.

'I believe so,' admitted Mahdoo. 'Which is strange indeed, for they
say she was once a dancing-girl from Kashmir. Yet for more than
two years she was the true ruler of the state, and at least she died a
Maharani.'

'She is dead?' exclaimed Ash, startled. Somehow it did not seem
possible. He had never even seen Janoo-Rani, yet her presence had
so dominated the Hawa Mahal that he found it difficult to believe
that the violent, ruthless woman who had ruled the old Rajah and
plotted Lalji's death—and his own—was no longer alive. It was as
though the fortress-palace itself had fallen, for she had seemed indestructible . . . 'Did they say how it happened, Cha-cha?'

Mahdoo's wise old eyes glinted in the faint glow from the hookah
as he looked sideways at Ash, and he said softly: 'She quarrelled
with her eldest son, and soon afterwards she died—from eating poisoned grapes.'

Ash caught his breath in a harsh gasp: 'You mean—? No. That I
will not believe. Not his own mother!'

'Have I said that he did it? *Nahin, nahin,*' Mahdoo wagged a
deprecatory hand. 'There was of course a *tálash* (inquiry) and it was
proved to be an accident; she herself had poisoned the grapes for the
purpose of ridding the garden of a plague of crows, and she must in
error have left a few of them on her own dish—'

The hookah chuckled slyly again, but Mahdoo had not finished: 'Did I not tell you that the ruler of Karidkote has suffered much misfortune? First his elder brother and then his father; and two years later, his mother. And before that there were also one or two small brothers and another sister who died when they were babes in a year of sickness, when cholera killed many children—and not a few grown men and women too. The Maharajah now has only the one brother left—the little prince who is here in the camp. And only one full sister, the younger of the two Rajkumaries who are being sent far away to be wed, for the elder is only a half-sister, the child of his father's second wife, who they say was a foreigner.'

'*Juli!*' thought Ash: and was stunned by the thought. That tall, veiled woman whom he had seen in the brides' pavilion two nights ago was the *Feringhi*-Rani's neglected little daughter, Anjuli; the child whom the *Nautch*-girl had scornfully likened to an unripe mango, and who had been known thereafter to everyone in the Palace of the Winds as 'Kairi-Bai'. It was Juli—and he had not known it.

He sat silent for a long time, staring into the starlight and re-living the past, while behind him the camp settled down to sleep. The voices of men and animals sank to a murmur that lost itself in the rustle of leaves as the night wind breathed through the branches of the banyan tree, and beside him Mahdoo's hookah bubbled a rhythmic accompaniment to the monotonous tunk-a-tunk of a distant tom-tom and the howl of a jackal-pack out on the plain. But Ash heard none of these sounds, for he was a long way away both in distance and in time, talking to a little girl in a balcony on a ruined tower that looked out upon the snows of the Dur Khaima . . .

How could he possibly have come to forget her almost completely, when she had been so much a part of his years in the Hawa Mahal? No—not forget her—he had forgotten nothing. He had merely pushed her into the back of his mind and not troubled to think of her: perhaps because he had always taken her for granted—

Later that night, after Mahdoo had gone, Ash unlocked the small tin cash-box that he had bought with his first pocket-money and in which he had kept his most treasured possessions ever since: a little silver ring that Sita had worn, his father's last and unfinished letter, the watch that Colonel Anderson had given him on the day they arrived at Pelham Abbas, his first pair of cuff-links and a dozen other trifles. He turned them over, looking for something, and finally emptied the contents of the box onto his camp bed. Yes, it was still there. A small flat square of yellowing paper.

He carried it over to the lamp, and unfolding it, stood looking at the thing it contained: a sliver of mother-of-pearl that was half of a Chinese counter shaped like a fish. Someone—the *Feringhi*-Rani, perhaps?—had bored a hole through the fish's eye and threaded a strand of twisted silk through it so that it could be worn as a medallion, as Juli had worn it. It had been Juli's most precious possession, yet she had given it to him for a keepsake and begged him not to forget her; and he had hardly ever thought of her again . . . there had been so many other and more urgent things to think of: and when Koda Dad had left Gulkote there had been no one to send him news of the palace, because no one else—not even Hira Lal—knew what had befallen him or where he had gone.

Ash slept little that night, and as he lay on his back looking up into the darkness, a hundred trivial incidents that had been lost with the years came trooping back again to dance before his mind's eye. A night full of fireworks and feasting that celebrated the birth of a son to Janoo-Rani—Nandu, who was now Maharajah of Karidkote. The names and faces of the boys he had played with in the streets of Gulkote—Gopi and Chitu, Jajat and Shoki and a dozen others. The death of Tuku the little mongoose, and Hira Lal telling him that he should be patient with Lalji, for he, Ashok, was more fortunate than his master. Juli bringing him a silver four-anna piece so that they could begin saving up for the house they would build in Sita's valley, and the two of them hiding the precious coin under a loose stone on the floor of the Queen's balcony. They had meant to add other coins to it from time to time, but had never been able to do so, and it was curious to think that unless Juli had taken it out after he had gone, it must still be there, hidden away and forgotten—like his half of her luck-piece that had lain so long in the bottom of the tin cash-box, out of sight and out of mind.

The stars were beginning to pale by the time he fell asleep, and just as his eyes closed, an odd fragment of a conversation returned to him out of the past—something that he himself had once said, though he could not recall the occasion, or why he should have said such a thing:

'*If I were you, Juli, I wouldn't get married at all. It's too dangerous.*'

Why dangerous? thought Ash drowsily as he drifted into sleep.

🦂 15

'Ahsti! Ahsti! Khabadar, Premkulli. *Shabash, mera moti—ab ek or. Bas, bas! Kya kurta, ooloo? . . . Nikal-jao! Arré! Arré! Hai! Hai! Hai! . . .'*

The camp was fording a river to the usual accompaniment of shouts, yells and confusion, and inevitably a cart had become bogged down half-way across and was being pulled out by one of the pad elephants.

Mulraj, who commanded the contingent of Karidkote State Forces, had ridden on ahead with Ash to test the depth of the ford, and now the two sat at ease on the far bank, and from the vantage point of a bluff overlooking the river, watched the unruly multitude straggle across.

'If they do not make haste,' observed Mulraj, 'it will be dark before the last is across. *Hai mai,* what a business they make of it!'

Ash nodded absently, his gaze still on the men splashing through the shallows or wading knee-deep in mid-river. Three days had passed since he had come face to face with Biju Ram and learned that the Princely State of Karidkote was one and the same as the Gulkote of his youth, and since then he had looked more closely at the men about him and found himself identifying several of them. There were more than half-a-dozen among the mahouts alone, men who had served in the elephant lines of the Hawa Mahal. And there were others too: palace officials, syces, members of the State Forces and a handful of servants and courtiers who four days ago would probably not have attracted his attention, but in the light of his new knowledge were suddenly familiar. Even the elephant, Premkulli, who was being exhorted by his mahout to be careful, was an old friend whom he had fed many times with sticks of sugar cane . . . The last rays of the sinking sun caught the river, glittering on the water in a blaze of gold that dazzled Ash's eyes so that he could no longer make out the faces of those who were crossing, and he turned away to discuss various matters of administration with Mulraj.

The servants and camp-followers, with the baggage animals, had been the first to cross, for there were tents to be pitched, fires lighted and food cooked. But the brides and their immediate entourage preferred to follow at a slower pace and delay their arrival until all was in readiness for them. They had picnicked today in a grove of trees half a mile from the ford, and knowing that their camp would be pitched at the first suitable spot on the far side of the river, had passed the afternoon there, waiting for the word to move on. But the trees had been full of birds coming home to roost by the time a messenger brought word that they might now proceed, and before they were ready to do so the sun had disappeared below the horizon. Accompanied by a rear guard of some thirty men of the State Forces, they had moved on at last in a leisurely manner that brought them to the ford in the twilight.

A covered cart full of waiting-women normally followed immediately behind the gaily caparisoned *ruth* in which the brides travelled, but tonight it had fallen some way behind, and when the *ruth* entered the water it was escorted only by a handful of soldiers and servants, and by the brides' uncle, who had announced his intention of walking the last mile, and having sent his palanquin on ahead, was dismayed to discover that the ford was not nearly as shallow as he had supposed.

On the far bank Ash had already called for his horse, and he was back in the saddle and moving down towards the level ground when a further outburst of shrieks and curses arose from the rapidly darkening river, and he stood up in his stirrups and saw that the near bullock of the *ruth* had fallen in midstream, snapping a shaft and throwing its driver into the water. Held fast by the traces, the animal was struggling and kicking in a frantic attempt to avoid drowning, and the *ruth* was already tilting over on one side. From behind its tightly laced curtains came the piercing shrieks of one of its occupants, while a dozen vociferous men milled about it in the dusk, pushing and pulling as the floundering bullock began to draw it towards deep water.

With night closing in it was difficult for the majority of those in the river to see what had happened, but looking down on the scene Ash had a clear picture of it, and he dug his heels into his horse's flanks and rode down the slope and into the river at a gallop, scattering the gaping crowd in the shallows. The shouting men who surrounded the *ruth* jumped back to give him room as he leaned from the saddle and wrenched at the curtain fastenings until they tore.

A soaked and screaming woman, lifted by a pair of firm, capable hands, seemed to leap at him from the darkness, and he snatched her out just as the off-side wheel broke and the *ruth* fell on its side and began to fill with water.

'Quick, Juli! Come on, get out!' Ash was unaware that he had called to the remaining occupant by name as he shouted to make himself heard above the tumult of yelling voices and the ominous sound of water rushing through the half-submerged *ruth,* but in fact his words had been lost in the din, for the small figure in his arms was clinging to him in a frenzy of terror and still shrieking at the top of her voice. He beat down the clutching hands and thrust her at the nearest person, who happened by good fortune to be her uncle, though it might just as easily have been a sowar or a bullock driver. The next second he was off his horse and in the river, with the water swirling above his waist.

'*Get out, girl!*'

There was a choking, spluttering sound from the darkness and a hand reached out between the torn curtains. Ash gripped it and dragged its owner up and out, and lifting her off her feet, carried her to the bank.

She was no light and fragile creature like the little sister whom she had thrust out of the *ruth* into his arms, nor did she scream or cling to him as the younger girl had done. But though she made no sound he could feel the quick rise and fall of her breast against his own, while the weight of her warm, wet body, and every slender curve and line of it, spoke eloquently of a woman and not of a child.

He was breathing a little unevenly himself by the time he reached dry land, though his reasons for doing so were not emotional but physical, and few men, called upon to carry approximately a hundred and twelve pounds across a river, with the current tugging at their knees and a crowd of excited spectators splashing and jostling alongside, would not have done the same. It seemed a long way to the shallows, and when he reached the bank there was no one to whom he could hand over his burden. He called for torches and the Rajkumaries' women and waited in the dusk, holding Anjuli's dripping figure in his arms while his syce set off to retrieve his horse, and far too many helpers struggled to free the bullocks and drag the broken *ruth* out of the way, so that the cart with the princesses' waiting-women could cross in safety.

Above him the stars came out one by one, and as the night wind arose and blew strongly off the river, the girl in his arms began to shiver in the cold air and Ash called for a blanket and wrapped it about her, drawing one end over her head to shield her from the gaze of the crowd as torches began to flower in the darkness and the women's cart creaked into view at last.

Judging from the noise, the younger bride was already inside it, though her shrieks had now given place to hysterical sobbing. But Ash did not pause to inquire after her. His muscles were beginning to ache, and he bundled Anjuli in without ceremony and stood back as the cart jolted on its way to the camp, aware for the first time that his clothes were soaking wet and that there was a distinct nip in the night air.

'*Mubarik ho,* that was well done, Sahib,' approved Mulraj, materializing out of the darkness. 'I owe you my life, I think. I and many others, for had you not been here the Rajkumaries might both have drowned, and then who knows what vengeance His Highness their brother would have taken on us his servants?'

'*Be-wakufi,*'* retorted Ash impatiently. 'They were never in the least danger of drowning. Only of getting wet. The river is not nearly deep enough there.'

'The driver of the *ruth* was drowned,' observed Mulraj dryly. 'The current took him into deep water and it seems that he could not swim. The Rajkumaries would have been trapped inside by the curtains and drowned also, but it was their good fortune that you should have been on horseback and watching—and most of all, that you are a Sahib, for no other man there, save only their uncle who is old and slow, would have dared to lay hands on the daughters of a Maharajah, and by the time I myself had seen what was toward and was in the saddle, it was all over. They should fill your hands with gold for this night's work.'

'At this moment I would rather have a hot bath and dry clothes,' said Ash with a laugh. 'And if anyone deserves praise it is Anjuli-Bai, for keeping her head and getting her younger sister out, instead of screaming and struggling to escape herself, when she must have known that the *ruth* was filling up with water. Where the devil is my syce? *Ohé,* Kulu Ram!'

'Here Sahib,' said a voice at his elbow: the horse's hooves had made no sound on the sandy ground. Ash took the reins and swung himself into the saddle, and having saluted Mulraj, touched the horse with his heel and cantered off between the clumps of pampas grass

---

* nonsense (literally, stupidity)

and the thorny *kikar* trees to where the lights of the camp made an orange glow in the night sky.

He turned in early, and the next day had been a busy one, for he had ridden off at dawn with Jhoti, Mulraj and Tarak Nath, a member of the camp's *panchayat,* and an armed escort of half-a-dozen sowars, to reconnoitre the next ford. The boy had been an unexpected addition to the party, having apparently teased Mulraj into bringing him. But as he proved to be an excellent rider, and was obviously eager to please and be pleased, he was no trouble to anyone. And it occurred to Ash that it would be no bad thing to get him away from his attendants and out into the fresh air, on horseback, as often as possible, for a day in the open had plainly done the little prince a world of good, and he already looked a different being from the pallid and anxious-eyed child of their first meeting.

The ford had proved impassable, and as it had been necessary to find out, by personal inspection, which of two alternative crossing places would save the most time and cause the least inconvenience, the sun was setting and the day almost over by the time they returned to the camp. Ash had intended to ask for an early start on the following morning, but this had been frustrated by Shushila-Bai, the younger princess, who sent word that she was suffering from shock and sickness and did not intend to move anywhere at all for at least two or three days—if not longer.

Her decision was not so tiresome as it would have been two days earlier, for food stocks were high and the river provided an unlimited supply of water. And as it happened, Ash himself was by no means averse to remaining in one place for a few days, for there were both black-buck and *chinkara* out on the plain, and he had seen snipe on a jheel near by and any amount of partridge in the scrubland. It would, he thought, be pleasant to go out shooting with Mulraj instead of shepherding this flock across country.

Having been informed that the Rajkumari Shushila was indisposed, he was surprised when a second messenger arrived with a politely worded request that he would pay the Maharajah's sisters the honour of visiting them. And as the messenger on this occasion had been no less a person than the brides' uncle, affectionately known throughout the camp as 'Kaka-ji Rao'*, it had been impossible for him to refuse, even though the hour was late and he would

* kaka = paternal uncle

have preferred bed to social conversation. However, there being no help for it, he duly changed into mess dress, and almost as an after-thought, slipped the broken half of the mother-of-pearl fish into his pocket before accompanying the Rao-Sahib through the lamp-lit camp.

The 'durbar tent' in which the princesses received guests was large and comfortable, and lined throughout with a rust-red cloth embroi-dered in gay colours and lavishly decorated with tiny circles of look-ing-glass that winked and glittered as the material billowed to the night breeze or the flames of the oil lamps swayed in a draught of air. The floor was strewn with Persian rugs and squabby silk and brocade cushions which served in place of chairs, and there were a number of low tables, carved from sandalwood and inlaid with ivory, on which an assortment of fruit and sweetmeats had been set out in silver dishes. But except for Kaka-ji Rao and the elderly duenna, Unpora-Bai, and two serving-women who sat in the shadows beyond the cir-cle of light, the only other persons present were the brides themselves and their younger brother, Jhoti.

The Rajkumaries were dressed much as they had been before. But with one noteworthy difference. Tonight they were both unveiled. 'It is because they owe their lives to you,' explained the little prince, coming forward to greet Ash and do the honours for his sisters. 'But for you, they would both have drowned. This very day their pyres would have been lit and the river received their ashes, and tomorrow we others should have returned home with our faces blackened. We have much to thank you for, and from now on you are as our brother.'

He waved away Ash's assertion that there had in fact been no danger, and his sisters rose to make their bows while Unpora-Bai made approving noises from behind her veil, and Kaka-ji observed that modesty was a virtue to be prized above valour, and that it was plain that Pelham-Sahib possessed both in full measure. One of the serving-women then shuffled forward with a silver tray that bore two ceremonial garlands fashioned out of tinsel ribbon ornamented with gold-embroidered medallions, and first Shushila and then Anjuli solemnly hung one about Ash's neck, where they glittered incon-gruously against the drab khaki of his mess jacket and gave him something of the appearance of an over-decorated General. After which he was invited to seat himself and plied with refreshments, and as a singular mark of favour (for it is pollution for those of high caste to eat with casteless men) the company ate with him—though not from the same dishes.

Once Shushila-Bai had been coaxed out of her shyness, the party relaxed and spent a very pleasant hour nibbling *halwa,* sipping sherbet and talking; and even cousin Unpora-Bai, while remaining closely veiled, contributed her mite to the conversation. It had not been easy to draw out the younger princess and persuade her to talk, but Ash, when he chose, had a way with him, and now he exerted himself to put the nervous child at her ease, and was eventually rewarded by a shy smile and then a laugh, and presently she was laughing and chattering as though she had known him all her life and he was indeed an older brother. It was only then that he felt free to turn his attention to her half-sister, Anjuli-Bai—and was startled by what he saw.

Anjuli had been sitting a little behind her sister when he entered, and directly under the shadow cast by the hanging lamp; and even when she rose to greet and garland him, he had not really been able to study her, for she had kept her head bent and wore the peak of her sari drawn so far forward that its broad edging of embroidery shadowed what little he could see of her face. Later, when they were all seated, he had been too occupied with his efforts to coax the younger princess into joining in the talk between himself and her brother and uncle to spare much attention for the elder one. That could wait. And though Anjuli had so far barely spoken, her silence neither suggested the nervous timidity that appeared to afflict her young half-sister, nor conveyed the impression that she was uninterested in what was being said. She sat quietly, watching and listening and occasionally nodding in agreement or shaking her head in smiling dissent, and Ash remembered that 'Kairi-Bai' had always been a good listener . . .

Looking fully at her at last, his first thought was that he had made a mistake. This was not Kairi. It was not possible that the thin, plain, shabby little creature who never seemed to have enough to eat, and who, as he had once complained, followed him around like a starving kitten, could have grown into a woman like this. Mahdoo had got it wrong, and this was not the daughter of the old Rajah's second wife, the *Feringhi*-Rani, but of someone else . . .

Yet because her head was no longer bent, her sari had slipped back a little, and the signs of her mixed blood were clearly to be seen. They were there in the colour of her skin and the structure of her bones; in the long, gracious lines of her body, the breadth of shoulder and hip, and the small, square-jawed face with its high cheek bones and broad brow; in the set of the wide-spaced eyes that were the colours of bog-water, the tilted tip of that short nose, and the lovely, generous mouth that was too large to suit the accepted standards of beauty that were so admirably personified by her half-sister.

By contrast, Shushila-Bai was as small and exquisite as a Tanagra figurine or the miniature of some legendary Indian beauty: golden-skinned and black-eyed, her face a flawless oval and her mouth a rose-petal. Her small-boned perfection made her seem as though she were fashioned from a different clay from the half-sister who sat beside and a little behind her—and who was not quite as tall as Ash's first impression of her, for standing, he had topped her by half a head. But then he was a tall man, and her co-bride, Shushila, stood barely four foot ten in her heelless silken slippers.

The elder girl lacked the delicacy of the East, but that did not prove that she was the *Feringhi*-Rani's daughter . . .

His gaze fell on a bare arm that was the colour of warm ivory, and there, just above the golden bangles, was a crescent-shaped scar: the mark left by the teeth of a monkey, many years ago . . . Yes, it is Juli all right, thought Ash. Juli grown up—and grown beautiful.

Long ago, during his first year at a public school, Ash had come across a line in one of Marlowe's plays that had caught his imagination and stuck fast in his memory ever since: Faust's words on seeing Helen of Troy: *'Oh thou art fairer than the evening air, clad in the beauty of a thousand stars!'* It had seemed to him then, and still did, the perfect description of beauty, and later he had applied it to Lily Briggs, who had giggled and told him that 'he wasn't 'alf a one', and later still to Belinda—who had reacted in a similar manner, though she had phrased her comment a little differently. Yet neither of them bore the least resemblance to the Maharajah of Karidkote's half-sister, Anjuli-Bai, for whom, thought Ash, astounded, those lines might have been expressly written.

Looking at Juli, it was as though he were seeing beauty for the first time in his life, and as though he had never realized before what it was. Lily had been blowsily attractive and Belinda had certainly been pretty—a great deal prettier than any of his previous loves. But then his ideal of feminine good looks had been shaped by his childhood in India, and unconsciously influenced by fashion—Victoria's England, as may be seen from countless paintings, picture-postcards and illustrated books of the period, still admired large eyes and a small rose-bud of a mouth in a smoothly oval face, to say nothing of sloping shoulders and a nineteen-inch waist. The era of Du Maurier's stately goddesses, who were to usher in an entirely new fashion in beauty, had not yet dawned; and it had never occurred to Ash that any form and face so diametrically opposed to the Victorian—and Indian—ideal could not only be immeasurably more arresting, but make the prettiness he had hitherto admired seem slightly insipid. But though his personal preference was still for dainty and delicately built women such as Shushila, Anjuli's looks, which threw back to her Russian great-grandmother, were a revelation to him, and he could not take his eyes off her.

Becoming aware of his regard and embarrassed by it, she half turned from him and drew the peak of her sari forward again so that her face was once more in shadow; and Ash suddenly realized that he had been staring—and also that Jhoti had just asked him a question and that he had no idea what it was. He turned quickly towards the boy, and for the next ten minutes became involved in a discussion on falconry; and only when Jhoti and Shushila began to tease their uncle to let them go hawking on the far side of the river was he able to turn back again to Anjuli.

The two elderly waiting-women were already beginning to yawn and nod, for it was getting late. But though he knew that it was time he took his leave, there was something he meant to do before he left. He put his hand in his pocket, and a moment or two later reached out and made believe to pick something off the carpet.

'Your Highness has dropped something,' said Ash, holding it out to Anjuli. 'This is yours, I think?'

He had expected her to look surprised or puzzled—probably the latter, for he thought it unlikely that after all these years she would remember either the luck-piece or the boy she had given it to. But she did neither. She turned her head when he spoke, and seeing the sliver of mother-of-pearl on his palm, took it with a smile and a brief murmur of thanks.

'*Shukr-guzari*, Sahib. Yes, it is mine. I do not know how it can have—'

She stopped on a gasp, for she had put a hand to her breast; and Ash knew in that moment that he had been wrong. Juli not only remembered, but she still wore her half of the luck-piece where she had always worn it, hanging from a strand of silk about her neck. And she had just realized that it was still there.

Ash was suddenly aware of a disturbing mixture of emotions that he did not wish to analyse, and turning to Shushila-Bai, he begged her forgiveness for keeping her up so late and asked for leave to withdraw. Yes, yes, agreed Kaka-ji, rising with alacrity, it was quite time they all retired to bed; the hour was late and though young people might be able to do without sleep, he himself could not. 'It has been a very pleasant evening. We must have other parties,' said Kaka-ji Rao.

Anjuli said nothing. Nor did she move. She sat quite still, holding the missing half of her luck-piece clenched in her hand and staring at Ash with wide, startled eyes. But Ash was already regretting the impulse that had made him give it to her, and as he said his farewells he avoided her gaze, and leaving the tent walked back through the camp feeling angry with himself and wishing that he had thrown away the piece of pearl shell—or at least had the sense to leave well alone. He had an uneasy feeling that he had started something, the end of which he could not see, like a man who carelessly flicks a pebble at an over-hanging ledge of snow, and thereby sets in motion an avalanche that may overwhelm some hamlet in a valley far below.

What if Juli were to talk of the strange return of the missing half of her luck-piece? He had no way of knowing how many people were in her confidence these days, or how much she had changed. Nor had he any idea where her loyalties now lay, for the sad little Kairi-Bai of his Gulkote days appeared to have nothing in common with this bejewelled princess of Karidkote who was being conveyed to her wedding with such pomp and splendour, and it was clear that her circumstances had altered surprisingly and everything turned out well for her. As for himself, he had no desire to be identified in any way with the boy who had been her brother's servant. Janoo-Rani might be dead, but Biju Ram was still very much alive; and, in all probability, just as dangerous. He at least would not have forgotten Ashok, and were he to hear the tale of Juli's luck-piece he might well take fright and decide to deal with this Sahib as he and Janoo-Rani had plotted to do all those years ago with Ashok. And for the same reason—for fear of what he might know or guess; and, now that Lalji was dead, of the ghosts that he might raise . . .

Thinking of all this, Ash was uneasily conscious of a cold feeling in the pit of his stomach and a compulsive urge to look over his shoulder as he walked back through the camp. He had been a fool and once again, as so often in the past, acted on impulse and without giving due thought to the possible consequences of the action; which was something he had sworn to himself that he would never do again.

That night he slept with the tent-flap laced shut and a revolver under his pillow, having made a mental note to pay more attention to the siting of his tent, which at present could be too easily approached from three sides without disturbing either Mahdoo or Gul Baz, or any of his personal servants. From now on he would have their tents pitched in a half-moon behind his own, with their guy-ropes interlocking, while the horses should be tethered to the right and left instead of bunched together in the rear. 'I'll see to it in the morning,' decided Ash.

But the morning was still several hours away when he was awakened from sleep by the sound of a hand trying the fastening of the tent-flap.

Ash had always been a light sleeper and the stealthy sound woke him instantly. He lay still, listening, and presently heard it repeated. Someone was trying to enter the tent, and it was not one of his own men; they would have coughed or spoken to attract his attention. Nor could it be a prowling dog or a jackal, for the sound did not come from ground level but from higher up. Ash slid a hand under his pillow and drew out his revolver, and was easing back the safety catch when someone again scratched softly but imperatively on the canvas and a whispering voice called: 'Sahib, Sahib.'

'*Kaun hai?*' (who is it?). 'What do you want?'

'No harm, Sahib. Indeed no harm. A word only—' The speaker's teeth chattered from cold, or possibly from fear or nervousness.

Ash said curtly: 'Speak then. I am listening.'

'The Rajkumari . . . my mistress, Anjuli-Bai, says . . .'

'Wait.'

Ash felt for the knot and unlacing the flap threw it back and saw that his visitor was a woman, a veiled and shrouded figure bundled in shawls, who was presumably one of the royal serving-women. He himself was more scantily clad, for his sole garment was a pair of loose cotton trousers, and the woman drew back with a startled gasp, disconcerted at being faced with a half-naked Sahib who clutched a revolver in one hand.

'Well, what is it?' demanded Ash impatiently. He did not relish being woken at such an hour and was ashamed of the fear that had stabbed through him in the moment of waking. 'What is it that your mistress wishes to know?'

'She wishes—she prays that you will tell her from whom you received a certain piece of pearl-shell, and asks if you can give her news of him . . . and of his mother also; and tell her where they may be found. That is all.'

And quite enough, thought Ash grimly. Was it only Juli who wanted this information, or had the return of the missing half of the luck-piece already been talked of in the camp, and could Biju Ram have sent this woman to question him?

He said brusquely: 'I cannot help the Rajkumari. Tell her that I am sorry, but I know nothing.'

He made as though to close the tent-flap, but the woman reached out and catching his arm said breathlessly: 'That is not true. You must surely know who gave it to you, and if so . . . Sahib, I beg of you! Of your charity, tell me only if they are alive and well.'

Ash looked down at the hand on his arm. The newly risen moon was in its last quarter, but its light was still bright enough to show him the shape of that hand, and he caught it about the wrist and holding it in a hard grasp, reached out and jerked aside the *chuddah* that hid the woman's face. She made one frantic attempt to free herself, and finding that she could not, stood quite still, staring at him and breathing a little quickly.

Ash laughed and made her a half bow. 'I am greatly honoured, Your Highness. But is this wise? As you see I am not dressed to receive visitors; and were you to be found here at such an hour it would cause great trouble for us both. Besides, you should not go unattended through the camp. It is too dangerous. You would have done better to send me one of your women. Let me advise you to return quickly before they awake and rouse the guard when they find you gone.'

'If it is for yourself that you are afraid,' said Anjuli sweetly, 'you have no cause to be, for I sleep alone and therefore no one will miss me. And if I feared for myself, I would not be here.'

Her voice was still barely more than a whisper, but there was so much scorn in it that the blood came up into Ash's face and for a fraction of a second his fingers tightened cruelly about her wrist.

'Why, you little bitch,' said Ash softly and in English. He laughed, and releasing her, stepped back and said: 'Yes, I am afraid. And if

Your Highness is not, I can only say that you should be. Myself, I cannot believe that your brothers or your uncle would treat such an escapade lightly; or your bridegroom, either. They might consider that it in some way touches your honour, and as I confess I have no wish to get a knife between my ribs one of these nights, I would urge you again, with all respect, to go quickly.'

'Not until you tell me what I wish to know,' said Anjuli stubbornly. 'I will stay here until you do, though as you well know, if I am found here it will go hard with me. Even my worst enemy could not wish me so much ill, and you have already saved my life. Only tell me what I ask and I will trouble you no more. I swear it.'

'Why do you want to know?'

'Because the thing you gave me tonight is the half of a luck-charm that once, very long ago, I myself gave to a friend; and when I saw it I—' A movement behind her made her spin round: a patter and a rustle in the stillness. 'There is someone there—!'

'It is only a *lakar bagha* (hyena)', said Ash.

The grotesque, shadowy creature that had been scavenging in the camp scuttled past and loped away across the plain, and the girl drew a deep, shuddering breath of relief and said haltingly: 'I thought it was . . . I thought I had—been followed.'

'So you *are* afraid after all,' said Ash unkindly. 'Well, if you wish to talk you had better come inside. It cannot be more dangerous than standing out here where anyone might see us.'

He stood back to let her enter the tent, and after a moment's hesitation she went in past him, and Ash closed the tent-flap and said: 'Don't move. I'll light a lamp.'

She heard him groping in the darkness and then a match flared, and when the wick of the hurricane lamp was burning steadily, he pulled up a canvas chair for her and, without waiting to see if she took it, turned away to put on his dressing gown and slippers. 'If we are going to be caught talking together at this hour of night,' observed Ash, tying the cord about his waist, 'it will look better if I am wearing a few more clothes. Won't you sit down? No? Then you won't mind if I do.' He seated himself on the end of the camp bed and looked up at her, waiting.

The carriage-clock on the table behind him ticked audibly in a silence that he made no attempt to break, and a moth that had found its way in from the night began to flutter around and around the lamp, throwing whirling, wavering shadows across the walls of the tent.

'I . . .' began Anjuli, and paused, biting her lip in a way that was suddenly and sharply familiar to Ash. It was a trick she had as a child and his mother used to scold her for it, saying that it would spoil the shape of her mouth.

'Go on,' said Ash unhelpfully.

'But I have already told you: I gave that charm to a friend many years ago, and I wish to know how you came by it because—because I would like to know what became of my friend and his mother, and where they are now. Is that so hard to understand?'

'No. But it is not enough. There must be more than that, or you would never have risked coming here. I want to know the whole. Also, before I answer your questions, I want to know whom you would tell.'

'Whom I would tell? I do not understand.'

'Don't you? Think—are there no others besides yourself who might also wish to know where this friend of yours is?'

Anjuli shook her head. 'Not now. Once, perhaps; for there was an evil woman who wished him ill and would have killed him if she could. But she is dead now and cannot harm him; and I think she had forgotten about him long ago. As for his friends, except for myself they left Gulkote, and I do not know where they are, or if they know where he is or what became of him. It may be that they too are dead. Or that they have forgotten him as everyone else has.'

'Except yourself,' said Ash slowly.

'Except myself. But then, you see . . . he was a brother to me—a true brother, as my own were not—and I do not remember my mother. She fell into disfavour before she died, and afterwards my father's new wife saw to it that I was kept out of his sight, so that he became a stranger to me. Even the servants knew that they need not treat me well, and only two were kind to me: one of my serving-women, and her son Ashok, a boy some few years older than myself who was in the service of my half-brother, the Yuveraj. Had it not been for Ashok and his mother I should have been friendless indeed, and you cannot know what their kindness meant to the child that I was . . .'

Her voice wavered uncertainly and Ash looked away from her, for there were tears in her eyes and once again he was ashamed because he had allowed himself to forget a little girl who had loved his mother and looked up to him as a friend and a hero, and whom he had left behind, friendless, in Gulkote and never thought of again . . .

'You see,' explained Anjuli, 'I had no one else to love, and when they went away I thought that I should die of grief and loneliness. They had no choice but to go . . . But I will not tell you that tale, for it is one I think you must know, or how else would you have known who had the other half of the luck-piece? I will only say that when we parted I gave the charm to Ashok for a keepsake, and he broke it in two and gave half back to me, promising that he would surely return one day and then—then we would join the two pieces together again. But I never learned what had become of him or even if he and his mother had escaped to safety, and there were times when I feared that they were both dead, for I could not believe that they would send me no word, or that Ashok would not come back. You see—he had promised. And then . . . and then tonight, when I saw that what you had given me was not my own half of the charm, but his, I knew that he was alive and that he must have asked you to give it to me. So I waited until all the camp was asleep, and came here to ask for news of him.'

The moth had fallen down the chimney of the oil lamp and set the wick flaring, and another clumsy night-flying insect was battering itself against the glass, making a monotonous sound that now Anjuli was no longer speaking seemed as loud as the beat of a drum in the silence. Ash rose abruptly and went over to trim the wick, standing with his back to her and apparently giving his whole attention to the task. He had not made any comment, and as the silence lengthened and he still did not speak, she said with a catch in her voice:

'Are they dead, then?'

Ash spoke without turning: 'His mother died many years ago. Not long after they left Gulkote.'

'And Ashok?' She had to repeat the question.

'He is here,' said Ash at last; and turned towards her, the light at his back falling full on her face and leaving his own in shadow.

'You mean—here in the camp?' Anjuli's voice was a startled whisper. 'Then why did he not . . . Where is he? What is he doing? Tell him—'

Ash said: 'Don't you know me, Juli?'

'Know you?' repeated Juli bewildered. 'Ah, do not make game of me, Sahib. It is not kind.'

She wrung her hands together in a gesture of despair and Ash said: 'I am not making game of you. Look at me, Juli–' he reached for the lamp and lifting it, held it so that the light fell on his face. 'Look carefully. Have I changed so much? Do you really not know me?'

Anjuli backed away from him, staring and whispering, 'No! no, no, no–' under her breath.

'Yes, you do. I can't have changed as much as all that: I was eleven. It was different with you. You were only a baby of six, or was it seven? I would never have recognized you if I hadn't known. But you still have the scar where the monkey bit you. Do you remember how my mother washed the bite and tied it up for you, and told you the story of Rama and Sita and how Hanuman and his monkeys helped them? And afterwards I took you to Hanuman's temple near the elephant lines? Have you forgotten the day that Lalji's marmoset ran away and we followed it into the *Mor Minar,* and found the Queen's balcony?'

'No,' breathed Anjuli, her eyes wide and enormous. 'No, it cannot be true. I do not believe it. It is a trick.'

'Why should I trick you? Ask me anything; something that only Ashok could know. And if I cannot answer–'

'He could have told you,' interrupted Anjuli breathlessly. 'You could be repeating things that you learned from him. Yes, that is it!'

'Is it? But why? There is nothing to be gained. Why should I trouble to tell you this if it were not true?'

'But–but you are a Sahib. An *Angrezi* Sahib. How can you be Ashok? I knew his mother. He was the son of my waiting-woman, Sita.'

Ash put the lamp back on the table and sat down again on the camp bed. He said slowly: 'So he always thought. But it was not so. And when she came to die, she told him that the woman who bore him was an *Angrezi* and the wife of an *Angrezi,* and that she, Sita, whose husband was his father's head syce, had been his foster-mother–his own having died at his birth. It was something that he– that I–did not wish to learn, for she had been, in every way but one, my real mother. But that did not make it any the less true, and truth is truth. I was, I am, Ashok. If you do not believe me you have only to send word to Koda Dad Khan, who lives now in his own village in the country of the Yusufzais, and whom you must surely remember.

Or to his son, Zarin, who is a Jemadar of the Guides, in Mardan. They will tell you that what I say is true.'

'Oh, no!' whispered Anjuli. Her voice failed, and turning from him she leaned her head against the tent pole and wept as though her heart would break.

It was, perhaps, the one reaction he was not prepared for, and it not only disconcerted him but left him feeling embarrassed and help-less, and more than a little indignant.

What on earth had she to cry about? *Girls!* thought Ash—not for the first time—and began to wish that he had kept his mouth shut. He had meant to do so; though admittedly only after it had occurred to him that others besides Anjuli-Bai might be interested in the fate of Ashok, and that it had probably been a grave mistake to resurrect the memory of that long-forgotten little boy. But the fact that Juli had remembered him and his mother with so much affection for so many years had melted his resolution, and it had suddenly seemed cruel not to tell her the truth, and allow her to believe, if it was any comfort to her, that he had kept a promise that, to be honest, he had forgotten all about until now. He had presumed that she would be pleased. Or at least excited. Not appalled and tearful.

What did she expect? thought Ash resentfully. What else could he have done? Fobbed her off with some cock-and-bull story of a stranger who had given him that piece of pearl-shell? Or refused to tell her anything and sent her away with a flea in her ear—which is what she deserved for behaving in this embarrassing manner. He scowled at the haze of insects that by now were circling the lamp and tried to shut his ears to the sound of that stifled sobbing.

The clock on the table by his bed struck three, and the small, brisk chimes made him start violently, not because they reminded him of the lateness of the hour, but because, subconsciously, his nerves were on the stretch. He had not realized until then just how apprehensive he was, but that involuntary spasm of alarm was a re-minder of the dangers of the present situation and the horrifying risk that Juli had taken in coming to see him. She had brushed it away lightly enough, but that did not make it any the less real; if she were missed, and found here, the consequences for them both did not bear thinking of.

For the second time that night Ash found himself thinking how easily he could be murdered (and Juli too, for that matter!) without anyone ever knowing, and his exasperation mounted. How like a woman to compromise them both and then, having landed them in this dangerous and ridiculous position, make matters worse by collapsing into floods of tears. He would like to shake her. Didn't she realize—?

He turned his head to look at her, still scowling, and his mood changed abruptly; for she was crying very quietly and there was something in her pose that reminded him vividly of the last time he had seen her cry. Even then it had been on his account—because he was in danger and was going away—and not because she herself would be left alone and friendless. And now once again he had made her cry. Poor Juli—poor little Kairi-Bai! He stood up and came to stand beside her, and after a moment or two said awkwardly: 'Don't cry, Juli. There isn't anything to cry about.'

She did not reply, but she shook her head in a helpless gesture that might have been either agreement or dissent, and for some reason that small, despairing gesture cut him to the heart and he put his arms about her and held her close, whispering foolish words of comfort and saying over and over again: 'Don't cry, Juli. Please don't cry. It's all right now. I'm here. I've come back. There isn't anything to cry about . . .'

For a minute or so the slender, shuddering body made no resistance. Her head lay passively against his shoulder and he could feel her tears soaking through the thin silk of his dressing-gown. Then all at once she stiffened in his arms and tore herself free. Her face was no longer beautiful: the lamplight showed it blurred and distorted with grief, and her lovely eyes were red and swollen. She did not speak; she merely looked at him. It was a chill and contemptuous look, as wounding as the lash of the whip, and turning from him, she ripped back the tent-flap and ran out into the night, and was swallowed up by the moonlight and the chequered shadows.

There was no point in following her, and Ash made no attempt to do so. He listened for a while, but hearing no sound of voices or any challenge from the direction of the camp, he went back into the tent and sat down again, feeling dazed and curiously breathless.

'No,' whispered Ash, arguing with himself in the silence. 'No of course not. It's ridiculous. It couldn't possibly happen like that . . . not in just one minute, between one breath and the next. It *couldn't* . . .'

But he knew that it could. Because it had just happened to him.

In obedience to the younger bride's wishes, the tents had not been struck on the following morning and word had gone out that there would be no further move for at least three days—a respite that was welcomed by all, for apart from a rest from marching it provided an opportunity for clothes to be washed and food to be cooked in a more leisurely manner, and a thousand repairs and re-adjustments made to tents, trappings and saddlery.

The banks of the river were soon lined with dhobis busied with piles of washing, mahouts bathing their elephants, and hordes of children splashing and playing in the shallows. Grass-cutters scattered in search of fodder and hunting parties rode out after game; and Jhoti and Shushila wheedled their uncle into arranging a day's hawking that the girls could attend without the necessity of keeping strict purdah.

Kaka-ji had needed a lot of persuading, but he had eventually given way on condition that they kept well out of sight of the camp, and a party had been made up that included Ash and Mulraj, half-a-dozen falconers, three of the brides' women and a small escort of palace guards and servants. It also included Biju Ram (who would be in attendance upon Jhoti) and Kaka-ji Rao, who announced that he himself would be accompanying them solely in order to keep an avuncular eye upon his nieces—which had deceived no one, for the old gentleman had a passion for falconry and they were all aware that he would not have missed it for anything; and also that he would have preferred to go without either of his nieces.

'It is not that they cannot ride well enough,' he explained to Ash in a burst of confidence, 'but they know little of falconry, which is a man's sport. A woman's wrist is not strong enough to support a hawk. Or at least, Shushila's is not, though with her half-sister it is different. But then Anjuli-Bai has no liking for the sport and Shushila tires too easily. I cannot think why they should wish to come with us.'

'Kairi did not wish to,' volunteered Jhoti, who had been listening to the conversation of his elders. 'She wanted to stay behind. But Shu-Shu said that if Kairi wouldn't go she would not go either, and she began to cry and say that she was so tired of the noise and the smells of the camp, and of being shut up in a *ruth* or a tent, and that if she didn't get away from it and out into the open air for a while she would die. *You* know what she is like. So of course Kairi had to agree to come. Oh, here they are at last—Good. Now perhaps we can start.'

They rode away across the plain, holding their horses to a sedate trot in order not to out-distance the cart containing the waiting women, who could not ride, or the Rajkumari Shushila, who in spite of what Kaka-ji had said was an indifferent horsewoman and rode on a lead-rein held by an elderly retainer.

Both girls wore light head scarves that concealed their faces and left only their eyes uncovered, but once clear of the camp and in open country they allowed the flimsy material to blow free. But Ash noted with interest that except for Jhoti and Kaka-ji, none of the men-folk —not even Mulraj, who was related to the royal family—ever looked directly at them even when replying to a question: an exhibition of good manners that impressed him, though he did not emulate it. Having been told to consider himself one of the family, he saw no reason why he should not claim an honorary brother's privilege and look as long and as openly as he pleased, and he had done so. But at Anjuli rather than at her younger sister; though little Shushila, laughing and excited by the sport and the heady taste of freedom, was well worth looking at: a princess from a fairy-tale, all gold and rose and ebony, and sparkling with gaiety.

'She will be ill tonight. You'll see,' said Jhoti cheerfully. 'She is always ill after she gets excited. Just like a see-saw, up in the air or down in the mud—*bump!* I think girls are silly, don't you? Fancy having to marry one.'

'Hmm?' said Ash, who was not listening.

'My mother,' confided Jhoti, 'had arranged a marriage for me, but when she died my brother Nandu broke it off, which was a good thing, for I did not wish to get married. He only did it to spite me— that I know well. He meant to do me an ill turn, and did me a good one by mistake, the silly owl. But I suppose I shall have to marry some day. One has to have a wife in order to get sons, does one not? Has yours given you any sons yet?'

Ash made another indeterminate noise and Mulraj, who was riding on the other side of him, answered on his behalf: 'The Sahib has no wife, Prince. His people do not marry young. They wait until they are old and wise. Is that not so, Sahib?'

'Umm?' said Ash. 'I'm sorry—I didn't hear what you said.'

Mulraj laughed and threw up a protesting hand. 'You see, my Prince?—he has heard nothing. His thoughts are far away today. What is it, Sahib? Is there something that troubles you?'

'No, of course not,' said Ash hastily. 'I was only thinking about something else.'

'That is plain—you have already missed a chance at three birds because of it. *Ohé!*—there goes another. A fine, fat pigeon. No . . . you are too late. The prince is before you.'

Jhoti had in fact been the first to see the pigeon, and before Mulraj had finished speaking his hawk was in the air and he himself spurring excitedly in pursuit.

'He has been well taught,' approved Mulraj, watching the child race away; 'and he rides like a Rajput. But I do not like the look of his saddle. It seems to me . . . Forgive me, Sahib.'

He set spurs to his horse and left at a gallop, abandoning Ash, who, left alone with his thoughts, was not ungrateful for a period of silence. He was not feeling at all sociable that morning; or particularly interested in the day's sport either, though he too had been well taught and the falcon on his wrist was a gift from Kaka-ji Rao. Normally he would have enjoyed nothing better than a day's hawking in such country, but today his mind was on other things.

The younger princess appeared to have shed a large part of her previous shyness, for she had talked gaily to him and obviously accepted him as a friend, but Anjuli had not spoken, and this time her silence was one of withdrawal and Ash discovered that he could not even make her look at him. He had tried to force her into conversation, only to find his questions answered with a slight gesture of the head or at best a faint polite smile, while her eyes continued to look past him as though he were not there. And she was not looking well. Her face was swollen and colourless and he suspected that she had not had enough sleep, which was not surprising considering that it was after three when she had left his tent. He did not think it would be possible for her to look ugly, for her beauty was bone deep, and the way her small square face was set on the column of her throat, the shortness of her upper lip and the width between her eyes, would always be there. But today, riding beside her little sister, she appeared almost plain, and he wondered why that should make no difference at all to the way she looked to him.

Months ago he had told Wally that he could never fall in love again because he was cured of love for ever—immunized to the disease like a man who has recovered from smallpox. And only a few hours ago, eight at most, he would have repeated that statement and been confident that it was true. He still could not understand why it should no longer be so, or how it had come about. His feelings for the child Juli, though protective, had certainly never been either fond or sentimental (small boys being seldom interested in, let alone deeply attached to, little girls much younger than themselves) and given the choice he would undoubtedly have preferred a playmate of his own age and sex. Besides, he had known who she was when he carried her through the river and stood holding her for an unconscionably long time in the dusk; yet his only emotion then had been impatience . . .

Two nights later, staring at her in the durbar tent and discovering with amazement that she was beautiful, his pulses had not quickened or his emotions been stirred; and when she came to his tent he had been suspicious, irritated and vaguely sentimental by turn, and ended up feeling angry and embarrassed. So why on earth should a few minutes in which she had sobbed in his arms, and the sight of her wet, distorted face, change the world for him? It did not make sense —yet it had happened, all the same.

One minute he had been furious with her for coming and wishing angrily that she would stop crying and go away—quickly. And thirty seconds later, holding her, he had known without a shadow of doubt that he had found the answer to that nagging feeling of emptiness that had bedevilled him for so long. It had gone for ever, and he had been made whole again, because he had found the thing that was lacking—it was here in his arms: Juli . . . his own Juli. Not part of his past, but quite suddenly, and for always, a part of his heart.

As yet he had no idea what, if anything, he intended to do about this. Prudence told him that he must put her out of his mind and do his best to avoid seeing or speaking to her ever again, because to do so could only end in disaster for them both: a point he had seen clearly enough last night and that was still as clear, if not clearer, in the harsh light of morning. The Rajkumari Anjuli was the daughter of a ruling prince, the half-sister of another, and soon to become the wife of a third. Nothing could alter that, so his wisest course—the only course—was to forget last night and be thankful that something he had said or done had succeeded in offending her so deeply that she obviously did not intend to have anything further to do with him. But then prudence had never been Ash's long suit; nor, for that matter, had caution. All he could think of at the moment was that he must and would talk to her, though that was going to be difficult enough to do even with her co-operation, and almost impossible without it. But he would manage it somehow. He must. There were still weeks of journeying ahead of them, and though up to the present he had done his best to hurry the camp forward and keep it on the move, this was something that could be altered.

From now on he would let the pace slow down, and stay longer at each stopping place—a day or two at least, which alone would add several weeks to the journey. And in order to ensure that Juli should not avoid him he would take special care to make friends with Shushila, Jhoti and Kaka-ji, who would invite him to the durbar tent, where Juli would have to join them. For judging from her little sister's dependence upon her, she would find it hard to refuse—and harder still to find a valid reason for doing so, as somehow he did not think she would be prepared to explain the true circumstances to her sister, or anyone else.

'*Hai mai!*' sighed Ash, and he did not know that he had spoken aloud until Kaka-ji, who had drawn rein beside him, said: 'What is it that troubles you?'

'Nothing of any importance, Rao-Sahib,' said Ash, flushing.

'No?' Kaka-ji's tone was gently teasing. 'Now I would have said, from the signs, that you were in love and had left your heart behind in Rawalpindi. For thus do young men look and speak and sigh when they think of the beloved.'

'You are too acute, Rao-Sahib,' said Ash lightly.

'Ah, but then I too have been young; though to look at me now, you might not believe that.'

Ash laughed and said: 'Did you ever marry, Rao-Sahib?'

'Assuredly—and when I was far younger than you. But she died of the cholera five years later, having given me two daughters; and now I have seven grandchildren—all girls, alas; though doubtless they will in time give me many great-grandsons. I must hope so.'

'You should have married again,' said Ash severely.

'So my friends said; and my family also. But at the time I was in no haste to add yet another woman to a household that seemed over-full of them. Then, later—much later—I fell in love . . .'

The last words had been spoken in such a lugubrious tone that Ash laughed again and said: 'To hear you speak, anyone would think that was the greatest of misfortunes.'

'To me, it was indeed so,' sighed Kaka-ji, 'for as she was not of my caste I knew that I should not think of her, and that my priests and my family would oppose it. But while I hesitated her father gave her in marriage to another man, who cared less for such matters than I; and afterwards . . . Afterwards I found that no other woman could take her place in my heart, or blot out her face from my mind. Therefore I could not bring myself to marry again, which was perhaps as well, for women can cause a great deal of trouble and noise, and when one is old, as I am, one requires peace and quiet.'

'And leisure to go hawking,' grinned Ash.

'True, true. Though with age one's skill at such pursuits grows less. Let me see now how you shape, Sahib . . .'

They talked no more of love, and Ash turned his attention to hawking, and during the next hour or so won golden opinions from Kaka-ji for his handling of the merlin-falcon. The mid-day meal was served in a large grove of trees near the edge of a *jheel,* and when it was over the brides and their women retired to take an afternoon siesta in a makeshift tent, while the men disposed themselves comfortably in the shade and prepared to sleep away the hottest part of the day.

By now the fresh breeze of the morning had dwindled to a mere breath of air that whispered among the branches but did not stir the dust below, and the chattering of the *saht-bai* and the little striped squirrels was stilled. Somewhere out of sight a pair of ring-doves kept up a soft, monotonous cooing that blended pleasantly with the drowsy rustle of the leaves and an occasional tinkle of bells as a hawk stirred and shook itself in the shadows. The soft combination of sounds was soothing enough to lull any average adult to sleep, and only Jhoti—who like most ten-year-olds considered sleeping in the afternoon a shocking waste of time—was alert and restless. Though not all his elders were asleep: Captain Pelham-Martyn, for one, was awake.

Comfortably settled between the roots of an ancient neem tree, his shoulders fitting snugly into a deep groove in the trunk, Ash was once again engaged in pondering the problems presented by Juli, while at the same time listening with one ear to a low-pitched conversation between two people whom he could not see, and who were presumably unaware that there was anyone else on the far side of the tree—unless they imagined him to be asleep. It was a singularly uninteresting conversation and only its content told him that one of the speakers was Jhoti, who apparently wished to go off on his own to try his hawk on the far side of the *jheel,* and was being discouraged from doing so by some un-cooperative adult. As Ash saw no reason to make his presence known and thereby be drawn into an argument in which both sides would appeal to him for support, he stayed where he was and kept silent, hoping that the two would soon go away and leave him in peace. The low-pitched voices interfered with his thoughts and made it impossible for him to concentrate, and he listened to them with increasing irritation.

'But I want to go,' said Jhoti. 'Why should I waste the whole afternoon snoring? If you don't want to come with me, you need not. I don't want you, anyway. I'd much rather go alone. I'm tired of being followed about as though I were a baby and never being allowed to do anything by myself. And I won't take Gian Chand, either. I can fly a hawk just as well as he can, and I don't need *him* to tell me how to do it.'

'Yes, yes, my Prince. Of course.' The whispering voice was soothing and placatory: 'Everyone knows it. But you cannot go about unattended. It is not fitting, and His Highness your brother would never permit it. Perhaps when you are older—'

'I am old enough now,' interrupted Jhoti hotly. 'And as for my brother, you know quite well that he would do anything to prevent me enjoying myself. He always has. He knew how much I wished to accompany my sisters to Bhithor, so of course he said I could not go just to spite me. But I tricked him finely and came after all.'

'You did, my Prince. But as I warned you then, it was a rash deed and one we may all live to regret, as he may yet send to fetch you back and revenge himself upon those of us who came with you. This escapade of yours has already put me in grave jeopardy, and were any harm to befall you on the journey, my head would surely pay for it.'

'Bah! That is child's talk. You said yourself that he would never have me dragged back for fear that it would create too much talk, and make him look foolish because I had out-witted him. Besides, you were in his service before you were in mine, so—'

'Nay, Prince, I was in your mother the Maharani's service. It was only by her orders that I served him; and by her order that I left his service for yours. Ah, she was a very great lady, the Maharani.'

'You do not need to tell *me* that,' said Jhoti jealously, 'she was my mother. And she loved me best—that I know. But because you were once in Nandu's household, you can always pretend that you only came away with me in order to see that I came to no harm.'

The reply was a curious giggling laugh that instantly identified the boy's companion and jerked Ash to sudden attention, for even after all these years he remembered that sound. Biju Ram had always giggled like that at Lalji's jokes and his own obscenities, or at the sight of any creature, human or animal, being tormented.

'Why do you laugh?' demanded Jhoti resentfully, his voice rising.

'Hush, Prince—you will wake the sleepers. I laughed because I was thinking of how your brother would look if I said any such thing to him. He would not believe it, though the gods know it is true. Yet you have shown him that you can think and act for yourself, and cannot be tied by the leg like one of his tame macaws, or followed about by women and old men crying "Take care", "Be careful", "Do not tire yourself", "Do not touch". *Hi-ya!* you are a true son of your mother. She ever took her own path and no one had the courage to gainsay her—not even your father.'

'They will not gainsay me either,' boasted Jhoti. 'And I am not going to be followed about any longer. I'm going to go out by myself and fly my own hawk; now, this minute, instead of lying around snoring. And you can't stop me.'

'But I can arouse your syce, and Gian Chand also. They will see that you come to no harm.'

'Don't you *dare!*' whispered Jhoti fiercely. 'I thought you were my friend. Why did you help me escape from my brother if you were going to behave just as he does and stop me from doing anything I want to do? You are just like everyone else. "Don't do this—don't do that. Take care. Be careful." '

'My Prince, I *beg* of you—'

'No! I will go. And I will go alone.'

'*Hazrat**,' sighed Biju Ram, capitulating. 'Well, if you will not let me go with you or take Gian Chand, at least do not ride Bulbul; he is too fresh today and may be hard to manage. Take Mela, who is quieter and will give you no trouble, and do not, I beg you, ride too

* Highness

far or too fast. Keep to a trot only and stay within sight of us, for if you were to fall—'

'Fall!' snorted Jhoti, outraged by the very idea. 'I have never fallen off a horse in my life!'

'There is always a first time,' observed Biju Ram sententiously, and giggled again as though to rob the platitude of offence.

Jhoti laughed, and a moment later Ash heard the pair move away between the trees. But though the afternoon was now silent he found himself oddly uneasy. There was something about the conversation he had overheard that did not ring true. Why, for instance, had Biju Ram, of all people, elected to side with the younger son against the elder, and carry his partisanship to the extent of helping to smuggle Jhoti out of Karidkote in defiance of the Maharajah's wishes? That his reasons were not altruistic could be taken for granted—unless his character had changed out of all knowledge during the past decade, which was something that Ash was not prepared to believe. Biju Ram had always known on which side his bread was buttered, and it was safe to assume that he still did so. On the other hand he had been Janoo-Rani's creature for many years, and if there was any truth at all in Mahdoo's slanderous hints as to the reason for her sudden demise, it was just possible that he might have turned against the parricide and transferred his allegiance to her younger son. Though not, decided Ash, unless there was a good chance of that son being able to reward him liberally one day for doing so.

Could there, then, be a move on foot to kill Nandu, the new Maharajah, and put Jhoti in his place? If so, then Biju Ram's behaviour was easily explained, as was his anxiety to keep the boy from running any risks. No wonder he too was attempting to molly-coddle the child, for if there was conspiracy against the Maharajah, it was possible that the Maharajah knew it and might kill his brother in order to deprive the plotters of a rallying point for revolt. And if Biju Ram's task was to remove the heir to a safe place until the throne was made vacant, it stood to reason that he would take very good care to see that the boy came to no harm.

Ash clasped his hands about his knees, and propping his chin on them, thought about Biju Ram and Karidkote. Ought he perhaps to send a word of warning to Mr Carter, the District Officer? or better still to the British Resident in Karidkote (there was bound to be one by now)? But then he had no proof. It would not be enough to say, 'I used to know Biju Ram, and therefore I know that if he is befriending young Jhoti it must be because he knows that Nandu is due to be murdered, and that Jhoti will soon be Maharajah.' No one would believe him. And in any case it might not be true. The whole thing was probably only a figment of his imagination; though Mahdoo had said . . . But then that too was merely a rumour, the idle gossip of some camp-follower and therefore no more reliable than his own random suspicions. There was obviously nothing he could do, and anyway the internal affairs of Karidkote were none of his business.

Ash yawned and leaning back against the tree trunk prepared to follow the example of the majority and go to sleep. But the afternoon was destined to be a disturbed one. The muffled clip-clop of a horse's hooves on thick dust was barely audible in the silence, but it was still loud enough to attract his attention, and he turned his head and saw Jhoti ride past, carrying a hooded falcon on one wrist and keeping his horse to a walk for fear of waking the sleepers in the grove. He was riding the bay gelding, Bulbul, and he was alone: proof enough that he had won his point against Biju Ram.

Ash could sympathize with the child's desire to escape from supervision, but watching him turn away from the *jheel* and head for the open country, he found himself in unexpected agreement with Biju Ram. This was probably the first time that Jhoti had ever ridden out alone, for up to now there must always have been several men in attendance on him, one of whom would ride ahead to make sure that he did not venture into country where there were such traps for the unwary as nullahs and concealed wells, patches of bog or unexpected outcrops of rock.

'It isn't safe,' thought Ash. 'Someone should have gone with him!' Hadn't Mahdoo said something about Lalji's father and a riding accident?—that the late Maharajah had been out hawking when his horse bolted and fell into a nullah, breaking both their necks? His uneasiness increased and he scrambled to his feet and began to walk quickly back through the trees to where his own horse, The Cardinal, was tethered.

There was no sign of Biju Ram, and falconers, syces and guards were all asleep. But Mulraj, who was not, saw him pass and inquired in an undervoice where he was going in such haste. Ash paused briefly to explain and Mulraj looked startled.

'So? Then I think I will go with you,' said Mulraj. 'We can pretend that we wished to spy out the land for game while the others slept, and took the same path as the boy by chance. Then he will not think that he has been followed. Let us be quick.'

Some of Ash's disquiet seemed to have communicated itself to Mulraj, for he began to run. They did not take long to saddle their horses, but to avoid rousing the others they rode through the grove at a walk, as Jhoti had done, and only when they were well clear of the trees did they break into a gallop. At first they could see no sign of the boy, for the plain shimmered under the mid-afternoon sun and the dancing heat-haze hid him from sight. But presently they caught sight of the little figure on horseback and reined their own mounts to a sedate canter.

Bulbul was still jerking his head and sidling impatiently, but Jhoti seemed to have no difficulty in controlling him. He was riding quite slowly through a patch of scrub, presumably in the hope of putting up a hare or a partridge, and Ash breathed a sigh of relief. The child had more sense than he had given him credit for and was evidently right when he asserted that he was quite old enough to look after himself. There had been no need at all for Mulraj and himself to go chasing off after the brat like a pair of anxious nursemaids, since he was plainly no milk-sop, and obviously at home on a horse. If he could only be persuaded to take more exercise and eat less *halwa,* and lose some of that puppy-fat, he would make a first-class rider one of these days; and as Mulraj had already pointed out, he knew how to handle a hawk.

'We're wasting our time,' observed Ash irritably. 'That child knows what he's doing and you and I are behaving like a pair of old women. It's just the sort of thing he complains of, and I don't blame him.'

'Look—' said Mulraj, who had not been listening, 'he has put up a partridge—no, a pigeon I think. Two of them!'

'Teal,' said Ash, whose eye-sight was keener. 'There must be grass among those bushes.'

They saw Jhoti rein in and heard his shrill, excited '*Hai-ai!*' as he rose in the saddle and flung up his arm to help the falcon take off. For a moment bird and boy were motionless: Jhoti standing in his stirrups to gaze upwards and the falcon hanging above him, threshing the air with its wings like a swimmer treading water, until, sighting its prey, it was away with the speed of an arrow. The boy plumped back into the saddle, and was almost unseated as his horse responded with a frenzied bound and plunged forward through the bushes to bolt wildly out onto the stony plain.

'What on earth—?' began Ash puzzled; and had no time to finish the sentence, for the next instant he and Mulraj together were racing in pursuit, using whip and spur in a desperate attempt to overtake the run-away.

There was no need for questions, as they could see clearly enough what had happened: Jhoti must have saddled his own horse to avoid waking the syces, and he had failed to pull the girth tight enough, for now the saddle was sliding over to one side, taking him with it and making it impossible for him to check Bulbul's headlong flight. But there was good blood in the boy—Rajput blood, than which there is no finer—and though his mother's birth had been lowly, she had possessed courage and a quick brain, and her youngest son had inherited both. Feeling the saddle slide to the right and finding himself unable to prevent it, he freed his right foot and stood in the left stirrup, and using that as a lever, flung himself forward onto his horse's neck where he clung like a monkey. The saddle swung over and crashed to the ground, striking against one of the flying hooves as it fell and putting the final touch to Bulbul's panic.

'Shabash, Raja-Sahib!' called Ash, yelling encouragement. 'Oh, well done.'

He saw Jhoti throw a quick glance over his shoulder and force a grin. The child's face was pallid with terror, but there was determination in it, and pride too: he was not going to be thrown if he could help it. In any case, to let go now would mean the certainty of breaking an arm or a leg, if not his backbone, for the ground was as hard as iron and he knew that the few bushes that grew on it were armed with thorns that were capable of tearing his eyes out. There was nothing for it but to hold on, and he did so with the tenacity of a limpet. But because his cheek was pressed to the horse's neck and Bulbul's mane blinded him, he did not see what both Ash and Mulraj now saw: the death-trap that yawned ahead of him. A wide, steep-sided nullah that the rains of many monsoons had scoured deep into the plain, dry now and thickly strewn with stones and water-worn boulders.

The horse had not seen it either, for in the manner of bolting horses it was crazed with panic and capable of running straight into a picket fence or over a cliff. It also had a long start on its pursuers and was carrying considerably less weight. But the child's head pressing against its neck made it bear to the left, which gave Ash and Mulraj an advantage, since they rode on a straight line—and on far better horses. Ash's roan, The Cardinal, had recently won two flat races and a point-to-point in Rawalpindi, while Mulraj's mare, Dulhan, had the reputation of being the finest horse in camp.

Yard by yard they narrowed the distance, but the lip of the nullah was barely ten paces away when at last Mulraj drew level and dropped his reins. Guiding Dulhan with his knees alone he leaned out, and gripping the child around the waist, snatched him away just as Ash, coming up on the opposite side, caught Bulbul's trailing reins and attempted to turn him.

As a horseman, Mulraj had few equals and no superior, though had he been riding any other horse that day the whole affair would even then have ended in disaster, if not tragedy. But man and horse had known each other for years and established a rare accord that made them seem, at times, to be part of a whole that was half equine, half human. Mulraj had made his calculations, and coming up on the left of the bolting horse was already riding on a line that would take him parallel to the nullah. Because of this, and despite the fact that he was hampered by the boy in his arms and unable to use his reins, he was still able to turn Dulhan away from the rim.

But Ash was unable to check The Cardinal, and the bay and the roan together tore on and over the lip of the nullah, to end up in kicking, threshing turmoil among the stones and boulders ten feet below.

Ash did not recover consciousness for some considerable time, which was just as well, because in addition to concussion and a large number of cuts and bruises, he had broken his collar-bone, cracked two ribs and dislocated a wrist; and under these circumstances, a jolting, three-mile journey in a bullock cart would have been almost as unpleasant as the subsequent setting of broken bones without the help of anaesthetics. Fortunately, however, he came through both ordeals without being aware of them.

Even more fortunately, Kaka-ji Rao's personal hakim was an expert bonesetter, for had Ash been left to the tender mercies of the Rajkumaries' doctor, whose services had been offered by Shushila-Bai, it would have gone hard with him, the royal physician being an elderly and old-fashioned practitioner who pinned his faith to herbal remedies and the curative properties of earth-currents and incantations, combined with offerings to the gods and various concoctions made from the dung and urine of the cow.

Luckily Kaka-ji, though a devout Hindu, had little faith in such medicines when it came to mending broken bones, and he had tactfully declined his niece's offer and sent his own doctor, Gobind Dass, to deal with the matter. Gobind had done so with great success; he knew what he was about and few college-trained European doctors could have done better. Aided by Mahdoo, Gul Baz, and one of the Rajkumari Anjuli's women, Geeta, who was a notable *dai* (nurse), he brought his patient safely through the two days and nights of high fever that had followed on the period of coma—in itself no small feat, for the sick man tossed and raved and had to be held down by force for fear that he should do himself further injury.

Ash was conscious of very little during those days, but once—it was at night—he thought he heard someone say, 'Is he going to die?' and opening his eyes saw a woman standing between him and the lamp. She was only a dark silhouette against the light, and he looked up into a face he could not see and muttered: 'I'm sorry, Juli. I didn't mean to offend you. You see, I—' But the words clotted on his tongue and he could not remember what it was he had meant to say; or to whom. And in any case the woman was no longer there, for he was looking at the unshaded lamp and he shut his eyes against the glare and sank back into blackness.

The fever left him on the third day and he slept the clock round, awaking to find that it was again night and the lamp was still burning, though its flame was shielded from him by something that threw a black bar of shadow across the bed. He wondered why he had not turned it out, and was still puzzling over this trivial point when he discovered that his mouth was as dry as a desert and that he was very thirsty, but when he attempted to move, the pain that shot through him was so unexpected that it wrenched a groan from him. The bar of shadow that lay across the upper half of his bed moved instantly.

'Lie still, child,' said Mahdoo soothingly. 'I am here . . . lie still, my son.'

The old man spoke in the voice of an adult addressing a child who has awakened from a nightmare, and Ash stared up at him, mystified by the tone and even more by Mahdoo's presence in his tent at such an hour.

'What on earth,' inquired Ash, 'are you doing here, Cha-cha-ji?'

The sound of his own voice surprised him as much as Mahdoo's had done, for it was no more than a hoarse croak. But Mahdoo's expression altered surprisingly and he threw up his arms and said wildly: 'Allah be praised! He knows me. Gul Baz—Gul Baz—send word to the Hakim that the Sahib is awake and in his right mind again. Go quickly. Praise be to Allah, the Merciful, the Compassionate—'

Tears rolled down the old man's cheeks and flashed in the lamplight, and Ash said weakly: 'Don't be an owl, Cha-cha. Of course I know you. For heaven's sake stop playing the fool and give me something to drink.'

But it was Gobind Dass, hurriedly aroused from sleep, who finally gave him a drink. Presumably one with a drug in it, because Ash fell asleep again, and when he awoke for the third time it was late afternoon.

The tent-flaps had been thrown back and through the open door he could see the low sunlight and the long shadows, and far away across the dusty plain, the faint line of the distant hills, already tinged with rose. There was a man squatting by the tent door and idly throwing dice, left hand against right, and Ash, watching him, was thankful to see that Mulraj at least had managed to avoid crashing into the nullah. The fog had lifted from his brain at last and he could remember what happened; and lying there he attempted to assess the extent of his injuries and was relieved to discover that his legs were not broken, and that it was his left arm and shoulder that was bandaged and not the right—proof that he had managed to fall on his left shoulder after all. He could remember thinking as The Cardinal plunged over into the nullah that he could not afford to lose the use of his right arm and must throw himself to the left, and there was a crumb of comfort in the fact that he had evidently managed to do this.

Mulraj gave a grunt of satisfaction at the fall of the dice, and glancing over his shoulder, saw that Ash's eyes were open and lucid.

'Ah!' said Mulraj, gathering up the dice and coming to stand beside the bed. 'So you are awake at last. It was time. How do you feel?'

'Hungry,' said Ash with the ghost of a grin.

'That is a good sign. I will send at once for the Rao-Sahib's Hakim, and it may be that he will permit you to have a little mutton broth—or a bowl of warm milk.'

He laughed at Ash's grimace of disgust and would have turned away to call a servant, but Ash reached out with his uninjured arm, and clutching a fold of his coat, said: 'The boy. Jhoti. Is he safe?'

Mulraj appeared to hesitate for a moment, and then said reassuringly that the child was well and Ash need not trouble his head about him. 'All you have to think of now is yourself. You must get well quickly; we cannot move camp until you have regained your strength, and we have already been here for nearly a week.'

'A *week?*'

'You were without your senses for a full night and day, and for the best part of the next three you raved like a madman. And since then you have been sleeping like a babe.'

'Good lord,' said Ash blankly. 'No wonder I'm hungry. What happened to the horses?'

'Jhoti's horse, Bulbul, broke his neck.'

'And mine?'

'I shot him,' said Mulraj briefly.

Ash made no comment, but Mulraj saw the betraying flicker of his eyelids and said gently: 'I'm sorry. But there was nothing else that I could do. He had broken both forelegs.'

'It was my fault,' said Ash slowly. 'I should have known that I couldn't turn that horse of Jhoti's. It was too late . . .'

Another man might have uttered consoling denials, but Mulraj had taken a liking to Ash and so he did not lie. He nodded instead and said: 'One makes these mistakes. But what is done is done, and there is no profit in bewailing what cannot be undone. Put it behind you, Pelham-Sahib, and give thanks to the gods that you are alive; for there was a time when we thought that you would surely die.'

The last words reminded Ash of something, and he frowned in an effort to remember what it was, and then said abruptly: 'Was there a woman in here one night?'

'Surely. The *dai*. She is one of the Rajkumaries' women and she has come every night; and will come for many more, being skilled in massage and the healing of torn ligaments and strained muscles. You owe her much—and the Hakim, Gobind, even more.'

'Oh,' said Ash, disappointed. And closed his eyes against the low sunlight.

Considering all things, he made a remarkably quick recovery; for which his constitution as much as Gobind's ministrations could take the credit. Those two hard years in the mountains beyond the North-West Frontier had paid dividends at last, for they had toughened him as nothing else could have done. The unorthodox nursing and insanitary conditions that prevailed in the camp—the dust and the flies, the cheerful disregard for even the most elementary rules of hygiene and the total lack of peace and quiet, all or any of which would have horrified a Western doctor—seemed almost luxurious to Ash when compared to the horrors and hardships that he had seen injured men endure in tribal territory. He considered himself lucky—and rightly so, because as Kaka-ji took care to point out, he could easily have been dead; or at the very least, crippled for life.

'Of all fool-hardy things to do!' scolded Kaka-ji severely. 'Would it not have been far better to let one horse die than to kill both, and but for a miracle, yourself as well? But then you young men are all alike—you do not think. Nevertheless, it was bravely done, Sahib, and I for one would willingly exchange all the caution and wisdom that the years have brought me for a little of such rashness and valour.'

Kaka-ji Rao was by no means Ash's only visitor. There were others, members of the camp's *panchayat* such as Tarak Nath and Jabar Singh, and old Maldeo Rai who was Kaka-ji's third cousin:

too many others, according to Mahdoo and Gul Baz, who disapproved of this stream of callers and did their best to keep them at bay. Gobind too had advocated quiet, but changed his mind when he saw that his patient was less restless when listening to gossip about Karidkote, or to any talk that kept him abreast of the day-to-day doings of the camp.

Ash's most frequent visitor was Jhoti. The boy would sit crosslegged on the floor, chatting away by the hour, and it was from him that Ash received confirmation of something that had occurred to him only as a vague suspicion. That Biju Ram, who for so many years had enjoyed the protection of Janoo-Rani—and during that time amassed a comfortable fortune in bribes, gifts and payments for unspecified services—had fallen on evil days.

It seemed that after the *Nautch*-girl's death, those who had stood highest in her favour had suddenly found themselves relegated by her son, Nandu, to positions of comparative unimportance and deprived of all their former influence, together with most of the perquisites of power, which had infuriated Biju Ram, who had grown vain and over-confident in the Rani's shadow. He had apparently been foolish enough to show his resentment, and the result had been an open quarrel, in the course of which Biju Ram had been threatened with arrest and the confiscation of all his property, and only saved himself by appealing to Colonel Pycroft, the British Resident, to intercede for him.

Colonel Pycroft had spoken to Nandu, who had said a great many rude things about his dead mother's stool-pigeon, but eventually agreed to accept a grovelling apology and a large fine, and forget the matter. But it was clear that Biju Ram had no confidence in Nandu doing any such thing, and when Nandu, barely a week after accepting that humiliating public apology, had refused permission for his Heir Apparent to accompany the bridal party to Bhithor, Biju Ram had instantly set about inciting the boy to revolt and planning Jhoti's escape—and his own.

For Ash had been right about that too. The idea had been Biju Ram's, and he and two of his friends, both of whom had been adherents of the late Rani and were now out of favour, had planned the escape and carried it through. 'He *said* it was because he was sorry for me,' said Jhoti, '—and because he and Mohun and Pran Krishna had always been loyal to my mother, and they knew she would have wished me to go to Shu-shu's wedding. But of course it was not that at all.'

'No? What then?' asked Ash, regarding his youthful visitor with increasing respect. Jhoti might be young, but he was obviously not gullible.

'Oh, because of the quarrel. My brother Nandu doesn't like any-one to disagree with him, and though he might pretend to forgive Biju Ram, he wouldn't: not really. So of course Biju Ram thought it would be safer to leave Karidkote as soon as possible, and to stay away as long as he could. I suppose he is hoping that in the end Nandu's anger may cool, but I don't think it will. Pran and Mohun only came with me because just now Nandu does not like any of the people who my mother appointed, and so they feel safer here too; and they have brought away all the money they could, in case they can't ever go back. I wish I didn't have to. I think I shall stay behind in Bhithor with Kairi and Shu-shu. Or perhaps I shall run away again and become a robber chief, like Kale Khan.'

'Kale Khan was caught and hanged,' observed Ash dampingly.

He did not intend to encourage Jhoti in any further forms of re-bellion; and in any case, he imagined that Biju Ram and his friends would be only too eager for Jhoti to extend his stay in Bhithor for as long as the Rana could be persuaded to have him. Unless, of course, news of Nandu's untimely demise was received even before they got there, in which case they would turn back at once and hurry homeward with the new Maharajah.

But Jhoti did not often talk of Karidkote. He much preferred to hear about life on the North-West Frontier; or better still, in Eng-land. He was an exhausting companion, for his thirst for knowledge forced Ash to talk a great deal at a time when talking was still some-thing of an effort. But though Ash would have been only too pleased to do without Jhoti's endless questions, it was one way of keeping him out of mischief; and a disturbing conversation with Mulraj had made him uneasy on the boy's behalf . . .

Mulraj had not intended to broach the subject until Ash was feel-ing stronger and better able to deal with such matters, but his hand had been forced, since despite all his efforts to change the conver-sation, Ash had persisted in discussing the accident and speculating upon its causes.

'I still can't make out,' said Ash, frowning at the tent pole, 'how that saddle came to fall off. I suppose it was Jhoti's fault for not fastening the girth properly. Unless Biju Ram or one of the syces did it for him. Who did? Do you know?'

Mulraj had not answered immediately, and Ash became aware that the older man had tried to avoid the whole subject. But he was tired of being treated as a feeble-minded invalid, so he scowled at Mulraj and repeated his question with a certain tartness, and Mulraj shrugged his shoulders, and bowing to the inevitable said: 'The child says that he alone saddled the horse, because Biju Ram refused to help him and went away, thinking that he could not do it single-handed and would therefore be prevented from going off alone, or be compelled to wake one of the syces, who would in turn rouse some servant who could not be prevented from following him.'

'Young idiot,' observed Ash. 'That'll teach him.'

'Teach him what?' inquired Mulraj dryly. 'To see that the straps on the girth are properly fastened? Or to look first—and very care-fully—at the underside of a saddle?'

'What do you mean by that?' demanded Ash, startled by something in Mulraj's face and voice rather than by the words themselves.

'I mean that the straps were securely fastened, but the girth itself broke. It had worn thin . . . and in a mere matter of hours, too. For by pure chance I examined the saddle earlier in the day. Do you remember how the boy flew his hawk at a pigeon that you had not even seen, your mind being elsewhere, and how I, watching him gallop away, thought that his saddle looked a trifle loose and rode after him?'

'Yes, now you mention it. You said something about not liking the look of it. But . . . Go on.'

'By the time we recovered his hawk and the pigeon,' continued Mulraj, 'we had outdistanced the rest of you and were alone, so I myself adjusted the girth; and I tell you, Sahib, that save for the fact that it could with advantage have been tighter, there was nothing wrong with it then. Yet only a few hours later it had become so worn that it broke when the horse began to gallop.'

'But that's impossible.'

'You are right,' agreed Mulraj grimly, 'it is not possible. Yet it happened. And there can be only two explanations: either that it was not the same girth, but an old and rotten one that had been substi-tuted for the other, or—which I myself think more likely—that while we ate and rested, someone had worked on it with a sharp knife, scraping it almost through, and so cunningly that it could be fastened without breaking or attracting notice, yet must part if too much strain were placed upon it . . . the strain, let us say, that would be occasioned by a bolting horse.'

Ash stared at him under frowning brows, and observed with some tartness that if it had broken while the boy was in the company of half-a-dozen others there wouldn't have been very much danger, and no one was to know that he would go off alone like that. Only Biju Ram, who for once was on the side of the angels and tried to stop him.

Mulraj shrugged in agreement, but added that there were certain things that the Sahib was not aware of: among them, that it was Jhoti's habit to gallop after his hawk, and that when he did so he hated to have someone riding at his heels. Therefore it would not have mattered how many people were out with him, because as soon as his hawk was away he would have spurred after it while everyone else would have waited and watched, and when his horse bolted, the extra strain on the girth would have made it part quickly; and as the speed of a run-away horse carrying little weight was likely to be greater, for a time, than one still under control and bearing a full-grown man, the chances were that the boy would have fallen before anyone could reach him. 'And to be thrown from a bolting horse in such country as this can kill a man, let alone a child. But those who planned it failed to make allowance for the boy's courage and quick thinking, nor did they foresee that his very size would enable him to cling on where a grown man could not.'

Ash made an impatient noise and inquired irritably how Mulraj imagined that 'they', whoever 'they' were, could possibly have foreseen that the horse would bolt? The whole thing hinged on that, and it was impossible.

Mulraj sighed and rising to his feet, stood looking down at Ash, his hands thrust through his belt and his face suddenly grim. He said very softly: 'You are wrong; that too was arranged. I could not understand why the horse should have bolted in that fashion, for Jhoti has always risen in his stirrups and cried aloud as he throws his hawk into the air, and Bulbul was as accustomed to that action as the child himself. Yet on this occasion we both saw the horse leap forward as though it had been shot. You recall?'

Ash nodded, and the pain of that incautious movement made him reply with more asperity than he had intended: 'Yes I do. And I also happen to remember that there was no one else within sight of us and no sound of a shot either. If you ask me, you've got a bee in your—'

He stopped suddenly, checked by a memory: the same that had sent him in search of his horse after seeing Jhoti ride off alone. Mahdoo's story of how the old Rajah had met his death while out hawking, and the old man's sly, sideways glance as he said: 'They think that perchance it may have been stung by a bee?'

Mulraj appeared to have followed this train of thought, for he said dryly: 'I see that you too have heard that tale. Well, it may even be true—who knows? But this time I meant to make sure, and therefore when I had dragged you from under your horse and found that you were not dead, I did not go to fetch help myself, but sent Jhoti instead. A risk, I own; though only a small one, for he would be riding Dulhan, who as you know is a horse in ten thousand and even a babe would be safe with her. When he was gone I went in search of his fallen saddle—'

'Go on,' said Ash tersely, for Mulraj had paused to look over his shoulder and appeared to be listening. 'It's only Mahdoo who is not near enough to hear and will cough if anyone else approaches.'

Mulraj nodded as though satisfied. But when he took up the tale it was in a voice that would not have carried beyond the walls of the tent: 'It was no bee this time, but the double thorn of a *kikar* tree which the boy drove home when he plumped back into the saddle after throwing up his hawk. It had been cunningly hidden in the padding in such a way that the movement of a rider would work it down, little by little, until in the end it must be driven into the horse's flesh. One day, when you are up and about again, I will show you how it is done. It is an old trick—and a very evil one, because no one can swear that such a thorn might not get there by chance. Have we not all, at some time or another, plucked such thorns out of our clothes and blankets and saddle cloths? Yet I will wager you my mare against a dhobi's donkey that this one did not find its way there by chance. The thorn alone—or the broken girth. But not both.'

There was a long silence in the tent, broken only by the buzz of flies, and when at last Ash spoke his voice was no longer sceptical: 'What have you done about it?'

'Nothing,' said Mulraj curtly. 'Except to try and keep a watch on the boy, which is no easy task, for he has his own people about him, and I am not one of them. I left the saddle where I found it and made no mention of the thorn—it being a thing I might well have missed seeing. As to the girth, which both you and I had seen break, I raised a great tumult about it when we returned to camp, berating the prince's syces for carelessness and saying that they must be dismissed. Had I not done this there are those who would have wondered why I kept silent; and that is something I do not desire.'

'But do you mean to say that you haven't told *anyone?*' demanded Ash incredulously.

'Whom should I tell? How do I know how many people, or how few, are involved in this matter?—or even the reason for it? Sahib, you have no knowledge of Karidkote, and you know nothing of the intrigues that infest the palace like a plague of flying-ants in the monsoon. Even here in the camp we are not free of it. I had not intended to speak of this matter to you until you were stronger, as worry is not good for a sick man; but now that I have done so I am glad, because two heads are better than one and together we may devise some way of protecting the child from his enemies.'

They had been able to talk no more about it that day, for the arrival of Gobind and Kaka-ji had put an end to the conversation. Gobind, declaring that his patient was looking feverish, had banned any further visitor for the remainder of that day, and Ash spent the rest of the afternoon and evening, and a good many hours of the following night, in worrying over the problem of Jhoti. Which was at least a change from worrying about Juli—though it did nothing towards improving his health or sweetening his temper. He found it intolerable to be tied to his bed at such a time, and it was then that he decided to encourage Jhoti to visit him as often and for as long as possible. A decision that he carried out in face of considerable opposition from Gobind, Mahdoo and Kaka-ji.

18

'You have been causing us all a great deal of trouble, you know,' remarked Jhoti chattily.

'*Afsos*, Highness,' murmured Ash; and placing his hands together in a mock gesture of abasement, added meekly that he was doing his best to get well as quickly as possible and should with luck be up and about in a few days.

'Oh, I didn't mean *that*,' said Jhoti. 'I meant with the priests.'

'The *priests . . . ?*' Ash looked blank.

'Yes. They have been very cross with my sisters. And with me and Mulraj too, and with my uncle most of all. And do you know why? Because they have been told that when you came to visit us in the durbar tent you sometimes sat on the same carpet as we did, and that when we offered you things to eat—fruit and sweets and things—we ate with you instead of just pretending to eat. They don't like that, because they are very strict, you know, so that they have been making a great fuss about it.'

'Have they, indeed?' said Ash, frowning. 'Yes . . . I suppose I ought to have thought of that. Does this mean that I am not to be asked to the durbar tent in future?'

'Oh no,' said Jhoti blithely, 'for when they complained to my uncle he got much crosser than they were, and told them to remember that you had saved us all from great shame and disaster—for of course it would have been terrible for everyone if Shu-shu had been drowned —and that, anyway, he took all responsibility for this. So after that there wasn't anything else they could say, because they know very well how devout he is, and how he spends hours every day at his *pujah*' (devotions), 'and gives alms to the poor and money and rich gifts to the temples. Besides, he *is* our father's brother. I was very cross too—with Biju Ram.'

'Why with Biju Ram?'

'Because he had asked me a lot of questions about what we did when you came to the durbar tent, and I told him; and then he went straight off and told the priests. He said he had only done it to protect me, because he was afraid that if it came to Nandu's ears, Nandu would spread it about to discredit me, and everyone would be angry with me for allowing it. As if I cared what Nandu or the bazaar-log think! Biju Ram interferes too much. He behaves as if he were my nurse, and I won't have it . . . Oh, here is my uncle coming to visit you. *Salaam,* Kaka-ji.'

'I might have known that I should find you here, tiring the Sahib with your chatter,' said Kaka-ji reprovingly. 'Run away now child, for Mulraj is waiting to take you out riding.'

He shooed his nephew away, and as Jhoti ran off, turned to shake an admonitory finger at the invalid. 'You are far too patient with that boy,' said Kaka-ji severely. 'How many times have I not told you so?'

'I have lost count,' admitted Ash with a grin. 'Have you only come here to scold me, Rao-Sahib?'

'You deserve to be scolded.'

'So it seems, for your nephew has been telling me that I have caused trouble for you with your priests.'

'*Chut!*' said Kaka-ji, annoyed. 'The child talks too much. There was no need to worry you with that matter. I have taken it on my own head, and it is now settled.'

'Are you sure? I would not wish to be the cause of any trouble between you and—'

'I have said that the matter is settled,' interrupted Kaka-ji firmly. 'If you wish to please me you will forget it; and also cease from allowing Jhoti to pester you. It is folly to permit him to tire you. You are letting that child worry you and giving your mind no rest.'

This was certainly true, though not in the sense that Kaka-ji meant. But Ash was not prepared to argue the point. His mind was very far from being at rest, and, as it happened, his worries on Jhoti's account had been greatly increased of late by certain things that Kaka-ji himself had let slip in the course of his frequent visits.

The old gentleman's intentions were admirable, and he would have been shocked to realize that his well-meant efforts to alleviate the invalid's boredom had proved far more disturbing than all Jhoti's questions put together. But there was no denying that Jhoti's uncle loved to talk, and Pelham-Sahib, immobilized by splints and bandages, proved an ideal audience. Kaka-ji had seldom found so good a listener—or Ash acquired so much valuable information by the simple expedient of keeping his mouth shut and looking interested. On the subject of Nandu, Maharajah of Karidkote, for instance, Ash had learned a great deal—far more, in all probability, than Kaka-ji had intended, for the old gentleman's tongue was apt to run away with him, and even when he was being discreet it was not difficult to read between the lines.

Janoo-Rani had undoubtedly been a clever woman, but as a mother she appeared to have been singularly unintelligent. Doting upon her sons, she had allowed no one to correct or punish them, and her first-born, Nandu, had been indulged to the point of foolishness, his easy-going father being too idle to take a hand in disciplining the boy. 'I do not think,' said Kaka-ji, 'that my brother really liked children, even when they were his own. He would tolerate their presence while they behaved well, but the moment they cried or were in any way troublesome he would send them from his presence and often refuse to see them again for many days, which he chose to believe was a punishment; though I do not think it was regarded as such by any save Lalji, who was his first-born and died many years ago. Lalji, I think, loved him greatly and would have given much for his father's favour; but the younger ones saw too little of him to love him, and though Jhoti might in time have taken his dead brother's place in his father's affections, Nandu was no horseman . . .'

This, it seemed, was once again Janoo-Rani's fault—one could hardly blame the boy, who was barely three years old when he took his first toss off a pony's back. Unaccustomed to being hurt, Nandu had screamed from fright and the pain of a few small scratches, and Janoo-Rani would not let the child ride again, insisting that he had suffered great injury and might easily have been killed. Even now he would not ride one if it could possibly be avoided. 'He uses elephants instead,' explained his uncle. 'Or drives out in a carriage—like a woman.'

Janoo would undoubtedly have done the same to his youngest brother had he not been made of different stuff, for the first time Jhoti took a fall he too screamed aloud. But when he had finished howling he insisted on mounting again and would not let the syce put him back on a leading rein, which delighted his father who had been watching—though Nandu, said Kaka-ji, was not so pleased. 'I think there has always been a certain jealousy there. It is not so unusual between brothers, when one has talents that the other lacks.'

Fortune had evidently favoured Nandu in many ways. Firstly, he was his mother's darling, her first-born and the favourite child. Then the death of his half-brother, Lalji, had made him heir to the throne, and now he was Maharajah of Karidkote. But it seemed that he could still be jealous, and that he was wholly the *Nautch*-girl's child both in character and physique. Like her he possessed a violent and ungovernable temper: and no one had ever made any attempt to control his rages, for his mother thought them royal and high-spirited and the servants were afraid of them, while his father, seeing little of him, was unaware of them. He had never excelled in any sport, and had not the build for it, being short and stout, like his mother; though, unlike her, he had few claims to beauty and was strangely dark-skinned for a northerner: A *'Kala-admi,'* said the citizens of Karidkote scornfully, a 'black man'. And they would cheer when Jhoti rode past, and keep silent when it was Nandu who drove through the city or the countryside.

'Jealousy is an ugly thing,' mused Kaka-ji, 'but alas, few if any of us can claim to be free of it. I myself was often afflicted by it in my youth, and though I am now old and should by rights have outgrown such unprofitable emotions, there are still times when I can feel its claws. Therefore I am afraid for Jhoti, whose brother is both jealous and powerful . . .'

The old man broke off to select another sugared plum from a box of candied fruit that he had brought as a present to the invalid, and the invalid inquired in a deceptively casual tone: 'And not above doing away with him, you think?'

'No, no, *no!* You must not think—I did not mean . . .' Kaka-ji swallowed the plum in his agitation and had to be restored with a drink of water, and Ash realized that he had made a grave mistake in trying to rush the old gentleman and put words into his mouth. There was nothing to be gained by such methods, and much by letting him ramble on unprompted. But if Kaka-ji was indeed afraid for Jhoti, what exactly was he afraid of? To what lengths did he think his nephew the Maharajah would go to injure a young brother of whom he was jealous, and who had had the temerity to flout him?

Ash was well aware that Jhoti had joined the bridal camp without permission and against his elder brother's expressed wishes. But the very fact that Jhoti had found it possible to ride after the camp, accompanied by at least eight persons and a not inconsiderable amount of baggage, proved that there could not have been any serious restriction of his liberty, and there was something about the whole affair that Ash did not understand; something that did not quite agree with his mental portrait of a jealous and tyrannical young ruler, who, for the pleasure of spiting his young brother, had banned him from accompanying his sisters to their wedding, and on hearing that the ban had been defied, flew into a fury and planned his assassination. There was, for instance, the question of time . . .

The Maharajah would not have heard of Jhoti's escapade (it could hardly be termed an 'escape') for several days. In fact it was probably much longer, because according to Kaka-ji, Nandu's reason for accompanying his sisters to the border of his state had been less a brotherly gesture than because it suited him to do so, it being on his route to the hunting grounds in the foothills to the north-east where he had planned a fortnight's sport, taking only a small party with him so that they could keep on the move, camping in a different spot each night and following the game by day. He did not often indulge in such expeditions, but when he did, he preferred to forget the affairs of state and shelve all such matters until he returned from the forest. Runners with messages were therefore discouraged, and as the hunting party was continually on the move, news of his little brother's behaviour was unlikely to catch up with him for some time. This fact was probably well known to Jhoti—and certainly known, thought Ash, to the men who had accompanied the boy on his flight from Karidkote, for however faithful and devoted to his interests they might be, they would hardly have agreed to take the risk of being stopped at the border or overtaken within a few miles of it, and ignominiously brought back to face the Maharajah while his anger was at white heat.

In Ash's opinion they would have been wiser not to have come at all, but Kaka-ji took a different view: they were all, said Kaka-ji, loyal members of Jhoti's household who had been appointed to his service by his mother the late Maharani, and it was not only their duty to obey him, but to their interest also; their fortunes being bound up with his.

'Besides,' admitted Kaka-ji, 'Jhoti too can be very obstinate, and I understand that when they attempted to dissuade him he threatened to go off alone, which of course they could not permit. The boy being in their care, it would have brought great shame on them had they allowed him to go alone and unattended; though I do not think that they would have dared accompany him had they not known that his brother would hear of his flight too late to stop him before he reached this camp. But once here, they can feel safe for a time, since they are no longer in the territory of the Maharajah but in that of the Raj. They are also under your protection, Sahib, and they reason that His Highness cannot know how you might regard an attempt to drag an unwilling child away from his sisters and return him to Karidkote to be punished—for all must know that Jhoti would never go willingly. Therefore his servants hope that His Highness will realize that there is nothing to be gained by sending men to arrest the child, particularly when he has only to wait until this wedding is over, as after that Jhoti will of course return. But by then we must all hope that the Maharajah's rage will have had time to cool, and he will be less inclined to deal harshly with something that is, let us admit it, only a boy's prank.'

Kaka-ji's words were optimistic, but the tone of his voice was less so, and he had changed the subject a little abruptly and begun to talk of other matters. However, he had already provided Ash with plenty of food for thought in the long night watches when the discomfort of splints and bandages kept sleep at bay.

The difficulties that he had foreseen, or been warned of in the prosaic, official atmosphere of Rawalpindi, had all had to do with such matters as provisioning or protocol and the possibility (considered to be negligible) of the camp being attacked by raiders in the remoter parts of the country through which it must pass. But neither he nor his military superiors had visualized the far more complicated and dangerous problems that now confronted him, and which, for the present at least, he had no idea how to deal with.

For this reason, if for no other, he had cause to be grateful for the injuries that tied him to his bed, as they not only gave him time for thought, but postponed the need for action. There was nothing he could do at the moment beyond encouraging Jhoti to spend as many hours as possible in his company, and trusting to Mulraj to keep an eye on the child for the rest of the day. Though there was always the night . . . But possibly Jhoti was safer then than at any other time, for he slept surrounded by his personal servants, all of whom, according to Kaka-ji, were devoted to him. Or if not to him, decided Ash cynically, at least to his interests, which must also be their own.

On the face of it, these men had taken a grave risk in order to let the little prince enjoy himself for a strictly limited time—possibly only for a day or two, supposing a search-party had set out at once to fetch him back, and at best a few months, since after that both he and they must return. How did they expect to be received on their return? Did they, like Kaka-ji, hope that the lapse of time would have cooled the Maharajah's wrath and allowed him to regard the episode as no more than a childish prank? Or was there some other plan? . . . Perhaps the murder of Nandu, who had as yet no son, and whose Heir Apparent was still his younger brother, Jhoti?

But then it was not Nandu but Jhoti who had very nearly been murdered—and here in the camp; though to the best of Ash's knowledge (it was a point on which he had taken the trouble to inquire) no one had followed after them or joined the camp since he himself had taken over from the District Officer in Deenagunj, nor had there been any messages from Karidkote. This suggested that the attempt had no connection with the boy's escape but must be the work of one of the rival party; some adherent of Nandu's, who, like Ash, concluded that there must be something more behind Jhoti's unexpected arrival than a 'boyish prank', and had decided to take no chances, but to scotch any further plotting by the simple expedient of killing the heir.

'If only I could talk to Juli,' thought Ash. She if anyone would know what went on inside the frowning walls and fretted wooden screens of the Hawa Mahal. The things that were whispered in its planless maze of rooms and corridors or gossiped about behind the purdahs of the Zenana Quarter . . . Juli would know, but there was no way of reaching her; and as Kaka-ji had taken fright, it would have to be Mulraj instead. At least Mulraj should know whom to watch, for the number of suspects must be limited to someone who was out with the hawking party that day. There had not been very many of them, and all those with alibis could be eliminated as a start.

Mulraj, however, had not proved helpful.

'What do you mean, "not very many of them"?' he demanded. 'It may have seemed a small party to you, but then your thoughts were not with us that day and you did not even see the game we put up—let alone who was there. Do you know how many there were? One hundred and eighteen, no less—and two thirds of them paid servants of the state, which means the Maharajah. Of what use to interrogate them? We should hear nothing but lies and would only succeed in putting the true assassins upon their guard.'

'Well, why not?' inquired Ash, ruffled by the impatience in Mulraj's voice. 'Once they realize that we know there has been an attempt on the boy's life, they may think twice before they make another. It will be too dangerous to try such tricks again, knowing that a watch will be kept.'

'Just so,' said Mulraj dryly. 'And were you dealing with your own people, your plan might be a good one. I myself have met few Sahibs, but I am told that it is their custom to go straight for an objective, looking neither to the right nor to the left. This is not so with us. You would not scare off those who meant to kill the child: you would only warn them. And being warned, they would, as you say, play no more tricks, but use instead such methods as would be less easy for us to guard against.'

'Such as?' asked Ash.

'Poison. Or a knife. Or perhaps a bullet. Any of those things would eliminate chance.'

'They would not dare. We are in British territory and there would be a strict inquiry. The authorities . . .'

Mulraj grinned derisively and said that naturally some more discreet method would be preferred, as plain murder would necessitate the provision of a scapegoat to pin the blame on, and there would also have to be a reason for the killing, one that would have no connection with the true one, and yet be acceptable as the truth. Neither of these things, in his opinion, would be impossible, but they would be a little more difficult to arrange, and as those who desired the boy's death would not want questions asked, an accident would serve them far better.

'And I am very sure that they will set about arranging another, provided they think that the first has gone unsuspected. I am also sure that knowing what we know, we shall be able to prevent it from being successful, and may even discover whose hand prepared it, and why: thereby putting an end to these attempts once and for all. It is our best chance. Perhaps our only one.'

Ash was forced to agree. Reason told him that Mulraj was right, and as the present state of his health debarred him from taking any action, he decided that the only thing to do was to try and collect more information as to the character and habits of Jhoti's elder brother; which sounded simple enough, but proved to be more difficult than he imagined. As he grew stronger the number of his visitors increased, and most of them remained to gossip; but although their talk was largely concerned with their home state, and certainly increased his knowledge of the politics and scandals of Karidkote, it taught him little more than he already knew about its ruler, and merely prevented him from having much private conversation with Kaka-ji or Mulraj—not that those two gentlemen appeared over-anxious to talk of the Maharajah either.

Jhoti, on the other hand, would have been only too willing to discuss his brother, but in such uncomplimentary terms that it was not safe to allow him to do so. There remained the *dai,* Geeta, a gaunt, pock-marked crone who under Gobind's orders continued to treat Ash's dislocated wrist and wrenched muscles, and to remain on watch for part of each night, squatting silently in the shadows in case her patient should wake and be in pain.

As a poor relation distantly connected to the late ruler's first wife, it was safe to assume that she would know all the gossip of the Zenana and prove a mine of information. But she had proved a sad disappointment, for she was far too timid; so much so that even a direct order from Shushila-Bai had not been able to persuade her to venture out except after dark and at an hour late enough to ensure that most of the camp would be asleep, and then only when shrouded in a cotton bourka such as Mohammedan women wear, for fear that a strange man should catch a glimpse of her face. (Ash, who had had that privilege, considered these precautions unnecessary, as he could not imagine any man in his senses wishing to spare her wrinkled and respectable visage so much as a passing glance.) Nevertheless he welcomed the lateness of her visits, for he found it difficult to get to sleep by the end of the day, and the *dai*'s belated appearance and skilful ministrations came at an opportune moment and always helped him to relax. But try as he would he could not coax her into talking. Her bony hands were firm and sure, but she was too shy and far too much in awe of the Sahib to do more than titter nervously when spoken to, or at most, reply in monosyllables.

Ash gave up the attempt, and deprived of more direct sources of information fell back on Mahdoo, who could be trusted to hold his tongue when necessary and at the same time collect a great deal of miscellaneous gossip from acquaintances in the camp. This he would relay of an evening when the lamps were lit and the visitors had gone, sucking at his hookah between the leisurely sentences while the smoke from the camp fires and the fragrance of cooking drifted out across the plain, and Gul Baz kept watch to see that no one crept near to listen.

Much of what he related could only have been apocryphal, and most of the rest was a hodge-podge of hearsay, speculation and scandal-mongering: the usual buzz of the bazaars, in which little credence could be placed. But here and there a nugget of useful information could be sifted from the spate of gossip, and these, put together, not only told Ash a good deal about the conditions that prevailed in the one-time state of Gulkote, but shed considerably more light on the temper and disposition of its present ruler. A score of anecdotes testified to his vanity and love of display, while many others hinted at a streak of cold-blooded and precocious cunning that had shown itself in childhood and grown with the years, and if even a fraction of the latter were true the picture that emerged was far from prepossessing.

Among the plethora of rumours, guess-work and gossip, two things stood out quite clearly: that Nandu could not endure to be defeated, and that he had very unpleasant ways of dealing with those who displeased him. An instance of this last was his treatment of a tame cheetah, one of a pair of hunting leopards that had been loosed after a buck on the plain below the Hawa Mahal, and which Nandu had backed with twenty gold mohurs to reach and pull down the quarry first. It had failed to do so and he had lost his money and his temper, and sending for a tin of kerosene oil, flung it over the wretched animal and set it alight.

This tale, unlike many others, was not based on hearsay, for a number of men in the camp had seen the cheetah burned alive. And though it had later been given out that its trainer had fled the state, few believed it. 'They say that he too died that same night,' said Mahdoo. 'But as to that, there is no proof; and though it is certain that the man was never seen again, that is not to say he is dead. It may be that he feared for his life and ran away. Who knows?'

'At a guess, the Maharajah,' said Ash grimly.

Mahdoo nodded in agreement. 'So it is believed. The Maharajah is young, but already he is greatly feared by his people. Yet it would be unwise to suppose that he is hated by all, for the people of Karidkote have never cared for weaklings, and many are pleased that their new ruler has shown himself both cunning and ruthless; taking this to be an assurance that they will not lose their independence and be swallowed up by the British, as other princely states have been. There are also many who admire him for those very qualities that make him the evil youth he is.'

'And many others, I suspect,' said Ash, 'who hate him enough to plot against him, and hope to pull him down so that they may set another in his place.'

'You mean the young prince?' Mahdoo pursed his lips and looked sceptical. 'Well, maybe. Yet if so, it is something I have not heard spoken of among the tents; and for myself, I do not think that in these times even the worst of the grumblers would desire to be ruled by a child.'

'Ah, but they would not be. That is the point. They would be ruled by that child's advisers, and it is certain that those advisers would be the ones who plotted to place him on the throne. It would be they and not the boy who would rule Karidkote.'

'Biju Ram,' murmured Mahdoo, as though considering the name.

'Why do you say that?' inquired Ash sharply. 'What have you heard about him?'

'Nothing good. He is not liked, and I have heard him called many evil names: scorpion, snake, jackal, spy and pander, and a dozen more. He is said to have been a creature of the late Maharani's and there is a tale . . . But that was many years ago and is of no consequence.'

'What tale?' demanded Ash.

Mahdoo shrugged his shoulders by way of reply and sucked at his pipe, brooding like an elderly parrot while the hookah bubbled gently in the silence. He refused to say anything more on the subject. But when Gul Baz came in to settle Ash for the night and he rose to take his leave, he returned to it briefly:

'Touching the matter we were discussing, I will make inquiry,' said Mahdoo, and went away to gather his nightly quota of gossip from around the camp fires that flickered in the darkness.

But the tittle-tattle of the camp produced nothing new, and Ash realized that if there was any more to be learned it must come from some other source, preferably from one of Nandu's immediate family—the Rajkumari Anjuli for choice. Juli was only a few months older than Nandu, and being the nearest to him in age must surely know more about him and be a better judge of his nature than anyone else in the camp. She had also known Biju Ram for many years, and she would not have forgotten Lalji . . .

'If only I could talk to her,' thought Ash for perhaps the twentieth time. 'Juli will know. I must manage it somehow . . . it can't be impossible. As soon as I can get on my feet again—'

But he did not have to wait as long as that.

19

'My sister Shushila,' announced Jhoti, presenting himself at Captain Pelham-Martyn's tent some two days later, 'says she wishes to see you.'

'Does she?' inquired Ash without much interest. 'What about?'

'Oh, just to talk, I think,' said Jhoti airily. 'She wanted to come with me to visit you, but my uncle said she must not: he does not think it would be proper. But he said that he would speak to Gobind, and if Gobind agreed, he did not see why you should not be carried across to the durbar tent this afternoon, where we can all eat and talk together.'

Ash's gaze ceased to wander and he was suddenly alert. 'Has Gobind agreed?'

'Oh, yes. He said you could be carried across in a *dhooli*. I told my sister that I did not think you would wish to go, because girls only giggle and chatter like a lot of parrots and never seem to have anything sensible to talk about. But she says that it is your talk she wishes to hear. My uncle says that this is because she is bored and afraid, and the things you speak of, being strange to her, cheer her up and make her laugh, so that she forgets her fears. Shu-shu has no courage at all: not one grain. She is even frightened of mice.'

'And your other sister?'

'Oh, Kairi is different. But then she is quite old, you know; and besides, her mother was a *feringhi*. She is strong too, and taller than my brother Nandu—a whole two inches taller. Nandu says she should have been a man, and I wish she had been; then she would have been Maharajah instead of him. Kairi would never have tried to stop me going to the wedding like my brother did—fat, spiteful bully that he is.'

Ash would have liked nothing better than to talk of Kairi-Bai, but he had no intention of allowing Jhoti to make uncomplimentary remarks about the Maharajah in his presence, particularly when there were at least two of the boy's attendants within call, not to mention several of his own. He therefore turned the conversation into less dangerous channels and spent the rest of the morning answering endless questions on the subject of cricket and football and similar pastimes of the *Angrezi-log,* until Biju Ram came to fetch Jhoti away for the mid-day meal.

Biju Ram had not stayed long, but to Ash even those few minutes had seemed interminable. It was all very well to come under that sly, hostile scrutiny by lamplight and in a crowded tent—and when one was wearing mess dress and presumably looking very much a foreigner and a Sahib. But it was quite a different matter to endure it in broad daylight while lying propped up and helpless on a camp bed, and as he looked up into the familiar face of his old enemy and listened to the smooth tones of that well-remembered voice mouthing glib compliments and inquiring solicitously after his health, Ash found it difficult to believe that the man could fail to recognize him.

Biju Ram himself had changed so little that seeing him again at close quarters the years dwindled away until the gap that separated the past from the present seemed negligible, and it was only the other day that a boy named Ashok had been the favourite butt of his malicious wit, and the victim of a hundred cruel and humiliating practical jokes that had made Lalji laugh and the courtiers snigger. Surely he could not have forgotten? But though Biju Ram's eyes were as crafty as ever, there was still no trace of recognition in them, and if his fulsome compliments were anything to go by, he seemed to be genuinely grateful for Ash's part in the rescue of Jhoti. This was not surprising if he were indeed out of favour with the Maharajah and hoping to lead a rival party, for Jhoti alive might one day prove to be a trump card, while Jhoti dead could only mean disaster for the handful of men who had accompanied him when he fled from Karidkote.

It occurred to Ash that probably the strangest aspect of the whole situation was that he and Biju Ram should find themselves on the same side of the fence—any fence. But although he would have preferred to do without such an ally, there was no denying that Biju Ram's ambition, combined with fears for his own skin, might in the end be a better guarantee of Jhoti's safety than any protection that Mulraj or he himself could devise. All the same, the very sight of the man had been enough to tighten his nerves and send a shudder down his spine, and it was a relief to turn his thoughts to the prospects of seeing Juli again in a few hours' time.

That she would do her best to avoid the meeting he was certain. But then he was equally certain that she would not succeed: Shushila would see to that, for the younger girl plainly leaned heavily on her half-sister for support and was unlikely to make any move without her. He was therefore not surprised to see her enter with her sister a few moments after he himself had been carried there, though what did surprise him was that she made no attempt to avoid his gaze, but looked gravely back at him, and with an interest as great as his own.

She had returned his greeting without a trace of embarrassment, and as she bowed to him in the graceful, conventional gesture of *namaste,* palm pressed to palm and lifted to touch her forehead, the slight sideways inclination of her head and the shape of her hands— those firm, square hands that were so different from the slender hands of most Indian women—were suddenly so familiar that he could not understand why he had not recognized her at sight.

Anticipating this meeting, he had been afraid she would be cold to him, if not openly hostile, and he had wondered how he could deal with this and made various plans for doing so. But there was neither coldness nor animosity in the eyes that he had likened to the 'fishpools of Heshbon', and no fear, merely interest. Evidently Juli had accepted the fact that he was, or had been, Ashok, and was studying him closely in an effort to trace in the features of a strange Englishman the face of a little Hindu boy she had once known; and as the evening wore on he also discovered that she was listening not so much to what he said as to the sound of his voice: testing it, per- haps against her memory of that boy's voice talking to her in the Queen's balcony long ago.

Ash had very little recollection of what he said during the earlier part of that evening, and he was uneasily conscious of talking at ran- dom. But with Juli sitting barely a yard away he found it almost im- possible to concentrate. She had always been a rather solemn little girl, unassuming and old beyond her years, and it was clear that she still retained much of that early gravity. It did not take much dis- cernment to see that here was a woman whose life was narrow and busy, and who had lost the habit (if she had ever possessed it) of at- taching any importance to her own feelings and desires because the needs of others pressed upon her and absorbed her to the exclusion of all else. An unassertive young person, completely unaware of her own beauty and already, in her attitude towards Shushila, over- burdened with a responsibility that seemed more akin to that of a mother or a devoted nurse rather than an older sister.

It did not surprise Ash that her unusual looks should be unappre- ciated by her people or herself, for they diverged too widely from the

Indian ideal. But he was disturbed by her acceptance of Shushila's dependence on her and all that it implied, though he did not know why it should make him so uneasy. He could not possibly be afraid of Shushila? He dismissed that thought almost before it entered his mind, and decided that it was because it offended him to think of Juli taking second place to the *Nautch*-girl's daughter, and cherishing and worrying over a spoilt, pretty, highly strung child, who could force her to do things she did not want to do by the simple expedient of bursting into tears and resorting to moral blackmail of the 'If you won't come with me, then I shan't go' variety. Yet there was nothing weak about Juli's firm chin or the line of her level brows. And that she was also quick-witted and courageous had been proved by the episode in the river.

He found it difficult to keep his gaze off her, and did not try very hard to do so, for it was refreshment beyond words merely to look at her. It was only when Jhoti tugged at his sleeve and inquired in a penetrating whisper why he kept staring at Kairi that he awoke to the unwisdom of his behaviour; and after that he was more careful. The hour that Kaka-ji had permitted passed very pleasantly and was an agreeable break from lying on a camp bed with nothing to look at, day after day, but the stretch of barren plain and sun-dried *kikar* trees that was all Ash could see through the open flaps of his own tent, and of which he was by now heartily tired. 'You will come again tomorrow,' said Shushila, her tone making the words a command rather than a query as he prepared to leave. And somewhat to Ash's surprise, Kaka-ji had seconded the invitation; though in fact the old man's reasons for doing so had been simple enough.

Kaka-ji was tired of listening to his youngest niece's woes. And tried, too, of attempting to soothe the nervous fears that had been temporarily forgotten in the novelty of meeting a foreigner, and the subsequent excitement of Jhoti's rescue and Pelham-Sahib's narrow escape from death, but that had now returned in force as a result of the boredom and inactivity of the past days.

His niece Kairi was accustomed to work, and even here there were numerous tasks that she was expected to do, such as dealing with the servants, listening to complaints and doing what she could to set matters right, supervising the waiting-women, settling quarrels, ordering meals, cooking and sewing—there was no end to it. But with Shushila it was different, for having been waited on all her days, she found the present state of affairs intolerable. As long as the camp was on the march she could at least count on there being something of interest in each day, and at least they would be moving—even though it was towards a future she dreaded. But owing to Pelham-Sahib's injuries the camp had remained static for far too long, and there was little to occupy a spoilt princess who must stay cooped up in tents that were hot and airless by day and draughty by night.

Anjuli had done her best to keep her little sister entertained, but such games as *chaupur* and *pachesi* soon began to pall, and Shushila complained that music made her head ache, and wept because she did not want to be married and because her cousin Umi, who was Kaka-ji's granddaughter, had died in childbirth, and she did not want to die in a strange country—or at all.

Kaka-ji, like his brother the late Maharajah, was a peaceable man, but he was rapidly being driven to the limit of exasperation by the tears, fears and megrims of his brother's youngest daughter, and by now was prepared to clutch at any straw that might help to alleviate them. Under normal circumstances he would not have considered it at all proper for any man outside the immediate family circle to continue to meet and converse with his nieces in such a relaxed and friendly fashion, but then the present situation was far from normal. They were, in effect, in the wilderness where every-day rules need not apply; and the man in question being a foreigner to whom they were greatly indebted, if his talk of *Belait* and the ways of foreigners amused Shushila and served to distract her attention from such things as homesickness and a morbid terror of the future, what harm? In any case, it was not as though he was ever likely to be alone with her; there would always be at least half a dozen others present, and this (and the fact that he was at the moment incapable of moving out of a chair without assistance and therefore could hardly be regarded as a threat to any woman), decided Kaka-ji to second Shushila's command that the Sahib should repeat his visit on the following day.

The Sahib had done so, and after that—though Kaka-ji was never quite sure how it had come about—it became an accepted thing that he should be carried to the durbar tent every evening, where he and Jhoti and Kaka-ji, and sometimes Muldeo Rai or Mulraj (who by virtue of his relationship and his office was permitted the entrée), would sit and talk with the brides and their women, or play foolish games and gamble for sweets or cowrie shells. It all helped to pass the time and ease Shushila's nervous tension, and she, like Jhoti,

delighted in Ash's descriptions of life in *Belait,* many of which struck
them as excruciatingly funny.

The two would explode into giggles over such things as hunt balls
and the absurdity of men and women prancing around in couples to
music; of Londoners groping through a pea-soup fog and families
bathing in the sea at Brighton; or descriptions of the ludicrously uncomfortable clothes that an *Angrezi* woman wore: her tight, high-
heeled, buttoned boots and tighter corsets—armoured with steel and
whalebone and laced to suffocation; the horse-hair bustles worn
under innumerable petticoats, the pads of wire and wool over which
her hair was rolled and pinned, and the hats that were skewered to
this edifice with yet more pins, and decorated with flowers, feathers
and fur; or even, on occasions, an entire stuffed bird.

Of them all, only Anjuli-Bai seldom spoke. But she listened, and
sometimes laughed, and though ostensibly Ash talked to the company at large, his conversation was in fact almost entirely directed at
Anjuli. It was Anjuli he exerted himself to please, and for her that he
tried to describe something of his life in England, so that she might
know what had happened to him and how he had lived in the years
since his escape from Gulkote.

He found it astonishingly easy to say things he knew would have
one meaning for the others but a different one for Juli, who because
of her special knowledge would be able to interpret it in a way that
no one else could have done; and often her smile or a faint movement of her head would tell him that she had understood an allusion
that had passed the others by. It was as though the clock had turned
back, and once again, as they had done in the presence of Lalji and
his courtiers, they were speaking to each other in code and using a
language that only the two of them understood, for in this respect, if
in no other, the rapport that had existed between the children they
had once been had survived the years.

The last time they had played that game Juli had been little more
than a baby, and until recently Ash himself had forgotten the way
they used to speak to Lalji, or pretend to talk to a pet monkey or one
of the macaws when they were in reality talking to each other—
exchanging news or arranging where and when they would meet, and
indicating times and other details by means of hand signals, coughs
or the rearranging of a vase or a cushion. He could even remember
their code word for the Queen's balcony: *Zamurrad* (emerald),

which was also the name given to the pampered peacock that lived with his harem in the Yuveraj's garden. The connection, a reference to the Peacock Tower, was easy to follow, and there had been a hundred ways in which one or other of them could bring that word into a conversation.

There had also been a word that stood for his mother's quarters, but he could not remember it: or their signals either, for though the outline of those remained, the details had been lost in the debris of the years and try as he would he could not recapture them. It was only when he had given up the attempt that suddenly, lying awake one night, the lost word slid unbidden into his mind: Hanuman. Of course: Hanuman the Monkey-God, whose legions had made a living bridge across the sea to Lanka, each holding his neighbour's tail so that Rama might cross in safety to rescue his wife Sita, kidnapped and held prisoner there by a Demon.

Did Juli remember that? Or had she been too young? Yet she had remembered so much—far more than he had done—and her response to his oblique conversation had made it clear that she had not forgotten their old method of communicating with each other when they were not alone. Perhaps he could make use of it again and press his advantage one step further. It was worth trying, thought Ash; and he had tried it on the following evening. But this time Juli had made no response, or given any sign that she understood him or remembered, and though she did not avoid his gaze, she could not have been said to return it.

Ash went back to his tent feeling tired and defeated, and was rude to Mahdoo and short with Gul Baz. And when later that night the *dai* scratched timidly on the canvas, he called out to her to go away, saying he was no longer in need of treatment and did not wish to see anyone. In proof of which he reached out and deliberately extinguished the lamp, knowing that she could not work in the dark and must accept the dismissal without argument—not that he imagined for a moment that she would think of arguing it. But apparently the *dai* possessed more obstinacy than he had credited her with, for the darkness thinned as the canvas was pushed aside and the bright bar of moonlight accompanied the familiar shrouded figure into the tent.

Ash raised himself on one elbow and repeated crossly that he did not need her that night and would she please go away and leave him in peace, and the woman said softly: 'But you yourself told me to come.'

It seemed to Ash as though his heart tried to jump into his throat so that for a moment he could not breathe or speak, and the next instant it had jerked back again and was hammering so wildly that he thought she must hear it. *'Juli—!'*

There was a ghost of a laugh; a familiar laugh but with an odd catch in it, and his uninjured hand shot out to clutch a fold of coarse cotton and grip it as though he was afraid she would vanish as silently as she had come.

Anjuli said: 'Did you not mean me to come? You spoke of Hanuman, and that was always our word for your courtyard.'

'My mother's,' corrected Ash involuntarily.

'Yours too. And as she is gone it could now have only meant one place. Your tent. That is right is it not?'

'Yes. But you were only a child—a baby. How could you possibly have remembered?'

'It was not difficult. Once you and your mother had gone, there was nothing else for me to do but remember.'

She had spoken quite matter-of-factly, but that brief sentence brought home to him as never before how lonely those years must have been for her, and once again he found that there was a lump in his throat and he could not speak.

Anjuli could not have seen his face, but she seemed to have followed his thought, for she said gently: 'Do not let it trouble you. I learned not to mind.'

Perhaps she had indeed done so. But he found that he minded—that he minded unbearably. It appalled him to think of the child Juli left cruelly alone and neglected, with nothing to live for but memories and the hope that he could keep his promise and return. How long had it been, he wondered, before she gave up hoping?

Anjuli said: 'And you too remembered.'

But that was not entirely true. In fact had it not been for Biju Ram, he might still not have known who she was, let alone recalled the old game of double-talk and the code-words that he himself had invented. Ash cleared his throat and spoke with an effort: 'Yes. But I did not know if you would remember . . . if you would understand.' And then, suddenly, panic gripped him as he realized for the first time the stupidity and selfishness of what he had done. 'You shouldn't have come here. It's too dangerous.'

'Then why did you ask me to?'

'Because I didn't dream that you would. That you *could*.'

'But it was very simple,' explained Anjuli. 'I had only to borrow one of old Geeta's bourkas and persuade her to let me come in her stead. She is fond of me because I once did her a favour. And I have come before, you know.'

'Then it *was* you—on the first night after the accident. I was sure it was, but Mulraj said it was only the *dai* and I—'

'He did not know,' said Anjuli. 'I came with Geeta because I had been angry with you for being—for behaving like a Sahib. And because you had not thought of me for years while I—I . . .'

'I know. I'm sorry, Juli. I thought you might never want to speak to me again.'

'Perhaps I would not have done if you had not been injured. But I thought you might be dying, and so I made Geeta bring me with her. I came with her more than once, and sat outside in the darkness while she worked over you.'

'Why, Juli? *Why?*' Ash's grip tightened on the fold of cloth, jerking at it imperatively, and Anjuli said slowly: 'I suppose—to hear your voice. So that I could be sure that you were really who you said you were.'

'Ashok.'

'Yes, my brother Ashok. My only brother.'

'Your—?'

'My bracelet-brother. Had you forgotten that? I had not. Ashok always seemed more my true brother than Lalji ever was—or Nandu or Jhoti. It was always as though he were my only brother.'

'Was it?' Ash sounded oddly disconcerted. 'And are you now sure that I am that same Ashok?'

'Of course. Would I be here if I were not?'

Ash pulled at the cotton bourka to draw her nearer, and said impatiently: 'Take this thing off and light the lamp. I want to look at you.'

But Anjuli only laughed and shook her head. 'No. That would indeed be dangerous; and very foolish too, for if someone were to surprise us they would only think that I was old Geeta, and as she seldom speaks, I would be safe. Loose me now, and I will sit here for a space and talk to you. It is easier to talk thus, in the dark; for while I cannot see your face, or you mine, we can make believe to be Ashok and Juli again, and not Pelham-Sahib, who is an *Angrezi,* or the Rajkumari Anjuli-Bai who is to be—'

338

She stopped a little abruptly, and leaving the sentence unfinished, subsided onto the carpet to sit cross-legged and comfortable beside the camp bed: a pale, shapeless form that might have been a ghost— or a bundle of washing.

Later on, trying to recall what they had talked of, it seemed to Ash that they had talked of everything. Yet no sooner had she gone than he remembered a hundred things he had meant to ask or forgotten to say, and he would have given anything to call her back. But he knew that he would see her again somehow, and there was enormous comfort in that. He had no idea how long she had stayed, for there had been so much to tell that they had lost count of time. But the bar of moonlight from the open tent-flap had crept upward until it showed him the small square of coarse mesh that concealed Juli's eyes, and he could catch a glint of them as she smiled or turned her head. A little later it lay in a pale lozenge on the roof above her head, and later still, as the moon reached its zenith, it vanished altogether, and left them in darkness with only the glimmer of stars showing in the segment of sky beyond the tent door.

They spoke in whispers for fear of arousing Ash's servants, and had it not been for the intervention of the *dai,* Geeta, who taking her courage in both hands had scuttled through the silent camp to find out why her mistress had not returned, it is possible that they might have talked on into the dawn and never noticed it. But Geeta's anxious voice had jerked them abruptly back from the past and to a realization of the lateness of the hour, and of the risk that they ran; for neither of them had heard her approach and it might well have been someone other than the old *dai* who tiptoed to the tent door while they talked.

Anjuli rose swiftly and moved to the doorway, blotting out the stars. 'I'm coming, Geeta. Goodnight, my brother. Sleep well.'

'But you will come again, won't you?'

'If it is possible. But even if not, we shall see each other often in the durbar tent.'

'What is the good of that? I can't talk to you there.'

'Oh yes you can. As we used to do in the old days, and as you did tonight. It is late, brother. I must go.'

'Juli, wait—' His hand went out in the darkness, but she had moved out of reach, and a moment later he could see the stars again and though he had heard no sound he knew that she had gone.

Ash leaned back against the pillows and stared out at the night sky, brooding with dismay on that word 'brother'. Was that really how she thought of him? He supposed that she must. And if that was why she felt free to visit him, he ought not to complain. But he did not think of her as a sister—though honesty compelled him to admit that he had certainly treated her as one, both in his neglect for her feelings and his forgetfulness of her existence. Yet the last thing he wanted from her now was sisterly affection, even though he realized that as long as she thought of him as a brother they were comparatively safe, while should their relationship change to anything deeper, the dangers ahead were incalculable.

He lay awake for a long time, making plans and discarding them, but when at last he fell asleep, only one thing was still clear to him: the need for caution. He would have to be very careful—for Juli's sake more than his own, though he was well aware of the peril in which he would lie should anyone suspect that his feelings towards one of the brides whom he had been charged with conveying to their wedding were far from detached.

He had not needed Mulraj to point out to him how easy it would be for young Jhoti to die on the march—ostensibly from an accident —without any inquiry being made by the British authorities; and he knew that it would be equally easy for his own death to be arranged. There were so many ways in which a man could die in India, and provided he were to do so at some stage in the journey where the camp was conveniently out of reach of an English doctor or anyone else capable of giving a professional opinion on his corpse before heat, vultures and jackals had effectively disposed of it, his murderers would run no risk of being found out. Nor would his death be a lingering one, as for their own sakes they would kill him quickly. But it would be otherwise with Juli.

Ash remembered the tale of the cheetah that Nandu had burned alive because it had lost him a wager, and he shivered at the thought of what might be done to Juli. Whatever happened, she must not risk coming to his tent again. They would have to find some other way of meeting—for if she imagined for a moment that he would be content to see her only in the presence of her relations and her women in the durbar tent, she was very much mistaken. Nevertheless, they must be careful . . .

On that decision, Ash fell asleep. And waking in the cheerful sunlight of another idle, cloudless morning, straightway abandoned it. The dangers that had been so easy to visualize in the darkness seemed far less menacing by daylight, and by the time he was carried to the evening meeting in the durbar tent and saw her smile at him as she sketched the familiar gesture of greeting, he had forgotten his good resolutions and decided that she must come just once more, if only so that he could explain to her why she must never come again, which was something that he found too difficult to convey to her by oblique and roundabout methods.

Three hours later she was seated on the end of his camp bed while old Geeta crouched in the shadows among the guy-ropes outside and kept watch, trembling with anxiety and muttering prayers to a variety of gods. But Ash had not succeeded in making Juli see the rashness of her behaviour.

'Are you afraid that Geeta will talk? I promise you she will not. And she is so deaf that we would have to talk much louder than this before she could hear what we were saying.'

'That is not the point, and you know it!' said Ash. 'What matters is that you are here, and you should not be. What could you say if you were discovered?'

Anjuli laughed at him and said lightly that there was not the least danger of her being discovered there, but that even if she were, no great harm would result from it. 'For has it not been agreed that you are now as our brother, having done us all great service in rescuing my sister and myself from the river, and injuring yourself in attempting to save our little brother from death? And should a sister not be permitted to visit a sick brother? Particularly when she comes after dark when strangers cannot gape at her, and is accompanied by an elderly and respectable widow.'

'But I am not your brother,' said Ash angrily. He would have liked to add that he had no wish to be, but as this did not seem to be an appropriate moment to say so, he said instead: 'You are talking like a child! and if you were still one this would not matter, but the trouble is that you are not. You are a woman grown, and it is not fitting that you should come to my tent alone. You must know that.'

'Surely,' agreed Anjuli; and though he could not see her face for the darkness and the bourka that she still wore, he knew that she was smiling. 'I am not entirely foolish. But if I am discovered here I can pretend to be. I shall say what I have just said to you, and though I shall be severely scolded and forbidden to come again, that is the worst that would happen.'

'To you, perhaps,' retorted Ash. 'But what about me? Would any-one believe that I—or any man for that matter—can see no harm in entertaining a woman in the privacy of my tent and by night?'

'But then you are not a man,' said Anjuli sweetly.

'I'm not—What the devil do you mean?' demanded Ash, justly in-censed.

'Only not in the way you meant,' explained Anjuli soothingly. 'Or not at present. My uncle himself has said that no woman could possi-bly consider herself endangered by the presence of an invalid who was trussed like a fowl in splints and bandages and incapable of moving freely.'

'Thank you,' observed Ash caustically.

'But it is true. When you are well again it will be different. But at present you could hardly be suspected of doing any harm to my vir-tue, even if you wished to.'

Ash could think of no adequate retort, though he knew that it was not as simple as all that, and that even the kindly Kaka-ji would not take a lenient view of his niece's behaviour, or his own either. But the temptation to let Juli stay was too great, and he made no further attempt to send her away or discourage any further visits. She had not stayed very long that night, nor had she allowed him to dispense with the *dai*'s treatment. She had sent the old lady in to knead and massage him while she herself waited outside in the moonlight, and the two had left together. But despite Geeta's ministrations, Ash had once again endured a wakeful night.

He was in no hurry to get the camp on the move again, but there were a great many disadvantages in letting it remain for too long in one place; not the least of them being the risk of depleting the sur-rounding countryside of food and fodder. He had no desire to risk a repetition of the situation that he had found on his arrival at Deena-gunj, and he also knew that the presence of so large a number of men and animals encamped in one spot would be bound to foul the locality to an extent that would soon become painfully noticeable. Already the wind blowing in through his tent door had brought him warning of this. Yet as long as they stayed there, Juli would probably continue to visit him, while once they moved on it might not be too easy. For that reason alone he would have given anything to stay, but he could not bring himself to disregard his responsibilities to the camp, and on the following morning he discussed the matter with Mulraj and informed Gobind that he was now perfectly capable of travelling; not on horseback, possibly, but in one of the baggage carts or on an elephant.

Gobind had been dubious, but after some argument had given way on condition that Pelham-Sahib allowed himself to be carried in a *palkee,* and a sedan having been procured, orders had gone out that the camp would march next day.

The decision had been generally welcomed, though not by the younger bride, who only a few days ago had been complaining of the inaction, yet now that they would shortly be on the move again, was reminded by all the bustle and preparation of what awaited her at their journey's end. Thinking of it, she wept and wrung her hands and clung to her sister for comfort, wailing that she felt ill and that the very thought of having to travel in that hot, stuffy *ruth* again was more than she could bear.

There had been no meeting in the durbar tent that evening, and later the *dai* had arrived alone and overcome her timidity sufficiently to whisper that Anjuli-Bai sent her salaams and regretted that she would not be able to visit the Sahib that night, or on the next one either. But during the following week she came nightly, though her visits were brief and she did not come alone, but always with Geeta, who would treat Ash and then retire out of earshot to wait while her mistress and the Sahib talked together.

The old lady's hearing might be poor, but her eyesight was still excellent, and her fears made her an admirable watch-dog, for the smallest movement attracted her attention. Her nervous little cough signalled a warning if anyone came too near, and the two in the tent would fall silent. But no one interrupted them, and Ash's servants, who would not have allowed anyone else to approach unchallenged, were used to the sight of the *dai* and the lateness of her visits, and being aware of her timidity were not surprised that she had taken to bringing a companion with her. They saw the women arrive and leave again, and were not troubled.

The friendly sessions in the durbar tent were no longer an accepted part of each day, for after long hours spent in a closed *ruth,* Shushila was often too weary for company. The roads, where they existed, were little better than cart-tracks between villages, and where there were none the surface of the plain was almost preferable. On both, the dust lay thick and the hooves of the trotting bullocks stirred it up in choking clouds that forced their way between the closely drawn curtains of the *ruth,* covering everything within, clothing, cushions, hands, faces and hair, with a thin grey film of grit.

Shushila coughed and wept and complained ceaselessly of the dust and the jolting and the discomfort, so that by the day's end Anjuli was often exhausted, and there were times when she came near to losing her patience and giving her little sister a good shaking. The fact that she did not do so was due to the habit of years as much as to her affection and sympathy for Shushila, for Juli had learned very early to control her emotions and hold her tongue. And to shoulder, without complaint, burdens that many an adult would have found hard to bear.

She had been six years old when Ashok and Sita fled from Gulkote, and during the next few months her position in the palace had been unenviable. But there came a day when by chance she succeeded in quietening little Shushila, who was cutting a tooth and had been screaming for hours on end, after everyone else had failed to do so. Her success was probably due to the fact that she happened to pick up the child at a moment when it had howled itself into exhaustion and was ready to stop anyway. But the equally exhausted Zenana thought otherwise, and Janoo-Rani, who while doting on her sons took little or no interest in a mere daughter, said carelessly that in future Kairi-Bai could make herself useful by helping to look after her half-sister.

There can be little doubt that the *Nautch*-girl derived a certain malicious satisfaction from seeing the *Feringhi*-Rani's daughter dancing attendance upon her own offspring, but Kairi-Bai had enjoyed the sudden sense of responsibility. Her days were no longer empty or aimless, for this latest of Janoo's children was a sickly and fretful little creature and its attendants had been only too willing to let someone else do their work for them—even when that someone was only a six-year-old child. Kairi-Bai was kept fully occupied, and it was not surprising that as the years went by Shushila should have come to look on her less as an older sister than a combination of nurse, playfellow and slave.

Kairi had been all those things: but her reward was love. A selfish, clinging, demanding love, it is true; but love all the same, which was something she had never had before—the poor *Feringhi*-Rani having died too soon to be remembered; and though Ashok had been kind to her and Sita had given her affection and understanding, she knew that those two loved only each other while Shushila, on the other hand, not only loved her, but needed her. To be needed was an equally novel experience, and such a comforting one that she did not begrudge the long hours of servitude that the idleness of the child's servants thrust upon her.

Had Kairi been given a free hand, it is even possible that she might have succeeded in bringing up her baby sister to be a tolerably healthy and well-adjusted young woman. But she was far too young and inexperienced to be able to combat the pernicious influence of the Zenana women, whose anxiety to curry favour with Janoo-Rani led them to make much of little Shushila, and vie with each other to pet and spoil the child.

The *Nautch*-girl's own treatment of her daughter was governed entirely by her moods. As these were unpredictable, little Shushila could never be certain if she would be received with a caress or a slap, and as a result she developed a morbid sense of insecurity which was aggravated by the fact that she admired her mother even more than she feared her, and craving as she did for her affection, the careless caresses could not compensate for the misery of being rebuffed. It was this that bred in her a passionate attachment for anything that was safe and familiar: the privacy and protection of the Zenana walls, the faces and voices of all those who peopled her small world, and the unchanging routine of each day. She had no interest in anything that lay beyond the Women's Quarters or in the world outside the Palace of the Winds, and no desire to venture there.

Kairi, who had watched her grow up, was aware of this, and perceptive enough to divine the reason for it, though Shushila herself would never have been able to put it into words, even supposing she had recognized the forces that drove her, which she did not. She was not given to analysing her emotions, any more than the women who pandered to them and by doing so encouraged her to be hysterical and selfish. It was only Kairi-Bai, made wise by harsh experience, who came to realize that her little sister's headaches and the attacks of nervous hysteria that caused so much anxiety in the Zenana were largely imaginary and always self-induced; and that these, together with her fear of the unfamiliar and her high-handed treatment of servants and the humbler members of the Zenana who were incapable of retaliation, were a form of revenge for the lack of interest that her fascinating and imperious mother showed towards her.

Nevertheless it seemed quite natural to Kairi, who was devoid of vanity, that Shu-shu's love for her mother should be immeasurably greater than her love for so unspectacular a person as herself—even though Janoo-Rani, apart from giving birth to her, had done nothing to earn it, while she herself had watched over her and waited on her with tireless devotion, played with her, comforted her and encouraged her, understood her and loved her. Yet with all her understanding, Kairi had never fully realized the depth of Shu-shu's idolatry until Janoo-Rani died.

Shushila's behaviour on that occasion had been so frenzied that the Zenana had confidently predicted that she would die of grief. She had wept and shrieked and tried to throw herself from one of the windows, and when Kairi had prevented this, turned on her half-sister like a wild cat, clawing at her face until the blood ran. Shut into a room with barred windows she had refused all food, and the fact that she had held out for five days proved conclusively that she possessed more stamina than her frail appearance and frequent illness had led anyone to suppose. To all Kairi's coaxing and efforts to console her she had turned a deaf ear, and in the end it had been Nandu who put a stop to the whole nerve-wracking business by storming in and berating his little sister in terms that only an angry and exasperated brother would have thought of using.

Astonishingly, it had worked, partly because as Maharajah of Karidkote as well as her elder brother he was doubly in authority over her, but mostly because he was a man, and as such, a magnificent and all-powerful being whose wishes must be regarded as law by any mere woman. Every Indian woman was taught that her first duty was obedience; and there was no woman, and no Zenana in all the land, that was not under the unquestioned control of some man. Shushila had meekly submitted to her brother's commands, his wrath having succeeded where Kairi-Bai's loving patience had failed, and peace had returned to the Zenana.

But as a result of Nandu's high-handed treatment of her, Shushila had somewhat unexpectedly transferred to him all the obsessive admiration she had felt for her mother; and the Zenana women, who had expected to see her half-sister's influence over her become greatly increased as a result of the Rani's death, were surprised (and in some cases relieved) to find that this was not so. Kairi-Bai's position in this respect remained unaltered, though in other ways it had changed a good deal; and for the better because Nandu had a keen sense of his own position and regarded any lack of respect shown to a member of his immediate family as a slight to his own dignity, and Kairi-Bai was a princess of the royal house and his own half-sister.

She did not look ahead, for she had learned long ago that it was better to live for the present and let the future rest in the lap of the gods, though she took it for granted that she would be married one day—marriage, after all, being the fate of every girl. But her father had been too indolent to bestir himself in the matter, and her step-mother too jealous to arrange a good match for her—yet too afraid of the Rajah to try marrying his eldest daughter to a nobody. The question of a husband for Kairi-Bai had therefore been shelved, and in time it began to seem unlikely that one would ever be found for her. After all, she was getting old: far too old for a bride.

When her father died, and later her step-mother, the old stumbling-block still remained; only now it was Nandu's pride that would not permit him to entertain the idea of giving his half-sister in marriage to anyone of inferior rank. Nor did he intend to let her take precedence over his full-sister even in such a matter as this: Shushila must be married first—and to a ruling prince. When that was done he would dispose of Kairi to some less important personage; though he realized that this might not be too easy, for as well as getting on in years she was no beauty: a tall, gawky woman with high cheek bones, a big mouth and the hands of a working woman—or a European. But his own father's daughter, nevertheless.

Little Shushila, on the other hand, gave promise of exceptional beauty, and already a number of offers had been made for her hand, though none so far had met with her brother's approval. Either their rank or their riches were not sufficiently impressive, or, in two cases where this was not an obstacle, the suitors' own lands lay too near to Karidkote.

Nandu had not forgotten how his father had acquired the disputed State of Karidarra, and he had no intention of providing any loophole that might one day allow some descendant of his sister Shushila's to lay claim to his own territories. He was nothing if not thorough. When, eventually, an offer had come from the Rana of

Bhithor, he had accepted it, though the match could hardly be termed a splendid one, Bhithor being a small and backward state with an unspectacular revenue, and its Rana a middle-aged man who had already been married and widowed twice over, and fathered no less than seven children—all of them girls. Both his previous wives had died in child-bed, the last one only a year ago (assisted, according to rumour, by poison), and of his seven daughters, the five who had survived their infancy were all considerably older than Shushila. But his lineage was superior to Nandu's and the gifts he had sent were impressively rich. Best of all, his state lay more than five hundred miles to the southward, which was much too far away from Karidkote to allow any future Rana to dream of annexing it. In Nandu's opinion it was a sensible and satisfactory match. But his little sister had been appalled.

Shushila had always known that she must marry one day, but now that the day was actually in sight she was overwhelmed by panic. The thought of leaving her home and all the safe, familiar people and surroundings that she had grown up amongst terrified her, while the prospect of travelling hundreds of miles across India to a strange place and a strange man—an old, middle-aged widower—was unendurable. She could not face it. She would not—she *would* not. She would rather die . . .

Once again hysterical shrieks and lamentations rang through the Zenana Quarters, and this time even Nandu at his angriest could not move her, though he had threatened to have her beaten within an inch of her life if she did not obey him. But then Nandu did not understand, as Anjuli did, that at the heart of her terror and resistance lay the dread of a far worse death. Death by fire. Against that, a beating seemed a trivial thing . . .

'It was the *Nautch*-girl's doing,' Anjuli had explained during one of those visits to Ash's tent. 'Janoo-Rani gave orders that her daughter should be strictly instructed in all those things that a well-born woman should know. Not only in religious observances and the proper ritual of *pujah*, but in all matters of ceremony and etiquette, and the duty of a wife towards her husband. This Shushila was taught almost from the time she could first speak, and she was only five when she was taken to see the hand-prints on the Suttee Gate—you remember it?—and told that if she herself were ever widowed, she must burn herself alive on her husband's pyre. Thereafter she was made to stir boiling rice with her little finger, in order to teach her to bear fire without flinching.'

Ash's comment had been savage and unprintable, and though he had spoken in English, Anjuli had not needed a translation; his tone had been enough and she had nodded agreement and said thoughtfully: 'Yes, it was cruel, and it did not serve its purpose, for it only succeeded in making Shu-shu more afraid. She became terrified of pain. She cannot endure it.'

Ash observed caustically that Janoo-Rani obviously could not endure it either, because she had certainly not practised what she preached when her own husband died, and he, for one, did not believe for a moment that anyone could have locked her in a room against her wishes. Or prevented her from doing anything else she wanted to do.

'That is true,' agreed Anjuli. 'I think she would not go to the pyre because she was very angry with my father for taking another wife, and she hated the woman so much that she would not even burn with her, for then their ashes would have mingled.'

Ash made a rude noise and said it was a good story, but it was obvious that she never had any intention of burning herself. As for Shushila, there was no need for her to worry, since suttee was now forbidden by law.

'An English law,' scoffed Anjuli. 'Have you really become so much an *Angrezi* that you believe your people have only to say "It is forbidden", for such old customs as this to cease immediately? Bah! —widows have burned themselves with their husbands for centuries, and the tradition will not die in a day—or a year or a score of years— at the bidding of *feringhis*. In places where there are large numbers of *Angrezis* and police and *pultons* to enforce the law, there will be those who will obey. But many others will not, and your Raj will never even know of it; for this is too vast a land for a handful of *feringhis* to keep watch over. Only when women themselves refuse to submit to this custom will it cease.'

Yet Anjuli knew that Shushila, for one, would never refuse. That early teaching had made too deep an impression on her, and though the very thought of such a death terrified her beyond words, it would not occur to her to avoid it, for she knew that not one of her father's predecessors had burned alone (those tragic prints on the Suttee Gate bore witness to that) and her father himself had been accompanied through the flames by his latest wife, the scheming little interloper, Lakshmi-Bai. It was the inescapable duty of a royal widow.

Had her prospective bridegroom been a boy of her own age, or even a youth in his teens, Shushila's reaction to the news of her betrothal might have been very different. But the Rana was almost forty and might die at any moment, and then her worst nightmare would come true and she would be burned alive. The finger with which she had been forced to stir that boiling rice had shrivelled to the bone, and she had learned to hide it very cleverly, looping the edge of her sari over it so that no one would ever have noticed it. But though it had become numb and nerveless long ago, she had never forgotten the agony of those early days; and if one small finger could cause such excruciating pain, what must it be like to have one's whole body thrust into a fire? It was this thought that now drove her to a hysterical frenzy and made her declare wildly that she would not marry the Rana—or anyone else.

Perhaps if she had explained this to Nandu he might have had some sympathy for her, though he would certainly not have changed his plans. But she could not bring herself to admit to anyone that it was not marriage that she was afraid of but widowhood, because that would mean that she, a Rajkumari and the daughter of a royal line, shrank from accepting a fate that millions of humbler women had accepted without question, and she would never disgrace herself by such an admission of cowardice. If Anjuli knew, it was not because Shushila had confided in her, but because she loved her, and therefore did not need words to explain the real cause of this stubborn and hysterical refusal to marry the husband that Nandu had chosen for her.

It had proved a trying time for almost everyone in the palace, not least for Anjuli. Patience and sympathy for the sufferer had very soon run out, and as the hysterical scenes continued, tempers had worn thin. Intimidation, bribery and entreaty had been tried in turn, but all to no effect, and eventually Nandu had carried out his threat and had his sister soundly beaten. Physical violence had won the day, for Shushila, as Anjuli had said, could not bear pain; and though there could be no comparison between a beating and being burned alive, the latter calamity was, after all, in the future (and might conceivably be avoided), whereas this—the cruel, cutting strokes of a bamboo cane that raised great weals on her tender flesh—was happening now, and she could not endure it. She had capitulated almost immediately. But not unconditionally. She would obey her dear brother and marry the Rana—but only if Kairi could go with her and remain with her. Were this granted, she promised to make no more trouble and to be a dutiful wife and do everything in her power to please her husband and her brother. But if it were not—

The prospect of more scenes was not to be borne, and Nandu was perceptive enough to recognize that despite her fragile appearance, beauty was not the only legacy that Shushila had inherited from their mother: somewhere inside that spoilt, highly strung and over-imaginative little girl there lurked a thin core of Janoo's own steel, and if driven too hard, she might well kill herself: not by poison or a knife, or anything that would involve too much pain, but by leaping from a window or into a well, which she would imagine to be quick and easy—or even by starving herself to death. She could be surprisingly obstinate when she chose, and once she had left Karidkote and was no longer under his eye there was no knowing what she might do, if she had left unwillingly. Obviously, then, it was better that she should go willingly; and if the Rana could be persuaded to take two brides instead of one, it would provide a neat solution to yet another problem: the question of a husband for Kairi-Bai.

The Rana's emissaries had been agreeable and Nandu had experienced the satisfaction of one who brings down two birds with one shot; though admittedly the dowry demanded for Kairi-Bai was greatly in excess of the sum he had had in mind, and there had been considerable argument on the subject, some of it verging on the acrimonious. The matter had eventually been settled to the advantage of the Rana, for as Nandu's current favourite had pointed out, it was only fair that Kairi-Bai's deficiency in the matter of breeding, age and beauty should be compensated for by a substantial dowry. And besides, the cost of a double wedding was bound to be less than two separate ones.

This last was certainly true, for Nandu had been able to economize in the matter of jewels and bride-clothes for his half-sister, giving as his excuse that it was only fitting that her trousseau should be smaller and less valuable than that of the more important bride, Shushila-Bai. Also the retinue he had sent to escort his two sisters to Bhithor would have been just as large and as lavish if only one of them had gone, it being, in reality, less a bridal procession than a public display of the might, splendour and importance of His Highness the Maharajah of Karidkote. For Nandu, as Mr Carter, the District Officer, had pointed out, was showing off.

All these arrangements had taken time, since the Rana himself had remained in Bhithor and the envoys he had sent to negotiate the marriage had not been able to accept an extra bride without consulting him. Messengers had ridden back and forth between the two widely separated states, and the journey being a slow and arduous one even for a rider with relays of fast horses, it was many months before Nandu's sisters at last set out for Bhithor.

Anjuli had had no say in all this: her future had been decided by her half-brother and his favourites, and there was nothing she could do about it. Even if her wishes had been consulted (and, even more unlikely, had carried any weight), she would never have dreamed of deserting Shushila. Shu-shu had always needed her, and now she needed her more than ever. It would have been unthinkable to let her go away alone, and Anjuli had quite simply not thought of it. She had not even given much thought to their future husband, or what her feelings might be for a man who was prepared to marry her solely in order to get her younger sister. That the bargain did not hold out much prospect of happiness for her was of minor importance, because Anjuli had never expected very much of marriage. It seemed to her a gamble in which the dice were heavily loaded in favour of the opposite sex, for no woman could choose her husband; yet, having married him, even though he proved to be cruel and unjust to her, or physically repulsive, she must worship him as a god, serving him and doing his will to her life's end, and if he died before her, immolating herself on his pyre. A bridegroom who was disappointed when he lifted his bride's veil and saw for the first time the face of the girl he had married could console himself with other women; but a disappointed bride had nothing but her sense of duty and the hope of children to sustain her.

In the circumstances, it did not do to build too heavily on the chance of a happy marriage, and Anjuli had not done so; partly, it must be admitted, because somewhere in the back of her mind there had lurked the hope that one day Ashok and his mother would come back for her, and she would be able to go away with them to live for the rest of her life in a valley among high mountains.

That hope had never quite faded; though it had grown fainter as the years passed and they had not returned. But as long as she remained unmarried it seemed to her that somewhere a door was still open: and as she grew up and left childhood behind her, and there was still no talk of a husband for her, she began to think that perhaps there never would be.

For Shushila of course, it would be different. Shu-shu was going to be as beautiful as her mother: that had been clear from the first. She was also a person of considerable importance, so an early and splendid marriage for her was a certainty. Anjuli had long ago resigned herself to the fact that it would separate them—perhaps for ever—and the news that this would not happen, and that they were to stay together after all, had compensated her for many things. For the closing of that door and the final abandonment of a dream. For having to leave Karidkote and live out her days in a hot and arid country far and far to the southward, where no one had ever seen a deodar or a rhododendron or a pine tree, and there were no mountains—and no snow . . .

She would never see the Dur Khaima again, or smell the scent of pine-needles when the wind blew in from the north. And if Ashok were now to keep his promise and return, it would be too late, for he would find her gone.

21

Not many people in the camp were able to sleep late. There was too much work to be done, and the majority rose early in order to feed and water animals, milk cows and goats, light fires and prepare the morning meal. Or, like Mahdoo and Kaka-ji, to pray.

Mahdoo's prayers did not take too long, but Kaka-ji's *pujah* was a protracted affair. The old man was keenly aware of the existence of God—though he confessed to being uncertain as to whether God was also aware of him. 'But one must hope,' said Kaka-ji. 'One must live in hope.' The Unseen was very real to him, and as he had no intention of allowing the fact that he was on a journey to interfere with his religious observances, he took to rising well before dawn in order that he might devote his customary two hours to his *pujah*.

His niece Shushila was one of the few who lay late abed, but her sister, Anjuli-Bai, rose almost as early as Kaka-ji; though for a different reason. Habit had something to do with it, but in the early days of the march she would be up by cockcrow in order to peer out between the tent-flaps and gaze at the mountains.

For a time the snow peaks of the Himalayas had remained clearly visible in the dawn, floating silver and serene in the cool air of morning. And though at mid-day the dust would hide them, when the day waned they would emerge again, rose-tipped now against the green of the evening sky. But as the weeks wore away, the snow-capped ranges receded, dwindling and growing fainter and further away, until finally they vanished. And Anjuli looked for them no more.

There came a day when the Punjab too, with its five great rivers, its friendly villages and fat crop-lands, was left behind. And with it, British India. They were crossing Rajputana now: Tod's fabled Rajasthan—the 'Country of the Kings'. A land of feudal states ruled over by the descendants of warrior princes whose deeds colour the chronicles of Hindustan with blood and violence and splendour, and whose names read like a fanfare of trumpets—Bikaner, Jodhpur, Gwalior and Alwar; Jaipur, Bhurtpore, Kotah and Tonk; Bundi, Dholpur, Udipore, Indore . . .

This was very different country from the fertile and densely populated Punjab. Here towns and villages no longer stood cheek-by-jowl, but were widely scattered, and the land itself was for the most part flat and featureless. A place of limitless horizons and little shade, where the light seemed harsher than in the north, and men, as though in compensation for the lack of colour in their surroundings, painted their houses blinding white or sugar-pink, and decorated their walls and gateways with gay murals of fighting elephants or legendary heroes. Even the horns of their cattle were often brightly tinted, and the country-women did not wear saris but favoured voluminous skirts in vivid tones of sapphire and scarlet, cerise, orange, grass-green and saffron, printed and bordered in black. With their tight, bright bodices and head-scarves of strongly contrasting colours, they were as brilliant as a flock of macaws, and they walked like queens, balancing vast brass cooking pots, water *chattis* or heavy loads of fodder on their heads with graceful ease, and moving always to the clash and jingle of silver, since every ankle and wrist bore its load of bracelets.

'Like dancing girls,' sniffed Mahdoo, disapprovingly.

'Like *Houris*,'* retorted Ash. 'Like peonies, or Dutch tulips.' The aridity of the landscape depressed him, but he approved of the gay garb of its women, and of the fact that this sandy and rock-strewn country was by no means as barren as it appeared at first sight, but supported more wild life than he had seen during all their days in the Punjab. Herds of black-buck and *chinkara* roamed the plain, and the scanty scrub seemed alive with partridge and quail and flocks of pigeons. And once, in the early dawn, he had seen a great cloud of sandgrouse that must have numbered many thousands, rising from a lonely pool of water in a treeless waste of sand. Apart from the beauty of these sights, it was a relief to realize that there would be no need for him to follow the example of such orthodox Hindus as Kaka-ji, and turn vegetarian.

A dâk-runner arrived in camp bearing a large packet of mail addressed to Captain Pelham-Martyn. Most of it was of little interest, and having skimmed through this dispiriting collection of waste paper and consigning it to its proper place, Ash turned gratefully to the only two items that interested him: a short letter from Zarin, and a much longer one from Wally, who was frankly envious and complained of the dullness of Rawalpindi and wished that he was in Ash's shoes.

'I told you those girls were bound to be beautiful, but you

* nymphs of the Mohammedan paradise

wouldn't believe it,' wrote Wally. 'They're wasted on you!' And then went on to belie his complaints by giving Ash a lyrical description of a Miss Laura Wendover, who unfortunately (or perhaps fortunately?) had turned out to be betrothed to a civil engineer. There was also a poem written to commemorate a fellow officer who had died of enteric, that began 'Lo, e'en ere his day had reached full morn', and ran to seven lengthy verses, each worse than the last.

Ash waded through the first two before crumpling it up and tossing it away, and as the wind caught the paper and carried it out of sight, wondered idly what a stranger, finding that effusion and unacquainted with Wally, would make of the poet. Any impressions gained from such turgid stuff would be nothing in the least like the writer, yet Wally's six-page letter conjured him up as though he were there in the flesh and talking aloud, and Ash laughed over it and re-read it, and for a moment almost wished himself back in Rawalpindi.

Zarin's letter, on the other hand, consisted of a single page and was a curious document. For one thing it had been written in English, which was surprising, as Zarin knew perfectly well that there was no longer any necessity for this, and Ash had received two letters from him while in Rawalpindi, both in Arabic script. This one like all the others had been dictated to a professional letter-writer, and apart from the usual flowery compliments and prayers for the recipient's health and prosperity, it contained only a few quite unimportant items of regimental news, and ended with the information that Zarin's mother was in excellent health and desired him to urge the Sahib to have a care for his own, and to take special precautions against such things as snakes, centipedes and scorpions—the latter being very prevalent in the wilds of Rajputana . . .

As Zarin's mother had been dead for a good many years, Ash came to the conclusion that Zarin too had made the belated discovery that Karidkote and Gulkote were one and the same, and was attempting to convey a warning. He would know that the use of her name would arrest Ash's attention and put him on his guard, supposing he had not already discovered this for himself, and that remark about scorpions was plainly a reference to Biju Ram, whose nickname in the Hawa Mahal had been *'Bichchhu'*, while the fact that the letter was written in English suggested that Zarin was taking precautions against the possibility of it being opened and read by someone else.

This last had obviously been a prudent move, as a close examination showed Ash that every single envelope that the dâk-runner had delivered to him had been tampered with—an unpleasant discovery, but one that did not worry him unduly, for he knew very well that there was no one in the Karidkote camp who could read English well enough to make much sense of them; and at least it proved that the risks that Zarin was trying to warn him against were not entirely imaginary.

Ash put Wally's letter aside, and tearing up Zarin's sent it to join the others in the waste-paper basket, and went out to exchange compliments with the local *Tulakdar* who had agreed to deliver a supply of sugar-cane to the elephant lines.

The camp had been on the march again for less than a week when he abandoned the sedan and insisted that he was now perfectly capable of riding once more, and impatient to try the paces of the mettlesome Arab, Baj Raj—'the Royal steed'—that Maldeo Rai, in the name of the *Panchayat,* had presented to him in replacement of his dead roan, The Cardinal.

That he was able to ride at all was a tribute to Gobind's skill and the ministrations of Geeta, the *dai;* and though his first day in the saddle had been more of a strain than he cared to admit, the next one had been better, and the next better still, and by the following week he was back to normal and feeling as fit as he had ever been. But the pleasure of being free of pain and bandages and on his feet again was not entirely unalloyed, because it also meant that there was no longer any need for the *dai*'s treatments; and once her visits ceased it became too dangerous for Juli to come alone.

For the time being there seemed no alternative to seeing her only in the durbar tent, which in Ash's view was a thoroughly unsatisfactory state of affairs and comparable to standing in the snow and looking through a plate-glass window at a warm room and a blazing fire. Besides, the evening meetings were still subject to the whims of Shushila, and now that the Sahib was no longer an invalid, Kaka-ji would have preferred to have discontinued them altogether, though he did not forbid them and appeared to enjoy them as much as anyone whenever Shushila happened to convene one. But Ash had become too used to being able to see Juli alone and talk with her freely to give that up, and he had no intention of doing so. There must be some other way in which they could meet.

Once again he lay awake at night making and discarding plans and weighing risks. But he could have saved himself the trouble and the hours of lost sleep, for Jhoti unwittingly solved the problem for him by complaining to Kaka-ji that his sisters were growing dull and tiresome and that even Kairi, who was never ill, had twice refused to play chess with him because she had a headache. And no wonder, declared Jhoti scornfully—what else did she expect?—cooped up for hours on end in a stuffy *ruth* when she wasn't shut up in a purdah tent, never taking the air or any exercise at all, and walking at most a dozen steps a day. At this rate, by the time they reached Bhithor she would be as bad as Shu-shu—always ill and no use to anyone.

As for Shu-shu, if she wasn't careful she wouldn't get there at all, for in addition to all the ailments she complained about, she was now not even eating properly, and if she went on like this she'd shrivel up and die, and then the Rana would find himself left with only Kairi, and probably refuse to have her. And *then,* added Jhoti, his imagination running away with him, they would all have to turn round and go back to Karidkote with nothing to show for all the trouble and expense, and Nandu would be so enraged that he would probably have everyone beheaded—or anyway sent to prison. Or perhaps he might even have a fit and fall down dead.

This final flight of fancy seemed to cheer Jhoti considerably. But there had been enough truth in his previous remarks to alarm Kaka-ji, and the next time he saw his nieces he looked at them with more attention and decided that Jhoti had been right. Kairi-Bai appeared tired and heavy-eyed and there was a listlessness in her manner that he had never noticed before. It alarmed him, for if she fell ill what would become of Shu-shu? None of the other women would be able to take her place, and it was easy to see that even she was finding the task of keeping her little sister's megrims within bounds a taxing one. The younger girl was also looking far from well, and Kaka-ji, studying her, decided that she was growing too thin and that it did not become her. She was beginning to look like . . . yes, like a skinny brown monkey, all eyes.

The thought shocked him profoundly, for until this moment he had always considered Shushila to be an exquisitely beautiful girl; and though he had no apprehensions that she might die before they reached Bhithor (as her little brother had so gloomily predicted) it would be almost as great a disaster if she were to lose her looks. After all, the Rana had not only been promised a beautiful bride but, as part of her bride-price, compelled to accept her much older half-sister as well; so there was no knowing how he might react were he to feel himself cheated on the deal. Something must be done at once, and Kaka-ji hurried away to see Pelham-Sahib; and spent the next half-hour discussing his predicament with an interested and sympathetic listener.

From Ash's point of view, the situation might have been tailor-made to suit his convenience, and seizing the opportunity with both hands he suggested that what both girls needed was more exercise. A daily ride, perhaps—preferably of an evening while the tents were being pitched and the air was cool and refreshing. Something of this nature could not fail to do them good, and coming at the end of a long day spent in the dusty discomfort of the *ruth,* it would provide a welcome relief for their cramped muscles and not only give them an appetite for the evening meal, but help to ensure a good night's sleep as well. He was sure that a quiet mount could be provided for the Rajkumari Shushila, and there would be no necessity for a guard to accompany them, for Kaka-ji, Mulraj and himself would be sufficient protection. Also it might be a good idea to encourage Jhoti to give his younger sister riding lessons, and there was even a chance that Shushila-Bai might become a good enough horsewoman to ride for some part of the journey instead of travelling the whole way in the *ruth.*

By using all the guile and diplomacy at his command he contrived to convey the impression that the whole scheme was in reality Kaka-ji's own idea from start to finish, and that all he, Ash, had done was to agree with it. With the result that later that evening, after consulting Gobind (who had agreed that the effect of exercise in moderation could be as beneficial as tonics and purges), the old gentleman had produced it to Mulraj as his own solution to the problem, and charged him with procuring suitable mounts for the brides and making any other arrangements that might be necessary.

Jhoti had been delighted at the prospect of showing off to Shushila, and was only too willing to instruct her. The plan had been put into effect on the very next day and been a success from the start; particularly from Ash's point of view, for the evening rides were an enormous improvement on those gatherings in the durbar tent, as they allowed far more latitude for private conversation and were free from the observant eyes of waiting-women.

The *ruth* would be stopped a mile short of the selected camping site, and Ash, with Jhoti, Mulraj and Kaka-ji, would ride back to meet it, taking two spare horses for the girls; a slow, sedate and well-mannered animal for Shushila-Bai and a more mettlesome one for Anjuli.

Sometimes they would bring hawks with them, and sometimes a shot-gun if there was a chance of game. But mostly they rode for exercise and pleasure. And as Shushila preferred to keep to a walk, or at most a gentle trot, while Jhoti, in the role of instructor, stayed close beside her with Mulraj to keep an eye on them both, and Kaka-ji was usually too tired by a day in the saddle to do more than jog along behind, Ash and Anjuli-Bai found it the easiest thing in the world to ride ahead and explore the countryside together without arousing any comment. Once again it became possible for them to talk freely, and this time without any fear that what they said might be overheard; for out in the open country they were safe and Ash could watch Juli's face as she talked, instead of only listening to a voice that whispered in the darkness from behind the folds of a bourka.

Jhoti had insisted on Shushila wearing male attire, as no one, he declared, could possibly manage to ride comfortably—let alone well—while swathed in a sari. And though Kaka-ji had protested at this, he had been over-ruled, for Shushila was enchanted at the prospect of dressing up, and Mulraj, who also considered a sari an impossible garment to ride in, pointed out that it would arouse less curiosity in any strangers they might happen to pass, if they gave the appearance of being a party of men out for an evening canter.

Dressed in borrowed clothing, Shushila made a charming boy and Anjuli a handsome young man. And even Kaka-ji had to admit that their costume could hardly be considered immodest, and was certainly more sensible; though he failed to notice that this change of dress resulted, inevitably, in an easier and far more informal atmosphere—a phenomenon that can be observed at any costume ball, where the mere donning of a false moustache or a farthingale seems to convince the wearers that they are no longer recognizable, and enables them to lose their inhibitions and frolic in a manner that they would never dream of doing on any other occasion.

The fact that his nieces were wearing what to them was fancy-dress made it possible for Anjuli-Bai to ride off with Pelham-Sahib in pursuit of a jackal, or to see what lay beyond a ridge of higher ground, without anyone, including himself, thinking that there was anything undesirable in it. For without the flowing lines of a sari to remind him of her sex, his elder niece seemed to shed her identity and become only an anonymous young person who could safely be allowed a certain amount of freedom. Harmless freedom naturally, for was not he there himself to keep a close eye on them all?

Kaka-ji congratulated himself on the success of his plan, because there was no doubt that the health and spirits of both girls had greatly improved. Shushila had already lost the wizened look that had so alarmed him and would soon be as pretty as ever, and her women assured him that her appetite was returning and her nerves were far better of late. He could also see that she enjoyed the riding lessons almost as much as Jhoti enjoyed giving them, and as he listened to his nephew's shrill little voice shouting advice and encouragement, and Shushila's answering laughter, Kaka-ji felt a glow of satisfaction at his own ingenious solving of a troublesome problem.

Much the same could be said of Ash, who had only one fault to find with the present situation: the fact that the evening rides were all too short and far too quickly over. The nights and the long, dusty days became no more than a preparation for that single hour in which he could be with Juli, even though he could not expect to spend more than a portion of the time with her, since caution and good manners forced them both to ride and talk with the others for at least some part of it. Nor was it always an hour, for like Ash, Jhoti and Mulraj and Kaka-ji had also ridden all day, and sometimes they too were tired—not that Ash, for one, would ever have admitted it. When that happened the hour would be cut by a quarter, or a half. But Ash was still grateful for every minute of it.

As the camp crawled southward across Rajputana like a vast and colourful circus procession (or, as it often seemed to Ash, an insatiable horde of locusts) the weather became warmer and he realized that the time would soon come when it would be too hot to march when the sun was high. But there was no need to start planning for that yet, as the temperature was still tolerable even at noon, and the nights remained mild.

The days slid into weeks almost without his noticing it, and he enjoyed every one of them: though it was far from being an idle time, for each day brought its own crop of difficulties, ranging from the routine ones of provisioning (which included dealing with claims for damages to crops and grazing-grounds by irate village headmen) to arbitrating in a wide variety of disputes within the camp, and, on more than one occasion, helping to beat off an attack by armed raiders. These and a hundred other matters kept him fully occupied.

But he would not have changed places with anyone in the world, for he found the constant and varying demands upon him stimulating, while the fact that there had been a serious attempt to murder young Jhoti—and would probably be others—added a spice of danger to the journey that offset any element of tedium. And at the end of each day there was always Juli, and riding beside her in the quiet hour before sunset he could relax and forget his responsibilities to the camp and to Jhoti, and become Ashok again instead of 'Pelham-Sahib'.

It was on one of these evenings—a hot, still evening at the end of an even hotter day—that he heard for the first time the story of how Hira Lal had accompanied Lalji and the old Rajah to Calcutta, and had vanished from his tent one night and never been seen again—taken, it was said, by a tigress, a notorious man-eater who was known to roam the district and had already accounted for more than a dozen villagers. The proof of this had been a fragment of Hira Lal's blood-stained clothing, found among the bushes. But there had been no pug-marks and no trace of the drag, and a local *shikari* (game hunter) had tactlessly insisted that he did not believe that this was the work of the man-eater—an opinion that was later borne out by the news that the tigress had killed a herdsman near a village some twenty-five miles away on the very night that Hira Lal disappeared . . .

'No one in the Hawa Mahal believed it either,' said Anjuli, 'and there were many who said he had been made away with by order of the Rani—though they did not say it out loud, but only in a whisper: very small whispers. I think, myself, that they were right; everyone knew that she had been enraged when she learned that my father had decided to take Lalji with him when he travelled to Calcutta to lay claim before the Viceroy to the throne of Karidarra, and it was no secret that it was Hira Lal who had persuaded him to do so—perhaps because he did not trust her not to bring about Lalji's death as soon as my father's back was turned. She was always jealous of Lalji.'

'And I imagine she made away with him in the end,' observed Ash grimly. 'Lalji and Hira Lal both. It almost makes one hope that there may be a hell after all; with a special section reserved for people like Janoo-Rani who do their murdering at second-hand.'

'*Don't!*' said Anjuli in a low voice, and shivered. 'You do not have to wish for that. The gods are just, and I think she paid in this life for all the evil she did—and more. Much more, for she did not die an easy death, and towards the end she shrieked out that it was Nandu himself who had poisoned her, though that is something I will not believe; no son could have done such a thing. Yet if she believed it, how terrible it must have been for her to die thinking that. There was no need for a hell after death for Janoo-Rani, for she found it here; and as we know that those whose conduct is evil attain an evil re-birth, she will also have to pay in her next life, and perhaps for many lives afterwards, for every ill deed that she committed in this one.'

'*"Take what you want," says God. "And pay for it,"*' quoted Ash. 'Do you really believe all that, Juli?'

'That we must pay for all we do? Of course.'

'No: that we are born over and over again. That you and I, for in-stance, have already lived many lives and will live many more.'

'If one has been born once, why not again?' asked Juli. 'Besides, the Upanishads* tell us that this is so, and according to that teaching it is only those who attain to the knowledge of the identity of the Soul of Brahma who reach "the way of the gods" and do not return to earth. Therefore it follows that you and I have not yet freed our-selves from the cycle of re-birth; and as I do not think either of us are seekers after holiness—or anyway, not yet—we shall surely be born again.'

'As a worm or a rat, or a pariah dog?'

'Only if we have committed some terrible sin in this life. If we are kind and just, and give to the poor—'

'And the priests,' interjected Ash derisively. 'Don't forget the priests.'

'And the priests also,' amended Anjuli gravely, 'then—who knows?—we may even be born as great ones. You a king or a famous warrior; or even a Mahatma. And I a queen—or a nun.'

'The gods forbid!' said Ash with a laugh.

But Anjuli did not smile and her face was suddenly sober as she said slowly, and almost as though she were speaking to herself: 'But I had forgotten . . . I will soon be a queen in this one. The Junior Rani of Bhithor . . .'

Her voice died out in a whisper and they rode on without speak-ing, until presently Ash reined in to sit watching the sun go down. He knew that Juli had drawn rein beside him, but though he would not look at her, he was acutely aware of her presence—of the faint fragrance of dried rose-petals that clung about her and the fact that

* part of the Vedic literature

he had only to move his hand a little way to touch hers. The sun slid below the horizon and was gone, and from the shelter of a patch of high grass a peacock called mournfully into the silence. Ash heard the girl beside him draw a slow breath and let it out on a sigh, and he said abruptly, still without looking at her: 'What are you thinking about, Juli?'

'The Dur Khaima,' said Juli unexpectedly. 'It is strange to think that I shall never see the Dur Khaima again. Or you either, once this journey is ended.'

The peacock cried again, its harsh call a loneliness in the gathering dusk. And like an echo of that sound came Jhoti's high-pitched voice calling to them that it was time to go back, and there had been nothing for it but to turn their horses and rejoin the others.

Ash had been noticeably silent as they rode back to the camp, and that night for the first time he took stock of the situation, and made a serious attempt to sort out his emotions and decide what, if anything, he meant to do about Juli. Or could do.

To the consternation of Gul Baz, he announced that he was going to take a long walk and would not be returning for some hours; and having brusquely refused to allow anyone to accompany him, he strode off into the darkness, armed only with a stout, iron-bound *lathi* (staff) such as country folk carry.

'Let him be, Gul Baz,' advised Mahdoo. 'He is young, and it is too hot for sleeping. Also I think there is something that troubles him, and it may be that the night air will serve to clear his mind. Go to bed, and tell Kunwar that I will be *chowkidar* tonight. There is no need for us both to wait up for the Sahib.'

The wait had proved much longer than Mahdoo expected, for the Sahib did not return until shortly before dawn; and long before that the old man fell asleep at his post, secure in the belief that Ash must arouse him in order to re-enter the tent, and untroubled by any serious fear for the safety of one who had learned caution on the Border and was well able to take care of himself. Any anxiety he felt was solely on the score of his Sahib's state of mind, which the old man had divined with far more accuracy than Ash would have given him credit for—or appreciated.

'Unless I am greatly mistaken, and I do not think I am,' mused Mahdoo, communing with himself before sleep overtook him, 'my boy is in love . . . and with someone he sees daily yet cannot win—which can only be one of the two Rajkumaris. Unless it is one of their women—that could well be. But whoever it is, there can be nothing in it but danger and disappointment for him; and let us hope that he has realized this, and that his night-walking will serve to cool his blood and permit prudence to prevail before matters go too far.'

Ash had not only realized it. He had seen the danger from the beginning and had not underrated it, but for one reason or another he had put off thinking about it. Stubbornly refusing to look ahead and see where all this was leading, or where it would end—perhaps because at the back of his mind he knew only too well, yet could not bring himself to face it.

He had, in effect, been indulging in a form of mental sleep-walking, and Juli's reminder that she would soon be a queen—'Junior Rani of Bhithor'—had acted as a dash of ice-cold water thrown in his face, awakening him at last to the discovery that the path he was on was no wide and level one, but a narrow ledge on the face of a precipice.

Her words had been a reminder, too, of another thing he had chosen to ignore: the swiftness with which the days were slipping by, and the fact that far more than two thirds of their journey was over. By now half Rajputana lay behind them; they had long since skirted the deserts of Bikanir, passed south of Ratangarh and Sikar, and from there marched north-eastward up through the harsh, rock-strewn ridges that guard the great Sambhar Lake and the approaches to Jaipur. Now, having crossed the Luni River and forded two tributaries of the Banas, they were facing south once more and it would not be long before they reached their journey's end; and then . . . Then he would attend the wedding ceremonies and watch Juli walk seven times round the sacred fire with the Rana of Bhithor, and when it was all over he would ride back to the Punjab alone, knowing that this time she was lost to him for ever.

It did not bear thinking of. But he would have to think of it now.

There was no moon that night, but Ash had always been cat-eyed in the dark, and grim necessity during his years in tribal territory had helped to sharpen his sight so that now he could walk confidently where many others would have had to grope forward with caution. He had brought the *lathi* with him as a walking-stick and not a weapon, for he had no fear of being attacked, and as for losing his way in unfamiliar country, there was little danger of that because he had ridden across it earlier that evening and noticed that half a mile away, in a direct line from his tent, the level ground narrowed to form a natural roadway between a wilderness of thorn-scrub and pampas grass and a wide belt of broken rock. As this provided the shortest and easiest way to reach the open country beyond, he was not likely to miss it even in the darkness, particularly with the lights of the camp providing a beacon that could be seen for miles across the plains.

The ground underfoot was hard and dry, and once his eyes had grown accustomed to the starlight he walked quickly; intent only on putting as much distance as possible between himself and the camp, because it seemed imperative to him that he should get beyond the range of the sound and smell of men and animals, and the sight of oil lamps and cooking fires, before he even began to think of Anjuli and himself.

Always, until now, the affairs of the camp had come between him and any serious consideration of personal matters, since he could not afford to be dilatory where his command was concerned but must deal promptly with every difficulty as it arose, however petty it might be, for unless solutions were found and arguments settled in the shortest possible time, chaos could easily result. But with Juli it had been different. The problem that she posed was a strictly personal one and so could be set aside to be dealt with later; there was no need to hurry, for he would be seeing her that evening—and tomorrow evening, and the evening after that . . . They had plenty of time . . .

But now, all at once, it could be put off no longer; time was running out, and if there was anything to decide he must decide now—one way or another.

The roar of the camp dwindled by degrees to a gentle hum and then a faint murmur that faded and was finally lost, and now at last the night was quiet: so quiet that for the first time in many weeks Ash found that he could hear the sough of the wind and a dozen small sounds that were suddenly audible in the silence. The whisper of dry grass and casurina fronds stirring in the breeze. The hoot of an owl and the scutter of some small nocturnal animal foraging around a clump of pampas. The chirr of a cricket and the flitter of a bat's wing, and from somewhere very far away, the sound that is the night-song of all India—the howl of a jackal-pack.

For a mile or so the plain remained level, and then it sloped sharply upwards, and Ash crossed a long, low ridge that was barely more than a spine of rock thrusting up from the naked earth, and once on the far side of it, found that he could no longer see the glow of the camp fires or any trace of human habitation. There was nothing now but the empty land and a sky full of stars; and there was no point in going any further. Yet he walked on mechanically, and might have done so for another hour if he had not come on a dry watercourse that was full of boulders and smooth, water-worn pebbles that slid treacherously underfoot.

To have crossed that by starlight would have been to risk a sprained ankle, so he turned aside, and selecting a patch of sand, settled down cross-legged in the classic Indian posture of meditation, to think about Juli . . . or at least, that was what he had meant to do. Yet now for no reason, he found himself thinking instead of Lily Briggs. And not only Lily, but her three successors: the soubrette of the seaside concert party, the red-haired barmaid of The Plough and Feathers and the provocative baggage from the hat-shop in Camberley, whose name he could no longer remember.

Their faces rose unbidden from the past and simpered at him. Four young women, all of whom had been older and far more experienced than he, and whose appeal to men had been unabashedly erotic. Yet not one of them had been mercenary, and it was ironic that he should have wished to marry Belinda Harlowe, who had the soul of a huckster, because by contrast she had seemed to epitomize all that was sweet and good and virginal—and was, in addition, a 'lady'. He had told himself that he loved her because she was 'different'—different from four over-generous wantons whose bodies he had known intimately but whose minds he had known nothing about and had never been interested in—and it had taken him more than a year to discover that he knew nothing about hers either, and that all the admirable qualities that he had believed her to possess had been invented by himself and forcibly bestowed on some mental image of his own devising.

'Poor Belinda!' thought Ash, looking back a little wryly at that pasteboard paragon of his own devising, and at the tedious young prig that he himself had been. It was not her fault that she had failed to live up to that idealized portrait; he doubted if anyone could have done so. The real Belinda had been no angel, but merely a very ordinary and rather silly young woman who happened to be pretty and was vain of her prettiness, and had been spoiled by too much flattery and adulation. He could see that quite clearly now, and realize, too, that the worldliness that had made her accept Mr Podmore-Smyth's offer, and the vindictive outburst that had destroyed poor George, could hardly be condemned as unusual failings when it was clear that a good many other people shared them. He himself would probably have shrugged off the first as a sensible if unromantic decision, and the second as a natural display of feminine pique at being lied to, had some other woman been involved. But because it was Belinda who had done these things he had chosen to regard it as a personal and appalling betrayal, and his revulsion had been so violent that for a time he had not been quite sane.

Even now the thought of what she had done to George gave him a momentary twinge of nausea. And George's face, as he had last seen it that hot Sunday afternoon in Peshawar, was still painfully clear in his memory. But Belinda's eluded him, and trying to recall her, Ash discovered that he could only remember that her eyes had been blue and her hair yellow; but not what she had actually looked like, or how she had spoken or moved or laughed. She seemed to have faded as an old daguerreotype will do if left too long in the sun, and considering all the emotional agonies he had suffered on her account, it was disconcerting to discover that he could remember Lily Briggs far more clearly. Though perhaps that was not so surprising for Lily had encouraged him to explore and caress every inch of her warm nakedness, while with Belinda, respect had kept his love-making strictly within bounds, and on those rare occasions when he had been permitted to take her befrilled and trimly corseted shape in his arms, his kisses could hardly have been more reverent had he been a Russian peasant kissing an ikon.

Sensuality had had no place in his affair with Belinda, while sensual pleasure had been the sole purpose of all the previous ones. With the result that, having experienced these two extremes, he had decided that he had now learned everything about women; and disliking what he knew, was cured for ever of falling in love (in the circumstances, an understandable reaction, though hardly an original one). Yet now, like many a disillusioned lover before him, he had fallen in love again. And it seemed like the first and only time: and would, he knew without any doubt, be the last.

There had been no joy in this discovery, for it was something that he would have given a great deal to avoid; and had there been any choice he would, even now, have elected to escape it, because he could see no solution that did not spell despair either for himself or Juli: or possibly for both of them. But as far as he was concerned, there was nothing he could do about it; it had been too late from the night that he had given her back his half of the little mother-of-pearl fish and had taken her into his arms, and known in the same instant that they belonged together just as surely as the two halves of the broken charm, and that it was not only Juli's luck-piece but he, Ash, who had been made whole again—and happy beyond words. He could not change that even if he would, nor could he analyse it or explain it away. It was simply there—like sight or sunlight or the air he breathed. An integral part of him . . .

Juli was as unlike any other woman he had ever known as a blue day in the Himalayas is unlike a grey one on Salisbury Plain. There was nothing that he could not tell her or that she would not understand, and to lose her now would be like losing his heart and his soul. And what man can live without the one, or hope for Heaven without the other?

'I cannot give her up,' thought Ash. 'I cannot . . . I *cannot!*'

A night-jar flitted down the dry watercourse and came to rest on a boulder, unaware that the motionless figure within a yard of it was a man, and a foraging mongoose paused, nose a-twitch, and deciding that the human was not dangerous, crept forward to investigate. But Ash was not aware of them: he was locked away in a private world, and so lost in thought that had there been dacoits abroad that night he might never have returned to camp, because the discovery that he could not face losing Juli was merely a first step on a long and dangerous road, and it was only when he had taken it that he began to see clearly how formidable were the barriers that separated them, and how difficult to surmount.

That Juli shared his own feeling of completeness and belonging was something he knew without having to be told; just as he knew that she was fonder of him than anyone else in the world—as she had always been. But fondness was not love, and if what she felt for him was only the same single-hearted devotion that had been given him by an adoring little girl who had trotted at his heels and thought him the wisest and best of all brothers, it was not enough, and unless he could change that into something deeper he would surely lose her . . .

It was not as her brother that he could ask her to throw in her lot with him and face the consequences: the disgrace and the difficulties, and the incalculable dangers that might follow. And his own love for her was not in the least brotherly; it was as a wife that he wanted her. But even if she had grown to love him in the same way, that too was only a first step, for she was still Anjuli-Bai: a princess and a Hindu. And though the question of rank might seem trivial to her, that of caste might prove too strong for her to overcome.

Ash's foster-mother had been a devout Hindu, and as her son he had been brought up with a proper knowledge of religious matters. He had studied the Rig-Veda and was familiar with the tale of the sacrifice of Purusha, the primeval man, from whose immolation came all creation, together with the four Hindu castes. From Purusha's breath had come the Brahmans, the priestly caste; from his arms, the warriors, or Kshatriyas; from his thighs, the Vaisyas—agriculturalists and traders; and from his feet the servile caste, the Sudras. All other men were outcasts; 'untouchables' whose very presence was defilement. Wherefore, to a Hindu, caste was the most important thing in life, for it decreed every person's social status and the work they were permitted to do, and affected in one way or another every aspect of living. Nothing could change it. A man born a Sudra, in the lowest caste, must live and die as one; no riches or power that he might acquire could raise him to a higher one, and his children and grandchildren, and their children after them to the end of time, would always be Sudras. Only a life of great piety and good works might, after his death, make it possible for him to be reborn as a member of a higher caste. But apart from that, there was no other way in which he could escape his destiny.

Sita's people had been farmers: hill-men, claiming Rajput blood. Her husband too had been a Vaisya, and she had brought Ash up as strictly as though he had been her son. Juli's mother, on the other hand, had been a half-caste, and therefore, in the eyes of orthodox Hindus, tainted by her foreign blood. But her father had belonged to the warrior caste, and like many Kshatriyas, considered that they, and not the Brahmans, should by rights hold pride of place. He also happened to be an autocrat, a Rajput and a Rajah. On these counts he regarded himself as being above caste, and had he wished to marry the daughter of the lowliest of Untouchables, he would probably have done so and carried it off with a high hand. Nevertheless, on the grounds of caste alone he would certainly not have considered the foster-child of the waiting-woman, Sita (and even less the only son of Professor Pelham-Martyn), in any way a suitable husband for his daughter by the *Feringhi*-Rani. Nor would his heir—that was something that Ash could be certain of, despite the lowly origins of

Nandu's own mother, or the fact that the dubious status of his half-sister, Anjuli-Bai, had caused so much argument and hair-splitting with the emissaries from Bhithor that only a lavish bribe and the promise of a munificent dowry had finally induced them to accept her as a suitable wife for their Rana.

At this date, however, the question of Nandu's approval or disapproval was wholly irrelevant; the fact remained that as the marriage contracts had been agreed and betrothal gifts exchanged, his sisters were to all intents and purposes already the legal property of the Rana, and the wedding ceremony would do no more than supply the final seal to a bargain that had been approved and was regarded as binding. So except for a miracle, there was no way out that would not involve a major scandal and considerable danger; and Ash was no believer in miracles.

Unless he could persuade Juli to run away with him, the wedding would take place. And once she was married to the Rana he would never be able to see her or speak to her again, for she would vanish into the sealed and secret world of the Women's Quarters, and be lost to him as surely as though she were dead. He would not even be able to write to her or to receive any news of her, unless, perhaps, through Kaka-ji—though that was highly unlikely, as Kaka-ji would not consider it proper to discuss the Rana's wife with another man, and the only information he would be likely to pass on would be the kind that would be unbearable to hear. That Anjuli-Bai had become a mother. Or was dead . . .

The thought of either was so intolerable that Ash flinched involuntarily as though ducking a blow, and the mongoose that had finally crept out across the sand to investigate this strange creature who sat so still, whisked away with a chatter of rage and vanished into the shadows.

Ash did not see it go, but the sound reminded him briefly of another mongoose: Tuku. It surprised him a little to find that after all these years he should still remember that name; and remember, too, the look of satisfied malice on Biju Ram's face, and the feel of Tuku's small body lying lifeless between his hands. But the memory of that day only served to bring his thoughts back to Juli, for it was she, 'Kairi-Bai', who had filled the void left by Tuku's death.

There were very few memories of the Hawa Mahal, now that he came to think of it, that did not include her; for though his attitude towards her had been a mixture of irritation and lordly condescension, she had come to be an integral part of his days, and but for her he would never have left the palace alive. Yes, he owed a great debt to Juli; and he had done nothing to repay her—unless possibly by forgetting his promise to come back for her, for honesty forced him to the conclusion that it might have been better for her if she had never seen him again and been able to think of him as dead. He remembered now that even as a child she had never questioned her fate but accepted it as inevitable—the decree of the gods—and had he not returned she would have come to terms with it, and at the very least have enjoyed a certain amount of comfort and security as the wife of a ruling prince. But what would her life be like if she ran away with a *feringhi*—a mere junior officer in the Guides—and just how far would they be allowed to run? That, after all, was the crux of the matter . . .

'Not very far, I imagine,' decided Ash grimly.

There was no blinking the fact that everyone in the camp, and in all India for that matter, would regard such an elopement as indefensible: a shameless and dishonourable betrayal that insulted Bhithor and brought black disgrace on both Karidkote and the Raj.

The British would take an equally strong view, though from a somewhat different angle. They would dismiss Juli's part in it with a careless shrug: 'What else can you expect from some illiterate little bint in purdah?' But there would be no mercy for Captain Ashton Pelham-Martyn, who had betrayed his trust and 'let his side down' by running off with a woman (and a 'native woman', at that) whom he had been charged with escorting across India and delivering safely into the care of her future husband.

'I would be cashiered,' thought Ash.

A year ago he had fully expected to face a Court Martial for his part in the affair of Dilasah Khan and the stolen carbines, and he knew that this had only been avoided by the narrowest of margins. But were he to run away with Juli there would be no question of avoiding it again. He would be court-martialled and dismissed from the army in disgrace: *'Her Majesty having no further use for his services.'*

He would never see Mardan again . . . or Zarin and Awal Shah—or Koda Dad. The men of his troop and his fellow officers, the Corps of Guides, and old Mahdoo, too . . . they would all be lost to him. And so would Wally; for even that inveterate hero-worshipper would not be able to condone this.

Wally might talk a great deal of nonsense about love and romance, but his views on such matters as duty were uncompromising, and he would see this in simple terms as a breach of trust: a sacred trust, because to Wally duty was sacred, and had he found himself in Ash's situation he would certainly have been able to say, like Lovelace: 'I could not love thee, dear, so much, loved I not honour more.' For it would never occur to him that Juli, or any woman in the world, could be worth more than honour . . .

'I should lose him, too,' thought Ash. And for the second time that night, flinched at a thought as though from a physical pain. Wally's friendship, and Wally's admiration, had come to mean so much to him that the withdrawal of both would leave a gap in his life that he would never be able to fill; or to forget. And there was another thing . . . why should he suppose that Juli would like living in England, when he himself had not?

The British in India invariably referred to their island as 'Home'. But it had never been home to him, and staring back into the past he knew very well that even if Juli went with him, he did not want to go back there. Yet they could not remain in India, for quite apart from the fact that they would be socially ostracized by British and Indians alike, the danger of reprisals from the offended rulers of Bhithor and Karidkote would be too great.

The former consideration carried little weight: Ash had never cared very much for social approval or the opinions of his fellow men. But for Juli's sake he could not risk the latter, so they would have to leave the country and live elsewhere—if not in England, then in America. No, not America . . . Americans, like 'memsahibs', held strong views on miscegenation, and even in the northern states Juli would be regarded as a 'coloured woman' and treated accordingly.

South America, then? Or perhaps Italy—or Spain?

But he knew in his heart that it would make no difference which country they chose, for wherever they went it would only mean one thing for both of them. Exile. Because India was their country: his as much as Juli's. And if they left it would be going into banishment just as surely as he had done once before, when he had sailed from Bombay as a forlorn twelve-year-old in the care of Colonel Anderson.

Only this time, he would know that he could never come home.

The night was almost gone when Ash at last rose stiffly to his feet, and having slapped the sand from his clothes and retrieved the *lathi,* turned to make his way back to the camp.

He had not meant to stay away for so long, and it was only when a small, cool wind arose and blew down the dry river-bed, stirring up the sand between the boulders and driving it into his eyes, that he realized how late it must be; for this was the wind that blows across Rajputana in the dark hour before the dawn, and dies before sunrise.

Standing once more on the crest of the ridge that had shielded him from sight of the camp, Ash saw that the myriad fires and lamps that had earlier made a red glow in the sky had burned out or been extinguished long ago, and now there were only a few scattered pin-points of light to show him where the camp lay. He would need them, as it was far darker now than it had been when he had set out; the stars had already begun to pale, and though there was now a segment of moon in the sky, it lay wan and lemon-coloured in the dregs of the night and gave little or no light.

The darkness forced him to walk slowly in order to avoid stumbling over rocks or into holes, but even this failed to prevent his brain from continuing to bedevil itself with the problem that had sent him out into the night some hours ago, and which he was now carrying back with him, still unsolved. It had not seemed particularly complicated when he set out—a mere matter of clearing his mind and deciding upon a course of action. It was only when he realized that he could not give Juli up, and began to plan ways and means of running away with her, that the appalling difficulties that would have to be faced and overcome rose up before him; and now as he made his way back to the camp, the problems seemed to multiply with every step . . .

Should they attempt to escape together they would certainly be followed: and this was not British India—this was Rajputana—'King's Country'; an amalgam of sovereign states ruled over by independent princes, where the writ of the Raj meant little. The hereditary rulers paid lip-service to the Queen-Empress, but apart from that they did very much as they pleased, and their rank protected them from prosecution in any court of law. A paternal Government provided them with 'advisers' in the form of Residents, Commissioners, Political Officers and an Agent-General, and decided such vexed questions as how many guns each should be entitled to have fired in salute on ceremonial occasions. But otherwise it made a point of not interfering with them unless actually forced to do so, and there would be little safety for a runaway princess and her lover in such country.

Once the word of their flight had gone out, every man's hand would be against them and no state in all Rajputana would give them refuge. So for the present there was nothing he could do but wait upon events and trust to the inspiration of the moment, hoping, like Mr Micawber, that something would turn up—a miracle, for preference, for he was beginning to think that they would need nothing less. 'Yet what have I ever done to deserve a miracle?' thought Ash.

He could find no answer to that, and when, half an hour later, something did indeed turn up, it was not the miracle he hoped for, but a confirmation of all his fears, and proof—if he had needed proof —that the dangers he had visualized were very far from imaginary.

Because the light was still poor enough to make the going treacherous, he had been keeping his eyes on the ground, and it had not occurred to him that his movements would be of any interest to anyone save Mahdoo and his own servants, or that he might be attacked.

The shot took him by surprise, and for a moment he did not realize that he had been the target. The bullet struck the *lathi* and spun it out of his hand in the same instant that he heard the report, and it was instinct alone made him throw himself flat among the stones; though even then it did not occur to him that he had done anything more than cross the line of fire of some local hunter who was shooting for the pot, and he raised his head and shouted angrily into the darkness.

The answer was a second shot that whipped above his head, missing him by less than an inch. The wind of its passing stirred his hair, but this time he made no sound, for though the first shot could have been accidental the second was not. He had seen the flash, and realized that the man who had fired was standing little more than fifteen yards away and could not possibly have failed to hear him call out, or mistaken his voice for that of a wounded animal. And in the next moment, as though to confirm this, he heard quite clearly in the silence the snick of a breech block as the man reloaded.

It was a frightening sound, and the cold deliberation of it made his heart lurch and miss a beat. But at the same time it seemed to clear his brain, and make him think a good deal more quickly and more concisely than he had done for many days. The vacillation of the past hours fell away from him and he found himself assessing the situation as coolly as though he were on a training exercise on the plains beyond Mardan.

The unknown man was certainly no wandering *budmarsh* shooting at a stranger for sport or viciousness; rifle bullets were far too valuable to waste without the certainty of reward, and he carried nothing worth stealing. His assailant was also plainly aware that his quarry was unarmed, for in spite of having fired twice, he had not troubled to move his position, but was standing confidently upright, concealed but in no way protected by the tall clump of pampas grass where he had been waiting for his victim to pass . . .

That last was something else of which Ash was suddenly certain, for this was the one place where the lie of the land dictated his route, and anyone wishing to waylay him would know that he must come this way, and had only to wait. Someone had known, and waited; and even in the darkness the shot must have been an easy one, since at that range the chance of missing was almost negligible. Moreover Ash had been walking very slowly and without troubling to move without noise, and had it not been for the *lathi* he would have died or been seriously wounded.

But the watcher with the gun would not know about the *lathi*, and having seen Ash fall, the chances were that he imagined the bullet to have gone home and that his victim was either dead or dying—the latter, probably: it had been a mistake to call out. On the other hand, many men did so at the moment of impact, and as he had made no further sound he could only hope that his assailant, thinking him dead, would refrain from wasting a third bullet on a corpse. It was not much of a chance, but the fact that the man must be reasonably confident that he had not missed was the only card that Ash held, and unless he could make good use of it he would die.

His assailant made no move for the best part of five minutes, but stood motionless in the shelter of the tall grass. Then at last he began to creep forward, treading as softly and as warily as a cat and pausing between every step to listen.

He was barely more than a dark outline against the shadowy background of pampas and thorn-scrub, but the sky was becoming lighter and objects that a few minutes ago had been unidentifiable were beginning to take shape and reveal themselves as rocks and bushes, and Ash could make out the barrel of the rifle that was still trained on him. From the angle at which it was held he knew that there was still a finger on the trigger, and that for his life's sake he must not move or breathe.

The wind had dropped with the approach of dawn, and the world was so quiet that he could hear the soft crunch of dry earth and pebbles under shoe leather, and presently, the sound of his would-be murderer's breathing, quick-drawn and uneven. The man was now less than a yard away. But that was still too far, for his rifle remained ready and unwavering and any premature movement would be the signal for a third bullet—fired this time at point-blank range. He was standing motionless, listening, and it seemed hardly possible that he could fail to hear his quarry's heart-beats when to Ash's own ears they sounded as loud as trip-hammers falling on iron. But apparently he did not, for after a moment or two he came forward and touched the supposed corpse with his foot. When it did not move, he kicked it, this time with some violence.

His foot was still in the air when a hand closed like a vice about his other ankle and jerked it savagely, and losing his balance he fell forward across something that appeared to be made of steel and whipcord.

The gun exploded in a deafening crash of sound and the bullet slammed into a rock and filled the air with a hornets' nest of flying splinters, one of which slashed across Ash's forehead, leaving a shallow cut that filled his eyes with blood.

But for this he would almost certainly have killed his adversary, because that kick had made him lose his temper with a thoroughness that he had never previously equalled, and driven anything he had ever been taught about Queensberry Rules out of his mind. He was intent only on killing—or being killed, though there was never much chance of the latter. His opponent might be dangerous with a gun in his hands, but deprived of it he proved to be no match for Ash, being not only shorter but inclined to stoutness, and judging from his frantic gasps for breath and the flabbiness of his muscles, sorely out of condition.

Nevertheless he fought hard for his life, scratching, clawing and biting with the desperation of a cornered rat as the two rolled over and over among the stones, until with a sudden frenzied wrench he was free. Ash, blinded by his own blood, grabbed at him but missed his hold, and was left clutching a handful of clothing that had torn in his grasp as their owner, sobbing and gasping, scrambled to his feet and bolted like a terrified animal for the cover of the pampas grass.

There had been no point in following him, for by the time Ash had cleared the blood out of his eyes the man had disappeared. And though the darkness had by now thinned to an indeterminate grey, there was still too little light to make tracking a fugitive through that maze of scrub and grass a feasible proposition, while any attempt to do so by ear alone would be equally fruitless, since the noise of his own passage would drown all other sounds. There was obviously nothing for it but to get back to the camp as quickly as possible and institute a few inquiries there.

Ash tied a make-shift bandage round his head to keep the blood out of his eyes and picked up his *lathi* and the fallen gun. The *lathi* had splintered and was of little further use, but the gun was evidence, and it should not be too difficult to trace the owner, for by the feel of it it appeared to be a modern sporting rifle similar to the one he himself owned. There could not be many other men in the camp who possessed such a weapon; and as only someone who was familiar with that type of rifle would think of using it for such a vital assignment as murder, the task would not have been given to a servant or an underling.

He did not doubt that the owner had come from the camp, and the rifle should be able to prove it. But he was daunted by the discovery that he possessed an enemy who was not only prepared to kill him, but had, to that end, kept so close a watch on him that when on the spur of the moment he had walked out on the plain that night, he had given the watcher an opportunity to put into practice a scheme that had probably been decided on much earlier—the death of Captain Ashton Pelham-Martyn.

Oddly enough, it had not occurred to Ash until now to wonder who had tried to kill him. But then the whole ugly incident, from the first shot to the moment when his assailant had wrenched himself free and escaped to the shelter of the thickets, had lasted no more than ten to fifteen minutes, and during that time he had had more urgent things to think of than the identity of the killer. But now the point seemed vitally important, and looking back on his own actions during the past two months, Ash wondered why it had not occurred to him before that he might have an enemy in the camp, when the person or persons who had attempted to murder Jhoti must still be with them, and could well hate him for his part in preventing it—and for the pains he had taken afterwards to keep an eye on the boy. Then, too, there was Juli . . .

It was not beyond the bounds of possibility that there were others besides the old *dai,* Geeta, who had learned of Juli's visits to his tent, and if so it might well be regarded as a matter of honour to kill him, since it would be assumed that he had seduced her. Or then again, there was always a chance that someone—possibly Biju Ram? —had somehow managed to trace a connection, through the Guides, with Zarin and Koda Dad, and from there to the Hawa Mahal, and had recognized the one-time servant of the late Yuveraj of Gulkote: the boy Ashok.

Ash considered this last and rejected it as unlikely. That trail was cold, and with Lalji and Janoo-Rani both dead there was no one in the newly named State of Karidkote who would derive any benefit from his death on that score, or even trouble to remember him. Nevertheless, after setting that aside, it was clear that there were several reasons to account for his having an enemy in the camp; and realizing that there was likely to be more than one, Ash took particular pains during the remainder of his return journey to keep well clear of any rock, bush or fold in the ground that might provide cover for a marksman, and registered a vow that never again would he go anywhere without a revolver.

The dawn light was flooding across the plain by the time he reached his tent, and Mahdoo, snoring peacefully, did not stir as he stepped over him. The lamp that hung from the tent pole had burned out, but he did not need it now; there was enough light to see by, and he stowed the rifle and the broken *lathi* under the bed, and having removed his shoes and coat, lay down in his shirt sleeves and was instantly asleep.

There had seemed no point in arousing Mahdoo, and it had not occurred to Ash that he would give the old gentleman the fright of his life, for he had not yet seen his own face in a looking-glass and had no idea of the spectacle he presented. But Mahdoo, waking half an hour later in the clear light of early morning and entering the tent to see if the Sahib had returned, imagined for one nightmare moment that he was looking at a corpse, and very nearly suffered a heart-attack on the spot.

Reassured by the sound of breathing, he tottered out to fetch Gul Baz, who came running and after a short inspection declared that there was no need for anxiety, as the Sahib was obviously not badly hurt.

'I think he has only been in a brawl,' observed Gul Baz reassuringly. 'Those marks on his cheeks are such as are made by fingernails and little stones. Also there is not much blood on the cloth about his head, and he is sleeping peacefully. It would be wiser not to wake him, and later we will get a piece of raw goat's meat to bind over his eye to reduce the discolouration and the swelling.'

The raw meat had been duly applied to an eye that by then had turned every colour of the rainbow, and may conceivably have done it some good. The rest of Ash's injuries were equally superficial and faded quickly, and within a week there was nothing to show that he had been in a fight but the ghost of a black eye and a faint scar that might have been mistaken for a frown line on his forehead. But however quickly these faded, the marks had been there and the man he had fought must have had similar ones: gravel rash, at least, and with luck an impressive collection of bruises, which should make it a simple matter to identify him.

It had not, however, been at all simple, because Ash had overlooked something: the fact that in a camp as vast as this one, any number of men incurred minor injuries every day of the week, and though the majority of cuts and bruises were due to carelessness or the normal hazards of daily life, a great many were acquired as a result of arguments that had ended in fights: 'and as for Gunga Dass,' reported Mahdoo, 'it seems that his wife and his wife's mother, finding that he had spent much money on one of the harlots, attacked him with cooking pots and broke a *chatti* on his head. Then there is Ram Lalla who . . .'

There were many such tales; too many. 'Were there only a hundred men in the camp, it would be a different matter,' said Mulraj. 'But there are thousands, and even if we should find the man we seek, he is sure to have a tale ready and a dozen witnesses to swear to its truth and tell how he came by such injuries; and who could disprove it?'

The only thing that had been easily proved was the ownership of the rifle, because as Ash had surmised, it was no old-fashioned musket but a modern, precision-made weapon, a Westley-Richards sporting rifle, capable of great accuracy up to a range of four hundred yards. He had felt sure that there could be few weapons of this type in the camp, and in this too he had been right: there was only one. His own.

To find that he had very nearly been murdered by his own rifle annoyed him even more than the attempt itself. The colossal impertinence of it added insult to injury, and he promised himself that when he found the man he would give him the thrashing of a lifetime. But the fact that the rifle had been removed from his tent under Mahdoo's very nose, and without one of his servants hearing a sound, was perhaps the most disturbing part of the affair, for it showed that he had little or no protection against assassination, and proved what he had already suspected: that someone, or possibly several people, had been keeping a close watch on him.

His attacker had obviously seen him start out last night, unarmed except for a *lathi,* and having overheard enough to know that he had intended to be away for several hours had been sufficiently cunning to realize the opportunity this offered. He must have seen the servants retire and Mahdoo settle down at the tent door to keep watch, and once the old man fell asleep it could not have been difficult to creep in at the back without disturbing him. The hurricane lamp would have been burning, but it would have been turned down low, providing only a glimmer of light that would have been enough to enable the thief to move without noise. And once in possession of the rifle he had only to leave as he had come, and following the same route that Ash had taken, lie up in the gully to wait, in the sure knowledge that his quarry would return that way.

Once again it occurred to Ash to wonder how many people had seen Juli come to his tent, and the very thought of it made him cold with fear and anger and a sudden sickening apprehension. If that attempt on his life had been on Juli's account, then he had made a serious mistake in mentioning it at all—let alone discussing it in detail with Mahdoo and Gul Baz and Mulraj, and speculating with them as to the possible reasons for it. He should have kept his mouth shut and invented some plausible story of a fall in the dark to account for that black eye and the other souvenirs of the night.

But then he had been in no state to concoct lies, or even consider whether or not to tell the truth when he had awakened late in the day, after hours of exhausted slumber, to find Mulraj staring down at him in frowning concern while Mahdoo and Gul Baz hovered anxiously in the background. He had merely explained the circumstances, and it had been the sight of his own face in the glass that had prompted him to remark that all they had to do was to keep a look-out for someone who bore similar marks—a man of medium height and inclined to plumpness, who was known to be a good marksman and . . .

It was at this point that Ash, turning towards his bed with the intention of producing the rifle, was side-tracked by a suggestion from Gul Baz that inquiries among the *dhobis* might prove profitable since one of them might remember washing a garment that was badly torn and stained. Ash had agreed, but the reference to washing reminded him that he himself was sorely in need of a bath, and as it was now late afternoon and he had eaten nothing since the previous evening, that he could also do with a meal.

The two servants had hurried off to see to the matter, and as luck would have it, a *bheesti* began to pour the bath just as Ash was groping under the bed for the rifle, with the result that he did not even look at it, but handed it to Mulraj and continued the conversation from the far side of a canvas partition while splashing in the tub and shaving.

Mulraj agreed that there could be few such weapons in the camp and that it should be a simple matter to trace the owner. 'For it is of the same pattern as the one that you yourself use to shoot black-buck. An *Angrezi* rifle,' said Mulraj, and replaced it under the bed. He was far more intrigued by the *lathi,* and after examining it, declared that the Sahib had clearly been born under a lucky star, for the bullet had struck one of the narrow iron rings that strengthened the stout bamboo, and with such force that although it had been deflected, the ring was almost flattened and the bamboo inside it reduced to a pulp. 'The gods were surely on your side last night,' commented Mulraj, and left, promising to lose no time in setting a few private inquiries on foot. So it was not until a full hour later, when Ash had dressed and done justice to a large and satisfying meal, that a closer inspection of the rifle disclosed its ownership; and by then it was too late for second thoughts.

He could hardly tell Mulraj, or even Mahdoo, that he had changed his mind and no longer wanted any help in tracking down the man who had tried to murder him, for they would want to know why; and the truth would not serve, because he could not explain that he was afraid that they might also uncover a motive—a motive for murder that had nothing whatever to do with Jhoti or jealousy (or even the fact that he, Pelham-Sahib, had once been a boy called Ashok) but was solely concerned with the Rajkumari Anguli-Bai and the honour of the royal houses of Karidkote and Bhithor . . .

It was a relief when both Mahdoo and Mulraj discovered, separately, that to try and find a man with a scratched and bruised face in a camp numbering close on eight thousand was like looking for one particular windfall in an apple-orchard after a stormy night. And also when Gul Baz's investigation failed for the same reason (according to the *dhobis,* so much clothing became torn and stained on the march that it was impossible to keep count of it).

Any inquiries, however artfully pursued, would inevitably arouse curiosity, and Ash was now thankful that he had not also thought to hand Gul Baz a piece of evidence that some *dhobi* might well have recognized. But then he himself had not realized—or not until much later—that the strip of pewter-grey cloth that he had used as a bandage was not his, but part of the man's clothing—the entire left front of a thin cotton coat that had torn away in his hands, and by doing so allowed his assailant to escape.

He must have tied it about his head without thinking, and on removing it, thrown it aside and never noticed it again until after he had found out about the rifle; by which time he could only feel grateful that no one else had shown any interest in it either, for the colour and material—a handwoven mixture of cotton and silk in two shades of grey that produced a 'shot' effect—was a valuable clue, and as such, the fewer people who knew about it, and the sooner it was destroyed, the better.

From now on he would keep quiet about any new clues, and with luck the investigation that he had so rashly set on foot would come to nothing, and the whole affair be forgotten—except by himself, for he had every intention of trying to discover the identity of the man who had attempted to kill him. But he would do it without assistance; this was something he must handle alone or not at all, and if the incident had done nothing else, it had at least forced him to make up his mind about Juli . . . he supposed he should be grateful for that.

The absurd, unformed hopes that had lurked for so long at the back of his mind, and that only yesterday had crystallized with startling suddenness in an urgent problem that must be solved without delay—all the fears and the wild plans that he had taken out onto the plain to wrestle with for the whole of one long night and carried back with him, still unresolved—had been settled by a bullet fired from his own gun; because it had brought home to him, as nothing else could have done, that he had been right to be afraid for Juli.

Ash had not been blind to the dangers of his own position in the camp, for unlike too many of his countrymen (and most of his countrywomen), who had already forgotten the lessons of the Mutiny, he knew that India as a whole had little love for the Raj. India had always respected strength, and she accepted the realities of power and was prepared to tolerate, if not enjoy, a situation that there seemed little prospect of putting an end to at present—and that on the whole happened to suit her fairly well. But she was like a bamboo thicket that sways to every breeze and bends gracefully before a gale yet never breaks, and hides among its canes a sleeping tiger that may awake at any moment, and kill.

As the sole representative of the authority of the Raj and the only European in camp, Ash's position was bound to be a little precarious, and he had taken certain precautions to safeguard himself. The siting of his tent, for instance, and its position in relation to his servants and his horses; the fact that he slept with a revolver under his pillow and an Afghan knife on the table by his bed, and that once his tent was pitched one or other of his servants would always be on guard unless he himself were in it. Yet despite all this his tent had been entered and his rifle stolen, and he himself had been spied upon, followed and ambushed as easily as though he had been a child, or a sheep. He meant to be a great deal more careful in future, but he knew that the advantage would always lie with the enemy, who could choose his time while he, the victim, even though forewarned, could not be perpetually on guard and suspicious of everyone. Sooner or later, not knowing who to suspect, there would come a time when the guard would be dropped; and then . . .

It was not his own body that Ash visualized lying sprawled and bleeding in the dust, but Juli's. And he knew that he could not bring her to her death. He must do nothing to prevent her marriage to the Rana, and perhaps after all she would find a measure of happiness— in motherhood, if in nothing else, though that thought still stabbed as cruelly as a dagger in the heart. But to picture Juli lying dead was infinitely worse; and at least in Bhithor she would be with Shushila, and as a Rani—even a Junior Rani—she would possess a certain amount of influence and considerable prestige, and live in comfort surrounded by waiting-women and servants. Her life might not be too unbearable, and though at first she would miss the mountains, the memory of them would fade; and in time she would forget the Peacock Tower and the Queen's balcony. And Ashok.

Juli would accept her fate and endure it without complaint. And at the worst, it would be better than death, for as long as one was alive there still was a chance, even though it might only be what Wally termed 'a fighting chance'—a chance of being able to twist fate to suit one's purpose, of making something out of the impossible, a chance that life might take a sudden unexpected turn, and disaster become victory. But to die and be buried, or burned . . . that was for the old, not for someone young and strong and beautiful, like Juli. Yet if she were to run away with him now, death would catch up with them very quickly.

They should have gone earlier, while they were still in British India . . . but it was too late to think of that now, and even if they had done so it would only have meant postponing the inevitable a little longer. Ash had not forgotten how the *Nautch*-girl's henchmen had once hunted him throughout the length and breadth of the peaceful Punjab, where there were British troops in a dozen cantonments and a police-post in every village, and he knew that they would almost certainly have caught him in the end if the Guides and Colonel Anderson had not turned him into a Sahib and whisked him out of the country.

Juli would be far easier to find than that little bazaar boy had been, and what chance would she have of getting safely out of the country if he himself were under arrest? There would be endless delays, and while officials argued and prevaricated, Nandu would act— that at least was something he could be certain of, as there was nothing in all the tales that Ash had heard about the new ruler of Karidkote to suggest that he would permit his half-sister to disgrace him in this fashion without taking immediate steps to wipe out the stain. And if Nandu was dilatory in exacting vengeance, there would still be the Rana to reckon with.

British India or no British India, they would hunt Juli down as remorselessly as a wolf pack on the trail of a hind, and long before Ash could arrange to get her out of the country they would have closed in for the kill.

Death, or the Rana? He would never know which one Juli would have chosen. Or whether she loved him enough to prefer the first, or still only thought of him as a favourite brother. But whichever way she chose, he would still have lost her.

Ash laid his head on his arms and sat motionless for a long time, looking into a future that was bleak and empty and devoid of all meaning. And that evening he did not join the riding party, but excused himself on the score of work.

When he did not go again, the rides were discontinued, though he was unaware of this. Shushila sent several times, inviting him to the durbar tent, but he pleaded a headache and did not go. He knew that he could not withdraw completely from that circle, but it was preferable to feign illness and pressure of work, or even to risk giving offence by appearing boorish, rather than to see too much of Juli.

The less they saw of each other the better it would be for both of them—particularly for her, if the attempt on his life had been on her account—but now that he no longer had the evening rides to look forward to the days seemed endless and the business of the camp an intolerable burden, and it became increasingly difficult to keep his temper and listen patiently to the innumerable complaints that were brought before him daily and that he was expected to settle. Because although Mulraj and his officers and such elder statesmen as Kaka-ji Rao dispensed justice in the camp, Ash had come to be regarded as the court of final appeal, and all too many cases came up before him for judgement.

Men quarrelled and came to blows, stole, lied and cheated, contracted debts that they did not pay, or accused each other of a variety of crimes that ranged from murder to giving short weight at the food stalls; and Ash would sit for hour after hour, looking attentive while accuser and accused produced their witnesses and talked interminably. And as often as not he would realize, suddenly, that he had not heard one word of what anyone had said and had no idea what the dispute was about. Then it would all have to be said over again; or, more frequently, he would set the case aside 'for further consideration' and go on to the next—and often hear very little of that too.

The effort not to think about his own affairs seemed to be affecting his ability to think about anything, though fatigue probably had a good deal to do with it. He was sleeping badly and was always tired; and the weather did not help, for each day it grew hotter, and already the *louh* had begun to blow—the hot wind that whines across Rajputana when the cold weather is over, and dries the moisture from ponds and plants and the bodies of men. Later, when the rivers

ran low and the countryside was parched with heat, there would be
dust-storms; dense, brown, smothering clouds that could blot out the
sun and turn noon-day into night; and though the season for such
storms still lay well ahead, the prospect of it provided Ash with yet
another reason for urging speed. Yet in the circumstances, any ex-
hortations to hurry were a waste of breath, since the camp no longer
marched in the daytime but moved only in the early hours of the
morning.

Each evening scouts rode on ahead to spy out the land and select
the best available stopping place for the following day, and the tents
were struck before first light so that the long procession could crawl
forward in the comparative coolness that preceded the dawn, to
stop again as soon as the sun was far enough above the horizon for
the heat of its rays to become unbearable. Very often the distance
between one camp site and the next would be no more than five
miles, and sometimes it was less, because their progress was governed by the need for water and shade—though the latter could, and
of necessity often was, dispensed with. But canvas and carts and
straw were a poor protection against the blazing sun; and only the
animals, tethered in the open and suffering torments from the heat,
had reason to be grateful for the scorching wind which at least kept
them free of flies. As the pace became slower and slower, men and
women alike became irritable and intolerant, and tempers flared; yet
however slowly they moved, each day's march brought them inexora-
bly nearer to the border of Bhithor, and it would not be long now
before they reached the end of their journey.

It could not be too soon for Ash, who had once wished that it
would never end and now only wanted to get it over quickly. The
physical discomforts of the march were becoming enough to try anyone's temper, but combined with acute mental stress and the mounting problems of the camp, they verged on the intolerable. On top of
which he now suffered from a disagreeable sense of insecurity, for
only three days after the attack on him, his tent had again been
burgled, this time in broad daylight, it having been the first occasion
on which the camp had moved off before dawn in order to avoid
marching in the heat, and stopped when the sun was high.

The site chosen that day had been near a shallow expanse of
weed-choked water that had evidently once been a man-made tank,
dug many centuries ago to supply some long-forgotten city, the
traces of which still surrounded it in the form of low mounds, crum-

bling sandstone blocks and the remains of ruined walls that were barely higher than the rustling, lion-coloured grass, and split by the roots of neem and *kikar* and *sal* trees.

As usual, Ash's tent had been pitched under a tree on the outskirts of the camp, with his servants' tents arranged in a half circle some way behind it. The waist-high grass had been cut or trampled down for twenty yards around to ensure that no one could approach unseen, yet some time during the hottest part of the day someone had done so.

No less than two of Ash's men had been on guard at the time, squatting in the shade of a neem tree at the edge of the clearing from where they could keep the tent under observation. But the fact that neither had seen anything suspicious was not altogether surprising—they had been up since four o'clock that morning, and having eaten their mid-day meal were replete and lulled into drowsiness by heat and the hot wind. Both had dozed off at intervals—secure in the conviction that their mere presence would be enough to deter any wrong-doer from approaching—and they had heard nothing to rouse them, for their ears had been filled with the dry rustle of leaves and grass in the wind.

Ash had been busy elsewhere, and he had returned to find his belongings in considerable disorder: the locks of his boxes forced and their contents strewn about the floor. Even his bed had been stripped, and the entire tent showed signs of being searched in great haste, yet with a thoroughness that he found oddly disquieting. Every piece of furniture had been moved and the matting rolled back to see if anything had been buried in the earth underneath it. His mattress had been slit open with a knife and both pillow-slips had been removed. But the search had proved unrewarding, as apart from a handful of small change—most of it copper—there had been neither money nor firearms in the tent, for Ash had taken to carrying his revolver, and had given the two cash boxes, the rifle and shot-gun and his spare ammunition to Mahdoo, who had hidden them in a shabby canvas bedding-roll which he added to his own luggage.

The only other mitigating circumstance—if it could be called that—was the fact that the thoroughness of the search seemed an indication that the thief had been looking for money, and was therefore not the man who had previously stolen the rifle. Ash drew what comfort he could from that, because although it was unpleasant enough to find that someone had managed to enter his tent without being seen, ransack it and leave again, all in broad daylight and with two of his servants in plain sight, it was better than wondering if once again one of his own weapons had been needed to use against him, and if so, why. To make a murder look like suicide?—or because suspicion would naturally fall on his servants if he were found shot with his own gun?

That last seemed the most likely explanation, as all the camp knew that the Sahib's tent stood apart and was not easy to approach unseen, so who but one of his own people would have been able to enter it and take the rifle? The reasoning would have appeared sound enough, and the majority would have accepted it because the alternative (that in a camp where there were literally thousands of firearms —muskets, muzzle-loaders and jezails without number, most of them easily stolen—a man bent on murder would go to immense trouble in order to steal the Sahib's gun) would seem absurdly far-fetched. The only question would be which one of the Sahib's servants was the murderer?

Ash would have liked to discuss this latest piece of unpleasantness with Mulraj, and had he been certain that the thief was only after money he would have done so and found it a great relief. But he was not certain, and so he said nothing. He told Mahdoo and Gul Baz that he did not wish it talked of, and Gul Baz had tidied up the tent without assistance, and later confided to Mahdoo that the sooner they were done with this wedding and free to return to Rawalpindi again, the better he would be pleased. 'I have had enough of Rajputana,' said Gul Baz. 'And more than enough of this camp. There is something here that I do not understand: some evil which threatens the Sahib, and perhaps others too. Let us pray that we may separate ourselves from these Karidkoties and turn our faces to the north before it overtakes us.'

Much the same thoughts were in Ash's mind, but with one difference, for he had few illusions about himself and knew that what he must pray for was patience and self-control.

He found that he could get through the days provided he filled every moment of them with some form of activity that would prevent his thinking of Juli, but the nights were a different matter; however hard he drove himself, and however tired he became, the moment he lay down to sleep her face rose before him and he could not banish it. He would turn and toss and stare into the darkness, or rise again to light the lamp and write unnecessary reports or check columns of figures—anything to shut her out of his mind, and Gul Baz, coming to wake him before first light with a mug of tea, would find him asleep at the table with his head on a pile of foolscap.

As the world turned pearl-grey before dawn and men and animals awoke reluctantly to a new day, he would climb wearily into the saddle and ride off to do what he could towards getting the camp on the move, while his servants struck his tent and loaded it with the rest of his belongings on to the bullock cart, where Mahdoo would already be ensconced among the cooking-pots, squatting comfortably on a pile of baggage that included a shabby canvas bedding-roll. The air would still be cool from the night, and at this hour there was no wind, for the *louh* did not blow before sunrise. But no one had leisure to notice, let alone enjoy it, for the uproar and activity that preceded departure, and the artificial heat of torches, oil lamps and cooking fires made an inferno of the early mornings.

As the crow flies, Bhithor was no great distance ahead. But now they were no longer crossing a featureless plain, and the country here was full of low, barren hills whose slopes were slippery with shale and dry grass and whose ridges were bare rock. A traveller on foot could cross them without much difficulty and thereby save himself many miles, but it was impossible for a cart to do so. The camp must go round them, winding to and fro along the wide, shallow valleys that meandered between the hills, and doubling on its tracks with monotonous regularity, as though caught in a maze. It was a particularly tedious form of progress, and when at last they came out into comparatively open country again no one was surprised when the younger bride put her foot down and demanded a halt of at least three days, announcing that if it were not granted she would refuse to move another step. She was, she said, aware that only a few more marches would bring them to the borders of Bhithor, but she had no intention of arriving in her new country ill from exhaustion, and unless she were allowed a few nights' uninterrupted sleep she would collapse.

Her ultimatum had been well timed, for that day's march had brought them to the banks of a river where there were trees in plenty; and no one, with the exception of Ash, was averse to a halt. It was an excellent site for a camp, and although the river had shrunk in the heat to no more than a narrow channel threading a shimmering waste of sandbanks, it was still capable of providing an inexhaustible supply of water, besides being easily fordable. Better still, on the far side there were several villages surrounded by cultivated land, and the inhabitants were eager to sell such things as grain and vegetables, milk, eggs and sugar-cane, while the country being more open here there would be plenty of fodder for the animals, as well as black-buck and *chinkara* on the plain, and fish in the river. As a camping site it could hardly have been improved upon, and Ash found no support when he wished to push on.

'What do a few days matter?' said Kaka-ji, fanning himself. 'There is no great need for haste, and we shall all of us benefit from a short rest. Yes, even you, Sahib! For I fear your health is not good these days. You have become much thinner, and have lost your spirits and no longer laugh, or talk and ride with us as before. No, no . . .' a raised hand checked Ash's apologies. 'It is the heat. The heat and this hot wind. We all suffer from it. You and Mulraj who are strong and I who am old, and Jhoti who is young—and pretends that it is the heat and not too many sweetmeats that have turned his stomach. Shushila too, for she has always been sickly, though I think that with her it is partly fear. Shu-shu is afraid of the future, and now that we are so nearly at Bhithor she would delay her arrival, even if only for a day or two.'

'You have only yourself to blame, Sahib,' shrugged Mulraj. There was an unaccustomed edge to his voice and his tone was unsympathetic. 'You know how it is with Shushila-Bai, and had she been kept amused and occupied she might have given less thought to the future—and found the heat easier to bear. But when first you and then Jhoti ceased to ride with us of an evening or join in the gatherings in the durbar tent, those things no longer amused her and she turned to fretting and complaining.'

'I have been too busy,' began Ash uncomfortably. 'There have been so many—' he broke off abruptly, and frowned: 'What's all this about Jhoti? Why did he stop coming?'

'To begin with, I suppose because you did. And when he was taken ill, he could not.'

'*Ill?* Since when? Why was I not told?'

Mulraj's brows lifted and for a moment he stared in astonishment; then his eyes narrowed and he said slowly: 'I see now: you were not even listening. I should have known as much when you did not ask after him or try to see him.'

His voice changed and was no longer unfriendly: 'I told you myself four days ago, and spoke of it again on the following morning.

When you said nothing, but only nodded your head, I thought that you no longer wished to be troubled with such things. I should have known better. What is the matter, Sahib? You have not been yourself of late. Not since that attack upon you. It is not pleasant to know that someone waits and watches for an opportunity to put a bullet through one's head or a knife in one's back; as I myself know only too well. Is it that, Sahib? Or is it something else that troubles you? If I can be of help, you have only to ask.'

Ash flushed and said hurriedly: 'I know. But there is nothing, only the weather, and you cannot change that. Now tell me about Shoti. Kaka-ji Rao said something about the heat being too much for him.'

'Not the heat,' said Mulraj dryly. '*Datura*—or so I think. Though one cannot be sure.'

Now *datura* is a plant that grows wild in many parts of India, though more especially in the south. Its white, lily-like flowers are sweetly scented and very beautiful. But its seed, which is round and green, is known as the 'apple of death', for it is exceedingly poisonous—and being easily obtained it has been used for centuries as a handy method of getting rid of unwanted husbands, wives or elderly relatives. It is one of the commonest of all poisons, and can be ground into a powder and mixed with almost any food (though bread is the usual choice) and death follows quickly or slowly, depending on the size of the dose or the amount that has been eaten. According to Mulraj, Jhoti must have eaten a good deal of it, but he had vomited most of it up and thereby saved himself. He had been moved to his sisters' tent, where he was making a rapid recovery under the care of the *dai*, Geeta . . .

'But where did he *get* it from?' demanded Ash. 'What was it in? Have you questioned the *khansamah* and the rest of his servants? Surely all his people eat the same food, don't they?—he can't have been the only one made ill by it.'

But it seemed that he was. The poison, said Mulraj, had apparently been in some *jellabies,* a form of fried sweetmeats that Jhoti was particularly fond of, and that he had found in his tent. Fortunately, he had gobbled the lot—more than enough to make any child sick without there being any sinister ingredients. And equally fortunately, one of his servants, alarmed by the excessive vomiting, had run at once for Gobind instead of losing his head like the rest of them.

'Did Gobind say it was *datura?*' asked Ash.

Mulraj made a gesture of negation with one hand. 'No. Only that it might be. The boy, as I have said, had eaten them all, even to licking the honey from the leaves on which they had lain, so that nothing remained. His own people said that it was only the excessive number and greasiness of the sweetmeats that was causing him to vomit.'

Apparently Gobind had not been so sure of that; and though he said nothing then of his suspicions, he had treated the child as though for poison and made inquiries among the servants as to where the sweets had come from. But as he told Mulraj later, even if there had been nothing wrong with the *jellabies* and they had been placed there as a small surprise by someone who was fond of the child and only meant to please him, the very fact that they had made him sick would ensure that the giver would deny all knowledge of them. So he had not been surprised when no one would admit to knowing anything about them.

'But someone must have seen the boy eating them. Did Gobind ask about that?'

'Of course. But those who saw supposed—or said they did—that the Rajkumar had brought the *jellabies* himself. And I myself was only told that in his opinion the child had been poisoned, probably with *datura,* and that had he not been so greedy he would have died. But all that grease would have helped to coat his stomach and prevent the poison from being too quickly absorbed, and the grease and the sweetness together had made him feel sick, so that he had vomited everything up before it was too late; or that is what Gobind thinks, though he says that it would be difficult to prove. After I had spoken to him, I arranged for Jhoti to be nursed by his sisters. The elder is a woman of sense, and it gives Shushila-Bai something to think of other than the heat and her own troubles.'

Ash said: 'But there is a guard on the boy's tent. How could anyone—' and stopped, recalling that there had been a guard on his own tent, yet it had twice been entered without anyone having been seen. He pushed a hand through his hair, looking harassed and angry, and said: 'I told you we should have spoken out about that first attempt to kill the boy, so that whoever was responsible for it would know that we knew and be afraid to try again. But you wouldn't have it, and now look what has happened. It's been tried again. This time you should have told everyone.'

'I told *you,* Sahib,' observed Mulraj dryly. 'But it seems that you had other things on your mind, and did not hear.'

Ash said nothing, for he knew that there had been too many occasions of late when, drunk with tiredness, he had only made a pretence of listening without taking in a single word that was being said. He had not let this disturb him overmuch, because he had been sure that if anything of real importance had been mentioned he would certainly remember it, and if he did not, it would only mean that the subject had been of no interest; yet Mulraj had spoken to him about Jhoti and he had not listened to a word. How much more had he missed? . . . how many other people had told him things that he had not listened to as he went about his duties in a daze, attempting not to think of his own troubles and thinking of nothing at all, and imagining himself to be doing useful work?

Mulraj, watching him, noticed for the first time how much thinner he seemed to have become; not only thinner, but older—which was something that Kaka-ji had noticed even earlier, and remarked on. But then Mulraj, like Ash, had had other things on his mind.

'I am sorry,' said Mulraj contritely, regretting his last remark. 'That was unkind.'

'It was deserved!' admitted Ash ruefully. 'I am the one who should apologize. I have been behaving like . . . like George!'

'George?' Mulraj looked puzzled. 'Who is George?'

'Oh . . . just someone I once knew. He used to dramatize himself. It's a bad habit. Now, what are we going to do about Jhoti?'

There was, when they came to discuss it, very little they could do towards protecting Jhoti from assassination, beyond what they had done already; which was not much.

It was not possible to police the boy for every minute of every hour, unless he was to be followed everywhere by a guard of picked men from the State Forces, and though Mulraj would not have admitted it, he could not be wholly certain that even among his own best men there might not be one or two who were untrustworthy. Nandu was, after all, their hereditary overlord and ruler of their state and their destinies, and their duty was to obey his orders. Besides, there would also be large rewards, for he would not be niggardly when it came to paying for something he desired—such as the death of his heir-presumptive.

Mulraj was no cynic, but he had few illusions on the subject of human nature. He knew that most men can be bought if the price is high enough, and had therefore decided to say nothing about that first attempt to kill the little Rajkumar, but instead to pray to the gods and hope that vigilance and fore-knowledge would be able to foil a second one.

But it seemed that the gods had not listened to him, and as it was no thanks to him, or to Ash either, that the second attempt had failed, this time they would have to speak out. There was obviously nothing to be gained by keeping silence, and though they had little to offer in the way of proof, the boy would at least be warned of his danger and would never again be careless as to what he ate or drank. It was the course that Ash had originally favoured; yet now that it came to the point, he opposed it. Because once again he remembered a face from the past, not George's this time, but the face of the frightened boy who had been Jhoti's half-brother and Yuveraj of Gulkote . . .

Lalji too had been threatened with assassination, and had lived in terror of it—starting at shadows and never knowing who if anyone he could trust. And though he had been warned (his old nurse, Dunmaya, had never ceased warning him) it had not saved his life. All that it had done was to make a hell of his short life, and his rages and cruelty and vindictiveness were a not unnatural reaction to a burden of fear that was too great for a child to bear.

Jhoti too was no stranger to fear. He had been afraid on the night when Ash had first seen him and been struck by his resemblance to another plump and pallid little boy. He had good reason to shake in his shoes, for he had just defied Nandu and run away, and he knew enough of his brother to be frightened—though not, Ash thought, of being murdered; only of being punished. But if he knew . . .

'It's no good. We can't do it,' said Ash harshly. 'It would be too cruel. He's only a child and it would scare him out of his wits to learn that there is someone here in this camp who means to kill him and who has not only nearly done so twice, but will certainly try again. He'll grow afraid of everything and everyone. Afraid of trusting anyone, or eating anything, or drinking or sleeping or riding. It's too much to expect any child to bear. But there's no reason why we shouldn't tell his sisters and Kaka-ji. They can see to it that his food is tasted by someone else before he touches it. And we'll get Gobind to tell him not to eat sweets, or anything else he finds lying around, because the ones that made him sick must have been stale, or fried in bad *ghee* or something like that. Gobind will know what to say, and he and the girls and Kaka-ji can all help to keep an eye on the boy. It's the best we can do.'

Mulraj frowned and pulled at his lip, and agreed that it would be kinder not to frighten the child, but that if they wished to keep him in ignorance they would not be able to tell either Kaka-ji or Shushila-Bai—particularly Shushila, who would never be able to keep it to herself. She would only work herself into a state of hysteria over it, and the tale would be all over the camp within a matter of hours. As for Kaka-ji, he was too old and frail to be worried by such violent matters, as well as being far too talkative—and too transparent. Which left only Anjuli-Bai . . .

'Jhoti is fond of her, and she of him,' said Mulraj. 'Also I know her to be a sensible woman and one who does not lose her head and become distracted by danger. I have not forgotten her behaviour on the night that the *ruth* foundered in the river and the driver of the bullocks was drowned. She did not shriek or show fear, but saw to it that her sister was saved; and I am very sure that she would do no less for her brother. It is a heavy responsibility to lay on one woman's shoulders, but we need help, and Anjuli-Bai is perhaps the best person to give it. At least we know that we can trust her. Which is more,' added Mulraj grimly, 'than can be said of very few others in this camp.'

Yes, Juli could be trusted, thought Ash. She would do everything in her power to protect her little half-brother from harm, and she would neither panic nor talk unwisely—or lose her head in a crisis. She was the obvious person to turn to for help, and it had been a mistake not to tell her the truth about Jhoti long ago, after that near-fatal riding accident. He had fully intended to do so, yet somehow he had not. He could not remember why.

Another thought struck him, and he said abruptly: 'But Anjuli-Bai is never alone, so how are you going to tell her?'

'*I?*' Mulraj sounded surprised. '*Nahin,* Sahib. It is you who will have to do that; if I did I would surely be overheard. But on our evening rides, which have lately ceased, it was your custom to gallop on ahead with the Rajkumari Anjuli, and if the rides are resumed you could do so again without occasioning any remark. It is the only way.'

Which is why Ash, despite all his good intentions, came to be riding beside Juli on the following evening . . .

He had, in point of fact, seen her on the previous day, as after speaking to Mulraj he had asked if he might see Jhoti, who was still convalescent and in his sister's care. The tent had been crowded with people, for the East has never believed in the theory that segregation and quiet are necessary to the sick, and in addition to the princesses and their women, both Kaka-ji and Muldeo Rai were present.

Jhoti was looking better than expected, and well on the way to recovery. But his greeting had contained a strong suggestion of reproach. He had obviously been hurt by Ash's failure to visit him earlier, and only forgave it when Ash cravenly put the blame on Gobind, who, he said, had forbidden him to do so until the patient was in better health. He had not stayed long, and there had been no opportunity to speak to Juli beyond the usual polite greetings. He thought she looked pale and tired, and when he met her gaze it was puzzled, and like Jhoti's, a little reproachful, and his heart contracted.

He did not look at her again, because he was afraid that if he did he would not be able to stop himself from reaching out in front of them all to smooth away that faint, bewildered frown, and tell her that he loved her and had only stayed away because he could not bear to endanger her. Turning away quickly he spoke instead to

Shushila, and afterwards he could not remember who had brought up the subject of a riding party on the following evening, or what arrangements had been made. He remembered only that he had agreed to go. And as he walked back to his tent, he realized that he should not have done so.

'But it is for Jhoti's sake,' thought Ash, arguing with himself. There were so many ways in which Juli could help—she *had* to be told about Jhoti, and because he, Ash, was the only one who could do it, he had no choice in the matter.

But there was a flaw in that argument, and he knew it. It was not that Juli could not help, because she could and would do more than anyone else to protect her young brother from harm, and her help would be invaluable; but there was a time limit to any help she could give, and it was a very short one. In a few days they would reach Bhithor, and then there would be the wedding; and once that was over she would not be able to help Jhoti any more, so there was not much point in telling her anything for the sake of what little she could do in the few days that were left . . .

'I should have told her long ago,' thought Ash. But he had not, and it was no good telling her now. It was too late . . . He ought to send word that he could not join the riding party tomorrow. He ought not to see her again . . . it would only make matters worse. He would not go.

But he knew that he would, because he could not resist seeing her and talking to her just once more. After all, it would be for the last time. The very last . . .

That night he fell asleep the moment his head touched the pillow and awoke next morning feeling enormously refreshed; and though the future, when analysed, remained as bleak as before, the fog of fatigue and despair that had enveloped him had lifted, and life did not seem so intolerable after all.

Even the weather had improved. As the sun moved up the sky and the temperature rose, the tents did not flap maddeningly or the trees and grass whine in the wind, and today there were no veils of sand hissing along the river-bed. For once, the *louh* was not blowing, and the relief of being free from its hot, fretting breath was as great as though a persistent drum had suddenly stopped beating. Men's nerves relaxed and the whole atmosphere of the camp changed and lightened, for the cessation of the wind was almost as great a boon as the prospect of a few days' rest in a spot where there was both shade and water. The camp settled down to enjoy both, and although by the afternoon the day had become airless and stifling and the hordes of flies that the wind had previously kept at bay were back in force, these were considered a small price to pay for rest and quiet.

The late afternoon continued breathlessly still, but as the shadows lengthened and the shimmering heat-haze that had danced all day above the sandbanks died away, a faint current of air stirred along the river and crept between the tents. 'It will be cooler out on the plain,' said Kaka-ji.

But it had not been cooler. If anything, it had been hotter, because apart from the belt of trees and the cultivated land that bordered the river, the plain beyond was dry and stony, and the low hills that surrounded it had been absorbing heat all day and were now giving it off again in the manner of a flat-iron that has just been removed from the stove.

To the riding party it felt as though they were moving towards an open furnace and away from what little there was of coolness and shade, and even the horses and the trotting bullocks that drew the *ruth* appeared reluctant to go forward. A sudden gust of wind, the first that had blown all that day, whipped up a small whirlwind of dust and dead leaves and sent it spinning across the plain like some fantastic ghostly top, and presently others arose, twirled briefly among the stones and died again. But otherwise the evening was very still, and except for the dust-devils nothing moved on the plain.

The spot chosen as a starting place for the ride lay over a mile from the camp and had been selected by Mulraj, who had ridden out at dawn accompanied by some of his officers and a local *shikari* to shoot black-buck for the pot, and had decided that it would suit them very well. It was out of sight of the camp and the villages and well away from any beaten track, and the *shikari* had told him that although men had once lived among the hills, that was long ago, before the river changed its course and left them waterless. No one now came this way except to shoot; and there would be no game to shoot of an evening, for as the day waned the black-buck moved off towards the river and the croplands and did not stay out on the plain.

Anjuli and her sister had left camp in the *ruth,* together with one of Shu-shu's women; their horses following behind in the charge of an elderly syce and two grey-bearded members of the body-guard, while Ash, Kaka-ji and Mulraj rode ahead. Jhoti had not come out with them, though he had meant to, insisting that he was quite recovered. But Gobind had produced a new and fascinating game that one played with coloured pegs, so he had decided at the last moment that he would prefer to stay behind after all, and that anyway it was too hot for riding: Shu-shu and Kairi must go without him.

The *ruth* came to a stop near a tall outcrop of rock near the mouth of a mile-wide amphitheatre where the hills made a half-circle about the plain, and syces and escort discreetly turned their faces away as the brides descended and the riding party set out across the level ground. Ash had been afraid that without Jhoti to keep her entertained, Shushila might insist on their all keeping together; but luckily Kaka-ji proved an excellent substitute. The old man rode beside her and complimented her on her progress, offered useful suggestions and chatted about various incidents in the camp, while Mulraj as usual kept near by. It was as easy as it had ever been for Ash and Juli to ride on ahead—though less easy to tell her about Jhoti, because the moment they were out of earshot she forestalled him by speaking first.

'Why have you kept away from us for so long?' demanded Anjuli. 'It was not because of work, and you have not been ill for I made Geeta make inquiries for me. There is something the matter. What is it, Ashok?'

Ash hesitated, taken off guard. Julie had always been direct, and he should have borne that in mind and been ready with an answer that would have satisfied her; but there was no time to think of one now—and he had already decided that he could not tell her the truth. The impulse to do so was suddenly so strong that he had to clench his teeth to keep back the words, and Anjuli must have seen it, for a small crease appeared between her brows—that same frown line that he had ached to smooth away last night, because he could not bear to see her troubled.

The sight of it was just as unbearable today, and he thought that if he had not known before that he loved her, he would know it now, if only because of the pain that that small shadow caused him. Once again he would have given anything to be able to smooth it away and to tell her that he loved her and that there was nothing he would not do to protect her from unhappiness. But because he could not do so he took refuge in anger, and told her furiously that he had had more important things to do than sit about making social conversation in the durbar tent, and though she might not be aware of it, there had already been two attempts to murder her young half-brother: the second of them by poison, and only a few days ago.

This was not in the least how he had planned to break the news to her and the sight of the white shock on her face made him ashamed of himself. But he could not unsay the words, and as it was too late now to try softening the blow, he told her the tale harshly and in detail, leaving nothing out. When he had finished she said only: 'You should have told me after the first time; not now, when I have so few days left.'

It was what Ash himself had thought; though it had certainly not occurred to him immediately—or to Mulraj at all, unless Mulraj considered that any help, for however short a period, was worth having. But Anjuli had seen it at once, and the crease between her brows deepened, though now it was no longer on Ash's account but on Jhoti's. She looked very white and shaken, and he saw for the first time that there were dark shadows under her eyes, as though she too had not been sleeping.

He said: 'I'm sorry, Juli.' And thought as he said it that in the circumstances it was a singularly useless statement to make—a polite and automatic expression of regret that could serve as an apology for overturning a tea-cup or inadvertently jostling someone in a doorway. But there did not seem to be anything else he could say, and he *was* sorry: deeply and sincerely sorry . . . and for so many more things than neglecting to tell her about Jhoti. Perhaps most of all for having given her back the broken half of her little mother-of-pearl fish, for if he had not done that . . .

The sound of Shushila's laughter, borne on another brief gust of wind, was a reminder that unless he quickened their present pace they would soon be overtaken, because as they talked they had unwittingly slowed to a walk. He said urgently, 'Come on,' and they spurred forward again and raced across the plain towards a gap in the encircling hills, and entering it, found themselves in a quiet valley that was awash with evening shadows.

The ground here was less rough and stony than on the open plain, but the hillsides were largely rock and there were caves among the tumbled boulders, some of which had clearly been occupied at some time or another by either men or cattle, for the rock faces bore the traces of old fires, and here and there on the ground about them were marks left by cow-droppings that had long since been dispersed by sun and wind and the dung-beetles. But though Ash looked closely, he could see no sign of present habitation, and having assured himself that they had not been followed and that the valley was untenanted, he drew rein, and once more both horses fell into a walk. But though there was no longer any danger of being overheard, he did not speak, and Anjuli too was silent.

The shadow of the hills to their right covered two thirds of the valley, and although those nearest them were still bright in the sunset and aglow with the heat of the burning afternoon, it was cooler here than it had been out on the plain. The wind that had whipped up the dust-devils was blowing more strongly now, and the occasional gust that swept in from the plain dried the sweat between their shoulders and put an end to the hot, brooding stillness that had prevailed all day. Ahead of them the sky was already green with the evening and the hills were no longer lion-coloured, but brilliant with rose and cerise and apricot where the sunlight still lingered, and deep blue and violet in the swift-gathering shadows below. But Ash had no eyes for such things . . .

He was looking at Juli and realizing that although he might see her again during the next few days, and once more, and finally, at her wedding, he would never again be alone with her and be able to look his fill.

She was dressed, as always for the evening rides, in men's clothing: trousers and *achkan* and a small muslin turban that covered her hair and showed only the deep widow's peak in the angle where its folds crossed. The severity of the headgear only served to heighten the beauty of her features, drawing attention to the lovely lines of cheek and chin and the size of the wide-set eyes with their heavy fringe of lashes, while its colour, a vivid ruby-red, deepened the ivory tones of her skin and was repeated in the warm curve of her lips and the caste-mark between her brows. She sat tall and straight-backed in the saddle, and her shoulders had nothing of the sloping delicacy of Shushila's, but were slim and square.

Any casual passer-by would have taken her to be a handsome youth, for she held her head erect like a man instead of submissively bent as becomes a gently nurtured woman. But to Ash, riding beside her, her present garb seemed to emphasize her femininity far more than the graceful folds of a sari. The straight lines of the *achkan* showed the swell of her breasts which a sari could hide, and her slender waist and rounded hips were not those of a boy—though her hands might well have been. So much of Juli's character, thought

Ash, was written in those hands. He studied them as they rested quietly against her horse's mane, the reins looped between the strong, square-tipped fingers. Dependable hands . . .

He had forgotten Jhoti. But Anjuli had not, and when she spoke at last it was in an undertone, as though she was thinking aloud: 'This is Nandu's doing,' said Anjuli quietly. 'It must be so, for who else could gain any profit from Jhoti's death, or have any reason for wishing to kill him? The camp is full of Nandu's men . . . though I cannot believe that there can be many who would be willing to kill a child. But then it would not need many, only one or two, and if we do not know who they are it will be difficult to guard him. We must decide who can be trusted and see to it that there is always one of them with him to keep watch.'

She turned to look at Ash, and said: 'Who else knows of this, besides Mulraj and yourself and my uncle's Hakim, Gobind Dass?'

'No one,' said Ash, and explained why it had seemed best that first time to keep the matter secret, and to tell only herself and Gobind now. Anjuli nodded and said thoughtfully: 'Yes, you were right. It would only frighten Shu-shu, and as she would never believe that Nandu could have ordered such a thing, she would see it as part of a plot to kill us all—our family. My uncle would believe, but what can he do? Besides, if he knew he would find it difficult to conceal his alarm from Shu-shu, or from Jhoti either. But there are others whom I think we can safely trust. Old Geeta, for one. And Jhoti's own body-servant, Ramji, who has been with him since he was born, and whose wife is one of my women. Ramji would surely know which, if any, of his fellow servants could be trusted. Let us think now . . .'

The horses wandered forward unchecked, pausing occasionally to crop a mouthful of parched grass and moving on again while their riders discussed ways and means of preventing the murder of a child, and behind them the sky darkened. Presently another and far stronger gust of wind swept down the valley, driving the dust before it and snatching the turban from Anjuli's head to send it bowling away, unwinding as it went. Her hair whipped about her face and streamed forward on the blast like sea-weed in a tide-rip, and both horses threw up their heads and snorted and began to trot.

'High time we turned back,' said Ash. 'You'd better tie something round your head or you won't be able to see where you're going. Here—'

He pulled a handkerchief from the pocket of his riding breeches and put it into her hand, and turning his horse caught his breath and said in English: 'Good God!'

They had both been too occupied to pay much attention to their surroundings, and neither of them had thought to look behind them or to wonder why the light seemed to be fading unusually quickly. The sky ahead had been clear and calm, and even now the last of the sun lay gold along the crest of the near hill. But as they turned they saw that behind them lay nothing but darkness: a brown, turgid curtain of darkness that spanned the horizon from left to right and was advancing with such speed that it had already blotted out the entrance to the valley. The wind that drove it forward was no longer blowing in gusts, but had steadied to a gale, and now they could smell the dust and see that the sky above them was turning brown. 'But it's too early,' thought Ash dazedly. 'A month too early . . . more!' He stared at the advancing dust-storm as though he could not believe what he saw.

Juli said: 'Shushila,' and caught her breath on a sob. 'Shushila—'

She dropped her hands and let the handkerchief that she had been trying to tie about her head vanish on the wind, and snatching up the reins, urged her horse to a gallop, riding headlong for the wall of darkness that had swallowed up the plain where they had left Shushila. But Ash had recovered himself and he was too quick for her. He had never before used more than the lightest touch of a spur on Baj Raj, but he used both now, and the horse bounded forward and was level with Anjuli's mare and riding it off, turning her back up the valley.

'No!' cried Anjuli. 'No—I must go to Shushila.'

She wrenched at the reins in an attempt to check the frantic animal, and Ash cut her across the wrists with his whip and called savagely: 'Don't be a fool. Mulraj will look after her'—and brought the whip down again, this time on Baj Raj, though the horse needed no urging, for the towering, boiling darkness that was sweeping down on them was something he had never seen before, and he desired to escape from it every bit as urgently as Ash did.

The mare too was galloping at full stretch, and it is doubtful if anyone could have turned her; but Anjuli made no further effort to do so, because she had realized even as he spoke that Ashok was right and that what she had meant to do would have been an act of madness. Once caught in the heart of such a storm she could have seen nothing and helped no one; and Mulraj was with Shu-shu. He and the others could be counted upon to see that no harm came to her, and in all probability they had seen the approaching storm long ago and ridden straight back to camp, and were safe by now. But she and Ashok . . .

Anjuli had never seen a dust-storm either, but she did not need to be told that it was not a thing to be caught in out in the open, and she settled down to ride as she had never ridden before, crouching over the saddle-horn with her weight thrown forward to help the labouring animal, and without any idea where they were going, for she was half blinded by her own hair blowing about her face in wild, black confusion.

Ash was making for a cave that he had noticed earlier that evening in the brief moment before the shadow of the far hills reached it. He would not have seen it if the sun had not been on it, for at the time it had been a good half mile ahead, and though they had been moving slowly towards it they had barely covered more than half that distance. But Ash had been trained among the Frontier hills, and in the sunlight there was a sharp difference between the work of nature and that of man . . .

Even at that range it had been possible to see that below a jutting overhang a rock someone, at some time, had closed in the front of a large cave with mud bricks, leaving an entrance large enough to admit a man or a cow. It was the shape of that doorway—a black, straight-sided oblong—and the bleached colour of the mud that did not quite match the surrounding hillside, that had caught Ash's attention and made him narrow his eyes and stare at it to make sure that the cave behind it was not occupied. But nothing had moved in the valley or on the hillsides, and he knew that if there had been any men about, there would have been smoke, for it was the time of the evening meal. The sunlight had retreated and the cave had been lost among the advancing shadows, and Ash had turned to look at Juli, and forgotten it: only to remember it again in the instant that he had realized the significance of that ominous pall of darkness.

There were other and nearer caves, but it was difficult to judge how deep they were, and a shallow one would offer no protection against such a storm as this. But one that had been worth blocking in with a mud wall was likely to run far back into the hillside, and that narrow doorway would keep out the worst of the dust—if only they could reach it in time, for Ash was sharply aware that if the storm overtook them before they did so they would never find their way to it, the air already being so thick with dust and flying fragments of dry grass and leaves that they seemed to be riding through a fog.

Had the ground been less level they might never have reached it; boulders would certainly have brought one or both of their horses down, and bushes would have slowed them, but mercifully there were neither, and the only difficulty had been preventing their horses from racing past it and on up the valley. But Ash, who was in the lead, reined in with a violence that forced Baj Raj back on his haunches, and was out of the saddle and leaping at the mare as it shot past, Anjuli tugging on the reins with all her strength.

The mare swerved wildly and came to a sliding, slithering stop, and Anjuli tumbled from the saddle, and picking herself up, ran to catch Baj Raj, who was trotting in an aimless circle stumbling over his reins, and led him through the empty doorway into the darkness beyond, to be followed a moment later by Ash with the mare.

There was not enough light to see how big the cave was, but judging by the hollow sound of the horses' hooves it was a large one; and they had reached it in time—but only just in time. The storm had been so close on their heels that even as they turned to face the entrance, a dark curtain appeared to be drawn across it and the daylight was blotted out as a churning, choking, maelstrom of dust whirled down the valley, driven by a wind that shrieked as though the Valkyries rode it, or witches from the Brocken.

The noise of the gale filled the quiet cave with sound and made the darkness reverberate with a hollow, high-pitched drone that seemed to come from all points of the compass at once, and dust poured in through the doorway until the close air within was suddenly so thick with it that breathing became difficult, and Anjuli began to cough and choke.

She heard Ash calling something, but the words were lost in the howl of the wind and the echoes that they awoke in the recesses of the cave. Then his hand closed upon her arm and he was shouting into her ear: 'Take your coat off and put it over your head. And get back into the cave—as far as you can.' He brushed away the silky hair that was getting into his mouth, and added: 'Carefully now, Larla; don't go falling over anything.'

The old endearment had slipped out unconsciously, and he did not know that he had used it, for he had other things on his mind; notably the horses, who were backing and snorting in an effort to escape from the stifling dust, and might panic at any moment and lash out in the darkness, injuring each other if not Juli or himself. And if the horses went lame it was going to mean a long walk back to camp—if there was still a camp. He did not want to think of what might be happening there, and in any case there was no point in worrying about a situation that was completely beyond his control. But at least he should be able to do something about Baj Raj and the mare.

He had given his handkerchief to Juli, so there was nothing for it but to remove his shirt and tear it into strips; and he did so—using his teeth to start it tearing and tying the first strip over his nose and mouth as a filter. It was easier to breathe after that, and he kept his eyes shut against the dust and did the rest by touch, soothing the horses and knotting up their reins out of harm's way, and finally fastening a loop of cloth between each animal's forelegs, just above the fetlock, in the time-honoured fashion of the Indian villager who slips a similar loop of grass rope on his pony so that it can only hobble, and lets it out to graze in the sure knowledge that it cannot stray too far or come to much harm.

That done, he turned his attention to exploring the cave in order to see if it went far enough back to allow them all to get out of this stifling smother and into cleaner air.

The wind was blowing slantwise down the valley and slightly away from the cave, and the overhang of rock helped in some small way to deflect it. But there was no way of blocking the entrance, and the dust fumed in through it like steam from a boiling kettle. The further away they could get from it the better for all of them, and Ash moved back cautiously into the darkness, feeling his way along one wall.

He had gone perhaps twenty yards when his hand touched something that was unmistakably metal, and further investigation showed that someone, presumably the long-ago occupant who had closed in the cave mouth with those mud bricks, had driven several short iron staples into the rock wall; though for what purpose was not clear. The staples were spaced in a long slanting line, and there were five of them, and may well have been others higher up the wall and out of reach. But at least four were at a reasonable level, and Ash blessed the unknown man who had put them there, for though they were corroded by rust and one snapped off in his hand, the others would serve his purpose, as the air in this part of the cave was more breathable than that by the open doorway.

He groped his way back to the horses and returned with Baj Raj, who was jerking his head wildly from side to side in an effort to escape the dust, and had to be coaxed to follow. But once out of the worst of the smother, and with his reins hitched to a staple in the wall, he stopped shivering and stood quietly, and Ash went back for the mare, and having tethered her in the same manner, wiped the caked dust from his eyes and opened them a fraction to see if there were any signs that the storm was abating. But the doorway still showed barely lighter than the surrounding blackness of the cave, and outside the wind still howled past with the racket of an express train whistling in a tunnel.

It looked, thought Ash, as though it was going to be a long business, and he wished that he had paid more attention when the headmen of villages in their line of march had spoken of hot winds and dust-storms and other vagaries of the Rajputana weather. But having learned that the season of such storms was still well ahead, he had not troubled to ask questions about them, imagining that that was something that could safely be left until later and need not concern the Karidkote camp until the wedding ceremonies were over and they were free to start north again. But he regretted now that he had not asked them earlier, for he had no idea how long a dust-storm could be expected to last. Hours?—or only minutes?

It seemed to him that this one had been raging for close on an hour already, but on reflection he revised that estimate. He could not have taken more than ten minutes to tear up his shirt and find those providential staples, and to tether the horses. Say fifteen at most, and surely there could not be enough dust in all Rajputana, dry as it was, to sustain such a storm as this for more than a limited period? Unless, of course it was blowing in a circle—which was something else he did not know. But at least it could not last indefinitely; as soon as the wind expended its first violence and began to die down, the clouds of dust would sink back to earth and it would be over. Though not, at this rate, until the sun had set.

There was a watch in the pocket of Ash's riding breeches, but he had not looked at it since he left the camp, and as he could not see it now he had very little idea of what time it was. But it occurred to him that the storm alone might not account for the fact that he could barely make out the entrance to the cave. Once the sun had set, the interval of twilight was very short, for here night did not come slowly, as in the West, but hastily, on the heels of day. And if the sun was already down they were going to have to find their way back in the dark, across unfamiliar country and through a maze of hills.

'Mulraj will send out men to search for us,' thought Ash; though with more hope than confidence, because it seemed to him only too likely that the camp would have been thrown into such appalling chaos that Mulraj and the rest of them would have their hands full and be forced to wait until daylight before sending out search-parties, by which time, with any luck, he and Juli would have got back on their own. Meanwhile, for as long as the storm raged they would have to stay where they were and make the best of it.

He pulled down the strip of cambric that he had tied over his nose and mouth, and sniffing the air, found that it was a good deal better than he had expected. It would probably be better still further back in the cave—particularly if, as the echoes suggested, there were side caves leading out of this one, which the dust would not have entered —and at least it was pleasantly cool in here. The heat of the sun's rays had not been able to penetrate this far into the hillside, and after the burning heat outside, the drop in temperature was considerable; he hoped that Juli would not catch a chill, for she was wearing only a thin cotton *achkan;* and possibly nothing under it.

He called out to her, and once again the cave filled with echoes that fought with the weird drone of the wind as a dozen voices shouted from different points in the darkness, some close and some far away, their words lost in the clamour. The echoes faded but the noise of the wind remained, and Ash did not know if Juli had answered him or not, for her voice would have been drowned in the medley of sounds. But suddenly and unreasonably, half-a-dozen hideous possibilities sprang into his mind, and his heart contracted in a spasm of sheer terror. He had warned her to be careful, but suppose there was a pit in the floor of the cave?—a well, even? Or some deep fissure that went far down into the rock, into which she could have fallen? Or were there other caves heading out of this one in a chain of caverns and passages going back and back into the hillside, branching and twisting so that anyone groping through them would soon become hopelessly lost . . . ? And supposing there were snakes . . .

Panic gripped him and he ran forward into the darkness, his hands outstretched, calling, 'Juli,—Juli. Where are you? Are you all right? Answer me, Juli!' And the echoes reverberated round him, mocking him; now fading, now rising above the deafening croon of the wind: *Juli . . . Juli . . . Juli . . .*

Once he thought he heard her answer; but he could not be sure where the sound had come from and he would, at that moment, have sold his soul for a light or a few seconds of silence. Straining to listen, he could hear nothing but the bagpipe drone of the wind and the maddening echoes of his own voice, and he stumbled on blindly, groping in the inky blackness and meeting only rock and rough earth, or emptiness.

He must have turned a corner into a side cave without knowing it, because all at once the volume of noise diminished as sharply as if a door had closed behind him, and the air was almost free from dust. He heard no new sound and the blackness was still as impenetrable; but suddenly he knew that it was from here that Juli had answered him, and that she was still here, for there was a faint fragrance of rose-petals in the stale, cool air. He turned towards it, and caught her in his arms.

Her arms and shoulders, her breasts and her slender waist were smooth and warm and naked against his own bare flesh, for having thrown the *achkan* over her head as a protection against the choking dust, she had pulled it away in order to call to him, and lost it somewhere in the darkness. The cheek that was pressed to his was wet with tears and she was breathing in hard gasps as though she had been running, for she had heard him shouting and had turned back to go to him, afraid that it had been a cry for help, because there had been so much urgency in the sound. But confused by the echoes she had lost her bearings and blundered round in the dark, bruising herself against unexpected outcrops of rock and sobbing and calling as she searched for him in the clamorous darkness.

They clung together for a long minute, not moving or speaking, and then Ash turned his head and kissed her.

24

If the dust-storm had not blown up so quickly . . . If they had noticed its approach earlier . . . If the cave had been smaller and they had been able to see; or hear . . .

Much later, Ash was to think of that and to wonder if it would have made any difference? Perhaps. Though not if old Uncle Akbar, after whom he had been named, had been right.

Uncle Akbar and Koda Dad had both assured him that all men are born into the world with their fate tied about their necks, and cannot escape it.

'*What is written, is written.*' How many times had he heard Koda Dad say that? And Akbar Khan had said it before him—once when Ash stood looking down at the dead body of a tiger, shot five minutes earlier from the machan where they had waited for hours; and again, on an equally memorable occasion, in the courtyard of Shah Jehan's great mosque in Delhi, where the crowd had been so great that two men had fallen from the gateway and been killed, and Ash had demanded explanations. But in the present instance, the question of predestination versus free-will was of purely academic interest; the fact remained that he had failed to notice the storm, and because the cave in which they had taken refuge had been very large and dark and full of noises, he had been seized by panic at the thought of Juli lost in it—breaking her neck by falling into some hideous underground cavern, or treading on a cobra in the dark.

Had he kept his head he would almost certainly have succeeded in keeping his good resolutions as well. In which case the two of them would have sat out the storm without touching each other, and set off for the camp the moment they heard the wind drop. Yet if they had done so they would have missed Kaka-ji and the *ruth,* and returned, innocent, to find themselves the centre of a major scandal and facing serious charges.

In the event, they had no idea of how long the storm lasted or when the wind dropped. It could have been an hour, or two hours, or ten. They had lost all count of time, and even the silence and the fact that they could hear each other's smallest whisper did not remind them of its passing.

'I never meant this to happen,' murmured Ash; which was true enough. But if there had been any hope at all of his making a last effort to avoid it, it was lost when Juli, found at last, had flung her arms about his neck and clung to him. And then he had kissed her— There was nothing of tenderness in that kiss. It was hard and violent, but though it bruised her lips and took the breath from her body, she did not draw back from it but clung closer, and the moment was almost one of desperation, as though they strove against each other as enemies, intent on inflicting pain and careless of receiving it.

The brief frenzy ended, and Juli's taut body relaxed as the panic ebbed away from her, leaving her soft and supple in his arms. Desperation died and gave place to a slow delight that burned its way through every vein and nerve and fibre. Her tears were salt on Ash's tongue, and he could feel the ripple of her hair all about him: long, silky strands that smelt of roses and slid over his skin like a cloak of feathers, or caught and clung to him as though they had a life of their own. Her lips were no longer tense with terror, but warm and eager and sweet beyond relief, and he kissed them again and again until at last they opened under his own, and he felt her whole body shiver with desire.

He would have lifted her then and laid her down on the floor of the cave, but even as his arm tightened, he checked himself and broke off that kiss to ask what seemed, in the circumstances, a superfluous question. Yet he too had been panic-stricken in the inky darkness, and knowing that Juli had been equally frantic, he had to be sure that her passionate response to his kisses was not merely an emotional reaction from terror. Therefore he spoke harshly, forcing himself to say the words, because he was suddenly afraid of how she might reply. 'Juli, do you love me?'

The cave, and caves beyond the cave, repeated it after him, again and again: *do you love me? . . . you love me . . . love me . . .* And Anjuli laughed very softly—but so lovingly that his heart seemed to turn over—and answered against his ear, too low for the echo to catch her voice: 'How can you ask me that when you know I have loved you all my life? Yes, always! From the very beginning.'

Ash's hands went up to grip her smooth shoulders, and he shook her roughly and said: 'As a brother. But that is no use to me. I want a lover—a wife. I want all of you—for my own, for always. Do you love me like that? Do you, Juli?'

She leaned her cheek against his left hand, rubbing it caressingly as it held her shoulder, and said slowly, as though she were reciting a poem or repeating a profession of faith: 'I love you. I have always loved you. I have always been yours and I always will be; and if I loved you first as a brother, it was not a brother that I waited for as I grew up and became a woman, but a lover. And—and—' She leaned forward to lay her cheek against his own and he felt the taut nipples touch his chest like light finger-tips: '—this you do not know: but when you returned again I loved you before ever I knew who you were, for when you lifted me out of the *ruth* that night in the river, and held me in your arms while we waited for my women, I could not breathe for the beating of my heart. And I was ashamed, because I thought you were a stranger. Yet something in my blood rejoiced to be held so, and would have had you hold me closer and closer. Like this—' She tightened her arms about his neck and kissed the hollow below his cheek bone, and said in a shaken whisper: 'Oh, my love! Love me—love me now, before it is too late for me.'

The whisper ended in a gasp as Ash's hands slid down from her shoulders to catch her again into a close embrace and pull her down with him onto the floor of the cave.

The dry, silver sand was cool and smooth and very soft, and Juli's black hair spread a silky coverlet over it as she lay in the darkness and felt Ash's hands strip away the only garment she still wore, and move up again slowly and caressingly: warm and firm and very sure. For a moment only she knew a pang of fear, but it passed as quickly as it had come, and when he said: 'I'm going to hurt you,' she tightened her arms about him, and did not cry out at the lovely cruelty that ended her girlhood.

'I never meant this to happen,' Ash had murmured. But that had been hours later—they did not know how many—and after it had happened again. And again . . .

'I did,' whispered Juli, lying quiet and relaxed in the curve of his arm, with her head pillowed on his shoulder.

'When, Larla?'

Juli did not answer immediately, but Ash was already thinking of something else, and the question had been an idle one for his mind had turned to plans. He was trying to visualize the large-scale Ordnance Maps that he had studied almost daily as the camp moved down across India, and decide which route would be the safest to

take. Because the sooner they quit Rajputana and the south, the better. They had their horses, but no money . . . They would need
money, yet they could not go back to the camp. He felt Juli move
her head, and the cool touch of the jewel in her ear reminded him
that the stones she wore that day were pigeon's-blood rubies, set in
gold, and not only in her ears, but as buttons on her *achkan*. If they
were careful they should be able to get a good price for them, and
they could dispose of them one by one as the need arose.

'A long time ago,' said Juli softly, answering his question at last. 'A
month or more; though I did not plan it this way. How could I know
that the gods would be so good to me as to send a storm in which we
two would be caught, and find refuge here, together? You will think
me shameless, but I planned to come if I could to your tent, and if
you would not take me willingly, to beg of you . . . because I was
desperate, and I thought that if only—'

'What are you talking about?' asked Ash, recalled abruptly from
his own plans.

'The Rana,' whispered Juli, and shivered. 'I—I could not endure to
think that I must lose my maidenhead to another man, one whom I
neither knew nor loved and who did not love me, yet who would use
me, by right—for lust or to beget heirs from my body. An old man
and a stranger . . .'

She shuddered convulsively and Ash tightened his arm about her,
holding her hard against him, and said: 'Don't, Larla. You don't
have to think of it any more. Ever.'

'But I must,' insisted Juli, her voice shaking. 'No—let me speak. I
want you to understand. You see, I knew from the beginning that I
must submit to him, and also that—that even if he did not find me
desirable he would use me, because I was a woman and his wife, and
he desires sons. That much I could not escape. But that he should be
the first—and the last . . . That I must be taken without love and
submit with loathing, and never, never know what it was to lie with a
lover and rejoice in being a woman—It was this that I could not endure, and therefore, Heart's-heart, I planned that I would ask you,
would beg of you if need be, to save me from it. Now you have done
so, and I am content. No one can ever take these hours away from
me, or spoil or defile them. And—who knows?—the gods may even
add to their kindness and permit me to conceive from this night. I
will pray to them that it may be so, and that my first-born will be

yours. But even if that is not granted me, at least I have known love
. . . and having known it I can endure the lust and the shame, and
not mind it too much.'

'You won't have to mind it at all!' said Ash violently. He pressed
his fingers through her hair and pulled her head back so that he
could kiss her: her eyes, her forehead, her temples, her cheeks and
chin and mouth. He kissed them in turn and spoke between the
kisses: 'My love . . . my foolish love. Do you really think I would
let you go now? I might have done so before, but not now. In spite
of everything, I couldn't now . . .'

He told her then how he had planned to ask her to run away with
him and been forced to decide that he must not do so, because the
danger was too great—for both of them, though for her most of all—
but that the dust-storm had changed all that. It was the miracle that
he had needed so badly and despaired of, since it gave them a way of
escaping unsuspected—and without any fear of pursuit. They had
horses with them, and if they set off as soon as the wind died down
they should be able to cover a good many miles that night, and by
sunrise be far beyond the reach of any search, for the confusion and
havoc that the storm must have wrought in the camp would make it
impossible to send out search parties to look for them before daylight. When they were not discovered it would be assumed that they
had lost their lives in the storm, and were lying dead and buried in
some sand drift among the hills; and the search for their bodies
would soon be abandoned because the country for miles around
would be changed by dust and blown sand, and too many gullies and
hollows would be newly silted up with it.

'They'll give up after a day or two, and go on to Bhithor,' said
Ash. 'They'll have to, because of the heat if nothing else. And we
don't even have to worry about money, for we can sell my watch and
your rubies—those earrings and the buttons on your coat. We can
live on those for months. Probably for years. Somewhere where no
one knows us: in Oudh, or among the foothills in the north, or in
Kulu Valley. And I can find work, and then when they have forgotten all about us—'

Anjuli shook her head. 'They would not. Me they might forget, for
I am of little worth to anyone. But with you it is different. You might
hide for a year, or for ten years; but when you showed your face
again, either here in Hind, or in *Belait,* and tried to claim your inheritance, you would still be an officer in the army of the Raj who had

run away without leave; and for that they would catch you and pun-ish you. And then all would become known.'

'Yes,' said Ash slowly. 'Yes; that's true.' There was a note of surprise in his voice as though he had made a new and disconcerting discovery. In the intoxication of the past hours he had genuinely for-gotten about the Guides. 'I could never go back. But—but we shall be together, and—'

He stopped, for Anjuli had laid a hand over his mouth.

'No, Ashok.' Her voice was a pleading whisper. 'Do not say any more. Please, please do not, because I cannot go with you . . . I cannot. I could not leave Shushila . . . I promised her that I would stay with her. I gave her my word, and I cannot go back on that . . .'

For a while Ash had not believed her. But when he tried to speak, her fingers pressed tighter against his mouth and her voice hurried on in the darkness, explaining, pleading. Each word a hammer blow. Shu-shu loved her and depended upon her, and had only agreed to marry the Rana on condition that she, Anjuli, stayed with her. She could not possibly abandon her little sister now and leave her to face the terrors of a new life alone. Ashok did not understand how fright-ened and homesick and unhappy Shu-shu was. How terrified of the prospect of marriage to a middle-aged stranger and of living among people whose ways would be different from hers, in surroundings that were so unlike those she had hitherto known and loved. Shu-shu was only a child still. A frightened and bewildered child—

'How could I ever be happy, knowing that I had deserted her?' whispered Anjuli. 'She is my little sister, whom I love; and who loves and trusts me—and needs me, too . . . she has always needed me, ever since she was a baby. Shu-shu gave me love in the years when I had nothing else, and if I failed her now, when her need is greatest, I would feel guilty all my days and never be able to forgive myself; or to forget that I had run away and left her . . . broken my word and —and betrayed her—'

Ash caught her wrist and wrenched her hand away: 'But *I* love you too. And *I* need you. Does that mean nothing to you? Do you care so much more for her than you do for me? Do you?'

'You know that I do not,' said Anjuli on a sob. 'I love you more than life. Beyond anyone and anything else. Beyond words—beyond shame! Have I not proved that to you tonight? But—but you are strong, Ashok. You will go on living and learn to put all this behind you and make yourself a good life without me; and one day—'

'Never. Never. *Never,*' broke in Ash vehemently.

'Yes, you will. And I too. Because—because we are both strong enough to do it. But Shu-shu is not; and if I am not there to give her courage when she is afraid, and to comfort her when she is ill or sad or wild with homesickness, she will die.'

'*Be-wakufi!*' said Ash roughly. 'She's probably a lot stronger than you suppose, and though she may be a child in some ways, she's her mother's daughter in a good many others. Oh, Juli, my darling, my Heart's-love—I know she's your sister and you're fond of her, but underneath all that shyness and charm she's a spoilt, selfish and demanding brat who likes her own way; and you've allowed her to have it, and to tyrannize over you for far too long. It's high time you let her stand on her own feet and realized that she isn't your baby sister any more, but a grown girl who will be a wife within a month and a mother inside a year. She isn't going to let herself die. Don't you believe it.'

Anjuli was silent for a moment or two, and then she said in a curiously flat and unemotional voice: 'If Shu-shu were told that I had perished in the storm, and that she must go on alone to Bhithor, she would go mad with grief and fear, and there would be no one who could control her. Nandu is not here, and only he was able to do so before. I tell you I know her; and you do not. And though I love her, I am not blind to her faults—or to my own. I know that she is spoilt and selfish and self-willed; and Janoo-Rani's daughter. But I also know her to be gentle and loving and very trusting, and I will not bring her to her death. If I did, how could you love me?—knowing that I too was selfish and self-willed, as well as faithless? And cruel, too! For I should be all those things if I were willing to jeopardize my little sister's life and reason for the sake of my own happiness.'

'And *my* happiness?' demanded Ash, his voice harsh with pain. 'Does mine not matter?'

But it had been no good. Nothing that he could say had made any difference. He had used every argument and every plea he could think of, and at last he had taken her again, ravaging her with an animal violence that had bruised and hurt, yet was still sexually skilful enough to force a response from her that was half pain and half piercing rapture. But when it was over and they lay spent and breathless, she could still say: 'I cannot betray her.' And he knew that Shushila had won, and that he was beaten. His arms fell away and he drew aside and lay on his back staring up into the darkness, and for a long time neither of them spoke.

The silence was so complete that he could hear the sound of his own breathing, and from somewhere in the outer cave the faint jingle of metal as one of the tethered horses moved restlessly. But it was not for an appreciable time that the significance of this dawned on him, and he realized that the wind had died, and that it must have done so some time ago, because he could not remember when he had last been aware of that vibrating drone. Not for at least an hour; and it was probably longer than that. In which case the sooner they made a start the better, for if they were going to return to the camp it would be wiser to do so under cover of darkness, and trust that in the general confusion their arrival would not be too public.

It was going to be bad enough, from Juli's point of view, to have been missing for several hours in the company of a single man. But the dust-storm would excuse that; and provided they returned as quickly as possible, scandal might be avoided by the mere fact that conditions had hardly been conducive to dalliance, and the camp it-self likely to be in such a state of disarray that few people would have any time to waste on idle gossip and speculation. With luck, Juli would escape with no more than a scolding for riding too far ahead of her sister and uncle, and no one would ever suspect . . . A thought struck Ash with jarring suddenness, and he said sharply: 'You can't go through with it, Juli. It's too dangerous. He's bound to know.'

'Who will know?' Anjuli's voice was muffled, as though she had been crying. 'Know what?'

'The Rana. He'll find out that you're not a virgin just as soon as he beds with you, and then there'll be the devil to pay. He isn't likely to forgive a thing like that, or take another man's leavings. He'll want to know who and when, and if you won't tell him he'll beat it out of you and send you back to your half-brother with your nose cut off, and without returning your dowry. And when your precious brother gets his hands on you, he'll either see to it that you die as painfully as possible, or he'll cut your feet off and let you live a crip-ple as a warning to other women. And what use are you going to be then to Shushila? You can't do it, Juli. You've burnt your boats now, and you can't go back.'

'I must and I can,' said Anjuli huskily. 'He will not know, because . . .' Her voice wavered and died, but she controlled herself with an effort: 'Because there are . . . ways.'

'What ways? You don't know what you are talking about. You couldn't possibly know—'

'Harlot's tricks? But I do'—he heard her swallow painfully. 'You forget that I was brought up by servants in the Women's Quarters of a palace, and that a Rajah keeps many women besides his wives: concubines who know every art and trick that can please a man or fool him, and who talk freely of these things because they have little else to talk of, and because they think it only right that all women should be instructed in them . . .' The young voice paused for a moment, and then went on again, very steadily: 'I do not like to tell you this, but had I not known that when the time came I could deceive the Rana, I would not have taken you for my lover.'

The words fell like drops of ice water into the darkness, and as the little echoes reverberated softly round the cave they sent a thin cold trickle through Ash's heart, and he said harshly and with deliberate cruelty: 'And I suppose you have thought too of what may happen to the child—my child—if you have one? Its legal father will be the Rana, and what if he chooses to bring it up to be another Nandu, or Lalji? Or appoints scorpions like Biju Ram to its service—perverts and panders who love to do evil? Have you thought of that?'

Anjuli said quietly: 'It was the *Nautch*-girl and not my father who appointed Biju Ram to Lalji's household. And—and I believe that it is a child's mother who can, if she chooses, shape its early years and set its feet on a given path, for it is to her that it will look when it is small, and not to its father. If the gods grant me your child I will not fail him: that I swear to you. I will see to it that he shall grow up to be a prince that we can be proud of.'

'Of what use will that be to me, when I shall never see or know him? When I may never even hear that he exists?' demanded Ash bitterly.

For a moment he thought that she was not going to answer him, and when she did it was in a whisper. 'I am sorry,' said Anjuli. 'I . . . I did not think—It was for myself, for my own comfort that . . . that I wished it. I have been selfish. . . .' Her breath caught on a sob, and then her voice steadied again: 'But it is done now: and what may come of it is out of our hands.'

'It is not! It is still in our hands. You can come away with me—for the child's sake, if not for mine. Promise me that if there should be a child you will come to me. Surely you can do that? I won't believe that Shu-shu means more to you than any child of mine could do, or that you would sacrifice its future for her sake. Promise me, Larla!'

Only the echoes answered him, for Anjuli did not speak. Yet her silence spoke for her, repeating, wordlessly, what she had told him before; that she had already given a promise to Shu-shu. And that a promise was sacred . . .

A tightness built up in Ash's throat but once again anger drove him to speech, and he forced words past the constriction and threw them viciously at that obdurate silence: 'Can't you understand what it will be like for me to have to live—as I may do—with the knowledge that my child, *my child,* is the property of another man to do what he likes with? To sell in marriage one day to whoever he chooses—as you and your sisters were?'

'You . . . will have other children—' whispered Anjuli.

'Never!'

'—and I shall not know,' continued Anjuli as though he had not spoken. 'It may even be that you have some already, for I know that men are careless of their seed. They think nothing of lying with harlots and light women, and do not trouble their minds as to what may come of such matings. Can you tell me that you yourself have never, until this night, lain with any other woman . . . ?' She paused briefly, and when he did not reply said sadly: 'No. I did not think I was the first. For all I know there may have been more than one; perhaps many. And if that is so, how can you be sure that there is not, somewhere, some child who could call you father? It is the custom for men to buy their pleasure, and when they have taken it and paid, to walk away and think no more of it. And though you say now that you will never marry—and you may not—I do not believe that it is in your nature to become an ascetic. Sooner or later, in the years to come, you will lie with other women and—it may be—father other children without knowing it, or caring. But I, if I should conceive one, will know . . . and care. I shall carry it in my body for many months and suffer all the discomforts that come from that, and at the end risk death and endure much pain to give it life. If I pay that price, surely you could not begrudge it me? . . . You could not.'

You could not, sobbed the echo. And he could not. For Juli was right. Men were careless with their seed, yet they reserved the right to pick and choose among the fruit of their matings: to ignore, repudiate or claim paternity as it suited them. It had never occurred to Ash before that he might have fathered a child, and now that it did he was horrified to realize that it was not only possible, but that he had not cared enough to take any precautions against it, presumably because he had always thought (if he had thought about it at all) that precautions were something for women to worry about and to deal with.

Yes, he supposed it was quite possible that there could be a child of his alive at this moment, living in 'Pindi Bazaar or some smoke-filled hut among the Border hills, or in the poorer quarters of London. And if that were so, and Juli were to bear one—braving the 'pains and perils of child-birth' to do so—then what possible right had he to lay claim to it? Or even to insist that he would make a better father than the unknown Rana?

He tried to speak and found that he could not, because his mouth was drawn as though he had swallowed acid; and because there was nothing left to be said. The echoes had faded and the silence shut down again, and presently he became aware of movements in the darkness and knew that Juli was drawing on the tight-fitting riding trousers that he had stripped off—how long ago? It seemed, suddenly, a life-time away, and he felt cold and defeated and drained of all emotion. The air in the cave struck so cold that he shivered, and the sharp, absurd sound of his own teeth chattering reminded him that unless they found Juli's *achkan* and the remnants of his shirt, there would be no hope of avoiding an appalling scandal, because they would both be forced to ride back to camp half-naked. He retrieved his riding breeches and boots and stood up tiredly to put them on, and having buckled the belt about his waist and made sure that he had dropped nothing from his pockets, spoke curtly into the darkness:

'What did you do with your coat?'

'I don't know'—her weariness was as vivid to him as though it had been his own. 'I had it over my head, and I must have dropped it when I heard you call.'

'Well, you can't go back without it, that's certain,' said Ash roughly. 'We'll just have to walk round in circles until we find it. Give me your hand. There's no point in losing each other in the dark.'

Her hand was cold and oddly impersonal. It did not clasp his, but remained entirely passive, and he held it as he would have held a stranger's: lightly and almost at arm's length, and solely as a means of keeping in touch in the inky darkness as they moved forward slowly, guiding themselves by the rock wall.

It took them nearly an hour to find the *achkan*. The shirt had been easier, as Ash had dropped it near the horses in the main cave, and now that the storm had passed, the entrance showed up as a grey, sharp-edged oblong that provided them with a landmark in the waste of blackness.

The depths of the cave had been cold, but the air outside was hot and still and heavy with the smell of dust, and the few stars that could be seen shone hazily, as though through a veil. The moon was either hidden by the hills or by dust clouds, and the valley was in shadow; but after the unrelieved darkness of the caves, both earth and sky seemed astonishingly light, and it was some time before Ash realized that this was not solely due to the fact that the storm had spread a pale-coloured shroud of dust and river sand over many miles of country, but because the dawn was near.

The discovery jolted him badly. He had never imagined for a moment that it could be as late as this, or that so many hours could have passed without his knowing it. He would have put it at two or three: four at most. Instead, it was almost a whole night, and his plan of smuggling Juli back into the camp under cover of darkness and confusion was useless, for by the time they reached it the sky would be light. No wonder there was no sign of the moon; it must have set hours ago. The stars were already fading and despite the dust there was a smell of morning in the air, that faint, indefinable smell that tells of a coming day as clearly as the growing light and the sound of a cock crowing.

'Hurry,' said Ash peremptorily, and urged Baj Raj into a gallop. But less than a minute later Juli's mare stumbled and slowed to an uneven trot, and he was forced to stop and turn back.

'I think it is only a pebble,' said Anjuli, dismounting to investigate. But it proved to be a piece of flint as sharp-edged as glass, and so deeply imbedded that lacking a knife and hampered by bad light, it had taken Ash the best part of ten minutes to remove it; and when he had done so the mare still limped, for the cut was a deep one.

'You'd better take Baj Raj and get back as fast as you can, and I'll come on later,' decided Ash. 'In fact it's probably a good idea in the circumstances for you to arrive back alone. You can pretend we got separated in the storm, and you spent the night alone in a cave and started back as soon as it began to get light. It will sound better that way. You can tell them you don't know where I am.'

'When I am riding your horse? And you mine? They would never believe it!' said Anjuli scornfully: 'Any more than they would believe that you would have permitted me to get lost.'

Ash grunted and said: 'No, I suppose not. It would take a lot of explaining and at the moment I can't think of a good enough story. Anyway, I suppose the fewer lies we tell the better.'

'We do not need to tell any,' said Anjuli curtly. 'We will tell the truth.'

'All of it?' inquired Ash dryly.

Anjuli did not answer, but remounted her horse in silence and they moved on again, this time at a walk. But although there was still very little light, and no sound but the creak of saddle-leather and the soft clop of hooves on thick dust, Ash knew that she was crying. Crying very quietly with her eyes wide open, as she used to do in the old days when she had been Kairi-Bai, and in trouble.

Poor little Kairi-Bai. Poor Juli . . . He had failed them both: forgetting the one, and now blaming the other because she had wanted to snatch a brief moment of glory out of the drabness and servitude that was her life, and had laid plans to keep it secret; not for her sake, but for Shushila's—because if she were to be cast off by the Rana and sent back in disgrace to Nandu, what would happen to her frail, hysterical, selfish little sister? It was unjust to blame Juli. But the descent from the heights of love and rapture and extravagant hope had been too violent, and that ugly picture of serving-women and concubines instructing their juniors in sexual tricks had so sickened him that for a dreadful instant he had wondered if the physical ecstasy he had experienced had been artfully heightened by what she herself had termed 'harlot's tricks', and if her own response had been real, or only simulated in order to add a sharper edge to his pleasure.

That suspicion had vanished as quickly as it had come. The intangible bond that linked them, and that made him aware at this moment that she was crying, could not have deceived him as they lay embraced, but something of the chill and the distaste still stayed with him. Enough, at least, to prevent him from further speech; though he had the grace to feel ashamed of himself for hurting her, and for keeping silent instead of apologizing and reaching out a hand to comfort her.

This was a sorry ending to an episode that she had risked a great deal for, and had hoped to treasure as a golden memory that would sustain her in the loveless years that lay ahead. He knew that if he let her go like this, without further words or even a touch of the hand, he would regret it until the end of his life. But at the moment he could not bring himself to do either, for his own disappointment was too bitter to be borne, and weariness and a crushing sense of failure pressed so heavily on him that he felt curiously numb and apathetic— as though he were a punch-drunk boxer, beaten to his knees on the canvas and vaguely aware of the necessity of getting to his feet before he was counted out, but unable to make any effort to do so. He would talk to Juli presently. Tell her he was sorry, and that he loved her and would always love her; even though she herself did not love him enough to desert Shushila for his sake . . . It was strange to think that although Janoo-Rani was dead she could still strike at both of them through her daughter, who was going to wreck their chance of happiness and ruin their lives . . .

The last star faded in a wash of pale light that crept slowly upward from the horizon and drained the darkness from the plain, turning it from black to a pearly grey in which the scattered boulders and occasional bushes cast no shadow. They were clear of the hills now, and ahead of them, in the far distance, a tall outcrop of rock thrust up out of the wide amphitheatre of plain, cutting a dark silhouette against the prevailing greyness. It was the spot where they had left the *ruth* and its escort on the previous evening, and Ash recognized it with relief, for he had paid little attention to the countryside yesterday and was not entirely sure where they were. But that jagged pile was the one unmistakable landmark in a colourless, treeless land where the outlines of the encircling hills presented few distinctive features, and once they reached it, they should be able to find their way back to the camp easily enough. But the sky was already beginning to turn yellow in the east and it would not be long now, thought Ash grimly, before the day broke and displayed them both in the merciless sunlight, dirty and dishevelled and still a long way from the camp.

He turned to look at Anjuli, and saw that she was drooping with fatigue and paying no attention to where she was going, but sitting slack in the saddle and allowing the limping horse to choose its own path between the stones and the low scrub. Even in that dim light her coat showed sadly crumpled and her attempt to confine the tangled mass of her hair into a single heavy plait, using her fingers for a comb, had not been particularly successful. Her head was turned away from him in order to hide the fact that she was crying, but even if he had not already known it intuitively the growing light would have betrayed her, for it glinted wetly on the outline of her averted face.

Perhaps a similar perceptiveness had made her aware of his gaze, because as he watched her she straightened her shoulders, and lifting a hand as though to push back her hair, brushed away the tell-tale wetness in a gesture that appeared so unstudied that anyone else would have been deceived.

It did not deceive Ash, and he felt his heart contract with love. There had been so much gallantry in that small, seemingly casual action, and in the determined straightening of her back. She had not asked for pity, and she would hide her grief and face the future with courage, and without complaining.

There was good Rajput blood in Juli, and the fire and rashness inherent in it had been cooled and balanced by a strong Cossack strain that was a legacy from her grandfather, old Sergei Vodvichenko—that hard-headed, aristocratic Soldier-of-Fortune who had sold his sword to the highest bidder and won battles for Ranjit Singh and Holkar and Scindia of Gwalior, and bequeathed his gold-flecked eyes and his high cheek bones to his granddaughter Anjuli, Princess of Karidkote.

Rajput and Cossack . . . it was a strange amalgam, and an unlikely one. But it had produced Juli, who was loving, faithful and passionate, and who possessed, in addition to courage, that particular brand of quiet fortitude that is rarer and far better than courage—together with the strength to keep a promise, once given, even if it meant the sacrifice of her own happiness.

Ash had once made her a promise and forgotten it. Though there was some excuse for that; he had, after all, been barely eleven at the time. Yet he was uncomfortably certain that had their positions been reversed and she had made him a similar promise, she would neither have forgotten it nor broken it. Juli, like Wally, took a disconcertingly literal view of such things; and it occurred to Ash that in some ways they were remarkably alike.

His mouth twisted in a wry grimace of self-contempt, and he reached out a hand to her. But he had left it too late, for even as he did so she reined in and pointed at something that moved in the half-light, separating itself from the shadowy bulk of the rocky outcrop ahead of them. An object that lurched away across the plain looking like a prehistoric animal with a double hump. It was the *ruth*.

'Look!' cried Anjuli. 'It is Shu-shu. So they did not get back either.'

But it was not Shu-shu. It was only Kaka-ji and the driver of the *ruth*.

Ash stood up in the stirrups and shouted out to them, and then spurred forward, leaving Anjuli to follow slowly in his wake coughing in the white clouds of dust that had been churned up by Baj Raj's galloping hooves. By the time she came up with them, Kaka-ji had told his own story and heard something of theirs, and there had been no need for Ash to make any suggestions, for one look at Anjuli had been enough for the old man.

'*Arré-bap!*' exclaimed Kaka-ji, startled. 'Get inside the *ruth* at once, my child.' He hurried to help her dismount, and then turning to peer at Ash, took in for the first time the enormity of that tattered shirt.

'It will be better,' decided Kaka-ji, looking from one dishevelled figure to the other, 'if we let it be supposed that we have all been together this past night. No'—he raised a peremptory hand to forestall any argument, and having bundled his niece into the *ruth*, turned to address the driver: 'Budoo, should anyone inquire, you will say that the Sahib returned with the Rajkumari only a moment or two after the dust overtook us, and that she took refuge in the *ruth* while we three men together lay beneath it. That is an order. And if I hear that there has been any talk to the contrary, I shall know who has spoken—and whom to punish. Is it understood?'

'*Hukum hai*, Rao-Sahib,' murmured the driver placidly, lifting a curved palm to his forehead in salute. He was an elderly man who had been promoted to his present employment after the original driver had drowned in the river, and having been in the service of the family for many years, he could be trusted to obey an order and keep his mouth shut.

'And you, Sahib,' said Kaka-ji authoritatively, turning back to Ash, 'you will take off those rags and wear my shirt in their stead. There are shawls in the *ruth* that will serve to cover me, but it is not fit that you should ride into the camp half-naked. The less talk we occasion the better, so do not argue with me.'

Ash had no intention of arguing, and the transfer having been accomplished, Kaka-ji joined his niece in the *ruth* and ordered the driver to proceed. The bullocks ceased chewing the cud and trotted obediently forward, while Ash took the mare on a leading-rein and followed behind, keeping well to one side and out of the dust; and as he listened to the rise and fall of Kaka-ji's voice re-telling the events of the past night to Juli, he realized that they were doubly fortunate, in that the old man was far more interested in his own experiences than in theirs.

Kaka-ji had accepted a brief and colourless account of their adventures without question, and embarked with enthusiasm on a description of his own trials, which had lost nothing in the telling. It seemed that neither he nor Mulraj, nor Shushila either, had noticed the approaching storm for some time; and when they did, it was only because Mulraj, like Ash, had happened to glance over his shoulder and seen that the sky behind them had become a dingy brown. The escort and the driver of the *ruth* were equally ignorant, for they were squatting in a shallow cleft among the rocks smoking and gossiping, facing an unclouded sky and well shielded from the wind and all view of the eastern horizon. At that time the storm was still some way off, but anyone could see that it was racing towards them with such alarming swiftness that if they hoped to get back to the camp before it struck, there was no time to be lost—and certainly no time to go chasing after the other two members of the riding party.

Kaka-ji had not actually said so in so many words, but it was perfectly clear to Ash that when the chips were down there was only one bride whose safety and well-being were vital to both Karidkote and Bhithor: young, lovely Shu-shu, whose beauty would compensate the Rana (together with that substantial bribe) for having to wed her plain, part-foreign half-sister as well. Neither Nandu nor the Rana was likely to lose much sleep over the loss of Kairi-Bai, but the loss of Shushila would spell disaster for them all, because even if Kairi-Bai survived, the Rana would never accept her in her sister's stead.

There would be no marriage, and the enormous sums that Nandu had spent on gifts and bribes and baksheesh, on clothes and jewels for his sisters' trousseaux and on the absurdly extravagant escort that he had sent to accompany them south would all have been wasted, and he would be mad with rage. Many heads would fall and both Mulraj and Kaka-ji knew it—and knew also that theirs would be among the first. With that ominous brown stain reaching up into the sky and spreading outward to span the horizon, there had been no time to waste in worrying over the whereabouts of Kairi-Bai and Pelham-Sahib, who would have to look after themselves. The important thing was to get Shushila back to the camp before the storm overtook them, for though she might just as easily come to harm in her own tent as out here among the rocks, at least if she did they would not be called upon to explain what she was doing there.

Mulraj had eyed the dust-cloud and made a swift calculation, and sacrificing convention and the proprieties, had taken Shushila up behind him and set off at full gallop, leaving Kaka-ji to follow with her riderless horse. The escort, still in ignorance of the approaching storm and seeing Mulraj racing towards them with the Rajkumari clinging to his waist like a monkey, had leapt up, expecting him to stop, and when he flashed past them, heading for the camp, they had barely waited for Kaka-ji's explanations before riding in pursuit, taking the waiting-woman with them.

Kaka-ji had not accompanied them. He had made them take Shushila's horse and his own, and had elected to stay behind with the *ruth,* whose driver, realizing that it could not possibly reach the camp ahead of the storm, was making hurried preparations to shelter his bullocks in a cleft among the rocks. 'We will wait here for my niece and the Sahib, who will shortly return and be dismayed if they find us all gone,' said Kaka-ji, peering anxiously in the direction of the hills. 'It is not fitting that the Rajkumari should be seen to return alone on horseback, accompanied only by the Sahib, and they cannot be long.'

But the minutes had passed and there was still no sign of the missing riders. Old Budoo, the driver, had backed the *ruth* as far as it would go between the rocks, and unyoking his bullocks had edged them past and tethered them in the cramped space behind it, after which he pulled out the rugs, shawls and bolsters that had cushioned the Rajkumaries and their women against jolting, and fastened them to form a rough-and-ready screen against the dust and sand that was roaring down on them. The smell of it was already in the air and now they could hear it; but still Kaka-ji waited, hoping to see horses galloping towards him. It was only when the bow-wave of dust struck the far side of the hillock of rock where they refuged that he allowed Budoo to drag him into the *ruth;* and there, deafened and half stifled, the two old men had crouched together while the storm raged outside.

Kaka-ji's account of his own sufferings was vivid in the extreme, and he had enjoyed telling it. But he too was uncertain how long the storm had lasted, and when it had passed and all was quiet again, he and Budoo had both fallen asleep and had not woken until the sky was beginning to pale. They had intended, he said, to set out in search of his niece and the Sahib, for whose safety he entertained the gravest fears, imagining that they would have been caught out in the open with no form of shelter; but they had barely started when they had heard the Sahib shouting aloud.

He had seen no reason to doubt Ash's story and he had not thought to question his niece, for having experienced all the discomforts of the storm himself, he was convinced that nothing of an improper nature could possibly have occurred between them. Not even the lustiest of men and the most ardent of young women would be likely to think of such things—let alone put them into practice—while fighting for breath with a cloth over the head, and eyes, mouth and nostrils full of grit. In Kaka-ji's opinion, a dust-storm was a more efficient guarantee of proper behaviour than a dozen duennas, though this did not prevent him from impressing on Anjuli that she must on no account let anyone suspect that she had not spent the night in the *ruth*. Not even Shu-shu.

'For you are shortly to be wedded,' said Kaka-ji, 'and it is most unseemly for a bride to go apart with any man, even if he be a Sahib. There are too many loose-tongued people who delight in slander, and if evil things were to be whispered about you, both the Rana and your brother would be gravely displeased. Therefore you will say only that you reached the *ruth* just as the storm struck, and stayed in it all night. And I and the Sahib and old Budoo will say the same.'

Anjuli could only nod wordlessly. She was too tired to speak—too tired to feel grateful for the way in which fate had played into her hands by letting her get caught in the storm with Ashok and then sending her uncle to save them both from scandal. Too tired even to think . . .

It was much lighter now, and presently, as the sun rose and a bright golden ray pierced between the embroidered curtains and lit up the dusty interior of the *ruth*, she fell asleep, and was still sleeping when they arrived at the camp.

Roused by Kaka-ji with the reassuring news that Shushila was safe, she stumbled out into the arms of Geeta and was instantly hurried off to bed.

25

The arrival of the *ruth* had created a small stir, but no more than that. For Ash had guessed right: the camp had been too badly hit for anyone to waste much thought on a single unusual incident when more than a hundred startling ones clamoured for attention.

Even the sudden and melodramatic return on the previous evening of Mulraj and the youngest bride had passed virtually unnoticed, for by then the whole camp was in a ferment and taking frantic measures to withstand the storm. Tent-pegs were being hammered home and guy-ropes tightened, and everything that was liable to be blown away was being battened down or otherwise secured. Syces, bullock-drivers and herdsmen were seeing to the safety of their animals, while the elephants had been hurried across the river and shackled to the stout trunks of a grove of palm trees in case they should grub up their pickets in panic and run amok through the camp.

Few people had leisure to spare even a glance for Mulraj and Shushila, galloping between the embattled tents only minutes before the storm whirled down upon the camp. And while it raged they could only crouch down under cover, with their mouths and noses bandaged against the dust, or struggle grimly to prevent their tents and carts and make-shift shelters from blowing away or being overturned.

When at last it was over, the havoc it had caused was so great that there was no time to think of anything but how to repair the damage, and the arrival of the brides' *ruth* shortly after sunrise, bearing the Rajkumari Anjuli and her uncle (who had been caught by the storm while out on the plain), had been greeted with relief, but aroused little curiosity. There were, as Ash had surmised, too many other things to think of, and his own arrival, jogging in slowly with the limping mare on a leading rein, had been unspectacular enough to attract no interest except among his own servants.

His tent was still standing, but unlike Anjuli, he had no sleep that day, because the damage to the camp was even worse than he had expected and it was clear that he and Mulraj, and every able-bodied man and woman in the place, were going to have their work cut out to repair it.

Considering the enormous number of men and animals in the

bridal retinue, it was a matter for congratulation that only three people had lost their lives in the storm, and of the hundred or so who
had been injured, most had received only minor cuts and bruises.
The animals had suffered far more severely, for the majority had
panicked in the choking dust, and the toll of broken necks and broken bones, and runaways who might or might not be recovered, was
high.

Inspecting the incredible profusion of assorted debris, the snapped
tent poles, torn canvas and tangled guy-ropes, and the endless drifts
of dust and sand that had silted up against the sides of everything
that had withstood the gale, Ash could only be grateful for the river,
which although it had helped to deluge them with sand, would at
least ensure that there was no shortage of water. To have had to con-
tend with that on top of everything else, and in this heat, would have
been the last straw. He gave thanks for small mercies, and went off
to find Mulraj and discuss ways and means of making good the
damage.

A large number of tents had been bodily uprooted or else blown
flat on their cowering occupants, but the palace guard had had the
sense to dismantle the big durbar tent and use its canvas to reinforce
the smaller ones in which Shushila and her women slept. They, and
Jhoti with them, had in consequence suffered less discomfort than
anyone else, and had never been in any real danger. But as they did
not know this, they made the most of their experiences, with the result that Anjuli, who had expected to face a barrage of questions,
found to her relief that they were all far more interested in telling her
everything that had happened to them, and there had been no need
for her to tell lies. Or, indeed, to say anything at all, for all that had
been required of her was to listen.

'You were lucky to have been out of it and safe in the *ruth*,' Shu-
shu told her, voicing the opinion of everyone present except Jhoti,
who commiserated with her for missing the fun.

'You've no idea how exciting it was, Kairi!' declared Jhoti. 'The
tent flapped and flapped and the dust came pouring up under it, and
I made Shu-shu get under my *charpoy* (bedstead), and covered it
with shawls because she howled and cried and said that the roof
would fall on us and we should all be smothered. Such a fuss.'

'I did not *howl!*' protested Shu-shu angrily.

'Yes, you did—like a jackal. Like six jackals!'

'I did not!'

'You *did!*' . . . The conversation relapsed into bickering, and neither then nor at any other time did anyone bother to ask Anjuli where she had been when the storm broke, and how or when she had managed to get back to Kaka-ji and the *ruth*.

There were to be no more evening rides, or any further meetings in the durbar tent. Both Ash and Mulraj were too busy to spare any time for social gatherings, and as Jhoti followed them about the camp all day, chattering incessantly and convinced that he was giving valuable assistance, he was tired enough by nightfall to welcome the prospect of early bed, which left only Kaka-ji, who continued to drop in for a chat with his nieces, but found it dull without the others, and did not stay long.

As though in apology for that unseasonable storm, the weather improved out of all knowledge. The day-time temperatures fell below ninety, while the nights were once again cool. But no one was prepared to risk getting caught by another dust-storm, and men toiled like galley slaves to repair the damage and get the camp ready to move again. And not only for fear of a second storm, for by now the vast majority were tired of this nomadic existence and only too anxious to stay in one place for a time, and to enjoy the fleshpots of Bhithor and all the festivities that would attend the wedding.

Most of the errant livestock had been rounded up, fresh fodder had been procured and food supplies, though still low, were adequate, Ash having ranged far afield to supplement the meagre amounts that the near-by villages, also hard hit by the storm, had been able to spare them. The camp rang with the sound of hammers and saws as tent poles and vehicles were repaired, but with the best will in the world it was obviously going to be at least a week before the order to march could be given.

It had, in fact, taken a little more than that, eight days, to be precise, and in all that time Ash had not had a glimpse of Juli, or of Shushila either. He had been too busy. But Kaka-ji and Jhoti gave him scraps of news about them, and he told himself that as soon as the camp was on the move again he would make a point of seeing them, if only to make his peace with Juli. That was something he could do no matter how many other people were present; there were words and ways that she would understand, and he could not endure the thought of parting from her without her knowing that he was sorry for being unkind to her, and that he would love her all his life. It was unthinkable to let her go without another word and with the bitter memory of his churlishness unerased, though had it not been for that, he would have avoided seeing her again, since to do so would only be driving a knife further into his own heart. And into hers also.

Ash had imagined that an opportunity to pay a call at the durbar tent would soon present itself, but there had been no suggestion that he should go there, and when he mentioned the matter to Kaka-ji, the old man had shrugged it aside and said that there was no need to trouble himself. 'You would find it very dull. My nieces are busy preparing for their arrival in Bhithor, and can talk of nothing now but what saris and which jewels they will wear.'

That did not sound like Juli, and Ash had been unable to resist saying so. Kaka-ji had agreed, but said with a chuckle that although it was Shu-shu who was exercised in her mind over the question of dress, he suspected Kairi of fostering it as a means of keeping her sister's mind off other matters. 'And she is quite right,' approved Kaka-ji. 'Anything that will distract Shu-shu's attention and keep her from tears and bewailing is a good thing for us all.'

Jhoti had echoed his uncle's opinion (though in cruder words as he had little sympathy with 'all this silly fussing about what to wear') while Mulraj had hinted that it might be better, now that they were so near Bhithor, for both the Sahib and himself to keep their distance from the durbar tent, as the Rana was known to be a stickler for etiquette.

Indirect methods having failed, Ash sent to ask when he might call upon the Rajkumaries, and received a flowery but evasive reply, intimating that Shushila-Bai did not feel strong enough at the moment to entertain visitors, and would therefore have to postpone the honour of receiving him until a later day. The refusal had been sweetened with a great many compliments; but it remained a refusal. Did Juli too, like Mulraj, consider it advisable for her sister and herself to retire into strict purdah now that they were almost within reach of their future husband's territory? Or did she really intend not to see him again? Either way it would mean that he would now never be able to put things right between them, and that the memory of the manner in which they had parted would be an unhealed wound all his days: a punishment—and a just one.

But he had misjudged Anjuli. It was not in her nature to be unforgiving, and she had not blamed him for that sudden repulsion. She had understood the reason for it as clearly as though he had spoken his thoughts aloud, and she knew him too well to imagine that it would last, or that he would not regret it; and perhaps wonder, too, if she blamed him. Well, there was still a way of telling him that she did not. A very simple one.

One evening, at the end of a long, tiring day in the saddle, a basket of oranges had been handed to Ash by one of the royal servants who explained that it was a gift from the Rajkumari Anjuli-Bai. The Rajkumari regretted that her sister's health prevented them from receiving the Sahib, but trusted that the Sahib himself would remain in excellent health, and that he would enjoy the fruit. Ash looked down at the oranges, and suddenly his heart was thudding violently and for a dizzy moment it was all he could do not to snatch the basket from the man's hands, and search it there and then for the message he was sure it would contain. But he managed to control himself, and having rewarded the bearer, carried the basket into his tent, and spilling the oranges onto his bed, found nothing.

But something must be there, otherwise why should Juli, of all people, have bothered to send him a conventional gift of fruit? It was not in character, and the polite verbal message that accompanied it had certainly not contained a hidden meaning. Ash picked up the oranges and examined them one by one. The skin of the fifth bore a small mark, as though a sharp knife had cut into it, and he broke it open and was immediately lifted out of despair. The malaise of the past days, the pain of guilt and self-loathing and the ache of loss were suddenly eased as he looked down at Juli's message, and felt hope return to him and the tiredness and strain fall away and be forgotten.

She had not written to him. There had been no need to, for she had sent him something that said more than the longest letter could have done. The half of the little mother-of-pearl fish that she had given him once before on the night that he had escaped from Gulkote.

Ash stood for a long time looking at it; not seeing it, because he was reliving that night. Remembering the silence and the fear and the whispering, urgent voices: seeing again the moonlight shimmering on the snow peaks of the Dur Khaima and flooding the Queen's balcony with a cold radiance that glinted on the pearl in Hira Lal's ear and turned to silver a little slip of carved shell that was Juli's most precious possession.

She had given it to him because he was her bracelet-brother, and to bring him luck; and because she loved him. And he had broken it in two and told her that they would each keep half, and that one day, when he came back, they would mend it and make it whole again. And now she sent him back his half, knowing that he would understand what she meant . . . that they themselves were still two halves of a whole, and that while they lived there would always be the hope that perhaps one day, far in the future and when their actions had ceased to be of any importance to anyone else, they might even be able to come together again. It was a tenuous hope at best; but to have any at all was like coming upon a spring of fresh water after wandering for days in a burning desert. And even if it were never realized, the piece of pearl-shell was in itself a tangible proof that Juli still loved him, and that she had forgiven him everything.

Ash touched it as gently as though it were a sentient thing, and saw it through a haze of tears. And it was only when his sight cleared that he realized that Juli had not sent him back the piece that he had originally possessed, but her own. The half that she had worn for so many years above her heart in the warm hollow between her breasts, and that still held the scent of her skin: a faint, faint fragrance of dried rose-petals. It was an additional message from her, as loving and as intimate as a kiss, and he held it to his cheek and was immeasurably comforted.

A discreet cough announced the return of Gul Baz and a *khidmatgar* with his evening meal, and Ash put the broken luck-charm in his pocket, hurriedly replaced the oranges, and went out to eat with a better appetite than he had shown for some time past.

Unless wind or weather prohibited it, he preferred to eat out of doors rather than in his tent, and this evening the table had been laid under a *kikar* tree whose yellow, mimosa-like blossoms diffused a dusty incense on the warm air and a film of pollen over table-cloth and dishes and Ash's dark head. The sky was still tinged with the sunset, but by the time the meal had been cleared away and the coffee drunk, it was full of stars; and Ash sat out under them, smoking a cigarette and thinking of Juli, and making a promise to her—and to himself. That he would never marry anyone else, and that even if he never saw her again he would always think of her as his wife, and in the words of the marriage service, 'Cleave only unto her as long as ye both shall live'.

A lamp glowed in the tent behind him and he could hear Gul Baz moving about, laying out his night shirt; and struck by a sudden thought, he called out to him to ask Mahdoo for the small japanned tin box that ever since the theft of his rifle had been in the old man's charge. Mahdoo himself brought it and stayed awhile to smoke and talk, and when he had gone Ash carried it into the tent and put it on the table, and took the luck-charm out of his pocket.

The strand of silk that it had hung from had been removed in order to insert it into the orange, and he would have to find another, as even the finest chain would probably end by breaking the shell. There was nothing in the tent that would serve and he would ask Gul Baz to find him something tomorrow, and in the meantime lock away Juli's half of the charm in the same place where his own had stayed, safe and out of mind, for so many years.

He removed the cheap brass key from his watch-chain and unlocked the box, and was surprised when the lid flew up as though it had been held by a spring. But there had not really been enough room for that piece of blood-stained material that he had crammed into it days ago; and he remembered now that he had had to force the lid to shut—though until this moment he had not spared another thought for the torn strip of cloth that he had hidden away from prying eyes and had meant to destroy.

At the time, the tin box had been the nearest thing to hand that was safe from inspection by Gul Baz, who had charge of all the other keys, so he had stuffed that ill-omened bandage into it and locked it, intending to take the thing out again at the first opportunity and burn it or bury it, or merely throw it away in open country. But then he had given the box to Mahdoo, together with his money and firearms and the spare ammunition, and forgotten all about it.

He took it out now and looked at it with a grimace of distaste, wondering again whom it had belonged to and what to do with it. He still could not burn it without the risk of bringing one of his servants at a run, imagining that his tent had caught fire. Nor could he drop it on the floor to be thrown away, for the sight of it would only remind Gul Baz of an episode that had best be forgotten. Probably the best course would be to take a short walk and discard it somewhere in the darkness beyond the range of the camp fires.

He crumpled it into a ball and was about to push it into his pocket, when he became aware of something that he remembered noticing, subconsciously, before. Something small and hard was attached to it, presumably a button or possibly a lead weight such as Indian tailors sometimes use to make a seam fall straight.

Apart from a cursory inspection Ash had never really examined that bit of torn material, for once having decided that it was a piece of evidence that he did not wish anyone else to see, he had been in too great a hurry to hide it before one of his servants, or Mulraj, should realize what it was and start asking questions that he did not want answered. Now for the first time he spread it out and looked at it more carefully.

The whole thing was blotched and stiff with blood, for that cut on his forehead had bled freely. But here and there between the stains it was possible to see that the grey, shadow-patterned material was a hand-woven mixture of silk and cotton that must have been expensive. The stuff was thin and unlined (the weather had been very hot) and it was the stitching and not the cloth that had parted; the entire left-hand front of the coat having come away along the seams, leaving collar and sleeve behind. There was a line of gaping button-holes and a single small breast-pocket on the inner side, rather oddly placed in that it was low down and below the armhole. The pocket had a double flap that prevented anything placed in it from falling out, and Ash, investigating, found that it had also been sewn up: presumably to ensure the safety of the small, hard object it contained.

Probably a jewel, thought Ash—a valuable one, if its owner had gone to the trouble of having his coats made with a special pocket in order to carry it about with him.

The stitches were caked with dried blood and as he picked at the thread he grinned to himself, picturing the would-be murderer's consternation on discovering his loss. All in all, an expensive evening for the gentleman in the grey coat, and it was to be hoped that it had taught him a salutary lesson. This, of course, explained that curious burglary and the meticulous manner in which his tent had been searched. He had been puzzled by that at the time, for it was obvious that the thief had been looking for something much smaller than a shot-gun or a box of cartridges, or even a bag of rupees. And but for the fact that only a few hours earlier the japanned tin box had been one of the things handed to Mahdoo for safe keeping, he would have found it.

'What I should have done,' thought Ash, giving up the attempt to break the stitches and looking around for a pair of nail-scissors, 'was to go back as soon as it was light and hide in the grass where I was ambushed. I bet that bastard went scuttling back as soon as he realized what he'd lost, and crawled over every inch of it—and serve him right: a nice piece of poetic justice if ever there was one.' But then at the time it had not occurred to him to go back for he did not know that his assailant had lost anything of value; and even if he had known, he would have been too late, because he had not woken until well into the afternoon. So much for hindsight.

Ash found the scissors, and without bothering to unpick the stitches, cut through the centre of the pocket. The trinket that it had contained fell out and rolled over the edge of the table onto the floor, where it lay in a pool of light thrown by the hurricane lamp that hung from a hook on the tent pole. A single pear-shaped jewel with the subtle, smoky iridescence of a pigeon's feather . . .

It was Hira Lal's earring.

Ash's body emptied itself of breath and he stood rigid, staring down at it for a full three minutes before he bent stiffly and picked it up.

It was incredible that after all these years he should actually have thought of this thing only an hour or so ago, and seen it clearly in his mind's eye. The fabulous black pearl that had so infuriated Biju Ram, who suspected—rightly—that it was worn in deliberate parody of the single earring that he himself wore, and that its rarity made his own diamond look flashy and meretricious by contrast.

The pearl glowed in the lamp-light as though it was alive, and looking at it Ash knew beyond any shadow of doubt who had killed Hira Lal. And who had ordered it.

Biju Ram would certainly have accompanied Lalji on that fateful visit to Calcutta, and Biju Ram had hated Hira Lal and envied his possession of the black pearl. The murder itself would have been the brain-child of Janoo-Rani, who had probably planned it down to the last detail before the travellers even set out, so that Biju Ram would only have had to wait until they were in tiger country—preferably in an area where there was known to be a man-eater—before putting it into operation. But Janoo should have known that he would never be able to resist keeping that priceless bauble, even though its retention would brand him a murderer and he would never dare wear it. Its beauty, as well as its rarity and value, had obviously overweighed those considerations and made it seem worth any risk, and Biju Ram must have carried it about with him ever since.

There must still be any number of people who even now would recognize that pearl on sight, as Ash had done, because no one who had seen it was likely to have seen another. It was doubtful if a pair to it could have been found in all India, and only greed—or hate?— could have made Biju Ram keep such a damning piece of evidence against himself. No wonder he had torn Ash's tent apart trying to find it. The thing was as dangerous as a *krait,* the little brown snake whose bite is swift death.

Ash weighed it thoughtfully in his hand and wondered why on earth he had not instantly known the identity of the man he had grappled with in the dark. Looking back on it there were so many things that should have told him, little things that should have made it perfectly clear, like size and shape—and smell. Biju Ram had always used scent, and the man who had ambushed him had smelled of orris-root. But at that time he had been far too angry to be conscious of anything except the desire to kill, and it was only now that he recalled the reek of orris-root, and realized, too, that Biju Ram no longer wore the vivid colours that he had been addicted to in the old days, but in conscious (or unconscious?) imitation of his dead rival, had taken to wearing grey. And only grey.

The blood-stained rag on the table smelt unpleasantly—though not of orris-root—and Ash tossed it out of the tent door and did not care who saw it or how many questions it evoked, because he knew now that it had nothing whatever to do with Juli. She had never come into it at all, and if he had not had a guilty conscience on her behalf he would have seen the real reason for that murderous attack long ago, and not wasted time concealing clues from his friends and hiding his own head in the sand for fear that any investigation must involve her.

The motive had been a very simple one. He had merely been looking at things the wrong way round, and it had taken the sight of Hira Lal's earring to set his brain working clearly. Now, suddenly, it was as though he had been presented with a mirror, and facing it, could make sense at last of something that had hitherto confused him because it had been written backwards . . .

Biju Ram had no interest at all in Anjuli-Bai, nor had he recognized, in Pelham-Sahib, the little boy who had once been the butt of his cruel jokes. He had meant to kill Ash for precisely the same reason that Janoo-Rani had meant to kill Ashok—because he had interfered, and was interfering, with a plot to assassinate the heir. It was as simple as that—and he had not seen it because he had been blinded by a preconceived idea.

Knowing that Biju Ram had been in the late Rani's pay for many years, and that it was she herself who had appointed him a member of Jhoti's personal suite, Ash had persisted in thinking of him as the *Nautch*-girl's creature—and Jhoti was the *Nautch*-girl's son. So, if it came to that, was Nandu. But then, if rumour was true, Nandu had murdered his mother and later (this at least was true, for there were a number of witnesses to prove it) he had quarrelled violently with Biju Ram. The enmity between them had reached such proportions that when Nandu had refused to allow his young brother to accompany the bridal party to Bhithor, Biju Ram had taken it upon himself to incite Jhoti to defy the order and escape, and had then metaphorically burned his boats by personally accompanying the runaway.

Taking all these events into consideration (and bearing in mind that Biju Ram was, in truth, about as trustworthy as a scorpion) Ash had decided that his old enemy was involved in a plot to have Nandu either murdered or deposed and replaced by Jhoti—who on account of his age would for some years be only a puppet ruler, and therefore could be used by the plotters to further their own ends and feather their own nests. It had seemed a reasonable assumption, since it fitted in with all the known facts—except one that Ash, from his knowledge of Biju Ram, should not have missed: that Biju Ram had always known on which side his bread was buttered, and that the moment it became clear that Nandu, and not the *Nautch*-girl, was going to be the real power in the state, he would have lost no time in changing his allegiance.

Looked at in this light, the pattern altered like the design in a kaleidoscope when the tube is twisted. The same pieces were there, but in a different order, and Ash saw now why there had had to be a loud and public quarrel, and why Jhoti had been refused permission to leave Karidkote and then allowed to escape. And why no one had been sent after him to fetch him back.

'I should have seen it before,' thought Ash bitterly, which was true enough, for the reasons were perfectly clear and would have been all along if only he had taken the trouble to question the evidence instead of accepting it at its face value. It was no consolation to realize that others had been equally gulled, for he, of all people, should have known better—and if this was what falling in love did to one, then perhaps there was something to be said after all for the official view, so infuriatingly expressed by his Commanding Officer and Major Harlowe when he had wanted to marry Belinda, that any junior officer who allowed himself to 'lose his head over a petticoat' was no use to the army and had better retire from active service and grow turnips.

Ash sat down on the end of his camp bed and looked at the evidence from another angle—something he should have done long ago . . .

Nandu regarded his brother as a rival and a possible focus for discontent, and therefore intended to get rid of him. But there had already been too much unpleasant speculation concerning the death of Janoo-Rani, and if Jhoti were also to die suddenly, the British Resident, who had shown a tendency to ask disagreeable questions after Janoo's death, would almost certainly ask a good many more; and then who knew what trouble might be stirred up? Better by far that Jhoti should leave Karidkote and meet with a fatal accident somewhere well beyond its borders; and just to underline Nandu's innocence and provide an additional artistic touch that should serve to disarm even the most suspicious, the boy must be shown to have left against his brother's wishes, and in circumstances that would prevent Nandu from hearing of his 'escape' in time to prevent it, or let it seem worth while sending after him to bring him back. Hence that convenient hunting party.

It had been a good plan, based on a sound knowledge of Jhoti's character and the assumption that no one was going to believe that a man who helped him to escape to his sister's camp, and accompanied him on the venture, could be anything but a sympathizer and a partisan. That last provided an alibi for Biju Ram, who would appear as an ally of the Heir Apparent (and by inference no friend of the Maharajah's), which would serve to clear him of all suspicion when the heir met with a fatal accident.

The details of the plan had obviously been thought out carefully, and Biju Ram would have had helpers—two at least, and possibly three. Ash thought it unlikely that there would have been more than that, for to involve too many would mean increasing the risk of discovery. Mohun and Pran Krishna, and perhaps Sen Gupta, he decided, making a mental selection from among the members of Jhoti's suite. The first two certainly, the latter probably. And the personal servants of all three would be open to bribery and therefore equally suspect.

Pran Krishna was a particular crony of Biju Ram's, and had always made a great show of admiring and sympathizing with their young master. He was also a superlative horseman, and had been a member of the hawking party on the day that Jhoti's saddle had been tampered with. He if anyone would have known how to play that trick; and had it succeeded he would have stood a good chance of being able to recover the evidence before anyone else thought to examine the saddle, for with Jhoti dead there would have been a good deal of confusion, and attention would have been centred on the boy and not the horse.

Ash remembered the conversation he had overheard on that afternoon, and realized now that far from dissuading Jhoti from going off to ride alone, Biju Ram had actually been using his knowledge of the child's character to goad him into doing so. And if Jhoti had not come back it would have been Biju Ram who would have raised the alarm and made a great to-do over it. He and Pran Krishna, with everyone else, would have galloped off to search for the boy, and had Jhoti been found dead, Biju Ram would have displayed extravagant grief and blamed the syce, while Pran Krishna disposed of the evidence under pretence of examining the saddle.

Few plans, however, are wholly water-tight, and this one was no exception; for though Jhoti could hardly avoid being thrown, he might only be injured and not killed. But that, too, had almost certainly been taken into account, and if his injuries alone had not been fatal, he could easily have been assisted to succumb to them by a surreptitious overdose of opium, or some similar draught that would have produced coma and death—something that, in the circumstances, was only to be expected and would therefore have aroused no suspicion. One way or another it stood a good chance of success— and then Ash had ruined everything by seeing the boy ride off alone, and not only deciding to follow him, but telling Mulraj, who had gone too. No wonder Biju Ram had been angry enough to turn his attentions to removing this meddler.

Both Nandu and Biju Ram must have known from the beginning that a British officer would be accompanying the camp to Bhithor, and they had probably considered it an excellent arrangement, because the presence of a Sahib would be a guarantee that any unfortunate accident that befell the Heir Apparent would be accepted by the authorities as just that and no more. And as their experience of Sahibs was small, they had probably expected some young and gullible junior officer with a limited knowledge of the languages and customs of the country, who would be easy to hoodwink.

But Pelham-Sahib had not resembled this comfortable picture, and to make matters worse he had interfered with a very well-laid plan, and followed it up by making friends with the intended victim and showing far too much interest in the boy's welfare. At this rate he might well develop into a serious stumbling block, and Biju Ram must have decided early on that it would be advisable to get rid of him, but only safe to do so when the camp had left British India and was in a part of the country where there were no towns large enough to warrant the presence of a British official, or anyone who might inquire too closely—or too soon—into an accident that involved the death of a Sahib. For it would, of course, be an accident.

Biju Ram had probably thought of several that might serve, and whenever the camp was in suitable territory had kept watch on this meddling *Angrezi*, in the hope of being presented with the right opportunity for putting one of them into practice. When it had come, he had seen it and seized it with frightening swiftness, and had Ash been found shot with his own rifle, then clearly he must have stumbled or been handling it carelessly and shot himself by mistake . . . And since Biju Ram's servants would not have been familiar with such a weapon, *Bichchhu* the scorpion would have had to play murderer himself.

Ash got up and went to stand in the open door of the tent and stare out into the night. But there were too many patches of shadow out there and it was impossible to tell if one of them concealed a watcher, though he himself must present an admirable target, outlined against the yellow lamp-light. Not that he was disturbed by that, for he was convinced that the last thing Biju Ram and his fellow-conspirators desired was to attract the attention of the British authorities: and the one thing that would attract an embarrassing amount of it would be the murder of a British officer. It must be an accident or nothing. And as another one had almost certainly been planned, he, Ash, would have to move very quickly indeed if he wished to reach Bhithor alive. But this time he must make certain that he was right and not merely guessing again. It was not enough to be sure in his own mind. He had been sure before; and wrongly so.

His gaze fell on the crumpled rag that he had thrown out of the tent door as something that need no longer be hidden, and presently he went out and picked it up, for he had suddenly thought of a use for it.

The start of the next day's march had been unduly delayed owing to an argument between a carter and the mahout of a baggage elephant over a redistribution of loads. A trivial matter, but tempers were short and both had attracted vociferous supporters, until eventually half the bullock-drivers and all the mahouts were involved in an exchange of insults that led, inevitably, to blows.

By the time the combatants had been separated and the dispute settled, a full two hours had been lost and it was plain that the next camping ground would not be reached until well after mid-day—an unpleasant prospect in that weather.

Their route that day followed a dry water-course that wound between high tussocks of grass, an occasional thorn tree and numerous tall ant-castles; and although the sun was still below the horizon when they at last set out, the freshness had already left the morning air and the day promised to be even hotter than the previous one. Sand rose in choking clouds from under the hooves of horses and bullocks, the wheels of carts and the plodding feet of men and elephants, and Shushila wept and complained until Jhoti, who was sharing his sister's *ruth,* lost his temper and slapped her.

'Anyone would think you are the only one who is hot and uncomfortable,' stormed Jhoti. 'Well, you're not! And if you think I am going to travel one more yard in this silly box with a whimpering ninny who makes more fuss than a sick goat, you're wrong.' With which he scrambled out into the dust, and ignoring all entreaties to return, sent for his horse and insisted on riding the rest of the way.

The slap and his sudden departure had a salutary effect upon Shushila, who was apt to react favourably to any display of male violence; and the incident also proved unexpectedly helpful to Ash, who, having gone to considerable trouble to avoid Biju Ram's society during the past weeks, was now wondering how to reverse the process without making it appear contrived.

Jhoti's sudden appearance on horseback solved this problem, because his entourage, who had of late been travelling in covered carts, were forced to abandon them in order to ride in attendance on their young master; and when he would have dismissed them, saying that he did not need them as he would be riding with the Sahib and

Mulraj, Ash had intervened with the suggestion that it might be useful if they stayed with him, as later on they could ride ahead to fetch food and drink. There being no chance of making camp in time for the mid-day meal, they would all have to eat by the wayside or not at all.

For once Jhoti had not argued, and they rode on together in a group, so that for the first time since the start of their journey Ash spent several hours in the company of Biju Ram, and even managed to speak to the man as if they were on easy terms with one another. Conversation had been desultory as the temperature did not encourage talk, but from Ash's point of view the situation could not have been bettered, as it had come about naturally and with no appearance of being contrived; and later on he had found it a simple matter to fall back well behind the tail of the procession, on the excuse that it was better to arrive last when all the tents had been pitched and the dust allowed to settle. But although this had meant keeping to a walk, no one—not even the horses—was feeling energetic, and they had all been content to amble along, staying well out of range of the dust-cloud raised by the shuffling marchers ahead.

The sun had been almost directly overhead before they found a suitable spot in which to stop for a meal, and Mohan and Biju Ram had ridden off to arrange for food to be brought to them. On their return they had reported that the camp site lay less than a mile ahead, and as the vanguard had reached it some time ago, most of the tents were already pitched and the remainder should be up within an hour.

Ash had hoped for a wind, but as luck would have it, that day the *louh* did not blow and the air was still; which in the long term might be no bad thing, though it meant that he would have to take extra care not to make the action he had planned appear contrived. Its success depended on an appearance of casualness, and it was just as important that the thing should look spontaneous as that Biju Ram should be watching; and almost equally important that the spot chosen should be easily recognizable and not too far from the camp—or too near, either.

He waited until the meal was over and they moved on again, for he could see, not too far ahead, a lone palm tree that rose above the waste of dusty ground and scattered grass clumps, and provided the landmark he needed. Beyond it, less than a mile away as the crow flies, a cloud of dust showed where the tents were rising, and soon they would be rejoining the camp. It was now or never—

Ash took a deep breath, and turned to Kaka-ji with a question about Karidkote that he knew would lead to general conversation and ensure that Biju Ram was paying attention. Then as they came abreast of the palm tree he removed his pith helmet, and remarking on the excessive heat, pulled a handkerchief from his pocket and began to mop the sweat off his neck and forehead. Only it was not a handkerchief. It was a torn and crumpled piece of material that had been part of an elegant grey *achkan* and was now stained with dark brown blotches. Ash drew attention to the fact by stopping in mid-sentence to look at it in blank surprise.

His expression suggested that he had never seen the thing before and could not understand how it had got there, and he stared at it, frowning, sniffed it and made a face of disgust, and without troubling to inspect it further, rolled it into a ball and tossed it away among the scattered clumps of pampas grass.

He did not even glance at Biju Ram until he had finished the sentence and hunted through his pockets for the conventional square of white linen that he had (supposedly) expected to find. Discovering this in an inner pocket of his riding coat, he dabbed his forehead with it, draped it over the back of his helmet to keep the sun off his neck, and continued the conversation, taking particular care to include Biju Ram in it so that there would be no chance of his turning back to retrieve that tattered piece of cloth before they reached the camp. Once there, it would be easy enough to see that he did not go in search of it too soon, for Ash had instructed Gul Baz to site his tent on this side of the perimeter, and facing this way, so that if Biju Ram went back to look for his late property by daylight he would have to do so in full view of Ash, who intended to sit out under an awning, ostensibly scanning the plain for black-buck with a pair of field glasses. Under these circumstances, it was unlikely that Biju Ram would risk it. Yet one thing at least was certain. Provided he had recognized that piece of material (and he had certainly been given every opportunity to do so) he would go back to look for it.

They reached the outskirts of the camp some fifteen minutes later, and the rest of the day passed uneventfully. The heat discouraged any unnecessary form of activity, and men and animals sought what shade they could find and drowsed away the slow hours until the sun was low in the sky and the temperature became more tolerable. Ash had kept a desultory watch on the plain where the solitary palm tree showed small as a toothpick against the bleached sky, but except that the landscape quivered continually to the waves of heat, nothing alive moved there. And when at length the camp aroused itself and set about its evening chores, the grass-cutters did not go that way, but avoiding the well-trodden route along which they had marched that morning, fanned out to left and right where the grass would be less thickly smothered in dust and sand.

As usual Ash ate in the open, though this evening he did not sit out late, but moved back into his tent as soon as the first stars showed, and having dismissed Gul Baz, waited until darkness fell and then turned out his lamp so that anyone who might happen to be interested in his movements would imagine that he had retired to bed. He had plenty of time at his disposal, for the moon was on the wane and would not be rising for another hour and more, but he was taking no chances. He preferred to be on the ground too early rather than risk being late, and the glass of the hurricane lamp had barely had time to cool before he slid out under the side of his tent, and lying flat on his stomach, wriggled across the open to the shelter of the grass clumps with a silence and celerity that even Malik Shah—who had taught him that trick—could not have bettered. Behind him the glow and glitter of lamps, torches and camp fires lit up the sky and turned night into day, but the plain ahead was a chartless sea of shadow dotted with rustling islands of grass, and even the nearest *kikar* trees were barely visible against the stars.

He paused for a while to make sure that he had not been seen or followed, and then set off into the darkness, guided by the line of the dry water-course whose sandy bed showed white in the starlight. The track he had ridden along earlier that day ran parallel to it, and though its windings added half as much again to the scant crow-flight mile that separated him from the spot where he had discarded the torn half of Biju Ram's *achkan,* it was easy to follow. So easy that almost before he knew it the dark column of the palm tree was looming up against the star-strewn sky.

Leaving the track he walked towards it, and once there, squatted down native-fashion to wait. The moon would not be up for well over half an hour, and as Biju Ram was unlikely to leave the camp until there was enough light to see by (and once started would take at least forty-five minutes to cover the distance) the wait promised to be a long one.

Ash had learned patience—painfully—but he would never find it easy to practise, and tonight proved to be no exception. For although he had been careful to memorize the place where he had thrown that piece of material, and would have said that he knew to within a yard or two where it lay, the islands of grass seemed to have taken on different shapes in the starlight, so that now he was less sure. And there was no way of telling whether it was still there or if a hawk or a prowling jackal had carried it away, and no point in searching for it in the darkness. If it was there Biju Ram would find it soon enough, while if it had gone it would not matter, because the mere fact that he had come in search of it would be proof enough. But when at last the moon came up over the plain he saw the thing itself, lying near a clump of pampas grass some ten paces to his left.

The moonlight also betrayed his own position, for now the palm tree no longer provided any shelter, and he rose and went over to the pampas grass, and having trodden out a rough-and-ready hide from where he could watch unseen, settled down once more to wait.

It proved to be an uncomfortable hiding place, as any unguarded movement made the grass rustle and the night was so still that the smallest sound was sharply audible. Yet the silence was to his advantage, for it meant that he would be warned of Biju Ram's approach long before he came in sight. But as the slow hours crawled by and nothing stirred, Ash began to wonder if he had made a mistake, not as to the ownership of the grey coat—he knew it to be one of Biju Ram's—but in the manner in which he had discarded it. Had he thrown it away too quickly and without allowing enough time for it to be recognized? Or so casually that the gesture had not even attracted a disinterested glance? Or had he overplayed the scene, so it rang false . . . ?

Biju Ram was no fool, and if he suspected a trap he would take no chances, no matter how alluring the bait. On the other hand, if he had been deceived by that performance this morning and accepted it at its face value, then nothing would keep him away; nor would he send a deputy or bring anyone with him. He would come alone or not at all. Yet by now the moon had been up for well over two hours and still there was no sign of him and no sound of anyone approaching. If he failed to appear it might well mean that he suspected a trap, in which case the likelihood of walking into an ambush on the way back to camp could not be disregarded.

Ash stirred restlessly and was tempted to abandon the vigil and return to his tent by a circuitous route, and go to bed. It must have been close on one o'clock by then, and in little more than three hours' time the camp would be astir in preparation for another early start. Besides it was not as if he needed any further proof that it was Biju Ram who had fired at him and whose coat had torn in his hands as they struggled together in the dark. Or, for that matter, that it was Biju Ram, on behalf of the *Nautch*-girl, who had engineered the disappearance of Hira Lal and the death of Lalji, and was now, at the bidding of a new master, striving to dispose of Jhoti as well. There was surely no need for anything more, and this quixotic conviction that he must, in all fairness, obtain at least one concrete piece of evidence to support his suspicions before taking any action, was absurd: what could it do but confirm what he knew already? And what had fairness ever had to do with Biju Ram?

'Nothing,' decided Ash angrily. *'Nothing'* . . .

Yet he knew that he could not leave until Biju Ram came. Or did not come. The conviction might be quixotic, but it was there and he could not free himself from it. The past was too strong for him. Hilary and Akbar Khan had, between them, sown better than they knew when they had impressed upon a small boy that the one unforgivable sin was injustice, and that he must at all costs be fair. And the very laws of England held that any accused person is presumed to be innocent until he is proven guilty.

'Ad vitam aut culpam,' thought Ash wryly, recalling one of Colonel Anderson's favourite tags, which the Colonel had chosen to translate as 'until some misconduct is proved'; while the Commandant of the Guides, discoursing on the same subject (the proper administration of justice), had been fond of quoting the opinion of Dickens's judge that 'what the soldier said was not evidence'. Yet the case against Biju Ram was founded on gossip and guess-work, strongly biased by a personal antipathy that dated back to the days of Ash's childhood, and he could not bring himself to condemn a man to death on suspicion alone.

To death . . . The words gave him an odd shock of surprise, for strangely enough it was the first time that he had consciously realized that he meant to kill Biju Ram. Yet here the influences of the Hawa Mahal and the Border tribes took over and Ash ceased to think as an Englishman . . .

Faced with a similar situation, ninety-nine out of a hundred British officers would have arrested Biju Ram and handed him over to be tried by the proper authorities, while the hundredth would probably have allowed Mulraj and the senior members of the Karidkote camp to deal with the matter. None would have dreamt of taking the law into their own hands, yet Ash saw nothing untoward in doing so.

If Biju Ram was guilty of murder and attempted murder, then there was nothing for it but to deal with him here and now—if he came. And if he did not? 'But he will,' thought Ash. 'He must. He won't be able to resist coming on the off-chance of finding that pearl.'

The shadows had shortened as the moon travelled up the sky, and by now the light was so bright that small print could have been read by it. A hot-weather moon over the plains of India has little in common with the cool silver globe that floats above colder lands, and even the smallest beetle scurrying across the dusty spaces between the grass clumps was as clearly visible as though it had been daylight. The torn piece of cloth with which Ash had baited his trap now lay starkly exposed as a dark blotch on the white dust, and the silence of the night was no longer unbroken.

A faint clattering sound announced the arrival of a young porcupine that had been attracted by the smell of stale blood, but having nosed the cloth and found it inedible, it scuttled off with an indignant rattle of quills. Far away a jackal pack broke into a wailing, yelping chorus that echoed across the plain and died on a long mournful howl, and shortly afterwards there was a patter and a rustle as a hyena loped past, making for the camp where there would be rich pickings for scavengers. But there was still no sound that suggested the approach of a man, and Ash flexed his stiffening muscles and longed for a cigarette. The moonlight was bright enough to neutralize the momentary flare of a match and he could easily conceal the glowing tip in his hand. But he could not risk lighting one; the scent of tobacco smoke would carry too far on the windless night, and Biju Ram would smell it and be warned.

Ash yawned tiredly and closed his eyes; and he must have dozed for a few minutes, for when he opened them again a little vagrant breeze was stirring the grasses with a sound like far-away surf on a pebble beach. And Biju Ram was standing in a patch of moonlight less than a dozen yards away . . .

For a moment it seemed to Ash that his hiding place had been discovered, for the man appeared to be staring straight at him. But Biju

Ram's gaze passed on. He was looking about him, glancing from the palm tree to the mile-distant camp and evidently calculating the line that he and the others had ridden along on the previous day. It was clear that he had no suspicion that he had walked into a trap or that anyone might be watching him, for he stood out in the open without any attempt at concealment and with his coat half unbuttoned to allow the breeze to cool his plump, bare chest.

Presently he began to move forward between the scattered clumps of knee-high grass and the tall islands of pampas, searching as he went. Once or twice he leant forward to peer more closely into the shadows and poke among them with the heavy silver-mounted walking-stick that he carried, and once he swooped to pick up something that he dropped again with a gesture of disgust, pausing to wipe his fingers on his coat sleeve before moving on again.

He was within a few feet of Ash's hiding place when he saw the thing that he came in search of, and his sudden in-drawn breath of satisfaction was audible even above the susurration of the grasses. For an appreciable length of time he stood wide-eyed and rigid, staring at it, and then he dropped his stick and ran forward to pick it up and crumple it between frantic hands.

An uncontrollable spurt of laughter proclaimed his discovery that there was still some small hard object hidden among its folds, and he tore at the concealed pocket in such a frenzy of haste that the earring leapt out and fell at his feet . . .

The diamonds in the tiny leaf glittered with a frosty brilliance and the black pearl lay like a drop of glowing darkness on the white dust, a thing of beauty and wonder that seemed to gather and reflect the moonlight. Looking down at it, Biju Ram laughed again—that familiar giggling laugh that had almost always been an expression of satisfied malice rather than honest amusement, and that now held an unmistakable note of triumph.

He had been too obsessed with his search for the lost jewel to sense the near presence of another human, and now, as he stooped to pick it up, he was not aware that though the breeze had died as suddenly as it had arisen, the grass was still rustling. And when he saw the shadow it was too late.

A hand like a steel trap closed about his wrist and twisted it so savagely that he cried out with pain and let go of the pearl, which fell back onto the dust.

Ash picked it up and put it in his pocket, and releasing his grip, stood back.

Biju Ram was quick and cunning, and he had shown himself capable of thinking very fast and of translating thought into action with equal speed. But this time he was taken off guard, for he had thought himself safe and the shock of Ash's sudden appearance drove him to incautious speech: 'Sahib! What—what do you do here? . . . I did not know . . . I came out to—to search for that trinket that I—that I lost this morning. Give it back to me, Sahib. It is mine.'

'Is it?' inquired Ash grimly. 'Then the coat that it was concealed in must also be yours. Which means that you have twice, to my knowledge, tried to kill me.'

'To kill you?' Biju Ram was recovering himself and his face and voice expressed complete bewilderment. 'I do not understand, Sahib. What coat?'

'This,' said Ash, touching it with his foot. 'You left this much of it in my hands when you escaped from me—having failed to kill me. And later you ransacked my tent looking for it, because you knew, as I did not, what it contained. But last night I too found out, and so I threw it down here for you to find, knowing that you would come back for it. I have watched you search for it and seen you take the pearl from it, so there is no need for you to waste breath pretending that you do not know what I am talking about, or that the coat was none of yours.'

A mixture of emotions compounded of rage, fear, indecision and wariness showed fleetingly on Biju Ram's face, to be succeeded by one of half-humorous deprecation as he smiled and spread out his hands in a gesture of resignation, and said wryly: 'Now I see that I shall have to tell all.'

'Good,' said Ash, surprised at this swift capitulation.

'I would have spoken long ago, Sahib, had I dreamt that you might suspect me. But such a thought did not enter my mind, so when my servant, Karam, confessed all and threw himself upon my mercy, and I learned that no grave harm had been done and no complaints raised, I foolishly agreed not to betray him—though you must not think that I did not punish him. I assure you I did, most severely. But he told me—and I believe him—that he never intended to steal the gun; only to borrow it so that he might shoot *kala hirren*' (black-buck) 'who come out to graze at night; there being those in our camp who eat meat and will pay good money for it. He had meant to replace the gun before it was missed, but in the darkness he mistook the Sahib for a buck, and fired, and on discovering his mistake was overcome with terror, for he said that until you leapt upon him he thought that he had killed you; and when at length he escaped from you, having dropped the gun and left a piece of clothing in your hands, he said nothing of all this but gave out that he had been injured in a fall. I myself would never have learned of it had it not been that only the day before I had given him an old coat of mine, forgetting that I had left an earring in one of the pockets, and when I realized what I had done I asked him for it, and it was then that he confessed all. Sahib—you may imagine my horror!'

He paused as though in expectation of some comment, and when Ash offered none, sighed deeply and shook his head over the recollection of that moment. 'I should have hauled him before you on the instant—I know it,' confessed Biju Ram magnanimously. 'But he begged me with tears to be merciful; and as you, Sahib, had made no report of the matter and by good fortune had been unharmed, I acceded to his request, and did not find it in my heart to denounce him. He promised, too, that he would find and return my earring, but had I known that he would search your tent for it, or that you had recognized the coat as mine and suspected me of being the culprit, I would have come to you at once and told you the truth, and you would have given me my earring and all would have been well. The fault was mine—I admit it—I was too lenient with my rascal of a servant, and for that I ask your pardon. But had you been in my place, and the offender one of your own men, would you not have done the same? I am sure of it! And now, Sahib, having told you all, I would beg leave to return to the camp. Tomorrow my *budmarsh* of a servant shall present himself before you to make full confession of his fault and receive whatever punishment you think fit. This I can promise you.'

'Yes, I am sure you can,' said Ash dryly. 'And I can also be sure that he will repeat what you have told me, word for word; because he will not dare to do otherwise. Also I imagine that you will see that he is well rewarded for acting as scapegoat.'

'The Sahib wrongs me,' protested Biju Ram, injured. 'I have spoken only the truth. Moreover, there are many who can bear witness that I did not leave my tent that night, and—'

'And that on the following morning your face showed no signs of cuts or scratches,' finished Ash. 'Of course. Though I think I have heard otherwise. But no matter—even if that could be proved I am sure that you and your friends would have some plausible story to account for it. Very well then. Since it seems that you can produce so many witnesses to swear that you speak truth, let us pretend that it was not you but one of your servants who stole my gun and tried to shoot me with it while wearing, by chance, a cast-off garment that you had generously given him only a day before. But what of the earring? Have you witnesses to prove that it is indeed yours?'

The moonlight betrayed the sudden, startled widening of Biju Ram's eyes, and Ash saw it and knew that he had been right in thinking that no one else would know about that pearl and that it could never be worn. To have admitted possessing it would have been to invite blackmail, if not murder. For even after all these years there would still be men who would recognize it, and recall how its owner's disappearance had never been satisfactorily explained. Biju Ram could bribe or threaten any number of people into giving false evidence, but he would not risk producing the black pearl in public or attempting to bribe anyone—even the most venal of his fellow conspirators—into testifying to his ownership of that jewel.

There was a noticeable interval before he replied to the question, and becoming aware of this he essayed a smile and said: 'The Sahib is pleased to jest. What need of witnesses? The trinket is mine, and surely the fact that I came here to search for it is proof enough, because had I myself not placed it for safe-keeping in an inner pocket of that coat, how could I have known it was there?—or what to look for? Besides, I doubt if even my servants would recognize it, as I have never worn it. It belonged to my father, who gave it to me as he lay dying, so it saddens me to see it, but I have carried it with me ever since in memory of him. I look upon it as a charm to remind me of a great and good man, and to keep me from harm.'

'Very filial of you,' commented Ash. 'And very interesting too. I would have said that he was not nearly old enough to be your father, as there cannot have been more than five years between you, if that. But then perhaps he was a particularly precocious child.'

Biju Ram's smile became a little fixed, but his voice remained smooth and once again he spread out his hands in a deprecatory gesture: 'You speak in riddles, Sahib, and I do not understand you. What can you know of my father?'

'Nothing,' said Ash. 'But I used to know the man who owned that earring and always wore it. His name was Hira Lal.'

The sharp hiss of indrawn breath was harshly audible in the silence as Biju Ram stiffened and stood rigid, and once again his eyes
were wide and revealing. But this time they reflected shock and disbelief, and the dawn of something that was half-way between rage
and terror. He ran his tongue over his lips as though they had suddenly become dry, and when he spoke at last it was in a grating
whisper that seemed forced from him against his will:

'*No,*' whispered Biju Ram. 'No . . . it is not true. You could not
. . . it is not possible . . .' A shudder went through him, and he appeared to wrench himself awake from the grip of a nightmare. His
voice shot up:

'Some enemy has told you lies about me, Sahib. Do not believe
them. There is no truth in this—none. This man you speak of, this
Mera—no, Hira Lal, was it not? There must be many of that name in
Karidkote. It is not an uncommon one, and it is possible that one of
them has an earring somewhat similar to this one of mine. But is that
any reason to accuse me of theft and falsehood? Sahib, you have
been misled by someone who wishes to ruin me, and if you are a just
man—and we know all Sahibs to be just—you will tell me the name of
this perjurer so that I may confront him and make him admit that he
lies. Who is it who accuses me?' demanded Biju Ram in throbbing
tones, 'and of what am I accused? If you know his name, speak,
Sahib. I demand justice!'

'You will get it,' promised Ash grimly. 'His name is Ashok. He
was once in the service of the late Yuveraj of Gulkote, and you of all
people should remember him well.'

'But—he is dead,' breathed Biju Ram. 'He could not . . . This is a
trick. A clumsy plot. You have been deceived by an impostor. That
boy died many years ago.'

'Did the men you sent to hunt him down tell you so? If so, they
lied. No doubt because they feared to return and admit that they had
failed. No, *Bichchhu-ji*'—Biju Ram jerked like a startled horse at the
old nickname—'your men lost him, and though his mother died, he
lived; and now he has come back to accuse you of the murder of his
friend Hira Lal, whose pearl you stole; and of the attempted murder
of the boy, Jhoti; and of myself, whom you would have shot. There
is also the matter of the death of Lalji, for though I cannot know if it
was your hand that thrust him from the battlements, I am very sure
that you contrived it—you and his step-mother, who between you

hastened the death of my mother, Sita, by hounding us back and forth across the Punjab until she died from exhaustion.'

'Us? . . . *your* mother–?'

'Mine, *Bichchhu*. Do you not recognize me? Look closer. Have I changed so much? You have not. I knew you again the moment I saw you–that first night in Jhoti's tent; as I knew the pearl too the instant it fell from the hidden pocket you had made for it in a coat that had torn in my hands.'

'But . . . but you are a Sahib,' whispered Biju Ram through dry lips, 'a Sahib–'

'Who was once Ashok,' said Ash softly.

Biju Ram stared and stared. His eyes seemed to stand out from his head, and great beads of sweat that had nothing to do with the warmth of the hot night formed on his forehead and glittered in the moonlight. 'No, it is not true'–the words were barely more than a breath of sound–'it cannot be . . . it is not possible . . . I do not believe . . .' But the muttered denials were contradicted by a dawning recognition on his face, and suddenly he said loudly: 'If it is true, there should be a scar, the mark of a branding–'

'It is still there,' said Ash, and pulled open his shirt to show the silvery-white ghost of a half-circle, still faintly visible against his brown, suntanned skin. A mark made long ago by the mouth of an old-fashioned blunderbuss.

He heard Biju Ram's involuntary *'Wah!'* and glanced down at the scar; which was unwise. He should have known better than to look aside from a man who had not been nicknamed 'the scorpion' for nothing and would not have ventured out unarmed. The heavy silver-mounted stick lay just out of Biju Ram's reach, but he carried a particularly deadly knife in a slit pocket in his *achkan,* and as Ash looked down he whipped it out and struck with the speed of his namesake.

The blow only missed its mark because Ash too could move swiftly; and though he had momentarily lowered his gaze he was aware of the quick movement and dodged instinctively, flinging himself to one side so that the thrust went harmlessly past his left shoulder. The force of it sent Biju Ram plunging forward, and Ash had only to put out a foot to trip him up and send him sprawling full length in the dust.

As he lay there, winded and gasping, Ash turned to snatch up the fallen knife and was tempted to plunge it between those heaving shoulders and be done with it. And had he indeed been of Zarin's blood he would have done so, for the sons of old Koda Dad had no pettifogging scruples in the matter of dealing with an enemy. But now, quite suddenly, Ash's ancestry and those tedious years at a public school betrayed him, for he could not bring himself to strike: not because to do so would have been murder, but for a more trivial reason—because he and his forebears had been taught that it is 'not cricket' to stab a man in the back or strike a fallen one; or to attack an unarmed man. It was the unseen presence of Uncle Matthew and a score of pastors and masters that stayed his hand and made him stand back and urge Biju Ram to get up and fight.

But it seemed that Biju Ram had no stomach for fighting, for when his breath returned to him and he began to scramble to his knees, the sight of Ash standing there, knife in hand, made him shrink back with a scream, and he fell on his face again to grovel in the dust and babble incoherent pleas for mercy.

The spectacle was not an edifying one, and though Ash had always known Biju Ram to be a vile creature, it had not occurred to him that the sadistic ogre of his childhood might be a coward at heart. It was a shock to discover that *Bichchhu*'s pleasure in inflicting pain was only equalled by his aversion to enduring it himself, and that he could go to pieces so completely when faced with a taste of his own medicine. Deprived of supporters and a weapon, the ogre had suddenly become a thing of straw.

Ash jeered and taunted, stirred the grovelling figure with a scornful foot and used every insult that he could lay his tongue to. But to no effect. Biju Ram refused to stand up, for instinct told him that once he rose to his feet the Sahib would attack him; and the Sahib not only held the knife, but was, by some terrifying wizardry, Ashok —Ashok returned from the dead. What were a few insults compared to that? A combination of superstitious awe and the fear of death kept Biju Ram flat on his face and deaf to abuse, until at last Ash turned away in disgust and told him roughly to get up and go back to camp.

'And tomorrow,' said Ash, 'you and your friends will make an excuse to part company with us. I do not care what excuse you use provided you leave, or where you go as long as it is not to Bhithor or back to Karidkote. But if I ever hear that you have been seen in either of these states I shall go straight to the authorities and tell everything that I know, and they will have you hanged or transported.

And if they should not, then I shall deal with you myself and kill you with my own hands. That is an oath! Now go—and quickly, before I change my mind and break your fat neck here and now, you lying, thieving, crawling murderer. Up and run, son of a swine. Go—*go!*'

His voice shot up and cracked with a rage which was directed at himself as much as the grovelling creature whom he had intended to kill, because he knew that this was no occasion for mercy; yet it seemed that he was not yet emancipated from the tradition of those hated schooldays and was still adrift in Limbo, neither wholly of the East nor of the West, and therefore still unable to react to any situation with an undivided heart.

Biju Ram stumbled to his feet, and with his gaze riveted to the knife in Ash's hand, began to back away cautiously, a step at a time. Evidently he found it difficult to believe that he was to be allowed to go free, and did not dare turn his back for fear that the knife would be driven home between his shoulder blades.

He had taken no more than three steps when he trod on the discarded walking-stick and tripped and almost fell, and Ash said scornfully: 'Take it up, *Bichchhu.* You will feel braver with a stick in your hand.'

Biju Ram obeyed, groping for it with his left hand while his eyes still watched the knife; and apparently Ash was right, for when he straightened up a measure of confidence seemed to have returned to him. He began to speak in a voice that was once again smooth and obsequious, addressing Ash as '*Huzoor'** and thanking him for his clemency, and assuring him that his orders would be obeyed to the letter. Tomorrow, with the dawn, he would take his departure from the camp—though the *Huzoor* misjudged him, for at no time had he ever intended harm to anyone. It was all a terrible mistake—a misunderstanding—and had he only known . . .

Still talking he continued to back away, and having edged crabwise past a clump of grass and put at least ten paces between himself and Ash, he paused and said with a shrug of the shoulders: 'But of what use are words? I am the *Huzoor*'s servant, and I will obey his orders and go. Farewell, Sahib—' He bowed deeply, bringing his hands together in the traditional manner.

The gesture was so familiar that the fact that he still held the stick appeared unimportant, and for the second time that night Ash was

* Your honour

caught off guard. For the stick was not all it seemed: it happened to be the work of a gunsmith who specialized in lethal toys for the rich, and it had been acquired by the late ruler of Karidkote, whose widow, shortly before her death, had given it to Biju Ram as a reward for unspecified services. But as Ash did not know this he was unprepared for what followed.

Biju Ram had been holding the stick in his left hand, and as he brought his two hands together the right twisted the silver-mounted top; and when he straightened up from his bow he held a slim-barrelled pistol.

The explosion shattered the moonlit silence with a brilliant flash of orange and a crack of sound, but though the range was a mere matter of six or seven yards, the events of the past quarter of an hour had so shaken Biju Ram that not only were his hands unsteady, but in the agitation of the moment he had forgotten that this particular weapon tended to throw to the left, and omitted to make allowances for it. As a result, the bullet that had been intended for Ash's heart did no more than scorch his shirtsleeve and flick a fragment of skin from his arm as it passed harmlessly by to be lost on the plain.

'*You bastard!*' said Ash viciously and in English; and flung the knife.

Rage does not make for good marksmanship and Ash's aim was no better than Biju Ram's had been—the knife point missed the throat and grazed a collar bone that was so well protected by fat that the blade came nowhere near reaching it. But as the knife fell to the ground and a small trickle of blood ran down from the wound, Biju Ram dropped the pistol and began to scream on a thin high-pitched note of pure terror.

There was something inhuman in the sound of that screaming, while the spectacle of a grown man reduced to a frenzy of fear by the sight of his own blood trickling from a cut that would hardly have discommoded a child was so nauseating that Ash's rage turned to scorn, and instead of leaping at Biju Ram to knock him down and beat him to a pulp with his own stick, he stayed where he was and began to laugh—not at the absurdity of the sight, but because it seemed incredible to him that this miserable craven should ever have been able to terrorize anyone. Seeing him now, it was difficult to believe that so lily-livered a thing could have murdered Hira Lal, and Ash's laughter was, in its way, as ugly a sound as those womanish screams.

The blood drew a thin dark line down Biju Ram's pale chest, and he stopped screaming and bent his head in a ludicrous attempt to suck the wound. But the cut was too high to allow his mouth to reach it, and when he realized this he shrieked again and began to run to and fro like a chicken that has had its head cut off, stumbling among the grass clumps and the scattered stones in an aimless frenzy of terror, until at last he tripped and fell, and once again lay writhing on the ground.

'I die!' wept Biju Ram. 'I die . . .'

'You deserve to,' said Ash unfeelingly. 'But I am afraid that scratch is unlikely to do more than give you a stiff shoulder for a day or two, and as I still dislike the idea of killing anyone as spineless as you in cold blood, you can stop play-acting and get up and start back to the camp. It's getting late. Stand up, *Bichchhu-baba*. No one is going to hurt you.'

He laughed again, but either Biju Ram did not trust him or the shock of that second failure had finally broken his nerve, for he continued to writhe and weep.

'Help me!' moaned Biju Ram. *'Marfkaro'* (have mercy), *'Marfkaro . . . !'*

His voice died on a curious gasping wail, and Ash walked over to him, still laughing but moving warily in case this was merely a trap designed to lure him within range of another unsuspected weapon. But a glance at Biju Ram's grey, contorted, sweat-drenched face checked his laughter. There was something here that he did not understand. He had heard that there are people who cannot endure the sight of their own blood and are literally overcome by it, but the man on the ground, while patently in the grip of fear, was also suffering from genuine physical agony. His body arched and twisted convulsively, and Ash bent down and said roughly: 'What is it, *Bichchhu?'*

'Zahr . . .' (poison), whispered Biju Ram. 'The knife . . .'

Ash straightened up with a jerk and took a quick step backwards, suddenly enlightened. So that was why the man had shrieked and cowered. He had misjudged Biju Ram: it was not fear of pain that had made him grovel on the ground, but the fear of death—swift and horrible death. Nor had he been afraid of Ash. His fear had been for the knife in Ash's hand—his own knife with a blade that was steeped in poison to ensure that any wound it inflicted would prove fatal. No wonder he had watched it with such hypnotized terror, and shrieked in panic when he saw that small bright trickle of blood. The wound was indeed a small one and 'no more than a scratch'. But, like Mercutio's it was enough: it would serve.

Biju Ram had been hoist with his own petard and there was nothing that Ash could do. It was already too late to try and suck the poison from the wound, and he had no antidote or any knowledge of what poison had been used. The camp was over a mile away, and even if it had been half that distance he could not have reached it and got back again in time to offer any help—if help were possible, which he doubted, for it was plain that the poison was a deadly one.

Biju Ram deserved to pay with his own life for the lives he had taken, or helped to take, and the irreparable harm that he had done. But even those who had most cause to hate him might have pitied him now. Yet Ash, watching him die, remembered Lalji's young, frightened face and haunted eyes—and a slab of sandstone that moved and slid as a boy in a blue satin coat rode under the Charbagh Gate in Gulkote bazaar. There were other memories too. Several carp floating belly upwards among the lily pads in a palace pool; a king cobra that had somehow found its way into the bedroom of the Yuveraj; Sita, dying of exhaustion under the rocks by the Jhelum River; Hira Lal, who had vanished in the jungle, and Jhoti—Jhoti who but for the grace of God would have died weeks ago, the innocent victim of another 'accident' arranged by Biju Ram.

Remembering all the evil that this man had done it was difficult to feel anything except that his fate was richly earned. And it was one that he had brought on himself, for Ash had not spoken idly when he had told him that he could go free provided he left the camp and kept away from Bhithor and Karidkote. Had he gone then he might have lived to wreak more harm and plan other murders for many years to come; but he had chosen instead to fire that shot, and it was this last act of treachery that had killed him. He had lived like a mad dog and it was only right that he should die like one, thought Ash. But he wished that it could have been over sooner, for it was not pleasant to watch, and had there been a second bullet in that ingenious pistol he would have used it unhesitatingly to put Biju Ram out of his misery. As he could not do so, he stayed, resisting the urge to turn and walk away, because it appalled him to think that anyone should have to die in this manner alone. At least he was another human being; and perhaps the fact that he was—or had been—an enemy did not matter any more.

He stayed until it was over. It did not in fact take long. Afterwards he stooped and closed the staring, sightless eyes, and retrieving the knife, cleaned it very thoroughly in the earth to remove any trace of poison. The pistol had fallen into a clump of grass and he had some difficulty in finding it, but having done so he fitted it back into place and laid the walking-stick down within reach of one of the dead man's hands.

Biju Ram would not be missed for some hours yet; and long before there was any chance of his body being found, the dawn wind would have swept the dust clear of footprints. There was therefore no point in leaving evidence that might suggest a quarrel and lead to questions being asked, and as it would be obvious that the cause of death was poison, it would be better, from every point of view, if it were put down to snake-bite.

Ash picked up the knife and having stained it with the fast-congealing blood, dropped it again and went off to search for one of the long double-pronged thorns that grow on *kikar* trees. Returning with this, he jabbed it into the dead man's flesh just below the wound. The two small punctures were almost exactly the marks that a striking snake would have made, and the cut above it would be taken for a fruitless attempt by the victim to stop the venom from spreading upwards. The only mystery would be why Biju Ram should have left the camp alone and at night, and strayed so far. But the heat would probably be blamed for that. They would decide that he could not sleep and so had gone out to walk in the moonlight, and that feeling tired he must have sat down to rest, and been bitten by a snake, which, remembering that Hira Lal's death had been arranged to look like the work of a tiger, was singularly apt. 'The gods, after all, are just,' thought Ash, 'for if it had been left to me, I would have been fool enough to let him go.'

There remained only Hira Lal's earring.

Ash took it out of his pocket and looked at it, and saw the black pearl gather and reflect the moonlight as it had done on that last, long-ago night in the Queen's balcony. And as he looked, the words that Hira Lal had spoken then came back to him, and it was almost as though the man himself was speaking to him again, very softly, and from very far away: '*Make haste, boy. It grows late and you have no time to waste. Go now—and may the gods go with you. Namaste!*'

Well, he—or perhaps the black pearl—had avenged Hira Lal. But the pearl held too many memories, and remembering how Biju Ram had come by it, it seemed to Ash a thing of ill-omen. Its possession could have brought little satisfaction to the thief, since to own it was proof of murder, so it had to be kept hidden away, with an ever-present risk of discovery, for as long as anyone remembered Hira Lal; and in the end it had brought only death. The pearl had done its work, and now Ash could not wait to be rid of it.

There was a rat hole near the clump of pampas grass in which he had lain in wait for Biju Ram, and judging from the lack of tracks about it, one that was no longer tenanted. Ash went back to it, and having dropped in the earring, filled it in with earth and small stones that he stamped hard down; and when he had scattered a handful of dust over the spot there was no longer any trace of the hole, or any indication that there had ever been one.

He stood for a moment or two looking down at the spot and thinking that perhaps, one day, someone as yet unborn would unearth the earring and wonder how it came there. But they would never know, and anyway, by then the thing would be almost valueless, for pearls too can die.

The dawn wind had begun to stir the grasses when Ash turned on his heel and started back to the camp. But the sun had been well above the horizon by the time that one of Biju Ram's servants (that same Karam who had been allotted the role of scapegoat) reported that his master was missing.

He would, explained Karam, have disclosed this much sooner had he not imagined that his master must have gone out unexpectedly early and would soon return. It was not his business to question his master's comings and goings, but he had become increasingly anxious when tent after tent came down and still his master had not returned to eat his morning meal or give any orders for the day. Tentative inquiries among the servants and the other members of the young prince's entourage having proved fruitless, Karam had finally reported the matter to an officer of the guard, who had raised the alarm.

The search for the missing man was complicated by the enormous size of the camp and the fact that it was by then on the move, and it is more than likely that Biju Ram's body would never have been found had it not been for the kites and the vultures. But the sun had not yet risen when the first winged scavenger dropped out of the skies, to be followed by another and another; and presently one of the searchers had seen them and ridden out to investigate.

The discovery had been made only just in time, for half an hour later there would have been nothing to show how Biju Ram had died, and there would have been talk of foul play and, inevitably, exhaustive inquiries. As it was, in spite of a good deal of damage from beak and claw it was still possible to see that his death was due to poison and that his body bore the mark of a snake's fangs—two small punctures near the collar bone. How or why he had come to be in that spot was less easy to explain, but as Ash had surmised, this was eventually put down to a combination of heat and insomnia, and this solution seemed to satisfy everyone.

Mulraj had sent word that the camp would halt until further orders, and later that day Biju Ram's remains were cremated with due ceremony on a pyre of *kikar* wood and dry grass, hastily collected from the surrounding country and drenched with *ghee*. Next morning, when the night wind had dispersed the ashes and the charred earth had cooled, the fragments of bone that remained were carefully collected in order that they could be taken to the Ganges and thrown into that sacred river. 'And as there are none of his relatives here, it is only right that his friends should take it upon themselves to perform this pious duty,' said Mulraj, straight-faced. 'Therefore I have arranged that Pran and Mohan, and Sen Gupta, with their servants and those of Biju Ram's, shall leave at once for Benares. For saving only Allahabad, there is no more sacred spot at which a man's ashes may be consigned to the waters of Mother Gunga.'

Ash received this Machiavellian announcement with a respect that verged on awe, for with Biju Ram dead, there was still the problem of how to rid the camp of those who had been his closest associates, and Ash could see no way out of it that would not involve argument and uproar and a good deal of dangerous speculation. Mulraj's solution was an admirably simple one, though there could be a flaw in it—

'What will Jhoti say to this?' inquired Ash. 'These men are of his party—or so he thinks—and he may not agree to let them go.'

'He has agreed already,' said Mulraj blandly. 'The prince sees clearly that it would not be fitting for the ashes of one of his entourage, a man of standing who served his late mother faithfully and for many years, should be thrown into any river and at any spot. Therefore he gives them leave to go.'

'But will they do so?'

'Assuredly. For how could they refuse?'

'Oh, *shabash*, Bahadur-Sahib,' murmured Ash in an under-voice. 'It is indeed well done. I salute you.'

He suited the action to the word, and Mulraj permitted himself a faint smile, and returning the salute said equally softly: 'And I you, Sahib.'

Ash looked a question and Mulraj held out his hand. In the palm lay a small shirt button made from pearl-shell—a common enough object, except that it was of European manufacture and had a metal shank.

'I found this by chance, within ten paces of the body,' said Mulraj quietly, 'my foot having struck against it where it lay hidden in the dust. Later I showed it to your bearer, saying that I had found it in my tent, and he claimed it as one of yours and said that he had noticed yesterday that one was missing from a shirt that you had worn the evening before. I told him I would return it to you myself—making a jest of it.'

Ash was silent for a moment or two, realizing that he must have jerked the button off when he pulled open his shirt to show the scar on his chest, and thinking that it was lucky that Mulraj and not one of Biju Ram's associates had found it—except that no one else would have seen anything in the least interesting in it. He reached out, and taking it said lightly: 'I must have lost it when we rode into camp.'

'Mayhap,' said Mulraj with a shrug. 'Though had I been asked I would have said that you wore a khaki shirt with horn buttons that morning. But no matter—it is better that I should know nothing. We will not speak of this again.'

They had not done so. Neither then nor later had Mulraj asked any questions, or Ash volunteered any information. Pran, Mohan and Sen Gupta, with their servants, had left before dawn on the following day, presumably for Benares, and the camp moved on again. But though it was too much to hope that it was now free of spies and plotters, those who remained were unlikely to do any serious harm, largely because they were now leaderless, but also, in part, because they would not be certain that the death of their leader and the sudden departure of his closest colleagues was merely a coincidence, and if it were not, how much had become known of their doings. Being unsure, they would lie very low and take no action, which meant that, for the time being at least, Jhoti was safe. Or as safe as he ever could be, decided Ash.

Anjuli remained invisible, and he knew that there was little chance of seeing her again save as a sari-shrouded figure on the occasion of her marriage; for with the Rana's territory only a few marches away the casual easy-going conditions that had prevailed for so long were abandoned, and rules that had been allowed to lapse were once again strictly enforced. He could not even send her a message, because the brides were now kept closely secluded. Additional guards surrounded their *ruth* on the march and kept watch on their tents at the stopping places, and there was nothing that he could do except wear the luck-charm openly at her wedding in the hope that she might see it, and knowing that he had found it, know too that he understood why she had sent it back to him.

The half of that little mother-of-pearl fish was not only a token of her forgiveness, but a reminder that the other half was still in her possession; and that perhaps some day—one day—they might come together again.

Ash took what comfort he could from that thought. It was not a great deal, yet it would have to do, for he had nothing else. But for the most part he tried not to think of Juli; or of the future. Because a future without her presented nothing more than a vista of empty, fruitless years, stretching away in front of him like an endless road that led nowhere, and the thought of it frightened him.

Book Four

Bhithor

With the low range of hills that formed the northern border of Bhithor clearly in sight, an embassy from the Rana rode into camp.

The emissaries brought gifts, garlands and messages of welcome, and were accompanied, somewhat disconcertingly, by what appeared at first sight to be a horde of masked bandits; though these turned out to be nothing more alarming than royal servants, who in accordance with a local custom wore the ends of their turbans wound about nose, mouth and chin in the manner of the veiled Tuaregs of the Sahara—an effect that was distinctly unnerving, in that it suggested footpads and violence, but was in fact (or so they were informed) a mark of respect in Bhithor—'a symbolic veiling of humble features from the effulgent glory of the countenances of the highly born'. All the same, the sight of that faceless horde was far from reassuring, and Ash was not the only one to wonder what sort of country they were entering. However, it was too late to worry about that now.

There was nothing for it but to go forward, and three days later the vast cavalcade that had set out from Karidkote so many weeks ago crossed into the Rana's territory, where they were greeted by an escort of State Cavalry and a number of dignitaries, headed by the Diwan—the Prime Minister—who presented more garlands and made more long and flowery speeches. But if Ash had imagined for one moment that his troubles were almost over, he was to be disappointed. They were, on the contrary, about to begin.

The Diwan having taken his leave, Ash and Mulraj and several of the senior members of the camp rode off with the Rana's men to be shown the place where they would pitch their tents for the duration of their stay, and where all but a handful of them would live until the time came for them to return to Karidkote. The site, which had been personally selected by the Rana himself, proved to be in a long, level valley, some three miles from the ancient walled city of Bhithor from which the state took its name. At first glance it seemed to be an admirable choice: it was large enough to accommodate the camp without any over-crowding, and was, moreover, bisected by a stream that would provide all the water they would need. Mulraj and the others had expressed approval, but Ash had been markedly silent.

As a Guides officer trained in Frontier warfare, the site appeared to him to possess certain drawbacks that more than outweighed its advantages. There were, for instance, no less than three forts in the valley. Two were clearly visible at the far end of it, crowning the hilltops that flanked the city, and not only guarding the approaches to the capital, but commanding the full stretch of the level ground. The third dominated the narrow, steep-sided gorge through which they had ridden in order to reach the valley, and even a casual observer (which Ash was not) could see that its ancient walls were still in an excellent state of repair and its bastions armed with a formidable number of heavy cannon.

These last, like Bhithor itself, were relics of an earlier and more barbarous age—great, green-bronze things that had been cast in the reign of Akbar, greatest of the Moguls and grandson of Barbur the Tiger, but still capable of hurling an iron cannon ball with deadly effect against anyone attempting to force a passage through the gorge.

Taking all this into consideration, the valley had the appearance of a trap, and Ash surveyed the terrain with a jaundiced eye and did not fancy the prospect of walking into it; for though he had no reason to distrust the Rana, he was well aware that last-minute disputes over such matters as the payment or non-payment of the bride-price, and similar monetary transactions connected with a marriage, were not uncommon. As witness the drama that had preceded Lalji's wedding, when the bride's relatives had suddenly demanded double the sum originally agreed upon.

His orders having expressly stated that he was to protect the interests of the Maharajah's sisters and see that the proper payments were made, it seemed unwise, to say the least of it, to allow them and their followers to make camp in such a vulnerable spot; because once under the Rana's guns, negotiation would be difficult if not impossible, and unless he wished to risk bloodshed he might well find himself forced to accept any settlement that the prospective bridegroom chose to make. It was a possibility that did not appeal to him, and to the unconcealed annoyance of the Bhithor dignitaries he had not only refused to move the bridal camp into the valley, but had actually withdrawn it to a position some two miles on the far side of the gorge that gave access to it, and dispatched a special messenger with a letter to the Political Officer responsible for that part of Rajputana, advising him of what he had done, and why.

The decision had been an unpopular one with all save Mulraj and some of the more cautious and level-headed elders, for the entire camp had been looking forward to roaming through the bazaars of Bhithor and seeing the sights of the city. They could still do so, but only at the cost of covering some sixteen miles there and back, and the days were very hot. Therefore they grumbled and protested, and the Rana sent two elderly relatives with another deputation of high-ranking officials to inquire why the Sahib would not permit the brides and their entourage to set up their tents within easy reach of the city, and on the excellent site that had been specially selected for them.

The deputation was plainly aggrieved, and Ash's reply that the camp did very well where it was did nothing to mollify them. They withdrew in so much dudgeon that Kaka-ji took fright and suggested that it might be wiser to fall in with the Rana's wishes, for if they offended him he might withdraw from the marriage contract altogether. Ash did not think this in the least likely—considering that half the bride-price had already been paid and that the preparations for the wedding must by now have cost the state a pretty penny. But Unpora-Bai and several of the elders had become infected by Kaka-ji's fears, and they urged him to reconsider.

Even Mulraj began to look a little doubtful, and when, eventually, a reply came from the Political Officer, it proved to be a frostily worded note that rebuked Captain Pelham-Martyn for being over-zealous and advised him to accept the proffered site without any further delay.

According to the Political Officer, such an uncalled-for display of caution could only offend the Rana, who was not in the least likely to back out of his obligations or attempt to dictate unacceptable terms, and therefore the sooner the camp was moved the better. The note, and its tone, was not something that Ash could afford to ignore, so bowing to the inevitable, he gave the order to march.

Two days later the last of the long column passed through the gorge under the guns of the fort crowning the ridge above it, to pitch their tents in the valley: and within a matter of hours Ash's fears were fully realized and the Political Officer's confidence proved groundless.

The Rana sent a junior minister to announce that the terms of the marriage contracts drawn up in the previous year with His Highness the Maharajah of Karidkote were, on reflection, adjudged to be unsatisfactory, and the council had therefore decided that they must be re-negotiated on a more realistic scale. If the Sahib and such of the elders who chose to accompany him cared to present themselves at the city palace, the Rana would be pleased to receive them and discuss the matter in more detail, after which they would undoubtedly see the justice of his claims, and the affair would be speedily settled to the satisfaction of all.

The minister sweetened his message with a few fulsome compliments, and having tactfully ignored the Sahib's statement that there was nothing whatever to discuss, set the time of the meeting for the following morning and removed himself with some haste.

'What did I tell you?' demanded Ash. The question was not untinged by a certain gloomy satisfaction, for he had not relished the barely concealed accusation of timidity that the Political Officer's strictures on 'undue and unnecessary caution' had inferred. Or the angry grumbling in the camp and the reiterated fears of those who had agreed with Kaka-ji that the Rana must not be annoyed.

'But he cannot do this to us,' exploded a senior official, finding his voice at long last. 'The terms were agreed. Everything was settled. He cannot in honour go back on them now.'

'Can't he?' returned Ash sceptically. 'Well, all we can do is wait and see what he has to say before we decide what we can do about it. With luck it may not turn out to be as bad as we think.'

On the following morning Ash, Kaka-ji and Mulraj, attended by a small escort of cavalry, had ridden to the city to meet the Rana.

The ride was not a pleasant one. The unshaded road was little more than a cart-track, inches deep in dust and full of ruts and potholes, and the sun was very hot. The valley must have been a good two miles wide at the point where their camp had been pitched, but nearer the city it narrowed until its sides were less than half that distance apart, the gap between them forming a natural gateway that gave on to a wide plain encircled by hills and containing the life-blood of Bhithor—the great Rani Talab, the 'Queen's Lake'. It was in the centre of this gap, midway between the two fort-crowned heights that flanked it, that the first Rana had built his capital in the reign of Krishna Deva Raya.

The city had changed very little since then. So little, that had its builders been able to return they would have found themselves on familiar ground, and still felt themselves at home, for here old customs and old ways still prevailed, and the lives of the inhabitants had altered almost as little as the solid sandstone of which their city was built or the jagged outline of the low hills that enclosed the valley. There were still only four gateways in the massive outer wall: the *Hathi Pol*—the 'Elephant Gate'—facing down the length of the valley, the Water Gate that looked eastward across the lake and the open country towards the far hills, and on the north and south, the *Mori* and the *Thakur* Gates, both of which faced an almost identical view —a belt of cultivated land three quarters of a mile wide, with beyond it the steep rise of a hillside topped by an ancient fort.

The cultivation gave the city the appearance of a rock standing in a river gorge and splitting the current into two streams: a green river made up of fields where the farmers grew grain and vegetables and sugar-cane, interspersed with groves of mango, papaya, lichi and palm trees. But the cultivated area did not stretch far, and beyond it the valley, grazing-grounds, plain and hills lay bleached and colourless under the glare of the sun, so that Ash was thankful to reach the shade of the great gateway, and more than grateful for the prospect of being able to dismount and sit in coolness and comfort in the Rana's palace, even though the accompanying interview might prove to be a trying one.

Just how trying it was likely to be was at once made clear by the behaviour of the guards at the gateway, who did not trouble to salute them, and the fact that the one person waiting there to conduct them to the palace was a very minor official who ranked little higher than a flunkey. This in itself was a discourtesy that verged on insult, and Mulraj spoke between his teeth in a muttered aside:

'Let us go back to the camp, Sahib. We will wait there until such time as these people' (*yeh-log*—the term is one of contempt) 'have learned manners.'

'Not so,' said Ash softly. 'We will wait here.' He lifted his hand, and as the escort clattered to a halt behind him, raised his voice and addressed the solitary courier:

'I fear that in our haste to greet the Rana we have arrived too early and caught him unprepared. Perhaps he has overslept, or his servants have been dilatory in attending to him. These things happen, and no court can be perfect. But we are in no hurry. You may tell your master that we will wait here in the shade until we hear that he is ready to receive us.'

'But—' began the man uncertainly.

Ash cut him short: 'No, no. Do not apologize, we shall find the rest pleasant. *Ijazat hai.*'*

He turned away and began to talk to Kaka-ji, and the man shifted uneasily and cleared his throat as though about to speak again, but Mulraj said curtly: 'You heard what the Sahib said—you have his leave to go.'

The man went, and for the next twenty minutes or so the delegation from Karidkote sat at ease in their saddles under the shadow of the great gateway, while their mounted escort held off an ever-growing crowd of interested citizens, and Mulraj favoured Kaka-ji with a long monologue (delivered sotto-voce but still clearly audible to most of the by-standers) deploring the muddle and disorganization, the shocking lack of discipline and total ignorance of polite procedure that was to be met with in many small and backward states.

The men of the escort grinned and murmured agreement, and Kaka-ji added injury to insult by rebuking Mulraj for being so hard on men who had not had his advantages and therefore knew no better. It was not their fault, said Kaka-ji, that being ignorant of the ways of the great world they lacked polish, and it was unkind to censure them for behaving in a manner that appeared uncouth to men of superior culture.

Mulraj acknowledged the justice of the reproof and complimented Kaka-ji on his charitable outlook and kindness of heart, and raising his voice began to admire the size of the gateway, the smartness of the guard and the arrangements that had been made for the comfort of the camp. He appeared to be enjoying himself, and the obvious discomfort of the guard, and those by-standers who had been near enough to overhear the preceding conversation, suggested that the Rana's slighting treatment of his guests—presumably designed to put them at a disadvantage and make them realize the weakness of their position—was proving a boomerang by making it appear instead that he and his courtiers and subjects were nothing but ignorant yokels, unversed in etiquette and lacking in courtesy.

Ash alone held his tongue, for he had no illusions as to their position. They might win a point by forcing the Rana to accord them an outward show of civility, but the victory would be a trivial one. The real struggle lay ahead, when the marriage settlements came to be discussed; and here the Rana held all the cards. It only remained to

* You have permission to go

be seen if he would dare to play them—and how far he could be bluffed.

A clatter of hooves announced the arrival of the Rana's personal bodyguard with two senior ministers and an elderly royal relative, who was profuse in his apologies for having mistaken the hour of the guests' arrival and thereby failed to be on time to receive them. It was all due to a sad mishap (it seemed he had been misinformed by an officious secretary) and he assured them that the man responsible for it would be severely punished, as not for the world would anyone in Bhithor have inconvenienced such honoured guests.

The honoured guests accepted the apologies and permitted themselves to be escorted in state through a maze of narrow streets towards the city palace, where the Rana awaited them.

Ash had not forgotten the Gulkote of his childhood, and he had, at one time or another, seen many Indian cities. But none of them had been in the least like this one. The streets and bazaars of Gulkote had been clamourous and colourful, and as crowded with people and full of life as the teeming rabbit-warren that was Peshawar, or the old walled cities of Delhi and Lahore with their shops and street-merchants and jostling, chattering citizens. But Bhithor was like something out of another age. An older and more dangerous age, full of menace and mystery. Its pale sandstone walls had an oddly bleached look, as though the burning suns of centuries had drained them of colour, while the sharp-edged shadows were grey rather than blue or black. The planless labyrinth of streets, and the blank and virtually windowless faces of the houses that hemmed them in gave Ash an uncomfortable feeling of claustrophobia. It seemed impossible that sunlight could ever penetrate into those narrow, man-made canyons, or the winds blow through them, or that ordinary people could live behind those barred doors and closely shuttered windows. Yet he was aware of eyes peering down through those shutters—women's eyes, presumably, for all over India the upper storeys of houses are woman's territory.

There were surprisingly few women in the shadowed streets however, and those few kept their faces hidden, holding their cotton head-cloths close so that once again nothing could be seen but eyes; wary and suspicious eyes. And though they wore the traditional dress of Rajputana, full-skirted and boldly patterned in black, their preferences seemed to be for such colours as rust-red, ochre and burnt orange, and Ash saw none of the vivid blues and greens that flaunted so gaily through the bazaars and by-ways of neighbouring states. As for the men, a number of these too gave the impression of being veiled, since even here in the city streets there were many who kept one end of their turbans wrapped about the lower part of their faces; and judging by their narrow gaze, a European was a novelty in Bhithor —and not a popular one, either.

The citizens stared at Ash as though he were some form of freak, and the expressions of those whose faces were uncovered betrayed more hostility than interest. It was, he thought, as though he were a dog walking down an alley full of cats, and he felt the hair on the back of his neck prickle in animal response to that silent antipathy— the enmity of closed minds towards all that is strange or new.

'One would think, to look at them, that we have come here for some evil purpose instead of for a wedding,' muttered Mulraj under his breath. 'This is an ill place, and one does not need to be told that they worship the Drinker-of-Blood. *Phew!* Look there—'

He jerked his head in the direction of a shrine to Kali, who is also Sitala the goddess of smallpox, that stood at the junction of two streets; and as they rode past it Ash caught a glimpse of the frightful goddess in whose honour the Thugs had strangled thousands of victims, and whose temples had benefited by a tithe of their loot. The nightmare deity, with her multiplicity of arms, her glaring eyeballs, protruding tongue and long necklace of human skulls, is worshipped throughout India as the wife of Shiva the Destroyer. A singularly appropriate patroness, thought Ash, for this sinister city.

A strong stench of corruption and a buzzing cloud of flies showed that her devotees were not backward in satisfying her thirst for blood, and it was a measure of his unease that he actually caught himself wondering if it were only goats that were being sacrificed to appease that thirst. He shook the thought from him with impatience, but was nevertheless inordinately relieved when at last they left the streets behind them, and dismounting in the entrance courtyard of the city palace, the 'Rung Mahal', were conducted through a maze of dusty rooms and dark stone passageways to meet the Rana. Though here too there was the same claustrophobic atmosphere that had been so noticeable in the streets: the same stillness and stifling heat, the same haunting sense of an unforgotten past . . . of old times and old evil, and the unquiet ghosts of dead kings and murdered queens.

Compared to the Palace of the Winds, the Rung Mahal—the 'Painted Palace'—was a modest building comprising half-a-dozen courtyards, a garden or two, and not more than sixty or seventy rooms (no one had ever counted those in the Palace of the Winds, though the number was believed to be in the region of six hundred). Possibly it was for this reason—among others—that its owner had begun by treating his guests in a manner calculated to damp any pretensions they might have, and now followed it up by simultaneously dazzling them with magnificence and chilling their blood with as barbaric a display of military strength as Ash, for one, had ever seen—or imagined.

It had been no surprise to find that the outer courtyards bristled with armed men, but the sight of the Rana's personal bodyguards, who policed the inner ones and lined the long dark corridors, had startled Ash considerably, not on account of their numbers, though there must have been several hundred of them, but because of their weird attire, and because here, once again, were masked faces.

The officers wore helmets of a pattern that the Saracens must have worn in the days of the Crusades. Antique iron casques with long flat nose pieces, damascened in gold and silver and deeply fringed with chain mail that protected the wearer's jaw and neck and partially concealed his cheeks, leaving only the eyes visible. The helmets of the rank and file, though similar in style, were fashioned of leather, and the effect in that half light was oddly inhuman, as though the macabre figures who lined the corridors were masked headsmen or the mummified bodies of dead warriors. Their surcoats too were of chain mail, and instead of swords they carried short spears. 'Like lictors,' thought Ash with a shiver.

He regretted that he had not brought his revolver with him, for the sight of these mailed figures brought home to him, as nothing else had done, that this was a place in which no rules—and no law as the West understood law—held sway. Bhithor was of another age and another world: she stood outside of present Time, and was a law unto herself.

In a final ante-chamber at least fifty servants, dressed in the Rana's colours of scarlet, sulphur-yellow and orange, divided to let the visitors through, and preceded by the royal relative with the senior officials bringing up the rear, they were ushered into the *Diwan-i-Am,* the 'Hall of Public Audience', where the Rana and his Prime Minister the Diwan, together with the councillors and courtiers, waited to receive them.

The *Diwan-i-Am* was a beautiful building, though at that season of the year unsuited for a morning audience, as it consisted of an open-sided pavilion formed by a triple row of columns, and was closed only at each end. With the sun blazing down upon it and no breath of breeze, the heat under the pillared arches was considerable, but its beauty made amends for any deficiencies in the way of comfort; and certainly the temperature did not appear to trouble the serried ranks of courtiers and noblemen who sat cross-legged on the uncarpeted floor, packed as closely as sardines in a tin, and dressed in their festive best.

At the far end of the hall a shallow flight of steps led up to a raised platform on which a central dais served as a throne for the ruler when he gave audience, received distinguished visitors or dispensed justice, and behind this stretched a solid wall of black marble with a polished surface that reflected the assembly as though in a mirror. The sides of the platform were enclosed by screens of pierced marble through which the ladies of the Zenana could watch the proceedings, but elsewhere the stonework had been plastered over with polished *chunam* and decorated in low relief with formal designs of beasts, birds and flowers that had once been brightly coloured, but had faded in the course of the slow centuries to pale ghosts of their former glory. Yet the *Diwan-i-Am* did not lack colour, since the Rana's courtiers, unlike his humbler subjects, were so gaily attired that a foreigner entering the hall might well have thought for a dazzled moment that he had walked into a flower-garden—or a fairground.

Turbans of scarlet and cerise, sulphur-yellow, sugar-pink and purple vied with *achkans* of every shade of blue and violet, turquoise, vermilion, grass-green and orange; while to add to the mass of colour, the centre aisle was kept clear by a double rank of crimson-turbaned retainers, gaudily uniformed in yellow muslin sashed with orange, and carrying huge, plumed fly-whisks made of horsehair that had been dyed a vivid shade of magenta.

There were more retainers on the raised platform, two of them standing behind the dais and plying fans of peacock feathers, and the remainder armed with naked tulwars—the long curved swords of Rajputana. And on the dais itself, cross-legged on a carpet sewn with pearls, ablaze with jewels and clad from top to toe in gold, sat the focal point of all this splendour: the Rana of Bhithor.

The warrior races of Rajputana are famous for their good-looks, and it is doubtful if any similar assembly of Western men could have matched the present one in the matter of physical beauty, distinction and panache. Even the grey-beards among them retained traces of the hawk-faced handsomeness they had possessed in youth, and held themselves as erect as though they sat in a saddle instead of cross-legged upon the ground. The white, tightly fitting jodhpurs and the sleek lines of flared, brocaded coats showed off each lean, broad-shouldered, slim-hipped figure to perfection, while the crisp folds of their brilliant turbans added inches to their height and made every man seem a giant. There were, of course, exceptions to the rule. Scattered here and there under the arched roof of the *Diwan-i-Am* were men who were fat or withered or ill-favoured, the most noticeable of these being their ruler himself.

The Rana's dress, jewels and diamond-hilted sword were magnificent. But his person did not do them credit, and Ash, gazing up at him from the bottom step of the stairs, was conscious of a violent sense of shock.

This—this misshapen baboon—was the bridegroom that Nandu had chosen for Juli. For Juli and Shushila . . . No, it could not be—there must be some mistake: the man on the dais could not possibly be in his late thirties. Why, he was *old*. Sixty, at least, if not seventy. Or if he was not, he certainly looked it, and Ash could only suppose that his way of life must have been singularly unsavoury to give him the appearance of old age before he was forty.

Discounting prejudice, the Rana was certainly an unprepossessing spectacle, and Ash could not have been the first person to be struck by his resemblance to a baboon. Anyone who had visited a zoo or been to Africa could hardly fail to notice it, and it was probably just as well that no citizens of Bhithor had ever done so and therefore did not realize how strikingly their ruler's facial structure, with its close-set eyes, abnormally long nose and wide, flaring nostrils, resembled a mandrill's—an old, sly, vicious mandrill, with an evil temper. As if that were not enough, the thin, hatchet-shaped and almost chinless face was deeply scored with the tell-tale lines of debauchery and self-indulgence, and the close-set eyes were as watchful and unblinking as a cobra's—their stillness in marked contrast to the ceaseless movement of the long, loose-lipped mouth; for the Rana was chewing *pan*. The betel-nut stained his lips and teeth and made small wet, red patches at the corners of his mouth, so that he might almost, like Kali, have been drinking blood.

In complexion he was fairer than most southern Europeans, for his lineage was impeccable (the royal house of Bhithor claimed descent from a god) but the pale golden tone of his skin was overlaid by an odd greyish tinge, and there were dark purple pouches, like bruises, under the cold, unblinking eyes. All in all, he presented a singularly unattractive picture, and the magnificence of his attire seemed to emphasize his physical shortcomings rather than detract from them.

Ash had been prepared for a good many things, but not this. The shock momentarily deprived him of words, and as the Rana remained silent it was left to Kaka-ji to step into the breach and fill the awkward pause with a graceful speech, to which the Rana replied a good deal less gracefully.

It was an inauspicious beginning, and the remainder of the morning did nothing to rectify it. The compliments proper to the occasion were duly exchanged—and at unconscionable length—and when at last they were over the Rana rose, and dismissing the assembled courtiers, retired to the 'Hall of Private Audience', the *Diwan-i-Khas,* accompanied by his Diwan, his senior councillors and the representatives of Karidkote.

The *Diwan-i-Khas,* unlike the *Diwan-i-Am,* was pleasantly cool. It consisted of a small marble pavilion set in the middle of a formal garden, and was surrounded by water channels in which fountains played—a setting that not only charmed the eye and reduced the temperature to comfortable limits, but ensured privacy, as no shrub was large enough to conceal an eavesdropper, and even if by some miracle an intruder had been able to enter the garden unseen, the splash of the fountains would have prevented him from hearing anything that was said inside the pavilion.

A chair had been provided for Ash, but the Rana occupied a cushioned and carpeted dais similar to the one in the *Diwan-i-Am,* while the remainder of the company disposed themselves comfortably on the cool marble floor. Uniformed servants dispensed glasses of cold sherbet, and for a short time the atmosphere seemed pleasantly friendly and informal; but it did not last. No sooner had the servants withdrawn than the Diwan, acting as the mouthpiece of the Rana, proceeded to justify Ash's worst fears.

He had approached his subject obliquely and wrapped it up in a wordy cloud of compliments and polite phrases. But shorn of irrelevant verbiage, the matter was plain: the Rana had no intention of paying the full bride-price for the Rajkumari Shushila, or of marrying her half-sister Anjuli-Bai, unless the bribe for doing so was increased to over three times the sum that had originally been offered (and pocketed), for after all, the girl's birth hardly qualified her to be the wife of such an exalted personage as the ruler of Bhithor, whose line was one of the oldest and most honourable in all Rajputana, and the Rana had already made a great concession in even considering the possibility of marrying her at all.

To be fair to the Rana, the sum that Nandu had demanded as a bride-price for Shushila had been very large. But then in view of her rank, her outstanding beauty and her impressive dowry, she was a valuable commodity in the marriage market and there were others who would have paid as much, if not more, for such a wife: several of them princes of far more consequence than the ruler of Bhithor. Nandu, for his own devious reasons, had decided in favour of the latter, and the Rana's ambassadors had not quibbled over the price or demurred at paying half of it in advance—or at giving a written promise on his behalf to pay the remainder as soon as the bride arrived in Bhithor, because large as the sum was, it had been drastically reduced by the bribe demanded as the price of the Rana's consent to take Anjuli-Bai as well as the lovely Shushila; and as any question of a second bride-price had been waived, the Rana had, in fact, got a bargain.

But it appeared that he was not content with it, and wanted more. Much more. The additional sum he now demanded for marrying the *Feringhi*-Rani's daughter came to a good deal more than half Shushila's bride-price, and if it were paid (and the half he himself still owed was not) it would mean that he would not only have acquired two brides, together with their dowries, for nothing, but would actually have made a handsome profit out of the transaction.

The demand was so outrageous that even Ash, who had been prepared for something of the kind, could not at first believe that he had heard aright—or if he had, that the Diwan had not exceeded his instructions. The man *could* not seriously mean what he said. But at the end of half an hour of argument and expostulation it was clear that the Diwan had done no more than speak his master's mind, and that the councillors were all in agreement with him. Plainly, now that the brides and their dowries were virtually in a trap, with their forces at the mercy of the guns and garrisons of two forts, and their camp confined to a valley from which the only exit was barred by a third, Bhithor saw no reason for keeping to the terms of the contract. The council not only approved the demand for a further extortionate bribe, but clearly considered that their ruler had shown himself to be a *chabuk sawi,* a smart fellow, who had successfully tricked a formidable opponent.

Ash could see no point in prolonging a discussion that could only lead to a loss of temper and a consequent loss of face by one or other of his own party—probably himself, for he had seldom felt angrier. It had been bad enough in all conscience to know that Juli was lost to him, without having to discover that her future husband was not only physically repulsive and prematurely aged by debauchery, but capable of going back on his word and resorting to blackmail; and not above insulting her in open council.

The fact that such a creature should dare to demand that he be paid for the privilege of making Juli his wife was beyond bearing, and Ash was aware that it was only a question of time before he lost his precarious hold on his temper, and spoke his mind in terms that would be both undiplomatic and quite unforgivable.

He therefore brought the proceedings to an abrupt close by announcing that—regrettably—the terms put forward by the Diwan were wholly unacceptable and would not be met: and forestalling further argument, rose to his feet, bowed curtly to the Rana, and withdrew in good order, followed by the fuming representatives of Karidkote.

The escort was waiting for them in the outer courtyard, and they mounted in grim silence, and did not speak as they rode back through the narrow streets and under the great archway of the Elephant Gate where the lounging sentries grinned openly as they passed.

The valley shimmered in the heat and there was no sign of life in the forts that looked down from the low hills to the left and right of the city, for the garrisons were taking their ease in the shade. But the mouths of the guns showed black against the sun-baked stone, and Ash stared up at them, and noting their number, spoke abruptly, his voice raw-edged with rage:

'It's my own fault. I should have backed my own judgement, instead of letting a pompous Political Officer give me orders and rap me over the knuckles for insulting a ruling prince with my unworthy suspicions. Much he knows! That treacherous old spider had it all planned, and we've done exactly what he meant us to do—walked meekly into his parlour.'

'It is terrible . . . terrible,' moaned Kaka-ji. 'I cannot believe . . . How is it possible that the Rana should refuse to pay? That *we* should pay . . . ?'

'Don't worry, Rao-Sahib. We won't,' said Ash shortly. 'He is merely bluffing.'

'You think so?' inquired Mulraj. '*Hmm.* I wish I could feel sure of that. He has enough guns in those forts to smash the valley into dust —and all of them trained on our camp. If it should come to a fight we would have no chance, since of what use are swords and muskets against stone walls and heavy cannon?'

'It will not come to a fight,' snapped Ash. 'He would not dare.'

'Let us hope that you are right. But I would not care to wager on it. The princes of Rajputana may think it prudent to pay lip-service to the Raj, but they still wield great power within their own states, and even the Sahibs of the Political Department—as you have seen— prefer to turn a deaf ear and a blind eye to much that they do.'

Ash observed tartly that it was going to be difficult to turn a blind eye to this, or a deaf ear either, as he intended to raise a considerable noise about it. He proposed to write a full account to the Political

Officer and have the letter sent off by special messenger that very afternoon.

'That would be as well,' agreed Mulraj. And added thoughtfully—'though I do not think your messenger will get through, for they have the roads well guarded. Moreover, my spies brought me a tale last night that I do not like: they say that the city and the forts can speak to each other without words.'

'You mean by semaphore?' inquired Ash, startled. 'Can they, by jove. I wonder where the devil they learned that?'

'You know of it, then? It is possible?'

'Of course. It's quite simple. It's done with flags: you make signs with them and— Oh, it would take too long to explain. I'll show you one day.'

'Ah, but this is not done with flags. This thing is done with the aid of small shields of polished silver that catch the light of the sun and flash warnings that can be seen from many miles away.'

'That for a tale,' scoffed Ash, losing interest. His scepticism was understandable, for though he had read that the Indians of North America had long since learned the trick of sending visual messages by means of smoke, the somewhat similar method of communication described by Mulraj, and that would become known as the heliograph, was as yet unknown to the Indian Army, nor would it be used by them for some years to come. He therefore dismissed it as a fabrication, and remarked that it did not do to believe everything one was told.

'Nor do I,' retorted Mulrag. 'But my spies tell me that it is no new thing in Bhithor and that it has been practised here for longer than anyone can remember. They say the secret of it was brought here by a merchant of this city who was a great traveller, and who learned the art from the *Chinni-log*' (he meant the Chinese) 'many years before the Company's Raj came to power. Be that as it may, it is certain that all our movements will be watched and reported on, and that no messenger that we send will leave unobserved. They will be ready and waiting for him. And even if one should succeed in slipping through their net, I will wager fifty gold mohurs to five rupees that the only answer he will bring back from the Political Sahib will be a request that you use great restraint and do nothing that might upset the Rana.'

'Done,' returned Ash promptly. 'You'll lose, because he'll have to take action on this.'

'I shall win, because, my friend, your Government does not wish to quarrel with the princes. To do so might lead to bloodshed and armed rising, and that would mean the dispatching of regiments and the expenditure of much money.'

Unfortunately, Mulraj had been right—on both counts.

Ash had sent off a detailed report of the latest developments, and it was only after the best part of a week had passed without any sign of his messenger with the reply that stringent inquiries and a strongly worded protest to the Diwan revealed that the man had got no further than the far end of the gorge, where he had been stopped and subsequently held prisoner in the fort on a trumped-up charge. (He had, it seemed, 'been mistaken for a notorious bandit' and the error was deeply regretted.) The second messenger did not go alone, but was accompanied by two armed troopers. They returned three days later, on foot, having been ambushed some twenty miles beyond the border by a party of dacoits who had stripped them of all they possessed, and taking their horses, left them naked, wounded and without food, to find their own way back.

Ash let it be known that he himself would be the next messenger, and that he would be taking an armed escort of over a dozen picked men of the Karidkote State Forces, all of them crack shots. And though he had not actually done this—being unwilling to leave the camp to its own devices with the Rana and his councillors in their present mood and tempers running high among their angry guests— he had made a pretence of doing so by riding with the original messenger and the escort until they were well outside Bhithor.

He did not see the warning sun signals that blinked frantically behind him from a high rooftop in the city and the outer walls of the two guardian forts. But Mulraj did, and he grinned as he watched them, for his spies had not been idle and the code was a very simple one—far more so than that complicated business of dots and dashes that the Sahib had called 'Morse' and tried to expound to him. The Bhithories had more sense than to waste time over such things, and like the Red Indians confined themselves to essentials. Their code was a model of simplicity, consisting of a single sustained flash for 'Enemy' or, alternatively, three long ones for 'Friend, do not molest', followed by short ones to indicate the numbers involved, up to a score; and if in excess of that, by a flurry of flashes. The addition of a side-to-side movement meant that the man or men in question were mounted, and not on foot, while several wide circular sweeps ordered 'stop them!'. To which the reply was seldom more than a single answering flash that could be translated as 'Message received and understood'. There were no other signals, Bhithor having found these more than adequate.

Mulraj watched the agitated flashes that commanded 'friends, do not molest', and his grin turned to a laugh, for he knew that Ash intended to turn back as soon as the border had been safely crossed—being reasonably certain that this time no plans would have been made to waylay the party, as the Rana would never risk attacking a well-armed band of men commanded by the Sahib himself, and by the time it was discovered that the Sahib was no longer with them, it would be too late to arrange yet another unfortunate accident.

All this had wasted a good many days. But they had not been spent in idleness. Those who did not possess tents had busied themselves constructing grass huts that would protect them from the burning sun and the night dews, and though wood was far from plentiful in Bhithor, Mulraj—visualizing a lengthy stay and anxious for the horses now that the hot weather had begun—had set men to work felling the broom-stick palms and the scarlet *dak* trees, and presently a score of stoutly built sheds arose, well thatched with palm-fronds and bundles of reeds from the lake.

Ash and his *panchayat,* for their part, had paid repeated visits to the city palace, where they conferred endlessly with the Diwan and one or other of the senior ministers, and occasionally with the Rana himself, in an effort to break the deadlock by persuading him to honour his bond or at least moderate his demands. They had also given a number of banquets for him and his courtiers, councillors and officials, and once, when the Rana had sent word that he was unable to attend because of a painful attack of boils (an affliction he was prone to), they had proffered the services of Gobind, in the hope that Kaka-ji's invaluable Hakim might be able to relieve the pain and thereby earn his good will.

Gobind had in fact not only succeeded in doing this, but had actually effected a cure, which was something that the Rana's own hakims had signally failed to do. But though the grateful patient had rewarded him with a handful of gold mohurs and presented Kaka-ji with a large ruby set in a gold thumb-ring, his attitude towards the marriage settlements had remained unchanged. For all the results that Ash and his colleagues achieved they might just as well have addressed their arguments to the pillars of the *Diwan-i-Am* and given banquets for the local pigeons; and when at last the messenger and his escort returned with the Political Officer's long-awaited reply, it proved to be almost exactly what Mulraj had predicted.

The Political Officer confessed to being greatly disturbed by Captain Pelham-Martyn's communication. He, Major Spiller, could only suppose that Captain Pelham-Martyn had either misunderstood the Rana's proposals or been less than patient in his handling of the ruler and his ministers. He was reluctant to believe that the Rana intended any breach of faith, but on the other hand he admitted the possibility of there being faults on both sides—each had probably misunderstood the other. He advised Captain Pelham-Martyn not to rush his fences but to proceed with the greatest caution, and having stressed the necessity for exercising Tact, Courtesy, and Forbearance, ended by saying that he looked to the Captain to do everything in his power to avoid antagonizing a ruling prince who had always been a loyal supporter of the Raj, and therefore . . .

Ash handed Mulraj five rupees without comment.

The ball was back in his own court, and he realized that he would have to negotiate a settlement without any help from the Political Department—or not for the time being, at all events. If he did so successfully, well and good. If not, then he and he alone would be blamed for bungling it. In short, Captain Pelham-Martyn would be convicted of 'failing to exercise tact, courtesy and forbearance', while the authorities, provided with this useful whipping-boy, would still be able to remain on excellent terms with both Karidkote and Bhithor. It was not a cheerful prospect.

'Heads, they win; tails, I lose,' concluded Ash bitterly.

He spent another sleepless night (there had been too many of them of late) wondering how he could get a message to Juli, and why she had not sent one to him when she could not fail to know how anxious he must be on her behalf. Was it a good sign that she had not done so, or a bad one? If only he knew, it would make it easier for him to hold to his present course. But while he did not, there would always be the fear that if he continued to conduct negotiations with the patience and caution recommended by the Political Officer, the delay might end by destroying Juli.

It was the time-factor that frightened him. By rights the wedding should have taken place within a few days of the brides' arrival in Bhithor, and it had obviously never occurred to Juli—any more than it had to him—that it might not. But already over three weeks had been wasted in fruitless talks, and by now it was almost two months since the night of the sandstorm. If her hopes had been fulfilled and she was pregnant, there would soon be very little chance of the child being accepted as a prematurely born offspring of the Rana's. And should there be any doubt at all on that score, both Juli and the child would die: that much was certain. It would be so easy. No one in authority would ask any questions, for death in childbed was all too common and the news that a junior Rani of Bhithor had died giving birth to a prematurely born infant would occasion no surprise. If only Juli would send him word. She *must* know by now—one way or another . . .

Ash did not close his eyes that night. He had watched the stars move slowly in their spheres and seen them pale in the yellow flush of another dawn, and when the sun was up he set out once more with Mulraj and the others for the city (it was the fourth time that week) to attend a meeting with the Diwan that proved no more fruitful than the preceding ones.

For the fourth successive time they were kept waiting in an anteroom for over an hour, and when they were eventually admitted, it was to no purpose. The situation remained at stalemate, because the Rana was confident that he held the upper hand and had no intention of retreating from what he plainly regarded as an impregnable position. On the contrary, there were signs that he might demand an even larger sum for marrying the 'foreigner's daughter', on the grounds that he would have to pay very highly to be 'purified' by the priests for taking such a woman to wife. The amount thus expended would, hinted the Diwan, be considerable, and in the circumstances the prospective bridegroom's demands could not be regarded as unreasonable.

Ash, replying on behalf of Karidkote, pointed out that all this had been discussed in full over a year ago. Nothing had been concealed, and the settlement that had been reached had been declared satisfactory by both sides. Were they then to conclude that the Rana's emissaries had not, after all, been empowered to speak for him? If so, why had they been sent? And if it was being claimed that they had exceeded their instructions, surely it would have been a simple matter for the Rana, on their return, to arrange for a *tar* (telegram) to be dispatched to Karidkote, breaking off the negotiations until someone more competent to carry out his wishes could be sent to reopen the discussions?—or at the very least, to halt the bridal train before they had travelled too far from the borders of their own state, instead of allowing them to complete the journey. Such conduct, implied Ash, was not compatible with either the dignity or the honour of a prince, and as the expense of the journey had been heavy, there could be no question of waiving the other half of the Princess Shushila's dowry, or of adding anything to the sum already paid on behalf of her half-sister, Anjuli-Bai.

The Diwan replied that he would relay these views to his master, and was sure that the matter would eventually be settled to everyone's satisfaction. And on that all-too-familiar note, the meeting ended.

'I wonder how long they will keep it up?' remarked Ash as they rode back to the camp.

Mulraj shrugged and said morosely: 'Until we give in.'

'Then it looks as though we are going to be here for a long time, because I do not intend to be blackmailed, and the sooner they realize that the better.'

'But what else can we do?' wailed Kaka-ji. 'Perhaps if we were to offer him—'

'Not one anna,' cut in Ash, brusquely interrupting the old man. 'Not one pi. The Rana is going to pay all that he owes. And more— much more.'

Mulraj grinned and said: '*Shabash*, Sahib. Bravely spoken! But may one ask how you mean to bring this about? It is not he, but we who are in a trap. And we cannot rush those forts, even by night.'

'I don't intend to rush anything—least of all the forts. *Or* my fences,' added Ash bitterly. 'No one is going to be able to say that I have acted precipitately or been too impatient. I mean to give the Rana all the time he wants, and see whose patience wears out first: his or mine. Or Bhithor's.'

'Bhithor's?'

'Certainly. Are we not all guests of the state? And as such, why should we pay for our keep? That is surely the privilege of a host. Presently the shopkeepers and the farmers and the cowherds, and all those who supply us with food and fuel and fodder, will demand payment. And they will not get it from us, that I promise you. The Rana and his councillors will soon find that it is costing them far more to keep us here than they bargained for, and after a time they may decide that it would be cheaper to make concessions.'

Mulraj laughed for the first time in several weeks, and the faces of the others cleared.

'*Arré*, that is true,' said Mulraj. 'I had not thought of it. Why, if we stay here long enough, those swindling sons of faithless mothers may even pay us to go away.'

'Or take what they want by force?' suggested Kaka-ji with a pessimistic nod in the direction of the nearest fort. 'Ah yes, Sahib'—here he shook his head at Ash—'I know that you think otherwise, and I wish that I was of your mind. But I cannot feel sure that the Rana will abstain from using violence once he finds that he cannot get what he desires by more peaceful means.'

'By blackmail and bluff, you mean,' retorted Ash. 'But bluff, my father, is a game that two can play at, which is something that these faithless apes have failed to take into account. Well, we will play it with them.'

He refused to be drawn further, for if the truth were known he had nothing in mind except a firm determination to resist the Rana's demands and see that he paid up to the last farthing. For the moment it behoved him to move cautiously, if only to show Major Spiller, the Political Officer, that he had done everything possible in the way of peaceful persuasion, and shown enough patience to arouse envy in Job. Once that point had been made, if the Rana continued to be intransigent then he, Ash, could hardly be blamed if he took more forceful measures to bring the bridegroom's party to their senses. But whatever happened, he must not lose his temper.

This last resolve came close to being broken two days later, when at yet another meeting in the Rung Mahal—convened to discuss 'new proposals'—the Diwan (who had again kept them waiting) announced in a confidential manner and with a great show of regret that as a result of further discussions with the priests on the religious aspect of the Rana's proposed marriage to his bride's half-sister, it had, unhappily, become necessary to ask for still more money in return for this favour. He mentioned a sum that made the previous extortionate demand seem almost paltry by contrast . . .

'These priests they are rapacious,' confessed the Diwan in a resigned, man-of-the-world voice. 'We have reasoned with them, but alas, to no avail. They have now demanded that my master build a new temple as the price of their consent to this marriage. It is iniquitous—but how can he refuse? He is a most religious man, and he cannot go against his priests. Yet to build a temple will cost a great deal of money; so you will see that he has no choice but to ask that His Highness of Karidkote should defray an expense that will have been incurred on behalf of His Highness's half-sister. It is all most unfortunate'—the Diwan wagged a regretful head and spread out his hands in a gesture of rueful deprecation—'but what can I do?'

Ash could think of several things. But the question was plainly rhetorical, and in any case he could not have answered it for the simple reason that he could not trust himself to speak, because it was Juli who was being subjected to insult by these contemptible, smirking blackmailers. He was aware, through a red haze of rage, that Kaka-ji was replying to the Diwan in a gentle, dignified voice; and presently that they were all out in the sunlight once more, mounting their horses and riding away again. But he still had no idea what answer the Diwan had received.

'Well, and what now, Sahib?' inquired Mulraj.

Ash did not reply, and Kaka-ji took up the question, repeating it and demanding to know what they could do in the face of this latest outrage.

Ash came out of his dream and said abruptly: 'I must speak to her.'

The old man stared at him in bewilderment. 'To Shu-shu? But I do not think—'

'To Anjuli-Bai. You must arrange it for me, Rao-Sahib. I must see her. And alone.'

'But that is impossible!' protested Kaka-ji, shocked. 'On the march, yes. There it did not matter too much. But not here in Bhithor. It would be most imprudent and I could not permit it.'

'You will have to,' insisted Ash tersely. 'For unless I do, I will take no further part in these negotiations, but send word to Spiller-Sahib that I can do no more and that he and the Rana must decide the matter between them.'

'But you cannot do that!' gasped Kaka-ji. 'What if he should give way to the Rana for the sake of peace?—which he might well do, as Mulraj has said. We should be undone, for how could we pay such a sum? Even if we had it—which we have not—it would beggar us, and without money we could not make the return journey. Nandu, I know, would never send us any more, for he would be mad with anger and—'

Agitation was making Kaka-ji speak with more frankness than he would normally have dreamt of using in public, and realizing it, he broke off to throw an anguished glance over his shoulder at the four other members of the party, who had fallen behind them, and was relieved to see that they were not only well out of earshot but engaged in an animated conversation of their own.

'Besides,' said Kaka-ji, lowering his voice and returning to his original argument, 'what good can you do by speaking to Anjuli-Bai? There is no way in which she can help us, and to tell her what the Rana has said would only be an unkindness, there being no way out for her or for Shu-shu.'

'All the same, I must see her,' said Ash implacably. 'She has a right to know how things stand. A right to be warned beforehand, in case . . .'

He hesitated, and Mulraj finished the sentence for him: 'In case the Rana refuses to wed her. Yes, I think you are right, Sahib.'

'No,' said Kaka-ji unhappily. 'It is not wise or proper that you should do so; and I cannot think that it is necessary. But as I see that you are both against me in this, I will tell her myself. Will that content you?'

Ash shook his head. 'No, Rao-Sahib, it will not. I must speak to her myself. It is not that I do not trust you, but there are things that I wish to say that you could not. But only you can arrange it.'

'Nay, Sahib. It is impossible. I cannot . . . It would become known. It would be too difficult . . .'

'Nevertheless you will do it for my sake. Because I ask it of you as a great favour. And because, or so I have heard, you and her grandfather, Sergei, were friends, and you knew her mother, who—'

Kaka-ji checked him with an uplifted hand: 'Enough, Sahib. You heard aright. I admired her grandfather the Russian very greatly when I was young. A strange man—a magnificent man—we feared him for his rages as much as we loved him for his laughter; and he laughed often. I have heard that even when he lay dying, he laughed and was not afraid . . .'

Kaka-ji sighed and was silent for a moment or two. And presently he said: 'Very well, Sahib, I will do what I can. But only on one condition. I myself must be present.'

Nothing that Ash could say would make him give way on that point. The old man was convinced that if it should come to the ears of the Rana and his council that Anjuli-Bai had talked alone with a young man who was unrelated to her, they might use it as an excuse to send her back from Bhithor in disgrace—and in all probability portionless as well. They were quite capable of impounding her dowry as 'compensation' for the loss of a bride, and the fact that the young man in question happened to be a Sahib whom the Government had placed in overall charge of the camp and empowered to negotiate the marriage settlements would be neither here nor there. The only factor of importance would be his sex, and a scandal would merely strengthen the Rana's hand and stiffen his attitude on the question of Shushila's bride-price.

'You have nothing to fear,' promised Kaka-ji. 'No word of what passes between you will ever be spoken afterwards by me: I will promise you that. But if by some evil chance news of it were to leak out, my niece must be safeguarded. I must be able to say that I, her uncle—brother to her father who was lately Maharajah of Karidkote —was present throughout. If you cannot agree to that, then I for my part cannot help you.'

Ash looked at him long and thoughtfully, recalling certain rumours he had heard about him, 'old, forgotten, far-off things' that might or might not be true. If they were . . . But there was obviously nothing to be gained by arguing with him now. Kaka-ji had meant what he said and would not go back on it; and as it was going to be impossible to have any speech with Juli without his help, there was nothing for it but to accept his terms. At least he could be trusted to keep his word and hold his tongue.

'I agree,' said Ash.

'Good. Then I will see what can be arranged. But I can make no promises on behalf of my niece. It may be that she may not wish to see you, and if that is so, I can do nothing.'

'You can try to persuade her,' said Ash. 'You can tell her . . . No. Just say that it is necessary, and that I would not have asked it of her—or of you—had it not been.'

Kaka-ji had arranged it. The meeting was to take place in his tent at one o'clock in the morning, at which time all the camp should be asleep. And as Ash would have to find his way there unseen, it would be as well, suggested Kaka-ji, if he disguised himself as a night-watchman, for it could be arranged that the *chowkidar* whose duty it was to patrol that part of the camp would be given a drug that night—something that would send him to sleep for an hour or so.

'Gobind will see to it,' said Kaka-ji; 'and also that no servant of mine is within sight of hearing. He is to be trusted, and it is necessary that I trust someone; but as we cannot be too careful, even he will not know who it is who comes to my tent by night. Now listen carefully, Sahib—'

Ash would have preferred a less complicated arrangement, and could see no reason for such elaborate precautions. But Kaka-ji was adamant, and on the score of secrecy, the meeting could not have gone better. No whisper of it had ever leaked out, and both his niece and the Sahib had come to his tent and left again without attracting any attention or arousing the least suspicion. But in all other respects it had been a sorry failure, and afterwards the old man was often to regret that he had gone back on his original refusal to have anything to do with it; and even more that having done so he had insisted on being present, as but for that he could have remained in happy ignorance of things that he would so much rather not have known.

His niece Anjuli had arrived first, shrouded in a dark cotton bourka and slipping into the tent as silently as a shadow, to be followed a few moments later by a tall, turbaned figure wearing a dingy shawl wrapped high about his mouth and nose in the time-honoured manner of *chowkidars,* who distrust the night air. Kaka-ji noted with approval that following his instructions the Sahib was carrying a night-watchman's *lathi* and the length of chain that is rattled at intervals to warn away evil-doers, and congratulated himself on his attention to detail. Now it only remained for the Sahib to say what he wanted without wasting words, and for Anjuli to refrain from unnecessary comments, and in less than a quarter of an hour the whole thing would be over and the two of them safely back in their own tents without anyone being the wiser.

Buoyed up by a warm feeling of complacency, Kaka-ji made himself comfortable on a pile of cushions and prepared to listen without interruption while the Sahib informed Anjuli of the Rana's demands and their possible consequence to herself.

The old man had been far too preoccupied with the impropriety and hazards of such a meeting to give much thought as to what exactly might be said at it, or why the Sahib should have been so insistent that only he could say it; which was unfortunate for Kaka-ji, as had he done so he might have been better prepared for what followed—or taken strong measures to prevent it altogether. As it was, that pleasant glow of complacency lasted only as long as the time it took Ash to adjust his eyes to the light and make out Anjuli's shrouded figure, standing motionless among the shadows beyond the lamp.

She had not removed her bourka and as its brown folds matched the canvas walls behind her, for a moment or two he did not realize that she was there, though he was aware of Kaka-ji sitting cross-legged and unobtrusive at the far side of the tent. The slight draught of his own entrance had set the pierced bronze lamp swaying, so that it sent a dazzle of golden stars across the walls and floor. The dancing points of light confused his eyes and made the shadows shift and sway and take on a dozen different shapes, and it was not until they steadied again that he saw that one of those shadows was Anjuli.

The sound of a *lathi* and a chain falling to the floor was disproportionately loud in that waiting silence, and though Kaka-ji was not an imaginative man, it seemed to him in that moment as though something vital and elemental quivered between those two silent figures: an emotion so intense as to be almost visible, and that drew them towards each other as irresistibly as a magnet and steel. He watched, rigid, as they moved on the same instant, and as they met, saw Ash put out a hand to lift the bourka and throw it back from Anjuli's face . . .

They neither spoke nor touched each other. They only looked, long and hungrily, and as though looking were enough and there was no one else in the tent, or in the world. And there was that in their faces that made speech unnecessary, for no words and no actions—not even the most passionate of embraces—could have conveyed love so clearly.

Kaka-ji caught his breath and attempted to rise, moved by some hazy notion of throwing himself between them and breaking the spell. But his legs refused to obey him and he was forced to stay where he was, cold with dismay and unable to do anything but stare in stunned disbelief; and when at last the Sahib spoke, to listen with horror.

Ash said softly: 'It's no good, my dear love. You cannot marry him. Even if it were safe for you to do so after so much delay; and that is something you have not told me yet. Would it have been safe?'

Anjuli did not pretend to misunderstand him. She nodded wordlessly: but the small gesture of negation was so desolate that he was ashamed of his own involuntary spasm of relief. He said: 'I'm sorry' —the words caught on a tightness in his throat and sounded dry and inadequate.

'I too,' whispered Anjuli. 'More than I can ever say.' Her lips quivered and she controlled them with a visible effort and bent her head so that her mouth and chin were in shadow: 'Is—is that why you wished to see me?'

'Partly. But there is something else. He does not want you, my Heart. He only agreed to take you because he could not get Shushila on any other terms, and because your brother bribed him to do so with a large sum of money, and asked no bride-price for you.'

'I know'—Anjuli's voice was as quiet as his own. 'I have known it from the first. There are few things that can be kept secret from the Women's Quarter.'

'And you did not mind?'

She raised her head and looked at him dry-eyed, but her lovely mouth was pinched and drawn. 'A little. But what difference does that make? You must know that I was given no choice—and that even if I had been, I should still have come.'

'For Shu-shu's sake. Yes, I know. But now the Rana says that the bribe he accepted from your brother was insufficient, and that unless nearly three times more is paid he will not wed you.'

Her eyes dilated and she put a hand up to her throat, but she did not speak, and Ash said harshly: 'Well, we have not that sum to spare, and even if we had, I could not authorize such payment without instructions from your brother, who from all I hear would never agree to pay it—and rightly. Yet I do not think that he will demand the return of both his sisters. The cost of this journey has been so great that I am very much afraid that when he has thought it over he will decide that it will be wiser in the long run to swallow the affront, and let the Rana's marriage with Shushila take place.'

'And . . . what of me?' asked Juli in a whisper.

'You would be sent back to Karidkote. But without your dowry, which the Rana is certain to claim as compensation for the loss of a bride that he does not want. That is, unless we are prepared to risk bloodshed to prevent him getting his hands on it.'

'But—but he cannot do that,' breathed Anjuli. 'It is against our law.'

'What law? The only law here in Bhithor is the Rana's.'

'I speak of Manu's law, which even he, as a Hindu, must obey. In that law it is laid down that a bride's jewels serve as her *istri-dhan* (inheritance) and may not be taken away from her. It was written by Manu that *"The ornaments which may be worn by women during their husband's life time, his heir shall not divide. Those who divide them shall be outcasts." '*

'But you are not his wife, so he need not regard that law. Nor will he do so,' said Ash grimly.

'But . . . I cannot go back. You *know* I cannot . . . I could not leave Shu-shu.'

'You will have no choice.'

'That is not true.' Her voice rose and she stepped back from him, and said breathlessly: 'The Rana may refuse to wed me, but he will not refuse to let me stay and take care of Shu-shu, as—as a waiting-woman, or an *ayah* if need be. If he keeps my dowry it will surely pay for what little food I eat, even if I should live to be old, and when he sees that unless I stay with her his wife will pine and die, he will be glad to keep me, while as for Nandu, I know very well that he will not want me back, for after this who is there who would wish to marry one whom the Rana of Bhithor has rejected?'

'There is one,' said Ash quietly.

Anjuli's face crumpled like a hurt child's, and she turned sharply away from him and said in a suffocated whisper: 'I know . . . But that cannot be, and therefore . . . you will tell any who ask that I will not go back to Karidkote and that no one can make me do so. And that if I cannot stay in Bhithor as my sister's co-wife, I will stay as her servant. That is all I have to say. Except . . . except to thank you for warning me, and for all . . .'

Her voice failed, and she moved her head in a small, helpless gesture that was more pitiful than words, and with shaking hands began to draw the bourka back into place.

For a moment—for just as long as a tear might take to gather and fall—Ash hesitated. Then he reached out and grasped her shoulders, and snatching away the bourka, pulled her round to face him. The sight of her wet cheeks sent a physical pain through his heart and made him speak with more violence than he had intended:

'Don't be a fool, Juli! Do you imagine for a moment that he will not bed you if you stay here as Shu-shu's servant instead of his wife? Of course he will. Once you are under his roof you will be just as much his property as if he had married you, but without the status of a Rani—or any status at all. He will be able to do exactly as he likes with you, and from what I have seen of him it will probably appeal to his vanity to use the daughter of a Maharajah as a concubine, having rejected her as a wife. Can't you see that your position would be intolerable?'

'It has often been that,' returned Anjuli with more composure. 'Yet I have borne with it. And I can do so again. But Shu-shu—'

'Oh, damn Shu-shu!' interrupted Ash explosively. His grip tightened and he shook her so savagely that her teeth chattered. 'It's no use, Juli. I won't let you. I thought I could, but I hadn't seen him then. You don't know what he's like. He's old—*old*. Oh, not in years, perhaps, but in every other way: in body and face, and in evil. He's rotted with vice. You cannot mate with a creature like that—a hideous, heartless, hairless ape who has shown himself to be without honour or scruples. Do you want to breed monsters? because that is what you'll do: misshapen monsters—and bastards at that. You cannot risk it.'

A spasm of pain contorted Anjuli's wet, tear-streaked face, but her voice was soft and steady and inflexible. 'I must. You know why. Even if you should be right about his vanity, it will surely satisfy him to be able to treat me as a servant without troubling himself to use me as he would a concubine, and my life will not be too unhappy. I shall at least be of help to my sister, whereas back in Karidkote there would be nothing for me: only disgrace and sorrow, for Nandu would vent his anger on me even more than he will on all those who will be returning there.'

'You speak as though you had no other choice,' said Ash. 'But that is not so, and you know it. Oh, my love—my Heart's-delight'—his voice broke—'come away with me. We could be so happy, and there is nothing for you here. Nothing but servitude and humiliation and—no, don't say it, I know that Shushila will be here—but I've told you before that you are wrong about her, that she's a spoilt child who has learned that tears and hysteria will get her almost everything she wants, and so she uses them as weapons, selfishly and ruthlessly to gain her own ends. And she won't even need you after a time, or even miss you—not when she is Rani of Bhithor with a host of women at her beck and call, or when she has children of her own to love and spoil, and play with. And what about me? What if *I* cannot live without you? . . . Shu-shu isn't the only one who needs you, Heart's-dearest—I need you too . . . far more than she does. Oh, Juli—'

The tears were running down Anjuli's cheeks, blinding her eyes and choking her voice so that for a time she could not speak; but she shook her head and presently she said in a broken whisper: 'You told me so before, and I said . . . I said then that you were strong but that Shu-shu is weak, and so . . . so I cannot betray her. And if the Rana is as you say, it will be worse for her. You know that I love you . . . more than anyone . . . more than life . . . But—I love her too; and you are wrong when you say she does not need me. She has always needed me. Now, more than ever. And so I cannot . . . I cannot . . .'

Once again her voice failed her, and Ash realized with a terrible, sick despair that he would have stood more chance if he had lied to her—made her believe that the Rana was handsome and fascinating, and that Shu-shu could not fail to fall madly in love with him and be far better off without any intrusive half-sister making a third in their blissful life together. Had Juli believed that she might have weakened. But the truth had been fatal because it had shown her only too clearly what lay in store for Shushila—for whom there was no prospect of escape. And being Juli, that was enough to stiffen her resolution and make it appear even more necessary, now, to stay and do everything possible to sustain and comfort and encourage the frightened little sister who must marry a monster. He should have known better, and he had not . . .

The realization of failure invaded his brain and body in a cold wave, taking his strength from him, so that his hands relaxed their grip and fell from Anjuli's shoulders and he could only stand and stare at her. She stood before him; tall and slender and lovely in the lamplight. And royal—a princess who would become a waiting-maid . . .

The silence began to fill with little sounds: the flutter of moths about the hanging lamp, the creak of a guy-rope and Anjuli's soft, sobbing breaths; and through them Ash could hear the thumping of his own heart and was surprised to find that it could still beat. Unless it was Juli's heart that he could hear. For an endless interval he studied her drawn face and wide, tear-blurred eyes in a passion of love and pain, until suddenly he could bear it no longer, and reaching out he snatched her into his arms and covered her face with desperate kisses, crushing her to him in the wild hope that physical contact might accomplish what words had failed to do, and break her resistance.

For a time it almost seemed as though he had won. Her arms flew up to circle his neck and he felt her hands pressing the back of his neck while she clung to him with a desperation that equalled his own, and turned up her mouth to meet and return those frantic kisses. Time stopped and stood still for them. They had forgotten Kaka-ji, and everything and everyone else. The world had narrowed down into a charmed and timeless circle in which they were alone together, clinging so closely that it seemed to the old man who watched them that their two figures had merged into one and become a single entity—a flame or a shadow, swayed by an invisible wind . . .

It was Anjuli who broke the spell. Her arms slid down and she leaned back, and forcing her hands between their two bodies, pressed her palms against Ash's breast to push him away from her. And though he could so easily have held her, he did not try to do so. He knew that he was beaten. Shushila's weakness had proved stronger than his love and his own need, and there was nothing left to say. And nothing else he could do, for he had long ago abandoned any idea of abducting Juli—recognizing that even with her consent the chances of success would be minimal and the risks appalling, while without it there could be no chance at all: only the certainty of death for both of them.

He released her and stood back, and watched her stoop to grope blindly for her bourka. Her hands were shaking so badly that she had difficulty in putting it on, and when she had done so she paused for a moment, holding back the voluminous folds from her face, to gaze at him with the terrible concentration of one who looks for the last time at a beloved face before the coffin-lid is closed upon it, as though she were imprinting him on her memory; learning him by heart so that she would never forget a single detail of feature or expression—the colour of his eyes and the slant of his brows, the set of a mouth that could be grave or grim or astonishingly tender, and the deep un-youthful lines that Belinda and George and life and death in the Border country beyond the North-West Frontier had scored on either side of it. The texture of his skin and the single dark lock of hair that habitually fell across his forehead and half hid a jagged, silvery scar that had been made by an Afghan knife—

Ash spoke in a flat, controlled voice: 'If you should ever need me, you have only to send me the luck-charm and I will come. Unless I am dead, I will come.'

'I know,' whispered Anjuli.

'Goodbye—' his voice broke suddenly—'Heart's-beloved—my dear

—my darling. I shall think of you every hour of every day, and be glad that I have known you.'

'And I you. Farewell . . . my lord and my life.'

The brown folds dropped into place and there was only a dark shrouded figure standing in the pool of light under the hanging lamp.

She went past him as noiselessly as a shadow, and he steeled himself to let her go and did not turn his head when he heard the rasp of canvas as she lifted the tent-flap, or when the lamp swayed once more to a faint draught of air and sprayed a shimmer of stars across the walls and ceiling. The flap fell with a soft thud that was, somehow, an unbelievably final sound. The lamp steadied and the stars were still: and Juli had gone.

Ash did not know how long he stood there, staring at nothing and thinking of nothing, because his mind was as empty as his arms—and his heart.

A movement in the shadows and the touch of a hand on his arm aroused him at last, and he turned slowly and saw Kaka-ji standing beside him. There was neither anger nor shock in the old man's face, only sympathy and understanding. And a great sadness.

'I have been blind,' said Kaka-ji quietly. 'Blind and foolish. I should have known that this might happen, and kept you apart. I am truly sorry, my son. But Anjuli has chosen wisely—for both of you, since had she consented to go with you I am very sure that you would both have died. Her brother Nandu is not one to forgive an injury and he would have hunted you to the death, the Rana aiding him, so it is better this way. And in time you will both forget. Being young, you will forget.'

'Did you forget her mother, then?' asked Ash harshly.

Kaka-ji caught his breath and for a fractional moment his fingers bit into Ash's arm: *'How did you—?'* he stopped abruptly.

His hand fell away and he released his breath in a long sigh. His gaze moved past Ash's shoulder to stare into the shadows as though he could see another face there, and his own face softened. 'No,' said Kaka-ji slowly. 'I did not forget. But then I . . . I was no longer a young man. I was already in my middle years when . . . *Chut!* no matter!—I put it away from me. There was no other course. Maybe if I had spoken earlier it would have been different, for her father and I had been friends. But she was younger than my own daughters, and having known her since she was a babe in arms she still seemed a child to me—too young for marriage, like the bud of the moon-flower that will wither unopened if it is plucked. Therefore I did not speak but waited instead for her to become a woman—not realizing that she had already become one. Then one day my brother, hearing rumours of her great beauty, contrived to see her: and seeing her, he loved her—and she him . . .'

Kaka-ji was silent for a space, and then he sighed again, very deeply, and said: 'After their marriage I left the state—my own children being wed—and went on a pilgrimage to the holy places, seeking enlightenment—and forgetfulness, which I did not find. And when at last I returned it was to find that she had died long since, and of a broken heart, leaving a little daughter for whom I could do nothing, because there was now a new Rani in the palace: an evil woman who had usurped that other's place, and by enslaving my brother's heart and bearing him sons had attained great power and influence over him—while I, who had once been close to him, had through my own folly become a stranger and of no account. Wherefore, finding that I could in no way help her child Anjuli, I withdrew to my own estates and seldom visited the court. And though it was urged upon me, I did not take a second wife because . . . because I could not forget *her*. I am now old; but still I cannot forget.'

'Yet you tell me that I shall do so,' said Ash bitterly.

'Ah, but then you, my son, are young, and many years of youth lie before you. It will be easier for you.'

'And what of her?—what of Anjuli? Will it be easier for her?'

Kaka-ji fended off the question with a helpless gesture of his small hands, and Ash said violently: 'You know it will not! Rao-Sahib, *listen* to me—you have just told me that you could do nothing to help her when she was a child, because of Janoo-Rani. But there is no one now who can stop you from helping her if you choose and you have seen enough of that vile creature who calls himself Rana of Bhithor to know what he is like and how little regard he has for honour or promises. No one could blame you, after all that has occurred, if you decided to withdraw from the contract and take both your nieces back to Karidkote.'

'But—but that is not possible,' gasped Kaka-ji, horrified. 'It would be madness. No, no, that I could not do.'

'*Why not?*' urged Ash. 'Who is there to prevent you? Rao-Sahib, I beg of you—for Shushila's sake as well as Anjuli's. No one would blame you. You need only—'

'*No!*' said Kaka-ji loudly. 'It is too late. You do not understand. You do not know Nandu.'

'He cannot be worse than the Rana.'

'You think not? But then as I have said you do not know him. Were we now to return, bringing back his sisters unwed and dowerless, having forfeited all that has already been paid and made ourselves a laughing stock throughout all India, Nandu's vengeance would fall terribly upon all of us. My own life is of little account, but there are others to be thought of: Mulraj and Maldeo Rai, and Suraj Ram and Bagwan Singh also, and many others besides. Even Unpora-Bai—'

'He would not dare kill them,' interrupted Ash impatiently. 'The British Resident—'

'*Bah!*' Kaka-ji's scornful expletive cut him short. 'You Sahib-log think your Raj can do many things that it cannot. Have I said that there would be a public slaying? There would be no need. There are other ways—many others. And even if we did not die, we and our families would forfeit all we had, even to the very roofs over our heads, while as for my nieces . . . who would there be after this who would wish to wed them when their names had become a byword and a jest because of this affair? I tell you, both would find their brother Nandu a crueller jailor than even the Rana of Bhithor, and end by wishing that we had let them be. If you do not believe that, ask Mulraj—ask Maldeo Rai. Either will bear me out. Sahib, what you suggest is not possible. We must make what terms we can with the Rana. That is all we can do.'

'Even though it means letting Anjuli sacrifice herself for the sake of the daughter of an evil woman—your own term, Rao-Sahib—who supplanted her mother and made her childhood a misery?' asked Ash bitterly.

'It is her own choice, my son,' Kaka-ji reminded him, forbearing to take offence. 'And if you think that I who am only her uncle could turn her from it, when you who love her, and whom it would seem that she loves, have failed to do so, then you cannot know her as I do.'

Ash's mouth twisted, and presently he said under his breath: 'I know her: I know her better than . . . anyone. Better even than myself . . .'

'Then you will know that I am right.'

Ash did not answer, but his face spoke for him. And reading that look, Kaka-ji said gently: 'I am sorry, my son: for both of you. But I have no choice—and she has made hers, and will abide by it despite anything you or I could say. The most we can do for her now is to see that she remains here as a wife and not as one of her sister's waiting-women; which the gods know is little enough when both of us have brought her so much sorrow—you by stealing her heart and thereby making the future sadder and more desolate for her, and I by my negligence and folly in permitting you to ride and talk with her, and being blind in that I did not perceive what might—what had —become of it. I am very greatly to blame.'

There was so much pain in the old man's voice that at any other time it must have awoken some response in Ash. But he was spent. His anger had drained out of him, and he was suddenly so tired that he could have dropped where he stood. He could not even think clearly, and though he knew that what Kaka-ji had said was true, and that between them they had done Anjuli a great disservice, his mind could only register the fact that he had made his last throw and lost. He could endure no more that night. Perhaps tomorrow . . . Tomorrow was another day. But a day without Juli—No more Juli for ever and ever. For ever and ever . . . *Amen.*

He turned away without another word, and stumbling out of the tent, made his way back through the silent camp, moving like a sleepwalker.

Maintaining a policy of patience, Ash allowed a full week to go by without making any move to re-open negotiations with the Rana, or to reply to his latest demand.

Messages and gifts of fruit and sweetmeats still arrived daily, and were received with polite expressions of thanks. But neither side suggested a further meeting, and it began to look as though the Rana, too, had decided on a waiting game.

'Having had his say, he is giving us time to realize that he means it. And to make up our minds to pay what he asks,' said Mulraj gloomily. To which Ash retorted that if this was what the Rana thought they were doing, he would soon find out that he was mistaken.

'Maybe,' shrugged Mulraj. 'But how if in the meantime we starve? The country folk and the merchants in the city are, as you foretold, demanding payment, and we have referred them to the Diwan and the council—who have sent them back to us. Now they are refusing to supply us with food-stuffs unless we pay beforehand, and if we do not pay we shall all go hungry, because they will withhold supplies; though the gods be thanked they cannot prevent us from cutting fodder for our animals, and we still have enough cattle and goats to provide a measure of milk and butter for all if we are careful.'

'And enough grain to keep us in bread for some little time,' added Ash with a fleeting grin. 'I have been hoarding it against just such a situation as this. Nevertheless, we will not touch it until we must, as a day may come when we need it more than we do now. Try these Bhithoris with fair words and promises, Mulraj, and see if they cannot be persuaded to give us credit for a little longer. And when they will do so no more, tell them that their bills and their demands must be given to us in writing. We must have written evidence to lay before this Political-Sahib who fears we may not be patient enough.'

'I will do that,' grinned Mulraj. 'When do you mean to ask for another meeting with the Rana or his Diwan?'

'I don't. This time we will wait until they ask us for one. In the meantime let us go out hawking, and while making pretence of searching for game, see if we cannot find some goat-tracks across these hills by which a few men could, if it became necessary, leave the valley unseen. It might come in useful.'

They had not succeeded in finding one, but a few days later the Rana had invited them to another meeting in the city palace, at which the same demands had been made and the same excuses put forward to justify them. These had once again been declared unacceptable, and the delegation from Karidkote had thereupon withdrawn in good order, leaving the position as before.

'Our turn next,' said Ash philosophically. And having allowed several days to elapse he requested a further audience with the Rana, and early in the following week presented himself at the Rung Mahal to argue the case all over again, though with no better results. After that there followed a short lull in the negotiations, and then as Bhithor appeared content to leave the initiative to Karidkote and the visitors were finding it increasingly difficult to obtain supplies on credit, Ash changed his tactics and took to calling daily at the palace to confer with the Rana, or if the Rana would not see him, with the Diwan, to press for more reasonable terms. He had even (with one eye on the Political Officer) offered a few small concessions, in order to avoid any future accusations by that gentleman and his department of inflexibility or of having made no attempt at bargaining or compromise. But the result of these efforts had, predictably, merely served to convince the Rana that the opposition was weakening, and that he had only to stand firm to have all his demands met.

This conviction was shared by his Diwan, who had actually had the temerity to hint that if his royal master's terms were not accepted soon, he might well reconsider them. The inference being that the price would go up, though Ash had affected to misunderstand him and observed gravely that he sincerely hoped so, as it was high time that he returned to Rawalpindi and his military duties. Which was true enough.

The double wedding had originally been planned for early spring, and even though the journey from Karidkote had taken longer than expected, it could still have taken place before the worst of the hot weather was upon them and the temperature was still tolerable. But six weeks having passed since the great bridal camp had pitched its tents in the valley, the hot weather was by now in full blast and the camping ground had become an inferno of heat and dust and flies, in which men and animals sweltered and suffered together. A scorching wind blew all day from dawn to dusk, stirring up the dust and setting every piece of canvas and every shred of rope flapping, thrumming and clattering so that there was never a moment of silence, and when it died at night-fall the dark hours were filled with the maddening drone of mosquitoes, the ululations of jackals and the yelping of pariah dogs who prowled between the tents in search of scraps.

Had it not been for the lake and the fact that the prevailing wind, blowing in from that direction, was several degrees cooler than in many parts of Rajputana, the situation of those in the camp would have been intolerable. As it was, it could be endured—though that was the most that anyone could say of it—and at least the wind helped to keep the flies at bay and enabled the more important personages in the camp to obtain a degree of comfort by the use of *kus-kus* tatties: thick mats of woven roots that were hung in the entrances of the tents, and kept drenched with water so that the wind passing through them blew cool and refreshing. But for those without tents or tatties it was an abominable time. More especially as all in the camp were hill-men and unused to temperatures that dwellers in Rajputana accepted as a matter of course.

'How much longer can we hold out?' groaned Kaka-ji, who was suffering an attack of acute depression.

The old man was looking as shrivelled and unhappy as a new-born monkey, for the wind blowing through the *kus-kus* tatties had given him a chill on the liver, and besides, he had much on his mind—and on his conscience.

'Do not fret yourself, Rao-Sahib,' said Ash. 'If all goes well, it should not be long before you and all in your charge will be installed in one of the guest-houses on the lake, where you will be able to live in more coolness and comfort.'

'*If*,' repeated Kaka-ji pessimistically. 'Yet I see no sign of the Rana relenting, and very soon now we may find ourselves short of water. Should the stream dry up—and my servants tell me that it is shrinking daily—what then? Are we to suffer thirst as well as hunger?'

'The stream will not dry up. It is fed by springs in the hills as well as by the lake, and though the lake is low, it is still deep and wide. Nevertheless it is time that we took action, for by now I do not believe that even the Political Agent-Sahib could accuse me of showing a lack of patience. We will speak with the Rana again tomorrow and see if his heart—if he has one—has changed.'

'You will find that it has not,' grunted Mulraj. 'Why waste our breath and our time?'

'In *Belait*,' said Ash, with a shrug, 'they have a saying, "If at first you don't succeed, try, try again".'

'*Bah!* We have tried a score of times—two score,' returned Mulraj disgustedly. '*Hai mai,* but I grow weary of this business.'

Nevertheless, on the morrow they had ridden yet again to the city —they were becoming all too familiar with that road—and after being kept waiting for an even longer time than usual, embarked on the same wearisome round of argument, with the same lack of success. But this time Ash had asked for the Rana's demands to be put in writing, in order, so he said, to cover himself (should he accede to them) in case His Highness the Maharajah of Karidkote, or the British authorities, refused to believe that they had actually been made, and suspected him of inventing the story to cover the fact that he and the other members of his party had misappropriated the additional sum and divided it among themselves.

'Unless we can show proof that such a sum was demanded of us, we dare not even consider paying it,' explained Ash. 'That is our difficulty, and you will, I am sure, understand that speaking for my companions, it would be as much as their lives were worth to return to Karidkote with nothing to support their word that they had expended this money on His Highness's behalf. I myself might be in great trouble with my superiors, so I would ask . . .'

To the Rana and his Diwan (and his entire council for that matter) such a request seemed perfectly sensible. Had the position been reversed, they themselves would certainly have reasoned along the same lines and taken similar steps to cover themselves, so what more natural than that the Maharajah and the Foreign and Political Department should, in their wrath, suspect the Sahib and his associates of theft and falsehood when they confessed to having parted with a sum greatly in excess of the agreed price? The Rana, scenting victory, had instantly agreed to furnish the Sahib with a written statement of his demands, and had even, at Ash's request, graciously appended his own thumbprint as proof that the document was not a forgery.

Ash read it over carefully, and having stowed it away in the inner breast pocket of his coat, thanked the Rana for his kindness with a cordiality that was, for once, quite genuine, though the Rana was wrong in supposing that it was a hopeful sign and an indication that the delegation from the camp had at last decided that they had no alternative but to capitulate to his demands.

'Well, and what have we gained by that?' inquired Mulraj as they rode out side by side through the Elephant Gate—Kaka-ji had not accompanied them that day, being confined to his bed with a chill.

'Proof,' replied Ash, slapping his breast pocket. 'This goes tonight with a covering letter to Spiller-Sahib, the Political Officer. And as soon as I am sure that he has received it, we will pull the Rana's nose. Even Spiller-Sahib cannot regard such an outrageous example of blackmail as something to be excused and given in to.'

The covering letter was written within the hour, and because Ash was angry and in haste, it was not as tactfully phrased as it might have been. Its curt sentences, while not actually rude, gave an impression of barely concealed irritation with official bumbling that was to cause deep offence and lead to unforeseen repercussions. But Ash did not know that.

Having finished it, he enclosed it in a sealed envelope, together with the paper setting out the Rana's demands, and once again accompanied the messenger to the frontier and set him on his way. Though this was probably an unnecessary precaution, since it would seem only natural to the Rana that the Sahib should send word to the Political Officer as a preliminary to capitulation, and it was therefore unlikely that on this occasion at least there would have been any attempt to prevent the messenger getting through. All the same, Ash preferred to take no chances, and he had watched the man ride away, and waited until he could see him no longer before turning back.

He knew very well that the action he had in mind was no more than a bluff, and that if it failed in its effect the result might be a disaster. But it was a gamble he had to take, the only alternative being to abandon Juli to the fate that must befall her if she were to be left behind in Bhithor unwed, and with no rights or privileges beyond those of any other waiting-woman in the Women's Quarters of the Rung Mahal. That was not to be thought of, for appalling as it was to leave her there at all, to leave her in such circumstances would be beyond all bearing, and he would do all in his power to ensure that she stayed as a Rani of Bhithor. That was the most he could do for her now.

He waited two days to give his messenger time to reach the Political Officer, and on the third day requested yet another audience, in order to warn the Rana not to cherish false hopes and give him one last chance to change his mind. The request having been granted, Ash rode to the Rung Mahal accompanied only by Mulraj and a small escort, and was received in a private room in the palace by the Rana and half-a-dozen of his councillors, and a few favourite courtiers.

The interview had been a short one: apart from the usual exchange of courtesies Ash had only spoken twice and the Rana once, and both had confined themselves to a few words. Ash had inquired if the Rana had reconsidered his demands, and was prepared to accept the terms that had originally been agreed upon in Karidkote by his representatives and His Highness the Maharajah, and the Rana had replied, in effect, that he had no intention of doing so, and in fact considered his demands to be not only just but exceedingly reasonable. His tone was insolent, and when his evil-genius prompted him to smile, the watching councillors, taking their cue, grinned appreciatively while one or two of the more sycophantic courtiers sniggered audibly. But it was to be the last time that any of them smiled that morning.

'In that case,' announced Ash curtly, 'we have no alternative but to remove our camp and refer the whole matter to the Government of India. Good-day, Rana-Sahib.'

He bowed briefly, and turning on his heel, left the room.

Mulraj followed, looking resigned; but they had not gone far when they were overtaken by a breathless councillor who brought a message from the Diwan. The Diwan, said the councillor, urgently desired to speak with them in private, and begged that they would grant him a few moments of their time. There being nothing to be gained by a refusal, they had turned back to find the Rana's Prime Minister waiting for them in a small ante-room near the one that they had left so unceremoniously a few moments before.

The Diwan was full of apologies for what he professed to regard as 'an unfortunate misunderstanding', and he had pressed refreshments on them, talking volubly the while. But it soon became clear that he had nothing new to offer in the way of concessions; or, for that matter, to add to the endless—and unconvincing—excuses that he had made before on the Rana's behalf. He had merely retraced his steps over the same ground that had already been covered to exhaustion during the past weeks, repeating the same arguments in support of his master's claims, until at last Ash's small remaining stock of patience had given out, and he had cut through the spate of words with the brusque announcement that if the Diwan had something fresh to offer they were prepared to listen. If not, they were merely wasting their time as well as his, and would bid him goodbye.

The Diwan seemed loth to let them go, but they were not prepared to wait any longer, and after further and protracted expressions of regret he had personally accompanied them as far as the gate into the outer courtyard, where he stayed talking to them while a servant was sent to fetch their horses and their escort, who were being entertained by men of the palace guard. It was therefore almost an hour after quitting the Rana's presence that they finally left the Rung Mahal, and as they rode out past the sentries, Mulraj said meditatively: 'Now what was the purpose of all that? The old villain had nothing to say, and this is the first time that my men have ever been offered hospitality by the guard at the palace. What do you suppose they hoped to gain?'

'Time,' said Ash succinctly.

'That much is clear. The old fox held us in talk for the best part of an hour, and then that servant took so long to fetch our men and our horses that it would not have surprised me to learn he had fallen asleep by the way. They wished to delay our departure—and they succeeded. But why? For what purpose?'

They had learned it within ten minutes of leaving the city.

The Rana had acted with considerable speed, for the twin forts that earlier that day had been garrisoned by no more than a handful of sentries were now manned by scores of artillery men who swarmed on the battlements and stood ready by their guns, a sight that the delegation from Karidkote, riding back to their camp, could not fail to take note of, and that must bring home to them the vulnerability and helplessness of their own position when faced with this threat of force.

The camp had already taken note, and anxious groups of men, who would normally have been taking an afternoon siesta in the shade, were standing about in the blinding sunlight to stare at the forts and speculate uneasily as to the reason for this ominous show of force. A dozen explanations, each one more alarming than the next, were in circulation among the tents, and presently a rumour arose that the Rana was about to open fire on the camp with the intention of killing everyone in it, so that he might seize the money and valuables that had been brought from Karidkote.

By the time Ash and Mulraj returned, panic had spread with the speed of a whirlwind, and only drastic action on the part of Mulraj, who set the pick of his troops to keep order with lances, musket butts and *lathis,* had averted a riot. But there was no denying that the situation looked exceedingly ugly, and within an hour of his return Ash had dispatched yet another message to the palace, requesting an audience on the following day—this time in public durbar.

'Why send so swiftly?' raged Mulraj, who, had he been consulted, would have preferred to save face by ignoring the threat for as long as possible. 'Could we not have waited at least until the morrow before begging that—that *dagabazik* (cheat, trickster) for an audience? Now everyone will think that his guns have thrown us into such terror that we dared not waste a moment for fear that he should loose them upon us.'

'Then they are due for a disappointment,' snapped Ash, whose hold on his temper was hourly becoming more precarious. 'They can think what they choose. But we have already wasted too many moments, and I do not intend to waste any more.'

'That would be good hearing,' sighed Kaka-ji, 'if only there was anything we could say to the Rana. But what is there left to say?'

'A good deal that should have been said long ago, had I had my way,' returned Ash shortly. 'And I trust that you will feel strong enough to accompany us tomorrow, Rao-Sahib, so that you too may hear it.'

They had all accompanied him: not only Kaka-ji, but all those who had attended the first durbar. And this time they had been required to present themselves at the city palace in the late afternoon. They had gone there dressed in their glittering best and escorted by thirty splendidly uniformed lancers. And despite the fact that the thermometer in his tent still registered 109 degrees, Ash himself had donned the fullest of full dress to ride with them through the sultry heat to the Rung Mahal, where they had been met by a minor official and conducted to the Hall of Public Audience. Here, as once before, they found the entire court awaiting them, seated in serried ranks between the painted arches.

Today the outer arches on the windward side were closed by *kus-kus* tatties and those on the opposite side by split-cane *chiks,* which while helping to reduce the temperature to something approaching coolness, filled the *Diwan-i-Am* with a shadowy gloom that seemed even deeper by contrast with the brightness outside. But even the combination of shadows and the low sunlight of the waning afternoon did not prevent Ash from seeing that every face in that crowded assembly room wore an expression of smug anticipation that was, in some cases, tinged with derision, and it was immediately clear to him that they were confidently expecting to witness the public humiliation of the emissaries from Karidkote and the foolish young Sahib who was their spokesman, and to enjoy the skill with which their crafty ruler had played his cards and out-witted his hapless guests. It was a pity, thought Ash sardonically, that they were to be disappointed on both counts. And dispensing with the accepted preliminaries of debate—the polite greetings, the compliments and the hollow expressions of mutual esteem and good-will that wasted so much time—he came straight to the point.

'I have noticed,' said Ash, addressing the Rana in a voice that none present had ever heard him use before, 'that Your Highness has seen fit to man all three forts that command the valley. For which reason I desired this meeting, so that I might inform you, in public durbar, that if so much as one of the guns that are trained upon our camp should be fired, your state will be taken over by the Government of India and you yourself will be deposed and sent away to spend the remainder of your life in exile. I will also inform you that I intend to strike camp and remove to our first site, outside the valley, where we shall remain until you are prepared to come to terms with us. *Our* terms. That is all I have to say.'

The grim certainty of his own voice surprised him, for his mouth was dry and he had, in fact, no confidence whatsoever in the Government's willingness to take such action—or indeed, give him any support. They were, he thought, more likely to reprimand him for making unauthorized threats in their name and 'exceeding his instructions'. But then the present company was not to know that. The Diwan's jaw had dropped and the Rana's face was a study in shock. And of a sudden it seemed as if every man in those close-packed ranks of men had caught his breath and was holding it; for though the wind still whined through the *kus-kus* tatties and rattled the swaying *chiks* with a maddening, monotonous tattoo, there was no other sound under the painted arches. Noting this, Ash realized that any further discussion could, at this point, rob the threat of half its effect, so without giving the Rana time to reply, he collected his own party with a jerk of the head and stalked out of the *Diwan-i-Am,* the jingle of his spurs and the clank of his sword sharply audible in the stunned silence.

This time no one had been sent hurrying after them, and there had been no attempt to delay their departure. The escort and their horses had been ready and waiting for them, and they had mounted without any words of farewell and clattered out of the courtyard and back through streets that were full of strolling citizens come out to 'eat the evening air'.

Kaka-ji had been the first to speak, but only after they were safely through the city gate and riding down the valley into the eye of the setting sun, and even then he had lowered his voice as though he were afraid of being overheard:

'Is it true, Sahib, what you told the Rana? Will the Sirkar (Government) indeed dispossess him if he uses his guns upon us?'

'I do not know,' confessed Ash with a wry grin. 'They should. But then one cannot tell how the affair would be reported to them, for how many of us would be left alive to tell the true tale? However, all that matters now is whether the Rana himself believes that they would do so; and that is something we shall find out as soon as we start moving off.'

'So you do mean us to move?' said Mulraj. 'When?'

'Now. At once. While they in the palace are still afraid that I may have spoken no more than the truth. We must be out of this valley and beyond the reach of those forts before the sun rises again.'

'But will that not be too great a risk?' demurred Kaka-ji, alarmed. 'What if they should fire upon us when they see us preparing to leave?'

'They will not do so while there is the least doubt in their minds as to how the Government may react; which is why we must not lose a moment, but move immediately, while they are still debating it. If there is a risk, it is one that we must take because there is nothing else we can do except give in and let the Rana have everything he asks. And that I will not consider. We march within the hour.'

'It will not be easy to move by night,' observed Mulraj, squinting at the setting sun. 'There is no moon.'

'All the better. To fire in the darkness at a moving target will not be easy either; also it might mean the destruction of much treasure—and perhaps of the brides also. Besides, in this heat a night march will at least be cooler than moving by day.'

By the time they reached the camp half the valley was in shadow and the wind had fallen with the approach of sunset. Cooking fires were already being lighted and smoke hung in the still air like a long scarf of grey gauze, spanning the valley floor and touching the flanks of the hills that hemmed it in on either side. Sunlight still lay along the heights, and its rays seemed to be concentrated on the sandstone walls of the nearest fort, turning them to burnished gold and striking blinding glints from bronze cannon and the barrels of muskets.

The opposite fort was only a dark violet shape against the evening sky, but its crouching bulk was no less menacing, and Ash felt a shiver run down his spine as he looked up at it. Supposing . . . just supposing he was wrong, and that his bluff had not deceived the Rana? Well, it was too late to worry about that now; and as he had told Kaka-ji, they would soon find out. He gave orders for the camp to be struck, and went off to change his uniform for clothing more suited to the work that lay ahead.

With less than an hour-and-a-half of daylight left, few men had found time for an evening meal, and those who had, had eaten it standing, the threat presented by the manning of the forts having been clear to all of them. They were as eager to quit the valley as Ash himself, and not only had no one queried the order to march or raised any objection on the score of short notice and the difficulties involved, but every man, woman and child had set to with feverish speed and worked with such a will that dusk had barely fallen when the first laden cart moved off towards the gorge, preceded by a picked band of cavalry.

By midnight the tail-end of the long column marched out, leaving the cooking fires still burning, as Ash had given orders that the fires were to be left to die out untouched so that watchers in the forts would be uncertain as to how many men had moved, and how many remained behind. The marchers themselves had been forbidden to carry lights, and seen from above and by starlight, they would be almost invisible, for as they plodded forward, the dust that rose up under their feet and made the going a torment served to screen them from view more effectively than anything else could have done, and made it difficult to guess at the numbers involved.

To Ash, riding in the thick of the press, the noise of their progress seemed appallingly loud; for though no one spoke except to give an order or urge on a reluctant animal—and then only in an undertone—

there were many other sounds that could not be avoided: the creak of wheels and the crack of whips, the tread of innumerable feet, the click of hooves and the jingle of harness, the wails of children and the grunts, squeals and grumbles of cattle, sheep, camels, horses and elephants. Not to mention a continual yapping from the horde of pi-dogs that had attached themselves to the camp and could not be persuaded to leave it.

Ash consoled himself with the reflection that deafening as it might sound at close quarters, from half a mile away even this amount of noise would be inaudible, and in any case there had never been any question of keeping the Rana's men in ignorance of the move. He had told them himself what he meant to do. All the same, he preferred to keep them guessing as to how long such an operation would take, for, if they under-estimated the speed with which it could be done, and were expecting to find at least two thirds of the camp still in the valley by morning, it might discourage them from taking any precipitate action that night. The critical part of the affair was going to be the passage through the gorge, for there progress was bound to be slow, and the fort that stood guard over it was over-close. He wondered how soon he would reach it and whether the small force that Mulraj had sent to lead the way had already done so, and were safely through it. And where Juli was . . .

He had seen the *ruth* move off, surrounded three-deep by an escort of armed guards and preceded and followed by a detachment of cavalry, together with the covered carts bearing the brides' women, servants and personal effects. Mulraj and Kaka-ji had ridden alongside it, and Jhoti had travelled with his sisters. Ash had seen the boy's excited face by the smoky light of a hurricane lamp as he climbed into the *ruth,* but the brides had been no more than a fleeting glimpse of two shrouded figures, indistinguishable from their women; and but for the fact that one of them was taller than the other he would not even have known which was Juli. A moment later the escort had closed about them and the *ruth* had jolted off into the darkness, and he could not even ride within sight of it. The most he had been able to do was to arrange that if the forts opened fire, or if it should come to a fight (as it would do if the Rana's soldiers attempted to close the gorge road), Juli, Shushila and Jhoti were to be snatched out of the mêlée by Mulraj and a small band of horsemen, who would circle back and attempt to find their way out across the hills, while he himself remained behind to cover their retreat and deal with the Rana in the morning.

It was a sketchy plan and far from foolproof. But if the worst came to the worst it would have to be tried, and Ash could only hope that it would not come to that; for though he and Mulraj had searched diligently during the past weeks, the only paths they had found among the hills were goat tracks that wandered aimlessly between outcrops of rock on the steep, grassy slopes, and appeared to lead nowhere. But there was no profit in worrying about that either. The die had been cast and by now the matter was out of his hands. There was nothing else he could do—except pray that he had convinced the Rana that any attempt at force would be fatal.

'If it does come to a fight,' thought Ash, 'there will be no wedding. They couldn't go ahead with it after that . . . Even Nandu would not consider doing so. Nor could the Government overlook such a thing—they'd have to take *some* action, even if they didn't actually take over the state . . . perhaps appoint another ruler, and see that Nandu was repaid some if not all of what he has spent on this sorry business . . . I ought not to have interfered. I should have left well alone, and then Juli would have . . .'

But he knew that he could not have done anything else. He could not have disregarded his orders and stood aside, leaving the bargaining and the decisions to Kaka-ji and his compatriots who would have been forced in the end to pay the blackmailer in full—as well as forfeiting Anjuli's dowry and leaving her behind, unwed. All the same he found himself listening for the sounds of battle and half hoping that the Rana's soldiers would deny them passage through the gorge, for a fight was the only thing that would put an end to any further talk of a wedding. Yet if it came to fighting, men would die. Probably a great many of them . . .

Ash was suddenly filled with a sick disgust of himself. Had he really fallen so low as to contemplate, even for a moment, the death of men he knew and liked, men in whose company he had travelled southward all the long way to Bhithor, merely because their deaths might help him achieve a purely personal desire? Juli, he knew, would never dream of buying happiness at such a price. And neither could he. With that thought it was as though she moved quietly away from him, as she had done when she left Kaka-ji's tent. The night noises ceased to whisper her name or the dust to hold a scent of roses, and as his mind emptied of her, he could listen once more to the many sounds about him with his ears alert to catch the crack of a distant musket.

It was no longer necessary to fear the cannon in the two forts behind him. If their crews had been going to open fire they would have done so before now, instead of waiting until the camp had moved out of range. The real danger lay ahead in the short half-mile of track that wound through the gorge below the third fort, where it would be only too easy to entrap a large part of the column, leaving all those who had not yet entered it with no alternative but to turn and retreat back into the larger trap of the valley.

'If they attack us there,' thought Ash, 'we are finished.'

But the threat of annexation and exile had destroyed the Rana's confidence. It did not occur to him that the Sahib could have spoken in that fashion on his own authority and without a shadow of official support. He presumed that the Sahib must be speaking as the mouthpiece of the Political Officer, who was himself the mouthpiece of the Raj; and he also knew that there had been many precedents for such action. Too many to allow him to count on the fact that as these had occurred in the days before the great uprising, when the East India Company ruled the land, they would not occur again under a Raj headed by a Viceroy representing the Padishah Victoria herself. If in the past such princely states as the great Kingdom of Oudh could be annexed, how could he be sure that a similar fate could not befall his own, which was small and by no means powerful? The Rana and his councillors had quailed at the thought, and urgent messages had been dispatched to the commanders of the forts, ordering them to abstain from any action that could possibly be construed as hostile.

The bridal camp passed unmolested through the gorge, and by the time the sun rose it was busily setting up tents and lighting new cooking fires on the old site, well out of range of the fort and in a position to defend itself against attack or, if necessary, to retreat over the border.

'Now let those sons of jackals try to threaten us,' said Mulraj viciously. '*Arré!* but I am weary. I am not a fearful man, and the gods know I would fight with the best against any odds in open battle. But I tell you, Sahib, I died a thousand deaths last night as we crept through that gorge in the darkness, knowing the slaughter that a mere handful of men on the cliffs above could have wrought on us, and expecting every moment to see the cannons speak and hear armed men pouring down to attack us. Ah well, it is over: we have broken out of the trap. But what happens now?'

'That is up to the Rana,' said Ash. 'We shall wait and see what he will do. But I am inclined to think that we shall have no further trouble from him and that he will pretend that it has all been . . . what was it the Diwan said? . . . "an unfortunate misunderstanding". Tomorrow, or perhaps today, he will send us a deputation bringing gifts and soothing messages, so we had better take what rest we can before they arrive. How is young Jhoti?'

'Asleep. And sadly disappointed in the Rana. He had been hoping that there would be a great battle.'

'Blood-thirsty brat,' commented Ash sourly. And added that he hoped the boy's uncle was also asleep, as the old man had had a great deal to put up with of late, and the events of the previous night must have tried him sorely.

'That is so,' agreed Mulraj, 'but it would take more than the discomforts of a night march to keep the Rao-Sahib from his prayers. He performs his *pujah,* and only when that is finished will he rest. As for myself, being less devout, I shall follow the young prince's example and take what sleep I can before these Bhithoris descend upon us with lies and excuses and false expressions of good-will.'

'And apologies also, one hopes—though I doubt that. But there is no need for us to break our rest for them. They have kept us waiting often enough and it will do them and their misbegotten ape of a Rana no harm to get a taste of their own medicine.'

'Oho! *Sahib ka mizaj aj bahut garum hai,*' quoted Mulraj with a grin, repeating a comment he had heard Gul Baz make in a muttered aside to Ash's syce.

'So would you be in a bad temper,' retorted Ash hotly, 'if you'd had to—' He broke off and laughed a trifle ashamedly: 'You are right. I'm in a foul mood, and at the moment I'd enjoy murdering the lot of them—starting with the Rana. The thought of having to pretend that all the insults and chicanery that we have been subjected to are forgiven and forgotten, and that the wedding can take place as though nothing had happened, sticks in my gullet, and when I think that . . . I'm sorry. I'd better get some sleep myself or I shall be in no fit state to conduct any further talks with anyone. Go on, get to your bed. *So-jana, bai,* and may your dreams be auspicious.'

He watched Mulraj walk tiredly away and was aware that he himself was tired beyond reason, not only physically but mentally—so tired that suddenly he could not feel angry any more. His anger, together with all the fears and hopes that had tormented him for so long, seemed to have drained out of him, leaving behind a vast emptiness. He had done all that he could for Juli. And also, which was ironical, for Nandu: he had saved Nandu's pride and his purse, together with Juli's honour, and (for what it was worth) the reputations of the Rana, the Political Officer and Captain Pelham-Martyn of the Guides. And none of it meant anything any more . . .

Ash turned and went into his tent, and a few minutes later the anxious Mahdoo, hastening in with a scalding cup of tea, found him stretched out on the camp bed, fully clothed and so deeply asleep that he did no more than grunt when Mahdoo and Gul Baz eased him out of his coat and riding boots before closing the tent-flap against the dazzle of the rising sun.

He was riding headlong across a stony plain that was bounded by
low, barren hills, and Anjuli was on the crupper behind him, clinging
to him and urging him to ride faster—faster. He could not see the
horsemen racing in pursuit, for when he looked back her unbound
hair, streaming out on the wind like a silken scarf, impeded his view.
But he could hear the thunder of galloping hoof-beats drawing nearer
and nearer, and he laughed because Juli's arms were about him and
nothing and no one could harm them as long as they were together.
And then suddenly he realized that the silken scarf was not black but
yellow, and he looked over his shoulder and saw with horror that it
was not Juli at all, but a silly simpering girl with blue eyes and blond
ringlets who pouted at him and said: 'Do hurry, Ashton. I don't
want Papa to catch us.' Belinda!—he had eloped with Belinda, and
now he would have to marry her and be saddled with her for the rest
of his life. For ever and always . . .

'No. Oh no,' cried Ash. And woke, sweating and shuddering, to
find Mahdoo bending over him and his tent once more lit by an oil
lamp. He had slept the clock round, and the messengers from the
Rana, who had arrived in the course of the morning, were still waiting to speak to him.

'The Sirdar Mulraj gave orders that neither you nor he were to be
disturbed,' said Mahdoo, 'but the Sirdar is still sleeping, and now the
Rao-Sahib sends to know what is to be done with them and whether
arrangements should be made for them to spend the night here.'

'Why here?' asked Ash, puzzled. His mind was still clouded with
the aftermath of nightmare and he was feeling absurdly shaken and
not yet fully awake.

'Because the hour is late, and the road to the city is a rough one in
the darkness,' explained Mahdoo.

Ash shook himself like a dog coming out of water, and his eyes
became focused and aware. He said shortly: 'That last we have good
reason to know. But if we could travel it, so can they. If the Rao-
Sahib's servant is without, I will speak to him. Call him.'

Mahdoo did so, and Kaka-ji's elderly major-domo entered and
salaamed.

'Tell the Rao-Sahib,' said Ash, 'that there is no reason why he should put himself out to offer hospitality to these people, and that I myself will send word to them that we much regret our inability to offer them any accommodation for the night, but owing to our own lack of sleep we have not yet had time to set our camp in order. So I suggest they now return to the city and visit us again tomorrow; or preferably the next day, when we shall be in a better state to receive them.'

He had done precisely that, and the Rana's envoys rode back to Bhithor by starlight in an extremely anxious frame of mind, having all wasted the greater part of a day without having been able to see or speak to a single person of consequence, or make any of the fulsome and placatory speeches they had been charged to deliver. At an early hour next morning they reported on the failure of their mission to the Diwan, who not unnaturally regarded this as proof positive that the Sahib was acting with the full approval of the Government of India—for otherwise how would he have dared to behave in this manner? The Rana fully agreed with this view, and after another urgent meeting with his councillors ordered the dispatch of large supplies of grain, fruit and fresh vegetables to the camp, as a personal gift from himself and a gesture of good-will from the citizens of Bhithor.

The arrival of these provisions relieved Ash of a major source of anxiety, for the stocks he had managed to hoard would not have lasted long, and had there been no way of augmenting them, the camp would have been forced to leave Bhithor and risk the possibility of not being invited to return, which would have spelt disaster for Karidkote. The long line of heavily laden carts that rumbled into the camp not only banished that fear, but showed that the Rana had lost his nerve and was metaphorically waving a white flag.

There had been no deputation from the palace that day, but on the following one the Diwan himself, accompanied by a number of senior councillors and nobles, had ridden into the camp and been received with all ceremony. It was immediately plain that there were to be no explanations or apologies, but that all the unpleasantness of the preceding weeks was to be treated as though it had never occurred. The Diwan had even managed to infer that any delay over the negotiations was only due to the fact that the Rana's family priest had not been in agreement with the priests of the city temple on the matter of an auspicious date for the wedding. But as this difficulty had at last been resolved, it remained only for the brides' relatives to choose which of two selected dates (both equally propitious) they preferred and the arrangements for the ceremony would at once be put in train.

No one on either side had made any reference to previous disagreements, and the talks had been conducted in an atmosphere of cordiality and sweet reason that could hardly have been exceeded among a band of bosom-friends. The Diwan had concluded by saying that the state guest-houses, together with the Moti Mahal, the Pearl Palace, were at the disposal of the brides and their entourage, and it was hoped that they would take up residence there at the earliest opportunity.

By now the entire camp had learned to place no trust in the Rana, and the thought of what he might do if he were allowed to gain possession of so many valuable hostages could not be avoided. Nevertheless, the offer had been accepted; largely because Ash considered that the danger was past and there would be no further attempts at blackmail or intimidation, but also because the Pearl Palace, and all three guest-houses, stood in the Ram Bagh, a large park on the banks of the lake and over a mile beyond the city.

'The Ram Bagh,' said Ash, 'has a wall about it. A high and well-built wall that we could defend if these faithless Bhithoris tried any further tricks. It is also shielded from the forts by the city, so that there will be no threat from their cannon, and we'll leave a third of our forces here, allowing it to be known that should any further "misunderstandings" occur, they have orders to fight their way out across the border and carry a full report of the matter to the Government. Yes, I think we may safely accept the offer.'

Kaka-ji and the elders had agreed, and after consulting his priest, Kaka-ji had declared in favour of the second of the two dates. That having been settled, two thirds of the camp had moved back through the gorge again, and marching down the length of the valley, had skirted the city and taken up residence in the royal park; the brides with their brother and uncle and their women in a little white marble palace on the lake's edge, Ash and Mulraj and other senior personages in the guest-houses, and the remainder in tents pitched under the shade of mango, neem and gold *mohur* trees.

The change was a welcome one, for now that the *louh* was failing the park was an infinitely cooler and more comfortable spot than the valley or the country beyond the gorge. Both palace and guest-houses were plentifully supplied with punkahs and *kus-kus* tatties, and what little breeze there was blew in off the lake and made the nights pleasant and the days far from intolerable. Nor could any fault be found with the behaviour of the Rana and his subjects, who now combined to see that the visitors lacked nothing. The Rana, with unexpected generosity, had actually decreed that the park was to be regarded as Karidkote territory for a period of six weeks, so that the brides' relatives and friends could look upon it as their home and, in effect, invite the *barat*—the bridegroom's party—to attend the wedding there.

'A truly thoughtful and courteous gesture,' approved Kaka-ji, adding hopefully that it showed the Rana had good qualities as well as bad ones, and possibly he had been influenced of late by evil advisers whom he had now found out and dismissed. 'It may be that in future he will be more just in his dealings,' said Kaka-ji. 'We must believe that this is so.'

Ash did not believe anything of the sort, but he could see no point in saying so. The old man was tired and anxious, and if it consoled him to hope that the Rana had suffered a change of heart, why not leave him to his daydreams? God knew that he, Ash, would have given much to share them, but he knew very well that the Rana's advisers merely echoed their master's wishes, and that there was only one ruler in Bhithor. If, at present, their ruler was on his best behaviour, it was merely because he had been badly frightened; but leopards did not change their spots, and once the wedding was over—and the interfering Pelham-Sahib had departed—the Rana would revert to normal. Of that Ash was confident.

But as there was nothing he could do about it he kept silent on that subject, though he pointed out somewhat acidly that the 'thoughtful and courteous gesture' of bestowing temporary territorial rights over the park to Karidkote was likely to prove an expensive one as far as Nandu was concerned, for by custom, the bride's family play host to the groom's party, the *barat,* during the three days of the marriage ceremonies. And though it is laid down that the *barat* must not exceed two hundred, in the present instance, as the wedding was to take place in the groom's own state, that number was, understandably, likely to be very much higher—a fact which had not troubled the bride's family at all, since they could hardly be expected to play host to their hosts. Now, however, as a result of the Rana's decree they must do that very thing—and pay heavily for the privilege.

Kaka-ji, who had hitherto failed to see this point, looked startled, and as its implications dawned on him, observed with grudging respect that the Rana was undoubtedly a cunning fellow and one to be reckoned with. 'Too cunning for an old man such as myself,' admitted Kaka-ji ruefully. 'Ah well, it would not have been possible for us to refuse his offer, so we must put a good face upon it. Nor do I feel that we need grudge him this little victory, seeing that we have defeated him so soundly in all other respects. Yet I hope you do not think that he has any further tricks in mind?'

Ash thought it only too likely: probably a round dozen. But he side-stepped the question by asking if the Rao-Sahib had yet learned how many people were likely to be in the bridegroom's party?—the durbar hall of the Pearl Palace, where the marriage ceremony would take place, was not overlarge, and . . .

The Rao-Sahib, instantly diverted, replied that only relatives and close friends would be in the durbar hall, but that several large *shamianahs* were already being erected in the gardens of the Moti Mahal to accommodate the remainder of the guests. He took Ash off to inspect them, and in the bustle and excitement of the preparations the Rana's 'minor victory' was tactfully forgotten.

There had been no more trouble over the payment of the bride-price, and now it seemed that nothing was too good for the visitors. The bride's brother and uncle, and anyone else who chose to do so, were pressed to stay on after the wedding for as long as it suited them—until the onset of the monsoon if they wished. The Pearl Palace would be placed at their disposal and no limit set to the number of attendants and other members of their entourage whom they might choose to keep with them, all of whom could be accommodated in the park.

The offer was a generous one, and Ash realized with dismay that it would probably be accepted, and that however much he personally disliked the idea of having to stay in Bhithor for even a day longer than he must, it would be no bad thing if it were, as there was no blinking the fact that the longer Jhoti stayed out of Nandu's reach the better. Biju Ram was dead and his servants and confederates banished from the camp, but there would still be men in Karidkote willing to do murder at a nod from their ruler, and it was Ash's hope (or had been, in the days before he met the Rana) that the boy's new brother-in-law might be persuaded to keep him in Bhithor until such time as he was old enough to guard himself from assassination—or until Nandu over-reached himself and was deposed, which was not so unlikely in view of the fact that the verbal report

Ash would be required to make on his return to Rawalpindi would include an account of the attempts on Jhoti's life, which would certainly result in a good deal of official attention being focused on Nandu's activities, both past and present.

There was also the welfare of the camp as a whole to be considered, and Ash knew very well that the great majority of its members, including the horses, elephants, pack animals and other livestock, would gain greatly from remaining in Bhithor until the arrival of the monsoon. If all had gone as planned, they would have been half-way home by now, but delays on the outward march and the protracted negotiations that had followed upon their arrival had totalled many weeks. The worst of the hot weather was already upon them, and to start the return journey in this heat would mean great hardship for all—the old in particular; and Kaka-ji, for one, was far from robust and unused to these high temperatures.

'They will have to stay,' thought Ash resignedly. They would all have to stay, himself included. He was tied to the camp until such time as they reached Deenagunj again. When the proposal was put to him he agreed to it, even though the thought of lingering in Bhithor within sight of the Rung Majal where Anjuli would be living, wedded and bedded to that shrivelled and unscrupulous satyr, was as near intolerable as makes no matter. He would have given ten years of his life to be able to turn his back on the place now, at once, and get as far away from it as possible; and a further ten to be able to forget that he had ever seen it.

But the news that they were to stay in Bhithor for a further month was received with delight by Jhoti, who now that the wedding day was imminent had begun to think of the future and to wonder what Nandu would do to him when he got back to Karidkote. The thought made him shiver, and he therefore greeted the Rana's invitation as a reprieve and, boy-like, forgot that it would at best be only a temporary one, and that the extra time granted him would pass all too soon. Instead, his spirits soared and he began to look upon the Rana as a benefactor instead of an ogre.

Kaka-ji was equally grateful. He had been dreading the rigours of a return journey at this season, and had not looked forward to exchanging the cool marble rooms of the Pearl Palace for an airless tent in the dust and the scorching heat of the empty plains. But Mulraj was less enthusiastic, though he agreed that as far as Jhoti and Kaka-ji were concerned, it was an excellent idea: 'But we cannot all stay. Our numbers are too great, and it would be a grave mistake to put so heavy a strain upon the Rana's hospitality; or his patience. Besides, there is no necessity for it. I would suggest that we divide our camp into two and that as soon as the festivities are over, one half should move off under the command of Hira Singh, who can be trusted to see to their safety and welfare, taking the heavy baggage and moving only by night—there being no need for haste. It is even possible that if the monsoon favours us, we who remain here may catch up with them before they reach the borders of Karidkote.'

Ash gave his consent to this plan, but made no move towards putting it into operation. The affairs of the camp had suddenly become so meaningless to him that he found it an effort to show even a cursory interest in them, and it was left to Mulraj and his officers to work out the details and deal with the hundred and one arrangements that must be made, while Ash spent his days shooting sandgrouse or riding through the narrow valleys between the hills. Anything to escape from the past and the Pearl Palace—and the sight and sound of men preparing for the celebration of a marriage; which was only possible far out on the plain or among the hills, since not only the city itself, but every village and hamlet in the state was a-flutter with banners and garlands, while the approaches to the park were spanned by arches decorated with tinsel and coloured paper and flowers.

By the day of the wedding the very alleyways of Bhithor smelled of marigolds and jasmine instead of the more familiar mixture of dust and refuse and boiling *ghee,* while the hum of the city was drowned by the din of *fu-fu* bands and the crackle of *patarkars.* In the Pearl Palace the centre portion of the durbar hall, normally open to the sky, had been roofed in by an awning, and below this four silver posts supported a canopy fashioned from thousands of marigold heads strung on gold wire, beneath which the sacred fire would be lighted and the officiating priests perform the *shadi,* the marriage ceremony.

The ground between the silver posts had been spread with fresh cow-dung that was patted and dried to form a smooth floor, eight foot square. On this a large circle and various good-luck signs were now drawn in a white paste made from rice flour . . . for at last the long awaited day was here.

In an inner room of the Pearl Palace the brides were being bathed and anointed with scented oil, the soles of their feet and the palms of their slender hands tinted with henna, their hair combed and braided by Unpora-Bai.

Their day had begun with a dawn-hour *pujah,* to pray for a hundred sons and a hundred daughters, and they had eaten nothing because they must fast until the marriage ceremony was over. Their women crowded about them, laughing and teasing and chattering like a flock of gaily coloured parakeets as they dressed the brides in the shimmering silks and gauzes of the wedding garments, painted their eyes with *kohl,* and hung them with jewels that were part of their dowries: diamonds, emeralds, pigeon's-blood rubies and ropes of pearls from the treasury of the Hawa Mahal.

The small room was dim and airless and heavy with the scent of sandalwood, jasmine and attar-of-roses, and Shushila's convulsive sobs were lost in the prevailing din of women's voices and went as unregarded as the dripping of a tap. Jhoti had been in to see his sisters and give them the benefit of his advice on what jewels they should wear, but as the mob of excited, shrill-voiced women who pressed about them had for once paid little attention to him, he had stayed only long enough to tell Shushila that if she didn't stop crying she would be the ugliest bride in all India—a brotherly piece of candour that only served to increase the flow of Shu-shu's tears and earned him an unexpectedly sharp slap from Unpora-Bai. Jhoti had withdrawn in some dudgeon, and run off to find Ash in order to show off his own wedding finery and complain of the silliness of women.

'It's true what I said, Sahib. She's done nothing but snivel until her eyes are all swollen and puffy and her nose is as red as her sari. She looks a fright and I expect the Rana will think we have cheated him on purpose and be angry with all of us. Do you suppose he'll beat her? I would, if she were my wife and all she could do was cry! And I shall tell her so. Except that Kairi said . . .'

But the Sahib was no longer listening.

Ash had been living of late in a curious half world, refusing to think and deliberately driving himself to exhaustion by means of hard exercise; or when that failed, working at reports or playing interminable games of chess with Kaka-ji or Mulraj, or of patience with himself. He had eventually managed to persuade himself that he was over the worst and could face this day, when it came, without any emotion. And now Jhoti had spoken of her, and the mention of the old nick-name had broken through his defences as though they were so much tissue paper, and clawed at his heart with a pain that was as sudden and as savage as the impact of a bullet smashing into flesh and bone. For a moment the room about him had turned dark and the walls and floor seemed to sway, and when they steadied again he became aware that Jhoti was still talking, though at first the words were no more than a jumble of meaningless sounds.

'Do you like my *achkan?*' demanded Jhoti, revolving slowly to show it off. 'I was going to wear a silver brocade one, but my uncle said he liked the gold one best. Do you think he was right, Sahib?'

Ash did not speak, and when Jhoti repeated the question, replied so much at random that it was clear that he had not been paying the least attention. 'Are you not feeling well?' inquired Jhoti solicitously. 'Is it the heat?'

'What . . . ?' Ash seemed to come back from a long way off. 'I'm sorry, Prince. I was thinking of something else . . . What did you say?'

'It is nothing,' said Jhoti, politely dismissing it with a wave of his small paw. He had seen men look and speak in a similar fashion after taking drugs, and presumed that the Sahib must have been dosing himself with opium against some sickness of the stomach. He had a fondness for Pelham-Sahib and was sorry that he should feel unwell, but there were so many exciting things to be seen and done that day that he did not waste time worrying over it, and ran off to show the gold brocade coat to Mulraj instead.

Ash was barely aware that he had gone; or that Gul Baz had entered the room and was saying something about it being time to go. Go where?

'The Rao-Sahib sends word that the bridegroom's procession is said to have left the Rung Mahal,' reported Gul Baz.

Ash nodded, and putting up an uncertain hand to wipe the sweat off his forehead, was startled to find his fingers shaking uncontrollably. He snatched them away and stared down at his hand, forcing it to steadiness with an effort of will, and when it was still again, reached for the elaborately braided and befrogged coat that Gul Baz was holding out to him, and that would today provide the only sober note among a rainbow of colours and the sheen of gold and silver thread.

Gul Baz had earlier helped him to pull on his boots and overalls and buckle on the webbed sword belt with its dangling straps about his waist; and now he shrugged himself reluctantly into the coat and adjusted the cross belt, feeling as stale and exhausted as though he had just returned from a route march instead of doing no more than rise from his bed and eat his breakfast. The high, tight collar of his uniform felt as though it would choke him, but though the day promised to be one of the longest and worst of his life, and was already abominably hot, as a Sahib and an officer he must sit through it sweltering in full-dress uniform, gloved, booted and spurred, and with a ceremonial sword clanking at his hip—which seemed, somehow, the last straw in the whole sorry business.

His hands were steady enough as he buckled on his sword, but when Gul Baz handed him the big white pith helmet that is worn with full dress, he took it and stood looking at it as he had looked at Jhoti, as though he did not see it.

Bands of blue and gold striped the pugaree-cloth about the crown, and the light glinted on the tall gilt spike that topped it and on the links of the chinstrap that custom decreed must be worn above and not below the chin. Gul Baz cleared his throat in a deprecatory cough that was a polite reminder that time was passing, and when that had no effect, said firmly: 'Put it on, Sahib. The sun is hot.'

Ash obeyed mechanically, and having adjusted the chinstrap, drew on his gloves and hitched forward the hilt of his sword, and straightening his shoulders as though he were about to face a firing squad, went out to join Kaka-ji and others who were already waiting to welcome the bridegroom and his party in a covered courtyard by the main gate of the Pearl Palace.

The courtyard was a large one, but it was stiflingly hot, and also exceedingly noisy, for in addition to the many people waiting there, a three-man band sat playing in a small balcony above the arch that led into the main block of the palace.

Garlands of roses and jasmine buds hung down from the balcony's edge and were looped across the marble screens, and the close air reeked with the cloying sweetness of *itr* and incense and fading flowers, the sharp smell of *pan* and cardamom seeds, and the less pleasing odour of perspiration. Ash could feel the sweat running down between his shoulder blades, and he surreptitiously unhooked the high collar of his coat and wished that the dignity of a Sahib did not entail his having to accept a chair instead of squatting Indian fashion on the floor as his companions were doing: the marble would at least be cool, whereas the plush upholstery of the chair that had been provided for him felt as though it had just come out of an oven. He shifted restlessly and wondered how long he would be called upon to endure it, and whether it was the heat or the lack of air or the intermittent bursts of ear-piercing music that was making his head ache so abominably.

In the event the wait turned out to be even longer than expected, for the report that the bridegroom and his *barat* had left the city palace and were on their way to the park had been over-optimistic. They had intended to leave a full two hours before noon, but Asia has little regard for Time and none at all for punctuality, and the afternoon was far advanced before the procession finally set out for the Ram Bagh; and when at last it reached the park the sun was well down in the sky and the worst of the heat was over.

They could hear it coming from a long way off. At first the tunk-a-tunk of drums and the joyous squeal of flutes, the braying of horns and the shouts of watching crowds were only a distant murmur barely louder than the cawing of crows and the crooning of doves and green pigeons among the trees of the Ram Bagh. But as the minutes slid past the sounds grew in volume, and at last Jhoti, who had scampered up to the roof from where he could catch a glimpse of the road across the intervening tree-tops, came pelting down to announce that the procession was entering the park gates, and where were the garlands? The assembled company rose to smooth down their *achkans* and straighten their turbans, and Ash refastened his collar, drew a deep breath, and setting his teeth, tried to think of nothing at all, and found himself thinking of Wally and Zarin, and the snow peaks of the Dur Khaima . . .

The bridegroom had not come on horseback from the city. He had been carried instead, seated on a platform that was draped and canopied with pearl-fringed cloth-of-gold and borne by twelve gorgeously liveried retainers. His dress too was gold, as on the occasion of that first durbar so many weeks ago, but today it was even more splendid, for the brocaded *achkan* was sewn with jewels. There were more jewels on his turban: a great crescent of diamonds and emeralds pinned an aigrette to the gold tissue, and ropes of pear-shaped diamonds looped about it in the manner of tinsel on a Christmas tree. Jewels flashed on his fingers and blazed on the solid gold of his sword belt, while the sword itself—the sword that a bridegroom wears to symbolize his readiness to defend his bride against all enemies—had a hilt encrusted with diamonds and topped by a single emerald the size of a rupee.

A stranger seeing that glittering figure seated on a golden platform and surrounded by liveried attendants and the gorgeously dressed members of the *barat* might well have taken it to be some Eastern idol being carried in procession by its worshippers, an impression heightened by the fact that its face was concealed by strings of marigold and jasmine buds that hung down from the turban, so that only the glint of eyes from behind the veil showed that the bedizened object was alive.

The music stopped on a long wailing note, and Kaka-ji's family priest went out to recite Vedic hymns and invoke the blessing of the gods, before calling the brides' uncle forward for the *milni,* officially the ceremony of the introduction between the fathers of the bride and groom, but today (both fathers being dead) between Kaka-ji and one of the Rana's maternal uncles. The two old gentlemen embraced, and Jhoti, as the brides' brother, assisted the bridegroom to alight and conducted him and his friends into the covered courtyard where the brides' party waited to garland the guests and present gifts to their opposite numbers in the *barat.*

Despite his dazzling dress the Rana appeared far less imposing on foot. Not even the over-large turban with its tall aigrette could disguise his lack of inches, and Kaka-ji Rao—no giant—topped him by half a head. Nevertheless the faceless figure still managed to convey a disquieting sense of power. 'And danger,' thought Ash.

It was as though a tiger, full-fed and therefore temporarily harmless, had come padding unconcernedly through a field full of sheep and cows, and the impression was so strong that Ash could almost have sworn that the man gave off a special smell: an animal smell, rank and menacing. He felt the hair at the base of his scalp prickle as though it were lifting, and recalled in a sudden flash of memory a long-forgotten scene: moonlight and the black shadows of trees and jungle grass, and a warning shiver that seemed to run through the silence like a cat's-paw of wind flitting across an expanse of still water, felt but not heard, and someone—was it Uncle Akbar?—saying in a whisper that was barely more than a breath of sound: *'Shere ahraha hai!'* (the tiger is coming).

The sweat that had soaked through his uniform was suddenly cold, and Ash shivered and heard his teeth chatter. Then the bridegroom had moved past him and was being escorted towards the arch below the balcony for the *jai-mala,* the garlanding of the groom by the bride.

The arch gave onto a narrow tunnel-like entrance hall where Shu-shila and her sister waited with the garlands that a bride must place round the groom's neck in token of her acceptance of him. Even now, at this eleventh hour, a wedding will be cancelled should the bride refuse to do this; and when there followed an unexplained pause in which the Rana waited and those behind him jostled and peered, Ash had a desperate moment of hope, the frantic foolish and utterly ludicrous hope that Shushila had changed her mind and meant to reject the marriage. But though the pause seemed a long one to those who could not see into the hallway and did not know the cause of the delay, it could not have lasted more than a minute or so, and then the groom bowed low, and when he straightened up the bride's garland was about his neck.

A moment later he bent again—though this time so slightly that it was more a brief inclination of the head than a bow—and those behind him saw a woman's hands lift a second garland high in order to clear the osprey plume on his gold turban. The hands were decked with jewels and the palms and finger nails had been tinted with henna and touched with gold leaf. But they were still square and capable—still unmistakably the hands of a little unloved girl who had been known as Kairi-Bai—and glimpsing them, Ash knew that he would, after all, be able to watch her go through the marriage rites and see her leave for her husband's house without flinching, because nothing that was to come could possibly hurt worse than that brief sight of Juli's hands . . .

With the garlanding over, the band struck up once more and the groom and guests entered the Pearl Palace to be feasted, the *barat* being fed before the brides' party, while all those for whom there was no room indoors filed out to take their places in the gaily decorated *shamianahs* where more bands played and servants hurried to and fro laden with dishes.

By now the sun was low and presently the evening breeze arose and blew gently across the lake, its breath bringing a welcome coolness to the park, though inside the Pearl Palace the air remained stifling, and now that the rich odour of food mingled with the scent of flowers and perfume the atmosphere was rapidly becoming un-breathable. Ash, however, was not called upon to endure it, this being one part of the ceremonies that he asked to be excused from attending, in order to save Kaka-ji the embarrassment of having to tell him what he already knew: that the Rana's caste forbade him from sitting down to eat with a foreigner.

Leaving the palace by a side door he walked back to his own quarters in one of the guest-houses, to eat his evening meal alone and to watch the sun go down behind the hills beyond the city and the stars come out one by one in a sky that darkened swiftly from dusty green to midnight blue: and not only stars, for tonight as the dusk deepened a myriad pin-points of light flowered on the walls and roof-tops and window-sills of Bhithor as the Rana's subjects lit thousands upon thousands of *chirags*—the little earthenware saucers filled with oil, in which a wisp of twisted cotton serves as a wick, that all over India are used for illuminations during times of festivity.

The park too was alive with lights that swayed and flickered or burned bright according to the whims of the breeze, and the Pearl Palace itself was outlined in twinkling gold, so that it shimmered against the night sky like some enchanted castle in a fairy tale. Even the forts had been decked with *chirags,* and presently the sky above the city began to blossom with showers of red and green and purple stars, as fireworks streaked upward to burst and blaze and fade slowly away on the darkness.

Ash watched them from the verandah outside his room, and wished that the Rana's caste had also prevented him from permitting a foreigner to be present during the actual marriage ceremony. But it seemed this was not so: and in any case, it would have been impossible to avoid attending, as apart from the fact that Kaka-ji and Mulraj had been particularly insistent that the Sahib should be present at the ceremony, the instructions issued to him in Rawalpindi had expressly stated that Captain Pelham-Martyn was to see the two sisters of His Highness the Maharajah of Karidkote safely married.

The actual wording was, of course, open to different interpretations. But in the circumstances it would be as well to take it literally, in case at some future date there should be any arguments as to the validity of at least one of the marriages, which was a point that Kaka-ji and Mulraj might also have had in mind.

Over an hour had passed since Gul Baz had removed the coffee tray and gone off to join in the merry-making, but the feasting was still in progress; and remembering Lalji's wedding, Ash realized that he might well have to wait for another hour or two before being summoned to witness the *shadi* ceremony. In the park and the palace, bands played on with unabated vigour, vying with the bang and crackle of fireworks and the throb of tom-toms in the city to turn the night into pandemonium, and Ash retreated to his room, and closing the doors against the noise, sat down to pass the time by writing to Wally and Zarin to let them know that he would be delayed in Bhithor for at least another month—more, if the monsoon were late— and there was small hope of his seeing either of them before the end of the summer at best.

He had finished both letters and begun a third, this time to the Political Officer, when Mulraj arrived to fetch him to the Pearl Palace where the *shadi* was about to take place; and as they walked back through the park, he saw that the moon was down, and knew that it must be close on midnight.

The durbar hall was crowded to capacity, and coming in from the night air the heat and the overpowering odour of sandalwood and incense and dying flowers met him like a tangible wave. But at least the bands were no longer playing, and except for the murmur of voices the hall was reasonably quiet. It was also surprisingly dark, for the lamps were all of coloured glass, and by now the oil in them had burned low so that it took him a moment or two to accustom himself to the dim light and be able to pick out his friends from among the sea of faces.

A chair had been placed for him near the door and in the shadow of a pillar, far back enough to make his presence unobtrusive, while allowing him to see over the heads of the men who sat cross-legged on the ground in close-packed rows in front of him. From it he could see not only the four silver posts with their golden canopy of marigolds, but the ground below it, where the circle drawn in rice-flour showed startling white against the smooth square of dry cow-dung. A brass cauldron in which the sacrificial fire would be lit stood ready, and beside it the priests had set up an altar on which they were busy arranging *pujah* vessels and bowls of Ganges water, lamps, godlings and incense-burners. And on low stools to one side of the square, their faces veiled by flowers, sat the bridegroom and the brides, together with Kaka-ji and Maldeo Rai (who were jointly deputizing for the brides' late father) and the shrouded figure of cousin Unpora-Bai, representing their deceased mothers—which was surely enough, thought Captain Pelham-Martyn sardonically, to cause the ashes of both ladies to rise in fury from the dust.

The rustle of talk sank to a whisper, and presently that too was silenced as one of the priests under the canopied enclosure began the *havan,* the lighting of the sacred fire. The flames illuminated his calm, smooth-shaven face so that it seemed to glow like burnished metal as he leaned forward to feed the fire with chips of scented wood and grains of incense. When it was well alight, silver platters heaped with perfumed salts were passed round to those who sat within reach of the circle, each of whom took a pinch and threw it at the fire. The salts sizzled and sputtered, giving off a strong, aromatic odour that set off a muffled chorus of coughing from the unseen women in the purdah gallery overlooking the hall. And in obedience to a signal, the Rana and Shushila rose and were led into the rice-flour circle.

A priest began to intone the *mantras,* but Ash sat too far away to catch more than an occasional word, and later, when the priest paused now and again for the bride and her groom to repeat the vows after him, only the Rana's voice could be heard. Shushila's was inaudible, but the vows were familiar to everyone present. The pair were promising to live according to their creed, to be true to each other and share each other's burdens, to beget sons and to remain firm and faithful as a rock . . .

Even standing beside her wizened groom, Shushila looked incredibly small and slight, like a child who has dressed up in its mother's finery. She was wearing scarlet as a bride should—red being the colour of rejoicing—and out of compliment to the groom, the traditional full-skirted dress of Bhithor, and all Rajasthan. The pigeon's blood rubies that circled her neck and wrists and decked her fingers caught the light of the flames and shone as though they were on fire, and though she kept her head bent and spoke her vows in a whisper, she performed her part in the ceremony without faltering: to the surprise (and no small relief) of her relatives and women, all of whom had fully expected a flood of tears if not a hysterical scene.

Ash could not help wondering if she would have behaved as well if she had been able to catch a glimpse of her bridegroom's face, or had any inkling of what that curtain of flower-buds concealed. But as custom decreed that a bridal pair must not look at each other until the wedding ceremony was over, and Shushila too wore a similar veil of flowers, it was not possible for her to see anything very much. The 'marriage ring'—a bracelet of iron—was placed on her arm, and the thread of happiness hung round her neck; and presently a corner of her sari was knotted to the end of her bridegroom's sash, and thus tied together they took the 'seven steps' round the fire: the *satapadi* that is the essential part of the whole ceremony, as without this the marriage is still revocable in law, while once the last step is taken it is established, and there can be no going back.

Shushila was now a wife and Rani of Bhithor, and her husband was addressing her in the words of the ancient Vedic hymn: *'Become thou my partner as thou has paced all the seven steps with me. Apart from thee I cannot live. Apart from me do thou not live. We shall share alike all goods and power combined. Over my house thou shalt bear full sway . . .'*

His voice ceased and the newly wedded pair returned to the sacred circle to receive the blessing of their older relatives, and that done, seated themselves once more. The fire was fed again with wood and incense, the *mantras* chanted and the silver trays passed round, and the whole ceremony repeated. But this time with more haste and with a different bride.

Anjuli had been seated on the far side of her half-sister and concealed from Ash's view by the stout shape of Unpora-Bai. But now she in her turn was led forward into the circle. The moment that he had dreaded for so long was upon him, and he must watch Juli being married.

Almost unconsciously he braced his body as though to face a physical assault. But there had, after all, been no need to do so. Perhaps it was the absence of hope that made it possible for him to relax his tense muscles and sit motionless and detached, feeling nothing—or almost nothing. For although he would have said that the ceremony of the garlanding had extinguished the last infinitesimal flicker of hope, a spark had survived: the chance that spoilt, highly strung Shu-shu, over-driven by the delays of the last weeks and her terror of marriage to a stranger in a strange land, might baulk at the last moment and refuse to go through with the ceremony.

It was unthinkable that a devout Hindu bride should refuse to take those final binding steps around the sacred fire, and such a thing could have happened only rarely—if at all. But then Shu-shu, by Western standards, was only a child: an over-emotional child whose reactions were often unpredictable, and who might well be capable of creating a scandalous precedent by refusing to perform the *satapadi*. But she had not done so; and as she took the seven steps, that last obstinate spark died, thereby releasing Ash from hope and enabling him to sit through that second ceremony with something approaching detachment.

He had been helped in this by the fact that there was nothing in the least familiar about the faceless and anonymous figure in the shimmering sari and a veil of flower buds. From where he sat it could have been any Indian woman; except that she was taller than most, and made her bridegroom appear wizened and stunted by comparison.

She was less splendidly dressed than her half-sister, which was understandable. But the choice of colour, jewels and material (for which Unpora-Bai had been responsible) was unfortunate, as the topaz and pearl ornaments did not show to advantage in the dim lighting, while the yellow and gold shot-silk that had seemed such an admirable foil for Shushila's scarlet paled into insignificance beside the brilliant gold of the bridegroom's coat. The material, too, was so stiff that it disguised the wearer's slenderness and grace and gave her an oddly clumsy appearance. There was nothing there of Juli: only a shapeless bundle of silk topped by a fringe of wilting marigold heads, repeating a series of actions that no longer seemed significant or charged with any emotion.

The priests hurried through the rites and the groom gabbled the final hymn, and it was all over. There followed a final ceremony in which the Rana led his wives out to introduce them to those members of the *barat* who had not been present at the wedding, in token that a bride is no longer a member of her own family but belongs from henceforth to her husband's. That being done, the two hungry and exhausted young women were free at last to return to their own rooms and take off their finery, and to eat the first food they had tasted in more than twenty-four hours.

Kaka-ji and the other men carried off the groom to a feast in the largest of the *shamianahs* in the park, and Ash went to bed and—surprisingly—slept through the din of bands and fireworks and rejoicing crowds as soundly as though he had been drugged.

The first day of the three-day ceremony had ended, and the second was several hours old and close to dawn before the bands and fireworks and voices ceased and the park was silent at last.

By tradition the two days that followed were given over to feasting the *barat*. But on the morning after the wedding Ash had excused himself from the celebrations and gone off shooting, accompanied by his syce, Kalu Ram, and a local *shikari*.

Returning in the dusk as the *chirags* were beginning to twinkle once more on rooftops and walls and the cattle strayed homeward from the grazing grounds around the city, he was met by a messenger who had arrived earlier in the day and who had been squatting by the door of his room, waiting for his return.

The man had ridden many miles and slept little during the past few days; but though he had accepted food he had refused to rest until he had given the letter he carried into the Sahib's own hand, as it had been impressed upon him that the matter was one of the greatest urgency—he would, he explained, have delivered it sooner if anyone had been able to tell him in which direction the Sahib had gone.

The envelope he proffered was heavily sealed, and recognizing the writing, Ash's heart sank. He had a guilty conscience over the tone of his last letter to the Political Officer, and half expected a sharp reprimand. Even without that, any communication from Major Spiller was bound to be depressing, and he wondered what he was going to be advised to do, or told not to do, this time. Well, whatever it was it was too late, for the wedding was over and done with and the bride-price had been paid.

He dismissed the messenger, and having handed over his shot-gun to Gul Baz and a brace of black partridge to Mahdoo, carried the letter into the lamp-lit sitting room and broke the seals with his thumb-nail. The envelope contained a single sheet of paper and he took it out and glanced at it, feeling bored and irritable. The message had clearly been written in haste, for it differed from any previous one he had received from the Political Officer, in that it was short and to the point. Yet he had to read it twice before he took it in, and then his first thought was that it had come too late. A week ago— even two days ago—it might have changed everything, but now there could be no going back; the thing was done. A cold tide of bitterness swelled up in him and he smashed his clenched fist against the wall and was grateful for the savage pain and the smart of bruised knuckles, because it served in some small way to counteract the less bearable pain in his heart.

He stood staring blindly before him for a long time, and it was only when Gul Baz came into the room and exclaimed at the sight of his injured hand that he roused himself and went off to wash it clean. The cold water seemed to clear his brain as well as the broken skin, and he realized that he was probably wrong in thinking that it would have made any difference if the news had arrived earlier, since after the expenditure of so much time and money and effort there would have been no question of turning back.

He allowed Gul Baz to bandage his knuckles, postponed his bath for half an hour, and having swallowed three fingers of brandy, retrieved the letter and went off to read it to Mulraj.

Mulraj had been dressing for that night's banquet when Ash walked in and demanded a few words with him in private, and he had taken one look at Ash's face and dismissed his servants. At first he too had been unable to credit the news that had first been sent, over a fortnight ago, to the Governor of the Punjab, passed on to the military authorities in Rawalpindi, from where it had been telegraphed to the Political Officer responsible for the affairs of Bhithor, who in turn forwarded it by the hand of a special messenger to Captain Pelham-Martyn, marked *Urgent. For Immediate Attention.*

Nandu, Maharajah of Karidkote, whose family had of late suffered more than their fair share of fatal accidents, had met with one himself: a genuine one, this time. He had been trying out some of the ancient muzzle-loading weapons in the old armoury of the Hawa Mahal, one of which had exploded in his face and killed him outright. As he had died childless, his younger brother, the Heir Apparent, was now Maharajah, and it was thought advisable that he should return immediately to take up his inheritance. Captain Pelham-Martyn was therefore instructed to escort His Highness back to Karidkote without delay. Speed being essential, they should travel light, taking with them only as many men as Captain Pelham-Martyn judged sufficient for the protection and comfort of his young charge, and it was left to his discretion to make what arrangements he considered necessary for the welfare of the remainder of the bridal camp, who would have to return in their own time and at their own pace . . .

'So it has all been useless,' said Ash bitterly.

'How so?' asked Mulraj, puzzled.

'The marriages. They were arranged by Nandu because he was afraid that if he married his sisters nearer home, a day might come when he found himself with a brother-in-law who might conceivably have designs on his throne, so he took care to choose one who lived too far away to make that possible. And now he is dead, and those poor girls have been tied to that—that offal for nothing!'

'That is not so,' said Mulraj. 'At least the boy is safe, and but for this journey to Bhithor he would not have been. If he had stayed in Karidkote his brother Nandu would have found a way to destroy him; and certainly the gods are on the boy's side, for while his brother lived he would not have been safe even here. There are always men who can be bribed to kill, provided the bribe is large enough.'

'And you do not think Nandu would have quibbled in the matter of blood money,' said Ash. 'Neither do I. Well, we have no need to worry ourselves over such questions any longer, because this news has solved all Jhoti's problems.'

It had also solved one of his own, for it meant that he could leave Bhithor at once instead of being forced to remain there for an indefinite period, within sight of the Rana's palace and with nothing to do but wait on the weather and eat his heart out for a girl who would be living less than a mile away—one who was for ever out of reach, but whose husband he might have to meet frequently and be polite to. It meant also that he would be spared the long, slow torment of a return journey without Juli, camping in familiar places that would be full of memories, and passing once more through country that they had ridden across side by side on those evening rides . . . He had dreaded that; but a small party, unencumbered by women and children and minus baggage carts, camp-followers, livestock or elephants, would be able to cut corners and move with far greater speed, and need not be tied to a route that had been dictated by the needs of a camp of thousands.

His eagerness to leave was so great that had it been at all possible, he would have gone that same night. This being out of the question, he had suggested they start on the following afternoon, but Mulraj had set his face against it: 'We cannot leave tomorrow,' said Mulraj.

'Why not? I know there will be much work to do, but if we set our minds to it we could be ready.'

'Perhaps. But you forget that tomorrow is the last day of the wedding festivities, and that at nightfall the brides will leave for their husband's house.'

Ash had not forgotten it, but he could hardly explain that it was precisely because he hoped to avoid that particular sight that he was so anxious to set out on the following afternoon. However, Mulraj insisted that to leave before the celebrations had ended would cause great offence to the Rana and his people. It would be neither seemly nor necessary to disrupt the festivity of the final day with preparations for departure, and as Nandu had already been dead for over two weeks it could make little difference if Jhoti started back in two days' time, or three or four.

'Also our preparations will be better if we do not make them too hastily,' said Mulraj. 'For as you say, there is much to be done.'

Ash had not been able to deny that, and they had eventually agreed to say nothing about the letter for another day so that the merry-making should not be marred by news that coming at such a time was bound to be regarded as ill-omened, and that however welcome it might be to some, would certainly cause grief and distress to Shushila, if to no one else. Time enough, said Mulraj, to disclose it on the morning after the brides' departure, when they themselves would be free to make their own arrangements to leave.

The banquet that night was given by Kaka-ji, who had politely invited the Sahib to attend and received an equally polite acceptance. Honour being satisfied, Ash had later sent a message regretting that a sudden and severe headache prevented him from being present, and when Mulraj had gone he went back to his own quarters and having sent for the camp records, spent the greater part of the night poring over lists of men, animals and transport, and deciding how many or how few to take with him, which to leave, and what was to be done about a score of other matters. All of this would of course have to be discussed with Mulraj and the *Panchayat*, but it was going to save a good deal of time if a detailed plan could be put forward for their approval as soon as the marriage festivities were over. His lamp was still burning when Kaka-ji's guests returned from the banquet, and the cocks were crowing before he turned it out and went to bed.

The third and last day of the ceremonies was again given over to feasting, but this time Ash did not leave the park to go off riding or shooting. He walked instead; and when at nightfall a message from Kaka-ji summoned him to the Pearl Palace, he put on his full-dress uniform again and went over to watch the final act of the tragi-comedy that Nandu had planned in order to guard against something that could only have been visualized by a mind as riddled with suspicion and jealousy as his own.

Certainly Jhoti would never have thought of it, and it occurred to Ash that if, as Mulraj seemed to think, the gods were on the boy's side, it was a pity that they had remained uninterested in the fate of his sisters, for had they removed Nandu a year earlier none of this would have happened. True, he himself would not have met Anjuli again—though in the circumstances, that would surely have been far better for both of them. But at least Shushila would have been happier and Biju Ram would still be alive; and as Jhoti took after his father's side of the family, he would not have worried his head over imaginary rivals or wasted the revenues of his state in showing off to his fellow princes—as Nandu had done when he sent that preposterously large bridal camp traipsing across half India.

Yet even now, waiting to see Anjuli leave for her husband's house, he could not feel sorry that he had met her again, and known her and loved her. The pain of loss and the prospect of the long, empty years ahead could not outweigh that, or make it less wonderful to him; and he knew that if he had been able to foresee the future when he first discovered the Rajkumari Anjuli of Karidkote, whom he was escorting to her wedding in Bhithor, was none other than little Kairi-bai of the Queen's balcony, it would have made no difference at all. He would still have handed her his half of the luck-charm—and accepted the consequences with gladness and gratitude.

Wally, who was always falling in and out of love, had been fond of quoting lines that some poet or other had written, to the effect that it was 'better to have loved and lost than never to have loved at all'. Well, Wally—and Tennyson, or whoever it was—had been right. It was better, infinitely better, to have loved Juli and lost her than not to have loved her at all. And if he did nothing worthwhile in the years ahead, life would still have been worth living because he had once loved and been loved by her . . .

It had taken him long enough to realize that, and it struck him as curious that he should not have done so until now, of all times, when he was waiting to catch a last glimpse of her. But it was enough that he had done so; and the knowledge brought him the same kind of relief that an exhausted swimmer feels when he reaches shallow water, and knows that he is not going to drown after all.

The departure of the brides and the groom had been a magnificent affair, and one that would surely have gratified the vanity of the late Maharajah of Karidkote if he could have seen it. His state elephants, gorgeously caparisoned, stood in the blaze of torchlight before the main entrance of the Pearl Palace, rocking gently from one foot to another as they waited for the procession to start. Their trunks and foreheads, their fringed ears and massive legs had been decorated with painted designs in brilliant colours, and their tusks ringed with bands of gold. The shimmering fringes of their velvet housings reached almost to the ground, and the embossed gold and silver-gilt of the howdahs gathered light from the bright flame of torches and the twinkling of innumerable *chirags.*

The start had already been held up by over an hour by the time Kaka-ji's message was delivered to Ash, and another hour went by without any sign of a move. Servants handed round *pan* and *itr,* and later, trays of little cakes to the patiently waiting crowd, and the guests munched and yawned and passed the time in desultory small-talk, until at last the groom's closest friends appeared on the steps of the palace. After that, things moved swiftly: a band struck up to signal the start, and as the elephants sank ponderously to their knees, an advance guard of gaily dressed horsemen set off with a clatter of hooves into the night. The Rana, ablaze with jewels and attended by a file of courtiers and uniformed servants, came through the gateway, closely followed by a small group of women—the Ranis of Bhithor and their ladies.

Tonight Shushila's sari was of flame-coloured gauze spangled and embroidered with gold, and though she wore it pulled far forward and held close to shield her face, the gems beneath it seemed to burn through it like fire. She walked without grace, supported by two attendants and almost tottering under the sheer weight of the jewels that decked every available inch of her slight body, and at each step the *rakhri* on her forehead trembled and its central stone, an enormous spinel ruby, glinted blood-red through the gauze.

Two paces behind her came Anjuli, tall and slender in green. Her sari was bordered with silver and seed pearls, but once again she was over-shadowed by Shushila's splendour. There was an emerald on her forehead, faintly visible through the woven silk that was fine enough to betray the hint of copper in her dark hair and the thin red line that coloured her parting—the streak of *kunkum* that only a wife may wear. Her hair had been threaded with pearls and braided into a thick plait that swung down almost to her knee, and as she passed him Ash caught the scent of dried rose-petals that he would always associate with her.

She must have known that he would be there among the other spectators, but she kept her head bent and did not glance to left or right. The Rana mounted a silver ladder held against the leading elephant by two scarlet-turbaned servants, and settled himself in the howdah. Shu-shu went next, half-pushed, half-carried by her women, and took her place at his side. And then Anjuli was mounting the steps, slim, straight and royal, a flash of green and silver and the end of a swinging plait of dark hair; narrow feet the colour of carved ivory and a glimpse of slender ankles circled with jewels.

The mahout shouted a word of command and the elephant lurched to its feet: and as it moved off, Anjuli looked down from her seat in the gilded howdah. Her eyes, dark-rimmed with *kohl,* appeared enormous above the close-held edge of her sari, and they did not search among the sea of faces below her, but went directly to Ash, as though the compulsion of his own intent gaze had been strong enough to tell her exactly where he stood.

For a long, long moment they looked at each other, straight and steadily. Looked with love and longing, and without grief, trying to say with their eyes all those things that did not need saying because they knew them already: 'I love you . . . I will always love you . . . Do not forget me.' And in Juli's wide eyes the words she had spoken long ago on a moonlit night, looking down on him as she was looking now—*Khuda hafiz*—God be with you. Then the attendants and the torch-bearers closed up on either side, another band struck up and the howdah swayed as the elephant swung slowly away, taking Juli and Shu-shu and the Rana down the avenue of shade trees towards the gates of the park and the mile-long road that led to the city and the Rung Mahal.

Ash remembered very little of what happened after that. He retained a confused impression of other elephants plodding majestically past him carrying the senior members of the *barat,* and had a vague recollection of helping Kaka-ji, Jhoti and Maldeo Rai into a gilded howdah, and seeing Mulraj and others of the Karidkote party climb into another and be borne away in their turn. After that it was a discordant blur of drums and flutes and horsemen, and of endless numbers of gaudily dressed men marching off into the night accompanied by files of linkmen bearing torches. The head of that long procession must have reached the Rung Mahal before the last of those who marched in it passed under the flower-decked arch leading out of the park, and Ash supposed that he must have stayed among the spectators outside the Pearl Palace and made polite conversation to the end, for it was long past midnight by the time he walked back through the hot night to his rooms in the airless guest-house.

The punkah-coolie who squatted in the verandah outside his bedroom, and whose task it was to pull the rope that set the heavy punkah swinging to and fro to create an artificial draught, was asleep at his post. So too was the *chowkidar* who lay, sheeted like a corpse, on a string bed that he had placed in the shelter of the porch. Ash did not wake them. He turned and trod softly away to where a flight of stone steps led upwards, and climbing them came out on the flat roof and went to lean on the parapet and look out at the lake and the city.

He had fought hard against thinking of Juli during the past weeks, and though he had not always been successful he had done his best, closing his mind against her with a deliberate effort of will whenever the thought of her slipped past his defences. But it had been a constant battle, and one that he knew he would have to continue fighting until time and old age came to his rescue, for he could not spend his days listening to echoes and living on memories. Life had to be lived, and he could not share his with Juli: he would have to come to terms with that—they both would. But tonight he could afford to devote a few hours to her, and who knew but that his thoughts might not be able to reach her across the scant mile that separated them, so that she would know that he was thinking of her, and be comforted.

The park below him was gradually sinking into silence. Dawn came early in these latitudes, and those who had not followed the procession were settling down to get what sleep they could before the birds awoke and another burning day was upon them. But torches still laid a jiggling ribbon of light along the road leading to the city, and Bhithor itself was ablaze with illuminations and noisy with bands and *patarkars*. High above the crowded houses, the sandstone roofs and cupolas of the Rung Mahal stood out against the night sky, glowing like burnished copper in the light of thousands of *chirags,* and Ash could picture the scene in the outer courtyard as one by one the elephants came in under the arch of the great gateway, and knelt to let their riders dismount. By now Juli would be in the Zenana Quarters and seeing for the first time the rooms in which she would spend the rest of her days: her women would be removing her jewels and laying away her gala dress, and very soon—

His imagination checked abruptly, but even as his mind winced from the thought, he realized that it would not be Juli but Shushila who would have to share the Rana's bed tonight. The Rana had never wanted Juli and perhaps he never would, and if so she might be left in peace and allowed to live out her life, busy and unregarded, taking care of Shu-shu and of Shu-shu's children; though it was a poor enough outlook for a girl like Juli, who was young and beautiful and formed for love . . .

To deprive her of motherhood and shut her away from life and happiness in the narrow world of the Zenana was as great a crime against heaven as the caging of a lark; but perhaps Shu-shu would come to realize the extent of that sacrifice, and repay it in the only possible way—with love. Ash could only hope so, though without much confidence, for Shu-shu had depended on her half-sister for so long that by now she took her devotion for granted—and it is only the thirsty or starving who are grateful for bread and water.

Juli was bread and water. But when there was rich food and wine and juicy fruits for the taking, Shu-shu might well lose her taste for plain fare and end by thinking it dull and unnecessary, and turn from it. One could not trust Shu-shu, that was the rub. She might mean well, but she had always been ruled by her emotions, and no one could tell in which direction they would drive her. And after all, she was still only a child and like most children, susceptible to flattery. Among these strangers there would be many who would spare no pains to ingratiate themselves with the new First Lady of the Palace —and several who would do their best to wean her away from her dependence on her half-sister and supplant Juli in her affections.

'Oh, my darling,' thought Ash, 'my dear, sweet, foolhardy love— what will become of you? What is to become of me?'

Once again the future yawned before him as lonely and dark and cold as outer space, and as endless as eternity, and there seemed no point in living if he must live without Juli. Bitterness and self-pity welled up in him, bringing its own weakness and making him less a man, so that glancing down at the drop below the parapet it occurred to him for the first time how easy it would be to put an end to it all.

The morbidness of the last thought suddenly struck him, and he grimaced at the picture of himself that it presented: a spineless coward, wallowing in self-pity. How Juli would despise him if she knew.

And she would be right to do so, for one thing was certain: living was going to be a lot easier for him than it would be for her. He was not condemned to stay in Bhithor, and there were many ways in which he could fill his life. The North-West Frontier was seldom quiet for long, and the Guides were more familiar with war than peace. There would be campaigns among the Border hills, and battles to be planned and fought and won; horses to ride and strange, wild places to explore; mountains to climb . . . and friends to talk and drink and laugh with—Zarin and Wally and Koda Dad, Mahdoo and Mulraj and Kaka-ji and many others. But for Juli there was only Shushila, and if Shu-shu were to fail her or turn against her, or fall ill and die, she would have nothing left . . .

The sky that had been dark when Ash came up onto the roof was beginning to pale, and there were no longer lights in the city, for the *chirags* had burned out or been extinguished by the dawn wind. The night was over and morning only a step away, and soon the cocks would begin to crow and a new day begin. It was time to go down to his room and try to snatch an hour's rest while the air was still faintly cool, because once the sun rose the heat would be too gruelling for sleep, and there was so much to be done and decided on in the coming day that it would be as well to avoid trying to deal with it while sodden with fatigue.

Ash straightened up tiredly and thrust his hands into his pockets, and as he did so his fingers encountered something round and rough. It was one of the small cakes that had been passed round among the guests on the steps of the Pearl Palace, and that he had accepted out of politeness and put in his pocket, meaning to throw it away later. He took it out, and looking at it was reminded of other days. A smile softened the grim weariness of his mouth and he crumbled it up and strewed it on the rim of the parapet; and when he had done that, he looked for the last time at the distant silhouette of the Rung Mahal and spoke very softly into the stillness.

It was not the prayer that he had used to say when he made offerings to the Dur Khaima but it was, in its way, a prayer. A prayer and a vow. 'Don't worry, my dear darling,' said Ash. 'I promise I won't forget you. I shall love you always and for ever. Goodbye, Juli. Goodbye, my dear and only love. *Khuda hafiz!* . . .'

He turned and walked back across the roof, and was asleep by the time the dawn broke in a wash of lemon yellow behind the dark line of the hills.

*   *   *

Two days later—which was one more than Ash had hoped for and several less than Mulraj had expected—the new Maharajah of Karidkote set out for home with a party of seventy men; twenty-four of them soldiers, a dozen officials, and the remainder syces and servants. They had received a royal send-off, being accompanied as far as the frontier of Bhithor by what appeared to be fully half the population of the state, headed by the Rana himself. And as they rode down the valley the guns of the three forts had thundered in salute.

Their departure had been preceded by three farewell interviews: an official one in the *Diwan-i-Khas,* another between Jhoti and his sisters, and a third, and private one, between Ash and Kaka-ji.

The official farewell had consisted largely of speeches and garlands, and Jhoti's had been a taxing experience. Shushila had genuinely admired her elder brother and already wept herself into a state of exhaustion on hearing of his death. Faced now with parting from the younger one, she had given way to hysteria and behaved in such a frenzied manner that Jhoti had finally been driven to slapping her. The blow having shocked her into silence he had seized the opportunity to deliver a brotherly lecture on the advantages of self-control, and made his escape before she could recover her powers of speech.

Ash's interview with Kaka-ji had been a much quieter affair. The old man had originally declared that he would of course accompany his nephew back to Karidkote, but Mulraj had managed to persuade him that his nieces must now be in sore need of his comfort and support, owing to the news of their elder brother's death, and when Ash, more bluntly, pointed out that his presence could only serve to slow down the speed of the return journey, Kaka-ji had given way and agreed (not without relief) to remain in Bhithor with the rest of the bridal camp until the monsoon broke. Later the two had spoken together alone when Ash came to say farewell before the advance party left.

'I have to thank you for many things, Rao-Sahib,' said Ash. 'For your friendship and understanding, but most of all for your great generosity. I know very well that you could have destroyed me with a word; and . . . and her also. Yet you did not, and for that I shall always be in your debt. If there should ever be anything that I can do to repay you, I will do it.'

Kaka-ji made a small deprecating gesture, and Ash laughed and said: 'That must sound like an empty boast, since at the moment I am not in a position to help anyone; as no one knows better than yourself, Rao-Sahib. Even my rank is only lent me because while I am here I represent the Raj, and as soon as my mission is completed I shall become a junior officer again, and of no importance to anyone. But I hope one day to be in a position to help my friends and repay my debts, and when that day comes—'

'Mother Gunga will long since have had my ashes,' finished Kaka-ji, smiling. 'You owe me nothing, my son. You have been courteous to an old man and I have taken pleasure in your company. Also it is we who are doubly in your debt: for saving my nieces from the river and also for saving their marriages; together with our honour which would have been lost had we been forced to return with them, empty-handed, to Karidkote. As for that other matter, I have put it out of my mind: and you, my son, would be well advised to do likewise.'

Ash's mouth quivered and the look on his face said all that he did not put into words. Kaka-ji replied to it as though he had spoken:

'I know. I know,' sighed Kaka-ji. 'Who should know better than I? But it is because I speak with a knowledge that was gained by my own mistakes that I can say to you now, "Do not look back." The past is the last refuge of the defeated—or the aged—and there is as yet no need for you to number yourself among either. Tell yourself that what is done is done, and put it away and forget it. Do not let yourself remember and try to live on memories. That is well enough for old men who have had their day, but it is bitter fare for the young. So be advised by me, my son, and look forward and not back, remembering always that life is a gift from the gods and therefore not a thing to be despised or wasted. Live it to the full: that is the best advice that I, who did not do so, can give you.'

'I will try, Rao-Sahib,' promised Ash. 'And now I must go. Will you give me your blessing?'

'Assuredly; though I fear it is of little worth. Yet for what it is, you have it. I will also make prayers to the gods that they grant you a safe and swift journey to Karidkote, and a quiet heart and happiness in the years to come. I will not say goodbye for it is my hope that we will meet again: many times, I trust.'

'I too,' said Ash. 'Will you come and visit me in Mardan, Rao-Sahib?'

'No, no. I have had my fill of journeying, and once I win home I shall not leave it again. But Jhoti I know has taken a great liking to you, and now that he is Maharajah he will certainly wish you to visit him. We shall surely see you in Karidkote.'

Ash did not contradict this statement, though he knew in his heart that he had no desire to set foot there again, and that once he had escorted Jhoti safely back to Karidkote, he would never return. But that was not something that he could explain to Kaka-ji.

He was wearing full uniform in deference to the official leave-taking at the Rung Mahal, but he forgot this and stooped instead in the manner of the East to touch the old man's feet.

'The gods go with you,' said Kaka-ji; and added softly: 'And rest assured that if at any time there should arise a . . . a need . . . I will send word to you.'

He did not have to add that the need would not be his own. That was understood. He embraced Ash, and there being no more to be said, dismissed him. They would see each other again that day, because Kaka-ji would be riding as far as the border with his nephew and the advance party, but there would be no further opportunity for private talk: or any necessity for it.

Two thirds of the returning party had left at dawn with the pack-horses, to set up camp some five miles on the far side of the border in readiness for the arrival of the more important members, whose departure was likely to be delayed by protocol and ceremony. In fact it had been delayed even longer than Ash had expected, for the sun had set by the time the motley cavalcade reached the frontier of Bhithor. As Ash turned in his saddle for a last look at Kaka-ji he saw by the flare of torchlight that there were tears on the old man's cheeks, and lifting a hand in salute, was astonished to find that his own eyes were wet.

'Goodbye, uncle!' shrilled Jhoti. 'Goodbye!'

The horses broke into a canter and the chorus of farewells became lost in the thunder of hoof-beats. And presently the yellow glow of the torches faded and they were riding through grey moonlight and the black shadows of the hills. The heartbreak and treachery and the claustrophobia of Bhithor lay behind them, and once again they were riding for the north.

Book Five

Paradise of Fools

32

'Two more days, if the gods are kind, and we shall be sleeping in our own beds again,' said Mulraj.

'Two more days. Two more days. Only two more days,' chanted Jhoti. 'In two days from now I shall be riding into the city—my own city—and entering my own palace, with all the people shouting and cheering as I pass. And after that I shall really be Maharajah.'

'Your Highness has been that ever since your brother died,' said Mulraj.

'I know. Only I don't *feel* as if I was. But when I am back in my own state I will. I mean to be a great king. A much better one than Nandu.'

'That last should not be too hard,' observed Mulraj dryly.

'Two more days . . .' thought Ash, and wished that he could share Mulraj's relief and Jhoti's enthusiasm.

The long ride up from the south had been remarkably free from incident. Considering the relentless heat that had forced them to move only between sunset and sunrise and snatch what rest they could during the burning day, they had made better time than any-one had expected; though it had been a gruelling ordeal for all of them, not least for the horses but most of all for Mahdoo, who had flatly refused to be left behind despite the fact that besides being eld-erly, he was an indifferent horseman.

The one person who had enjoyed every moment of the journey had been Jhoti. They had all been anxious on his account and worried that the pace might be too much for him, but he seemed to thrive on heat and hard exercise—so much so that there were times when his high spirits made Ash feel at least a hundred years old, though on the whole he had enjoyed Jhoti's lively company and un-inhibited conversation and endured the never-ending stream of ques-tions with commendable patience. The boy had shed his fears along with his plumpness and his pasty complexion, and became a different person from the apprehensive run-away whom Biju Ram had so skil-fully goaded into 'escaping' from Karidkote, and it occurred to Ash as he watched and listened to him that the denizens of Karidkote were likely to be very fortunate in their new ruler.

Jhoti talked continuously of their arrival and the state entry he meant to make into his capital (still apparently known as Gulkote) and was full of plans for the ceremonies that would attend his installation as Maharajah. But as they neared their journey's end Ash became increasingly aware that he himself had no desire to see Gulkote again, let alone enter the Hawa Mahal.

He had never felt any great urge to return there, for he had always known that it would be unwise to do so while the *Nautch*-girl lived; and in any case his memories of the place were far from pleasant. His first years in the city had, indeed, been happy ones; but they had been overshadowed by the misery, fear and humiliation of the later ones in the Hawa Mahal, and though there had been compensations even there, in the main he remembered the Palace of the Winds as a prison from which he had escaped only just in time to save his life, and Gulkote as a place that he and Sita had fled from by night in terror of capture and death.

There was no longer anything left to draw him back there—apart from a cluster of snow peaks that he used to say his prayers to and the memory of a little girl whose devotion had consoled him in some small degree for the loss of his pet mongoose—and the prospect of returning, now of all times, had begun to fill him with something like panic. But as there was no way by which he could avoid doing so, he would have had to set his teeth and go through with it; and if Kaka-ji was right about the past being the last refuge of the defeated, then the sooner he faced it and stared it down the better.

By now the fertile plains were behind them and they were among the bad-lands: a rough and desolate region of boulders, ridges and ravines where little grew except camel-thorn and rank grasses. But ahead of them lay the foothills and behind the foothills were the mountains, no longer a dimly seen barrier along the horizon but near and blue and solid, towering above them; and sometimes the scorching, dust-laden air carried a clean smell of pine-needles, and in the early dawn, or towards evening, Ash could see the snow peaks of the Dur Khaima.

This was the country through which Sita had brought him after their escape from Delhi in the Black Year of the Mutiny. But in those days there had been no road, and Deenagunj (it had been Deena then) had consisted of half-a-dozen mud huts, huddled together on the only level spot between the plains and the river that formed the southern boundary of Gulkote. Yet despite its inhospitable surroundings, Deenagunj was now a thriving town, for when the territories of Gulkote and Karidarra had been amalgamated under the rule of Lalji's father, the Government had sent a British Resident to advise His Highness on matters of finance and policy, and followed this up by building a road through the bad-lands and a bridge of boats across the river. The Government's road-building had brought prosperity to the twenty-odd villagers of Deena, who had seen their tiny hamlet grow into a town of no mean size, and Ash, looking about him, was no longer surprised that he had failed, in the previous autumn, to recognize the frontiers of Gulkote when he rode along that wide and well-trodden road on his way to take over command of a bridal camp from a state whose name was unfamiliar to him for the mountains had been hidden by heaped haze and clouds.

Today, for the first time since leaving Bhithor, they had broken camp at dawn instead of sundown, and were riding by daylight. The thermometer still registered a temperature of 102° at noon, but the past night had been pleasantly cool, and now Deenagunj was almost within sight. They could have reached it before midnight, but by common consent they did not press on, but made camp as darkness fell, and slept for the first time in many days by starlight.

Rising with the dawn, rested and refreshed, they bathed and prayed and ate a frugal morning meal. After which they sent a messenger ahead to announce their arrival, and having dressed themselves in their best, as befitted the escort of a Maharajah, rode into Deenagunj at an easy pace, where they were met by the District Officer and a deputation of senior citizens, and what appeared to be the entire population of the town, eager to witness any form of *tamarsha*.

There were several familiar faces among the waiting deputation; men who had presented bills or brought complaints when Ash had last been in Deenagunj. But the District Officer's was not one of them: Mr Carter had apparently suffered yet another attack of malaria with the onset of the hot weather, and was on sick-leave in Murree. His replacement, a Mr Morecombe, informed Ash that the British Resident, together with the members of his staff and at least fifty nobles of Karidkote, were waiting to receive the new Maharajah in a camp that had been set up on the far side of the bridge of boats, where it had been arranged that His Highness would spend the night. The state entry into the capital would take place on the following day; but unfortunately Captain Pelham-Martyn would not be able to see it, for he was ordered to return immediately to Rawalpindi.

A letter confirming this was handed to him by the District Officer, who commiserated with him under the mistaken impression that it would be a disappointment. 'Rotten bad luck,' said the District Officer over a glass of country-brewed beer. 'Seems a bit hard, bringing that boy all this way and then being done out of the show, and what's the betting that when you do get to 'Pindi, you'll find there was no need at all to go chasing back there in such a tearing hurry? But that's G.H.Q. all over.'

Ash thought it only too likely—and was deeply grateful to whoever was responsible for sending off the order for his return. Nevertheless, for politeness' sake he did his best to appear disappointed, though not sufficiently so to encourage Jhoti to insist on his staying:

'No. Your Highness cannot send a *tar* to the *Jung-i-lat* Sahib, demanding that I remain,' said Ash firmly. 'Or to the Viceroy or the Governor of the Punjab either. It would do me no good. I know that you are now a Maharajah, but I am still a soldier; and as Mulraj will tell you, a soldier must obey the orders of his senior officers. The General-Sahibs in Rawalpindi have commanded my return, and even for Your Highness I cannot disobey them. But I hope that you will write and tell me about the ceremonies and rejoicings, and I promise that I will write to you as often as I can.'

'And visit me, too,' insisted Jhoti.

'And visit you too,' agreed Ash, hoping that he might be forgiven the lie—if it was a lie. Perhaps it was not. Perhaps one day he would feel differently about returning to Gulkote and the Hawa Mahal, and if so . . .

He said his farewells, and realized as he did so how much he was going to miss them all: Mulraj and Jhoti, Kaka-ji and Gobind—and so many others . . . It was not only Juli whom he was going to miss and to think of in the years to come.

'It is my hope that we shall meet again many times,' said Mulraj. 'You will come here on *chutti* (leave) and we will take you out hawking on the flat lands and show you good sport among our mountains. And when I am an old man and you are a General-Sahib, we shall still meet and talk over old times together. Therefore I do not say "Good-bye", but "Come again soon".'

They had accompanied Ash for a mile and more down the road, and looking back to wave a last farewell, he knew a momentary regret that he was riding away instead of going on with them to

Gulkote. If he could have changed his mind then, he might well have turned back. But it was too late for that now.

A turn of the road hid them from sight and he knew in his heart that in spite of Mulraj's confident prediction, he was unlikely to see them again, because his only hope lay in taking Kaka-ji's advice and turning his back on the past. The old man had been right: he must strive to put it all behind him and to forget; he must learn not to think of Juli at all, and as visiting Gulkote would only serve to bring back the past, he must not go there—not now, or for many years—if ever. Because were he to do so the sense of ease and comradeship that had existed between himself and those in whose company he had spent these last months could be destroyed.

In the camp he had been the only European, and because no one there spoke his language it had been possible for him to forget at times that he was a *feringhi*. But he would not be allowed to forget it in Karidkote; not now that there was a British Resident there, supported by a large staff of Europeans and possibly a guard of British troops. There would also be many old and orthodox Hindus who would strongly disapprove of his being treated with the casual familiarity that had been accorded to him on the march, and inevitably, his relations with Jhoti and Mulraj would suffer. The ease and camaraderie of the camp would be replaced by politeness, and there would, in all probability, be relief when he left—which was something he did not even like to think of.

No; much better to stay away and let them think of him with affection as someone they had known and liked, and hoped to see again some day. And then perhaps when he was old—when they were all old, and nothing mattered very much any longer because life was nearly over and the bad parts of it forgotten—he might go back for a short visit to talk over old days with any who might still remember him. And to make a last offering to the Dur Khaima.

Later, as the light began to fade and the dusk turn green about him, he reined in and turned to look back at the mountains that were already in shadow and sharply violet against the hyacinth of the darkening sky. One cluster of peaks still held a last gleam of the sunset: the crown of the Dur Khaima, rose-pink in the twilight . . . the far pavilions . . . The warm colour faded from them as he looked, and peak after peak turned from rose to lavender until at last only *Tara Kilas,* the 'Star Tower', held the light. Then suddenly that too had gone, and the whole long range lost its sharpness of outline and merged into a night that was brilliant with stars.

Memories crowded upon him, choking him; and almost without knowing it, he dismounted, and placing his palms together as he used to do long ago, he bowed his head and repeated the old prayer of the Queen's balcony that asks forgiveness for 'three sins that are due to human limitations'.

'. . . Thou art everywhere,' murmured Ash, 'but I worship thee here: Thou art without form, but I worship thee in these forms: Thou needest no praise, yet I offer thee these prayers and salutations . . .'

The first breath of the night wind sighed through the parched thorn bushes and brought him the scent of pine trees and woodsmoke, and mounting again, he turned his horse's head and rode slowly on to join Mahdoo and Gul Baz and Kulu Ram the syce, who had ridden on ahead and would by now have selected a camp site and set about preparing the evening meal.

Had they travelled as swiftly as they had done on the way up from Bhithor, they would have reached Rawalpindi in well under a week. But there was no longer, in Ash's opinion, any pressing need for haste; and as the temperature in the plains never fell below 110° in the daytime and 102° in the coolest part of the night, and Mahdo was very tired and saddle-sore, they moved at a leisurely pace, rising at two o'clock in the morning to ride until just before the sun rose, when they would make camp and rest until the same hour on the following day.

In this way, averaging no more than twenty-five miles a day, they covered the last lap of their journey. And in the early dawn of the last day of May they came within sight of Rawalpindi, and found Wally waiting, as he had waited every morning for the past eight days, by the third mile-stone on the 'Pindi–Jhelum Road.

Ash had been away for eight months, during which time he had spoken English perhaps half-a-dozen times at most, and for the rest had talked, thought and dreamed in the language of his adoptive mother, Sita.

'Pindi in June is a place to be avoided. Heat and glare and dust combine to turn it into an inferno, and those whose duty keeps them tied to an office or to barracks and parade ground are liable to fall victim to a tedious variety of hot-weather ills ranging from heat-stroke to sandfly fever.

In the compound of Wally's bungalow the giant neem tree was grey with the dust of the scorching plain, and when the hot wind blew, its leaves did not rustle but clicked instead like dice in a leather shaker, or rattled like dry bones: nor could Ash any longer see the hills, for they were hidden by the dust-clouds and the heat haze.

'How does it feel like to be a lowly Lieutenant again after eight months of peacocking about as a lordly Captain in command of countless thousands?' asked Wally curiously.

'Dull,' said Ash. 'Dull but peaceful. How many pairs of socks do you think I'd better take?'

The best part of a week had passed since Ash's return from his travels, and he was preparing to move again, but this time on leave. He had duly presented himself at Army Headquarters, where he had given a brief report of his mission and a detailed account of the Rana's misbehaviour to a Colonel Dorton, whose habit of falling asleep during office hours had earned him the nick-name of Dormouse. The Colonel had run true to form and sat through the interview with closed eyes, only opening them (after Ash had been silent for a full two minutes) to stare vaguely into the middle-distance and remark that Mr Pelham-er-Martyn had better report to the Adjutant General's Department, where Major Boyle would assign him to some new duty.

But the prediction made by the District Officer at Deenagunj proved correct. There had been no special reason for Ash's recall. Major Boyle had gone down with a severe attack of dysentery and no one else in the Adjutant General's department appeared to have heard of Lieutenant (lately Captain) Pelham-Martyn, let alone have any orders for him. On the face of it he might just as well have stayed away, for apart from demoting him from the honorary rank he had held for the past eight months (and sending an immediate memo to this effect to the Pay Department) no one seemed to know what to do with him. Ash had asked to be allowed to return to his Regiment, but had been told somewhat tartly that this was a matter for the Commandant of the Guides, who would send for him when he thought fit.

All in all, it had been a depressing home-coming, and but for Wally, he might well have resigned his commission on the spot and set off to explore Tibet or enlist as a deck-hand on a cargo boat—

anything that would take him away from the monotony of cantonment life and let him work off the gnawing restlessness that had possessed him ever since his last sight of Juli outside the Pearl Palace in Bhithor. The speed of the journey back across Rajputana and the Punjab to Deenagunj had temporarily assuaged it, but here in Rawalpindi where there was little or nothing to do it returned to torment him, and only Wally's cheerful presence and lively interest in every detail of the Karidkote–Bhithor venture kept it within bounds.

To Wally, Ash retold the story that had aroused so little interest in the somnolent Colonel Dorton, but this time in more detail and leaving less out, though he held back the truth about Juli, and, oddly enough, did not mention the fact that Karidkote had turned out to be the Gulkote of his childhood. Even to this close friend he would not —could not—talk about Juli, and if he could have left her out of the story altogether, he would have done so. That being impossible, he referred to her only when he must, and as though she were less an individual than an abstract problem that had to be solved between the ruler of Bhithor and himself. Though why he should have remained silent on the other matter was something that he could not explain even to himself. It was, after all, the most surprising thing about the whole affair, and Wally, who already knew the saga of those early years in Gulkote, would have been enthralled to hear that the State of Karidkote was the self-same place that Ash had described to him over a year ago on a moonlit night among the ruins of Taxila.

Yet Ash had kept back that vital piece of information, and without it the tale of Biju Ram's death lost much of its point. The rest posed no special problems, and Wally had listened and asked questions as avidly as Jhoti had done; and with much the same enthusiasm.

Compared with these stirring adventures, Wally declared that his own doings during the same period had been deplorably tame. He had, predictably, fallen in and out of love with several charming young women, written a vast amount of bad poetry, broken his collar-bone playing polo and lost a month's pay in a single evening at poker. But his most important piece of news had been kept until the last.

Having finally passed for his Lieutenancy, he had been offered, and accepted, a commission in the Guides, and would be joining the Corps in August.

Wally added, after congratulations, that he had delayed putting in for joining leave in the hope that Ash would return in time for the two of them to spend it together. 'Because of course you must be due for some too. You haven't had any since last summer, so it stands to reason they'll give it you without a murmur if you ask for a couple of months off now.'

This was something that had not occurred to Ash, largely because he had felt himself to be enjoying a glorified form of leave during a good two thirds of his time with the Karidkote camp, and to demand more now smacked of extortion. But taking into account the fact that the Adjutant General's Department appeared to have no orders for him and Major Boyle was still on the sick-list, he could see no harm in asking. They could only refuse, and might even welcome the chance of getting rid of him for a further spell.

He therefore immediately put in for six weeks' leave, and far from being refused, was told that he could take eight—the extra two being in the nature of a bonus, in consideration of the fact that he had been constantly on duty for a period that included the New Year, the Christian holidays of Christmas, Whitsun and Easter, the Hindu festival of Diwali, and the Moslem celebration of Id-ul-Fitre.

He was not particularly grateful for the extra two weeks once he discovered that the ban on his entry into the North-West Frontier Province was still in force, because it meant that he would not be able to visit Mardan and that unless Zarin could manage to get a few days' leave and ride over to Rawalpindi, he might not see him for another year—possibly even longer, should the Commandant of the Guides decide that it would be wiser to extend the ban for a further period.

Ash returned to the bungalow to tell Wally the news and to write three letters: one to the Commandant, Colonel Jenkins, asking to be allowed to return to his unit, another to Wigram Battye, begging him to put in a good word on his behalf, and the third to Zarin. Colonel Jenkins had been away on leave and unable to reply, but his Second-in-Command wrote to say that Ash's request had been noted and would, he felt sure, receive the Commandant's sympathetic consideration as soon as he returned to Mardan, while Wigram, in a friendly letter full of regimental news, promised to do all he could to speed Ash's recall. Zarin did not write, but he sent a verbal message by an itinerant horse-dealer, well known to them both, making an assignation to meet Ash at a certain house on the outskirts of Attock. 'The Resaidar' (Zarin had been promoted) 'cannot take his *chutti* at this time,' explained the horse-dealer. 'But as it is permitted that he absent himself for a day, he will set out at nightfall on the coming Friday, and if all goes well should reach Attock by midnight. If this should not be convenient, the Sahib has only to send a *tar.*'

The messenger salaamed and was about to leave when he remembered something and turned back: '*Chut!* I had almost forgotten: Zarin Khan called after me to say that if the Sahib wishes to bring Ashok with him, all can be arranged. Would that be one of the Sahib's syces? I have heard that many down-country men make good horse-boys. My own . . .' Here he embarked on a discussion of the merits and demerits of horse-boys in general, thereby saving Ash from the necessity of answering such an awkward question, because the purport of Zarin's apparently casual afterthought was clear. The little town of Attock lies on the east bank of the Indus, and one has only to cross the river to enter the North-West Frontier Province. It would therefore be wiser if Ash were not seen there, as it might look as though he intended to defy the ban, which at the present moment could easily prejudice his chances of being allowed to return to the Guides in the near future. Yet as Zarin could only spare a day, if they could meet at Attock rather than in Rawalpindi or some halfway house, they would have more time together.

Wally put in for his leave as soon as he heard that Ash's had been granted, but whereas Ash had been told that he could take his immediately, Wally was informed that he might go on leave in ten days' time, and not a day before: 'I tried everything, but the old scutt was adamant,' explained Wally sadly. 'It seems that they cannot spare their blue-eyed boy at present, because Johnnie Reeves has chosen this moment to join the ranks of the great majority.'

'Dead?' asked Ash, startled.

'No. Dysentery. That makes six of 'em so far. Ah well, it can't be helped, so I'm thinking you'd better go on ahead. We can arrange to meet somewhere as soon as I can get away.'

As it happened, this programme could not have suited Ash better, since it gave him a free hand for the next few days, and absolved him from explaining about his own plans to visit Attock, which was something he preferred not to discuss with Wally. The two agreed to meet at Murree and go on from there, on foot, to Kashmir; taking only Wally's bearer Pir Baksh, and hiring any other servants they might need, so that all those who had accompanied Ash to Bhithor could take leave.

Both Mahdoo and Gul Baz had protested that they had no wish to take *chutti,* but in the end they had allowed themselves to be persuaded, and Ash had engaged a seat in the mail-tonga bound for Abboatabad, and seen Mahdoo aboard: 'And when you return, we will engage an assistant for you, Cha-cha-ji. One you can instruct, and who will learn to cook so well that all you will need to do will be to oversee him. It is time you had more leisure and someone to take the bulk of the work off your shoulders.'

'It is not necessary,' growled Mahdoo. 'I am not yet so old that I cannot earn my wage. Or are you no longer satisfied with me?'

Ash laughed and told him not to talk nonsense for he knew very well that he was indispensable.

Gul Baz and Kulu Ram and the others left for their respective homes that same day, and when darkness fell Ash went out into the Mall, and hailing a passing *ekka,* told the driver to take him to a house in the Rawalpindi bazaar where he had some business to transact. He did not get back to the bungalow until long past midnight, and some five hours after breakfasting with Wally, he left again by tonga, taking a modest amount of luggage and bound, ostensibly, for Murree.

There were several rest-houses on the Murree road, and Ash stopped at the least frequented of these, where having paid off the tonga and selected the least stifling room, he stretched himself out on the bare *narwar* bed and made up for lost sleep. Awakened in the late afternoon by the sound of two horsemen riding into the compound, he went out to greet a friend of his, one Kasim Ali, whose father owned half the cloth shops in Rawalpindi bazaar, and whom it seemed that he had been expecting.

The two exchanged a few words, and the second rider having dismounted, Ash took over his horse and told the *khansamah* of the rest-house that he would be away for a couple of nights, but that his friend's servant would remain to keep an eye on his luggage, and must be provided with bed and food. The horse carried a small bundle strapped to the back of the saddle, and once safely out of sight of the rest-house Ash stopped in the first clump of trees to change into the clothes it contained, before riding on across country in the guise of a Kashmiri pundit.

Reaching Hasan Abdal in the twilight, he bought food at a wayside stall and let his horse rest and graze while he ate his evening meal on a grassy hillside overlooking the tomb of Lalla Rookh. There was still another thirty-odd miles to be covered, but as Zarin would not be leaving Mardan before sunset there was no need for haste. He lingered by the quiet tomb, listening to the horse cropping the parched grasses and watching the light fade from the far hills while the sky bedecked itself with stars, until at last the moon rose in the hot dust-scented dark. With that bone-white glare lighting the road, it was possible to press on at a fair pace, and the rest and the cooler air had put so much heart into the horse that it brought Ash to the tall old house on the outskirts of Attock in far less time than he had anticipated.

The house stood in a large walled garden, and its owner, Koda Dad's sister Fatima-Begum, was an elderly widow who had often entertained her nephews and their friends there, and this would not be the first time that Ash had stayed under that hospitable roof. Tonight the old lady had already retired, for the hour was late, and as the gatekeeper said that the Risaidar-Sahib Zarin Khan had not yet arrived, Ash left his horse to be stabled and walked on down through the sleeping town, past the walls of the Emperor Akbar's great stone fort that had guarded the ferry for close on two centuries. The descendants of the first ferry-men still plied the trade of their forefathers, but they would soon be gone, for the English had constructed a bridge of boats over the Indus and nowadays nine tenths of the traffic crossed by that.

Ash stopped on a turn of the road from where he could see the bridge, and squatted down in a patch of shadow to wait for Zarin. Few people were abroad at that hour, and except for a sentry on duty at the bridgehead, only Ash seemed to be awake; and listening. The resonant voice of the 'Father of Rivers' as it foamed through the Attock gorge filled the night with thunder, but the sound of horses' hooves carried far, and Ash's ears caught that beat above the water noises.

As it came nearer it changed to a hollow drumming on the wooden planks of the bridge, and he saw that there was not one horseman, but two. Zarin (there was no mistaking the set of that head I 47

and shoulders) had brought someone with him. But despite the brightness of the moonlight it was not until they breasted the rise that Ash realized who the other rider was, and leaping up he ran down the road to grasp Koda Dad's stirrup with both hands and touch his forehead to the old man's foot.

'I came to assure myself that all was well with you, my son,' said Koda Dad, leaning down to embrace him.

'And also to hear news of that which was once Gulkote,' grinned Zarin, dismounting.

'That too,' said Koda Dad in a tone of reproof. 'But I have been anxious for you ever since we learned too late what manner of folk it was whom you were escorting across Hind. If anyone had recognized you there might still have been great danger, and it is good to see that you are safe and well.'

It was like a homecoming, thought Ash, as he walked up the moon-blanched road with Zarin on one side of him and Koda Dad riding at a foot's pace on the other. After the thirsty wastes of Rajputana the very sound of the river was both refreshment and reassurance; and best of all was the knowledge that he was in the company of two people with whom he could talk freely of Gulkote, for both had been so intimately linked with his childhood that there was little they did not know about it.

Except for certain facts connected with Juli, there was nothing that he could not tell them about the happenings of the last eight months; and that alone, apart from his pleasure at seeing them again, brought him an enormous feeling of relief. The need to unburden himself to someone who would fully understand the complexities of his situation had been building up in him for many weeks, though until a few days ago he had not realized how strong it had become, or how necessary it was to his peace of mind to be able to pour it all out and rid himself of doubts and guilt and anxieties—and ghosts.